Johnny Ludlow by Mrs Henry Wood

The Fourth Series

"God sent his Singers upon earth
With songs of sadness and of mirth,
That they might touch the hearts of men,
And bring them back to heaven again."

I0668931

Ellen Price was born on 17th January 1814 in Worcester.

In 1836 she married Henry Wood, whose career in banking and shipping meant living in Dauphiné, in the South of France, for two decades. During their time there they had four children.

Henry's business collapsed and he and Ellen together with their four children returned to England and settled in Upper Norwood near London.

Ellen now turned to writing and with her second book 'East Lynne' enjoyed remarkable popularity. This enabled her to support her family and to maintain a literary career.

It was a career in which she would write over 30 novels including 'Danesbury House', 'Oswald Cray', 'Mrs. Halliburton's Troubles', 'The Channings' and 'The Shadow of Ashlydyat'.

Sadly, her husband, Henry died in 1866.

Ellen though continued to strive on. In 1867, she purchased the magazine 'Argosy', founded two years previously by Alexander Strahan. She was a prolific writer and wrote much of the magazine herself although she had some very respected contributors, amongst them Hesba Stretton and Christina Rossetti. Although she would gradually pare down writing for the magazine she continued to write novel after novel. Such was her talent that for a time she was, in Australia, more popular than Charles Dickens.

Apart from novels she was an excellent translator and a writer of short stories. 'Reality or Delusion?' is a staple of supernatural anthologies to this day.

Ellen Wood died of bronchitis on 10th February 1887. He estate was valued at a very considerable £36,000.

She is buried in Highgate Cemetery, London.

A monument to her in Worcester Cathedral was unveiled in 1916.

Index of Contents

A MYSTERY

I

"Look here, Johnny Ludlow," said Darbyshire to me—Darbyshire being, as you may chance to remember, our doctor at Timberdale—"you seem good at telling of unaccountable disappearances: why don't you tell of that disappearance which took place here?"

I had chanced to look in upon him one evening when he was taking rest in his chimney-corner, in the old red-cushioned chair, after his day's work was over, smoking his churchwarden pipe in his slippers and reading the story of "Dorothy Grape."

"We should like to see that disappearance on paper," went on Darbyshire. "It is the most curious thing that has happened in my experience."

True enough it was. Too curious for any sort of daylight to be seen through it; as you will acknowledge when you hear its details; and far more complicated than the other story.

The lawyer at Timberdale, John Delorane, was a warm-hearted and warm-tempered man of Irish extraction. He had an extensive practice, and lived in an old-fashioned, handsome red-brick house in the heart of Timberdale, with his only daughter and his sister, Hester.

You may have seen prettier girls than Ellin Delorane, but never one that the heart so quickly went out to. She was too much like her dead mother; had the same look of fragile delicacy, the same sweet face with its pensive sadness, the soft brown eyes and the lovely complexion. Mrs. Delorane had died of decline: people would say to one another, in confidence, they hoped Ellin might escape it.

The largest and best farm in the neighbourhood of Timberdale, larger than even that of the Ashtons, was called the Dower Farm. It belonged to Sir Robert Tenby, and had been occupied for many years by one Roger Brook, a genial, pleasant gentleman of large private means apart from his success in farming. Rich though he was, he did not disdain to see practically after his work himself; was up with the lark and out with his men, as a good farmer ought to be. Out-of-doors he was the keen, active, thorough farmer; indoors he lived as a gentleman. He had four children: three boys and one girl, who were all well and comprehensively educated.

But he intended his sons to work as he had worked: no idleness for him; no leading of indolent and self-indulgent lives. "Choose what calling you please," he said to them; "but stick to it when chosen, and do your very best in it." The eldest son, Charles, had no fancy for farming, no particular head for any of the learned professions; he preferred commerce. An uncle, Matthew Brook, was the head of a mercantile house in New York; he offered a post in it to Charles, who went out to him. The second son, Reginald, chose the medical profession; after qualifying for it, he became assistant to a doctor in London to gain experience. William, the third son, went to Oxford. He thought of the Church, but being conscientious, would not decide upon it hastily.

"So that not one of you will be with me," remarked Mr. Brook. "Well, be it so. I only want you to lead good and useful lives, striving to do your duty to God and to man."

But one of those overwhelming misfortunes, that I'm sure may be compared with the falling of an avalanche, fell on Mr. Brook. In an evil hour he had become a shareholder in a stupendous undertaking which had banking for its staple basis; and the thing failed. People talked of "swindling." Its managers ran away; its books and money were nowhere; its shareholders were ruined. Some of the shareholders ran away too; Roger Brook, upright and honourable, remained to face the ruin. And utter ruin it was, for the company was one of unlimited liability.

The shock was too much for him: he died under it. Every shilling he possessed was gone; harpies (it is what Timberdale called them) came down upon his furniture and effects, and swept them away. In less time almost than it takes to tell of, not a vestige remained of what had been, save in memory: Sir Robert Tenby had another tenant at the Dower Farm, and Mrs. Brook had moved into a little cottage-villa not a stone's throw from Darbyshire's. She had about two hundred a-year of her own, which no adverse law could touch. Her daughter, Minnie, remained with her. You will hardly believe it, but they had named her by the romantic name of Araminta.

William Brook had come down from Oxford just before, his mind made up not to be a clergyman, but to remain on the farm with his father. When the misfortunes fell, he was, of course, thrown out; and what to turn his hand to he did not at once know. Brought up to neither profession nor trade, no, nor to farming, it was just a dilemma. At present, he stayed with his mother.

One day he presented himself to Mr. Delorane. "Can you give me some copying to do, sir?" he asked: "either at your office here, or at home. I write a good clear hand."

"What do you mean to do, Master William?" returned the lawyer, passing over the question. The two families had always been intimate and much together.

"I don't know what; I am waiting to see," said William. He was a slender young fellow of middle height, with gentle manners, a very nice, refined face, and a pair of honest, cheery, dark-blue eyes.

"Waiting for something to turn up, like our old friend Micawber!" said the lawyer.

"If I could earn only a pound a-week while I am looking out, I should not feel myself so much of a burden on my mother—though she will not hear me say a word about that," the young man went on. "You would not take me on as clerk and give me that sum, would you, Mr. Delorane?"

Well, they talked further; and the upshot was, that Mr. Delorane did take him on. William Brook went into the office as a clerk, and was paid a pound a-week.

The parish wondered a little, making sundry comments over this at its tea-tables: for the good old custom of going out to real tea was not out of fashion yet in Timberdale. Every one agreed that William Brook was to be commended for putting his shoulder to the wheel, but that it was a grave descent for one brought up to his expectations. Mr. St. George objected to it on another score.

Years before, there had arrived in England from the West Indies a little gentleman, named Alfred St. George. His father, a planter, had recently died, and the boy's relatives had sent him home to be educated, together with plenty of money for that purpose. Later, when of an age to leave school, he was articled to Mr. Delorane, and proved an apt, keen pupil. Next he went into the office of a renowned legal firm in London, became a qualified lawyer and conveyancer, and finally accepted an offer made him by Mr. Delorane, to return to Timberdale, as his chief and managing clerk. Mr. Delorane paid him a handsome salary, and held out to him, as report ran, hopes of a future partnership.

Alfred St. George had grown up a fine man; tall, strong, lithe and active. People thought his face handsome, but it had unmistakably a touch of the tar-brush. The features were large and well formed, the lips full, and the purple-black hair might have been woolly but for being drilled into order with oils. His complexion was a pale olive, his black eyes were round, showing a great deal of the whites, and at times they wore a very peculiar expression. Take him for all in all, he was a handsome man, with a fluent tongue and persuasive eloquence.

It was Mr. St. George who spoke against William Brook's being taken on as clerk. Not that his objection applied to the young man himself, but to his probable capacity for work. "He will be of no use to us, sir," was the substance of his remonstrance to Mr. Delorane. "He has had no experience: and one can hardly snub Brook as one would a common clerk."

"Don't suppose he will be of much use," carelessly acquiesced Mr. Delorane, who was neither a stingy nor a covetous man. "What could I do but take him on when he asked me to? I like the young fellow; always did; and his poor father was my very good friend. You must make the best of him, St. George: dare say he won't stay long with us." At which St. George laughed good-naturedly and shrugged his shoulders.

But William Brook did prove to be of use. He got on so well, was so punctual, so attentive, so intelligent, that fault could not be found with him; and at the end of the first year Mr. Delorane voluntarily doubled his pay—raising it to two pounds per week.

Timberdale wondered again: and began to ask how it was that young Brook, highly educated, and reared to expect some position in the world, could content himself with stopping on, a lawyer's clerk? Did he mean to continue in the office for ever? Had he ceased to look out for that desirable something that was to turn up? Was he parting with all laudable ambition?

William Brook could have told them, had he dared, that it was not lack of ambition chaining him to his post, but stress of love. He and Ellin Delorane had entered a long while past into the mazes of that charming dream, than which, as Tom Moore tells us, there's nothing half so sweet in life, and the world was to them as the Garden of Eden.

It was close upon the end of the second year before Mr. Delorane found it out. He went into a storm of rage and reproaches—chiefly showered upon William Brook, partly upon Ellin, a little upon himself.

"I have been an old fool," he spluttered to his confidential clerk. "Because the young people had been intimate in the days when the Brooks were prosperous, I must needs let it go on still, and never suspect danger! Why, the fellow has had his tea here twice a-week upon an average!—and brought Ellin home at night when she has been at his mother's!—and I—I—thought no more than if it had been her brother! I could thrash myself! And where have her aunt Hester's eyes been, I should like to know!"

"Very dishonourable of Brook," assented St. George, knitting his brow. "Perhaps less harm is done than you fear, sir. They are both young, can hardly know their own minds; they will grow out of it. Shall you part them?"

"Do you suppose I shouldn't?" retorted the lawyer.

William Brook was discharged from the office: Ellin received orders to give up his acquaintanceship; she was not to think of him in private or speak to him in public. Thus a little time went on. Ellin's bright face began to fade; Aunt Hester looked sick and sorry; the lawyer had never felt so uncomfortable in his life.

Do what he would, he could not get out of his liking for William Brook, and Ellin was dear to him as the apple of his eye. He had been in love himself once, and knew what it meant; little as you would believe it of a stout old red-faced lawyer; knew that both must be miserable. So much the better for Brook—but what of Ellin?

"One would think it was you who had had your lover sent to the right-about!" he wrathfully began to Aunt Hester, one morning when he came upon her in tears as she sat at her sewing. "I'd hide my face if I were you, unless I could show a better."

"It is that I am so sorry for Ellin, John," replied Aunt Hester, meekly wiping her tears. "I—I am afraid that some people bear sorrow worse than others."

"Now what do you mean by that?"

"Oh, not much," sighed Aunt Hester, not daring to allude to the dread lying latent in her own mind—that Ellin might fade away like her mother. "I can see what a sharp blow it has been to the child, John, and so—and so I can but feel it myself."

"Sharp blow! Deuce take it all! What business had young Brook to get talking to her about such rubbish as love?"

"Yes indeed, it is very unfortunate," said Aunt Hester. "But I do not think he has talked to her, John; I imagine he is too honourable to have said a single word. They have just gone on loving one another in secret and in silence, content to live in the unspoken happiness that has flooded their two hearts."

"Unspoken fiddlestick? What a simpleton you are, Hester!"

Mr. Delorane turned off in a temper. He knew it must have been a "sharp blow" to Ellin, but he did not like to hear it so stated to his face. Banging the door behind him, he was crossing the hall to the office—which made a sort of wing to the house—when he met William Brook.

"Will you allow me to speak to you, sir?" asked the young man in a tone of deprecation. And, though the lawyer had the greatest mind in the world to tell him NO and send him head-foremost out again, he thought of Ellin, he thought of his dead friend, Roger Brook; so he gave a growl, and led the way into the dining-room.

In his modest winning way, William Brook spoke a little of the trouble that had come upon their family— how deeply sorry he was that Ellin and he should have learnt to care for one another for all time, as it was displeasing to Mr. Delorane—

"Hang it, man," interrupted the lawyer irascibly, too impatient to listen further—"what on earth do you propose to yourself? Suppose I did not look upon it with displeasure?—are you in a position to marry her?"

"You would not have objected to me had we been as we once were—prosperous, and—"

"What the dickens has that to do with it!" roared the lawyer. "Our business lies with the present, not the past."

"I came here to tell you, sir, that I am to leave for New York to-night. My brother Charles has been writing to me about it for some time past. He says I cannot fail to get on well in my uncle's house, and attain to a good position. Uncle Matthew has no sons: he will do his best to advance his nephews. What I wish to ask you, sir, is this—if, when my means shall be good and my position assured, you will allow me to think of Ellin?"

"The man's mad?" broke forth Mr. Delorane, more put about than he had been at all. "Do you suppose I should let my only child go to live in a country over the seas?"

"No, sir, I have thought of that. Charles thinks, if I show an aptitude for business, they may make me their agent over here. Oh, Mr. Delorane, be kind, be merciful: for Ellin's sake and for mine! Do not send me away without hope!"

"Don't you think you possess a ready-made stock of impudence, William Brook?"

The young man threw his earnest, dark-blue eyes into the lawyer's. "I feared you would deem so, sir. But I am pleading for what is dearer to me and to her than life: our lives will be of little value to us if we must spend them apart. Only just one ray of possible hope, Mr. Delorane! It is all I ask."

"Look here; we'll drop this," cried the lawyer, his hands in his pockets, rattling away violently at the silver in them, his habit when put out, but nevertheless calming down in temper, for in spite of prejudice he did like the young man greatly, and he was not easy as to Ellin. "The best thing you can do is to go where you are going—over the Atlantic: and we'll leave the future to take care of itself. The money you think to make may turn out all moonshine, you know. There; that's every word I'll say and every hope I'll give, though you stop all day bothering me, William Brook."

And perhaps it was as much as William Brook had expected: any way, it did not absolutely forbid him to hope. He held out his hand timidly.

"Will you not shake hands with me, sir—I start to-night—and wish me God speed."

"I'll wish you better sense; and—and I hope you'll get over safely," retorted Mr. Delorane: but he did not withhold his hand. "No correspondence with Ellin, you understand, young man; no underhand love-making."

"Yes, sir, I understand; and you may rely upon me."

He quitted the room as he spoke, to make his way out as he came—through the office. The lawyer stood in the passage and looked after him: and a thought, that had forced itself into his mind several times since this trouble set in, crossed it again. Should he make the best of a bad bargain: give Brook a chief place in his own office and let them set up in some pleasant little home near at hand? Ellin had her mother's money: and she would have a great deal more at his own death; quite enough to allow her husband to live the idle life of a gentleman—and William was a gentleman, and the nicest young fellow he knew. Should he? For a full minute Mr. Delorane stood deliberating—yes, or no; then he took a hasty step forward to call the young man back. Then, wavering and uncertain, he stepped back again, and let the idea pass.

"Well, how have you sped?" asked Mr. St. George, as William Brook reappeared in the office. "Any hope?"

"Yes, I think so," answered William. "At least, it is not absolutely forbidden. There's a line in a poem my mother would repeat to us when we were boys—'God and an honest heart will bear us through the roughest day.' I trust He, and it, will so bear me and Ellin."

"Wish I had your chance, old fellow!"

"My chance!" repeated William.

"To go out to see the world; to go out to the countries where gold and diamonds are picked up for the stooping—instead of being chained, as I am, between four confined walls, condemned to spend my life over musty parchments."

William smiled. "I don't know where you can pick up gold and diamonds for the stooping. Not where I am going."

"No, not in New York. You should make your way to the Australian gold-fields, Brook, or to the rich Californian mines, or to the diamond mountains in Africa, and come back—as you would in no time—with a sack of money on your shoulders, large enough to satisfy even Delorane."

"Or lose my health, if not my life, in digging, and come home without a shirt to my back; a more common result than the other, I fancy," remarked William. "Well, good-bye, old friend."

St. George, towering aloft in his height and strength, put his arm around William's shoulder and walked thus with him to the street-entrance. There they shook hands, and parted. Ellin Delorane, her face shaded behind the drawing-room curtain from the October sun, watched the parting.

There was to be no set farewell allowed to her. She understood that. But she gathered from Aunt Hester, during the day, that her father had not been altogether obdurate, and that if William could get on in the future, perhaps things might be suffered to come right. It brought to her a strange comfort. So very slight a ray, no bigger than one of the specks that fall from the sky, as children say, will serve to impart a most unreasonable amount of hope to the troubled heart.

Towards the close of the afternoon, Ellin went in her restlessness to pay a visit to her friend Grace at the Rectory, who had recently become Herbert Tanerton's wife, and sat talking with her till it was pretty late. The moon, rising over the tops of the trees, caused her to start up with an exclamation.

"What will Aunt Hester say?"

"If you don't mind going through the churchyard, Ellin," said Grace, "you would cut off that corner, and save a little time." So Ellin took that route.

"Ellin!"

"William!"

They had met face to face under the church walls. He explained that he was sparing a few minutes to say farewell to his friends at the Rectory. The moon, coming out from behind a swiftly passing cloud, for it was rather a rough night, shone down upon them and upon the graves around them. Wildly enough beat the heart of each.

"You saw papa to-day," she whispered unevenly, as though her breath were short.

"Yes, I saw him. I cannot say that he gave me hope, Ellin, but he certainly did not wholly deny it. I think—I believe—that—if I can succeed in getting on, all may be well with us yet."

William Brook spoke with hesitation. He felt trammelled; he could not in honour say what he would have wished to say. This meeting might be unorthodox, but it was purely accidental; neither he nor Ellin had sought it.

"Good-bye, my darling," he said with emotion, clasping her hands in his. "As we have met, there cannot be much wrong in our saying it. I may not write to you, Ellin; I may not even ask you to think of me; I may not, I suppose, tell you in so many words that I shall think of you; but, believe this: I go out with one sole aim and end in view—that of striving to make a position sufficiently fair to satisfy your father."

The tears were coursing down her cheeks; she could hardly speak for agitation. Their hearts were aching to pain.

"I will be true to you always, William," she whispered. "I will wait for you, though it be to the end of life."

To be in love with a charming young lady, and to have her all to yourself in a solitary graveyard under the light of the moon, presents an irresistible temptation for taking a kiss, especially if the kiss is to be a farewell kiss for days and for years. William Brook did not resist it; very likely did not try to. In spite of Mr. Delorane and every one else, he took his farewell kiss from Ellin's lips.

Then they parted, he going one way, she the other. Only those of us—there are not many—who have gone through this parting agony can know how it wrings the heart.

But sundry superstitious gossips, hearing of this afterwards, assured Ellin that it must be unlucky to say farewell amidst graves.

The time went on. William Brook wrote regularly to his people, and Minty whispered the news to Ellin Delorane. He would send kind remembrances to friends, love to those who cared for it. He did not dislike the work of a mercantile life, and thought he should do well—in time.

In time. There was the rub, you see. We say "in time" when we mean next Christmas, and we also say it when we mean next century. By the end of the first year William Brook was commanding a handsome salary; but the riches that might enable him to aspire to the hand of Miss Delorane loomed obscurely in the distance yet. Ellin seemed strong and well, gay and cheerful, went about Timberdale, and laughed and talked with the world, just as though she had never had a lover, or was not waiting for somebody over the water. Mr. Delorane thought she must have forgotten that scapegrace, and he hoped it was so.

It was about this time, the end of the first year, that a piece of good luck fell to Mr. St. George. He came into a fortune. Some relative in the West Indies died and left it to him. Timberdale put it down at a thousand pounds a-year, so I suppose it might be about five hundred. It was thought he might be for giving up his post at Mr. Delorane's to be a gentleman at large. But he did nothing of the kind. He quitted his lodgings over Salmon's shop, and went into a pretty house near Timberdale Court, with a groom and old Betty Huntsman as housekeeper, and set up a handsome gig and a grey horse. And that was all the change.

As the second year went on, Ellin Delorane began to droop a little. Aunt Hester did not like it. One of the kindest friends Ellin had was Alfred St. George. After the departure of young Brook, he had been so tender with Ellin, so considerate, so indulgent to her sorrow, and so regretful (like herself) of William's absence, that he had won her regard. "It will be all right when he comes back, Ellin," he would whisper: "only be patient."

But in this, the second year, Mr. St. George's tone changed. It may be that he saw no hope of any happy return, and deemed that, for her own sake, he ought to repress any hope left in her.

"There's no more chance of his returning with a fortune than there is of my going up to the moon," he said to Tod confidentially one day when we met him striding along near the Ravine.

"Don't suppose there is—in this short time," responded Tod.

"I'm afraid Ellin sees it, too: she seems to be losing her spirits. Ah, Brook should have done as I advised him—gone a little farther and dug in the gold-fields. He might have come back a Croesus then. As it is— whew! I wouldn't give a copper sixpence for his chance."

"Do you know what I heard say, St. George?—that you'd like to go in for the little lady yourself."

The white eye-balls surrounding St. George's dark orbs took a tinge of yellow as they rolled on Tod. "Who said it?" he asked quietly.

"Darbyshire. He says you are in love with her as much as ever Brook was."

St. George laughed. "Old Darbyshire? Well, perhaps he is not far wrong. Any way, love's free, I believe. Were I her father, Brook should prove his eligibility to propose for her, or else give her up. Good-day, Todhetley; good-day, Johnny."

St. George went off at a quick pace. Tod, looking after him, made his comments. "Should not wonder but he wins her. He is the better man of the two—"

"The better man!" I interrupted.

"As to means, at any rate: and see what a fine upright free-limbed fellow he is! And where will you find one more agreeable?"

"In tongue, nowhere; I admit that. But I wouldn't give up William Brook for him, were I Ellin Delorane."

That St. George was in love with her grew as easy to be seen as is the round moon in harvest. Small blame to him. Who could be in the daily companionship of a sweet girl like Ellin Delorane, and not learn to love her, I should like to know? Tod told St. George he wished he had his chance.

At last St. George spoke to her. It was in April, eighteen months after Brook's departure. Ellin was in the garden at sunset, busy with the budding flowers, when St. George came to join her, as he sometimes did, on leaving the office for the day. Aunt Hester sat sewing at the open glass-doors of the window.

"I have been gardening till I am tired," was Ellin's greeting to him, as she sat down on a bench near the sweetbriar bush.

"You look pale," said Mr. St. George. "You often do look pale now, Ellin: do you think you can be quite well?"

"Pray don't let Aunt Hester overhear you," returned Ellin in covert, jesting tones. "She begins to have fancies, she says, that I am not as well as I ought to be, and threatens to call in Mr. Darbyshire."

"You need some one to take care of you; some one near and dear to you, who would study your every look and action, who would not suffer the winds of heaven to blow upon your face too roughly," went on St. George, plunging into Shakespeare. "Oh, Ellin, if you would suffer me to be that one—"

Her face turned crimson; her lips parted with emotion; she rose up to interrupt him in a sort of terror.

"Pray do not continue, Mr. St. George. If—if I understand you rightly, that you—that you—"

"That I would be your loving husband, Ellin; that I would shelter you from all ill until death us do part. Yes, it is nothing less than that."

"Then you must please never to speak of such a thing again; never to think of it. Oh, do not let me find that I have been mistaking you all this time," she added in uncontrollable agitation: "that while I have ever welcomed you as my friend—and his—you have been swayed by another motive!"

He did not like the agitation; he did not like the words; and he bit his lips, striving for calmness.

"This is very hard, Ellin."

"Let us understand each other once for all," she said—"and oh, I am so sorry that there's need to say it. What you have hinted at is impossible. Impossible: please not to mistake me. You have been my very kind friend, and I value you; and, if you will, we can go on still on the same pleasant terms, caring for one another in friendship. There can be nothing more."

"Tell me one thing," he said: "we had better, as you intimate, understand each other fully. Can it be that your hopes are still fixed upon William Brook?"

"Yes," she answered in a low tone, as she turned her face away. "I hope he will come home yet, and that—that matters may be smoothed for us with papa. Whilst that hope remains it is simply treason to talk to me as you would have done," she concluded with a spurt of anger.

"Ellin," called out Aunt Hester, putting her head out beyond the glass-doors, "the sun has set; you had better come in."

"One moment, Ellin," cried Mr. St. George, preventing her: "will you forgive me?"

"Forgive and forget, too," smiled Ellin, her brow smoothing itself. "But you must never recur to the subject again."

So Mr. St. George went home, his accounts settled—as Tod would have said: and the days glided on.

"What is it that ails Ellin?"

It was a piping-hot morning in July, in one of the good old hot summers that we seem never to get now; and Aunt Hester sat in her parlour, its glass-doors open, adding up the last week's bills of the butcher and the baker, when she was interrupted by this question from her brother. He had come stalking upon her, rattling as usual, though quite unconsciously, the silver in his trousers pockets. The trousers were of nankeen: elderly gentlemen wore them in those days for coolness.

"What ails her!" repeated Aunt Hester, dropping the bills in alarm. "Why do you ask me, John?"

"Now, don't you think you should have been a Quaker?" retorted Mr. Delorane. "I put a simple question to you, and you reply to it by asking me another. Please to answer mine first. What is it that is the matter with Ellin?"

Aunt Hester sighed. Of too timid a nature to put forth her own opinion upon any subject gratuitously in her brother's house, she hardly liked to give it even when asked for. For the past few weeks Ellin had been almost palpably fading; was silent and dispirited, losing her bright colour, growing thinner; might be heard catching her breath in one of those sobbing sighs that betoken all too surely some secret, ever-present sorrow. Aunt Hester had observed this; she now supposed it had at length penetrated to the observation of her brother.

"Can't you speak?" he demanded.

"I don't know what to say, John. Ellin does not seem well, and looks languid: of course this broiling weather is against us all. But—"

"But what?" cried the lawyer, as she paused. "As to broiling weather, that's nothing new in July."

"Well, John—only you take me up so—and I'm sure I shouldn't like to anger you. I was about to add that I think it is not so much illness of body with Ellin as illness of mind. If one's mind is ransacked with perpetual worry—"

"Racked with perpetual worry," interrupted Mr. Delorane, unconsciously correcting her mistake. "What has she to worry her?"

"Dear me! I suppose it is about William Brook. He has been gone nearly two years, John, and seems to be no nearer coming home with a fortune than he was when he left. I take it that this troubles the child: she is losing hope."

Mr. Delorane, standing before the open window, his back to his sister, turned the silver coins about in his pockets more vehemently than before. "You say she is not ailing in body?"

"Not yet. She is never very strong, you know."

"Then there's no need to be uneasy."

"Well, John—not yet, perhaps. But should this state of despair, if I don't use too strong a word, continue, it will tell in tune upon her health, and might bring on—bring on—"

"Bring on what?" sharply asked the lawyer.

"I was thinking of her mother," said poor Aunt Hester, with as much deprecation as though he had been the Great Mogul: "but I trust, John, you won't be too angry with me for saying it."

Mr. Delorane did not say whether he was angry or not. He stood there, fingering his sixpences and shillings, gazing apparently at the grass-plat, in reality seeing nothing. He was recalling a past vision: that of his delicate wife, dying of consumption before her time; he seemed to see a future vision: that of his daughter, dying as she had died.

"When it comes to dreams," timidly went on Aunt Hester, "I can't say I like it. Not that I am one to put faith in the foolish signs old wives talk of—that if you dream of seeing a snake, you've got an enemy; or, if you seem to be in the midst of a lot of beautiful white flowers, it's a token of somebody's death. I am not so silly as that, John. But for some time past Ellin has dreamt perpetually of one theme—that of being in trouble about William Brook. Night after night she seems to be searching for him: he is lost, and she cannot tell how or where."

Had Aunt Hester suddenly begun to hold forth in the unknown tongue, it could not have brought greater surprise to Mr. Delorane. He turned short round to stare at her.

"Seeing what a wan and weary face the child has come down with of late, I taxed her with not sleeping well," continued Aunt Hester, "and she confessed to me that she was feeling a good bit troubled by her dreams. She generally has them towards morning, and the theme is always the same. The dreams vary, but the subject is alike in all—William Brook is lost, and she is searching for him."

"Nonsense! Rubbish!" put in Mr. Delorane.

"Well, John, I dare say it is nonsense," conceded Aunt Hester meekly: "but I confess I don't like dreams that come to you persistently night after night and always upon one and the same subject. Why should they come?—that's what I ask myself. Be sure, though, I make light of the matter to Ellin, and tell her her digestion is out of order. Over and over again, she says, they seem to have the clue to his hiding place, but they never succeed in finding him. And—and I am afraid, John, that the child, through this, has taken up the notion that she shall never see him again."

Mr. Delorane, making some impatient remark about the absurdity of women in general, turned round and stood looking into the garden as before. Ellin's mind was getting unhinged with the long separation, she had begun to regard it as hopeless, and hence these dreams that Brook was "lost," he told himself, and with reason: and what was he to do?

How long he stood thus in perfect silence, no sound to be heard but the everlasting jingling of the loose silver, Aunt Hester did not know; pretty near an hour she thought. She wished he would go; she felt very uncomfortable, as she always did feel when she vexed him—and here were the bills waiting to be added up. At length he turned sharply, with the air of one who has come to some decision, and returned to the office.

"I suppose I shall have to do it myself," he remarked to Mr. St. George.

"Do what, sir?"

"Send for that young fellow back, and let them set up in some little homestead near me. I mean Brook."

"Brook!" stammered St. George.

"Here's Ellin beginning to fade and wither. It's all very well for her aunt to talk about the heat! I know. She is pining after him, and I can't see her do it; so he must come home."

Of all the queer shades that can be displayed by the human countenance, about the queerest appeared in that of Mr. St. George. It was not purple, it was not green, it was not yellow; it was a mixture of all three. He gazed at his chief and master as one gazes at a madman.

"Brook can come into the office again," continued Mr. Delorane. "I don't like young men to be idle; leads 'em into temptation. We'll make him head clerk here, next to you, and give him a couple of hundred a-year. If—what's the matter?"

For the strange look on his manager's face had caught the eye of Mr. Delorane. St. George drew three or four deep breaths.

"Have you thought of Miss Delorane, sir—of her interests—in planning this?" he presently asked.

"Why, that's what I do think of; nothing else. You may be sure I shouldn't think of it for the interest of Brook. All the same, I like the young man, and always shall. The child is moping herself into a bad way. Where shall I be if she should go into a decline like her mother? No, no; she shall marry and have proper interests around her."

"She could do that without being sacrificed to Brook," returned St. George in a low tone. "There are others, sir, of good and suitable position, who would be thankful to take her—whose pride it would be to cherish her and render every moment of her life happy."

"Oh, I know that; you are one of 'em," returned Mr. Delorane carelessly. "It's what all you young sparks are ready to say of a pretty girl, especially if she be rich as well. But don't you see, St. George, that Ellin does not care for any of you. Her heart is fixed upon Brook, and Brook it must be."

Of course this news came out to Timberdale. Some people blamed Mr. Delorane, others praised him. Delorane must be turning childish in his old age, said one; Delorane is doing a good and a wise thing, cried another. Opinions vary in this world, you know, and ever will, as proved to us in the fable of the old man and his ass.

But now—and it was a strange thing to happen the very next day Mr. Delorane received a letter from William Brook, eight closely written pages. Briefly, this was its substance. The uncle, Matthew Brook of New York, was about to establish a house in London, in correspondence with his own; he had offered the managership of it to William, with a small share of profits, guaranteeing that the latter should not be less than seven hundred a-year.

"And if you can only be induced to think this enough for us to begin upon, sir, and will give me Ellin," wrote the young man, "I can but say that I will strive to prove my gratitude in loving care for her; and I trust you will not object to her living in London. I leave New York next month, to be in England in September, landing at Liverpool, and I shall make my way at once to Timberdale, hoping you will allow me to plead my cause in person."

"No no, Master William, you won't carry my daughter off to London," commented Mr. Delorane aloud, when he had read the letter—not but that it gratified him. "You must give up your post, young man, and settle down by me here, if you are to have Ellin. I don't see, St. George, why Brook should not make himself into a lawyer, legal and proper," added he thoughtfully. "He is young enough—and he does not dislike the work. You and he might be associated together after I am dead: 'Brook and St. George.'"

Mr. St. George's face turned crusty: he did not like to hear his name put next to Brook's. "I never feel too sure of my own future," he said in reply. "Now that I am at my ease in the world, tempting visions come often enough across me of travelling out to see it."

Mr. Delorane wrote a short, pithy note in answer to the appeal of William Brook, telling him he might come and talk to him as soon as he returned. "The young fellow may have left New York before it can reach him," remarked the lawyer, as he put the letter in the post; "but if so, it does not much matter."

So there was Timberdale, all cock-a-hoop at the prospect of seeing William Brook again, and the wedding that was to follow. Sam Mullet, the clerk, was for setting the bells to ring beforehand.

Some people think September the pleasantest month in the year, when the heats of summer have passed and the frosts of winter have not come. Never a finer September than we had that autumn at Timberdale; the skies looked bright, the leaves of the trees were putting on their tints of many colours, and the land was not yet quite shorn of its golden grain.

All the world was looking out for William Brook. He did not come. Disappointment is the lot of man. Of woman also. When the third week was dragging itself along in expectancy, a letter came to Mrs. Brook from William. It was to say that his return home was somewhat delayed, as he should have to take Jamaica en route, to transact some business at Kingston for his uncle. He should then proceed direct from Kingston by steamer to Liverpool, which place he hoped to reach before the middle of October. "Tell all my friends this, that they may not wonder at my delay," the letter concluded; but it contained no intimation that he had received the answer written by Mr. Delorane.

A short postscript was yet added, in these words: "Alfred St. George has, I know, some relatives living in, or near Kingston—planters, I believe. Tell him I shall call upon them, if I can make time, to see whether they have any commands for him."

Long before the middle of October, Ellin Delorane became obviously restless. A sort of uneasy impatience seemed to have taken possession of her: and without cause. One day, when we called at Mr. Delorane's to take a message from home, Ellin was in the garden with her outdoor things on, waiting to go out with her aunt.

"What a ridiculous goose you are!" began Tod. "I hear you have taken up the notion that Sweet William has gone down in the Caribbean Sea."

"I'm sure I have not," said Ellin. "Aunt Hester must have told you that fable when she was at Crabb Cot yesterday."

"Just so. She and the mater laid their gossiping caps together for the best part of an hour—and all about the foolishness of Miss Ellin Delorane."

"Why, you know, Ellin," I put in, "it is hardly the middle of October yet."

"I tell myself that it is not," she answered gravely. "But, somehow, Johnny, I don't—don't—expect—him."

"Now, what on earth do you mean?"

"I wish I knew what. All I can tell you is, that when his mother received that letter from William last month, saying his return was delayed, a sort of foreboding seized hold of me, an apprehension that he would never come. I try to shake it off, but I cannot. Each day, as the days come round, only serves to make it stronger."

"Don't you think a short visit to Droitwich would do you good, Ellin?" cried Tod, which was our Worcestershire fashion of recommending people to the lunatic asylum.

"Just listen to him, Johnny!" she exclaimed, with a laugh.

"Yes, 'just listen to him'—and just listen to yourself, Miss Ellin, and see which talks the most sense," he retorted. "Have you got over those dreams yet?"

Ellin turned her face to him quickly. "Who told you anything about that, Aunt Hester?"

Tod nodded. "It's true, you know."

"Yes, it is true," she slowly said. "I have had those strange dreams for some weeks now; I have them still."

"That William Brook is lost?"

"That he is lost, and that we are persistently searching for him. Sometimes we are seeking for him in Timberdale, sometimes at Worcester—in America, in France, in places that I have no knowledge of. There always seems to be a sadness connected with it—a sort of latent conviction that he will never be found."

"The dreams beget the dreams," said Tod, "and I should have thought you had better sense. They will soon vanish, once Sweet William makes his appearance: and mind, Miss Ellin, that you invite me to the wedding."

Ellin sighed—and smiled. And just then Aunt Hester appeared attired in her crimson silk shawl with the fancy border, and the primrose feather in her Leghorn bonnet.

A day or two went on, bringing no news of the traveller. On the nineteenth of October—I shall never forget the date—Mr. and Mrs. Todhetley and ourselves set off in the large open phaeton for a place called Pigeon Green, to spend the day with some friends living there. On this same morning, as it chanced, a very wintry one, Mr. St. George started for Worcester in his gig, accompanied by Ellin Delorane. But of this we knew nothing. He had business in the town; she was going to spend a few days with Mary West, formerly Mary Coney.

Ellin was well wrapped up, and Mr. St. George, ever solicitous for her comfort, kept the warm fur rug well about her during the journey: the skies looked grey and threatening, the wind was high and bitterly cold. Worcester reached, he drove straight through the town, left Ellin at Mrs. West's door, in the Foregate Street, and then drove back to the Hare and Hounds Inn to put up his horse and gig.

II

I shall always say, always think, it was a curious thing we chanced to go that day, of all days, to Pigeon Green. It is not chance that brings about these strange coincidences.

"There's a divinity that shapes our ends,
Rough-hew them how we will."

Pigeon Green, a small colony of a dozen houses, formed a triangle, as may be said, with Timberdale and Evesham, being a few miles distant from each. Old Mr. and Mrs. Beele, life-long friends of the Squire, lived here. Their nephew had brought his newly-married wife from London to show her to them, and we were all invited to dinner. As the Squire did not care to be out in the dark, his sight not being what it used to be, the dinner-hour was fixed for two o'clock. We started in the large open phaeton, the Squire driving his favourite horses, Bob and Blister. It was the nineteenth of October. Mrs. Todhetley complained of the cold as we went along. The lovely weather of September had left us; early winter seemed to be setting in with a vengeance. The easterly wind was unusually high, and the skies were leaden.

On this same wintry morning Mr. St. George left Timberdale in his gig for Worcester, accompanied by Ellin Delorane. St. George had business to transact with Philip West, a lawyer, who was Mr. Delorane's agent in Worcester. Philip West lived in the Foregate Street, his offices being in the same house. Ellin was very intimate with his wife, formerly Mary Coney, and was invited to spend a few days with her. It was Aunt Hester who had urged the acceptance of this invitation: seeing that Ellin was nervous at the non-arrival of her lover, William Brook, was peeping into the newspapers for accounts of shipwrecks and other calamities at sea. So they set off after breakfast, Ellin well wrapped up, in this stylish gig of Mr. St. George's. There are gigs and gigs, you know, and I assure you some gigs were yet fashionable vehicles in those days.

It was bitterly cold. St. George, remarking that they should have snow as soon as the high wind would let it come down, urged his handsome grey horse to a fleet pace, and they soon reached Worcester. He drove straight to Foregate Street, which lay at the other end of the town, set down Ellin, and then went back again to leave his horse and gig at the Hare and Hounds in College Street, the inn at which he generally put up, retracing his steps on foot to Mr. West's.

And now I must return to ourselves.

After a jolly dinner at two o'clock with the Beeles, and a jolly dessert after it, including plenty of fresh filberts and walnuts, and upon that a good cup of tea and some buttered toast, we began to think about getting home. When the phaeton came round, the Squire remarked that it was half-an-hour later than he had meant to start; upon which, old Beele laid the fault of its looking late to the ungenial weather of the evening.

We drove off. Dusk was approaching; the leaden skies looked dark and sullen, the wind, unpleasantly high all day, had increased to nearly a hurricane. It roared round our heads, it whistled wildly through the trees and hedges, it shook the very ears of Bob and Blister; the few flakes of snow or sleet beginning then to fall were whirled about in the air like demons. It was an awful evening, no mistake about that; and a very unusual one for the middle of October.

The Squire faced the storm as well as he could, his coat-collar turned up, his cloth cap, kept for emergencies in a pocket of the carriage, tied down well on his ears. Mrs. Todhetley tied a knitted grey shawl right over her bonnet. We, in the back seat, had much ado to keep our hats on: I sat right behind the Squire, Tod behind Mrs. Todhetley. It was about the worst drive I remember. The wild wind, keen as a knife, stung our faces, and seemed at times as if it would whirl us, carriage and horses and all, in the air, as it was whirling the sleet and snow.

Tod stood up to speak to his father. "Shall I drive, sir?" he asked. "Perhaps you would be more sheltered if you sat here behind."

Tod's driving in those days was regarded by the Squire with remarkable disparagement, and Tod received only a sharp answer—which could not be heard for the wind.

We got along somehow in the teeth of the storm. The route lay chiefly through by-ways, solitary and unfrequented, not in the good, open turnpike-roads. For about a mile, midway between Pigeon Green and Timberdale, was an ultra dreary spot; dreary in itself and dreary in its associations. It was called Dip Lane, possibly because the ground dipped there so much that it lay in a hollow; overgrown dark elm-trees grew thickly on each side of it, their branches nearly meeting overhead. In the brightest summer's day the place was gloomy, so you may guess how it looked now.

But the downward dip and the dark elm-trees did not constitute all the dreariness of Dip Lane. Many years before, a murder had been committed there. The Squire used to tell us of the commotion it caused, all the gentlemen for miles and miles round bestirring themselves to search out the murderers. He himself was a little fellow of five or six years old, and could just remember what a talk it made. A wealthy farmer, belated, riding through the lane from market one dark night, was attacked and pulled from his horse. The assailants beat him to death, rifled his pockets of a large sum, for he had been selling stock, and dragged him through the hedge, making a large gap in it. Across the field, near its opposite side, was the round, deep stagnant piece of water known as Dip Pond (popularly supposed to be too deep to have any bottom to it); and it was conjectured that the object of the murderers, in dragging him through the hedge, was to conceal the body beneath the dark and slimy water, and that they must have been disturbed by some one passing in the lane. Any way, the body was found in the morning lying in the field a few yards from the gap in the hedge, pockets turned inside out, and watch and seals gone. The poor frightened horse had made its way home, and stayed whinnying by the stable-door all night.

The men were never found. A labourer, hastening through the lane earlier in the evening, with some medicine from the doctor's for his sick wife, had noticed two foot-pads, as he described them, standing under a tree. That these were the murderers, then waiting for prey, possibly for this very gentleman they attacked, no one had any doubt; but they were never traced. Whoever they were, they got clear off with their booty, and—the Squire would always add when telling the story to a stranger—with their wicked consciences, which he sincerely hoped tormented them ever afterwards.

But the most singular fact in the affair remains to be told. From that night nothing would grow on the spot in the hedge over which the murdered man was dragged, and on which his blood had fallen. The blood-stains were easily got rid of, but the hedge, though replanted more than once, never grew again; and the gap remained in it still. Report went that the farmer's ghost haunted it—that, I am sure, you will not be surprised to hear, ghosts being so popular—and might be seen hovering around it on a moonlit night.

And amidst the many small coincidences attending the story (my story) which I am trying to place clearly before you, was this one: that the history of the murder was gone over that day at Mr. Beele's. Some remark led to the subject as we sat round the dessert-table, and Mrs. Frank Beele, who had never heard of it, inquired what it was. Upon that, the Squire and old Beele recounted it to her, each ransacking his memory to help the other with fullest particulars.

To go on with our homeward journey. Battling along, we at length plunged into Dip Lane—which, to its other recommendations, added that of being inconveniently narrow—and Tod, peering outwards in the gloomy dusk, fancied he saw some vehicle before us. Bringing his keen sight to bear upon it, he stood up to reconnoitre, and made it out to be a gig, going the same way that we were. The wind was not quite so bad in this low spot, and the snow and sleet had ceased for a bit.

"Take care, father," said Tod: "there's a gig on ahead."

"A gig, Joe?"

"Yes, it's a gig: and going at a strapping pace."

But the Squire was going at a strapping pace also, and driving two fresh horses, whereas the gig had but one horse. We caught it up in no time. It slackened speed slightly as it drew close to the hedge on that side, to give us room to pass. In a moment we saw it was St. George's gig, St. George driving.

"Halloa!" called Tod, as we shot by, and his shout was loud enough to frighten the ghost at the gap, which lively spot we were fast approaching, "there's William Brook! Father, pull up: there's William Brook!"

Brook was sitting with St. George. His coat was well buttoned up, a white woollen comforter folded round his neck and chin, and a low-crowned, wide-brimmed hat pulled down over his brows. I confess that but for Tom's shout I should not have recognized him—muffled up in that way.

Anxious to get home, out of the storm, the Squire paid no heed to Tod's injunction of pulling up. He just turned his head for a moment towards the gig, but drove on at the same speed as before. All we could do was to call out every welcome we could think of to William Brook as we looked back, and to pull off our hats and wave them frantically.

William Brook pulled off his, and waved it to us in return. I saw him do it. He called out something also, no doubt a greeting. At least, I thought he did; but the wind swept by with a gust at the moment, and it might have been St. George's voice and not his.

"Johnny, lad, it's better than nuts," cried Tod to me, all excitement for once, as he fixed his hat on his head again. "How glad I am!—for Nelly's sake. But what on earth brings the pair of them—he and St. George—in Dip Lane?"

Another minute or so, and we reached the gap in the hedge. I turned my eyes to it and to the pond beyond it in a sort of fascination; I was sure to do so whenever I went by, but that was seldom; and the conversation at the dessert-table had opened the wretched details afresh. Almost immediately afterwards, the gig wheels behind us, which I could hear above the noise of the wind, seemed to me to come to a sudden standstill. "St. George has stopped," I exclaimed to Tod. "Not a bit of it," answered he; "we can no longer hear him." Almost close upon that, we passed the turning which led out of the lane towards Evesham. Not heeding anything of all this, as indeed why should he, the Squire dashed straight onwards, and in time we gained our homestead, Crabb Cot.

The first thing the Squire did, when we were all gathered round the welcome fire, blazing and crackling with wood and coal, and the stormy blasts beat on the window-panes, but no longer upon us, was to attack us for making that noise in Dip Lane, and for shouting out that it was Brook.

"It was Brook, father," said Tod. "St. George was driving him."

"Nonsense, Joe," reprimanded the Squire. "William Brook has not landed from the high seas yet. And, if he had landed, what should bring him in Dip Lane—or St. George either?"

"It was St. George," persisted Tod.

"Well, that might have been. It looked like his grey horse. Where was he coming from, I wonder?"

"Mr. St. George went to Worcester this morning, sir," interposed Thomas, who had come in with some glasses, the Squire having asked for some hot brandy-and-water. "Giles saw his man Japhet this afternoon, and he said his master had gone off in his gig to Worcester for the day."

"Then he must have picked up Brook at Worcester," said Tod, in his decisive way.

"May be so," conceded the Squire, coming round to reason. "But I don't see what they could be doing in Dip Lane."

The storm had disappeared the following morning, but the ground was white with a thin coating of snow; and in the afternoon, when we started for Timberdale to call on William Brook, the sky was blue and the sun shining. Climbing up from the Ravine and crossing the field beyond it to the high-road, we met Darbyshire, the surgeon, striding along as fast as his legs would carry him.

"You seem to be in a hurry," remarked the Squire.

"Just sent for to a sick patient over yonder," replied Darbyshire, nodding to some cottages in the distance. "Dying, the report is; supposed to have swallowed poison. Dare say it will turn out to be a case of cucumber."

He was speeding on when Tod asked whether he had seen William Brook yet. Darbyshire turned to face him, looking surprised.

"Seen Brook yet! No; how should I see him? Brook's not come, is he?"

"He got home last night. St. George drove him from Worcester in his gig," said Tod, and went on to explain that we had passed them in Dip Lane. Darbyshire was uncommonly pleased. Brook was a favourite of his.

"I am surprised that I have not seen him," he cried; "I have been about all the morning. St. George was in Worcester yesterday, I know. Wonder, though, what induced them to make a pilgrimage through Dip Lane!"

Just, you see, as the rest of us had wondered.

We went on towards Mrs. Brook's. But in passing Mr. Delorane's, Aunt Hester's head appeared above the Venetian blind of the dining-room. She began nodding cordially.

"How lively she looks," exclaimed the Squire. "Pleased that he is back, I take it. Suppose we go in?"

The front-door was standing open, and we went in unannounced. Aunt Hester, sitting then at the little work-table, making herself a cap with lace and pink ribbons, got up and tried to shake hands with all three of us at once.

"We are on our way to call on William Brook," cried the Squire, as we sat down, and Aunt Hester was taking up her work again.

"On William Brook!—why, what do you mean?" she exclaimed. "Has he come?"

"You don't mean to say you did not know it—that he has not been to see you?" cried the Squire.

"I don't know a thing about it; I did not know he had come; no one has told me," rejoined Aunt Hester. "As to his coming to see me—well, I suppose he would not feel himself at liberty to do that until Mr. Delorane gave permission. When did he arrive? I am so glad."

"And he is not much behind his time, either," observed Tod.

"Not at all behind it, to speak of, only we were impatient. The truth is, I caught somewhat of Ellin's fears," added Aunt Hester, looking at us over her spectacles, which she rarely wore higher than the end of her nose. "Ellin has had gloomy ideas about his never coming back at all; and one can't see a person perpetually sighing away in silence, without sighing a bit also for company. Did he get here this morning? What a pity Ellin is in Worcester!"

We told Aunt Hester all about it, just as we had told Darbyshire, but not quite so curtly, for she was not in a hurry to be off to a poisoned patient. She dropped her work to listen, and took off her spectacles, looking, however, uncommonly puzzled.

"What a singular thing—that you should chance to have been in Dip Lane just at the time they were!— and why should they have chosen that dreary route! But—but—"

"But what, ma'am?" cried the Squire.

"Well, I am thinking what could have been St. George's motive for concealing the news from me when he came round here last night to tell me he had left Ellin safely at Philip West's," replied she.

"Did he say nothing to you about William Brook?"

"Not a word. He said what a nasty drive home it had been in the teeth of the storm and wind, but he did not mention William Brook. He seemed tired, and did not stay above a minute or two. John was out. Oh, here is John."

Mr. Delorane, hearing our voices, I suppose, came in from the office. Aunt Hester told him the news at once—that William Brook was come home.

"I am downright glad," interrupted the lawyer emphatically. "What with one delay and another, one might have begun to think him lost: it was September, you know, that he originally announced himself for. What do you say?"—his own words having partly drowned Aunt Hester's—"St. George drove him home last night from Worcester? Drove Brook? Nonsense! Had St. George brought Brook he would have told me of it."

"But he did bring him, sir," affirmed Tod: and he went over the history once more. Mr. Delorane did not take it in.

"Are these lads playing a joke upon me, Squire?" asked he.

"Look here, Delorane. That we passed St. George in Dip Lane is a fact; I knew the cut of his gig and horse. Some one was with him; I saw that much. The boys called out that it was William Brook, and began shouting to him. Whether it was he, or not, I can't say; I had enough to do with my horses, I can tell you; they did not like the wind, Blister especially."

"It was William Brook, safe enough, sir," interposed Tod. "Do you think I don't know him? We spoke to him, and he spoke to us. Why should you doubt it?"

"Well, I suppose I can't doubt it, as you speak so positively," said Mr. Delorane. "The news took me by surprise, you see. Why on earth did St. George not tell me of it? I shall take him to task when he comes in. Any way, I am glad Brook's come. We will drink his health."

He opened what was in those days called the cellaret—and a very convenient article it was for those who drank wine as a rule—and put on the table some of the glasses that were standing on the sideboard. Then we drank health and happiness to William Brook.

"And to some one else also," cried bold Tod, winking at Aunt Hester.

"You two boys can go on to Mrs. Brook's," cried the Squire; "I shall stop here a bit. Tell William I am glad he has surmounted the perils of the treacherous seas."

"And tell him he may come to see me if he likes," added the lawyer. "I expect he did not get a note I wrote to him a few months back, or he'd have been here this morning."

Away we went to Mrs. Brook's. And the first thing that flabbergasted us (the expression was Tod's, not mine) was to be met by a denial of the servant's. Upon Tod asking to see Mr. William, she stared at us and said he was not back from his travels.

"Come in," called out Minty from the parlour; "I know your voices." She sat at the table, her paint-box before her. Minty painted very nice pieces in water-colours: the one in process was a lovely bit of scenery taken from Little Malvern. Mrs. Brook was out.

"What did I hear you saying to Ann about William—that he had come home?" she began to us, without getting up from her work—for we were too intimate to be upon any ceremony with one another. "He is not come yet. I only wish he was."

"But he is come," said Tod. "He came last night. We saw him and spoke to him."

Minty put down her camel-hair pencil then, and turned round. "What do you mean?" she asked.

"Mr. St. George drove William home from Worcester. We passed them in the gig in Dip Lane."

Minty retorted by asking whether we were not dreaming; and for a minute or two we kept at cross-purposes. She held to it that they had seen nothing of her brother; that he was not at Timberdale.

"Mamma never had a wink of sleep last night, for thinking of the dreadful gale William must be in at sea. Your fancy misled you," went on Minty, calmly touching-up the cottage in her painting—and Tod looked as if he would like to beat her.

But it did really seem that William had not come, and we took our departure. I don't think I had ever seen Tod look so puzzled.

"I wish I may be shot if I can understand this!" said he.

"Could we have been mistaken in thinking it was Brook?" I was beginning; and Tod turned upon me savagely.

"I swear it was Brook. There! And you know it as well as I, Mr. Johnny. Where can he be hiding himself? What is the meaning of it?"

It is my habit always to try to account for things that seem unaccountable; to search out reasons and fathom them; and you would be surprised at the light that will sometimes crop up. An idea flashed across me now.

"Can Brook be ill, Tod, think you?—done up with his voyage, or something—and St. George is nursing him at his house for a day or two before he shows himself to Timberdale?" And Tod thought it might be so.

Getting back to Mr. Delorane's, we found him and the Squire sitting at the table still. St. George, just come in, was standing by, hat in hand, and they were both tackling him at once.

"What do you say?" asked St. George of his master, when he found room for a word. "That I brought William Brook home here last night from Worcester! Why, what can have put such a thing into your head, sir?"

"Didn't you bring him?" cried the Squire. "Didn't you drive him home in your gig?"

"That I did not. I have not seen William Brook."

He spoke in a ready, though surprised tone, not at all like one who is shuffling with the truth, or telling a fable, and looked from one to another of his two questioners, as if not yet understanding them. The Squire pushed his spectacles to the top of his brow and stared at St. George. He did not understand, either.

"Look here, St. George: do you deny that it was you we passed in Dip Lane last night—and your grey horse—and your gig?"

"Why should I deny it?" quietly returned St. George. "I drew as close as I could to the hedge as a matter of precaution to let you go by, Squire, you were driving so quickly. And a fine shouting you greeted me with," he added, turning to Tod, with a slight laugh.

"The greeting was not intended for you; it was for William Brook," answered Tod, his voice bearing a spice of antagonism; for he thought he was being played with.

St. George was evidently at a loss yet, and stood in silence. All in a moment, his face lighted up.

"Surely," he cried impulsively, "you did not take that man in the gig for William Brook!"

"It was William Brook. Who else was it?"

"A stranger. A stranger to me and to the neighbourhood. A man to whom I gave a lift."

Tod's face presented a picture. Believing, as he did still, that it was Brook in the gig, the idea suggested by me—that St. George was concealing Brook at his house out of good-fellowship—grew stronger and stronger. But he considered that, as it had come to this, St. George ought to say so.

"Where's the use of your continuing to deny it, St. George?" he asked. "You had Brook there, and you know you had."

"But I tell you that it was not Brook," returned St. George. "Should I deny it, if it had been he? You talk like a child."

"Has Brook been away so long that we shouldn't know him, do you suppose?" retorted quick-tempered Tod. "Why! as a proof that it was Brook, he shouted back his greeting to us, taking off his hat to wave it in answer to ours. Would a strange man have done that?"

"The man did nothing of the kind," said St. George.

"Yes, he did," I said, thinking it was time I spoke. "He called back a greeting to us, and he waved his hat round and round. I should not have felt so sure it was Brook but for seeing him without his hat."

"Well, I did not see him do it," conceded St. George. "When you began to shout in passing the man seemed surprised. 'What do those people want?' he said to me; and I told you were acquaintances of mine. It never occurred to my mind, or to his either, I should imagine, but that the shouts were meant for me. If he did take off his hat in response, as you say, he must have done it, I reckon, because I did not take off mine."

"Couldn't you hear our welcome to him? Couldn't you hear us call him 'Brook'?" persisted Tod.

"I did not distinguish a single word. The wind was too high for that."

"Then we are to understand that Brook has not come back: that you did not bring him?" interposed the Squire. "Be quiet, Joe; can't you see you were mistaken? I told you you were, you know, at the time. You and Johnny are for ever taking up odd notions, Johnny especially."

"The man was a stranger to me," spoke St. George. "I overtook him trudging along the road, soon after leaving Worcester; it was between Red Hill and the turning to Whittington. He accosted me, asking which of the two roads before us would take him to Evesham. I told him which, and was about to drive on when it occurred to me that I might as well offer to give the man a lift: it was an awful evening, and that's the truth: one that nobody would, as the saying runs, turn a dog out in. He thanked me, and got up; and I drove him as far as—"

"Then that's what took you round by Dip Lane, St. George?" interrupted Mr. Delorane.

"That's what took me round by Dip Lane," acquiesced St. George, slightly smiling; "and which seems to have led to this misapprehension. But don't give my humanity more credit than it deserves. Previously to this I had been debating in my own mind whether to take the round, seeing what a journey was before me. It was about the wildest night I ever was out in, the horse could hardly make head against the wind, and I thought we might feel it less in the small and more sheltered by-ways than in the open road. Taking up the traveller decided me."

"You put him down in Dip Lane, at the turning that leads to Evesham," remarked the Squire.

"Yes, I put him down there. It was just after you passed us. He thanked me heartily, and walked on; and I drove quickly home, glad enough to reach it. Who he was, or what he was, I do not know, and did not ask."

Tod was still in a quandary; his countenance betrayed it. "Did you notice that he resembled William Brook, St. George?"

"No. It did not strike me that he resembled any one. His face was well wrapped up from the cold, and I did not get a clear view of it: I am not sure that I should know it again. I should know his voice, though," he added quickly.

Poor Aunt Hester, listening to all this in dismay, felt the disappointment keenly: the tears were stealing down her face. "And we have been drinking his health, and—and feeling so thankful that he was safely back again!" she murmured gently.

"Hang it, yes," added Mr. Delorane. "Well, well; I dare say a day or two more will bring him. I must say I thought it odd that you should not have mentioned it to me, St. George, if he had come."

"I should have thought it very odd, sir," spoke St. George.

"Will you take a glass of wine?"

"No, thank you; I have not time for it. Those deeds have to be gone over, you know, sir, before post-time," replied St. George; and he left the room.

"And if ever you two boys serve me such a trick again—bringing me over with a cock-and-bull story that people have come back from sea who haven't—I'll punish you," stuttered the Squire, too angry to speak clearly.

We went away in humility; heads down, metaphorically speaking, tails between legs. The Squire kept up the ball, firing away sarcastic reproaches hotly.

Tod never answered. The truth was, he felt angry himself. Not with the Squire, but with the affair altogether. Tod hated mystification, and the matter was mystifying him utterly. With all his heart, with all the sight of his eyes, he had believed it to be William Brook: and he could not drive the conviction away, that it was Brook, and that St. George was giving him house room.

"I don't like complications," spoke he resentfully.

"Complications!" retorted the Squire. "What complications are there in this? None. You two lads must have been thinking of William Brook, perhaps speaking of him, and so you thought you saw him. That's all about it, Joe."

The complications were not at an end. A curious addition to them was at hand. The Squire came to a halt at the turning to the Ravine, undecided whether to betake himself home at once, or to make a call first at Timberdale Court, to see Robert Ashton.

"I think we'll go there, lads," said he: "there's plenty of time. I want to ask him how that squabble about the hunting arrangements has been settled."

So we continued our way along the road, presently crossing it to take the one in which the Court was situated: a large handsome house, lying back on the right hand. Before gaining it, however, we had to pass the pretty villa rented by Mr. St. George, its stable and coach-house and dog-kennel beside it. The railway was on ahead; a train was shrieking itself at that moment into the station.

St. George's groom and man-of-all-work, Japhet, was sweeping up the leaves on the little lawn. Tod, who was in advance of us, put his arms on the gate. "Are you going to make a bonfire with them?" asked he.

"There's enough for't, sir," answered Japhet. "I never see such a wind as yesterday's," he ran on, dropping his besom to face Tod, for the man was a lazy fellow, always ready for a gossip. "I'm sure I thought it 'ud ha' blowed the trees down as well as the leaves."

"It was pretty strong," assented Tod, as I halted beside him, and the Squire walked on towards the Court. "We were out in it—coming home from Pigeon Green. There was one gust that I thought would have blown the horses right over."

"The master, he were out in it, too, a coming home from Worcester," cried Japhet, taking off his old hat to push his red hair back. "When he got in here, he said as he'd had enough on't for one journey. I should think the poor horse had too; his coat were all wet."

Tod lifted up his head, speaking impulsively. "Was your master alone, Japhet, when he got home? Had he any one with him?"

"Yes, he were all alone, sir," replied the man. "Miss Delorane were with him when he drove off in the morning, but she stayed at Worcester."

Had Tod taken a moment for thought he might not have asked the question. He had nothing of the sneak in him, and would have scorned to pump a servant about his master's movements. The answer tended to destroy his theory of Brook's being concealed here, and to uphold the account given by Mr. St. George.

Quitting the railings, we ran to catch up the Squire. And at that moment two or three railway passengers loomed into view, coming from the train. One of them was Ellin Delorane.

She came along briskly, with a buoyant step and a smiling face. The Squire dropped us a word of caution.

"Now don't go telling her of your stupid fancy about Brook, you two: it would only cause her disappointment." And with the last word we met her.

"Ah ha, Miss Ellin!" he exclaimed, taking her hands. "And so the truant's back again!"

"Yes, he is back again," she softly whispered, with a blush that was deep in colour.

The Squire did not quite catch the words. She and he were at cross-purposes. "We have but now left your house, my dear," he continued. "Your aunt does not expect you back to-day; she thought you would stay at Worcester till Saturday."

Ellin smiled shyly. "Have you seen him?" she asked in the same soft whisper.

"Seen whom, my dear?"

"Mr. Brook."

"Mr. Brook! Do you mean William Brook? He is not back, is he?"

"Yes, he is back," she answered. "I thought you might have seen him: you spoke of the return of the truant."

"Why, child, I meant you," explained the Squire. "Nobody else. Who says William Brook is back?"

"Oh, I say it," returned Ellin, her cheeks all rosy dimples. "He reached Worcester yesterday."

"And where is he now?" cried the Squire, feeling a little at sea.

"He is here, at Timberdale," answered Ellin. "Mr. St. George drove him home last night."

"There!" cried Tod with startling emphasis. "There, father, please not to disparage my sight any more."

Well, what do you think of this for another complication? It took me aback. The Squire rubbed his face, and stared.

"My dear, just let us understand how the land lies," said he, putting his hand on Ellin's shoulder. "Do you say that William Brook reached Worcester yesterday on his return, and that St. George drove him home here at night?"

"Yes," replied Ellin. "Why should you doubt it? It is true."

"Well, we thought St. George did drive him home," was the Squire's answer, staring into her face; "we passed his gig in Dip Lane and thought that it was Brook that he had with him. But St. George denies this. He says it was not Brook; that he has not seen Brook, does not know he has come home; he says the man he had with him was a stranger, to whom he was giving a lift."

Ellin looked grave for a moment; then the smiles broke out again.

"St. George must have been joking," she cried; "he cannot mean it. He happened to be at Worcester Station yesterday when Mr. Brook arrived by the Birmingham train: we suppose he then offered to drive him home. Any way, he did do it."

"But St. George denied that he did, Ellin," I said.

"He will not deny it to me, Johnny. Gregory West, returning from a visit to some client at Spetchley, met them in the gig together."

The Squire listened as a man dazed. "I can't make head or tail of it," cried he. "What does St. George mean by denying that he brought Brook? And where is Brook?"

"Has no one seen him?" questioned Ellin.

"Not a soul, apparently. Ellin, my girl," added the Squire, "we will walk back with you to your father's, and get this cleared up. Come along, boys."

So back we went to turn the tables upon St. George, Tod in a rapture of gratification. You might have thought he was treading upon eggs.

We had it out this time in Mr. Delorane's private office; the Squire walked straight into it. Not but that "having it out" must be regarded as a figure of speech, for elucidation seemed farther off than before, and the complications greater.

Mr. Delorane and his head-clerk were both bending over the same parchment when we entered. Ellin kissed her father, and turned to St. George.

"Why have you been saying that you did not drive home William Brook?" she asked as they shook hands.

"A moment, my dear; let me speak," interrupted the Squire, who never believed any one's explanation could be so lucid as his own. "Delorane, I left you just now with an apology for having brought to you a cock-and-bull story through the misleading fancies of these boys; but we have come back again to tell you the story's true. Your daughter here says that it was William Brook that St. George had in his gig. And perhaps Mr. St. George"—giving that gentleman a sharp nod—"will explain what he meant by denying it?"

"I denied it because it was not he," said Mr. St. George, not appearing to be in the least put out. "How can I tell you it was Brook when it was not Brook? If it had been—"

"You met William Brook at the Worcester railway-station yesterday afternoon," interrupted Ellin. "Mrs. James Ashton saw you there; saw the meeting. You were at the station, were you not?"

"I was at the station," readily replied St. George, "and Mrs. James Ashton may have seen me there, for all I know—I did not see her. But she certainly did not see William Brook. Or, if she did, I didn't."

"Gregory West saw you and him in your gig together later, when you were leaving Worcester," continued Ellin. "It was at the top of Red Hill."

St. George shook his head. "The person I had in my gig was a stranger. Had Gregory West come up one minute earlier he would have seen me take the man into it."

"William has come," persisted Ellin.

"I don't say he has not," returned St. George. "All I can say is that I did not know he had come and that I have not seen him."

Who was right, and who was wrong? Any faces more hopelessly puzzled than the two old gentlemen's were, as they listened to these contradictory assertions, I'd not wish to see. Nothing came of the interview; nothing but fresh mystification. Ellin declared William Brook had arrived, had been driven out of Worcester for Timberdale in St. George's gig. We felt equally certain we had passed them in Dip Lane, sitting together in the gig; but St. George denied it in toto, affirming that the person with him was a stranger.

And perhaps it may be as well if I here say a word about the routes. Evesham lay fifteen miles from Worcester; Timberdale not much more than half that distance, in a somewhat different direction, and on a different road. In going to Timberdale, if when about half-way there you quitted the high-road for by-ways you would come to Dip Lane. Traversing nearly the length of the lane, you would then come to a by-way leading from it on the other side, which would bring you on the direct road to Evesham, still far off. Failing to take this by-way leading to Evesham, you would presently quit the lane, and by dint of more by-ways would gain again the high-road and soon come to Timberdale. This is the route that Mr. St. George took that night.

We went home from Mr. Delorane's, hopelessly mystified, the Squire rubbing up his hair the wrong way; now blowing us both up for what he called our "fancies" in supposing we saw William Brook, and now veering round to the opposite opinion that we and Ellin must be alike correct in saying Brook had come.

Ellin's account was this: she passed a pleasant morning with Mary West, who was nearly always more or less of an invalid. At half-past one o'clock dinner was served; Philip West, his younger brother Gregory, who had recently joined him, and Mr. St. George coming in from the office to partake of it. Dinner over, they left the room, having no time to linger. In fact, Gregory rose from table before he had well finished. Mary West inquired what his haste was, and he replied that he was off to Spetchley; some one had been taken ill there and wanted a will made. It was Philip who ought to have gone, who had been sent for; but Philip had an hour or two's business yet to do with Mr. St. George. Mrs. West told St. George that she would have tea ready at five o'clock, that he might drink a cup before starting for home.

Later on in the afternoon, when Ellin and Mrs. West were sitting over the fire, talking of things past and present, and listening to the howling of the wind, growing more furious every hour, James Ashton's wife came in, all excitement. Her husband, in medical practice at Worcester, was the brother of Robert Ashton of Timberdale. A very nice young woman was Marianne Ashton, but given to an excited manner. Taking no notice of Mrs. West, she flew to Ellin and began dancing round her like a demented Red Indian squaw.

"What will you give me for my news, Ellin?"

"Now, Marianne!" remonstrated Mrs. West. "Do be sensible, if you can."

"Be quiet, Mary: I am sensible. Your runaway lover is come, Ellin; quite safely."

They saw by her manner, heard by her earnest tone, that it was true. William Brook had indeed come, was then in the town. Throwing off her bonnet, and remarking that she meant to remain for tea, Mrs. James Ashton sat down to tell her story soberly.

"You must know that I had to go up to the Shrub Hill Station this afternoon," began she, "to meet the Birmingham train. We expected Patty Silvester in by it; and James has been since a most unearthly hour this morning with some cross-grained patient, who must needs go and be ill at the wrong time. I went up in the brougham, and had hardly reached the platform when the train came in. There was a good deal of confusion; there always is, you know; passengers getting out and getting in. I ran about looking for Patty, and found she had not come: taken fright at the weather, I suppose. As the train cleared off, I saw a figure that seemed familiar to me; it was William Brook; and I gave a glad cry that you might have heard on the top of St. Andrew's spire. He was crossing the line with others who had alighted, a small black-leather travelling-bag in his hand. I was about to run over after him, when a porter stopped me, saying a stray engine was on the point of coming up, to take on the Malvern train. So, all I could do was to stand there, hoping he would turn his head and see me. Well: just as he reached the opposite platform, Mr. St. George stepped out of the station-master's office, and I can tell you there was some shaking of hands between the two. There's my story."

"And where is he now?"

"Oh, they are somewhere together, I suppose; on their way here perhaps," rejoined Mrs. James Ashton carelessly. "I lost sight of them: that ridiculous stray engine the man spoke of puffed up at the minute, and stopped right in front of me. When it puffed on again, leaving the way clear, both he and St. George had vanished. So I got into the brougham to bring you the news in advance, lest the sudden sight of William the deserter should cause a fainting-fit."

Ellin, unable to control herself, burst into glad tears of relief. "You don't know what a strain it has been," she said. And she sat listening for his step on the stairs. But William Brook did not come.

At five o'clock punctually the tea was brought in, and waited for some little time on the table. Presently Mr. West appeared. When they told him he was late, he replied that he had lingered in the office expecting Mr. St. George. St. George had left him some time before to go to the Shrub Hill Station, having business to see to there, and had promised to be back by tea-time. However, he was not back yet. Mr. West was very glad to hear of the arrival of William Brook, and supposed St. George was then with him.

Before the tea was quite over, Gregory West got back from Spetchley. He told them that he had met St. George just outside the town, and that he had a gentleman in his gig. He, Gregory West, who was in his brother's gig, pulled up to ask St. George whether he was not going home earlier than he had said. Yes, somewhat, St. George called back, without stopping: when he had seen what sort of a night it was going to be, he thought it best to be off as soon as he could.

"Of course it was William Brook that he had with him, Gregory!" exclaimed Mary West, forgetting that her brother-in-law had never seen William Brook.

"I cannot tell," was the only answer the young lawyer could give. "It was a stranger to me: he wore a lightish-coloured over-coat and a white comforter."

"That's he," said Mrs. James Ashton. "And he had on new tan-coloured kid gloves: I noticed them. I think St. George might have brought him here, in spite of the roughness of the night. He is jealous, Ellin."

They all laughed. But never a shadow of doubt rested on any one of their minds that St. George was driving William Brook home to Timberdale. And we, as you have heard, saw him, or thought we saw him, in Dip Lane.

III

I scarcely know how to go on with this story so as to put its complications and discrepancies of evidence clearly before you. William Brook had been daily expected to land at Liverpool from the West Indies, and to make his way at once to Timberdale by rail, viâ Birmingham and Worcester.

In the afternoon of the 19th of October, Mrs. James Ashton chanced to be at the Worcester Station when the Birmingham train came in. Amidst the passengers who alighted from it she saw William Brook, whom she had known all her life. She was not near enough to speak to him, but she watched him cross the line to the opposite platform, shake hands there with Mr. St. George, and remain talking. Subsequently, Gregory West had met St. George leaving Worcester in his gig, a gentleman sitting with him; it was therefore assumed without doubt that he was driving William Brook to Timberdale, to save him the railway journey and for companionship.

That same evening, at dusk, as we (not knowing that Brook had landed) were returning home from Pigeon Green in the large phaeton, amid a great storm of wind, and slight sleet and snow, Mrs. Todhetley sitting with the Squire in front, Tod and I behind, we passed St. George's gig in Dip Lane; and saw William Brook with him—as we believed, Tod most positively. We called out to Brook, waving our hats; Brook called back to us and waved his.

But now, Mr. St. George denied that it was Brook. He said the gentleman with him was a stranger to whom he had given a lift of three or four miles on the road, and who bore no resemblance to Brook, so far as he saw. Was it Brook, or was it not? asked every one. If it was Brook, what had become of him? The only one point that seemed to be sure in the matter was this—William Brook had not reached Timberdale.

The following, elaborated, was Mr. St. George's statement.

He, as confidential clerk, soon to be partner, of Mr. Delorane, had a good deal of business to go through that day with Philip West at Worcester, and the afternoon was well on before it was concluded. He then went up to the station at Shrub Hill to inquire after a missing packet of deeds, which had been despatched by rail from Birmingham to Mr. Delorane and as yet could not be heard of. His inquiries over, St. George was traversing the platform on his way to quit the station, when one of the passengers, who had then crossed the line from the Birmingham train, stopped him to ask if he could inform him when the next train would leave for Evesham. "Very shortly," St. George replied, speaking from memory: but even as he spoke a doubt arose in his mind. "Wait a moment," he said to the stranger; "I am not sure that I am correct"—and he drew from his pocket a time-table and consulted it. There would not be a train for Evesham for more than two hours, he found, one having just gone. The stranger remarked that it was very unfortunate; he had not wanted to wait all that time at Worcester, but to get on at once. The stranger then detained him to ask, apologizing for the trouble, and adding that it was the first time he had been in the locality, whether he could get on from Evesham to Cheltenham. St. George told him that he could, but that he could also get on to Cheltenham from Worcester direct. "Ah," remarked the stranger, "but I have to take Evesham on my way." No more passed, and St. George left him on the platform. He appeared to be a gentleman, spoke as a cultured man speaks, St. George added when questioned on these points: and his appearance and attire tallied with that given by Mrs. Ashton. St. George had not observed Mrs. James Ashton on the opposite platform; did not know she was there.

Perceiving, as he left the station, how bad the weather was getting, and what a wild night might be expected, St. George rapidly made up his mind to start for home at once, without waiting for tea at Philip West's or going back at all to the house. He made his way to the Hare-and-Hounds through the back streets, as being the nearest, ordered his gig, and set off—alone—as soon as it was ready. It was then growing dusk; snow was falling in scanty flakes mixed with sleet, and the wind was roaring and rushing like mad.

Gaining the top of Red Hill, St. George was bowling along the level road beyond it, when some wayfarer turned round just before him, put up his hand, and spoke. By the peculiar-coloured coat—a sort of slate—and white comforter, he recognized the stranger of the railway-station; he also remembered the voice. "I beg your pardon a thousand times for stopping you," he said, "but I think I perceive that the road branches off two ways yonder: will you kindly tell me which of them will take me to Evesham? there seems to be no one about on foot that I can inquire of." "That will be your way," St. George answered, pointing with his whip. "But you are not thinking of walking to Evesham to-night, are you?" he added. "It is fifteen miles off."

The stranger replied that he had made up his mind to walk, rather than wait two hours at Worcester station: and St. George was touching his horse to move on, when a thought struck him.

"I am not going the direct Evesham road, but I can give you a lift part of the way," he said. "It will not cut off any of the distance for you, but it will save your legs three or four miles." The stranger thanked him and got up at once, St. George undoing the apron to admit him. He had the same black bag with him that St. George had noticed at the station.

St. George had thus to make a detour to accommodate the stranger. He was by no means unwilling to do it; for, apart from the wish to help a fellow-creature, he believed it would be less rough in the low-lying lands. Driving along in the teeth of the furious wind, he turned off the highway and got into Dip Lane. We saw him in it, the stranger sitting with him. He drove on after we had passed, pulled up at the proper place for the man to descend, and pointed out the route. "You have a mile or two of these by-ways," he said to him, "but keep straight on and they will bring you out into the open road. Turn to your left then, and you will gain Evesham in time—and I wish you well through your walk."

Those were St. George's exact words—as he repeated them to us later. The stranger thanked him heartily, shook hands and went on his way, carrying his black bag. St. George said that before parting with the traveller, he suggested that he should go on with him to Timberdale, seeing the night was so cold and wild, put up at the Plough-and-Harrow, where he could get a comfortable bed, and go on to Evesham in the morning. But the stranger declined, and seemed impatient to get on.

He did not tell St. George who he was, or what he was; he did not tell his name, or what his business was in Worcestershire, or whether he was purposing to make a stay at Evesham, or whither he might be going when he left it: unless the question he had put to St. George, as to being able to get on to Cheltenham, might be taken for an indication of his route. In fact, he stated nothing whatever about himself; but, as St. George said, the state of the weather was against talking. It was difficult to hear each other speak; the blasts howled about their ears perpetually, and the sharp sleet stung their faces. As to his bearing the resemblance to Brook that was being talked of, St. George could only repeat that he did not perceive it; he might have been about Brook's height and size, but that was all. The voice was certainly not Brook's, not in the least like Brook's, neither was the face, so far as St. George saw of it: no idea of the kind struck him.

These were the different statements: and, reading them, you have the matter in a nutshell. Mrs. James Ashton continued to affirm that it was William Brook she saw at the station, and could not be shaken out of her belief. She and William had played together as children, they had flirted together, she was pleased to declare, as youth and maiden, and did anybody suppose she could mistake an unknown young man for him in broad daylight? An immense favourite with all the world, Marianne Ashton was fond of holding decisively to her own opinions; all her words might have begun with capital letters.

I also maintained that the young man we saw in St. George's gig in Dip Lane, and who wore a warm great-coat of rather an unusual colour, something of a grey—or a slate—or a mouse, with the white woollen comforter on his neck and the soft low-crowned hat drawn well on his brows, was William Brook. When he took off his hat to wave it to us in response, I saw (as I fully believed) that it was Brook; and I noticed his gloves. Mrs. Todhetley, who had turned her head at our words, also saw him and felt not the slightest doubt that it was he. Tod was ready to swear to it.

To combat this, we had Mr. St. George's cool, calm, decisive assertion that the man was a stranger. Of course it outweighed ours. All the probabilities lay with it; he had been in companionship with the stranger, had talked with him face to face: we had not. Besides, if it had been Brook, where was he that he had not made his way to Timberdale? So we took up the common-sense view of the matter and dismissed our own impressions as fancies that would not hold water, and looked out daily for the landing of the exile. Aunt Hester hoped he was not "lost at sea:" but she did not say it in the hearing of Ellin Delorane.

The days went on. November came in. William Brook did not appear; no tidings reached us of him. His continued non-appearance so effectually confirmed St. George's statement, that the other idea was exploded and forgotten by all reasonable minds. Possibly in one or two unreasonable ones, such as mine, say, a sort of hazy doubt might still hover. But, doubt of what? Ay, that was the question. Even Tod veered round to the enemy, said his sight must have misled him, and laid the blame on the wind. Both common sense and uncommon said Brook had but been detained in Jamaica, and might be expected in any day.

The first check to this security of expectation was wrought by a letter. A letter from New York, addressed to William Brook by his brother there, Charles. Mrs. Brook opened it. She was growing vaguely uneasy, and had already begun to ask herself why, were William detained in the West Indies, he did not write to tell her so.

And this, as it proved, was the chief question the letter was written to ask. "If," wrote Charles Brook to his brother, "if you have arrived at home—as we conclude you must have done, having seen in the papers the safe arrival of the Dart at Liverpool—how is it you have not written to say so, and to inform us how things are progressing? The uncle does not like it. 'Is William growing negligent?' he said to me yesterday."

The phrase "how things are progressing," Mrs. Brook understood to apply to the new mercantile house about to be established in London. She sent the letter by Araminta to Mr. Delorane.

"Can William have been drowned at sea?" breathed Minty.

"No, no; I don't fear that; I'm not like that silly woman, Aunt Hester, with her dreams and her fancies," said Mr. Delorane. "It seems odd, though, where he can be."

Inquiries were made at Liverpool for the list of passengers by the Dart. William Brook's name was not amongst them. Timberdale waited on. There was nothing else for it to do. Waited until a second letter came from Charles Brook. It was written to his mother this time. He asked for news of William; whether he had, or had not, arrived at home.

The next West Indian mail-packet, steaming from Southampton, carried out a letter from Mr. St. George, written to his cousin in Kingston, Jamaica, at the desire of Mr. Delorane: at the desire, it may with truth be said, of Timberdale in general. The same mail also took out a letter from Reginald Brook in London, who had been made acquainted with the trouble. Both letters were to the same purport—an inquiry as to William Brook and his movements, more particularly as to the time he had departed for home, and the vessel he had sailed in.

In six or eight weeks, which seemed to some of us like so many months, Mr. St. George received an answer. His relative, Leonard St. George, sent rather a curious story. He did not know anything of William Brook's movements himself, he wrote, and could not gain much reliable information about them. It appeared that he was to have sailed for England in the Dart, a steamer bound for Liverpool, not one of their regular passenger-packets. He was unable, however, to find any record that Brook had gone in her, and believed he had not: neither could he learn that Brook had departed by any other vessel. A friend of his told him that he feared Brook was dead. The day before the Dart went out of port, a young man, who bore out in every respect the description of Brook, was drowned in the harbour.

Comforting news! Delightfully comforting for Ellin Delorane, not to speak of Brook's people. Aunt Hester came over to Crabb Cot, and burst into tears as she told it.

But the next morning brought a turn in the tide; one less sombre, though uncertain still. Mrs. Brook, who had bedewed her pillow with salt tears, for her youngest son was very dear to her heart, received a letter from her son Reginald in London, enclosing one he had just received from the West Indies. She brought them to Mr. Delorane's office during the morning, and the Squire and I happened to be there.

"How should Reginald know anything about it?" demanded St. George, in the haughty manner he could put on when not pleased; and his countenance looked dark as he gazed across his desk at Mrs. Brook, for which I saw no occasion. Evidently he did not like having his brother's news disputed.

"Reginald wrote to Kingston by the same mail that you wrote," she said. "He received an introduction to some mercantile firm out there, and this is their answer to him."

They stated, these merchants, that they had made due inquiries according to request, and found that William Brook had secured a passage on board the Dart; but that, finding himself unable to go in her, his business in Kingston not being finished, he had, at the last moment, made over his berth and ticket to another gentleman, who found himself called upon to sail unexpectedly: and that he, Brook, had departed by the Idalia, which left two days later than the Dart and was also bound for Liverpool.

"I have ascertained here, dear mother," wrote Reginald from London, "that the Idalia made a good passage and reached Liverpool on the 18th of October. If the statement which I enclose you be correct, that William left Jamaica in her, he must have arrived in her at Liverpool, unless he died on the way. It is very strange where he can be, and what can have become of him. Of course, inquiries must now be made in Liverpool. I only wish I could go down myself, but our patients are all on my hands just now, for Dr. Croft is ill."

The first thought, flashing into the mind of Mr. Delorane, was, that the 18th of October was the eve of the day on which William Brook was said to have been seen by Mrs. James Ashton. He paused to consider, a sort of puzzled doubt on his face.

"Why, look you here," cried he quickly, "it seems as though that was Brook at Worcester Station. If he reached Liverpool on the 18th, the probabilities are that he would be at Worcester on the 19th. What do you make of it?"

We could not make anything. Mrs. Brook looked pale and distressed. The Squire, in his impulsive good-nature, offered to be the one to go, off-hand, to make the inquiries at Liverpool. St. George opposed this: he was the proper person to go, he said; but Mrs. Delorane reminded him that he could be ill spared just then, when the assizes were at hand. For the time had gone on to spring.

"I will start to-night," said the Squire, "and take Johnny with me. My time is my own. We will turn Liverpool upside down but what we find Brook—if he is to be found on earth."

That the Squire might have turned Liverpool "upside down" with the confusion of his inquiries was likely enough, only that Jack Tanerton was there, having brought his own good ship, the Rose of Delhi, into port but a few days before. Jack and William Brook had been boys together, and Jack took up the cause in warm-hearted zeal. His knowledge of the town and its shipping made our way plain before us. That is, as plain as a way can be made which seems to have neither inlet nor outlet.

The Idalia was then lying in the Liverpool docks, not long in again from the West Indies. We ascertained that William Brook had come in her the previous autumn, making the port of Liverpool on the 18th of October.

"Then nothing happened to him half-way?" cried the Squire to the second mate, a decent sort of fellow who did all he could for us. "He was not lost, or—or—anything of that sort?"

"Why no," said the mate, looking surprised. "He was all right the whole of the voyage and in first-rate spirits—a very nice young fellow altogether. The Idalia brought him home, all taut and safe, take our word for that, sir; and he went ashore with the rest, and his luggage also: of which he had but little; just a big case and the small one that was in his cabin."

All this was certain. But from the hour Brook stepped ashore, we were unable to trace anything certain about him. The hotels could not single him out in memory from other temporary sojourners. I think it was by no means a usual occurrence in those days for passing guests to give in their names. Any way, we found no record of Brook's. The railway porters remembered no more of him than the hotels—and it was hardly likely they would.

Captain Tanerton—to give Jack his title—was indefatigable; winding himself in and out of all kinds of places like a detective eel. In some marvellous way he got to learn that a gentleman whose appearance tallied with Brook's had bought some tan-coloured kid gloves and also a white comforter in a shop in Bold Street on the morning of the 19th of October. Jack took us there that we might question the people, especially the young woman who served him. She said that, while choosing the gloves, he observed that he had just come off a sea-voyage and found the weather here very chilly. He wore a lightish great-coat, a sort of slate or grey. She was setting out the window when he came in, and had to leave it to serve him; it was barely eight o'clock, and she remarked that he was shopping betimes; he replied yes, for he was going off directly by train. He bought two pair of the gloves, putting one pair of them on in the shop; he next bought a warm knitted woollen scarf, white, and put that on. She was quite certain it was the 19th of October, and told us why she could not be mistaken. And that was the last trace we could get of Brook in Liverpool.

Well, well; it is of no use to linger. We went away from Liverpool, the Squire and I, no better off than we were when we entered it. That William Brook had arrived safely by the Idalia, and that he had landed safely, appeared to be a fact indisputable: but after that time he seemed to have vanished into air. Unless, mark you, it was he who had come on to Worcester.

The most concerned of all at our ill-luck was Mr. St. George. He had treated the matter lightly when thinking Brook was only lingering over the seas; now that it was proved he returned by the Idalia, the case was different.

"I don't like it at all," he said to the Squire frankly. "People may begin to think it was really Brook I had with me that night, and ask me what I did with him."

"What could you have done with him?" dissented the Squire.

"Not much—that I see. I couldn't pack him up in a parcel to be sent back over seas, and I couldn't bury him here. I wish with all my heart it had been Brook! I won't leave a stone unturned now but what I find him," added St. George, his eyes flashing, his face flushing hotly. "Any way, I'll find the man who was with me."

St. George set to work. Making inquiries here, there, and everywhere for William Brook, personally and by advertising. But little came of it. A porter at the Worcester railway-station, who had seen the traveller talking with St. George on the platform, came forward to state that they (the gentleman and Mr. St. George) had left the station together, walking away from it side by side, down the road. St. George utterly denied this. He admitted that the other might have followed him so closely as to impart a possible appearance of their being together, but if so, he was not conscious of it. Just as he had denied shaking hands with the stranger, which Mrs. James Ashton insisted upon.

Next a lady came forward. She had travelled from Birmingham that afternoon, the 19th of October, with her little nephew and niece. In the same compartment, a first-class one, was another passenger, bearing, both in attire and person, the description told of—a very pleasant, gentlemanly young man, nice-looking, eyes dark blue. It was bitterly cold: he seemed to feel it greatly, and said he had recently come from a warmer climate. He also said that he ought to have got into Worcester by an earlier train, but had been detained in Birmingham, through missing his luggage, which he supposed must have been put out by mistake at some intermediate station. He had with him a small black hand-bag; nothing else that she saw. His great-coat was of a peculiar shade of grey; it did not look like an English-made coat: his well-fitting kid gloves were of fawn (or tan) colour, and appeared to be new. Once, when the high wind seemed to shake the carriage, he remarked with a smile that one might almost as well be at sea; upon which her little nephew said: "Have you ever been to sea, sir?" "Yes, my little lad," he answered; "I landed from it only yesterday."

The only other person to come forward was a farmer named Lockett, well known to us all. He lived on the Evesham Road, close upon the turning, or by-way, which led up from Dip Lane. On the night of the storm, the 19th of October, he went out about ten o'clock to visit a neighbour, who had met with a bad accident. In passing by this turning, a man came out of it, walking pretty sharply. He looked like a gentleman, seemed to be muffled up round the neck, and carried something in his hand; whether a black bag, or not, Mr. Lockett did not observe. "A wild night," said the farmer to him in salutation. "It is that," answered the other. He took the road to Evesham, and Mr. Lockett saw him no more.

St. George was delighted at this evidence. He could have hugged old Lockett. "I knew that the truth would be corroborated sooner or later," he said, his eyes sparkling. "That was the man I put out of my gig in Dip Lane."

"Stop a bit," cried Mr. Delorane, a doubt striking him. "If it was the same man, what had he been doing to take two or three hours to get into the Evesham Road? Did he bear any resemblance to William Brook, Lockett?—you would have known Brook."

"None at all that I saw. As to knowing Brook, or any one else, I can't answer for it on such a night as that," added the farmer after a pause. "Brook would have known me, though, I take it, daylight or dark, seeing me close to my own place, and all."

"It was the other man," affirmed St. George exultantly, "and now we will find him."

An advertisement was next inserted in the local newspapers by Mr. St. George, and also in the Times.

"Gentleman Wanted. The traveller who got out of the Birmingham train at Worcester railway-station on the 19th of last October, towards the close of the afternoon, and who spoke to a gentleman on the platform respecting the trains to Evesham and to Cheltenham, and who was subsequently overtaken a little way out of Worcester by the same gentleman and given a few miles' lift in his gig, and was put down in a cross-country lane to continue his walk to Evesham: this traveller is earnestly requested to give an address where he may be communicated with, to Alfred St. George, Esquire, Timberdale, Worcester. By doing so, he will be conferring a great favour."

For two long weeks the advertisements brought forth no reply. At the end of that time there came to Mr. St. George a post-letter, short and sweet.

"Tell me what I am wanted for.—R. W."

It was dated Post Office, Cheltenham. To the Post Office, Cheltenham, St. George, consulting with Mr. Delorane, wrote a brief explanation. That he (R. W.) had been mistaken by some people who saw him that night in the gig, for a gentleman named Brook, a native of Timberdale, who had been missing since about that time. This, as R. W. might perceive, was not pleasant for himself, St. George; and he begged R. W. to come forward and set the erroneous idea at rest, or to state where he could be seen. Expenses, if any, would be cheerfully paid.

This letter brought forth the following answer:—

"DEAR SIR,

"I regret that your courtesy to me that stormy night should have led to misapprehension. I the more regret it that I am not able to comply with your request to come forward. At present that is impossible. The truth is, I am, and have been for some months now, lying under a cloud, partly through my own credulous fault, chiefly through the designing faults of another man, and I dare not show myself. It may be many more months yet before I am cleared: that I shall be, in time, there exists no doubt, and I shall then gladly bear personal testimony to the fact that it was I myself who was with you. Meanwhile, perhaps the following statement will suffice: which I declare upon my honour to be true.

"I was hiding at Crewe, when I received a letter from a friend at Evesham, bidding me go to him without delay. I had no scruple in complying, not being known at all in Worcestershire, and I started by one of the Liverpool trains. I had a portmanteau with me containing papers principally, and this I missed on arriving at Birmingham. The looking for it caused me to lose the Worcester train, but I went on by the next. Upon getting out there, I addressed the first person I saw after crossing the line—yourself. I inquired of you when the next train would start for Evesham. Not for two hours, you told me: so I set off to walk, after getting some light refreshment. Barely had I left Worcester when, through the dusk of evening, I thought I saw that the road before me branched off two ways. I did not know which to take, and ventured to stop a gig, then bowling up behind me, to ask. As you answered me I recognized you for the gentleman to whom I had spoken at the station. You offered to take me a few miles on my road, and I got into the gig. I found that you would have to go out of your way to do this, and I expressed concern; you laughed my apologies off, saying you should probably have chosen the way in any case, as it was more sheltered. You drove me as far as your road lay, told me that after I got out of the cross-lanes my way would be a straight one, and I left you with hearty thanks—which I repeat now. I may as well tell you that I reached Evesham without mishap—in process of time. The storm was so bad, the wind so fierce, that I was fain to turn out of the lane close upon leaving you, and shelter myself for an hour or two under a hay-rick, hoping it would abate. How it was possible for mortal man to see enough of me that night in your gig to mistake me for some one else, I am at a loss to understand. I remember that carriage passing us in the narrow line, the people in it shouted out to you: it must have been they, I conclude, who mistook me, for I do not think we saw another soul. You are at full liberty to show them this letter: but I must ask you not to make it absolutely public. I have purposely elaborated its details. I repeat my sacred declaration that every word of it is true—and I heartily regret that I cannot yet testify to it personally.

"R. W."

This letter set the matter at rest. We never doubted that it was genuine, or anything but a plain narrative of absolute facts. But the one great question remained—where was William Brook?

It was not answered. The disappearance, which had been a mystery at the beginning, seemed likely to remain a mystery to the end.

Another autumn had come round. Ellin Delorane, feeble now, sat in the church-porch, the graveyard lying around her under the hot September sun, soon herself to be laid there. Chancing to take that way round from buying some figs at Salmon's for Hugh and Lena, I saw her, and dashed up the churchyard path.

"You seem to have set up a love for this lively spot, Ellin! You were sitting here the last time I passed by."

"The sun is hot yet, and I get tired, so I come across here for a rest when out this way," she answered, a sweet smile on her wan face and a hectic on her thin cheeks. "Won't you stay with me for a little while, Johnny?"

"Are you better, Ellin?" I asked, taking my place on the opposite bench, which brought my knees near to hers, for the porch was not much more than big enough for a coffin to pass through.

She gently shook her head as she glanced across at me, a steadfast look in her sad brown eyes. "Don't you see how it is, Johnny? That I shall never be better in this world?"

"Your weakness may take a turn, Ellin; it may indeed. And—he may come back yet."

"He will never come back: rely upon that," she quietly said. "He is waiting for me on the Eternal shores."

Her gaze went out afar, over the gravestones and the green meadows beyond, almost (one might fancy) into the blue skies, as if she could see those shores in the distant horizon.

"Is it well to lose hope, Eileen mavourneen?"

"The hope of his returning died out long ago," she answered. "Those dreams that visited me so strangely last year, night after night, night after night, seemed to take that from me. Perhaps they came to do it. You remember them, Johnny?"

"I cannot think, Ellin, how you could put faith in a parcel of dreams!"

"It was not in the dreams I put faith—exactly. It was in the mysterious influence—I hope I don't speak profanely—which caused me to have the dreams. A silent, undetected influence that I understood not and never grasped—but it was there. Curious dreams they were," she added, after a pause; "curious that they should have come to me. William was always lost, and I, with others, was always searching for him—and never, never found him. They lasted, Johnny, for weeks and months; and almost from the time of their first setting-in, the impression, that I should never see him again, lay latent in my heart."

"Do they visit you still?"

"No. At least, they have changed in character. Ever since the night that he seems to have been really lost, the 19th of October. How you look at me, Johnny!"

"You speak so strangely."

"The subject is strange. I was at Worcester, you know, at Mary West's, and we thought he had come. That night I had the pleasantest dream. We were no longer seeking for him; all the anxiety, the distress of that was gone. We saw him; he seemed to be with us—though yet at a distance. When I awoke, I said in my happiness, 'Ah, those sad dreams will visit me no more, now he is found.' I thought he was, you see. Since then, though the dreams continue, he is never lost in them. I see him always; we are often talking, though we are never very close together. I will be indoors, perhaps, and he outside in the garden; or maybe I am toiling up a steep hill and he stands higher up. I seem to be always going towards him and he to be waiting for me. And though I never quite reach him, they are happy dreams. It will not be very long first now."

I knew what she meant—and had nothing to say to it.

"Perhaps it may be as well, Johnny," she went on in speculative thought. "God does all things for the best."

"Perhaps what may be as well?"

"That he should never have come back to marry me. I do not suppose I should have lived long in any case; I am too much like mamma. And to have been left a widower—perhaps—no, it is best as it is."

"You don't give yourself a chance of getting better, Ellin—cherishing these gloomy views."

"Gloomy! They are not gloomy. I am as happy as I can be. I often picture to myself the glories of the world I am hastening to; the lovely flowers, the trees that overshadow the banks of the pure crystal river, whose leaves are for the healing of the nations, and the beautiful golden light shed around us by God and the Lamb. Oh, Johnny, what a rest it will be after the weary sorrow here—and the weakness—and the pain!"

"But you should not wish to leave us before your time."

"I do not wish it; it is God who is taking me. I think if I had a wish it would be to stay here as long as papa stays. For I know what my death will be to him. And what it will be to you all," she generously added, holding out her hands to me, as the tears filled her eyes.

I held them for a minute in mine. Ellin took up her parasol, preparatory to moving away; but laid it down again.

"Johnny, tell me—I have often thought I should like to ask you—what do you think could have become of William? Have you ever picked up an idea, however faint, of anything that could tend to solve the mystery?"

It was a hard question to answer, and she saw my hesitation.

"I cannot admit that I have, Ellin. When looking at the affair in one light, I whisper to myself, 'It might have been this way;' when looking at it in another, I say, 'It might have been that.' Difficulties and contradictions encompass it on all sides. One impediment to elucidation was the length of time that elapsed before we began the search in earnest. Had we known from the first that he was really lost, and gone to work then, we might have had a better chance."

Ellin nodded assent. "Marianne Ashton still maintains that it was William she saw that day at the railway-station."

"I know she does. She always will maintain it."

"Has it ever struck you, Johnny, in how rather remarkable a way any proof that it was he, or not he, seems to have been withheld?"

"Well, we could not get at any positive proof, one way or the other."

"But I mean that proof seems to have been withheld," repeated Ellin. "Take, to begin with, the traveller's luggage: but for its being lost (and we do not know that it was ever found), the name, sure to have been on it, would have told whether its owner was William Brook, or not. Then take Marianne Ashton: had she gained the platform but a few seconds earlier, she would have met the traveller face to face, avoiding all possibility of mistake either way. Next take the meeting of the two gigs that evening when Gregory West was returning from Spetchley. Gregory, a stranger to Worcester until recently, did not know William Brook; but had Philip West himself gone to Spetchley—as he ought to have done—he would have known him. Again, had Philip's groom, Brian, been there, he would have known him: he comes from this neighbourhood, you know. Brian was going with the gig that afternoon, but just as it was starting Philip got a message from a client living at Lower Wick, and he had to send Brian with the answer, so Gregory went alone. You must see how very near proof was in all these moments, yet it was withheld."

Of course I saw it. And there was yet another instance: Had the Squire only pulled up when we passed the gig in Dip Lane, instead of driving on like the wind, we should have had proof that it was, or was not, Brook.

"If it was he," breathed Ellin, "it must have been that night he died. He would not, else, keep away from Timberdale."

My voice dropped to a lower key than hers. "Ellin! Do you really think it was he with St. George?"

"Oh, I cannot say that. If any such thought intrudes itself, I drive it away. I do not like St. George, but I would not be unjust to him."

"I thought St. George was one of your prime favourites."

"He was never that. He used to be very kind to me, especially after William went away, and I liked him for it. But latterly I have taken a most unreasonable dislike to him—and really without any justifiable cause. He worries me—but it is not that."

"Worries you!"

"In pressing me to be his wife," she sighed. "Of course I ought to be grateful: he tells me, he tells papa, that with a new life and new scenes, which he would carry me to, my health might be re-established. Poor papa! Only the other day he said to me, 'My dear, don't you think you might bring yourself to try it,' and I was so silly as to burst into tears. The tears came into papa's eyes too, and he promised never to suggest it to me again."

The tears were trickling down her cheeks, now as she spoke. "What a world of crosses and contradiction it is!" she cried, smiling through them as she rose. "And, Johnny, all this is between ourselves, remember."

Yes, it was between ourselves. We strolled across the churchyard to a tomb that stood in a corner facing the western sun. It was of white marble, aromatic shrubs encircling it within ornamental railings, and an inscription on it to her who lay beneath—"Maria, the beloved wife of John Delorane."

Ellin lingered on through the frosts of winter. Except that she grew thinner and weaker and her cheeks brighter, there really did not seem to be much the matter. Darbyshire saw her every day, other medical men occasionally, but they could not save her. When the snowdrops were peeping from the ground, and the violets nestled in their mossy shelters, and the trees and hedges began to show signs of budding, tokens of the renewal of life after the death of winter, Ellin passed away to that other life, where there is no death and the flowers bloom for ever. And another inscription was added to the white tombstone in the churchyard—"Ellin Maria, the only child of John and Maria Delorane."

"You should have seen St. George at the funeral," said Tom Coney to us, as we turned aside after church one hot summer's day to look at the new name on grave, for we were away from Crabb Cot when she died. "His face was green; yes, green—hold your tongue, Johnny!—green, not yellow; and his eyes had the queerest look. You were right, Todhetley; you used to say, you know, that St. George was wild after poor Ellin."

"Positive of it," affirmed Tod.

"And he can't bear the place now she's gone out of it," continued Tom Coney. "Report says that he means to throw up his post and his prospects, and run away for good."

"Not likely," dissented Tod, tossing his head. "A strong man like St. George does not die of love nowadays, or put himself out of good things, either. You have been reading romances, Coney."

But Tom Coney was right. When the summer was on the wane St. George bade a final adieu to Timberdale. And if it was his love for Ellin, or her death, that drove him away, he made no mention of it. He told Timberdale that he was growing tired of work and meant to travel. As he had a good income, Timberdale agreed that it was only natural he should grow tired of work and want to travel. So he said adieu, and departed: and Mr. Delorane speedily engaged another head-clerk in his place, who was to become his partner later.

St. George wrote to Sir. Delorane from Jamaica, to which place he steamed first, to take a look at his cousins. The letter contained a few words about William Brook. St. George had been instituting inquiries, and he said that, by what he could learn, it was certainly William Brook who was drowned in Kingston harbour the day before he ought to have sailed for England in the Dart. He, St. George, felt perfectly assured of this fact, and also that if any man had sailed in the Idalia under Brook's name, it must have been an impostor who had nefariously substituted himself. St. George added that he was going "farther afield," possibly to California: he would write again from thence if he arrived without mishap.

No other letter ever came from him. So whether the sea swallowed him up, as, according to his report, it had swallowed his rival, none could tell. But it would take better evidence than that, to convince us William Brook had not come home in the Idalia.

And that is all I have to tell. I know you will deem it most unsatisfactory. Was it William Brook in the gig, or was it not? We found no trace of him after that stormy night: we have found none to this day. And, whether that was he, or was not he, what became of him? Questions never, as I believe, to be solved in this life.

There was a peculiar absence of proof every way, as Ellin remarked; nothing but doubt on all sides. Going over the matter with Darbyshire the other evening, when, as I have already told you, he suggested that I should relate it, we could not, either of us, see daylight through it, any more than we saw it at the time of its occurrence.

There was the certainty (yes, I say so) that Brook landed at Liverpool the evening of the 18th of October; he would no doubt start for home the morning of the 19th, by rail, which would take him through Birmingham to Worcester; there was also what the shopwoman in Bold Street said, though hers might be called negative testimony, as well as the lady's in the train. There was Mrs. James Ashton's positive belief that she saw him arrive that afternoon at Worcester by the Birmingham train, shake hands with St. George and talk with him: and there was our recognition of him an hour or two later in St. George's gig in Dip Lane—

"Hold there, Johnny," cried Darbyshire, taking his long clay pipe from his mouth to interrupt me as I went over the items. "You should say supposed recognition."

"Yes, of course. Well, all that points to its having been Brook: you must see that, Mr. Darbyshire. But, if it was in truth he, there's a great deal that seems inexplicable. Why did he set off to walk from Worcester to Timberdale—and on such a night!—why not have gone on by rail? It is incredible."

"Nay, lad, we are told he—that is, the traveller—set off to walk to Evesham. St. George says he put him down in Dip Lane; and Lockett, you know, saw somebody, that seems to answer the description, turn from the lanes into the Evesham road."

I was silent, thinking out my thoughts. Or, rather, not daring to think them out. Darbyshire put his pipe in the fender and went on.

"If it was Brook and no stranger that St. George met at Worcester Station, the only possible theory I can form on that point is this, Johnny: that St. George then proposed to drive him home. He may have said to him, 'You walk on, and I will get my gig and overtake you directly:' it is a lame theory, you may say, lad, but it is the only one I can discern, and I have thought of the matter more than you suppose. St. George started for home earlier than he had meant to start, and this may have been the reason: though he says it was because he saw it was going to be so wild a night. Why they should not have gone in company to the Hare-and-Hounds, and started thence, in the gig together, is another question."

"Unless Brook, being done up, wished not to show himself at Worcester that day—to get on at once to Timberdale."

Darbyshire nodded: the thought, I am sure, was not strange to him. "The most weighty question of all remains yet, lad: If St. George took up Brook in his gig, what did he do with him? He would not want to be put down in Dip Lane to walk to Evesham."

He caught up his churchwarden pipe, relighted it at the fire, and puffed away in silence. Presently I spoke again.

"Mr. Darbyshire, I do not like St. George. I never did. You may not believe me, perhaps, but the first time I ever saw his face—I was a little fellow—I drew back startled. There was something in its expression which frightened me."

"One of your unreasonable dislikes, Johnny?"

"Are they unreasonable? But I have not taken many such dislikes in my life as that one was. Perhaps I might say any such."

"St. George was liked by most people."

"I know he was. Any way, my dislike remained with me. I never spoke of it; no, not even to Tod."

"Liking him or disliking him has nothing to do with the main question—what became of Brook. There were the letters too, sent by the traveller in answer to St. George's advertisements."

"Yes, there were the letters. But—did it ever occur to you to notice that not one word was said in those letters, or one new fact given, that we had not heard before? They bore out St. George's statement, but they afforded no proof that his statement was true."

"That is, Mr. Johnny, you would insinuate, putting it genteelly, that St. George fabricated the answers himself."

"No, not that he did, only that there was nothing in the letters to render it impossible that he did."

"After having fabricated the pretty little tale that it was a stranger he picked up, and what the stranger said to him, and all the rest of it, eh, Johnny?"

"Well"—I hesitated—"as to the letters, it seemed to me to be an unaccountable thing that the traveller could not let even one person see him in private, to hear his personal testimony: say Mr. Delorane, or a member of the Brook family. The Squire went hot over it: he asked St. George whether the fellow thought men of honour carried handcuffs in their pockets. Again, the stranger said he should be at liberty to come forward later, but he never has come."

Darbyshire smoked on. "I'd give this full of gold," he broke the silence with, touching the big bowl of the clay pipe, "to know where Brook vanished to."

My restless fingers had strayed to his old leaden tobacco jar, on the table by me, pressing down its heavy lid and lifting it again. When I next spoke he might have thought the words came out of the tobacco, they were so low.

"Do you think St. George had a grudge against Brook, Mr. Darbyshire?—that he wished him out of the way?"

Darbyshire gave me a look through the wreathing smoke.

"Speak out, lad. What have you on your mind?"

"St. George said, you know, that he stopped the gig in Dip Lane at the turning which would lead to Evesham, for Brook—I mean the traveller—to get out. But I thought I heard it stop before that. I was almost sure of it."

"Stop where?"

"Just about opposite the gap in the hedge; hardly even quite as far as that. We had not reached the turning to Evesham ourselves when I heard this. The gig seemed to come to a sudden standstill. I said so to Tod at the time."

"Well?"

"Why should he have stopped just at the gap?"

"How can I tell, lad?"

"I suppose he could not have damaged Brook? Struck him a blow to stun him—or—or anything of that?"

"And if he had? If he (let us put it so) killed him, Johnny, what did he do with—what was left of him? What could he do with it?"

Darbyshire paused in his smoking. I played unconsciously with the jar. He was looking at me, waiting to be answered.

"I suppose—if that pond had been dragged—Dip Pond—if it were to be dragged now—that—that—nothing would be found—"

"Hush, lad," struck in Darbyshire, all hastily. "Walls have ears, people tell us: and we must not even whisper grave charges without sufficient grounds; grounds that we could substantiate."

True: and of course he did right to stop me.

But we cannot stay rebellious thought: and no end of gruesome ideas connected with that night in Dip Lane steal creepingly at times into my mind. If I am not mistaken they steal also into Darbyshire's.

All the same they may be but phantoms of the imagination, and St. George may have been a truthful, an innocent man. You must decide for yourselves, if you can, on which side the weight of evidence seems to lie. I have told you the story as it happened, and I cannot clear up for you what has never yet been cleared for Timberdale. It remains an unsolved mystery.

SANDSTONE TORR

I

What I am going to tell of took place before my time. But we shall get down to that by-and-by, for I had a good deal to do with the upshot when it came.

About a mile from the Manor, on the way to the Court (which at that time belonged to my father) stood a very old house built of grey stone, and called Sandstone Torr: "Torr," as every one knew, being a corruption of Tower. It was in a rather wild and solitary spot, much shut in by trees. A narrow lane led to it from the highway, the only road by which a carriage could get up to it: but in taking the field way between the Court and Dyke Manor, over stiles and across a running rivulet or two, you had to pass it close. Sandstone Torr was a rambling, high, and ugly old building, once belonging to the Druids, or some ancient race of that kind, and said to have been mighty and important in its day. The points chiefly remarkable about it now were its age, its lonesome grey walls, covered with lichen, and an amazingly lofty tower, that rose up from the middle of the house and went tapering off at the top like an aspiring sugar loaf.

Sandstone Torr belonged to the Radcliffes. Its occupier was Paul Radcliffe, who had inherited it from his father. He was a rather unsociable man, and seemed to find his sole occupation in farming what little land lay around the Torr and belonged to it. He might have mixed with the gentry of the county, as far as descent went, for the Radcliffes could trace themselves back for ages—up to the Druids, I think, the same as the house: but he did not appear to care about it. Who his wife had been no one knew. He brought her home one day from London, and she kept herself as close as he did, or closer. She was dead now, and old Radcliffe lived in the Torr with his only son, and a man and maid servant.

Well, in those days there came to stay at Dyke Manor a clergyman, named Elliot, with his daughter Selina. Squire Todhetley was a youngish man then, and he and his mother lived at the Manor together. Mr. Elliot was out of health. He had been overworked for the past twenty years in the poor London parish of which he was curate; and old Mrs. Todhetley asked them to come down for a bit of a change. Change indeed it brought to Mr. Elliot. He died there. His illness, whatever it was, took a sudden and rapid stride onwards, and before he had been at Dyke Manor three weeks he was dead.

Selina Elliot—we have heard the Squire say it many a time—was the sweetest-looking girl that ever the sun shone on. She was homeless now. The best prospect before her was that of going out as governess. The Elliots were of good descent, and Selina had been thoroughly well educated; but of money she had just none. Old Mrs. Todhetley bid her not be in any hurry; she was welcome to stay as long as she liked at Dyke Manor. So Selina stayed. It was summer weather then, and she was out and about in the open air all day long: a slight girl, in deep mourning, with a shrinking air that was natural to her.

One afternoon she came in, her bright face all aglow, and her shy eyes eager. Soft brown eyes they were, that had always a sadness in them. I—a little shaver—can remember that, when I knew her in later years. As she sat down on the stool at Mrs. Todhetley's feet, she took off her black straw hat, and began to play nervously with its crape ends.

"My dear, you seem to be in a heat," said Mrs. Todhetley; a stout old lady, who sat all day long in her easy-chair.

"Yes, I ran home fast," said Selina.

"Home from whence? Where have you been?"

"I was—near the Torr," replied Selina, with hesitation.

"Near the Torr, child! That's a long way for you to go strolling alone."

"The wild roses in the hedges there are so lovely," pleaded Selina. "That's why I took to go there at first."

"Took to go there!" repeated the old lady, thinking it an odd phrase. "Do you see anything of the Torr people? I hope you've not been making intimate with young Stephen Radcliffe," she added, a thought darting into her mind.

"Stephen? that's the son. No, I never saw him. I think he is away from home."

"That's well. He is by all accounts but a churlish lout of a fellow."

Selina Elliot bent her timid face over the hat, smoothing its ribbons with her restless fingers. She was evidently ill at ease. Glancing up presently, she saw the old lady was shutting her eyes for a doze: and that hastened her communication.

"I—I want to tell you something, please, ma'am. But—I don't like to begin." And, with that, Selina burst into unexpected tears, and the alarmed old lady looked up.

"Why, what ails you, child? Are you hurt? Has a wasp been at you?"

"Oh no," said Selina, brushing the tears away with fingers that trembled all over. "I—if you please—I think I am going to live at the Torr."

The old lady wondered whether Selina was dreaming. "At the Torr!" said she. "There are no children at the Torr. They don't want a governess at the Torr."

"I am going there to be with Mr. Radcliffe," spoke Selina, in her throat, as if she meant to choke.

"To be with old Radcliffe! Why, the child's gone cranky! Paul Radcliffe don't need a governess."

"He wants to marry me."

"Mercy upon us!" cried the old lady, lifting both hands in her amazement. And Selina burst into tears again.

Yes, it was true. Paul Radcliffe, who was fifty years of age, if a day, and had a son over twenty, had been proposing marriage to that bright young girl! They had met in the fields often, it turned out, and Mr. Radcliffe had been making his hay while the sun shone. Every one went on at her.

"It would be better to go into a prison than into that gloomy Sandstone Torr—a young girl like you, Selina," said Mrs. Todhetley. "It would be sheer madness."

"Why, you'd never go and sacrifice yourself to that old man!" cried the Squire, who was just as outspoken and impulsive and good-hearted then as in these latter years. "He ought to be ashamed of himself. It would be like June and December."

But all they said was of no use in the end. It was not that Selina, poor girl, was in love with Mr. Radcliffe—one could as well have fancied her in love with the grizzly old bear, just then exhibiting himself at Church Dykely in a travelling caravan. But it was her position. Without money, without a home, without a resource of any kind for the future, save that of teaching for her bread, the prospect of becoming mistress of Sandstone Torr was something fascinating.

"I do so dislike the thought of spending my whole life in teaching!" she pleaded in apology, the bitter tears streaming down her face. "You cannot tell what it is to feel dependent."

"I'd rather sweep chimneys than marry Paul Radcliffe if I were a pretty young girl like you," stormed the old lady.

"Since papa died you don't know what the feeling has been," sobbed Selina. "Many a night have I lain awake with the misery of knowing that I had no claim to a place in the wide world."

"I am sure you are welcome to stay here," said the Squire.

"Yes; as long as I am here myself," added his mother. "After that—well, I suppose it wouldn't be proper for you to stay."

"You are all kindness; I shall never meet with such friends again; and I know that I am welcome to stay as long as I like," she answered in the saddest of tones. "But the time of my departure must come sometime; and though the world lies before me, there is no refuge for me in it. It is very good of Mr. Radcliffe to offer to make me his wife and to give me a home at the Torr."

"Oh, is it, though!" retorted the Squire. "Trust him for knowing on which side his bread's buttered."

"He is of good descent; he has a large income—"

"Six hundred a-year," interrupted the Squire, slightingly.

"Yes, I am aware that it cannot appear much to you," she meekly said; "but to me it seems unbounded. And that is apart from the house and land."

"The house and land must both go to Stephen."

"Mr. Radcliffe told me that."

"As to the land, it's only a few acres; nothing to speak of," went on the Squire. "I'd as soon boast of my gooseberry bushes. And he can leave all his money to Stephen if he likes. In my opinion, the chances are that he will."

"He says he shall always behave fairly by me," spoke poor Selina.

"Why, you'd have a step-son older than yourself, Selina!" put in the old lady. "And I don't like him—that Stephen Radcliffe. He's no better than he should be. I saw him one day whipping a poor calf almost to death."

Well, they said all they could against it; ten thousand times more than is written down here. Selina wavered: she was not an obstinate girl, but tractable as you please. Only—she had no homestead on the face of the earth, and Mr. Radcliffe offered her one. He did not possess youth, it is true; he had never been handsome: but he was of irreproachable descent—and Selina had a little corner of ambition in her heart; and, above all, he had a fairly good income.

It was rather curious that the dread of this girl's life, the one dread above all other dreads, was that of poverty. In the earlier days of her parents, when she was a little girl and her mother was alive, and the parson's pay was just seventy pounds a-year, they had had such a terrible struggle with poverty that a horror of it was implanted in the child's mind for ever. Her mother died of it. She had become weaker and weaker, and perished slowly away for the want of those comforts that money alone could have bought. Mr. Elliot's stipend was increased later: but the fear of poverty never left Selina: and now, by his death, she was again brought face to face with it. That swayed her; and her choice was made.

Old Mrs. Todhetley and the Squire protested that they washed their hands of the marriage. But they could only wash them gingerly, and, so to say, in private. For, after all, excepting that Paul Radcliffe was more than old enough to be Selina's father, and had grizzly hair and a grown-up son, there was not so much to be said against it. She would be Mrs. Radcliffe of Sandstone Torr, and might take her standing in the county.

Sandstone Torr, dull and gloomy, and buried amidst its trees, was enough to put a lively man in mind of a prison. You entered it by a sort of closed-in porch, the outer door of which was always chained back in the daytime. The inner door opened into a long, narrow passage, and that again to a circular stone hall with a heavy ceiling, just like a large dark watch-box. Four or five doors led off from it to different passages and rooms. This same kind of round place was on all the landings, shut in just as the hall was, and with no light, except what might be afforded from the doors of the passages or rooms leading to it. It was the foundation of the tower, and the house was built round it. All the walls were of immense thickness: the rooms were low, and had beams running across most of them. But the rooms were many in number, and the place altogether had a massive, grand air, telling of its past importance. It had one senseless point in it—there was no entrance to the tower. The tower had neither staircase nor door of access. People said what a grand view might be obtained if you could only get to the top of it, or even get up to look through the small slits of windows in its walls. But the builder had forgotten the staircase, and there it ended.

Mr. Radcliffe took his wife straight home from the church-door. Selina had never before been inside the Torr, and the gloominess of its aspect struck upon her unpleasantly. Leading her down the long passage into the circular hall, he opened one of its doors, and she found herself in a sitting-room. The furniture was good but heavy; the Turkey carpet was nearly colourless with age, but soft to the feet; the window looked out only upon trees. A man-servant, who had admitted them, followed them in, asking his master if he had any orders.

"Send Holt here," said Mr. Radcliffe. "This is the parlour, Selina."

A thin, respectable woman of middle age made her appearance. She looked with curiosity at the young lady her master had brought in: at her wedding-dress of grey silk, at the pretty face blushing under the white straw bonnet.

"Mrs. Radcliffe, Holt. Show your mistress her rooms."

The woman curtsied, and led the way through another passage to the stairs; and into a bedroom and sitting-room above, that opened into one another.

"I've aired 'em well, ma'am," were the first words she said. "They've never been used since the late mistress's time, for master has slept in a little chamber near Master Stephen's. But he's coming back here now."

"Is this the drawing-room?" asked Selina, observing that the furniture, though faded, was prettier and lighter than that in the room downstairs.

"Dear no, ma'am! The drawing-room is below and on t'other side of the house entirely. It's never gone into from one month's end to another. Master and Mr. Stephen uses nothing but the parlour. We call this the Pine Room."

"The Pine Room!" echoed Selina. "Why?"

"Because it looks out on them pines, I suppose," replied Holt.

Selina looked from the window, and saw a row of dark pines waving before the higher trees behind them. The view beyond was completely shut in by these trees; they were very close to the house: it almost seemed as though a long arm might have touched them from where she stood. Anything more dull than this aspect could not well be found. Selina leaned from the window to look below: and saw a gravel-path with some grass on either side it, but no flowers.

It was a week later. Mr. Radcliffe sat in the parlour, busily examining some samples of new wheat, when there came a loud ring at the outer bell, and presently Stephen Radcliffe walked in. The father and son resembled each other. Both were tall and strongly built, and had the same rugged cast of features: men of few words and ungenial manners. But while Mr. Radcliffe's face was not an unpleasing one, Stephen's had a most sullen—some might have said evil—expression. In his eyes there was a slight cast, and his dull brown hair was never tidy. Some time before this, when the father and son had a quarrel, Stephen had gone off into Cornwall to stay with his mother's relations. This was his first appearance back again.

"Is it you, Stephen!" cried Mr. Radcliffe, without offering to shake hands: for the house was never given to ceremony.

"Yes, it's me," replied Stephen, who generally talked more like a boor than a gentleman, particularly in his angry moods. "It's about time I came home, I think, when such a notice as this appears in the public papers."

He took a newspaper from his pocket, and laid it before his father, pointing with his fore-finger to an announcement. It was that of Mr. Radcliffe's marriage.

"Well?" said Mr. Radcliffe.

"Is that true or a hoax?"

"True."

Stephen caught the paper up again, tore it in two, and flung it across the room.

"What the devil made you go and do such a thing as that?"

"Softly, Ste. Keep a civil tongue in your head. I am my own master."

"At your age!" growled Stephen. "There's no fool like an old fool."

"If you don't like it, you can go back to where you came from," said Mr. Radcliffe quietly, turning the wheat from one of the sample-bags out on the table.

Stephen went to the window, and stood there looking at that agreeable prospect beyond—the trees—his hands in his pockets, his back to his father, and swearing to himself awfully. It would not do to quarrel implacably with the old man, for his money was at his own disposal: and, if incensed too greatly, he might possibly take the extreme step of leaving it away from him. But Stephen Radcliffe's heart was good to turn his father out of doors there and then, and appropriate the money to himself at once, if he only had the power. "No fool like an old fool!" he again muttered. "Where is the cat?"

"Where's who?" cried Mr. Radcliffe, looking up from his wheat.

"The woman you've gone and made yourself a world's spectacle with."

"Ste, my lad, this won't do. Keep a fair tongue in your head, as I bid you; or go where you may make it a foul one. For by Heaven!"—and Mr. Radcliffe's passion broke out and he rose from his seat menacingly—"I'll not tolerate this."

Stephen hardly ever remembered his father to have shown passion before. He did not like it. They had gone on so very quietly together, until that quarrel just spoken of, and Stephen had had his own way, and ruled, so to say, in all things, for his father was easy, that this outbreak was something new. It might not do to give further provocation then.

He was standing as before in sullen silence, his hands in his trousers' pockets and the skirts of his short brown velveteen coat thrown back, and Mr. Radcliffe had sat down to the bags again, when the door opened, and some one came in. Stephen turned. He saw a pretty young girl in black, with some books in her delicate hands. Just for an instant he wondered who the young girl could be: and then the thought flashed over him that "the woman" his father had married might have a grown-up daughter. Selina had been unpacking her trunks upstairs, and arranging her things in the drawers and closets. She hesitated on her way to the book-case when she saw the stranger.

"My son Stephen, Selina. Ste, Mrs. Radcliffe."

Stephen Radcliffe for a moment forgot his sullenness and his temper. He did nothing but stare. Was his father playing a joke on him? He had pictured the new wife (though he knew not why) as a woman of mature age: this was a child. As she timidly held out the only hand she could extricate from the load of books, he saw the wedding-ring on her finger. Meeting her hand ungraciously and speaking never a word, he turned to the window again. Selina put the books down, to be disposed in their shelves later, and quitted the room.

"This is even worse folly than I dreamed of," began Stephen, facing his father. "She's nothing but a child."

"She is close upon twenty."

"Why, there may be children!" broadly roared out Stephen. "You must have been mad when you did such a deed as this."

"Mad or sane, it's done, Stephen. And I should do it again to-morrow without asking your leave. Understand that."

Yes, it was done. Rattling the silver in his pockets, Stephen Radcliffe felt that, and that there was no undoing it. Here was this young step-mother planted down at the Torr; and if he and she could not hit it off together, it was he who would have to walk out of the house. For full five minutes Stephen mentally rehearsed all the oaths he remembered. Presently he spoke.

"It was a fair trick, wasn't it, that you should forbid my marrying, and go and do the same thing yourself!"

"I did not object to your marrying, Ste: I objected to the girl. Gibbon's daughter is not one to match with you. You are a Radcliffe."

Stephen scoffed. Nobody had ever been able to beat into him any sense of self-importance. Pride of birth, pride in his family were elements unknown to Stephen's nature. He had a great love of money to make up for it.

"What's good for the goose is good for the gander," he retorted, plunging into a communication he had resolved to make. "You have been taking a wife on your score, and I have taken one on mine."

Mr. Radcliffe looked keenly at Stephen. "You have married Gibbon's girl?"

"I have."

"When? Where?"

"In Cornwall. She followed me there."

The elder man felt himself in a dilemma. He did care for his son, and he resented this alliance bitterly for Stephen's sake. Gibbon was gamekeeper to Sir Peter Chanasse, and had formerly been outdoor servant at the Torr; and this daughter of his, Rebecca—or Becca, as she was commonly called—was a girl quite beneath Stephen. Neither was she a lovable young woman in herself; but hard, and sly, and bony. How it was that Stephen had fancied her, Mr. Radcliffe could not understand. But having stolen a march on Stephen himself, in regard to his own marriage, he did not feel much at liberty to resent Stephen's. It was done, too—as he had just observed of his own—and it could not be undone.

"Well, Stephen, I am more vexed for your sake than I care to say. It strikes me you will live to repent it."

"That's my look out," replied Stephen. "I am going to bring her home."

"Home! Where?"

"Here."

Mr. Radcliffe was silent; perhaps the assertion startled him.

"I don't want Gibbon's daughter here, Stephen. There's no room for her."

"Plenty of room, and to spare."

So there was; for the old house was large. But Mr. Radcliffe had not been thinking of space.

"I can't have her. There! You may make your home where you like."

"This is my home," said Stephen.

"And it may be still, if you like. But it's not hers. Two women in a house, each wanting to be mistress, wouldn't do. Now no noise, Ste, I won't have Gibbon's girl here. I've not been used to consort with people who have been my servants."

It is one thing to make a resolution, and another to keep it. Before twelve months had gone by, Mr. Radcliffe's firmly spoken words had come to naught; and Stephen had brought his wife into the Torr and two babies—for Mrs. Stephen had presented him with two at once. Selina was upstairs then with an infant of her own, and very ill. The world thought she was going to die.

The opportunity was a grand one for Madam Becca, and she seized upon it. When Selina came about again, after months spent in confinement, she found, so to say, no place for her. Becca was in her place; mistress, and ruler, and all. Stephen behaved to her like the lout he was; Becca, a formidable woman of towering height, alternately snapped at, and ignored her. Old Radcliffe did not interfere: he seemed not to see that anything was amiss. Poor Selina could only sit up in that apartment that Holt had called the Pine Room, and let her tears fall on her baby-boy, and whisper all her griefs into his unconscious ear. She was refined and timid and shrinking: but once she spoke to her husband.

"Treat you with contempt?—don't let you have any will of your own?—thwart you in all ways?" he repeated. "Who says it, Selina?"

"Oh, it is so; you may see that it is, if you only will notice," she said, looking up at him imploringly through her tears.

"I'll speak to Stephen. I knew there'd be a fuss if that Becca came here. But you are not as strong to bustle about as she is, Selina: let her take the brunt of the management off you. What does it matter?"

What did it matter?—that was Mr. Radcliffe's chief opinion on the point: and had it been only a question of management it would not have mattered. He spoke to Stephen, telling him that he and his wife must make things pleasanter for Mrs. Radcliffe, than, as it seemed, they were doing. The consequence was, that Stephen and Becca took a convenient occasion of attacking Selina; calling her a sneak, a tell-tale, and a wolf in sheep's clothing, and pretty nearly frightening her into another spell of illness.

From that time Selina had no spirit to retaliate. She took all that was put upon her—and it was a great deal—and bore it in silence and patience. She saw that her marriage, taking one thing with another, had turned out to be the mistake her friends had foretold that it would be. Mr. Radcliffe, growing by degrees into a state of apathy as he got older, was completely under the dominion of Stephen. He did not mean to be unkind to his wife: he just perceived nothing; he was indifferent to all that passed around him: had they set fire to Selina's petticoats before his eyes, he'd hardly have seen the blaze. Now and again Selina would try to make friends with Holt: but Holt, though never uncivil, had a way of throwing her off. And so, she lived on, a cowed, broken-spirited woman, eating away her heart in silence. Selina Radcliffe had found out that there were worse evils in the world than poverty.

She might have died then but for her boy. You never saw a nicer little fellow than he—that Francis Radcliffe. A bright, tractable, loving boy; with laughing blue eyes, and fair curls falling back from his pretty face. Mr. and Mrs. Stephen hated him. Their children, Tom and Lizzy, pinched and throttled him: but the lad took it all in good part, and had the sweetest temper imaginable. He loved his mother beyond telling, and she made him as gentle and nearly as patient as she was. Virtually driven from the parlour, except at meal-times, their refuge was the Pine Room. There they were unmolested. There Selina educated and trained him, doing her best to show him the way to the next world, as well as to fit him for this.

One day when he was about nine years old, Selina was up aloft, in the little room where he slept; which had a better view than some of the rooms had, and looked out into the open country. It was snowy weather, and she caught sight of the two boys in the yard below, snowballing each other. Opening the window to call Francis in—for he always got into the wars when with Tom, and she had learnt to dread his being with him—she saw Stephen Radcliffe crossing from the barn. Suddenly a snowball took Stephen in the face. It came from Tom; she saw that; Francis was stooping down at the time, collecting material for a fresh missive.

"Who flung that at me?" roared out Stephen, in a rage.

Tom disclaimed all knowledge of it; and Stephen Radcliffe seized upon Francis, beating him shamefully.

"It was not Francis," called out Selina from the window, shivering at the sight; for Stephen in his violence might some time, as she knew, lame the lad. "Its touching you was an accident; I could see that; but it was not Francis who threw it."

The cold, rarefied air carried her words distinctly to the ear of Stephen. Holding Francis by one hand to prevent his escape, he told Mrs. Radcliffe that she was a liar, adding other polite epithets and a few oaths. And then he began pummelling the lad again.

"Come in, Francis! Let him come in!" implored the mother, clasping her hands in her bitter agony. "Oh, is there no refuge for him and for me?"

She ran down to their sanctum, the Pine Room. Francis came up, sore all over, and his face bleeding. He was a brave little lad, and he strove to make light of it, and keep his tears down. She held him to her, and burst into sobs while trying to comfort him. That upset him at once.

"Oh, my darling, try and bear! My poor boy, there's nothing left for us both but to bear. The world is full of wrongs and tribulation: but, Francis, it will all be made right when we get to heaven."

"Don't cry, mamma. It didn't hurt me much. But, indeed, the snowball was not mine."

At ten years old the boys were sent to school. Young Tom, allowed to have his own way, grew beyond every one's control, even his father's; and Stephen packed him off to school. Selina besought her husband to send Francis also. Why not, replied Mr. Radcliffe; the boy must be educated. And, in spite of Stephen's opposition, Francis was despatched. It was frightfully lonely and unpleasant for Selina after that, and she grew to have a pitiful look on her face.

The school was a sharp one, and Francis got on well; he seemed to possess his grandfather Elliot's aptitude for learning. Tom hated it. After each of the half-yearly holidays, it took Stephen himself to get him to school again: and before he was fourteen he capped it all by appearing at home uncalled for, a red-hot fugitive, and announcing an intention of going to sea.

Tom carried his point. After some feats of skirmishing between him and his father, he was shipped off as "midshipman" on board a fine merchantman bound for Hong Kong. Stephen Radcliffe might never have given a consent, but for the certainty that if he did not give it, Tom would decamp from the Torr, as he did from school, and go off as a common seaman before the mast. It was strange, with his crabbed nature, how much he cared for those two children!

"You'll have that other one home now," said sullen Stephen to his father. "No good to be paying for him there."

And most likely it would have been so; but fate, or fortune, intervened. Francis had a wind-fall. A clergyman, who had known Mr. Elliot, died, and left Francis a thousand pounds. Selina decided that it should be spent, or at least a portion of it, in completing his education in a more advanced manner—though, no doubt, Stephen would have liked to get hold of the money. Francis was sent up to King's College in London, and to board at the house of one of the masters. In this way a few more years passed on. Francis chose the Bar as a profession, and began to study law.

"The Bar!" sneered Stephen. "A penniless beggar like Francis Radcliffe! Put a pig to learn to spell!"

A bleak day in winter. The wind was howling and crying round Sandstone Torr, tearing through the branches of the almost leafless trees, whirling the weather-cock atop of the lofty tower, playing madly on the window-panes. If there was one spot in the county that the wind seemed to favour above all other spots, it was the Torr. It would go shrieking in the air round about there like so many unquiet spirits.

In the dusk of evening, on a sofa beside the fire in the Pine Room lay Mrs. Radcliffe, with a white, worn face and hollow eyes. She was slowly dying. Until to-day she had not thought there was any immediate danger: but she knew it all now, and that the end was at hand.

So it was not that knowledge which had caused her, a day or two ago, to write to London for Francis. Some news brought in by Stephen Radcliffe had unhinged and shocked her beyond expression. Francis was leading a loose, bad life, drinking and gambling, and going to the deuce headlong, ran the tales, and Stephen repeated them indoors.

That same night she wrote for Francis. She could not rest day or night until she could see him face to face, and say—Is this true, or untrue? He might have reached the Torr the previous day; but he did not. She was lying listening for him now in the twilight gloom amidst the blasts of that shrieking wind.

"If God had but taken my child in infancy!" came the chief thought of her troubled heart. "If I could only know that I should meet him on the everlasting shores!"

"Mother!"

She started up with a yearning cry. It was Francis. He had arrived, and come upstairs, and his opening of the door had been drowned by the wind. A tall, slender, bright-faced young fellow of twenty, with the same sunny hair as in his childhood, and a genial heart.

Francis halted, and stood in startled consternation. The firelight played on her wasted face, and he saw—what was there. In manners he was still almost a boy; his disposition open, his nature transparent.

She made room for him on the sofa; sitting beside him, and laying her weary head for a moment on his shoulder. Francis took a few deep breaths while getting over the shock.

"How long have you been like this, mother? What has brought it about?"

"Nothing in particular; nothing fresh," she answered. "I have been getting nearer and nearer to it for years and years."

"Is there no hope?"

"None. And oh, my darling, but for you I should be so glad to die. Sitting here in my loneliness for ever, with only heaven to look forward to, it seems that I have learnt to see a little already of what its rest will be."

Francis pushed his hair from his brow, and left his hand there. He had loved his mother intensely, and the blow was cruel.

Quietly, holding his other hand in hers, she spoke of what Stephen Radcliffe had heard. Francis's face turned to scarlet as he listened. But in that solemn hour he could not and would not tell a lie.

Yes, it was true; partly true, he said. He was not always so steady as he ought to be. Some of his acquaintances, young men studying law like himself, or medicine, or what not, were rather wild, and he had been the same. Drink?—well, yes; at times they did take more than might be quite needful. But they were not given to gambling: that was false.

"Francis," she said, her heart beating wildly with its pain, "the worst of all is the drink. If once you suffer yourself to acquire a love for it, you may never leave it off. It is so insidious—"

"But I don't love it, mother; I don't care for it—and I am sure you must know that I would tell you nothing but truth now," he interrupted. "I have only done as the others do. I'll leave it off."

"Will you promise me that?"

"Yes, I will. I do promise it."

She carried his hand to her lips and kissed it. Francis had always kept his promises.

"It is so difficult for young fellows without a home to keep straight in London," he acknowledged. "There's no good influence over us; there's no pleasant family circle where we can spend our evenings: and we go out, and get drawn into this and that. It all comes of thoughtlessness, mother."

"You have promised me, Francis."

"Oh yes. And I will perform."

"How long will it be before you are called to the Bar?" she asked, after a pause.

"Two years."

"So much as that?"

"I think so. How the wind howls!"

Mrs. Radcliffe sighed; Francis's future seemed not to be very clear. Unless he could get on pretty quickly, and make a living for himself—

"When I am gone, Francis," she said aloud, interrupting her own thoughts, "this will not be any home for you."

"It has not been one for me for some years now, mother."

"But if you do not get into work soon, and your own funds come to an end, you will have no home but this to turn to."

"If I attempted to turn to it, Stephen would soon make it too hot for me, I expect."

"That might not be all; not the worst," she quickly answered, dropping her voice to a tone of fear, and glancing around as one in a fever.

Francis looked round too. He supposed she was seeking something.

"It is always scaring me, Francis," she whispered. "There are times when I fancy I am going to see it enacted before my eyes. It puts me into a state of nervous dread not to be described."

"See what enacted?" he asked.

"I was sitting here about ten days ago, Francis, thinking of you, thinking of the future, when all at once a most startling prevision—yes, I call it so—a prevision came upon me of some dreadful ill in store for you; ill wrought by Stephen. I—I am not sure but it was—that—that he took your life," she added, scarcely above her breath, and in tones that made Francis shiver.

"Why, what do you mean, mother?"

"Every day, every day since, every night and nearly all night, that strange conviction has lain upon me. I know it will be fulfilled: when the hand of death is closing on us, these previsions are an instinct. As surely as that I am now disclosing this to you, Francis, so surely will you fall in some way under the iron hand of Stephen."

"Perhaps you were dreaming, mother dear," suggested Francis: for he had his share of common sense.

"It will be in this house; the Torr," she went on, paying no attention to him; "for it is always these rooms and the dreary trees outside that seem to lie before me. For that reason, I would not have you live here—"

"But don't you think you may have been dreaming?" repeated Francis, interrupting the rest.

"I was as wide awake as I am now, Francis, but I was deep in thought. It stole upon me, this impression, without any sort of warning, or any train of ideas that could have led to it; and it lies within me, a sure and settled conviction. Beware of Stephen. But oh, Francis! even while I give you this caution I know that you will not escape the evil—whatever it may turn out to be."

"I hope I shall," he said, rather lightly. "I'll try, at any rate."

"Well, I have warned you, Francis. Be always upon your guard. And keep away from the Torr, if you can."

Holt, quite an aged woman now, came in with some tea for her mistress. Francis took the opportunity to go down and see his father. Mr. Radcliffe, in a shabby old coat, was sitting in his arm-chair at the parlour fire. He looked pleased to see Francis, and kept his hand for a minute after he had shaken it.

"My mother is very ill, sir," said Francis.

"Ay," replied the old man, dreamily. "Been so for some time now."

"Can nothing be done to—to—keep her with us a little longer, father?"

"I suppose not. Ask Duffham."

"What the devil!—is it you! What brings you here?"

The coarse salutation came from Stephen. Francis turned to see him enter and bang the door after him. His shoes were dirty, his beaver gaiters splashed, and his hair was like a tangled mop.

"I came down to see my father and mother," answered Francis, as he held out his hand. But Stephen did not choose to see it.

Mrs. Stephen, in a straight-down blue cloth gown and black cap garnished with red flowers, looking more angular and hard than of yore, came in with the tea-tray. She did as much work in the house as a servant. Lizzy had been married the year before, and lived in Birmingham with her husband, who was curate at one of the churches there.

"You'll have to sleep on the sofa to-night, young man," was Mrs. Stephen's snappish salutation to Francis. "There's not a bed in the house that's aired."

"The sofa will do," he answered.

"Let his bed be aired to-morrow, Becca," interposed the old man. And they stared in astonishment to hear him say it.

Francis sat down to the tea-table with Stephen and his wife; but neither of them spoke a word to him. Mr. Radcliffe had his tea in his arm-chair at the fire, as usual. Afterwards, Francis took his hat and went out. He was going to question the doctor; and the wind came rushing and howling about him as he bore onwards down the lane towards Church Dykely.

In about an hour's time he came back again with red eyes. He said it was the wind, but his subdued voice sounded as though he had been crying. His father, with bent head, was smoking a long pipe; Stephen sat at the table, reading the sensational police reports in a low weekly newspaper.

"Been out for a stroll, lad?" asked old Radcliffe—and it was the first voluntary question he had put for months. Stephen, listening, could not think what was coming to him.

"I have been to Duffham's," answered Francis. "He—he—" with a stopping of the breath, "says that nothing can be done for my mother; that a few days now will see the end of it."

"Ay," quietly responded the old man. "Our turns must all come."

"Her turn ought not to have come yet," said Francis, nearly breaking down.

"No?"

"I have been looking forward at odd moments to a time when I should be in work, and able to give her a happy home with me, father. It is very hard to come here and find this."

Old Radcliffe took a long whiff; and, opening his mouth, let the smoke curl upwards. "Have a pipe, Francis?"

"No, thank you, sir. I am going up to my mother."

As he left the room, Stephen, having finished the police reports, was turning the paper to see what it said about the markets, when his father put down his pipe and began to speak.

"Only a few days, he says, Ste!"

"What?" demanded Stephen in his surly and ungracious tones.

"She's been ailing always; and has sat up there away from us, Ste. But we shall miss her."

"Miss her!" retorted Ste, leaving the paper, and walking to the fire. "Why, what good has she been? Miss her? The house'll have a good riddance of her," he added, under his breath.

"It'll be my turn next, Ste. And not long first, either."

Stephen took a keen look at his father from beneath his overhanging, bushy eyebrows, that were beginning to turn grey. All this sounded very odd.

"When you and me and Becca's left alone here by ourselves, we shall be as easy as can be," he said.

"What month is it, Ste?"

"November."

"Ay. You'll have seen the last o' me before Christmas."

"Think so?" was Stephen's equable remark. The old man nodded; and there came a pause.

"And you and Becca'll be glad to get us out, Ste."

Stephen did not take the trouble to gainsay it. He was turning about in his thoughts something that he had a mind to speak of.

"They've been nothing but interlopers from the first—she and him. I expect you to do what's right by me, father."

"Ay, I shall do what's right," answered the old man.

"About the money, I mean. It must all come to me, father. I was heir to it before you ever set eyes on her; and her brat must not be let stand in my way. Do you hear?"

"Yes, I hear. It'll be all right, Ste."

"Take only a fraction from the income, and how would the Torr be kept up?" pursued Stephen, plucking up his spirits at the last answer. "He has got his fine profession, and he can make a living for himself out of it: some o' them counsellors make their thousands a-year. But he must not be let rob me."

"He shan't rob you, Ste. It will be all right."

And covetous Stephen, thus reassured and put at ease, strolled into the kitchen, and ordered Becca to provide his favourite dish, toasted cheese, for supper.

The "few days" spoken of by Mr. Duffham, were slowly passing. There was not much difference to be observed in Selina; except that her voice grew weaker. She could only use it at intervals. But her face had a beautiful look of peace upon it, just as though she were three parts in heaven. I have heard Duffham say so many a time since; I, Johnny Ludlow.

On the fifth day she was so much better that it seemed little short of a miracle. They found her in the Pine Room early, up and dressed: when Holt went in to light the fire, she was looking over the two books that lay on the round table. One of them was the Bible; the other was a translation of the German tale "Sintram," which Francis had brought her when he came down the last summer. The story had taken hold of her imagination, and she knew it nearly by heart.

Down went Holt, and told them that the mistress (for, contradictory though it may seem, Selina had been always accorded that title) had taken a "new lease of life," and was getting well. Becca, astonished, went stalking up: perhaps she was afraid it might be true. Selina had "Sintram" in her hand as she sat: her eyes looked bright, her cheeks pink, her voice was improved.

"Oh," said Becca. "What have you left your bed for at this early hour?"

"I feel so well," Selina answered with a smile, letting the book lie open on the table. "Won't you shake hands with me?—and—and kiss me?"

Now Becca had never kissed her in all the years they had lived together, and she did not seem to care about beginning now. "I'll go down and beat you up an egg and a spoonful of wine," said she, just touching the tips of Selina's fingers, in response to the held-out hand: and, with that, went away.

Stephen was the only one who did not pay the Pine Room a visit that day. He heard of the surprising change while he was feeding the pigs: for Becca went out and told him. Stephen splashed some wash over the side of the trough, and gave a little pig a smack with the bucket, and that was all his answer. Old Radcliffe sat an hour in the room; but he never spoke all the time: so his company could not be considered as much.

Selina crept as far as the window, and looked out on the bare pines and the other dreary trees. Most trees are dreary in November. Francis saw a shiver take her as she stood, leaning on the window-frame; and he went to give her his arm and bring her back again. They were by themselves then.

"A week, or so, of this improvement, mother, and you will be as you used to be," said he cheerfully, seating her on the sofa and stirring up the fire. "We shall have our home together yet."

She turned her face full on his, as he sat down by her; a half-questioning, half-wondering look in her eyes.

"Not in this world, Francis. Surely you are not deceived!" and his over-sanguine heart went down like lead.

"It is but the flickering of the spirit before it finally quits the weary frame; just as you may have seen the flame shoot up from an expiring candle," she continued. "The end is very near now."

A spasm of pain rose in his throat. She took his hands between her own feeble ones.

"Don't grieve, Francis; don't grieve for me! Remember what my life has been."

He did remember it. He remembered also the answer Duffham gave when he had inquired what malady it was his mother was dying of. "A broken heart."

"Don't forget, Francis—never forget—that it is a journey we must enter on, sooner or later."

"An uncertain and unknown journey at the best!" he said. "You have no fear of it?"

"Fear! No, but I had once."

She spoke the words in a low, sweet tone, and pointed with a smile to the book that still lay open on the table. Francis's eyes fell on the page.

"When death is drawing near,
And thy heart shrinks with fear,
And thy limbs fail,
Then raise thy hands and pray
To Him who cheers the way
Through the dark vale.

"Seest thou the eastern dawn?
Hears't thou, in the red morn,
The angel's song?
Oh! lift thy drooping head,
Thou who in gloom and dread
Hast lain so long.

"Death comes to set thee free;
Oh! meet him cheerily,
As thy true friend;
And all thy fears shall cease,
And in eternal peace
Thy penance end."

Francis sat very still, struggling a little with that lump in his throat. She leaned forward, and let her head rest upon him, just as she had done the other day when he first came in. His emotion broke loose then.

"Oh, mother, what shall I do without you?"

"You will have God," she whispered.

Still all the morning she kept up well; talking of this and that, saying how much of late the verses, just quoted, had floated in her mind and become a reality to her; showing Holt a slit that had appeared in the table-cover and needed darning: telling Francis his pocket-handkerchiefs looked yellow and should be bleached. It might have been thought she was only going out to tea at Church Dykely, instead of entering on the other journey she had told of.

"Have you been giving her anything?" demanded Stephen, casting his surly eyes on Francis as they sat opposite to each other at dinner in the parlour. "Dying people can't spurt up in this manner without drugs to make 'em."

Francis did not deign to answer. Stephen projected his fork, and took a potato out of the dish. Frank went upstairs when the meal was over. He had left his mother sitting on the sofa, comparatively well. He found her lying on the bed in the next room, grappling with death. She lifted her feeble arms to welcome him, and a ray of joyous light shone on her face. Francis made hardly one step of it to the bed.

"Oh, my darling, it will be all right!" she breathed. "I have prayed for you, and I know—I know I have been heard. You will be helped to put away that evil habit; temptation may assail, but it will not finally overcome you. And, Francis, when—" Her voice failed.

"I no longer hear what you say, mother," cried Francis in an agony.

"Yes, yes," she repeated, as if in answer to something he had said. "Beware of Stephen."

The hands and face alike fell. Francis rang the bell violently, and Holt came up. All was over.

Stephen attended the funeral with the others. Grumbling wofully at having to do it, because it involved a new suit of black clothes. "They'll be ready for the old man, though," was his consoling reflection: "he won't be long."

He was even quicker than Stephen thought. On the very day week that they had come in from leaving Selina in the grave, Mr. Radcliffe was lying as lifeless as she was. A seizure carried him off. Francis was summoned again from London before he had well got back to it. Stephen could not, at such a season, completely ignore him.

He did not foresee the blow that was to come thundering down. When Mr. Radcliffe's will came to be opened, it was found that his property was equally divided between the two sons, half and half: Stephen of course inheriting the Torr; and Squire Todhetley being appointed trustee for Francis. "And I earnestly beg of him to accept the trust," ran the words, "for the sake of Selina's son."

Francis caught the glare of Stephen as they were read out. It was of course Stephen himself, but it looked more like a savage wild-cat. That warning of his mother's came into Francis's mind with a rush.

II

It stood on the left of the road as you went towards Alcester: a good-looking, red-brick house, not large, but very substantial. Everything about it was in trim order; from the emerald-green outer venetian window-blinds to the handsome iron entrance-gates between the enclosing palisades; and the garden and grounds had not as much as a stray worm upon them. Mr. Brandon was nice and particular in all matters, as old bachelors generally are; and he was especially so in regard to his home.

Careering up to this said house on the morning of a fine spring day, when the green hedges were budding and the birds sang in the trees, went a pony-gig, driven by a gentleman. A tall, slender young fellow of seven-and-twenty, with golden hair that shone in the sun and eyes as blue and bright as the sky. Leaving the pony to be taken care of by a labouring boy who chanced to be loitering about, he rang the bell at the iron gates, and inquired of the answering servant whether Mr. Brandon was at home.

"Yes, sir," was the answer of the man, as he led the way in. "But I am not sure that he can see you. What name?" And the applicant carelessly took a card from his waistcoat-pocket, and was left in the drawing-room. Which card the servant glanced at as he carried it away.

"Mr. Francis Radcliffe."

People say there's sure to be a change every seven years. Seven years had gone by since the death of old Mr. Radcliffe and the inheritance by Francis of the portion that fell to him; three hundred a-year. There were odd moments when Frank, in spite of himself, would look back at those seven years; and he did not at all like the retrospect. For he remembered the solemn promise he had made to his mother when she was dying, to put away those evil habits which had begun to creep upon him, more especially that worst of all bad habits that man, whether young or old, can take to—drinking—and he had not kept the promise. He had been called to the Bar in due course, but he made nothing by his profession. Briefs did not come to him. He just wasted his time and lived a fast life on the small means that were his. He pulled up sometimes, turned his back on folly, and read like a house on fire: but his wild companions soon got hold of him again, and put his good resolutions to flight. Frank put it all down to idleness. "If I had work to do, I should do it," he said, "and that would keep me straight." But at the close of this last winter he had fallen into a most dangerous illness, resulting from the draughts of ale, and what not, that he had made too free with, and he got up from it with a resolution never to drink again. Knowing that the resolution would be more easy to keep if he turned his back on London and the companions who beset him, down he came to his native place, determined to take a farm and give up the law. For the second time in his life some money had come to him unexpectedly; which would help him on. And so, after a seven years' fling, Frank Radcliffe was going in for a change.

He had never stayed at Sandstone Torr since his father's death. His brother Stephen's surly temper, and perhaps that curious warning of his mother's, kept him out of it. He and Stephen maintained a show of civility to one another; and when Frank was in the neighbourhood (but that had only happened twice in the seven years), he would call at the Torr and see them. The last time he came down, Frank was staying at a place popularly called Pitchley's Farm. Old Pitchley—who had lived on it, boy and man, for seventy years—liked him well. Frank made acquaintance that time with Annet Skate; fell in love with her, in fact, and meant to marry her. She was a pretty girl, and a good girl, and had been brought up to be thoroughly useful as a farmer's daughter: but neither by birth nor position was she the equal of Frank Radcliffe. All her experience of life lay in her own secluded, plain home: in regard to the world outside she was as ignorant as a young calf, and just as mild and soft as butter.

So Frank, after his spell of sickness and reflection, had thrown up London, and come down to settle in a farm with Annet, if he could get one. But there was not a farm to be let for miles round. And it was perhaps a curious thing that while Frank was thinking he should have to travel elsewhere in search of one, Pitchley's should turn up. For old Pitchley suddenly died. Pitchley's Farm belonged to Mr. Brandon. It was a small compact farm; just the size Frank wanted. A large one would have been beyond his means.

Mr. Brandon sat writing letters at the table in his library, in his geranium-coloured Turkish cap, with its purple tassel, when his servant went in with the card.

"Mr. Francis Radcliffe!" read he aloud, in his squeaky voice. "What, is he down here again? You can bring him in, Abel—though I'm sure I don't know what he wants with me." And Abel went and brought him.

"We heard you were ill, young man," said Mr. Brandon, peering up into Frank's handsome face as he shook hands, and detecting all sorts of sickly signs in it.

"So I have been, Mr. Brandon; very ill. But I have left London and its dissipations for good, and have come here to settle. It's about time I did," he added, with the candour natural to him.

"I should say it was," coughed old Brandon. "You've been on the wrong tack long enough."

"And I have come to you—I hope I am first in the field—to ask you to let me have the lease of Pitchley's Farm."

Mr. Brandon could not have felt more surprised had Frank asked for a lease of the moon, but he did not show it. His head went up a little, and the purple tassel took a sway backwards.

"Oh," said he. "You take Pitchley's Farm! How do you think to stock it?"

"I shall take to the stock at present on it, as far as my means will allow, and give a bond for the rest. Pitchley's executors will make it easy for me."

"What are your means?" curtly questioned old Brandon.

"In all, they will be two thousand pounds. Taking mine and Miss Skate's together."

"That's a settled thing, is it, Master Francis?"—alluding to the marriage.

"Yes, it is," said Frank. "Her portion is just a thousand pounds, and her friends are willing to put it on the farm. Mine is another thousand."

"Where does yours come from?"

"Do you recollect, Mr. Brandon, that when I was a little fellow at school I had a thousand pounds left me by a clergyman—a former friend of my grandfather Elliot?"

Mr. Brandon nodded. "It was Parson Godfrey. He came down once or twice to the Torr to see your mother and you."

"Just so. Well, his widow has now recently died; she was considerably younger than he; and she has left me another thousand. If I can have Pitchley's Farm, I shall be sure to get on at it," he added in his sanguine way. For, if ever there was a sanguine, sunny-natured fellow in this world, it was Frank Radcliffe.

Old Brandon pushed his geranium cap all aside and gave a flick to the tassel. "My opinion lies the contrary way, young man: that you will be sure not to get on at it."

"I understand all about farming," said Frank eagerly. "And I mean to be as steady as steady can be."

"To begin with a debt on the farm will cripple the best man going, sir."

"Oh, Mr. Brandon, don't turn against me!" implored Frank, who was feeling terribly in earnest. "Give me a chance! Unless I can get some constant work, some interest to occupy my hands and my mind, I might be relapsing back to the old ways again from sheer ennui. There's no resource but a farm."

Mr. Brandon did not seem to be in a hurry to answer. He was looking straight at Frank, and nodding little nods to himself, following out some mental argument. Frank leaned forward in his chair, his voice low, his face solemn.

"When my poor mother was dying, I promised her to give up bad habits, Mr. Brandon. I hope—I think—I fully intend to do so now. Won't you help me?"

"What do you wish me to understand by 'bad' habits, young man?" queried Mr. Brandon in his hardest tones. "What have been yours?"

"Drink," said Frank shortly. "And I am ashamed enough to have to say it. It is not that I have been a constant drinker, or that I have taken much, in comparison with what very many men drink; but I have, sometimes for weeks together, taken it very recklessly. That is what I meant by speaking of my bad habits, Mr. Brandon."

"Couldn't speak of a worse habit, Frank Radcliffe."

"True. I should have pulled up long ago but for those fast companions I lived amongst. They kept me down. Once amidst such, a fellow has no chance. Often and often that neglected promise to my mother has lain upon me, a nightmare of remorse. I have fancied she might be looking down upon earth, upon me, and seeing how I was fulfilling it."

"If your mother was not looking down upon you, sir, your Creator was."

"Ay. I know. Mr. Brandon"—his voice sinking deeper in its solemnity, and his eyes glistening—"in the very last minute of my mother's life—when her soul was actually on the wing—she told me that she knew I should be helped to throw off what was wrong. She had prayed for it, and seen it. A conviction is within me that I shall be—has been within me ever since. I think this—now—may be the turning-point in my life. Don't deny me the farm, sir."

"Frank Radcliffe, I'd let you have the farm, and another to it, if I thought you were sincere."

"Why—you can't think me not sincere, after what I have said!" cried Frank.

"Oh, you are sincere enough at the present moment. I don't doubt that. The question is, will you be sincere in keeping your good resolutions in the future?"

"I hope I shall. I believe I shall. I will try with all my best energies."

"Very well. You may have the farm."

Frank Radcliffe started up in his joy and gratitude, and shook Mr. Brandon's hands till the purple tassel quivered. He had a squeaky voice and a cold manner, and went in for coughs and chest-aches, and all kinds of fanciful disorders; but there was no more generous heart going than old Brandon's.

Business settled, the luncheon was ordered in. But Frank was a good deal too impatient to stay for it; and drove away in the pony-gig to impart the news to all whom it might concern. Taking a round to the Torr first, he drove into the back-yard. Stephen came out.

Stephen looked quite old now. He must have been fifty years of age. Hard and surly as ever was he, and his stock of hair was as grizzled as his father's used to be before Frank was born.

"Oh, it's you!" said Stephen, as civilly as he could bring his tongue to speak. "Whose chay and pony is that?"

"It belongs to Pitchley's bailiff. He lent it me this morning."

"Will you come in?"

"I have not time now," answered Frank. "But I thought I'd just drive round and tell you the news, Stephen. I'm going to have Pitchley's Farm."

"Who says so?"

"I have now been settling it with Mr. Brandon. At first, he seemed unwilling to let me have it—was afraid, I suppose, that I and the farm might come to grief together—but he consented at last. So I shall get in as soon as I can, and take Annet with me. You'll come to our wedding, Stephen?"

"A fine match she is!" cried cranky Stephen.

"What's the matter with her?"

"I don't say as anything's the matter with her. But you have always stuck up for the pride and pomp of the Radcliffes: made out that nobody was good enough for 'em. A nice comedown for Frank Radcliffe that'll be—old Farmer Skate's girl."

"We won't quarrel about it, Stephen," said Frank, with his good-humoured smile. "Here's your wife. How do you do, Mrs. Radcliffe?"

Becca had come out with a wet mop in her hands, which she proceeded to wring. Some of the splashes went on Frank's pony-gig. She wore morning costume: a dark-blue cotton gown hanging straight down on her thin, lanky figure; and an old black cap adorning her hard face. It was a great contrast: handsome, gentlemanly, well-dressed, sunny Frank Radcliffe, barrister-at-law; and that surly boor Stephen, in his rough clothes, and his shabby, hard-working wife.

"When be you going back to London?" was Becca's reply to his salutation, as she began to rinse out the mop at the pump.

"Not at all. I have been telling Stephen. I am going into Pitchley's Farm."

"Along of Annet Skate," put in Stephen; whose queer phraseology had been indulged in so long that it had become habitual. "Much good they'll do in a farm! He'd like us to go to the wedding! No, thank ye."

"Well, good-morning," said Frank, starting the pony. They did not give him much encouragement to stay.

"Be it true, Radcliffe?" asked Becca, letting the mop alone for a minute. "Be he a-going to marry Skate's girl, and get Pitchley's Farm?"

"I wish the devil had him!" was Stephen's surly comment, as he stalked off in the wake of the receding pony-gig, giving his wife no other answer.

No doubt Stephen was sincere in his wish, though it was hardly polite to avow it. For the whole of Frank's life, he had been a thorn in the flesh of Stephen: in the first years, for fear their father should bequeath to Frank a share of the inheritance; in the later years, because Frank had had the share! That sum of three hundred a-year, enjoyed by Frank, was coveted by Stephen as money was never yet coveted by man. Looking at matters with a distorted mind, he considered it a foul wrong done him; as no better than a robbery upon him; that the whole of the money was his own by all the laws of right and wrong, and that not a stiver of it ought to have gone to Frank. Unable, however, to alter the state of existing things, he had sincerely hoped that some lucky chance—say the little accident of Frank's drinking himself to death—would put him in possession of it; and all the rumours that came down from London about Frank's wild life rejoiced him greatly. For if Frank died without children, the money went to Stephen. And it may as well be mentioned here, that old Mr. Radcliffe had so vested the three hundred a-year that Frank had no power over the capital and was unable to squander it. It would go to his children when he died; or, if he left no children, to Stephen.

Never a night when he went to bed, never a morning when he got up, but Stephen Radcliffe's hungry heart gave a dismal groan to that three hundred a-year he had been deprived of. In truth, his own poor three hundred was not enough for him. And then, he had expected that the six would all be his! He had, he said, to work like a slave to keep up the Torr, and make both ends meet. His two children were for ever tugging at his purse-strings. Tom, quitting the sea, had settled in a farm in Canada; but he was always writing home for help. Lizzy would make her appearance at home at all kinds of unseasonable times; and tell pitiful stories of the wants of her scanty ménage at Birmingham, and of her little children, and of the poor health and short pay of her husband the curate. Doubtless Stephen had rather a hard life of it and could very well have done with a doubled income. To hear that Frank was going to settle down to a sober existence and to marry a wife, was the worst news of all to Stephen, for it lessened his good chances finely.

But he had only the will to hinder it, not the power. And matters and the year went swimmingly on. Francis entered into possession of the farm; and just a week before Midsummer Day, he married Annet Skate and took her home.

The red June sunset fell full on Pitchley's Farm, staining the windows a glowing crimson. Pitchley's Farm lay in a dell, about a mile from Dyke Manor, on the opposite side to Sandstone Torr. It was a pretty little homestead, with jessamine on the porch, and roses creeping up the frames of the parlour-windows. Just a year had gone by since the wedding, and to-morrow would be the anniversary of the wedding-day. Mr. and Mrs. Francis Radcliffe were intending to keep it, and had bidden their friends to an entertainment. He had carried out his resolution to be steady, and they had prospered fairly well. David Skate, one of Annet's brothers, a thorough, practical farmer, was ever ready to come over, if wanted, and help Francis with work and counsel.

Completely tired with her day's exertions, was Annet, for she had been making good things for the morrow, and now sat down for the first time that day in the parlour—a low room, with its windows open to the clustering roses, and the furniture bright and tasty. Annet was of middle height, light and active, with a delicate colour on her cheeks, soft brown eyes, and small features. She had just changed her cotton gown for one of pink summer muslin, and looked as fresh as a daisy.

"How tired I am!" she exclaimed to herself, with a smile. "Frank would scold me if he knew it."

"Be you ready for supper, ma'am?" asked a servant, putting in her head at the door. The only maid kept: for both Frank and his wife knew that their best help to getting on was economy.

"Not yet, Sally. I shall wait for your master."

"Well, I've put it on the table, ma'am; and I'm just going to step across now to Hester Bitton's, and tell her she'll be wanted here to-morrow."

Annet went into the porch, and stood there looking out for her husband, shading her eyes with her hand from the red glare. Some business connected with stock took him to Worcester that day, and he had started in the early morning; but Annet had expected him home earlier than this.

There he was, riding down the road at a sharpish trot; Annet heard the horse's hoofs before she saw him. He waved his hand to her in the distance, and she fluttered her white handkerchief back again. Thorpe, the indoor man, appeared to take the horse.

Francis Radcliffe had been changing for the better during the past twelvemonth. Regular habits and regular hours, and a mind healthily occupied, had done great things for him. His face was bright, his blue eyes were clear, and his smile and his voice were alike cheering as he got off the horse and greeted his wife.

"You are late, Frank! It is ever so much past eight."

"Our clocks are fast: I've found that out to-day, Annet, But I could not get back before."

He had gone into the parlour, had kissed her, and was disincumbering his pockets of various parcels: she helping him. Both were laughing, for there seemed to be no end to them. They contained articles wanted for the morrow: macaroons, and potted lampreys, and lots of good things.

"Don't say again that I forget your commissions, Annet."

"Never again, Frank. How good you are! But what is in this one? it feels soft."

"That's for yourself," said Frank. "Open it."

Cutting the string, the paper flew apart, disclosing a baby's cloak of white braided cashmere. Annet laughed and blushed.

"Oh, Frank! How could you?"

"Why, I heard you say you must get one."

"Yes—but—not just yet. It may not be wanted, you know."

"Stuff! The thing was in Mrs. What's-her-name's window in High Street, staring passers-by in the face; so I went in, and bought it."

"It's too beautiful," murmured Annet, putting it reverently into the paper, as if she mistook it for a baby. "And how has the day gone, Frank? Could you buy the sheep?"

"Yes; all right. The sheep—Annet, who do you think is coming here to-morrow? Going to honour us as one of the guests?"

At the break in the sentence, Frank had flung himself into a chair, and thrown his head back, laughing. Annet wondered.

"Stephen! It's true. He had gone to Worcester after some sheep himself. I asked whether we should have the pleasure of seeing them here, and he curtly said that he was coming, but couldn't answer for Mrs. Radcliffe. Had the Pope of Rome told me he was coming, I should not have been more surprised."

"Stephen's wife took no notice of the invitation."

"Writing is not in her line: or in his either. Something must be in the wind, Annet: neither he nor his wife has been inside our doors yet."

They sat down to supper, full of chat: as genial married folks always are, after a day's separation. And it was only when the house was at rest, and Annet was lighting the bed-candle, that she remembered a letter lying on the mantel-piece.

"Oh, Frank, I ought to have given it to you at once; I quite forgot it. This letter came for you by this morning's post."

Frank sat down again, drew the candle to him, and read it. It was from one of his former friends, a Mr. Briarly; offering on his own part and on that of another former friend, one Pratt, a visit to Pitchley's Farm.

Instincts arise to all of us: instincts that it might be well to trust to oftener than we do. A powerful instinct, against the offered visit, rushed into the mind of Francis Radcliffe. But the chances are, that, in the obligations of hospitality, it would not have prevailed, even had the chance been afforded him.

"Cool, I must say!" said Frank, with a laugh. "Look here, Annet; these two fellows are going to take us by storm to-morrow. If I don't want them, says Briarly, I must just shut the door in their faces."

"But you'll be glad to see them, won't you, Frank?" she remarked in her innocence.

"Yes. I shall like well enough to see them again. It's our busy time, though: they might have put it off till after harvest."

As many friends went to this entertainment at Pitchley's Farm as liked to go. Mr. Brandon was one of them: he walked over with us—with me, and Tod, and the Squire, and the mater. Stephen Radcliffe and his wife were there, Becca in a black silk with straps of rusty velvet across it. Stephen mostly sat still and said nothing, but Becca's sly eyes were everywhere. Frank and his wife, well dressed and hospitable, welcomed us all; and the board was well spread with cold meats and dainties.

Old Brandon had a quiet talk with Annet in a corner of the porch. He told her he was glad to find Frank seemed likely to do well at the farm.

"He tries his very best, sir," she said.

"Ay. Somehow I thought he would. People said 'Frank Radcliffe has his three hundred a-year to fall back upon when he gets out of Pitchley's': but I fancied he might stay at Pitchley's instead of getting out of it."

"We are getting on as well as we can be, sir, in a moderate way."

"A moderate way is the only safe way to get on," said Mr. Brandon, putting his white silk handkerchief corner-wise on his head against the sun. "That's a true saying, He who would be rich in twelve months is generally a beggar in six. You are helping Frank well, my dear. I have heard of it: how industrious you are, and keep things together. It's not often a good old head like yours is set upon young shoulders."

Annet laughed. "My shoulders are not so very young, sir. I was twenty-four last birthday."

"That's young to manage a farm, child. But you've had good training; you had an industrious mother"—indicating an old lady on the lawn in a big lace cap and green gown. "I can tell you what—when I let Frank Radcliffe have the lease, I took into consideration that you were coming here as well as he. Why!—who are these?"

Two stylish-looking fellows were dashing up in a dog-cart; pipes in their mouths, and portmanteaus behind them. Shouting and calling indiscriminately about for Frank Radcliffe; for a man to take the horse and vehicle, that they had contrived to charter at the railway terminus; for a glass of bitter beer apiece, for they were confoundedly dry—there was no end of a commotion.

They were the two visitors from London, Briarly and Pratt. Their tones moderated somewhat when they saw the company. Frank came out; and received a noisy greeting that might have been heard at York. One of them trod on Mr. Brandon's corns as he went in through the porch. Annet looked half frightened.

"Come to stay here!—gentlemen from London!—Frank's former friends!" repeated old Brandon, listening to her explanation. "Fine friends, I should say! Frank Radcliffe,"—laying hold of him as he was coming back from giving directions to his servant—"how came you to bring those men down into your home?"

"They came of their own accord, Mr. Brandon."

"Friends of yours, I hear?"

"Yes, I knew them in the old days."

"Oh. Well—I should not like to go shouting and thundering up to a decent house with more aboard me than I could carry. Those men have both been drinking."

Frank was looking frightfully mortified. "I am afraid they have," he said. "The heat of the day and the dust on the journey must have caused them to take more than they were aware of. I'm very sorry. I assure you, Mr. Brandon, they are really quiet, good fellows."

"May be. But the sooner you see their backs turned, the better, young man."

From that day, the trouble set in. Will it be believed that Frank Radcliffe, after keeping himself straight for ever so much more than a year, fell away again? Those two visitors must have found their quarters at Pitchley's Farm agreeable, for they stayed on and on, and made no sign of going away. They were drinkers, hard and fast. They drank, themselves, and they seduced Frank to drink—though perhaps he did not require much seduction. Frank's ale was poured out like water. Dozens of port, ordered and paid for by Briarly, arrived from the wine-merchant's; Pratt procured cases of brandy. From morning till night liquor was under poor Frank's nose, tempting him to sin. Their heads might be strong enough to stand the potions; Frank's was not. It was June when the new life set in; and on the first of September, when all three staggered in from a day's shooting, Frank was in a fever and curiously trembling from head to foot.

By the end of the week he was strapped down in his bed, a raving madman; Duffham attending him, and two men keeping guard.

Duffham made short work with Briarly and Pratt. He packed them and their cases of wine and their portmanteaus off together; telling them they had done enough mischief for one year, and he must have the house quiet for both its master and mistress. Frank's malady was turning to typhus fever, and a second doctor was called in from Evesham.

The next news was, that Pitchley's Farm had a son and heir. They called it Francis. It did not live many days, however: how was a son and heir likely to live, coming to that house of fright and turmoil? Frank's ravings might be heard all over it; and his poor wife was nearly terrified out of her bed.

The state of things went on. October came in, and there was no change. It was not known whether Annet would live or die. Frank was better in health, but his mind was gone.

"There's one chance for him," said Duffham, coming across to Dyke Manor to the Squire: "and that is, a lunatic asylum. At home he cannot be kept; he is raving mad. No time must be lost in removing him."

"You think he may get better in an asylum?" cried the Squire, gloomily.

"Yes. I say it is his best chance. His wife, poor thing, is horrified at the thought: but there's nothing else to be done. The calmness of an asylum, the sanatory rules and regulations observed there, will restore him, if anything will."

"How is she?" asked the Squire.

"About as ill as she can be. She won't leave her bed on this side Christmas. And the next question is, Squire—where shall he be placed? Of course we cannot act at all without your authority."

The Squire, you see, was Frank Radcliffe's trustee. At the present moment Frank was dead in the eye of the law, and everything lay with the Squire. Not a sixpence of the income could any one touch now, but as he pleased to decree.

After much discussion, in which Stephen Radcliffe had to take his share, according to law and order, Frank was conveyed to a small private asylum near London. It belonged to a Dr. Dale: and the Evesham doctor strongly recommended it. The terms seemed high to us: two hundred pounds a-year: and Stephen grumbled at them. But Annet begged and prayed that money might not be spared; and the

Squire decided to pay it. So poor Frank was taken to town; and Stephen, as his nearest male relative—in fact, his only one—officially consigned him to the care of Dr. Dale.

And that's the jolly condition things were in, that Christmas, at Pitchley's Farm. Its master in a London madhouse, its mistress in her sick-bed, and the little heir in Church Dykely churchyard. David Skate, like the good brother he was, took up his quarters at the farm, and looked after things.

It was in January that Annet found herself well enough to get upon her legs. The first use she made of them was to go up to London to see her husband. But the sight of her so much excited Frank that Dr. Dale begged her not to come again. It was, he said, taking from Frank one chance of his recovery. So Annet gave her promise not to do so, and came back to Pitchley's sobbing and sighing.

Things went on without much change till May. News came of Frank periodically, chiefly to Stephen Radcliffe, who was the recognized authority in Dr. Dale's eyes. On the whole it was good. The improvement in him, though slow, was gradual: and Dr. Dale felt quite certain now of his restoration. In May, the cheering tidings arrived that Frank was all but well; and Stephen Radcliffe, who went to London for a fortnight about that time and saw Frank twice, confirmed it.

Stephen's visit up arose in this way. One Esau D. Stettin (that's how he wrote his name), who owned land in Canada, came to this country on business, and brought news to the Torr of Tom Radcliffe. Tom had every chance of doing well, he said, and was quite steady—and this was true. Mr. and Mrs. Stephen were almost as glad to hear it as if a fortune had been left them. But, to ensure his doing well and to make his farm prosperous, Tom wanted no end of articles sent out to him: the latest improvements in agricultural implements; patent wheelbarrows, and all the rest of it. For Stephen to take the money out of his pocket to purchase the wheelbarrows was like taking the teeth from his head; but as Esau D. Stettin—who was above suspicion—confirmed Tom's need of the things, Stephen decided to do it. He went up to London, to buy the articles and superintend their embarkation, and it was during that time that he saw Frank. Upon returning to the Torr, he fully bore out Dr. Dale's opinion that Frank was recovering his mind, was, in fact, almost well; but he privately told the Squire some other news that qualified it.

Frank's health was failing. While his mind was resuming its tone, his body was wasting. He was, Ste said, a mere shadow; and Dr. Dale feared that he would not last very long after complete sanity set in.

How sorry we all were, I need not say. With all his failings and his instability, every one liked Frank Radcliffe. They kept it from Annet. She was but a shadow herself: had fretted her flesh to fiddlestrings; and Duffham's opinion was that she stood a good chance of dwindling away till nothing was left of her but a shroud and a coffin.

"Would it be of any use my going up to see him, poor fellow?" asked the Squire, sadly down in the mouth.

"Not a bit," returned Stephen. "Dale would be sure not to admit you: so much depends on Frank's being kept free from excitement. Why, he wanted to deny me, that Dale; but I insisted on my right to go in. I mean to see him again, too, before many days are over."

"Are you going to London again?" asked the Squire, rather surprised. It was something new for Stephen Radcliffe to be a gad-about.

"I shall have to go, I reckon," said Stephen, ungraciously. "I've to see Stettin before he sails."

Stephen Radcliffe did go up again, apparently much against his will, to judge by the ill words he gave to it. And the report he brought back of Frank that time was rather more cheering.

The Squire was standing one hot morning in the yard in his light buff coat, blowing up Dwarf Giles for something that had gone wrong in the stables, when a man was seen making his way from the oak-walk towards the yard. The June hay-making was about, and the smell of the hay was wafted across to us on the wings of the summer breeze.

"Who's that, Johnny?" asked the pater: for the sun was shining right in his eyes.

"It—it looks like Stephen Radcliffe, sir."

"You may tell him by his rusty suit of velveteen," put in Tod; who stood watching a young brood of ducklings in the duck-pond, and the agonies of the hen that had hatched them.

Stephen Radcliffe it was. He had a stout stick in his hand, and his face was of a curious leaden colour. Which, with him, took the place of paleness.

"I've had bad news, Mr. Todhetley," he began, in low tones, without any preliminary greeting. "Frank's dead."

The Squire's straw hat, which he chanced to have taken off, dropped on the stones. "Dead! Frank!" he exclaimed in an awestruck tone. "It can't be true."

"Just the first thought that struck me when I opened the letter," said Stephen, drawing one from his pocket. "Here it is, though, in black and white."

His hands shook like anything as he held out the letter. It was from one of the assistants at Dale's—a Mr. Pitt: the head doctor, under Dale, Stephen explained. Frank had died suddenly, it stated, without warning of any kind, so that there was no possibility of apprising his friends; and it requested Mr. Radcliffe to go up without delay.

"It is a dreadful thing!" cried the Squire.

"So it is, poor fellow," agreed Stephen. "I never thought it was going to end this way; not yet awhile, at any rate. For him, it's a happy release, I suppose. He'd never ha' been good for anything."

"What has he died of?" questioned Tod.

The voice, or the question, seemed to startle Stephen. He looked sharply round, as if he hadn't known Tod was there, an ugly scowl on his face.

"I expect we shall hear it was heart disease," he said, facing the Squire and turning his back upon Tod.

"Why do you say that, Mr. Radcliffe? Was anything the matter with his heart?"

"Dale had some doubts of it, Squire. He thought that was the cause of his wasting away."

"You never told us that."

"Because I never believed it. A Radcliffe never had a weak heart yet. And it's only a thought o' mine: he might have died from something else. Laid hands on himself, maybe."

"For goodness' sake don't bring up such an ill thought as that," cried the pater explosively. "Wait till you know."

"Yes, I must wait till I know," said Stephen, sullenly. "And a precious inconvenience it is to me to go up at this moment when my hay's just cut! Frank's been a bother to me all his life, and he must even be a bother now he's dead."

"Shall I go up for you?" asked the Squire: who in his distress at the sudden news would have thought nothing of offering to start for Kamschatka.

"No good if you did," growled Stephen, folding up the letter that the pater handed back to him. "They'd not as much as release him to be buried without me, I expect. I shall bring him down here," added Stephen, jerking his head in the direction of the churchyard.

"Yes, yes, poor fellow—let him lie by his mother," said the Squire.

Stephen said a good-morrow, meant for the whole of us; and had rounded the duck-pond on his exit, when he stopped, and turned back again to the pater.

"There'll be extra expenses, I suppose, up at Dale's. Have I your authority to discharge them?"

"Of course you have, Mr. Radcliffe. Or let Dale send in the account to me, if you prefer it."

He went off without another word, his head down; his thick stick held over his shoulder. Tho Squire rubbed his face, and wondered what on earth was the next thing to do in this unhappy crisis.

Annet was in Wales with her mother at some seaside place. It would be a dreadful shock to her. Getting the address from David Skate, the Squire wrote to break it to them in the best manner he could. But now, a mischance happened to that letter. Welsh names are difficult to spell; the pater's pen put L for Y, or X for Z, something of that sort; and the letter went to a wrong town altogether, and finally came back to him unopened. Stephen Radcliffe had returned then.

Stephen did not keep his word, instead of bringing Frank down, he left him in London in Finchley Cemetery. "The heat of the weather," he pleaded by way of excuse when the Squire blew him up. "There was some delay; an inquest, and all that; and unless we'd gone to the expense of lead, it couldn't be done; Dale said so. What does it signify? He'll lie as quiet there as he would here."

"And was it the heart that was wrong?" asked the pater.

"No. It was what they called 'effusion on the brain,'" replied Stephen. "Dale says it's rather a common case with lunatics, but he never feared it for Frank."

"It is distressing to think his poor wife did not see him. Quite a misfortune."

"Well, we can't help it: it was no fault of ours," retorted Stephen: who had actually had the decency to put himself into a semblance of mourning. "The world 'ud go on differently for many of us, Squire, if we could foresee things."

And that was the end of Francis Radcliffe!

"Finchley Cemetery!" exclaimed Mr. Brandon, when he heard it. "That Stephen Radcliffe has been at his stingy tricks again. You can bury people for next to nothing there."

Poor Annet came home in her widow's weeds, In health she was better; and might grow strong in time. There was no longer any suspense: she knew the worst; that was in itself a rest. The great doubt to be encountered now was, whether she could keep on Pitchley's Farm. Mr. Brandon was willing to risk it: and David Skate took up his abode at the farm for good, and would do his best in all ways. But the three hundred a-year income, that had been the chief help and stay of herself and Frank, was gone.

It had lapsed to Stephen. Nothing could be said against that in law, for old Mr. Radcliffe's will had so decreed it; but it seemed a very cruel thing for every shilling to leave her, an injustice, a wrong. The tears ran down her pale face as she spoke of it one day at Pitchley's to the Squire: and he, going in wholesale for sympathy, determined to have a tussel with Stephen.

"You can't for shame take it all from her, Stephen Radcliffe," said the Squire, after walking over to Sandstone Torr the next morning. "You must not leave her quite penniless."

"I don't take it from her," replied Stephen, rumpling up his grizzled hair. "It comes to me of right. It is my own."

"Now don't quibble, Stephen Radcliffe," said the Squire, rubbing his face, for he went into a fever as usual over his argument, and the day was hot. "The poor thing was your brother's wife, and you ought to consider that."

"Francis was a fool to marry her. An unsteady man like him always is a fool to marry."

"Well, he did marry her: and I don't see that he was a fool at all for it. I wish I'd got the whip-hand of those two wicked blades who came down here and turned him from his good ways. I wonder how they'll answer for it in heaven."

"Would you like to take a drop of cider?" asked Stephen.

"I don't care if I do."

The cider was brought in by Eunice Gibbon: a second edition, so far as looks went, of Mrs. Stephen Radcliffe, whose younger sister she was. She lived there as servant, the only one kept. Holt had left when old Mr. Radcliffe died.

"Come, Stephen Radcliffe, you must make Annet some allowance," said the Squire, after taking a long draught and finding the cider uncommonly sour. "The neighbours will cry out upon you if you don't."

"The neighbours can do as they choose."

"Just take this much into consideration. If that little child of theirs had lived, the money would have been his."

"But he didn't live," argued Stephen.

"I know he didn't—more's the pity. He'd have been a consolation to her, poor thing. Come! you can't, I say, take all from her and leave her with nothing."

"Nothing! Hasn't she got the farm-stock and the furniture? She's all that to the good. 'Twas bought with Frank's money."

"No, it was not. Half the money was hers. Look here. Unless she gets help somewhere, I don't see how she is to stay on at Pitchley's."

"And 'twould be a sight better for her not to stay on at Pitchley's," retorted Stephen. "Let her go back to her mother's again, over in the other parish. Or let her emigrate. Lots of folks is emigrating now."

"This won't do, Stephen Radcliffe," said the Squire, beginning to lose his temper. "You can't for shame bring every one down upon your head. Allow her a trifle, man, out of the income that has lapsed to you: let the world have to say that you are generous for once."

Well, not to pursue the contest—which lasted, hot and sharp, for a couple of hours, for the Squire, though he kept getting out of one passion into another, would not give in—I may as well say at once that Stephen at last yielded, and agreed to allow her fifty pounds a-year. "Just for a year or so," as he ungraciously put it, "while she turned herself round."

And it was so tremendous a concession for Stephen Radcliffe that no one believed it at first, the Squire included. It must be intended as a thanksgiving for his brother's death, said the world.

"Only, Ste Radcliffe is not the one to offer thanksgivings," observed old Brandon. "Take care that he pays it, Squire."

And thus things fell into the old grooves again, and the settling down of Frank Radcliffe amongst us seemed but as a very short episode in Church Dykely life. Stephen Radcliffe, in funds now, bought an adjoining field that was to be sold, and added it to his land: but he and his wife and the Torr kept themselves more secluded than ever. Frank's widow took up her old strength by degrees, and worked and managed incessantly: she in the house, and David Skate out of it; to keep Pitchley's Farm together. And the autumn drew on.

The light of the moon streamed in slantwise upon us as we sat round the bay-window. Tod and I had just got home for the Michaelmas holidays: and we sat talking after dinner in the growing dusk. There was always plenty to relate, on getting home from school. A dreadful thing had happened this last quarter:

one of the younger ones had died at a game of Hare and Hounds. I'll tell you of it some time. The tears glistened in Mrs. Todhetley's eyes, and we all seemed to be talking at once.

"Mrs. Francis Radcliffe, ma'am."

Old Thomas had opened the door and interrupted us. Annet came in quietly, and sat down after shaking hands all round. Her face looked pale and troubled. We asked her to stay tea; but she would not.

"It is late to come in," she said, some apology in her tone. "I meant to have been here earlier; but it has been a busy day, and I have had interruptions besides."

This seemed to imply that she had come over for some special purpose. Not another word, however, did she say. She just sat in silence, or next door to it: answering Yes and No in an abstracted sort of way when spoken to, and staring out into the moonlight like any one dreaming. And presently she got up to leave.

We went out with her and walked across the field; the pater, I, and Tod. Nearly every blade of the short grass could be seen as distinctly as in the day. At the first stile she halted, saying she expected to meet David there, who had gone on to Dobbs the blacksmith on some errand connected with the horses.

Tod saw a young hare scutter across the grass, and rushed after it, full chase. The moon, low in the heavens, as autumn moons mostly are, lighted up the perplexity on Annet's face. It was perplexed. Suddenly she turned it on the Squire.

"Mr. Todhetley, I am sure you must wonder what I came for."

"Well, I thought you wanted something," said the Squire candidly. "We are always pleased to have you; you ought to have stayed tea."

"I did want something. But I really could not muster courage to begin upon it. The longer I sat there— like a statue, as I felt—the more my tongue failed me. Perhaps I can say it here."

It was a curious thing she had to tell, and must have sounded to the Squire's ears like an incident out of a ghost story. The gist of it was this: an impression had taken hold of her mind that her husband had not been fairly dealt with. In plain words, had not come fairly by his end. The pater listened, and could make no sense of it.

"I can't tell how or when the idea arose," she said; "it seems to have floated in my mind so long that I do not trace the beginning. At first it was but the merest shadow of a doubt; hardly that; but it has grown deeper and darker, and I cannot rest for it."

"Bless my heart!" cried the Squire. "Johnny, hold my hat a minute."

"Just as surely as that I see that moon in the sky, sir," she went on, "do I seem to see in my mind that some ill was wrought to Frank by his brother. Mrs. Radcliffe said it would be."

"Dear me! What Mrs. Radcliffe?"

"Frank's mother. She had the impression of it when she was dying, and she warned Frank that it would be so."

"Poor Selina! But—my dear lady, how do you know that?"

"My husband told me. He told me one night when we were sitting alone in the parlour. Not that he put faith in it. He had escaped Stephen's toils until then, he said in a joking tone, and thought he could take care of himself and escape them still. But I fear he did not."

"Now what is it you do fear?" asked the Squire. "Come."

She glanced round in dread, and then spoke with considerable hesitation and in a low whisper.

"I fear—that Stephen—may have—murdered him."

"Mercy upon us!" uttered the Squire, recoiling a step or two.

She put her elbow on the stile and raised her hand to her face, showing out so pale and distressed under its white net border.

"It lies upon me, sir—a great agony. I don't know what to do."

"But it could not be," cried the Squire, collecting his scared senses. "Your imagination must run away with you, child. Frank died up at Dr. Dale's; Stephen Radcliffe was down here at the time."

"Yes—I am aware of all that, sir. But—I believe it was as I fear. I don't pretend to account for it; to say what Stephen did or how he did it—but my fears are dreadful. I have no peace night or day."

The Squire stared at her and shook his head. I am sure he thought her brain was touched.

"My dear Mrs. Frank, this must be pure fancy. Stephen Radcliffe is a hard and griping man, not sticking at a trick or two where his pocket is concerned, but he wouldn't do such a thing as this. No, no; surly as he may be, he could not be guilty of murder."

She took her arm off the stile, with a short shiver. David Skate came into sight; Tod's footsteps were heard brushing the grass.

"Good-night, sir," she hurriedly said; and was over the stile before we could help her.

III

When the rumours first began, I can't tell you. They must have had a beginning: but no one recollected when the beginning was. It was said that curious noises were heard in the neighbourhood of Sandstone Torr. One spoke of it, and another spoke of it, at intervals of perhaps a month apart, until people grew accustomed to hearing of the strange sounds that went shrieking round the Torr on a windy night. Dovey, the blacksmith, going up to the Torr on some errand, declared he had heard them at mid-day: but he was not generally believed.

The Torr was so remote from the ordinary routes of traffic, that the noises were not likely to be heard often, even allowing that there were noises to hear. Shut in by trees, and in a lonely spot, people had no occasion to pass it. The narrow lane, by which it was approached from Church Dykely, led to nowhere else; on other sides it was surrounded by fields. Stephen Radcliffe was asked about these noises; but he positively denied having heard any, except those caused by the wind. That shrieked around the house as if so many witches were at work, he said, and it always had as long as he could remember. Which was true.

Stephen's inheritance of all the money on the death of his young half-brother Francis—young, compared with him—seemed to have been only the signal for him and his wife to become more unsociable, and they were bad enough before. They shut themselves up in the Torr, with that sister of hers, Eunice Gibbon, who acted as their servant, and saw no one. Neither visitors nor tradespeople were encouraged there; they preferred to live without help from any one: butcher or baker or candlestick maker. The produce of the farm supplied ordinary daily needs, and anything else that might be wanted was fetched from the village by Eunice Gibbon—as tall and strapping a woman as Mrs. Stephen, and just as grim and silent. Even the postman had orders to leave any letters that might arrive, addressed to the Torr, at Church Dykely post-office to be called for. Possibly it was a sense of their own unfitness for society that caused them to keep aloof from it. Stephen Radcliffe had always been a sullen, boorish man, in spite of his descent from the ancient Druids—or whatever the high-caste tribes might be, that he traced back from; and as to his wife, she was just as much like a lady as a pig's like a windmill.

The story of the queer noises gained ground, and in the course of time it coursed about pretty freely. One evening in the late spring—but the report had been abroad then for months and months—a circumstance caused it to be discussed at Dyke Manor. Giles, our groom, strolling out one night to give himself an airing, chanced to get near the Torr, and came home full of it. "Twere exactly," he declared, "like a lot o' witches howling in the air." Just as Stephen Radcliffe had said of the wind. The Squire told Giles it must be the owls; the servants thought Mr. Radcliffe might be giving his wife a beating; Mrs. Todhetley imagined it might be only the bleating of the young lambs. Giles protested it could come from neither owls nor lambs: and as to Radcliffe's beating 'Becca, he'd be hardly likely to try it on, for she'd beat back again. Tod and I were at school, and heard nothing of it till we got home in summer.

"Johnny! There's the noise!"

We two had been over to the Court to see the Sterlings; it was only the second day of our holidays; and were taking the cross-cut home through the fields, which led us past Sandstone Torr. It was the twilight of a summer's evening. The stars were beginning to show themselves; in the north-west the colours were the most beautiful opal conceivable; the round silver moon sailed in the clear blue sky. Crossing the stile by the grove of trees that on three sides surrounded the Torr, we had reached the middle of the next field, when a sort of faint wailing cry, indescribably painful, brought us both to a standstill.

"It must be the noise they talk of," repeated Tod.

Where did it come from? What was it? Standing on the path in the centre of the open field, we turned about and gazed around; but could see nothing to produce or cause it. It seemed to be overhead, ever so far up in the air: an unearthly, imploring cry, or rather a succession of cries; faint enough, as if the sound spent itself before it reached us, but still distinct; and just as much like what witches might be supposed to make, witches in pain, as any cries could be. I'd have given a month's pocket-money not to have heard it.

"Is it in the Torr?" exclaimed Tod, breaking the silence. "I don't see how that could be, though."

"It is up in the air, Tod."

We stood utterly puzzled; and gazing at the Torr. At as much of it, at least, as could be seen—the tops of the chimneys, and the sugar-loaf of a tower shooting up to its great height amidst them. The windows of the house and its old stone walls, on which the lichen vegetated, were hidden by the clustering old trees, in full foliage then.

"Hark! There it is again!"

The same horrible, low, distressing sound, something between a howl and a wail; enough to make a stout man shiver in his shoes.

"Is it a woman's cry, Tod?"

"I don't know, lad. It's like a person being murdered and crying out for help."

"Radcliffe can't be tanning his wife."

"Not he, Johnny. She'd take care of that. Besides, they've never been cat-and-dog. Birds of a feather: that's what they are. Oh, by Jove! there it comes again! Just listen to it! I don't like this at all, Johnny. It must be witches, and nothing else."

Decidedly it must be. It came from the air. The open fields lay around, white and still under the moonlight, and nothing was on their surface of any kind, human or animal. Now again! that awful cry, rising on the bit of breeze there was, and dying away in pain to a faint echo.

"Let us go to the Torr, Johnny, and ask Radcliffe if he hears it!"

We bounded forward under the cry, which rose again and again incessantly; but in nearing the house it seemed to get further off and to be higher than ever in the air. Leaping the gate into the lane, we reached the front-door, and seized the bell-handle. It brought Mrs. Radcliffe; a blue cap and red roses adoring her straggling hair. Holding the candle above her head, she peered at us with her small, sly eyes.

"Oh, is it you, young gentlemen? Do you want anything? Will you walk in?"

I was about to say No, when Tod pushed me aside and strode up the damp stone passage. They did not make fires enough in the house to keep out the damp. As he told me afterwards, he wanted to get in to listen. But there was no sound at all to be heard; the house seemed as still as death. Wherever the cries might come from, it was certainly not from inside the Torr.

"Radcliffe went over to Wire-Piddle this afternoon, and he's not back yet," she said; opening the parlour-door when we got to the hall. "Did you want him? You must ha' been in a hurry by the way you pulled the bell."

She put the candle down on the table. Her work lay there—a brown woollen stocking about half-way knitted.

"There is the most extraordinary noise outside that you ever heard, Mrs. Radcliffe," began Todd, seating himself without ceremony on the old-fashioned mahogany sofa. "It startled us. Did you hear it in here?"

"I have heard no noise at all," she answered quietly, taking up the stocking and beginning to knit standing. "What was it like?"

"An awful shrieking and crying. Not loud; nearly faint enough for dying cries. As it is not in your house—and we did not think it was, or could be—it must be, I should say, in the air."

"Ay," she said, "just so. I can tell you what it is, Mr. Joseph: the night-birds."

Tod looked at her, plying the knitting-needles so quickly, and looked at me, and there was a silence. I wondered what was keeping him from speaking. He suddenly bent his head forward.

"Have you heard any talk of these noises, Mrs. Radcliffe? People say they are to be heard almost any night."

"I've not heard no talk, but I have heard the noise," she answered, whisking out a needle and beginning another of the three-cornered rows. "One evening about a month ago I was a-coming home up the lane, and I hears a curious kind o' prolonged cry. It startled me at the moment, for, thinks I, it must be in this house; and I hastens in. No. Eunice said she had heard no cries: as how should she, when there was nobody but herself indoors? So I goes out again, and listens," added Mrs. Radcliffe, lifting her eyes from the stocking and fixing them on Tod, "and then I finds out what it really was—the night-birds."

"The night-birds?" he echoed.

"'Twas the night-birds, Mr. Joseph," she repeated, with an emphatic nod. "They had congregated in these thick trees, and was crying like so many human beings. I have heard the same thing many a time in Wiltshire when I was a girl. I used to go there to stay with aunt and uncle."

"Well, I never heard anything like it before," returned Tod. "It's just as though some unquiet spirit was in the air."

"Mayhap it sounds so afore you know what it is. Let me give you young gentlemen a drop o' my home-made cowslip wine."

She had taken the decanter of wine and some glasses off the sideboard with her long arms, before we could say Yes or No. We are famous for cowslip wine down there, but this was extra good. Tod took another glass of it, and got up to go.

"Don't be frighted if you hear the noise again, now that you know what it is," she said, quite in a motherly way. "For my part I wish some o' the birds was shot. They don't do no good to nobody."

"As there is not any house about here, except this, the thought naturally arises that the noise may be inside it—until you know to the contrary," remarked Tod.

"I wish it was inside it—we'd soon stop it by wringing all their necks," cried she. "You can listen," she added, suddenly going into the hall and flinging wide every door that opened from it and led to the different passages and rooms. "Go to any part of the house you like, and hearken for yourselves, young gentlemen."

Tod laughed at the suggestion. The passages were all still and cold, and there was nothing to hear. Taking up the candle, she lighted us to the front-door. Outside stood the woman-servant Eunice, a basket on her arm, and just about to ring, Mrs. Radcliffe inquired if she had heard any noise.

"Only the shrieking birds up there," she answered readily. "They be in full cry to-night."

"They've been startling these gentlemen finely."

"There bain't nothing to be startled at," said the woman, roughly, turning a look of contempt upon us. "If I was the master I'd shoot as many as I could get at; and if that didn't get rid of 'em, I'd cut the trees down."

"They make a queerer noise than any birds I ever heard before," said Tod, standing his ground to say it.

"They does," assented the woman. "That queer, that some folks believes it's the shrieks o' the skeleton on the gibbet."

Pleasant! When I and Tod had to pass within a few yards of its corner. The posts of the old gibbet were there still, but the skeleton had mouldered away long ago. A bit of chain, some few inches long, adhered to its fastening in the post still, and rattled away on windy nights.

"What donkeys we were, Johnny, not to know birds' cries when we heard them!" exclaimed Tod, as we tumbled over the gate and went flying across the field. "Hark! Listen! There it is again!"

There it was. The same despairing sort of wail, faintly rising and dying on the air. Tod stood in hushed silence.

"Johnny, I believe that's a human cry!—I could almost fancy," he went on, "that it is speaking words. No bird, that ever I met with, native or foreign, could make the like."

It died away. But still occurred the obvious question, What was it, and where did it come from? With nothing but the empty air above and around us, that was difficult to answer.

"It's not in the trees—I vow it," said Tod; "it's not inside the Torr; it can't rise up from under the ground. I say, Johnny, is it a case of ghost?"

The wailing arose again as he spoke, as if to reprove him for his levity. I'd rather have met a ghost; ay, and a real ghost; than have carried away that sound to haunt me.

We tore home as fast as our heels could take us, and told of the night's adventure. After the pater had blown us up for being late, he treated us to a dose of ridicule. Human cries, indeed? Ghosts and witches? I might be excused, he said, being a muff; but Joe must be just going back to his childhood. That settled Tod. Of all disagreeable things he most hated to be ridiculed.

"It must have been the old birds in those trees, after all, Johnny," said he, as we went up to bed. "I think the moon makes people fanciful."

And after a sound night's rest we woke up to the bright sunshine, and thought no more of the cries.

That morning, being close to Pitchley's Farm, we called in to see Mrs. Frank Radcliffe. But she was not to be seen. Her brother, David Skate, just come in to his mid-day dinner, came forward to meet us in his fustian suit. Annet had been hardly able to keep about for some time, he said, but this was the first day she had regularly broken down so as to be in bed.

"It has brought on a touch of fever," said he, pressing the bread-and-cheese and cider upon us, which he had ordered in.

"What has?" asked Tod.

"This perpetual torment that she keeps her mind in. But she can't help it, poor thing, so it's not fair to blame her," added David Skate. "It grows worse instead of better, and I don't see what the end of it is to be. I've thought for some time she might go and break up to-day."

"Why to-day?"

"Because it is the anniversary of her husband's death, Master Johnny. He died twelve months ago to-day."

Back went my memory to the morning we heard of it. When the pater was scolding Dwarf Giles in the yard, and Tod stood laughing at the young ducks taking to the water, and Stephen Radcliffe loomed into sight, grim and surly, to disclose to us the tidings that the post had brought in—his brother Frank's death.

"Has she still that curious fancy in her, David?—that he did not come by his death fairly."

"She has it in her, and she can't get it out of her," returned David. "Why, Master Johnny, it's nothing but that that's killing her. Ay, and that's not too strong a word, sir, for I do believe she'll die of it, unless something can be done to satisfy her mind, and give her rest," he added earnestly. "She thinks there was foul play used in some way, and that Stephen Radcliffe was at the bottom of it."

We had never heard a word about the fancy since that night when Annet first spoke of it at the stile, and supposed she had forgotten it long ago. The Squire and Mrs. Todhetley had often noticed how ill she looked, but they put it down to grief for Francis and to her anxiety about the farm.

"No, she has said no more since then," observed David. "She took up an idea that the Squire ascribed it to a wandering brain; and so has held her peace since."

"Is her brain wandering, do you think?" asked Tod.

"Well, I don't know," returned David, absently making little cuts at the edge of the cheese with the knife. "In all other respects she is as sane as sane can be; there's not a woman of sounder sense, as to daily matters, anywhere. But this odd fancy has got hold of her mind; and it's just driving her crazy. She says that her husband appears to her in her dreams, and calls upon her to help and release him."

"Release him from what? From his grave in Finchley Cemetery?"

"From what indeed!" echoed David Skate. "That's what I ask her. But she persists that, sleeping or waking, his spirit is always hovering near her, crying out to her to avenge him. She declares that it is no fancy. Of course it is, though."

"I never met with such a case," said Tod, forgetting the good cider in his astonishment. "Frank Radcliffe died up at Dr. Dale's in London. Stephen could not have had anything to do with his death: he was down here at the time."

"Well, Annet has the notion firmly fixed in her mind that he had, and there's no turning her," said David. "There will be no turning her this side the grave, unless we can free her from it. Any way, the fancy has come to such a pitch now, and is telling upon her so seriously, that something must be done. If it were not that just the busiest time has set in; the hay cut, and the wheat a'most ready to cut, I'd take her to London to Dr. Dale's. Perhaps if she heard the account of Frank's death from his own lips, and that it was a natural death, it might help her a bit."

We went home full of this. The Squire was in a fine way when he heard it, and brimming over with pity for Annet. He had grown to like her; and he had always looked on Francis as in some degree belonging to him.

"Look here," said he, in his impulsive good nature, "it will never do to let this go on: we shall have her in a mad-house too. That's not a bad notion of David Skate's; and if he can't leave to take her up to London just now, I'll take her."

"She could not go," said Tod. "She is in bed with low fever."

"Then I'll go up by myself," stamped the Squire in his zeal. "And get Dr. Dale to write out all the particulars, and hurry down again with them to her as fast as the train will bring me. Poor thing! her disease must be a sort of mania."

"Now, Johnny, mind you don't make a mistake in the omnibus. Use your eyes; they are younger than mine."

We were standing at Charing Cross in the hot afternoon sun, looking out for an omnibus that would take us westward. The Squire had lost no time in starting for London, and we had reached it an hour before. He let me come up with him, as Tod had gone to Whitney Hall.

"Here it is, sir. 'Kensington,—Hammersmith,—Richmond.' This is the right one."

The omnibus stopped, and in we got; for the Squire said the sun was too fierce for the outside; and by-and-by, when the houses became fewer, and the trees and fields more frequent, we were set down near Dr. Dale's. A large house, standing amidst a huge grass-plat, shut in by iron gates.

"I want to see Dr. Dale," said the pater, bustling in as soon as the door was opened, without waiting to be asked.

The servant looked at him and then at me; as if he thought the one or the other of us was a lunatic about to be left there. "This way, sir," said he to the Squire and put us into a small square room that had a blue and drab carpet, and a stand of plants before the window. A little man, with deep-set dark eyes, and the hair all gone from the top of his head, soon made his appearance—Dr. Dale.

The Squire plunged into explanations in his usual confusing fashion, mixing up many things together. Dr. Dale knitted his brow, trying to make sense of it.

"I'm sure I should be happy to oblige you in any way," said he—and he seemed to be a very pleasant man. "But I do not quite understand what it is you ask of me."

"Such a dreadful thing, you know, if she has to be put in a mad-house too!" went on the pater. "A pretty, anxious, hard-working little woman she is, as ever you saw, Dr. Dale! We think the account in your handwriting might ease her. I hope you won't mind the trouble."

"The account of what?" asked the doctor.

"Only this," explained the Squire, laying hold, in his zeal, of the doctor's button-hole. "Just dot down the particulars of Francis Radcliffe's death. His death here, you know. I suppose you were an eye-witness to it."

"But, my good sir, I—pardon me—I must repeat that I do not understand. Francis Radcliffe did not die here. He went away a twelvemonth ago, cured."

"Goodness bless me!" cried the Squire, staggering back to a chair when he had fully taken in the sense of the words, and staring about him like a real maniac. "It cannot be. I must have come to the wrong place."

"This is Dale House, and I am Dr. Dale. Mr. Francis Radcliffe was under my charge for some months: I can't tell exactly how many without referring to my books; seven or eight, I think; and he then left, cured, or nearly so."

"Johnny, hand me my handkerchief; it's in my hat. I can't make top or tail of this."

"I did not advise his removal," continued Dr. Dale, who, I do believe, thought the Squire was bad enough for a patient. "He was very nearly, if not quite well, but another month here would have established his recovery on a sure basis. However, his brother insisted on removing him, and I had no power to prevent it."

"What brother?" cried the Squire, rubbing his head helplessly.

"Mr. Radcliffe, of Sandstone Torr."

"Johnny, I think we must all be dreaming. Radcliffe of the Torr got a letter from you one morning, doctor—in June, I think; yes, I remember the hay-making was about—saying Francis had died; here in this house, with you: and bidding him come up to see you about it."

"I never wrote any such letter. Francis Radcliffe did not die here."

"Well, it was written for you by one of your people. Not die! Why, you held a coroner's inquest on him! You buried him in Finchley Cemetery."

"Nothing of the sort, Mr. Todhetley. Francis Radcliffe was taken from this house, by his brother, last June, alive and well."

"Well I never!—this beats everything. Was he not worn away to a skeleton before he went?—had he not heart disease?—did he not die of effusion on the brain?" ran on the Squire, in a maze of bewilderment.

"He was thin certainly: patients in asylums generally are; but he could not be called a skeleton; I never knew that he had heart disease. As to dying, he most assuredly did not die here."

"I do think I must be lost," cried the Squire. "I can't find any way out of this. Can you let me see Mr. Pitt, your head assistant, doctor? Perhaps he can throw some light on it. It was Pitt who wrote the letter to Mr. Radcliffe."

"You should see him with pleasure if he were still with me," replied the doctor. "But he has left."

"And Frank did not die here!" commented the Squire. "What can be the meaning of it?"

The meaning was evidently not to be found there. Dr. Dale said he could tell us no more than he had told, if he talked till night—that Francis Radcliffe was taken out by his brother. Stephen paid all charges at the time, and they went away together.

"And of course, Johnny, he is to be believed," quoth the pater, turning himself round and round on the grass-plot, as we were going away, like a teetotum. "Dale would not deceive us: he could have no object in doing that. What in the world does it all mean?—and where is Francis? Ste Radcliffe can't have shipped him off to Canada with the wheelbarrows!"

How the Squire whirled straight off to the train, finding one on the point of starting, and got down home again, there's no space to tell of. It was between eight and nine, as the station clock told him, but he was in too much excitement to let the matter rest.

"Come along, Johnny. I'll have it out with Stephen before I sleep."

And they had it out in that same gloomy parlour at the Torr, where Tod and I had been a night or two before; frightfully gloomy to-night, for the dusk was drawing on, and hardly a bit of light came in. The Squire and Stephen, sitting opposite each other, could not see the outline of one another's faces. Ste brazened it out.

"You're making a hullabaloo for nothing," said he, doggedly. "No, it's true he didn't die at the mad-house; he died within a week of coming out of it. Why didn't I tell the truth about it? Why, because I knew I should get a heap o' blame thrown back at me for taking him out—and I wished I hadn't took him out; but 'twas no good wishing then. How was I to know that the very self-same hour he'd got his liberty, he would begin drinking again?—and drink himself into a furious fever, and die of it? Could I bring him to life again, do you suppose?"

"What was the meaning of that letter you brought to me, purporting to come from Dr. Dale? Answer that, Stephen Radcliffe."

"I didn't bring you a letter from Dr. Dale. 'Twas from Pitt; Dr. Dale's head man. You read it yourself. When I found that Frank was getting unmanageable at the lodgings, I sent to Pitt, asking if he'd be good enough to come and see to him—I knew no other doctor up there; and Pitt was the best I could have, as he understood his case. Pitt came and took the charge; and I left Frank under him. I couldn't afford to stay up there, with my grass waiting to be cut, and all the fine weather wasting itself away. Pitt stayed with him; and he died in Pitt's arms; and it was Pitt that wrote the letter to tell me of it. You should ha' gone up with me, Squire," added Stephen, with a kind of sneer, "and then you'd have seen where he was for yourself, and known as much as I did."

"It was an infamous deceit to put upon me, Stephen Radcliffe."

"It did no harm. The deceit only lay in letting you think he died in the mad-house instead of out of it. If I'd not thought he was well enough to come out, I shouldn't have moved him. 'Twas his fault," sullenly added Stephen. "He prayed me to take him away from the place; not to go away without him."

"And where was it that he did die?"

"At my lodgings."

"What lodgings?"

"The lodgings I stayed at while I was shipping off the things to Tom. I took Frank there, intending to bring him down home with me when I came, and surprise you all. Before I could come he was drinking, and as mad again as a March hare. Pitt had to strap him down to his bed."

"Are you sure you did not ship him off to Tom also, while you were shipping the things?" demanded the Squire. "I believe you are crafty enough for it, Stephen Radcliffe—and unbrotherly enough."

"If I'd shipped him off, he could have shipped himself back again, I take it," returned Stephen, coolly.

"Where are these lodgings that he died at?"

"In London."

"Whereabouts in London? I didn't suppose they were in New York."

"'Twas near Cow Cross."

"Cow Cross! Where in the name of wonder is Cow Cross?"

"Up towards Smithfield. Islington way."

"You give me the address, Stephen Radcliffe. I insist upon knowing it. Johnny, you can see—take it down. If I don't verify this matter to my satisfaction, Mr. Radcliffe, I'll have you up publicly to answer for it."

Stephen took an old pocket-book out of his coat, went to the window to catch what little light came in, and ran his finger down the leaves.

"Gibraltar Terrace, Islington district," read he. "That was all the address I ever knew it by."

"Gibraltar Terrace, Islington district," repeated the pater. "Take it down, Johnny—here's the back of an old letter. And now, Mr. Radcliffe, will you go with me to London?"

"No. I'll be hanged if I do."

"I mean to come to the bottom of this, I can tell you. You shan't play these tricks on honest people with impunity."

"Why, what do you suspect?" roared Stephen. "Do you think I murdered him?"

"I'm sure I don't know what you did," retorted the pater. "Find out a man in one lie, and you may suspect him of others. What was the name of the people, at these lodgings?"

Stephen Radcliffe, sitting down again, put his hands on his knees, apparently considering; but I saw him take an outward glance at the Squire from under his grey eyebrows—very grey and bushy they were now. He could see that for once in his life the pater was resolute.

"Her name was Mapping," he said. "A widow. Mrs. Mapping."

"Put that down, Johnny. 'Mrs. Mapping, Gibraltar Terrace, Islington district.' And now, Mr. Radcliffe, where is Pitt to be found? He has left Dale House."

"In the moon, for aught I can tell," was the insolent answer. "I paid him for his attendance when we came back from the funeral—and precious high his charges were!—and I know nothing of him since."

We said good-night to Stephen Radcliffe with as much civility as could be called up under the circumstances, and went home in the fly. The next day we steamed up to London again to make inquiries at Gibraltar Terrace. It was not that the Squire exactly doubted Stephen's word, or for a moment thought that he had dealt unfairly by Frank: nothing of that sort: but he was in a state of explosion at the deceit Stephen Radcliffe had practised on him; and needed to throw the anger off. Don't we all know how unbearable inaction is in such a frame of mind?

Well. Up one street, down another, went we, in what Stephen had called the Islington district, but no Gibraltar Terrace could we see or hear of. The terrace might have been in Gibraltar itself, for all the sign there was of it.

"I'll go down to-morrow, and issue a warrant against Ste Radcliffe," cried the Squire, when we got in, tired and heated, to the Castle and Falcon—at which inn, being convenient to the search, he had put up. "I will, Johnny, as I'm a living man. It is infamous to send us up here on a wild-goose chase, to a place that has no name, and no existence. I don't like the aspect of things at all; and he shall be made to explain them."

"But I suppose we have not looked in all parts of Islington," I said. "It seems a large place. And—don't you think, sir—that it might be as well to ascertain where Pitt is? I dare say Dr. Dale knows."

"Perhaps it, would, Johnny."

"Pitt would be able to testify to the truth of what Stephen Radcliffe says. We might hear it all from him."

"And need not bother further about this confounded Gibraltar Terrace. The thought did not strike me before, Johnny. We'll go up to Dale's the first thing after breakfast."

The Squire chartered a cab: he was in too much of a fever to look out for an omnibus: and by ten o'clock Dr. Dale's was reached. The doctor was not at home, but we saw some one that the servant called Mr. Lichfield.

"Pitt?" said Mr. Lichfield—who was a tall, strong young man in a tweed suit of clothes, and had black hair parted down the middle—"Oh, he was my predecessor here. He has left."

"Where's he gone?" asked the Squire.

"I don't know, I'm sure. Dr. Dale does not know; for I have once or twice heard him wonder what had become of Pitt. Pitt grew rather irregular in his habits, I fancy, and the doctor discharged him."

"How long ago?"

"About a year, I think. I have not the least idea where Pitt is now: would be happy to tell you if I knew."

So, there we were again—baffled. The Squire went back in the cab to the Castle and Falcon, rubbing his face furiously, and giving things in general a few hard words.

Up to Islington again, and searching up and down the streets and roads. A bright thought took the pater. He got a policeman to show him to the district sorting-house, went in, and inquired whether such a place as Gibraltar Terrace existed, or whether it did not.

Yes. There was one. But it was not in Islington; only on the borders of it.

Away we went, after getting the right direction, and found it. A terrace of poor houses, in a quiet side-street. In nearly every other window hung a card with "Lodgings" on it, or "Apartments." Children played in the road: two men with a truck were crying mackerel.

"I say, Johnny, these houses all look alike. What is the number we want?"

"Stephen Radcliffe did not give any number."

"Bless my heart! We shall have to knock at every one of them."

And so he did. Every individual door he knocked at, one after the other, asking if Mrs. Mapping lived there. At the very last house of all we found her. A girl, whose clothes were dilapidated enough to have come down from Noah's Ark, got up from her knees, on which she was cleaning the door-flag, and told us to go into the parlour while she called Mrs. Mapping. It was a tidy threadbare room, not much bigger than a closet, with "Lodgings" wafered to the middle pane of the window.

Mrs. Mapping came in: a middle-aged, washed-out lady, with pink cheeks, who looked as if she didn't have enough to eat. She thought we had come after the lodgings, and stood curtsying, and rubbing her hands down her black-silk apron—which was in slits. Apparently a "genteel" person who had seen better days. The Squire opened the ball, and her face took a puzzled look as she listened.

"Radcliffe?—Radcliffe?" No, she did not recollect any lodger of the name. But then, nine times out of ten, she did not know the names of her lodgers. She didn't want to know them. Why should she? If the gentlemen's names came out incidental, well and good; if not, she never presumed to inquire after them. She had not been obliged to let lodgings always.

"But this gentleman died here—died, ma'am," interrupted the Squire, pretty nearly beside himself with impatience. "It's about twelve months ago."

"Oh, that gentleman," she said. "Yes, he did die here, poor young man. The doctor—yes, his name was Pitt, sir—he couldn't save him. Drink, that was the cause, I'm afeard."

The Squire groaned—wishing all drink was at the bottom of the Thames. "And he was buried in Finchley Cemetery, ma'am, we hear?"

"Finchley? Well, now yes, I believe it was Finchley, sir," replied Mrs. Mapping, considering—and I could see the woman was speaking the truth according to her recollection. "The burial fees are low at Finchley, sir."

"Then he did die here, ma'am—Mr. Francis Radcliffe?"

"Sure enough he did, sir. And a sad thing it was, one young like him. But whether his name was Radcliffe, or not, I couldn't take upon myself to say. I don't remember to have heard his name."

"Couldn't you have read it on the coffin-plate?" asked the Squire, explosively. "One might have thought if you heard it in no other way, you'd see it there."

"Well, sir, I was ill myself at the time, and in a good deal of trouble beside, and didn't get upstairs much out of my kitchen below. Like enough it was Radcliffe: I can't remember."

"His brother brought him—and lodged here with him—did he not?"

"Like enough, sir," she repeated. "There was two or three of 'em out and in often, I remember. Mr. Pitt, and others. I was that ill, myself, that some days I never got out of bed at all. I know it was a fine shock to me when my sister came down and said the young man was dead. She was seeing to things a bit for me during my illness. His rantings had been pitiful."

"Could I see your sister, ma'am?" asked the Squire.

"She's gone to Manchester, sir. Her husband has a place there now."

"Don't you recollect the elder Mr. Radcliffe?" pursued the Squire. "The young man's brother? He was staying up in London two or three times about some shipping."

"I should if I saw him, sir, no doubt. Last year I had rare good luck with my rooms, never hardly had 'em empty. The young man who died had the first-floor apartments. Well, yes, I do remember now that some gentleman was here two or three times from the country. A farmer, I think he was. A middle-aged man, sir, so to say; fifty, or thereabouts; with grey hair."

"That's him," interrupted the Squire, forgetting his grammar in his haste. "Should know the description of him anywhere, shouldn't we, Johnny? Was he here at the time of the young man's death, ma'am?"

"No, sir. I remember as much as that. He had gone back to the country."

Mrs. Mapping stood, smoothing down the apron, waiting to hear what we wanted next, and perhaps not comprehending the drift of the visit yet.

"Where's that Mr. Pitt to be found?"

"Law, sir! as if I knew!" she exclaimed. "I've never set eyes on him since that time. He didn't live here, sir; only used to come in and out to see to the sick young man. I never heard where he did live."

There was nothing more to wait for. The Squire slipped half-a-crown into the woman's hand as we went out, and she curtsied again and thanked him—in spite of the better days. Another question occurred to him.

"I suppose the young man had everything done for him that could be? Care?—and nourishment?—and necessary attendance?"

"Surely, sir. Why not? Mr. Pitt took care of that, I suppose."

"Ay. Well, it was a grievous end. Good-morning, ma'am."

"Good-day to you, gentlemen."

The Squire went looming up the street in the dumps; his hands in his pockets, his steps slow.

"I suppose, Johnny, if one tried to get at Pitt in this vast London city, it would be like looking for a needle in a bottle of hay."

"We have no clue to him, sir."

"No. And I don't know that it would answer any purpose if we did get at him. He could only confirm what we've heard. Well, this is fine news to take back to poor Annet Radcliffe!"

"I should think she had better not be told, sir."

"She must know it some time."

The Squire sent for David Skate when we got home, and told him what we knew; and the two marched to the Torr in the blazing June sun, and held an interview with Stephen Radcliffe. Ste was sullen and reserved, and (for him) haughty. It was a mistake, of course, as things turned out, his having taken Frank from the asylum, he admitted that, admitted he was sorry for it, but he had done it for the best. Frank got drinking again, and it was too much for him; he died after a few days of delirium, and Pitt couldn't save him. That was the long and the short of the history; and the Squire and Skate might make the best and the worst of it.

The Squire and Skate were two of the simplest of men; honest-minded themselves, and unsuspicious of other people. They quitted the Torr for the blazing meadows, on their road home again.

"I shall not say anything about this to Annet," observed David Skate. "In her present frame of mind it would not do. The fever seems better, and she is up, and about her work again. Later perhaps we may tell her of it."

"I wish we could have found Pitt," said the Squire.

"Yes, it would be satisfactory to hear what he has to say," replied David. "Some of these days, when work is slack, I'll take a run up to London and try and search him out. Though I suppose he could not tell us much more than the landlady has told."

"There it is," cried the Squire. "Even Johnny Ludlow, with his crotchets about people and his likes and dislikes, says he's sure Mrs. Mapping might be trusted; that she was relating facts."

So matters subsided, and the weeks and our holidays went on together. Stephen Radcliffe, by this act of deceit, added another crooked feather to his cap of ills in the estimation of the neighbourhood; though that would not be likely to trouble him. Meeting Mr. Brandon one day in the road, just out of Church Dykely, Stephen chanced to say that he wished to goodness it was in his power to sell the Torr, so that he might be off to Canada to his son: that was the land to make money at, by all accounts.

"You and your son might cut off the entail, now poor Francis is gone," said old Brandon, thinking what a good riddance it would be if Stephen went.

"I don't know who'd buy it—at my price," growled Stephen. "I mean to get shut o' them birds, though," he added, as an afterthought. "They're not entailed. They've never cried and shrieked as they do this summer. I'd as soon have an army of squalling cats around the place."

"The noise is becoming a subject of common talk," said old Brandon.

Ste Radcliffe bit his lips and turned his face another way, and emitted sundry daggers from his looks. "Let folks concern themselves with their own business," said he. "The birds is nothing to them."

Four weeks had gone by, and the moon was nearly at the full again. Its light streamed on the hedges, and flickered amidst the waving trees, and lay on the fields like pale silver. It was Sunday evening, and we had run out for a stroll before supper, Tod and I.

On coming out of church, Duffham had chanced to get talking of the cries. He had heard them the previous night. They gave him the shivers, he said, they were so like human cries. This put it into our heads to go again ourselves, which we had not done since that first time. How curiously events are brought about!

Leaping the last stile, the Torr was right before us at the opposite side of the large field, the tops of its chimneys and its towering sugar-loaf tower showing out white in the moonlight. The wind was high, blowing in gusts from the south-west.

"I say, Johnny, it's just the night for witches. Whirr! how it sweeps along! They'll ride swimmingly on their broomsticks."

"The wind must have got up suddenly," I answered. "There was none to-day. It was too hot for it. Talking of witches and broomsticks, Tod, have you read—"

He put his arm out to stop my words and steps, halting himself. We had been rushing on like six, had traversed half the field.

"What's that, Johnny?" he asked in a whisper. "There"—pointing onwards at right angles. "Something's lying there."

Something undoubtedly was—lying on the grass. Was it an animal?—or a man? It did not look much like either. We stood motionless, trying to make the shape out.

"Tod! It is a woman."

"Gently, lad! Don't be in a hurry. We'll soon see."

The figure raised itself as we approached, and stood confronting us. The last pull of wind that went brushing by might have brushed me down, in my surprise. It was Mrs. Francis Radcliffe.

She drew her grey cloak closer round her and put her hand upon Tod's arm. He went back half a step: I'm not sure but he thought it might be her ghost.

"Do not think me quite out of my mind," she said—and her voice and manner were both collected. "I have come here every evening for nearly a week past to listen to the cries. They have never been so plain as they are to-night. I suppose the wind helps them."

"But—you—were lying on the grass, Mrs. Francis," said Tod; not knowing yet what to make of it all.

"I had put my ear on the ground, wondering whether I might not hear it plainer," she replied. "Listen!"

The cry again! The same painful wailing sound that we heard that other night, making one think of I know not what woe and despair. When it had died away, she spoke further, her voice very low.

"People are talking so much about the cries that I strolled on here some evenings ago to hear them for myself. In my mind's tumult I can hardly rest quiet, once my day's work is done: what does it matter which way I stroll?—all ways are the same to me. Some people said the sounds came from the birds, some said from witches, some from the ghost of the man on the gibbet: but the very first night I came here I found out what they were really like—my husband's cries."

"What!" cried Tod.

"And I believe from my very soul that it is his spirit that cries!" she went on, her voice taking as much excitement as any voice, only half raised, can take. "His spirit is unable to rest. It is here, hovering about the Torr. Hush! there it comes again."

It was anything but agreeable, I can assure you, to stand in that big white moonlit plain, listening to those mysterious cries and to these ghostly suggestions. Tod was listening with all his ears.

"They are the very cries he used to make in his illness at the farm," said Mrs. Radcliffe. "I can't forget them. I should know them anywhere. The same sound of voice, the same wail of anguish: I could almost fancy that I hear the words. Listen."

It did seem like it. One might have fancied that his name was repeated with a cry for help. "Help! Frank Radcliffe! Help!" But at such a moment as this, when the nerves are strung up to concert pitch, imagination plays us all sorts of impossible tricks.

"I'll be shot if it's not like Frank Radcliffe's voice!" exclaimed Tod, breaking the silence. "And calling out, too."

"Thank you," said Mrs. Francis. "I shall not be able to bear this long: I shall have to speak of it to the world. When I say that you have recognized his voice also, they will be less likely to mock at me as a lunatic. David did, when I told him. At least, I could make no impression on him."

Tod was lying down with his ear to the ground. But he soon got up, saying he could not hear so well.

"Did Stephen kill him, do you think?" she asked, in a dread whisper, drawing closer to us. "Why, else, should his poor unquiet spirit haunt the region of the Torr?"

"It is the first time I ever heard of spirits calling out in a human voice," said Tod. "The popular belief is, that they mostly appear in dumb show."

He quitted us, as he spoke, and went about the field with slow steps, halting often to look and listen. The trees around the Torr in particular seemed to attract his attention, by the length of time he stared up at them. Or, perhaps, it might be at the tops of the chimneys: or perhaps at the tapering tower. We waited in nearly the same spot, shivering and listening. But the sounds never came so distinctly again: I think the wind had spent itself.

"It is a dreadful weight to have to carry about with me," said poor Annet Radcliffe as we walked homewards. "And oh! what will be the ending? Will it be heard always?"

I had never seen Tod so thoughtful as he was that night. At supper he put down his knife and fork perpetually to fall into a brown study; and I am sure he never knew a word of the reading afterwards.

It was some time in the night, and I was fast asleep and dreaming of daws and magpies, when something shook my shoulder and awoke me. There stood Tod, his nightshirt white as snow in the moonlight.

"Johnny," said he, "I have been trying to get daylight out of that mystery, and I think I've done it."

"What mystery? What's the matter?"

"The mystery of the cries. They don't come from Francis Radcliffe's ghost, but from Francis himself. His ghost! When that poor soft creature was talking of the ghost, I should have split with laughter but for her distress."

"From Francis himself! What on earth do you mean?"

"Stephen has got him shut up in that tower."

"Alive?"

"Alive! Go along, Johnny! You don't suppose he'd keep him there if he were dead. Those cries we heard to-night were human cries; words; and that was a human voice uttering them, as my ears and senses told me; and my brain has been in a muddle ever since, all sleep gone clean out of it. Just now, turning and twisting possibilities about, the solution of the mystery came over me like a flash of lightning. Ste has got Frank shut up in the Torr."

He, standing there upright by the bed, and I, digging my elbow into the counterpane and resting my cheek on my hand, gazed at one another, the perplexity of our faces showing out strongly in the moonlight.

IV

Mr. Duffham the surgeon stood making up pills and powders in his surgery at Church Dykely, the mahogany counter before him, the shelves filled with glass bottles of coloured liquids behind him. Weighing out grains of this and that in the small scales that rested beside the large ones, both sets at the end of the counter, was he, and measuring out drops with a critical eye. The day promised to be piping-hot, and his summer house-coat, of slate-coloured twill, was thrown back on his shoulders. Spare and wiry little man though he was, he felt the heat. He was rather wondering that no patients had come in yet, for people knew that this was the time to catch him, before he started on his rounds, and he generally had an influx on Monday morning.

Visitor the first. The surgery-door, standing close to the open front one, was tapped at, and a tall, bony woman entered, dressed in a big straw bonnet with primrose ribbons, a blue cotton gown and cotton shawl. Eunice Gibbon, Mrs. Stephen Radcliffe's sister.

"Good-morning, Mr. Duffham," she said, lodging her basket on the counter. "I'm frightfully out o' sorts, sir, and think I shan't be right till I've took a bottle or two o' physic."

"Sit down," said the doctor, coming in front of the counter, preparatory to inquiring into the symptoms.

She sat down in one of the two chairs: and Duffham, after sundry questions, told her that her liver was out of order. She answered that she could have told him that, for nothing but "liver" was ever the matter with her. He went behind the counter again to make up a bottle of some delectable stuff good for the complaint, and Eunice sat waiting for it, when the surgery-door was pushed open with a whirl and a bang, and Tod and I burst in. To see Eunice Gibbon there, took us aback. It seemed a very curious coincidence, considering what we had come about.

"Well, young gentlemen," quoth Duffham, looking rather surprised, and detecting our slight discomfiture, "does either of you want my services?"

"Yes," said Tod, boldly; "Johnny does: he has a headache. We'll wait, Mr. Duffham."

Leaning on the counter, we watched the progress of the making-up in silence, Duffham exchanging a few words with Eunice Gibbon at intervals. Suddenly he opened upon a subject that caused Tod to give me a private dig with his elbow.

"And how were the cries last night?" asked Duffham. "Did you hear much of them?"

"There was no cries last night," answered Eunice—which brought me another dig from Tod. "But wasn't the wind high! It went shrieking round the Torr like so many mad cats. Two spoonfuls twice a-day, did you say, sir?"

"Three times a-day. I am putting the directions on the bottle. You will soon feel better."

"I've been subject to these bilious turns all my life," she said, speaking to me and Tod. "But I don't know when I've had as bad a one as this. Thank ye, sir."

Taking the bottle of physic, she put it into her basket, said good-morning, and went away. Duffham came to the front, and Tod jumped on the counter and sat there facing us, his long legs dangling. I had taken one of the chairs.

"Mr. Duffham, what do you think we have come about?" began Tod, dropping his voice to a mysterious key. "Don't you go and faint away when you hear it."

"Faint away!" retorted old Duffham.

"I'll be shot if it would not send some people into a faint! That Gibbon woman has just said that no cries were to be heard last night."

"Well?"

"Well, there were cries; plenty of them. And awful cries they were. I, and Johnny, and Mrs. Frank Radcliffe—yes, she was with us—stood in that precious field listening to them till our blood ran cold. You heard them, you know, on Saturday night."

"Well?" repeated Duffham, staring at Tod.

"Look here. We have found it out—and have come over to tell you—and to ask you what can be done," went on Tod earnestly, jumping off the counter and putting his back against the door to make sure of no interruption. "The cries come from Frank Radcliffe. He is not dead."

"What?" shouted Duffham, who had turned to face Tod and stood in the middle of the oil-cloth, wondering whether Tod was demented.

"Frank is no more dead than I am. I'd lay my life upon it. Stephen Radcliffe has got him shut up in the tower; and the piteous cries are his—crying for release."

"Bless my heart and mind!" exclaimed Duffham, backing right against the big scales. "Frank Radcliffe alive and shut up in the tower! But there's no way to the tower. He could not be got into it."

"I don't care. I know he is there. That huzzy, now gone out, does well to say no cries were abroad last night; her business is to throw people off the scent. But I tell you, Duffham, the cries never were so loud or so piteous, and I heard what they said as distinctly as you can hear me speak now. 'Help! Frank Radcliffe! Help!' they said. And I swear the voice was Frank's own."

"If ever I heard the like of this!" ejaculated Duffham. "It is really not—not to be credited."

"The sound of the cries comes out on the air through the openings in the tower," ran on Tod, in excitement. "Oh, he is there, poor fellow, safe enough. And to think what long months he has been kept there, Stephen's prisoner! Twelve. Twelve, as I'm alive. Now, look you here, Duffham! you are staring like an unbeliever."

"It's not altogether that—that I don't believe," said Duffham, whose wide-open eyes were staring considerably. "I am thinking what is to be done about it—how to set the question at rest."

Tod left the door unguarded and flung himself into the other chair. He went over the whole narrative quietly: how Mrs. Frank Radcliffe—who had been listening to the cries for a week past—had first put him into a puzzle, how he had then heard the words and the voice, and how the true explanation came flashing into his mind later. With every sentence, Duffham grew more convinced, and at last he believed it as much as we did.

"And now how is he to be got out?" concluded Tod.

Holding a council together, we decided that the first step must be to get a magistrate's order to search the Torr. That involved the disclosure of the facts to the magistrate—whosoever he might be. Mr. Brandon was pitched upon: Duffham proposed the Squire at first; but, as Tod pointed out, the Squire would be sure to go to work in some hot and headlong manner, and perhaps ruin all. Let Stephen

Radcliffe get only half an inkling of what was up, and he might contrive to convey Frank to the ends of the earth.

All three of us started at once, Duffham leaving his patients for that one morning to doctor themselves, and found Mr. Brandon at breakfast. He had been distracted with face-ache all night, he said, which caused him to rise late. The snow-white table-cloth was set off with flowers and plate, but the fare was not luxurious. The silver jug held plenty of new milk, the silver tea-pot a modicum of the weakest of tea, the silver rack the driest of dry toast. A boiled egg and the butter-dish remained untouched. One of the windows was thrown up wide to the summer air, and to the scent from the clustering flower-beds and the hum of the bees dipping over them to sip their sweets.

Breaking off little bits of toast, and eating them slowly, Mr. Brandon listened to the tale. He did not take it in. That was check the first. And he would not grant a warrant to search the Torr. That was check the second.

"Stephen Radcliffe is bad enough in the way of being sullen and miserly," said he. "But as to daring such a thing as this, I don't think he would. Pass his brother off to the world for dead, and put him into his house and keep him there in concealment! No. No one of common sense would believe it."

Tod set on again, giving our experience of the past night, earnestly protesting that he had recognized Frank's voice, and heard the words it said—"Help! Frank Radcliffe!" He added that Annet Radcliffe, Frank's widow—or wife, whichever it might turn out to be—had been listening to the cries for days past and knew them for her husband's: only she, poor daft woman, took them to come from his ghost. Mr. Brandon sipped his tea and listened. Duffham followed on: saying that when he heard the cries on Saturday night, in passing the Torr on his way from the Court, he could then almost have staked his existence upon their being human cries, proceeding from some human being in distress, but for the apparent impossibility of such a thing. And I could see that an impression was at length made on Mr. Brandon.

"If Stephen Radcliffe has done so infamous an act, he must be more cruel, more daring than man ever was yet," remarked he, in answer. "But I must be more satisfied of it before I sign the warrant you ask for."

Well, there we sat, hammering at him. That is, they did. Being my guardian, I did not presume to put in a word edgeways, so far as pressing him to act went. In all that he thought right, and in spite of his quiet manner and his squeaky voice, old Brandon was a firm man, not to be turned by argument.

"But won't you grant this warrant, sir?" appealed Tod for the tenth time.

"I have told you, no," he replied. "I will not at the present stage of the affair. In any case, I should not grant it without consulting your father—"

"He is so hot-headed," burst in Tod. "He'd be as likely as not to go off knocking at the Torr door without his hat, demanding Frank Radcliffe."

"Mr. Todhetley was Frank Radcliffe's trustee, and he is your father, young man; I do not stir a step in this matter without consulting him," returned old Brandon, coolly persistent.

Well, there was nothing for it now but to go back home and consult the pater. It seemed like a regular damper—and we were hot and tired besides. Tod in his enthusiasm had pictured us storming the Torr at mid-day, armed with the necessary authority, and getting out Frank at once.

Mr. Brandon ordered his waggonette—a conveyance he did not like, and scarcely ever used himself, leaving it to the servants for their errands—and we all drove back to Dyke Manor, himself included. To describe the astonishment of the pater when the disclosure was made to him would take a strong pen. He rubbed his face, and blustered, and stared around, and then told Tod he was a fool.

"I know I am in some things," said Tod, as equably as old Brandon could have put it; "but I'm not in this. If Frank Radcliffe is not alive in that tower of Stephen's, and calling out nightly for his release, you may set me down as a fool to the end of my days, Father."

"Goodness bless us all!" cried the poor bewildered Squire. "Do you believe this, Brandon?"

Mr. Brandon did not say whether he believed it or not. Both of them shook their heads about granting a warrant: upon which, Tod passionately asked whether Francis Radcliffe was to be left in the tower to die. It was finally decided that we should go in a body that night to the field again, so as to give the two doubters the benefit of hearing anything there might be to hear. And Mr. Brandon stayed with us for the day, telling his coachman to come back at night with the small pony-gig to take him home.

The moon was just as bright as on the previous night, and we started on our expedition stealthily. Tod and I went first; Duffham came strolling next; and the Squire and Mr. Brandon afterwards. Should Stephen Radcliffe or any of his people catch sight of the whole of us moving together, he might suspect there was something in the wind.

Annet did not make her appearance, which was a great relief. For we could talk without restraint; and it would never have done to let her know what we suspected: and so raise wild hopes within her that might not be fulfilled. We knew later that her mother was at Pitchley's Farm that evening, and it kept Annet at home.

Was Heaven interfering in Frank's behalf? It does interfere for the oppressed, you know; ay, more often than we heedless and ungrateful mortals think for. Never had the cries been so plain as they were this night, though there was no wind to waft them downwards, for the air was perfectly still: and the words were distinctly heard. "Help! Help! Frank Radcliffe."

"Mercy upon us!" exclaimed the Squire, under his breath. "The voice does sound like Frank's."

Mr. Brandon was standing with his hand to his ear. Duffham leaned on his gold-headed cane, his face lifted upwards.

Tod stood by in dudgeon; he was angry with them for not having believed him at first.

"I think we may grant a search-warrant, Squire," said Mr. Brandon.

"And send old Jones the constable, to execute it," assented the Squire.

Tod flung back his head. "Old Jones! Much use he'd be! Why, father, Eunice Gibbon alone could settle old Jones with his shaky legs. She'd pitch him out at the first window."

"Jones can take help, Joe."

It was the breakfast hour at the Torr, eight o'clock. The meal was being taken in the kitchen. Less semblance of gentility than even in the former days was kept up; all usages of comfort and refinement had departed with old Mr. Radcliffe and Selina. Stephen was swallowing his eggs and rashers of bacon quickly. Tuesday is Alcester market-day, and he was going in to attend it, expecting to sell some of his newly-gathered crop of hay. Mrs. Stephen sat opposite him, eating bacon also; and Eunice Gibbon stood at the dresser, mixing some meal for the fattening of fowls. Miserly though Stephen was by nature, he liked a good table, and took care to have it.

"Could you bring some starch home, master?" asked Eunice, turning her head round to speak.

"Why can't you get your starch here?" retorted Stephen.

"Well, it's a farthing less a pound at Alcester than it is at Church Dykely," said Eunice. "They've rose it here."

Farthings were farthings in Stephen's eyes, and he supposed he might as well bring the starch. "How much is wanted of it?" he growled.

"We'd better have a pound," interposed Becca. "Half pounds don't get the benefit of the farthing: you can't split a farthing in two. Shall you be home early?" she continued to her husband.

"Don't know. Not afore afternoon."

"Because we shall want some of the starch to-day. There's none to go on with, is there, Eunice?"

"Yes, there's a bit. I can make it do."

"You'll have to wait till you get it," remarked Stephen as he pushed his plate away and rose from table. "And mind you don't forget to give the pigs their dinner."

"What'll be wanted up there to-day?" inquired Becca, pointing towards some invisible place over-head, possibly intending to indicate the tower.

"Nothing but dinner," said Stephen. "What should there be? I shall be back afore tea-time."

He went out at the back-door as he spoke, gave a keen look or two around his yard and premises generally, to see that all was right, and presently trotted away on horseback. A few minutes later, Jim, the only regular man kept, was seen to cross the yard towards the lane with the horse and cart.

"Where be you off to, Jim?" demanded Becca, stalking to the door and speaking at the top of her voice.

"Master ordered me to go after that load o' manure," called back Jim, standing upright in the cart and arresting the horse for a moment.

"What, this morning?"

"It's what he told me."

"Well, don't go and make a day's work of it," commanded Mrs. Stephen. "There's a sight o' things a-waiting to be done."

"I can't be back afore two, hasten as I 'ool," returned Jim, giving the horse his head and clattering off.

"I wonder what the master sent him to-day for, when he's away himself?" cried Becca to her sister, returning to the table in the kitchen.

"Well, he got a message last night to say that if he didn't send for it away to-day it wouldn't be kept for him," said Eunice. "It's a precious long way to have to go for a load o' manure!"

"But then we get it for the fetching; there's naught to pay," returned Becca.

She had begun to wash up the breakfast-things, and when that was done she put the kitchen to rights. Eunice seemed to be at all sorts of jobs, indoors and out, and went stalking about in pattens. The furnace had been lighted in the brewhouse, for Eunice had a day's washing before her. Becca went up to make the beds, and brought down sundry armfuls of clothes for the wash. About ten o'clock she appeared in the brewhouse with her bonnet and shawl on. Eunice was standing at the tub in her pattens, rubbing away at the steaming soap-suds.

"Why, where be you going?" she exclaimed in evident surprise.

"I'm a-going over to Dick's to fetch Beccy," replied Mrs. Stephen. "It's a long while since she was here. Ste don't care to see children about the place. The child shall stop to dinner with us and can go home by herself in the afternoon. What's the matter now, Eunice Gibbon? Don't it please ye?"

"Oh, it pleases me well enough," returned Eunice, who was looking anything but pleased, and splashing both hands desperately about in the water, over one of Stephen's coloured cotton handkerchiefs. "The child can come, and welcome, for me. 'Tain't that."

"It's some'at else then," remarked Becca.

"Well, I'd wanted to get a bit o' talk with ye," said Eunice. "That's what it is. The master's safe off, and it was a good opportunity for it."

"What about?"

Eunice Gibbon took her hands out of the soap-suds and rested them on the sides of the tub, while she answered—coming to the point at once.

"I've been a-thinking that I can't stop on here, Becca. I bain't at ease. Many a night lately I have laid awake over it. If anything comes out about—you know what—we might all of us get into trouble."

"No fear," said Becca.

"Well, I says there is fear. Folks have talked long enough; but it strikes me they won't be satisfied with talking much longer: they'll be searching out. Only yesterday morning when I was waiting at Duffham's while he mixed up the stuff, he must begin upon it. 'Did ye hear the cries last night?' says he—or something o' that. 'No,' says I in answer; 'there was none to hear, only the wind.' Them two young gents from the Manor was there, cocking up their ears at the words. I see 'em."

Rebecca Radcliffe remained silent. Truth to tell, she and Stephen were getting afraid of the cries themselves. That is, of what the cries might result in.

"He ought to be got away," resumed Eunice.

"But there's no means o' getting him away."

"Well, I can't feel comfortable, Becca; not safe, you know. So don't you and the master be put out if I walks myself off one o' these here first fine days. When I come here, I didn't bargain for nothing o' this sort."

"There's no danger of ill turning up," flashed Becca, braving out the matter with scorn. "The cries is took to come from the birds: who is to pick up any other notion, d'ye suppose? I'll tell ye what it is, Eunice: that jaundiced liver of yours is tormenting you. You'll be afeared next of your own shadda."

"Perhaps it is," acknowledged Eunice, dropping the argument and resuming her rubbing. "I know that precious physic of old Duffham's is upsetting me. It's the nausiousest stuff I ever took."

Mrs. Stephen stalked out of the kitchen and betook herself across the fields, towards her brother's. Richard Gibbon had succeeded to his late father's post of gamekeeper to the Chavasses. The gamekeeper's lodge was more than a mile away; and Mrs. Stephen strode off, out of sight, unconscious of what was in store for the Torr.

Eunice went on with her washing, deep in thought. She had fully made up her mind to quit the Torr; but she meant to break the fact by degrees to its master and mistress. Drying her hands for the temporary purpose of stirring-up and putting more slack on the furnace fire, she was interrupted by a gentle ring at the front-door bell.

"Why, who on earth's that?" she exclaimed aloud. "Oh, it must be Lizzy," with a flash of recollection: "she sent word she should be over to-day or to-morrow. How early she have got here!"

Free of all suspicion, glancing at no ill, Eunice went through the passages and opened the front-door. Quite a small crowd of people stood there, and one or two of them pushed in immediately. Mr. Duffham, Tod, I, the Squire, old Jones, and old Jones's man, who was young, and active on his legs. The Squire would come, and we were unable to hinder him.

"In the Queen's name!" cried old Jones—who always used that formula on state occasions. And Eunice Gibbon screamed long and loud.

To oppose our entrance was not to be thought of. We had entered and could not be thrust back again. Eunice took to her heels up the passage, and confronted us at the parlour-door with a pair of tongs. Duffham and Tod disarmed her. She then flew to the kitchen, sat down, and went into hysterics. Old Jones read out the authority for the search, but she only screamed the louder.

They left her to get out of the screaming at her leisure, and went up, seeking the entrance to the tower. It was found without much difficulty: Tod was the one to see it first. A small door (only discovered by Stephen Radcliffe since his father's death, as we heard later) led from a dark and unused lumber-room to the narrow stairs of the tower. In its uppermost compartment, a little, round den, sat Frank Radcliffe, chained to the wall.

Not at once could we take in the features of the scene; for, all the light came in through the one long narrow opening, a framed loophole without glass, that was set in the deep round wall of the tower. A mattress was spread on the floor, with a pillow and blankets; one chair stood close to a box that served for a table, on which he no doubt eat his meals, for there were plates and food on it; another box, its lid open, was in a corner, and on the other chair sat Frank. That was every earthly article the place contained. It was through that opening—you could not call it a window—that Frank's cries for help had gone forth to the air. There he sat, the chain round his waist, turning his amazed eyes upon us.

And raving mad, you ask? No. He was all skin and bone, and his fair hair hung down like that of a wild man of the woods, but he was as sane as you or I. He rose up, the chain clanking, and then we saw that it was long enough to admit of his moving about to any part of the den.

"Oh, God bless you, Frank!—we have come to release you," burst forth the Squire, impetuously seizing both his hands. "God help you, my poor lad!" And Frank, what with surprise and the not being over stout, burst into joyous tears.

The ingenious scheme of taking possession of Frank, and representing him as dead, that he might enjoy all the money, had occurred to Stephen Radcliffe when he found Frank was recovering under Dr. Dale's treatment. During the visits Stephen paid to London at that time, he and Pitt, Dr. Dale's head man, became very intimate: and when Pitt was discharged from Dr. Dale's they grew more so. Stephen Radcliffe would not perhaps have done any harm to Frank in the shape of poison or a dagger, being no more of a killer and slayer of men than were his neighbours; but to keep him concealed in the Torr, so as to reap the benefit himself of all the money, he looked upon as a very venial crime indeed—quite justifiable, so to say. Especially, if he could escape being found out. And this fine scheme he perfected and put in practice, and successfully carried through.

How much of it he confided to Pitt, or how much he did not, will never be known. Certain it was, that Pitt wrote the letter announcing Frank's death; though we could not find out that he had helped it in any other way. But a very curious coincidence attended the affair; one that aided Stephen's plans materially; and but for its happening I do not see that they could have succeeded when inquiries were made. In the London house where Stephen lodged (Gibraltar Terrace, that I and the Squire had a two days' hunt to find) there came to live a young man, who was taken ill close upon his entrance with a malady arising from his habits of drinking. Pitt, coming often to Gibraltar Terrace then with Stephen Radcliffe, took to attend on the young man out of good nature, doing for him all that could be done. It was this young man who died, and was buried in Finchley Cemetery; and of whose death the landlady with the faded face and black silk apron spoke to the Squire, thereby establishing in our minds the misapprehension that it was Francis Radcliffe. Stephen did not take Frank to the lodgings at all; he brought him straight down to the Torr when he was released from Dr. Dale's, taking care to get out at a remote country station in the dusk of evening, where his own gig, conveyed thither by Becca, was in waiting. He laid his plans well, that crafty Stephen! And, once he had got Frank securely into that upper den, he might just have kept him there for life, but for that blessed outlet in the wall, and no one been any the wiser.

Stephen Radcliffe did not bargain for that. It nearly always happens that in doing an ill deed we overreach ourselves in some fatal way. Knowing that no sound, though it were loud enough to awaken the seven sleepers, could penetrate from that upper room through the massive walls of the house, and be heard below, Stephen thought his secret was safe, and that Frank might call out, if he would, until Doomsday. It never occurred to him that the cries could get out through that unglazed window in the tower wall, and set the neighbourhood agog with curiosity. They did, however: and Stephen, whatever amount of dread it might have brought his heart, was unable to stop them. Not until Frank had been for some months chained in his den, did it occur to himself to make those cries, so hopeless was he of their being heard below to any good purpose. But one winter night when the wind was howling outside, and the sound of it came booming into his ears through the window, it struck him that he might be heard through that very opening; and from that time his voice was raised in supplication evening after evening. Stephen could do nothing. He dared not brick the opening up lest some suspicion or other should be excited outside; he could not remove Frank, for there was no other secret room to remove him to, or where his cries would not have been heard below. He ordered Frank to be still: he threatened him; he once took a horsewhip to him and laid it about his shoulders. All in vain. When Frank was alone, his cries for release never ceased. Stephen and his household put it upon the birds and the wind, and what not; but they grew to dread it: and Stephen, even at this time, of discovery, was perpetually ransacking his brains for some safe means of departing for Canada and carrying Frank with him. The difficulty lay in conveying Frank out of the Torr and away. They might drug him for the bare exit, but they could not keep him perpetually drugged; they could not hinder him coming in contact with his fellow-men on the journey and transit, and Frank had a tongue in his head. No: Stephen saw no hope, no safety, but in keeping him where he was.

"But how could you allow yourself to be brought up here?—and fastened to a stake in this shameful fashion?" was nearly the first question of the Squire when he could collect his senses: and he asked it with just a touch of temper, for he was beginning to think that Frank, in permitting it, must have been as simple as the fool in a travelling circus.

"He got me up by stratagem," answered Frank, tossing his long hair back from his face. "While we were sitting at supper the night we arrived here, he began talking about the wonderful discovery he had made of the staircase and opening to the tower. Naturally I was interested; and when Stephen proposed to show it me at once, I assented gladly. Becca came with us, saying she'd carry the candle. We got up here, and were all three standing in the middle of the floor, just where we are standing now, when I suddenly had a chain—this chain—slipped round my waist, and found myself fastened to the wall, a prisoner."

"But why did you come to the Torr at all?" stamped the Squire, while old Jones stretched out his hands, as if putting imaginary handcuffs on Stephen's. "Why did you not go at once to your own home—or come to us? When you knew you were going to leave Dale's, why didn't you write to say so?"

"When events are past and gone we perceive the mistakes we have made, though we do not see them at the time," answered Frank, turning his blue eyes from one to the other of us. "Dr. Dale did not wish me to quit his house quite so soon; though I was perfectly well, he said another month there would be best for me. I, however, was anxious to get away, more eager for it than I can tell you—which was only natural. Stephen whispered to me that he would accomplish it, but that I must put myself entirely in his hands, and not write to any one down here about it. He got me out, sooner than I had thought for: sooner, as he declared, than he had thought for himself; and he said we must break the news to Annet very cautiously, for she was anything but strong. He proposed to take me to the Torr for the first night of my return, and give me a bed there; and the following day the communication could be made to Annet at Pitchley's Farm, and then I might follow it as soon as I pleased. It all seemed to me feasible; quite the right way of going to work; in fact, the only way: I thanked Stephen, and came down here with him in all confidence."

"Good patience!" cried the Squire. "And you had no suspicions, Frank Radcliffe!—knowing what Stephen was!"

"I never knew he would do such a dastardly deed as this. How could I know it?"

"Oh, come along!" returned the Squire, beginning to stumble down the narrow, dark stairs. "We'll have the law of him."

The key of the chain had been found hanging on a nail outside the door, out of poor Frank's reach. He was soon free; but staggered a little when he began to descend the stairs. Duffham laid hold of him behind, and Tod went before.

"Thank God! thank God!" he broke out with reverent emotion, when the bright sun burst upon him through the windows, after passing the dark lumber-room. "I feared I might never see full daylight again."

"Have you any clothes?" asked Duffham. "This coat's in rags."

"I'm sure I don't know whether I have or not," replied Frank. "The coat is all I have had upon me since coming here."

"Becca's a beast," put in Tod. "And I hope Stephen will have his neck stretched."

Eunice Gibbon was nowhere to be seen below. The premises were deserted. She had made a rush to her brother's, the gamekeeper's lodge, to warn Becca of what was taking place. We started for Dyke Manor, Frank in our midst, leaving the Torr, and its household gods, including the cackling fowls and the dinnerless pigs, to their fate. Mr. Brandon met us at the second field, and he took Frank's hand in silence.

"God bless you, lad! So you have been shut up there!"

"And chained to a stake in the wall," cried the Squire.

"Well, it seems perfectly incredible that such a thing should take place in these later days. It reads like an episode of the dark ages."

"Won't we pay out Master Radcliffe for 't!" put in old Jones, at work with his imaginary handcuffs again. "I should say, for my part, it 'ud be a'most a case o' transportation to Botany Bay."

Frank Radcliffe was ensconced within Dyke Manor (sending Mrs. Todhetley into hysterics, for she had known nothing), and Duffham undertook the task of breaking it to Frank's wife. Frank, when his hair should have been trimmed up a little, was to put himself into a borrowed coat and to follow on presently.

Pitchley's Farm and Pitchley's roses lay hot and bright under the summer sunshine. Mr. Duffham went straight in, and looked about for its mistress. In the sitting-rooms, in the kitchen, in the dairy: he and his cane, and could not see her.

"Missis have stepped out, sir," said Sally, who was scrubbing the kitchen table. "A fearful headache she have got to-day."

"A headache, has she!" responded Duffham.

"I don't think she's never without one," remarked Sally, dipping her brush into the saucer of white sand.

"Where's Mr. Skate?"

"Him? Oh, he be gone over to Alcester market, sir."

"You go and find your mistress, Sally, and say I particularly wish to speak with her. Tell her that I have some very good news for her."

Sally left her brush and her sand, and went out with the message. The doctor strolled into the best parlour, and cribbed one of the many roses intruding their blooming beauty into the open window. Mr. Duffham had to exercise his patience. It seemed to him that he waited half-an-hour.

Annet came in at last, saying how sorry she was to have kept him: she had stepped over to see their carter's wife, who was ill, and Sally had only just found her. She wore her morning gown of black and white print, with the small net widow's cap on her bright hair. But for the worn look in her face, the sad eyes, she was just as pretty as ever; and Duffham thought so.

"Sally says you have some good news for me," she observed with a poor, faint smile. "It must be a joke of yours, Mr. Duffham. There's no news that could be good for me."

"Wait till you hear it," said he. "You have had a fortune left you! It is so good, Mrs. Frank Radcliffe, that I'm afraid to tell you. You may go into a fit; or do some other foolish thing."

"Indeed no. Nothing can ever have much effect on me again."

"Don't you make too sure of that," said Duffham. "You've never felt quite sure about that death of your husband, up at Dales, have you? Thought there was something queer about it—eh?"

"Yes," she said. "I have thought it."

"Well, some of us have been looking into it a little. And we find—in short, we are not at all sure that—that Frank did die."

"Oh!"—her hands lifting themselves in agitation—"what is it, sir? You have come to disclose to me that my husband was murdered."

"The contrariness of woman!" exclaimed Duffham, giving the floor a thump with his cane. "Why, Mrs. Frank Radcliffe, I told you as plainly as I could speak, that it was good news I brought. So good, that I hardly thought you could bear it with equanimity. Your husband was not murdered."

Poor Annet never answered a word to this. She only gazed at him.

"And our opinion is that Frank did not die at all; at Dale's, or elsewhere. Some of us think he is alive still, and—now don't you drop down in a heap."

"Please go on," she breathed, turning whiter than her own cap. "I—shall not drop down."

"We have reason to think it, Mrs. Frank. To think that he is alive, and well, and as sane in mind as you'd wish him to be. We believe it, ma'am; we all but know it."

She let her head fall back in the chair. "You, I feel sure, would not tell me this unless you had good grounds for it, Mr. Duffham. Oh, if it may but be so! But—then—what of those cries that we heard?" she added, recollecting them. "I am sure they were his."

"Very likely. Stephen may have had him shut up in the tower, and Frank cried out to let the world know he was there. Oh, I dare say that was it. I should not wonder, Mrs. Frank, but your husband may be here to-day."

She rose from her seat, face lightening, hands trembling. She had caught sight through the window of a small knot of people approaching the house-door, and she recognized the cut of Frank's fair Saxon face amongst them, and the gleam of his golden hair. Duffham knew no more till she was in Frank's arms, sobbing and crying.

Ring! knock! shake! Shake! knock! ring! It was at the front-door of the Torr, and old Jones was doing it. He had gone there to apprehend Stephen Radcliffe, a whole posse of us at his tail—where we had no business to be—and the handcuffs in his side-pocket.

By the afternoon of the day just told of, the parish was up in arms. Had Frank Radcliffe really risen from the dead, it could scarcely have caused more commotion. David Skate, for one, was frightened nearly out of his senses. Getting in from Alcester market, Sally accosted him, as he was crossing the yard, turning round from the pump to do it, where she was washing the summer cabbage for dinner.

"The master be in there, sir."

"What master?" asked David, halting on the way.

"Why, the master hisself, Mr. Frank. He be come back again."

To hear that a dead man has "come back" again and is then in the house you are about to enter, would astonish most of us. David Skate stared at Sally, as if he thought she had been making free with the cider barrel. At that moment, Frank appeared at the door, greeting David with a smile of welcome. The sun shone on his face, making it look pale, and David verily and truly believed he saw Frank's ghost. With a shout and a cry, and cheeks all turned to a sickly tremor, he backed behind the pump and behind Sally. Sally, all on the broad grin, enjoyed it.

"Why, sir, it be the master hisself. There ain't nothing to be skeered at."

"David, don't you know me?" called out Frank heartily; and came forth with outstretched hands.

But David did not get his cheeks right again for a good quarter-of-an-hour. And he was in a maze of wonder all day.

A warrant had been issued for the apprehension of Stephen Radcliffe of the Torr, and old Jones started off to the Torr to execute it. As if Stephen was likely to be found there! Ringing the bell, knocking at the door, shaking the handle, stood old Jones; the whole string of us behind burning to help him. It was not answered, and old Jones went at it again. You might have heard the noise over at Church Dykely.

Presently the door was drawn slowly back by Stephen Radcliffe's daughter—the curate's wife. She was trembling all over and looking fit to drop. Lizzy had come over from Birmingham and learned what had taken place. Naturally it scared her. She had always been the best of the bunch; and she had, of course, not known the true secret of the cries.

"I want to see Mr. Radcliffe, if you please, ma'am," began old Jones, putting his foot inside, so that the door should not be closed again.

"My father is not here," she answered, shaking and shivering.

"Not here!" repeated old Jones, surreptitiously stealing one hand round to feel the handcuffs.

"There's no one in the house but myself," she said. "When I got here, an hour or two ago, I found the place deserted."

"I should like to see that for myself, ma'am," returned incredulous old Jones.

"You can," she answered, drawing back a little. For she saw how futile it would be to attempt to keep him out.

Old Jones and some more went in to the search. Not a living creature was there but herself and the dog. Stephen Radcliffe had never been back since he started for Alcester in the morning.

In fact, Stephen was not to be found anywhere, near or distant. Mrs. Stephen was not to be found. Eunice Gibbon was not to be found. They had all made themselves scarce. The women had no doubt contrived to convey the news to Stephen while he was at Alcester, and he must have lost no time in turning his back on Warwickshire.

In a day or two, a rumour arose that Stephen Radcliffe and his wife had sailed for Canada. It proved to be true. "So much the better," said old Jones, regaling himself, just then, with cold beef in the Squire's kitchen. "Let him go! Good shut of bad rubbish!"

Just the sentiments that prevailed generally! Canada was the best place for Stephen the crafty. It spared us further sight of his surly face and saved the bother of a prosecution. He took only his own three hundred a-year with him; the Squire, for Frank, had resumed the receipt of the other three. And Lizzy, the daughter, with a heap of little ones at her skirts, remained in possession of the Torr until it should be taken. She had charge to let it as soon as might be.

Pitchley's Farm resumed its bustle and its sounds of everyday, happy life. The crowds that flocked to it to shake hands with Frank and welcome his wonderful resuscitation were beyond telling. Frank had sworn a solemn oath never to drink again: he never would, God helping him. He knew that he never should, he whispered one day to Mr. Brandon, a joyous light in his face as he spoke. His mother praying for him in dying, had told him that he would overcome; she had seen that he would in that last solemn hour, for the prayer had been heard, bringing her peace. He had overcome now, he said, and he would and should overcome to the end.

And Mr. Brandon, reading the faith and the earnestness, felt as sure of it as Frank did.

Frank kept his word. And, two years later, there he was, back at the Torr again. For Stephen had died of a severely cold winter in Canada, and his son Tom had died, but not of cold, and the Torr was Frank's.

Mrs. Stephen came back again, and took up her abode at her brother's. She would enjoy the three hundred a-year for life, by Stephen's will; it would then go to her daughter Lizzy—who would want it badly enough with her flock of youngsters. Becca and Eunice turned their attention to poultry, and sent rare fowls to shows, and gained prizes for them. Eunice returned long before Mrs. Stephen. She had never been out of England at all; and, finding it safe for her, put in an appearance, one winter day, at the gamekeeper's lodge.

Frank began to make alterations at the Torr as soon as he entered it, cutting down trees, and trying to render it a little less gloomy. Annet, with a calm face of sweet content, was much occupied at that time with a young man who was just getting on his legs, propelling him before her by the help of some safety reins that she called "backstrings," a fair child, who had the frank face and the golden curls of his father. And in all the country round about, there was not a gentleman more liked and respected than Francis Radcliffe of Sandstone Torr.

CHANDLER AND CHANDLER

I

Standing at right angles between North Crabb and South Crabb, and from two to three miles distant, was a place called Islip. A large village or small town, as you might please to regard it; and which has not a railroad as yet.

Years and years before my days, one Thomas Chandler, who had served his articles to a lawyer in Worcester, set up in practice for himself at Islip. At the same time another lawyer, one John Paul, also set up at Islip. The two had no wish to rival one another; but each had made his arrangements, and neither of them would give way. Islip felt itself suddenly elevated to pride, now that it could boast of two established lawyers, when until then it had not possessed one, but concluded that both of them would come to grief in less than a twelve-month. At the twelve-month's end, however, each was bearing steadily onwards, and had procured one or two valuable land agencies; in addition to the legal practice, which, as yet, was not much. So they kept themselves afloat: and if they had sometimes to eat bread-and-cheese for dinner, it was nothing to Islip.

In the second or third year, Mr. Chandler took his brother Jacob, who had qualified for a solicitor, into the office; and subsequently made him a partner, giving him a full half share. Islip thought it was an extravagantly generous thing of Mr. Chandler to do, and told him he had better be careful. And, after that, the years went on, and the Chandlers flourished. The business, what with the land agencies and other things, increased so much that it required better offices: and so Mr. Chandler, who had always lived on the premises, moved into a larger and a handsomer house some doors further up the street. Jacob Chandler had a pretty little place called North Villa, just outside Crabb, and walked to and fro night and morning. Both were married and had children. Their only sister, Mary Ann Chandler, had married a farmer in Gloucestershire, Stephen Cramp. Upon his death, a year or two afterwards, she came back and settled herself in a small farm near Islip, where she hoped to get along, having been left but poorly off. And that is enough by way of explanation.

I was only a little shaver, but I remember the commotion well. We were staying for the autumn at Crabb Cot; and, one afternoon, I, with Tod and the Squire, found myself on the Islip Road. I suppose we were going for a walk; perhaps to Islip; but I know nothing about that. All in a moment we saw a gig coming along at a frightful pace. The horse had run away.

"Here, you boys, get out of harm's way!" cried the Squire, and bundled us over the fence into the field. "Bless my heart and mind, it is Chandler!" he added, as the gig drew nearer. "Chandler and his brother!"

Mr. Chandler was driving: we could see that as the gig flew past. He was a tall, strong man; and, perched up on the driving-cushion, looked like a giant compared with Jacob, who seemed no bigger than a shrimp beside him. Mr. Chandler's face wore its usual healthy colour, and he appeared to retain all his presence of mind. Jacob sat holding on to the driving-cushion with his right hand and to the gig-wing with the left, and was just as white as a sheet.

"Dear me, dear me, I hope and trust there will be no accident!" groaned the Squire. "I hope Chandler will be able to hold in the horse!"

He set off back to North Crabb at nearly as fleet a pace as the horse, Tod after him, and I as fast as my small legs would take me. At the first turning we saw what had happened, for there was a group lying in the road, and people from the village were running up to it.

The horse had dashed at the bank, and turned them over. He was not hurt, the wretched animal. Jacob stood shivering in the highway, quitte pour la peur, as the French say; Mr. Chandler lay in a heap.

Jacob's house was within a stone's-throw, and they carried Mr. Chandler to it on a hurdle, and sent for Cole. The Squire went in with the rest; Tod and I sat on the opposite stile and waited. And if I am able to tell you what passed within the doors, it is owing to the Squire's having been there and staying to the end. No need was there for Cole to tell Thomas Chandler that the end was at hand: he knew it himself. There remained no hope for him: no hope. Some complicated injury had been done him inwardly, through that fiend of a horse trampling on him; and neither Cole nor all the doctors in the world could save him.

He was carried into one of the parlours and laid upon a mattress, hastily placed upon the carpet. Somebody got another gig and drove fiercely off to fetch his wife and son from Islip. He had two sons only, Thomas and George. Thomas, sixteen years old now, was in the office, articled to his father; George was at school, too far off to be sent for. Mrs. Chandler was soon with him. She had been a farmer's daughter, and was a meek, patient kind of a woman, who gave you the idea of never having a will of her own. The office clerks went posting about Islip to find Tom; he having been out when the gig and messenger arrived.

It chanced that Jacob Chandler's wife had gone abroad that day, taking her daughters; so the house was empty, save for the two maid-servants. The afternoon wore on. Cole had done what he could (which was nothing), and was now waiting in the other parlour with the clergyman; who had also done all that was left to do. The Squire stayed in the room; Chandler seemed to wish it; they had always liked one another. Mrs. Chandler knelt by the mattress, holding the dying hand: Jacob stood leaning against the book-case with folded arms and looking the very picture of misery: the Squire sat on the other side, nursing his knees.

"There's no time to alter my will, Betsy," panted poor Chandler, who could only speak by snatches: "and I don't know that I should alter it if I had the time. It was made when the two lads were little ones. Everything is left to you without reserve. I know I can trust you to do a mother's part by them."

"Always," responded Mrs. Chandler meekly, the silent tears rolling down her cheeks.

"You will have enough for comfort. Thoughts have crossed me at times of making a fortune for you and the lads: I was working on and laying by for it. How little we can foresee the future! God alone knows what that will be, and shapes it out. Not a day, not a day can we call our own: I see it now. With your own little income, and the interest of what I have been able to put by, you can live. There will also be money paid to you yearly from the practice—"

He was stopped by want of breath. Could not go on.

"Do not trouble yourself to think of these things," she said, catching up a sob, for she did not want to give way before him. "We shall have quite plenty. As much as I wish for."

"And when Tom is out of his articles he will take my place, you know, and will be well provided for and help you," said Mr. Chandler, taking up the word again. "And George you must both of you see to. If he has set his heart upon being a farmer instead of a clergyman, as I wished, why, let him be one. 'If you are a clergyman, Georgy, you will always be regarded as a gentleman,' I said to him the other day when he was at home, telling me he wanted to be a farmer. But now that I am going, Betsy, I see how valueless these distinctions are. Provided a man does his duty in the world and fears God, it hardly matters what his occupation in it is. It is for so short a time. Why, it seems only the other day that I was a boy, and now my few poor years are over, and I am going into the never-ending ages of immortality!"

"It shall all be as you wish, Thomas," she whispered.

"Ay," he answered. "Jacob, come here."

Jacob let his arms drop, and left the book-case to stand close over his brother. Mr. Chandler lifted his right hand, and Jacob stooped and took it.

"When we drew up our articles of partnership, Jacob, a clause was inserted, that upon the death of either of us, the survivor should pay a hundred and fifty pounds a-year out of the practice to those the other should leave behind him, provided the business could afford it. You remember that?"

"Yes," said Jacob. "I wish it had been me to go instead of you, Thomas."

"The business will afford it well, as you know, and more than afford it: you might well double it, Jacob. But I suppose you will have to take an additional clerk in my place, some efficient man, and he must be paid. So we will let it be at the hundred and fifty, Jacob. Pay that sum to my wife regularly."

"To be sure I will," said Jacob.

"And when Tom shall be of age he must take my place, you know, and draw his full half share. That was always an understood thing between you and me, Jacob, if I were taken. Your own son will, I suppose, be coming in shortly: so that in later years, when you shall have followed me to a better world, the old firm will be perpetuated in them—Chandler and Chandler. Tom and Valentine will divide the profits equally, as we have divided them."

"To be sure," said Jacob.

"Yes, yes; my mind is at rest on the score of worldly things. I would that all dying men could be as much at ease. God bless and prosper you, Jacob! You'll give a fatherly eye over Tom and George in my place, and lead them in straightforward paths."

"That I will," said Jacob. "I wish with all my heart this dreadful day's work had never happened!"

"And so will I too," put in the Squire. "I'll look a bit after your two boys myself, Chandler."

Mr. Chandler, drawing his hand from his brother, held it towards the Squire. At that moment, a suppressed stir was heard outside, and an eager voice. Tom had arrived: having run all the way from Islip.

"Where's papa?—where's he lying? Is he hurt very much?"

Cole appeared, marshalling him in. A well-grown young fellow for sixteen, with dark eyes, a fresh colour, and a good-natured face; altogether, the image of his father. Cole took a look down at the mattress, and saw how very much nearer something was at hand than it had been only a few minutes before.

"Hush, Tom," he said, hastily pouring some drops into half a wine-glass of water. "Gently, lad. Let me give him this."

Poor Tom Chandler, aghast at what he beheld, was too frightened to speak. A sudden stillness fell upon him, and he knelt down by the side of his mother. Cole's drops did no good. There could be only a few last words.

"I never thought it would end thus—that I should not have time granted me for even a last farewell," spoke the dying man in a faint voice and with a gasp between every word, as he took Tom's hand. "Tom, my boy, I cannot say to you what I would."

Tom gave a great burst as though he were choking, and was still the next minute.

"Do your duty, my boy, before God and man with all the best strength that Heaven gives you. You must some time lie as I am lying, Tom; it may be with as little warning of it as I have had: at the best, this life will last such a little while as compared with life eternal. Fear God; find your Saviour; love and serve your fellow-creatures. Make up your accounts with your conscience morning and evening. And—Tom—"

"Yes, father; yes, father?" spoke poor Tom, entreatingly, as the voice died away, and he was afraid that the last words were dying away too and would never be spoken.

"Take care of your mother and be dutiful to her. And do you and George be loving brothers to each other always: tell him I enjoined it with my closing breath. Poor George! if I could but see him! And—and—and—"

"Yes, oh yes, I will; I will indeed! What else, father?"

But there was nothing else. Just two or three faint words as death came in, and a final gasp to close them.

"God be with you ever, Tom!"

That was all. And the only other thing I recollect was seeing the sister, Mrs. Cramp, come up in a yellow chaise from the Bell at Islip, and pass into the house, as we sat on the gate. But she was just too late.

You may be sure that the affair caused a commotion. So grave a calamity had never happened at North Crabb. Mr. Chandler and his brother had started from Islip in their gig to look at some land that was going to be valued, which lay a mile or two on the other side Crabb on the Worcester Road. They had driven the horse a twelvemonth and never had any trouble with him. It was supposed that something must have been wrong with the harness. Any way, he had started, kicked, backed, and finally run away.

I saw the funeral: standing with Tod in the churchyard amidst many other spectators, and reading the inscriptions on the grave-stones while we waited. Mr. Chandler had been taken back to his house at Islip, and was brought from thence to Crabb to be buried. Tom and George Chandler came in the first mourning-coach with their Uncle Jacob and his son Valentine. In the next sat two other relatives, with the Squire and Mr. Cole.

Changes followed. Mrs. Chandler left the house at Islip, and Jacob Chandler and his family moved into it. She took a pretty cottage at North Crabb, and Tom walked to the office of a morning and home again at night. Valentine, Jacob's only son, was removed from school at once to be articled to his father. He was fifteen, just a year younger than Tom.

Years passed on. Tom grew to be four-and-twenty, Valentine three-and-twenty. Both of them were good-looking young men, tall and straight; but Tom had the pleasanter face, address, and manners. Every one liked him. Crabb had thought when Tom attained his majority, and got his certificate as a solicitor, that his uncle would have taken him into partnership. The Squire had said it publicly. Instead of that, old Jacob gave him a hundred a-year salary to start with, and said to him, "Now we shall go on comfortably, Tom." Tom, who was anything but exacting, supposed his uncle wished him to add a year or two to his age and some more experience, before taking him in. So he thanked old Jacob for the hundred a-year, and was contented.

George Chandler had emigrated to Canada. Which rather gave his mother a turn. Some people they knew had gone out there, purchased land, and were doing well on it; and George resolved to follow them. George had been placed with a good farmer in Gloucestershire and learnt farming thoroughly. That accomplished, he began to talk to his mother about his prospects. What he would have liked was, to take a farm on his own account. But he had no money to stock it, and his mother had none to give him. Her income, including the hundred and fifty paid to her from the business, was about four hundred pounds, all told: home living and her sons' expenses had taken it all, leaving no surplus. "There's nothing for me but going to Canada, mother," said George: "I don't see any opening for me in England. I shall be sure to get on, over there. I am healthy and steady and industrious; and those are the qualities that make way in a new country. If the worst comes to the worst, and I do not succeed, I can but come back again." His arguments prevailed at length, and he sailed for Canada, their friends over there promising to receive and help him.

All this while Jacob Chandler had flourished. His practice had gradually increased, and he had become a great man. Great in show and expense. It was not his fault; it was that of his family: of his own will, he would never have put a foot forward out of his plain old groove. Mrs. Jacob Chandler, empty-headed, vain, and pretty, had but two thoughts in the world: the one to make her way amidst fashionable people, the other to marry her daughters well. Originally a small tradesman's daughter in Birmingham, she was now ridiculously upstart, and put on more airs and graces in an hour than a lady born and bred would in a lifetime. Mrs. Jacob Chandler's people had sold brushes and brooms, soaps and pickles: she had occasionally stood behind the counter and served out the soap with her own hands; and Mrs. Jacob now looked down upon Birmingham itself and every one in it.

North Villa had not been given up, though they did move to Islip. Jacob Chandler held a long lease of it, and he sub-let it for three or four years. At the end of that period it occurred to Mrs. Jacob that she should like to keep it for herself, as a sort of country house to retire to at will. As she was the grey mare, this was done; though Jacob grumbled. So North Villa was furbished up, and some new furniture put into it; and the garden, a very nice one, improved: and Mrs. Jacob, with one or other or all three of her daughters, might be frequently seen driving her pony-carriage with its handsome ponies between North Villa and Islip, streamers flying, ribbons fluttering: you would have taken it for a rainbow coming along. The girls were not bad-looking, played and sang with open windows loud enough to frighten the passers-by, and were given to speak to one another in French at table. "Voulez-vouz donner-moi la sel, Clementina?" "Voulez-vous passer-moi le moutarde, Georgiana?" "Voulez-vous envoyer-moi les poivre, Julietta?" For, as Mrs. Jacob would have told you, they had learnt French at school; and to converse in it was of course only natural to themselves, and most instructive to any visitor who might chance to be present. Added to these advantages Mrs. and the Miss Chandlers adored dress, their out-of-door toilettes being grander than a queen's.

All this: the two houses and the company received in them; the ponies and the groom; the milliners' bills and the dress-makers', made a hole in Jacob Chandler's purse. Not too much of a hole in one sense of the word; Jacob took care of that: but it prevented him from putting by all the money he wished. He made plenty of it: more than the world supposed.

In this manner matters had gone on since the departure of George Chandler for Canada. Mrs. Chandler living quietly in her home making it a happy one for her son Tom, and treasuring George's letters from over the sea: Mrs. Jacob Chandler and her daughters keeping the place alive; Valentine getting to be a very fine gentleman indeed; old Jacob sticking to business and pocketing his gains. The first interruption came in the shape of a misfortune for Mrs. Chandler. She lost a good portion of her money through a calamity that you have heard of before—the bursting-up of Clement Pell. It left her with very little, save the hundred and fifty pounds a-year paid to her regularly by Jacob. Added to this was the hundred a-year Tom earned, and which his uncle had not increased. And this brings us down to the present time, when Tom was four-and-twenty.

Jacob Chandler sat one morning in his own room at his office, when a clerk came in and said Mrs. Chandler from Crabb was asking to see him. Cordiality had always subsisted between the two families, though they were not much together; Mrs. Chandler disliking their show; Mrs. Jacob and her daughters intensely despising one who wore black silk for best, and generally made her puddings with her own fingers. "So low-lived, you know, my dears," Mrs. Jacob would say, with a toss of her bedecked head.

Jacob heard his clerk's announcement with annoyance; the lines on his brow grew deeper. He had always been a shrimp of a man, but he looked like a shrivelled one now. His black clothes sat loosely upon him; his white neckcloth, for he dressed like a parson, seemed too large for his thin neck.

"Mrs. Chandler can come in," said he, after a few moments' hesitation. "But say I am busy."

She came in, putting back her veil: she had worn a plain-shaped bonnet with a white border ever since her husband died. It suited her meek, kind, and somewhat homely face, on which the brown hair, streaked with grey, was banded.

"Jacob, I am sorry to disturb you, especially as you are busy; but I have wanted to speak to you for some time now and have not liked to come," she began, taking the chair that stood near the table at which he sat. "It is about Tom."

"What about him?" asked Jacob. "Has he been up to any mischief?"

"Mischief! Tom! Why, Jacob, I hardly think there can be such another young man as he, for steadiness and good conduct; and, I may say, for kindness. I have never heard anything against him. What I want to ask you is, when you think of making a change?"

"A change?" echoed Jacob, as if the words puzzled him, biting away at the feather of his pen. "A change?"

"Is it not time that he should be taken into the business? I—I thought—and Tom I know also thought, Jacob—that you would have done it when he was twenty-one."

"Oh, did you?" returned Jacob, civilly.

"He is twenty-four, you know, now, Jacob, and naturally wishes to get forward in life. I am anxious that he should; and I think it is time—forgive me for saying it, Jacob—that something was settled."

"I was thinking of raising Tom's salary," coolly observed Jacob; "of giving him, say, fifty pounds a-year more. Valentine has been bothering me to do the same by him; so I suppose I must."

The fixed colour on Mrs. Chandler's thin cheeks grew a shade deeper. "But, Jacob, it was his father's wish, you know, that he should be taken into partnership, should succeed to his own share of the business; and I thought you would have arranged it ere this. An increase of salary is not the thing at all: it is not that that is in question."

"Nothing can be so bad for a young man as to make him his own master too early," cried Jacob. "I've known it ruin many a one."

"You promised my husband when he was dying that it should be so," she gently urged. "Besides, it is Tom's right. I understood that when he was of a proper age, he was to come in, in accordance with a previous arrangement made between you and poor Thomas."

Jacob bit the end of the pen right off and nearly swallowed it. "Thomas left all things in my hands," said he, coughing and choking. "Tom must acquire some further experience yet."

"When do you propose settling it, then? How long will it be first?"

"Well, that depends, you know. I shall see."

"Will it be in another year? Tom will be five-and-twenty then."

"Ay, he will: and Val four-and-twenty. How time flies! It seems but the other day that they were in jackets and trousers."

"But will it be then—in another year? You have not answered me, Jacob."

"And I can't answer you," returned Jacob. "How can I? Don't you understand me when I say I must wait and see?"

"You surely will do what is right, Jacob?"

"Well now, can you doubt it, Betsy? Of course I shall. When did you hear from George?"

Mrs. Chandler rose, obliged to be satisfied. To urgently press any interest of her own was not in her nature. As she shook hands with Jacob she was struck with the sickly appearance of his face.

"Are you feeling quite well, Jacob? You look but poorly."

"I have felt anything but well for a long time," he replied, in a fretful tone. "I don't know what ails me: too much work, perhaps, but I seem to have strength for nothing."

"You should give yourself a rest, Jacob, and take some bark."

"Ay. Good-day."

Now it came to pass that in turning out of the house, after nodding to Tom and Valentine, who sat at a desk side by side in the room to the left, the door of which stood open, Mrs. Chandler saw the Squire on the opposite side of the street, and crossed over to him. He asked her in a joking way whether she had been in to get six and eightpenceworth of law. She told him what she had been in for, seeing no reason for concealing it.

"Bless me, yes!" cried he, in his impulsive way. "I'm sure it's quite time Tom was in the firm. I'll go and talk to Jacob."

And when he got in—making straight across the street with the words, and through the passage, and so to the room without halt or ceremony—he saw Jacob leaning back in his chair, his hands thrust into his black side-pockets, and his head bent on his chest in deep thought. The Squire noticed how deep the lines in his brow had grown, just as Mrs. Chandler had.

"But you know, Jacob Chandler, that it was an agreement with the dead," urged the Squire, in his eagerness, after listening to some plausible (and shuffling) remarks from Jacob.

"An agreement with the dead!" repeated Jacob, looking up at the Squire for explanation. They were both standing on the matting near the fender: which was filled with an untidy mass of torn and twisted scraps of paper. "What do you mean, Squire? I never knew before that the dead could make an agreement."

"You know what I mean," cried the Squire, hotly. "Poor Thomas was close upon death at the time you and he had the conversation: he wanted but two or three minutes of it."

"Oh, ah, yes; that's true enough, so far as it goes, Squire," replied Jacob, pulling up his white cravat as if his throat felt cold.

"Well," argued the Squire. "Did not you and he agree that Tom was to come in when he was twenty-one? Both of you seemed to imply that there existed a previous understanding to that effect."

"There never was a word said about his coming in when he was twenty-one," contended Jacob.

"Why, bless my heart and mind, do you suppose my ears were shut, Jacob Chandler?" retorted the Squire, beginning to rub his head with his red silk handkerchief. "I heard the words."

"No, Squire. Think a bit."

Jacob spoke so calmly that the Squire began to rub up his memory as well as his head. He had no cause to suppose Jacob Chandler to be other than an honourable man.

"'When Tom shall be of age, he must take my place:' those were I think the very words," repeated the Squire. "I can see your poor brother's face now as he lay down on the floor and spoke them. It had death in it."

"Yes, it had death in it," acquiesced Jacob, in a tone of discomfort. "What he said was this, Squire: 'When Tom shall be of an age.' Meaning of course a suitable age to justify the step."

"I don't think so: I did not hear it so," persisted the Squire. "There was no 'an' in it. 'When Tom shall be of age:' that was it. Meaning when he should be twenty-one."

"Oh dear, no; quite a mistake. You can't think my ears would deceive me at such a time as that, Mr. Todhetley. And about our own business too."

"Well, you ought to know best, of course, though my impression is that you are wrong," conceded the Squire. "Put it that it was as you say: don't you think Tom Chandler is now quite old enough for it to be acted upon?"

"No, I don't," replied Jacob. "As I have just told his mother, nothing can be more pernicious for a young man than to be made his own master too early. Nine young fellows out of every ten would get ruined by it."

"Do you think so?" asked the Squire, dubiously.

"I am sure so, Squire. Tom Chandler is steady now, for aught I know to the contrary; but just let him get the reins into his hands, and you'd see what it would be. That is, what it might be. And I am not going to risk it."

"He is as steady-going a young man as any one could wish for; diligent, straightforward. Not at all given to spending money improperly."

"Because he has not had it to spend. I have known many a young blade to be quiet and cautious while his pockets were empty; and as soon as they were filled, perhaps all at once, he has gone headlong to rack and ruin. How do we know that it would not be the case with Tom?"

"Well, I—I don't think it would be," said the Squire, with hesitation, for he was coming round to Jacob's line of argument.

"But I can't act upon 'thinking,' Squire; I must be sure. Tom will just stay on with me at present as he is; so there's an end of it. His salary is going to be raised: and I—I consider that he is very well off."

"Well, perhaps he'll be none the worse for a little longer spell of clerkship," repeated the Squire, coming wholly round. "And now good-morning. I'm rather in a hurry to-day, but I thought it right to put in a word for Tom's sake, as I was present when poor Thomas died."

"Good-morning, Mr. Todhetley," answered Jacob, as he sat down to his desk again.

But he did not get to work. He bent his head on his neckcloth as before, and set on to think. What had just passed did not please him at all: for Jacob Chandler was not devoid of conscience; though it was an elastic one, and he was in the habit of deadening it at will. It was not his intention to take his nephew into partnership at all; then or later. Almost ever since the day of his brother's funeral he had looked at matters after his own fashion, and soon grew to think that Tom had no manner of right to a share in the business; that as Thomas was dead and gone, it was all his, and ought to be all his. He and Thomas had shared it between them: therefore it was only just and proper that he, the survivor, should take it. That's how Jacob Chandler, who was the essence of covetousness, had been reasoning, and his mind was made up.

It was therefore very unpleasant to be pounced upon in this way by two people in one morning. Their application as regarded Tom himself would not have troubled him: he knew how to put disputants off civilly, saying neither yes nor no, and promising nothing: but what annoyed him was the reminiscence they had called up of his dying brother. Jacob intended to get safely into the world above, some day, by hook or by crook; he went to church regularly, and considered himself a model of good behaviour. But these troublesome visitors had somehow contrived to put before his conscience the fact that he might be committing a lifelong act of injustice on Tom; and that, to do so, was not the readiest way of getting to heaven. Was that twelve o'clock? How the morning had passed!

"Uncle Jacob, I am going over to Brooklands about that lease. Have you any particular instructions to give me?"

It was Tom himself who had entered. A tall, good-looking, fresh-coloured young man, who had honesty and kindliness written on every line of his open face.

Jacob lifted his bent head, and drew his chair nearer his table as if he meant to set to work in earnest. But his mouth took a cross look.

"Who told you to go? I said Valentine was to go."

"Valentine has stepped out. He asked me to go for him."

"Where has he stepped to?"

"He did not say," replied Tom, evasively. For he knew quite well where Valentine was gone: to the Bell inn over the way. Valentine went to the Bell a little too much, and was a little too fond of the Bell's good liquor.

"I suppose you can go, then. No, I have no instructions: you know what to say as well as I do. We don't give way a jot, mind. Oh, and—Tom!" added Jacob, calling him back as he went out.

"Yes, sir."

"I am intending to raise your salary. From the beginning of next month, you will have a hundred and fifty a-year."

"Oh, thank you, Uncle Jacob."

Tom spoke as he in his ready good-nature felt—brightly and gratefully. Nevertheless, a shade of disappointment did cross his mind, for he thought his position in the house ought to be a different one.

"And I am sure it is quite as much as I ought to do for him," argued Jacob with his conscience. And he put away unpleasant prickings and set to work like a house on fire.

It was one o'clock when Valentine came in. He had an excuse ready for his father: the latter, turning out of the clerks' room, chanced to see him enter. "He had been down to Tyler's to see if he could get that money from them." It was an untruth, for he had stayed all the while at the Bell; and his father noticed that his face was uncommonly flushed. Old Jacob had had his suspicions before; yes, and spoken of them to Valentine: he now motioned him to go before him into the private room.

"You have been drinking, sir!"

"I!—good gracious, no," returned Valentine, boldly, his blue eyes fearlessly meeting his father's. "What fancies you do pick up!"

"Valentine, when I was your age I never drank a drop of anything till night, and then it was only a glass of beer with my supper. It seems to me that young men of the present day think they can drink at all hours with impunity."

"I don't drink, father."

"Very well. Take care you do not. It is a habit more easily acquired than left off. Look here: I am going to give you fifty pounds a-year more. Mind you make it do: and do not spend it in waste."

It was not very long after this that Jacob Chandler had a shock: a few months, or so. During that time he had been growing thinner and weaker, and looked so shrivelled up that there seemed to be nothing left of him. Islip, small place though it was, had a market-day—Friday;—when farmers would drive or walk in and congregate at the Bell. One afternoon, just as the ordinary was over, Jacob went to the inn, as was his general custom: he had always some business or other to transact with the farmers; or, if not, something to say. His visit to them over, he said good-day and left: but the next minute he turned back, having forgotten something. Some words fell on his ear as he opened the door.

"Ay. He is not long for this world."

They were spoken by old Farmer Blake—a big, burly, kind-hearted man. And Jacob Chandler felt as certain that they were meant to apply to himself as though his name had been mentioned. He went into a cold shiver, and shut the door again without entering.

Was it true, he asked himself, as he walked across the street to his office: was it indeed a fact that he was slowly dying? A great fear fell upon him: a dread of death. What, leave all this beautiful sunshine, this bright world in which he was so busy, and pass into the cold dark grave! Jacob turned sick at the thought.

It was true that he had long been ailing; but not with any specific ailment. He could not deny that he was now more like a shadow than a man, or that every day seemed to bring him less of strength. Passing into his dining-parlour instead of into his private business room, he drank two glasses of wine off at once, and it seemed to revive him. He was a very abstemious man in general.

Well, if Farmer Blake did say it—stupid old idiot!—it was not obliged to be true, reflected Jacob then. People judged by his spareness: he wished he could get a little fatter. And so he reasoned and persuaded himself out of his fears, and grew sufficiently reassured to transact his business, always pressing on a Friday.

But that same evening, Jacob Chandler drove to North Villa in his gig, telling his wife he should sleep there for a week or two, for the sake of the fresh air. And the next morning, before he went to Islip, he sent for the doctor—Cole.

"People are saying you won't live!" repeated Cole, having listened to Jacob's confidential communication. "I don't see why you should not live. Let's examine you a bit. You should not take up fancies."

Cole could find nothing particular the matter with him. He recommended him rest from business, change of air, and a generous diet. "Try it for a month," said he.

"I can't try it—except the diet," returned Jacob. "It's all very well for you to talk about rest from business, Cole, but how am I to take rest? My business could not get on without me. Business is a pleasure to me; it's not a pain."

"You want rest from it all the same," said Cole. "You have stuck closely to it this many a year."

"My mother died without apparent cause," said Jacob, dreamily. "She seemed just to drift out of life. About my age, too."

"That's no reason why you should," argued Cole.

Well, they went on, talking at one another; but nothing came of it. And Cole left, saying he would send him in some tonics to take.

By the evening it was known all over the place that Jacob Chandler was ill and had sent for Cole. People talked of it the next morning as they went to church. Jacob appeared, looking much as usual, and sat down in his pew. The next to come in was Mrs. Cramp; who walked over to our church sometimes. She stayed to dine with the Lexoms, and went to call at North Villa after dinner; finding Mrs. Jacob and the rest of them at dessert with a guest or two. Jacob was somewhere in the garden.

Mrs. Cramp found him in the latticed arbour, and sat down opposite to him, taking up her brown shot-silk gown, lest the seat should be dusty. When she told him it was the hearing of his illness which had brought her over to Crabb, he turned cross. He was not ill, he said; only a trifle out of sorts, as every one else must be at times and seasons. By dint of questioning, Mrs. Cramp, who was a stout, comely woman, fond of having her own way, got out of him all Cole had said.

"And Cole is right, Jacob: it is rest and change you want," she remarked. "You are sure you do not need it? don't tell me. A stitch in times saves nine, remember."

"You know nothing about it, Mary Ann."

"I know that you look thinner and thinner every time I see you. Be wise in time, brother."

"Cole told me to go away to the seaside for a month. Why, what should I do, mooning for a whole month in a strange place by myself? I should be like a fish out of water."

"Take your wife and the girls."

"I dare say! They would only worry me with their fine doings. And look at the expense."

"I will go with you if you like, Jacob, rather than you should go alone, though it would be an inconvenience to me. And pay my own expenses."

"Mary Ann, I am not going at all; or thinking of it. It would be impossible for me to leave my business."

Mrs. Cramp, turning over matters in her mind, determined to put the case plainly before him, and did so; telling him that it would be better to leave his business for a temporary period now, than to find shortly that he must leave it for ever. Jacob sat gazing out straight before him at the Malvern Hills, the chain of which lay against the sky in the distance.

"If you took my advice, brother, you would retire from business altogether. You have made enough to live without it, I suppose—"

"But I have not made enough," he interrupted.

"Then you ought to have made it, Jacob."

"Oughts don't go for much."

"What I mean is, that you ought to have made it, judging by the style in which you live. Two houses, a carriage and ponies (besides your gig), expensive dress, parties: all that should never be gone into, brother, unless the realized income justifies it."

"It is the style we live in that has not let me put by, Mary Ann. I don't tell you I have put nothing by: I have put a little by year by year; but it is not enough to live upon."

"Then make arrangements for half the proceeds of the business to be given over to you. Let the two boys take to it, and—"

"Who?" cried Jacob.

"The two boys, Tom and Valentine. It will be theirs some time, you know, Jacob: let them have it at once. Tom's name must be first, as it ought to be. Valentine—"

"I have no intention of doing anything of the kind," interposed Jacob, sharply. "I shall keep the business in my own hands as long as I live. Perhaps I may take Valentine into it: not Tom."

Mrs. Cramp sat for a full minute staring at Jacob, her stout hands, from which the gloves had been taken, and her white lace ruffles lying composedly on her brown gown.

"Not take Tom into the business!" she repeated, in a slow, astonished tone. "Why, Jacob, what do you mean?"

"That," said Jacob. "Tom will stay on at a good salary: I shall increase it, I dare say, every two years, or so; but he will not come into the firm."

"You can't mean what you say."

"I have meant it this many a year past, Mary Ann. I have never intended to take him in."

"Jacob, beware! No luck ever comes of fraud."

"Of what? Fraud?"

"Yes; I say fraud. If you deprive Tom of the place that is justly his, it will be a cheat and a fraud, and nothing short of it."

"You have a queer way of looking at things, Mrs. Cramp. Who has kept the practice together all these years, but me? and added to it little by little, and made it worth double what it was; ay, and more than double? It is right—right, mind you, Mary Ann—that my own son should succeed to it."

"Who made the practice in the first place, and took you into it out of brotherly affection, and made you a full partner without your paying a farthing, and for seventeen or eighteen years was the chief prop and stay of it?" retorted Mrs. Cramp. "Why, poor Thomas; your elder brother. Who made him a promise when he was lying dying in that very parlour where your wife and children are now sitting, that Tom should take his proper place in the firm when he was of age, and his half-share with it, according to agreement? Why you. You did, Jacob Chandler."

"That was all a mistake," said Jacob, shuffling his thin legs and wrists.

"I will leave you," said Mrs. Cramp. "I don't care to discuss questions while you are in this frame of mind. Is this all the benefit you got from the parson's sermon this morning, and the text he gave out before it? That text: think of it a bit, brother Jacob, and perhaps you'll see your way to acting differently. Remember," she added, turning back to him for the last word, which she always had, somehow, "that cheating never prospers in the long run. It never does, Jacob; never: for where it is crafty cheating, hidden away from the sight of man, it is seen and noted by God."

Her brown skirts (all the shades of a copper tea-kettle) disappeared round the corner by the mulberry-tree, leaving Jacob very angry and uncomfortable. Angry with her, uncomfortable in himself. Do what he would, he could not get that text out of his mind—and what right had she to bring it cropping up to him in that inconvenient way, he wondered, or to speak to him about such matters at all. The verse was a beautiful verse in itself; he had always thought so: but it was not pleasant to be tormented by it—and all through Mary Ann! There it was haunting his memory again!

"Keep innocency, and take heed unto the thing that is right: for that shall bring a man peace at the last."

Jacob Chandler grew to look a little fresher, though not stouter, as the weeks went on: the drive, night and morning, seemed to do him good. Meeting Cole one day, he told him he felt stronger, and did not see why he should not live to be ninety. With all his heart, Cole answered, but most people found seventy long enough.

All at once, without warning, a notice appeared in the local papers, stating that Jacob Chandler had taken his son Valentine into partnership. Mrs. Chandler read it as she sat at breakfast.

"What does it mean, Tom?" she asked.

"I don't know what it means, mother. We have heard nothing about it at the office."

"Tom, you may depend your uncle Jacob has done it, and that he does not intend to take you in at all," spoke Mrs. Chandler, in her strong conviction. "I shall go to him."

She finished her breakfast and went off there and then, catching Jacob just as he was turning out of the white gate at North Villa to mount his gig: for he still came over to Crabb to sleep. The newspaper was in her hand, and she pointed to the advertisement.

"What does it mean, Jacob?" she asked, just as she had a few minutes before asked of Tom.

"Mean!" said Jacob. "It can't have more than one meaning, can it? I've thought it best to let Val's name appear in the practice, and made over to him a small share of the profits. Very small, Betsy. He won't draw much more than he has been drawing as salary."

"But what of Tom?" questioned poor Mrs. Chandler.

"Of Tom? Well, what of him?"

"When is he to be taken in?"

"Oh, there's time enough for that. I can't make two moves at once; it could not be expected of me, Betsy. My son is my son, and he had to come in first."

"But—Jacob—don't you think you ought to carry out the agreement made with Tom's father—that you are bound in honour?" debated Mrs. Chandler, in her meek and non-insisting way.

"Time enough, Betsy. We shall see. And look there, my horse won't stand: he's always fresh in the morning."

Shaking her hand hastily, he stepped up, took the reins from the man, and was off in a trice, bowling along at a quicker pace than usual. The poor woman, left standing there and feeling half-bewildered, saw Mrs. Jacob at one of the open windows, and crossed the lawn to speak.

"I came up about this announcement," she said. "It is so strange a thing; we can't understand it at all. Jacob should take Tom into partnership. Especially now that he has taken Valentine."

"Do you think so?" drawled Mrs. Jacob; who wore a pink top-knot and dirty morning wrapper, and minced her words more than usual, for she thought the more she minced them the finer she was. "Dear me! I'm sure I don't know anything about it. All well at home, I hope? I won't ask you in, for I'm going to be busy. My daughters are invited to a garden-party this afternoon, and I must give directions about the trimming of their dresses. Good-morning."

Back went Mrs. Chandler, and found her son watching for her at the door, waiting to hear what news she brought, before setting out on his usual walk.

"Your uncle slips through it like an eel, Tom," she began. "I can make nothing of him one way or another. He does not say he will not take you in, but he does not say he will. What is to be done?"

"Nothing can be done that I know of, mother," replied Tom; "nothing at all. Uncle Jacob holds the power in his own hands, you see. If it does not please him to give me my lawful share, we cannot oblige him to do it."

"But how unjust it will be if he does not!"

"Yes. I think so. But, it seems to me there's little else but injustice in the world," added Tom, with a light smile. "You would say so if you were in a lawyer's office and had to dive into the cases brought there. Good-bye, mother mine."

Pretty nearly a year went on after this, bringing no change. "Jacob Chandler and Son, Solicitors, Conveyancers, and Land Agents," flourished in gilt letters on the front-door at Islip, and Jacob Chandler and Son flourished inside, in the matter of business. But never a move was made to take in Tom. And when Jacob was asked about it, as he was once or twice, he civilly shuffled the topic off.

But, before the year had well elapsed, Jacob was stricken down. To look at him you would have said he had been growing thinner all that while, only that it seemed impossible. This time it was for death. He had not much grace given him, either: just a couple of days and a night.

He went to bed one night as well as usual, but the next morning did not get up, saying he felt "queer," and sent for Cole. Jacob Chandler was a rare coward in illness. That fining-down process he had been going through so long had not troubled him: he thought it was only his natural constitution: and when real illness set in his fears sprang up.

"You had better stay in bed to-day," said Cole. "I will send you a draught to take."

"But what is it that's the matter with me?" asked Jacob.

"I don't know," said Cole.

"Is it ague? Or intermittent fever coming on? See how I am shaking."

"N—o," hesitated Cole, either in doubt, or else because he would not say too much. "I'll look in again by-and-by."

Towards midday Jacob thought he'd get up, and see what that would do for him. It seemed to do nothing, except make him worse; and he went to bed again. Cole looked in three times during the day, but did not say what he thought.

In the middle of the night a paroxysm of illness came on again, and a servant ran to knock up the doctor. Jacob was shaking the very bed, and seemed in awful fear.

And in the morning he appeared to know that he had not many hours to live. Knew it by intuition, for Cole had not told him. An express went flying to Worcester for Dr. Malden: but Cole knew—and told it later—that all the physicians in the county could not save him.

And the state of mind that Jacob Chandler went into with the knowledge, might have read many a careless man a lesson. It seemed to him that he had a whole peck of suddenly-recollected sins on his head, and misdeeds to be accounted for. He remembered Tom Chandler then.

"I have not done by him as I ought; it lies upon me with an awful weight," he groaned. "Valentine, you must remedy the wrong. Take him in, and give him his proper share. I should like to see Tom. Some one fetch him."

Tom had to be fetched from Islip. He came at once, his long legs skimming over the ground quickly; and he entered the sick-chamber with the cordial smile on his open face, and took his uncle's hand.

"It shall all be remedied, Tom; all the injustice; and you shall have your due rights. I see now how unjust it was: I don't know what God's thinking of me for it. I wanted to make a good provision for my old age, you see; to be able to live at ease; and now there is no old age for me: God is taking me before it has come on."

"Don't distress yourself, Uncle Jacob; it will be all right. And I'm sure I have not thought much about it."

"But others have," groaned Jacob. "Your mother; and Mary Ann; and—and Squire Todhetley. They have all been on at me at times. But I shut my ears. Oh dear! I wish God would let me live a few years over again! I'd try and be different. What shall I do? Oh, what shall I do?"

And that was how he kept on the best part of the day. Then he called out that he wanted his will altered. Valentine brought in pen and ink, but his father motioned him away and said it must be done by Paul. So Paul the lawyer was got over from Islip, and was shut up alone with the sick man for a quarter-of-an-hour. Next the parson came, and read some prayers. But Jacob still cried out his piteous laments, at having no time to redeem the past, until his voice was too weak to speak. At nine o'clock in the evening all was over.

The disease that killed him must have been making silent progress for a good while, Cole said, when the truth was ascertained: but he had never seen it develop itself with so little warning, or prove fatal so quickly as in the case of Jacob Chandler.

II

Jacob Chandler, solicitor, conveyancer, and land-agent, had died: and his son Valentine (possibly taking a leaf out of the history of Jonas Chuzzlewit) determined that he should at least be borne to the grave with honours, if he had never had an opportunity to specially bear them in life. Crabb churchyard was a show of mutes and plumes, and Crabb highway was blocked up with black coaches. As it is considered a compliment down with us to get an invitation to a funeral, and a great slight on the dead to refuse it, all classes, from Sir John Whitney, down to Massock, the brickmaker, and little Farmer Bean, responded to Valentine Chandler's notes. Some people said that it was Valentine's mother, the new widow, who wished for so much display; and probably they were right.

It took place on a Saturday. I can see the blue sky overhead now, and the bright sun that shone upon the scene and lighted up the feathers. It was thought he must have died rich, and that the three daughters he left would have good portions. His son Valentine had the practice: so, at any rate, he was provided for. Tom Chandler, the nephew, made one of the mourners: and the spectators talked freely enough in an undertone, as he passed them in his place when the procession walked up the churchyard path. It seemed but the other day, they said, that his poor father was buried, killed by that lamentable accident. Time flew. Years passed imperceptibly. But Jacob—lying so still under that black and white pall, now slowly disappearing within the church—had not done the right thing by his dead brother's son. The practice had been made by Thomas, the elder brother. Thomas took Jacob into full partnership without fee or recompense; and there was an understanding entered into between them later (but no legal agreement) that if the life of either failed his son should succeed to his post. If Thomas, the elder, died, his son Tom was to take his father's place as senior partner in due time. Thomas did die; died suddenly; but from that hour to this, Jacob had never attempted to carry out the agreement: he had taken his own son, Valentine, into partnership, but not Tom. And Crabb knew, both North and South, for such things get about curiously, that the injustice had troubled Jacob when he was dying, and that he had charged Valentine to remedy it.

Sunday morning was not so fine: leaden clouds, threatening rain, had overshadowed the summer sky. But all the family mourners came to church, Valentine wearing his long crape hatband and shoulder scarf (for that was our custom); the widow in her costly mourning, and the three girls in theirs. The mourning was furnished, Miss Timmens took the opportunity of whispering to Mrs. Todhetley, from a fashionable black shop at Worcester: and, to judge by the frillings and furbelows, very fashionable indeed the shop must have been. Mrs. Chandler and her son Tom sat together in their own pew, Mrs. Cramp, Jacob's sister, with them. It chanced that we were staying at Crabb Cot at the time of Jacob's death, just as we had been at Thomas's, and so saw the doings and heard the sayings, and the Squire was at hand for both funerals.

The next morning, Monday, Valentine Chandler took his place in the office as master for the first time, and seated himself in his late father's chair in the private room. He and his mother had already held some conversation as to arrangements for the future. Valentine said he should live at the office at Islip: now that there was only himself he should have more to do, and did not want the bother of walking or driving to and fro morning and evening. She would live entirely at North Villa.

Valentine took his place in his father's room; and the clerks, who had been hail-fellow-well-met with him hitherto, put on respect of manner, and called him Mr. Chandler. Tom had an errand to do every Monday morning connected with the business, and did not enter until nearly eleven o'clock. Before settling to his desk, he went in to Valentine.

They shook hands. In times of bereavement we are apt to observe more ceremony than at others. Tom sat down: which caused the new master to look towards him inquiringly.

"Valentine, I want to have a bit of talk with you. Upon what footing am I to be on here?"

"How do you mean?" asked Valentine: who was leaning back in the green leather chair with the air of his new importance full upon him, his elbows on the low arms, and an ivory paper-knife held between his fingers.

"My uncle Jacob told me that from henceforth I was to assume my right place here, Valentine. I suppose it will be so."

"What do you call your right place?" cried Valentine.

"Well, my right place would be head of the office," replied Tom, speaking, as he always did, cordially and pleasantly. "But I don't wish to be exacting. Make me your partner, Valentine, and give me the second place in the firm."

"Can't do it, old fellow," said Valentine, in tones which seemed to say he would like to joke the matter off. "The practice was my father's, and it is now mine."

"But you know that part of it ought to have been mine from the first, Valentine. That is, from the time I have been of an age to succeed to it."

"I don't know it, I'm sure, Tom. If it 'ought' to have been yours, I suppose my father would have given it to you. He was able to judge."

Tom dropped his voice. "He sent for me that last day of his life, you know, Valentine. It was to tell me he had not done the right thing by me, but that it should be done now: that he had charged you to do it."

"Ah," said Valentine, carelessly, "worn-out old men take up odd fancies—fit for a lunatic asylum. My poor father must have been spent with disease, though not with age: but we did not know it."

"Will you make me your partner?"

"No, Tom, I can't. The practice was all my father's, and the practice must be mine. Look here: on that same day you speak of he sent for John Paul to add a codicil to his will. Now it stands to reason that if he had wished me to take you into the firm, he would have mentioned it in that codicil and bound me down to do it."

"And he did not?"

"Not a word of it. You are quite welcome to read the will. It is a very short and simple one: leaving what property he had to my mother, and the business and office furniture to me. The codicil Paul wrote was to decree that I should pay my mother a certain sum out of the profits. Your name is not mentioned in the will at all, from beginning to end."

Tom made no reply. Valentine continued.

"The object of his tying me down to pay over to my mother a portion of the profits is, because she has not enough to live on without it. There need be no secret about it. I am to give her a third of the income I make, whatsoever it may be."

"One final word, Valentine: will you be just and take me in?"

"No, Tom, I cannot. And there's another thing. I don't wish to be mean, I'm sure; it's not in my nature: but with all my own expenses upon me and this third that I must hand over to my people, I fear I shall not be able to continue to give your mother the hundred and fifty a-year that my father has allowed her so long."

"You cannot help yourself, Valentine. That much is provided for in the original partnership deed, and you are bound by it."

"No," dissented Valentine, flicking a speck off the front of his black coat. "My father might have been bound by it, but I am not. Now that the two original partners are dead, the deed is cancelled, don't you see. It is not binding upon me."

"I think you are mistaken: but I will leave that question for this morning. Is your decision, not to give me a share, final?"

"It is."

"Let me make one remark. You say the codicil stipulates that you shall pay a third of the profits to your mother—and it is a very just and right thing to do. Valentine, rely upon it, that your father's last intentions were that, of the other two-thirds left, one of them should be mine."

Valentine flushed red. He had a florid complexion at all times, something like salmon-colour. Very different from Tom's, which was clear and healthy.

"We won't talk any more about it, Tom. How you can get such crotchets into your head, I can't imagine. If you sit there till midday, I can say no more than I have said: I cannot take you into partnership."

"Then I shall leave you," said Tom, rising. He was a fine-looking young fellow, standing there with his arm on the back of the client's chair, in which he had sat; tall and straight. His good, honest face had a shade of pain in it, as it gazed straight out to Valentine's. He looked his full six-and-twenty years.

"Well, I wish you would leave me, Tom," replied Valentine, carelessly. "I have heaps to do this morning."

"Leave the office, I mean. Leave you for good."

"Nonsense!"

"Though your father did not give me the rights that were my just due, I remained on, expecting and hoping that he would give them some time. It was my duty to remain with him; at least, my mother told me so; and perhaps my interest. But the case is changed now. I will not stay with you, Valentine, unless you do me justice; I shall leave you now. Now, this hour."

"But you can't, Tom. You would put me to frightful inconvenience."

"And what inconvenience—inconvenience for life—are you putting me to, Valentine? You take my prospects from me. The position that ought to be mine, here at Islip, you refuse to let me hold. This was my father's practice; a portion of it, at least, ought to be mine. I will not continue to be a servant where I ought to be a master."

"Then you must go," said Valentine.

Tom held out his hand. "Good-bye. I do not part in enmity."

"Good-bye, Tom. I'm sorry: but it's your fault."

Tom Chandler went into the office where he had used to sit, opened his desk, and began putting up what things belonged to him. They made a tolerable-sized parcel. Valentine, left in his chair of state, sat on in a brown study. All the inconvenience that Tom's leaving him would be productive of was flashing into his mind. Tom had been, under old Jacob, the prop and stay of the business; knew about everything, and had a clear head for details. He himself was different—and Valentine was never more sure of the fact than at this moment. There are lawyers and lawyers. Tom was one, Valentine was another. He, Valentine, had never much cared for business; he liked pleasure a great deal better. Indulged always by both father and mother, he had grown up self-indulgent. It was all very fine to perch himself in that chair and play the master; but he knew that, without Tom to direct things, for some time to come he should be three-parts lost. But, as to making him a partner and giving him a share? "No," concluded Valentine emphatically, "I won't do it."

Tom, carrying his paper parcel, left the house and crossed the road to the post-office, which was higher up the street, to post a letter he had hastily written. It was addressed to a lawyer at Worcester. A week or two before, Tom, being at Worcester, was asked by this gentleman if he would take the place of head clerk and manager in his office. The question was put jokingly, for the lawyer supposed Tom to be a fixture at Islip: but Tom saw that he would have been glad for him to take the berth. He hoped it might still be vacant. What with one thing and another, beginning with the injustice done him at the old place and his anxiety to get into another without delay, Tom felt more bothered than he had ever felt in his life. The tempting notion of setting-up somewhere for himself came into his mind. But it went out of it again: he could not afford to risk any waste of time, with his mother's home to keep up, and especially with this threat of Valentine's to stop her hundred and fifty pounds a-year income.

"How do you do, Mr. Chandler?"

At the sound of the pretty voice, Tom turned short round from the post-office window, which was a stationer's, to see a charming girl all ribbons and muslins, with sky-blue eyes and bright hair. Tom took the hand only half held out to him.

"I beg your pardon, Emma: I was reading this concert bill. The idea of Islip's getting up a concert!"

She was the only child of John Paul the lawyer, and had as fair a face as you'd wish to see, and a habit of blushing at nothing. To watch her as she stood there, the roses coming and going, the dimples deepening, and the small white teeth peeping, did Tom good. He was reddening himself, for that matter.

"Yes, it is to be given in the large club-room at the Bell to-night," she answered. "Shall you come over for it?"

"Are you going to it, Emma?"

"Oh yes. Papa has taken twelve tickets. A great many people are coming in to go with us."

"I shall go also," said Tom decidedly. And at that the roses came again.

"What a large parcel you are carrying!"

Tom held the brown-paper parcel further out at the remark.

"They are my goods and chattels," said he. "Things that I had at the office. I have left it, Emma."

"Left the office!" she repeated, looking as though she did not understand. "You don't mean really left it?—left it for good?"

"I have left it for good, Emma. Valentine—"

"Here's papa," interrupted Emma, as a stout, elderly gentleman with iron-grey hair turned out of the stationer's; neither of them having the least idea he was there.

"Is it you, Tom Chandler?" cried Mr. Paul.

"Yes, it is, sir."

"And fine to be you, I should say! Spending your time in gossip at the busiest part of the day."

"Unfortunately I have to-day no business to do," returned Tom, smiling in the old lawyer's face. "And I was just telling Miss Paul why. I have left the office, sir, and am looking out for another situation."

Mr. Paul stared at him. "Why, it is your own office. What's that for?"

"It ought to be my own office in part, as it was my father's before me. But Valentine cannot see that, sir. He tells me he will not take me into partnership; that I ought not to expect it. I refuse to remain on any other terms; and so I have left him for good. These are my rattletraps. Odds and ends of things that I am bringing away."

Mr. Paul continued to look at Tom in silence for a minute or two. Tom thought he was considering what he should next say. It was not that, however. "How well he would suit me! How I should like to take him! What a load of work he'd lift off my shoulders!" Those were the thoughts that were running rapidly through Mr. Paul's mind.

But he did not speak them. In fact, he had no intention of speaking them, or of taking on Tom, much as he would have liked to do it.

"When Jacob Chandler lay dying only yesterday, as it were, he told me you would join his son; that the two of you would carry on the practice together."

"Yes, he said the same thing to me," replied Tom. "But Valentine refuses to carry it out. So I told him I would not be a servant where I ought to be a master, and came away."

"And what are you going to do, young man?"

Tom smiled. He was just as much a lawyer as Mr. Paul was. "I should like to set up in practice for myself," he answered; "but I do not yet see my way sufficiently clear to do so. There may be a chance for me at Worcester, as managing clerk. I have written to ask if the place is filled up. May I join your party to the concert to-night, sir?" he asked.

"I don't mind—if you are going to it," said the old lawyer: "but I can't see what young men want at concerts?"

Tom caught Miss Emma's eye and her blushes, and gave her a glance that told her he should be sure to come.

But, before the lapse of twenty-four hours, in spite of his non-intention, Mr. Paul had taken on Tom Chandler and, looking back in later years, it might be seen that it had been on the cards of destiny that Tom should be taken.

"There's a divinity that shapes our ends,
Rough-hew them how we will."

Lawyer Paul was still in his dining-room that evening in his handsome house just out of Islip, and before any of his expected guests had come, when Tom arrived to say he could not make one, and was shown into the drawing-room. Feasting his eyes with Miss Emma's charming dress, and shaking her hand longer than was at all polite, Tom told her why he could not go.

"My mother took me to task severely, Emma. She asked me what I could be thinking of to wish to go to a public concert when my uncle was only buried the day before yesterday. The truth is, I never thought of that."

"I am so sorry," whispered Emma. "But I am worse than you are. It was I who first asked whether you meant to go. And it is to be the nicest concert imaginable!"

"I don't care for the concert," avowed Tom. "I—I should like to have gone to it, though."

"At least you—you will stay and take some tea," suggested Emma.

"If I may."

"Would you please loose my hand?" went on Emma. "The lace has caught in your sleeve-button."

"I'll undo it," said Tom. "What pretty lace it is! Is it Valenciennes? My mother thinks there's no lace like Valenciennes."

"It is only pillow," replied Emma, bending her face over the lace and the buttons. "After you left this morning, papa said he wished he had remembered to ask you where he could get a prospectus of those water-works. He—"

"Mrs. and Miss Maceveril," interrupted a servant, opening the door to show in some ladies.

So the interview was over; and Tom took the opportunity to go to the lawyer's dining-room, and tell him about the water-works.

"You have come over from Crabb to go to this fine concert!" cried Mr. Paul, sipping his port wine; which he always took out of a claret-glass. Though never more than one glass, he would be half-an-hour over it.

"I have come to say I can't go to it," replied Tom. "My mother thinks it would not be seemly so soon after Uncle Jacob's death."

"Quite right of her, too. Why don't you sit down? No wine? Well, sit down all the same. I want to talk to you. Will you come into my office?"

The proposal was so sudden, so unexpected, that Tom scarcely knew what to make of it. He did not know that Mr. Paul's office wanted him.

"I have been thinking upon matters since I saw you this morning, Tom Chandler. I am growing elderly; some people would say old; and the thought has often crossed me that it might be as well if I had some one about me different from an ordinary clerk. Were I laid aside by illness to-morrow the conduct of the business would still lie upon me; and lie it must, unless I get a confidential manager, who is a qualified lawyer: one who can act in my place without reference to me. I offer you the post; and I will give you, to begin with, two hundred a-year."

"I should like it of all things," cried Tom in delight, eyes and face sparkling. "I am used to Islip and don't care to leave it. Yes, sir, I will come with the greatest pleasure."

"Then that's settled," said old Paul.

Just about two years had gone on, and it was hot summer again. In the same room at North Villa where poor Thomas Chandler had died, sat Valentine Chandler and his mother. It was evening, and the window was open to the garden. In another room, its window also open, sat the three girls, Georgiana, Clementina, and Julietta; all of them singing and playing and squalling.

"Not talk about business on a Sunday night! You must have grown wonderfully serious all on a sudden!" exclaimed Mrs. Chandler, tartly. "I never get to see you except on a Sunday: you know that, Valentine."

"It is not often I can get time to come over on a week-day," responded Valentine, helping himself to some spirits and water, which had been placed on the table after supper. "Business won't let me."

"If all I hear be true, it is not business that hinders you," said Mrs. Chandler. "Be quiet, Valentine: I must speak. I have put it off and off, disliking to do it; but I must speak at last. Your business, as I am told, is falling off alarmingly; that a great deal of it has gone over to John Paul."

"Who told you?"

"That is beyond the question, Valentine, and I am not going to make mischief. Is it true, or is it not true?"

"A little of the practice went over to Paul when Tom left me. It was not much. Some of the clients, you see, had been accustomed to Tom at our place, and they followed him. That was a crafty move of John Paul's—getting hold of Tom."

"I am not alluding to the odds and ends of practice that left you then, Valentine. I speak chiefly of this last year. Hardly a week has passed in it but some client or other has left you for Paul."

"If they have, I can't help it," was the careless reply. "How those girls squall!"

"I suppose there is no underhand influence at work, Valentine?" she said dubiously. "Tom Chandler does not hold out baits for your clients, and so fish them away from you?"

"Well, no, I suppose not," repeated the young lawyer, draining his glass. "I accused Tom of it one day, and for once in his life he flew into a passion, asking me what I had ever seen in him to suspect he could be guilty of such a thing."

"No. I fear it is as I have been given to understand, Valentine: that the cause lies with you. You spend your time in pleasure instead of being at business. When clients go to the office, three times out of every five they do not find you. You are not there. You are over at the Bell, playing at billiards, or drinking in the bar."

"What an unfounded calumny!" exclaimed Valentine.

"I have been told," continued Mrs. Chandler, sinking her voice, "that you are getting to drink frightfully. It is nothing for clients now to find you in a state incapable of attending to them."

"Now, mother, I insist upon knowing who told you these lies," spluttered Valentine, getting up and striding to the window. "Let anybody come forward and prove that he has found me incapable—if he can."

"I heard that Sir John Whitney went in the other day and could make neither top nor tail of what you said," continued his mother, disregarding his denial. "You are agent for the little bit of property he owns here: he chanced to come over from Whitney Hall, and found you like that."

"I'll write to Sir John Whitney and ask what he means by saying it."

"He did not say it—that I know of. Others were witnesses of your state as well as he."

"If my clerks tell tales out of my office, I'll discharge them from it," burst forth Valentine, too angry to notice the tacit admission his words gave. "Not the clerks, you say? Then why don't you—"

"Do be still, Valentine. Putting yourself out like this will do no good. I hope it is not true: if you assure me it is not, I am ready to believe you. All I spoke for was, to caution you, and to tell you what is being said, that you may be on your guard. Leave off going to the Bell; stick to business instead: people will soon cease talking then."

"I dare say they will!" growled Valentine.

"If you are always at your post, ready to confer with clients, they would have no plea for leaving you and going to Paul. For all our sakes, Valentine, you must do this."

"And so I do. If—"

"Hush! The girls are coming in. I hear them shutting the piano."

Valentine dashed out a second supply, and drank it, not caring whether it contained most brandy or water. We are never so angry as when conscience accuses us: and it was accusing him.

In came the young ladies, laughing, romping, and pushing one another; Georgiana, Clementina, and Julietta, arrayed in all the colours of the rainbow. The chief difference Sunday made to them was, that their smartest clothes came out.

Mrs. Chandler's accusations were right, and Valentine's denials wrong. During the past two years he had been drifting downwards. The Bell was getting to possess so great a fascination for him that he could not keep away from it more than a couple of hours together. It was nothing for him to be seen playing billiards in the morning, or lounging in the parlour or the bar-room, drinking. One of his clerks would come interrupting him with news that some client was waiting at the office, and Valentine would put down his cue or his glass, and go flying over. But clients, as a rule, don't like this kind of reception: they expect to find their legal advisers cool and ready on the spot.

The worst of all was the drink. Valentine had made a friend of it so long now, that he did not attempt to do without it. Thought he could not. Where he at first drank one glass he went on to drink two glasses, and the two gave place to three, or to more. Of course it told upon him. It told now and then upon his manner in the daytime: which was unfortunate. He could leave his billiards behind him and his glass, but he could not leave the effects of what the glass had contained; and it was no uncommon thing now for his clients, when he did go rushing in to them, to find his speech uncertain and his brains in a muddle. As a natural result, the practice was passing over to John Paul as fast as it could: and Tom, who was chief manager at Paul's now, had been obliged to take on an extra clerk. Every day of his life old Paul told himself how lucky his move of engaging Tom had turned out. And this, not for the extra business he had gained: a great deal of that might have come to him whether Tom was with him or not: but because Tom had eased his shoulders of their hard work and care, and because he, the old man, had grown to like him so much.

But never a word had Mr. Paul said about raising Tom's salary. Tom supposed he did not intend to raise it. And, much as he liked his post, and, for many reasons, his stay at Islip, he entertained notions of quitting both. Valentine had stopped the income his father had paid to Mrs. Chandler; and Tom's two hundred a-year, combined with the trifle remaining to her out of her private income, only just sufficed to keep the home going.

It chanced that on the very same Sunday evening, when they were talking at North Villa of Valentine's doings, Tom broached the subject to his mother. They were sitting out of doors in the warm summer twilight, sniffing the haycocks in the neighbouring field. Tom spoke abruptly.

"Should you mind my going to London, mother?"

"To London!" cried Mrs. Chandler. "What for?"

"To live."

"You—you are not leaving Mr. Paul, are you?"

"I am thinking of it. You see, mother mine, there is no prospect of advancement where I am. It seems to me that I may jog on for ever at two hundred a-year—"

"It is enough for us, Tom."

"As things are, yes: but nothing more. If—for instance—if I wanted to set up a home of my own, I have no means of doing it. Never shall have, at the present rate."

Mrs. Chandler turned and looked at Tom's face. "Are you thinking of marrying, Tom?"

"No. It is of no use to think of it. If I thought of it ever so, I could not do it. Putting that idea aside, it occurs to me sometimes to remember that I am eight-and-twenty, and ought to be doing better for myself."

"Do you fancy you could do better in London?"

"I am sure I could. Very much better."

Opening the Bible on her lap, Mrs. Chandler took out the spectacles that lay between the leaves, and put them into their case with trembling fingers.

"Do whatever you think best, Tom," she said at length, having waited to steady her voice. "Children leave their parents' home for one of their own; this Book tells us that they should do so. Had Jacob Chandler done the right thing by you, you would never have needed to leave Islip: had his son done the right thing by me, I should not be the burden to you that I am. But now that George has taken to sending me money over from Canada—"

"Burden!" interrupted Tom, laughingly. "Don't you talk treason, Mrs. Chandler. If I do go to London, you will have to come with me, and see the lions."

That night, lying awake, Tom made his mind up. He had been offered a good appointment in London to manage a branch office for a large legal firm—four hundred a-year salary. And he would never for a moment have hesitated to take it, but for not liking to leave old Paul and (especially) old Paul's daughter.

Walking to Islip the next morning, he thought a bit about the best way of breaking it to Mr. Paul—who would be sure to come down upon him with a storm. By midday he had found no opportunity of speaking: people were perpetually coming in: and in the afternoon Tom had to go a mile or two into the country. In returning he overtook Emma. She was walking along the field-path under the hedge, her hat hanging on her arm by its strings.

"It is so warm," said she, in apology, as Tom shook hands. "And the trees make it shady here. I went over to ask Mary Maceveril to come back with me and dine: but they have gone to Worcester for the day."

"So much the better for me," said Tom. "I want to tell you, Emma, that I am going to leave."

"To leave!"

"I have had a very good place offered me in London. Mr. Paul knows nothing about it yet, for I did not make up my mind till last night, and I could not get a minute alone with him this morning."

She had turned her face suddenly to the hedge, seemingly to pick a wild rose. Tom saw that the pink roses on her cheek had turned to white ones.

"I shall be very sorry to leave Islip, Emma. But what else can I do? Situated as I am now, I cannot even glance at any plans for the future. By making this change, I may be able to do so. My salary will be a good one and enable me to put by: and the firm I am going to dropped me a hint of a possible partnership."

"I wish these dog-roses had no thorns! And I wish they would grow double, as the garden roses do!"

"So that I—having considered the matter thoroughly—believe I shall do well to make the change. Perhaps then I may begin to indulge dreams of a future."

"There! all the petals are off!"

"Let me gather them for you. What is the matter, Emma?"

"Matter? Nothing, sir. What should there be?"

"Here is a beauty. Will you take it?"

"Thank you. I never thought you would leave papa, Mr. Chandler."

"But—don't you perceive my reasons, Emma? What prospect is there for me as long as I remain here? What hope can I indulge, or even glance at, of—of settling in life?"

"I dare say you don't want to settle."

"I do not put the question to myself, because it is so useless."

"I shall be late for dinner. Good-bye."

She took a sudden flight to the little white side-gate of her house, which opened to the field, ran across the garden, and disappeared within doors. Tom, catching a glimpse of her face, saw that it was wet with tears.

"Yes, it's very hard upon her and upon me," he said to himself. "And all the more so that I cannot in honour speak, even just to let her know that I care for her."

Continuing his way towards the office, he met Mr. Paul, who was just leaving it. Tom turned with him, having to report to him of the business he had been to execute.

"I expected you home before this, Chandler."

"Willis was out when I arrived there, and I had to wait for him. His wife gave me some syllabub."

"Now for goodness' sake don't mix up syllabubs with law!" cried the old gentleman, testily. "That's just you, Tom Chandler. Will Willis do as I advise him, or will he not?"

"Yes, he is willing; but upon conditions. I will explain to-morrow morning," added Tom, as Mr. Paul laid his hand upon the handle of his front-gate, to enter.

"You can come in and explain now: and take some dinner with me."

Emma did not know he was there until she came into the dining-room. It gave her a sort of pleasant shock. They were deep in conversation about Willis, and she sat down quietly.

"I am glad he has asked me," thought Tom. "It will give me an opportunity of telling him about myself after dinner."

Accordingly, when the port wine was on the table and Emma had gone, for she never stayed after the cloth was removed, Tom spoke. Old Paul was pouring out his one large glass. The communication was over in a few words, for Tom did not feel it a comfortable one to make.

"Oh!" said old Paul, after listening. "Want to better yourself, do you? Going to London to get four hundred a-year, with a faint prospect of partnership? Have had it in your mind some time to make a change? No prospects here at Islip? Can only just keep your mother? Perhaps you want to keep a wife as well, Tom Chandler?"

Tom flushed like a school-girl. As the old gentleman saw, peering at him from under his bushy grey eyebrows.

"I should very much like to be able to do it, sir," boldly replied Tom, playing with his wine-glass. "But I can't. I can't as much as think of it under present circumstances."

"Who is the young lady? Your cousin Julietta?"

Tom burst into laughter. "No, that it is not, sir."

"Perhaps it is Miss Maceveril? Well, the Maceverils are exclusive people. But faint heart, you know, never won fair lady."

Tom shook his head. "I should not be afraid of winning her." But it was not Miss Maceveril he was thinking of.

"What should you be afraid of?"

"Her friends. They would not listen to me."

"Thinking you are not rich, I suppose?"

"Knowing I am not, sir."

"The young lady may have money."

"There's the evil of it," said Tom, impulsively. "If she had none, it would be all straight and smooth for us. I would very soon make a little home for her in London."

"It is the first time I ever heard of money being an impediment to matrimony," observed old Paul, taking the first sip at his wine.

"Not when the money is on the wrong side, sir."

"Has she much?"

"I don't know in the least. She will be sure to have some: she is an only child."

"Then it is Mary Maceveril!" nodded the old man. "You look after her, Tom, my boy. She will have ten thousand pounds."

"Miss Maceveril would not look at me, if I wanted her ever so. She is as proud as a peacock."

"Tut, tut! Try. Try, boy. Why, what could she want? As my partner, you might be a match for even Miss Maceveril."

"Your what, sir?" cried Tom, in surprise, lifting his eyes from the blue-and-red checked table-cover.

"I said my partner, Tom. Yes, that is what I intend to make you: have intended it for some time. We will have no fly-away London jaunts and junkets. Once my partner, of course the world will understand that you will be also my successor: and I think I shall soon retire."

Tom had risen from his seat: for once in his life he was agitated. Mr. Paul rose and put his hand on Tom's shoulder.

"With this position, and a suitable income to back it, Tom, you are a match for Mary Maceveril, or for any other good girl. Go and try her, boy; try your luck."

"But—it is of no use," spoke Tom. "You don't understand, sir."

"No use! Go and try,"—pushing him towards the door. "My wife was one of the proud Wintertons, you know: how should I have gained her but for trying? I did not depreciate myself, and say I'm not good enough for her: I went and asked her to have me."

"But suppose it is not Mary Maceveril, sir?—as indeed it is not. Suppose it is somebody nearer—nearer home?"

"No matter. Go and try, I say."

"I—do—think—you—understand—me, sir," cried Tom, slowly and dubiously. "I—hope there is no mistake!"

"Rubbish about mistake!" cried old Paul, pushing him towards the door. "Go and do as I bid you. Try."

He went to look for Emma, and saw her sitting under the acacia tree on the bench, which faced the other way. Stepping noiselessly over the grass, he put his arms on her shoulders, and she turned round with a cry. But Tom would not let her go.

"I am told to come out and try, Emma. I want a wife, and your father thinks I may gain one. He is going to make me his partner; and he says he thinks I am a match for any good girl. And I am not going to London."

She turned pale and red, red and pale, and then burst into a fit of tears and trembling.

"Oh, Tom, can it be true! Oh, Tom, Tom!"

And Tom kissed her for the first time in his life. But not for the last.

The news came out to us in a lump. Tom Chandler was taken into partnership and was to marry Emma. We wished them good luck. She was not to leave her home, for her father would not spare her: she and Tom were to live with him.

"I had to do it, you know, Squire," said old Paul, meeting the Squire one day. "Only children are apt to be wilful. Not that I ever found Emma so. Had I not allowed it, I expect she'd have dutifully saddled herself, an old maid, upon me for life."

"She could not have chosen better," cried the Squire, warmly. "If there's one young fellow I respect above another, it's Tom Chandler. He is good to the back-bone."

"He wouldn't have got her if he were not; you may rely upon that," concluded old Paul, emphatically.

So the wedding took place at Islip in the autumn, and old Paul gave Tom a month's holiday, and told him he had better take Emma to Paris; as they both seemed, by what he could gather, red-hot to see it.

Drizzle, drizzle, drizzle, came down the rain, dropping with monotonous patter on the decaying leaves that strewed the garden. Not the trim well-kept garden it used to be, but showing signs of neglect. What with the long grass, and the leaves, and the sloppy roads, and the November skies, nothing could well look more dreary than the world looked to-day, as seen from the windows of North Villa.

Time had gone on, another year, bringing its events and its changes; as time always does bring. The chief change, as connected with this little record, lay in Valentine Chandler. He had gone to the dogs. That was Islip's expression for it, not mine. A baby had come to Tom and Emma.

Little by little, step by step, Valentine had gone down lower and lower. Some people, who are given to bad habits, make spasmodic efforts to reform; but, so far as Islip could see, Valentine never made any. He passed more time at the Bell, or at less respectable public-houses, and drank deeper: and at last neglected his business almost entirely. Enervated and good for nothing, he would lie in bed till twelve o'clock in the day. To keep on the office seemed only a farce. Its profits were not enough to pay for its one solitary clerk. Valentine was then pulled up by an illness, which confined him to his bed, and left him in a shaky state. The practice had quite gone then, and the clerk had gone; and Valentine knew that, even though he had had sufficient energy left to try to bring them back, no clients would have returned to him.

He was going to emigrate to Canada. His friends hoped he would be steady there, and redeem the past: he gave fair promises of it. George Chandler (Tom's brother, who was doing very well there now, with a large farm about him, and a wife and children) had undertaken to receive Valentine and help him to employment. So he would have to begin life over again.

It was all so much gall and bitterness to his mother and sisters, and had been for a long while. The tears were dropping through the fingers of Mrs. Chandler now, as she leaned on her hand and watched the dreary rain on the window-panes. With all his faults, she had so loved Valentine. She loved him still, above all the trouble he had brought; and it seemed, this afternoon, just as though her heart would break.

When the business fell off, of course her income fell off also. Valentine was to have paid her a third of the profits, but if he did not make any profits, he could not pay her any. She had the private income, two hundred a-year, which Jacob had secured to her: but what was that for a family accustomed to live in the fashion? There is an old saying that necessity has no law: and Mrs. Jacob Chandler and her daughters had proved its truth. One of the girls had gone out as a governess; one was on a prolonged visit to her aunt Cramp; and Julietta and her mother were to move into a smaller house at Christmas. The practice and the other business, once Valentine's, and his father's before him, had all gone over to the other firm, Paul and Chandler.

"I'm sure I don't know what Georgiana means by writing home for money amidst all our troubles!" cried Mrs. Chandler, fretfully. "She has fifteen pounds a-year salary, and she must make that do."

"She says her last quarter's money is all spent, and she can't possibly manage without a new mantle for Sunday," returned Julietta.

"I can't supply it; you know I can't. I am not able to pay my own way now. Let her write to Mrs. Cramp."

"It would be of no use, mamma. Aunt Mary Ann will never help us to clothes. She says we have had too many of them."

"Well, I don't want to be worried with these matters: it's enough for me to think of poor Valentine's things. Only two days now before he starts. And what wretched weather it is!"

"Valentine says he shall not take much luggage with him. He saw me counting his shirts, and he said they were too many by half."

"And who will supply him with shirts out there, do you suppose?" demanded Mrs. Chandler. "You talk nothing but nonsense, Julietta. Where is Valentine? He ought to be here, with all this packing to do. He must have been gone out these two hours."

"He said he had business at Islip."

Mrs. Chandler looked gloomy at the answer. She hated the very name of Islip: partly because they held no longer any part in the place, partly because the Bell was in it.

But Valentine had not gone to the Bell this time. His visit was to his cousin Tom; and his errand was to beg of Tom to give or lend him a fifty-pound note before sailing.

"I shall have next to nothing in my pocket, Tom, when I land," he urged, as the two sat together in Tom's private room. "If I get on over there, I will pay you back. If I don't—well, perhaps you won't grudge having helped me for the last time."

For a moment Tom did not answer. He sat before his desk-table, Valentine near him: just as Valentine had one day sat at his desk in his private room, and Tom had been the petitioner, not so many years gone by. Valentine looked upon the silence as an ill-omen.

"You have all the business that once was mine in your fingers now, Tom. It has left me for you."

"But not by any wish or seeking of mine, Valentine; you know that," spoke Tom readily, turning his honest eyes and kindly face on the fallen man. "I wish you were in your office still. There's plenty of work for both of us."

"Well, I am not in it; and you have got it all. You might lend me such a poor little sum as fifty pounds."

"Of course I mean to lend it: but I was thinking. Look here, Valentine. I will not give it you now; you cannot want it before sailing: and you might lose it on board," he added laughing. "You shall carry with you an order upon my brother George for one hundred pounds."

"Will George pay it?"

"I will take care of that. He shall receive a letter from me by the same mail that takes you out. Stay, Valentine. I will give you the order now."

He wrote what was necessary, sealed it up, and handed it over. Valentine thanked him.

"How is Emma?" he asked as he rose. "And the boy?"

"Quite well, thank you: both. Will you not go in and see them?"

"I think not. You can say good-bye for me. I don't much care to trouble people."

"God bless you, Valentine," said Tom, clasping his hand. "You will begin life anew over there, and may have a happy one yet. One of these days you will be coming back to us, a prosperous man."

Valentine went trudging home through the rain, miserable and dispirited, and found a visitor had arrived—Mrs. Cramp. His mother and sister were upstairs then, busy over his trunks; so Mrs. Cramp had him all to herself. She had liked Valentine very much. When he went wrong, it put her out frightfully, and since then she had not spared him: which of course put out Valentine.

"Yes, it will be a change," he acknowledged, in reply to a remark of hers. "A flourishing solicitor here, and a servant there. For that's what I shall be over yonder, I conclude; I can't expect to be my own master. You don't know how good the business was, Aunt Mary Ann, at the time my father died. If I could only have kept it!"

"You could not expect to keep it," said Mrs. Cramp, who sat facing him, her bonnet tilted back from her red and comely face, her purple stuff gown pulled up above her boots.

"I should have kept it, but for now and then taking a little drop too much," confessed poor Valentine: who was deeper in the dumps that day than he had ever been before.

"I don't know that," said Mrs. Cramp. "The business was a usurped one."

"A what?" said Valentine.

"There is an overruling Power above us, you know," she went on. "I am quite sure, Valentine—I have learnt it by experience—that injustice never answers in the long run. It may seem to succeed for a time; but it does not last: it cannot and it does not. If a man rears himself on another's downfall, causing himself that downfall that he may rise, his prosperity rests on no sure foundation. In some way or other the past comes home to him; and he suffers for it, if not in his own person, in that of his children. Ill-gotten riches bring a curse, never a blessing."

"What a growler you are, Aunt Mary Ann!"

"I don't mean it for growling, Valentine. It is true."

"It's not true."

"Not true! The longer I live the more examples I see of it. A man treads another down that he may rise himself: and there he stands high and flourishing. But wait a few years, and look then. He is gone. Gone, and no trace of his prosperity left. And when I mark that, I recall that verse in the Psalms of David: 'I went by, and lo, he was gone: I sought him, but his place was nowhere to be found.' That verse is a true type of real life, Valentine."

"I don't believe it," cried Valentine. "And where's the good of having the Psalms at your finger-ends?"

"You do believe it. Why, Valentine, take your own case. Was there ever a closer exemplification? Tom was injured; put down; I may say, crushed by you and your father. Yes, crushed: crushed out of his rights. His father made the business; and the half of it, at any rate, ought to have been Tom's. Instead of that, your father deposed him and usurped it. He repented when he was dying, and charged you to remedy the wrong. But you did not; you usurped it. And what has it ended in?"

"Ended in?" cried Valentine vacantly.

"You are—as you are; ruined in character, in purse, in reputation; and Tom is respected and flourishing. The business has left you and gone to him; not through any seeking of his, but through your own doings entirely; the very self-same business that his father made has in the natural course of time and events gone back to him—and he is not thirty yet. It is retribution, nephew. Justice has been righting herself; and man could neither stay nor hinder it."

"What nonsense!" debated Valentine testily. "Suppose I had been steady: would the business have left me for Tom then?"

"Yes. In some inscrutable way, that we see not, it would. I am sure of it. You would no more have been allowed to triumph to the end on your ill-gotten gains, than I could stand if I went out and perched myself on yonder weathercock," affirmed Mrs. Cramp, growing warm. "Your father kept his place, it is true; but what a miserable man he always was, and without any ostensible cause."

"I wonder you don't set up for a parson, Aunt Mary Ann! This is as good as a sermon."

"Then carry the sermon in your memory through life, Valentine. Our doings, whether they be good or ill, bring back their fruits. In some wonderful manner that we cannot understand, events are always shaping onwards their own true ends, their appointed destiny, and working out the will of Heaven."

That's all. And the Squire seemed to take a leaf out of Mrs. Cramp's book. For ever so long afterwards, he would tell us to read a lesson from the history of the Chandlers, and to remember that none can deal unjustly in the sight of God without having to account for it sooner or later.

VERENA FONTAINE'S REBELLION

I

You have been at Timberdale Rectory two or three times before; an old-fashioned, red-brick, irregularly-built house, the ivy clustering on its front walls. It had not much beauty to boast of, but was as comfortable a dwelling-place as any in Worcestershire. The well-stocked kitchen-garden, filled with plain fruit-trees and beds of vegetables, stretched out beyond the little lawn behind it; the small garden in front, with its sweet and homely flowers, opened to the pasture-field that lay between the house and the church.

Timberdale Rectory basked to-day in the morning sun. It shone upon Grace, the Rector's wife, as she sat in the bow-window of their usual sitting-room, making a child's frock. Having no little ones of her own to work for—and sometimes Timberdale thought it was that fact that made the Rector show himself so crusty to the world in general—she had time, and to spare, to sew for the poor young starvelings in her husband's parish.

"Here he comes at last!" exclaimed Grace.

Herbert Tanerton looked round from the fire over which he was shivering, though it was a warm and lovely April day. A glass of lemonade, or some such cooling drink, stood on the table at his elbow. He was always catching a sore throat—or fancied it.

"If I find the delay has arisen through any neglect of Lee's, I shall report him for it," spoke the Rector severely. For, though he had condoned that one great mishap of Lee's, the burning of the letter, he considered it his duty to look sharply after him.

"Oh but, Herbert, it cannot be; he is always punctual," cried Grace. "I'll go and ask."

Mrs. Tanerton left the room, and ran down the short path to the little white gate; poor old Lee, the letterman, was approaching it from the field. Grace glanced at the church clock—three-quarters past ten.

"A break-down on the line, we hear, ma'am," said he, without waiting to be questioned, as he put one letter into her hand. "Salmon has been in a fine way all the morning, wondering what was up."

"Thank you," said Grace, glancing at the letter; "we wondered too. What a beautiful day it is! Your wife will lose her rheumatism now. Tell her I say so."

Back ran Grace. Herbert Tanerton was standing up, impatient for the letter he had been specially expecting, his hand stretched out for it.

"Your letter has not come, Herbert. Only one for me. It is from Alice."

"Oh!" returned Herbert, crustily, as he sat down again to his fire and his lemonade.

Grace ran her eyes quickly over the letter—rather a long one, but very legibly written. Her husband's brother, Jack Tanerton—if you have not forgotten him—had just brought home in safety from another voyage the good ship Rose of Delhi, of which he was commander. Alice, his wife, who generally voyaged with him, had gone immediately on landing to her mother at New Brighton, near Liverpool; Jack remaining with his ship. This time the ship had been chartered for London, and Jack was there with it.

Grace folded the letter slowly, an expression of pain seated in her eyes. "Would you like to read it, Herbert?" she asked.

"Not now," groaned Herbert, shifting the band of flannel on his throat. "What does she say?"

"She says"—Grace hesitated a moment before proceeding—"she says she wishes Jack could leave the sea."

"I dare say!" exclaimed Herbert. "Now, Grace, I'll not have that absurd notion encouraged. It was Alice's cry last time they were at home; and I told you then I would not."

"I have not encouraged it, Herbert. Of course what Alice says has reason in it: one cannot help seeing that."

"Jack chose the sea as his profession, and Jack must abide by it. A turncoat is never worth a rush. Jack likes the sea; and Jack has been successful at it."

"Oh yes: he's a first-rate sailor," conceded Grace. "It is Alice's wish, no doubt, rather than his. She says here"—opening the letter—"'Oh, if Jack could but leave the sea! All my little ones coming on!—I shall not be able to go with him this next voyage. And I come home to find my little Mary and my mother both ill! If we could but leave the sea!'"

"I may just as well say 'If I could but leave the Church!'—I'm sure I'm never well in it," retorted Herbert. "Jack had better not talk to me of this: I should put him down at once."

Grace sighed as she took up the little frock again. She remembered, though it might suit her husband to forget it, that Jack had not, in one sense of the word, chosen the sea; he had been deluded into it by Aunt Dean, his wife's mother. She had plotted and planned, that woman, for her daughter's advancement, and found out too late that she had plotted wrongly; for Alice chose Jack, and Jack, through her machinations, had been deprived of the greater portion of his birthright. He made a smart sailor; he was steady, and stuck to his duty manfully; never a better merchant commander sailed out of port than John Tanerton. But, as his wife said, her little ones were beginning to grow about her; she had two already; and she could not be with them at New Brighton, and be skimming over the seas to Calcutta, or where not, in the Rose of Delhi. Interests clashed; and with her whole heart Alice wished Jack could quit the sea. Grace sighed as she thought of this; she saw how natural was the wish, though Herbert did not see it: neither could she forget that the chief portion of the fortune which ought to have been Jack's was enjoyed by herself and her husband. She had always thought it unjust; it did not seem to bring them luck; it lay upon her heart like a weight of care. Their income from the living and the fortune, comprised together, was over a thousand pounds a-year. They lived very quietly, not spending, she was sure, anything like half of it; Herbert put by the rest. What good did all the money bring them? But little. Herbert was always ailing, fretful, and grumbling: the propensity to set the world to rights grew upon him: he had ever taken pleasure in that, from the time when a little lad he would muffle himself in his step-father's surplice, and preach to Jack and Alice. Poor Jack had to work hard for what he earned at sea; he had only a hundred and fifty pounds a-year, besides, of the money that had been his mother's; Herbert had the other six hundred and fifty of it. But Jack, sunny-natured, ever-ready Jack, was just as happy as the day was long.

Lost in these thoughts, her eyes bent on her work, Alice did not see a gentleman who was coming across the field towards the house. The click of the little gate, as it swung to after him, caused her to look up, but hardly in time. Herbert turned at the sound.

"Who's come bothering now, I wonder?"

"I think it is Colonel Letsom," answered Grace.

"Then he must come in here," rejoined Herbert. "I am not going into that cold drawing-room."

Colonel Letsom it was; a pleasant little man with a bald head, who had walked over from his house at Crabb. Grace opened the parlour-door, and the colonel came in and shook hands.

"I want you both to come and dine with me to-night in a friendly way," spoke he; "no ceremony. My brother, the major, is with us for a day or two, and we'd like to get a few friends together to meet him at dinner."

Herbert Tanerton hesitated. He did not say No, for he liked dinners; he liked the importance of sitting at the right or left hand of his hostess and saying grace. He did not say Yes, for he thought of his throat.

"I hardly know, colonel. I got up with a sore throat this morning. Very relaxed indeed it is. Who is to be there?"

"Yourselves and the Fontaines and the Todhetleys: nobody else," answered the colonel. "As to your throat—I dare say it will be better by-and-by. A cheerful dinner will do you good. Six o'clock sharp, mind."

Herbert Tanerton accepted the offer, conditionally. If his throat got worse, of course he should have to send word, and decline. The colonel nodded. He felt sure in his own mind the throat would get better: he knew how fanciful the parson was, and how easily he could be roused out of his ailments.

"How do you like the Fontaines?" questioned he of the colonel. "Have you seen much of them yet?"

"Oh, we like them very well," answered the colonel, who, in his easy nature, generally avowed a liking for everybody. "They are connections of my wife's."

"Connections of your wife's!" repeated Herbert quickly. "I did not know that."

"I'm not sure that I knew it myself, until we came to compare notes," avowed the colonel. "Any way, I did not remember it. Sir Dace Fontaine's sister married—. Stop; let me consider—how was it?"

Grace laughed. The colonel laughed also.

"I know it now. My wife's sister married a Captain Pym: it is many years ago. Captain Pym was a widower, and his first wife was a sister of Dace Fontaine's. Yes, that's it. Poor Pym and his wife died soon; both of them in India: and so, you see, we lost sight of the connection altogether; it slipped out of memory."

"Were there any children?"

"The first wife had one son, who was, I believe, taken to by his father's relatives. That was all. Well, you'll come this evening," added the colonel, turning to depart. "I must make haste back home, for they don't know yet who's coming and who's not."

A few days previously to this, we had taken up our abode at Crabb Cot, and found that some people named Fontaine had come to the neighbourhood, and were living at Maythorn Bank. Naturally the

Squire wanted to know who they were and what they were. And as they were fated to play a conspicuous part in the drama I am about to relate, I must give to them a word of introduction. Important people need it, you know.

Dace Fontaine belonged to the West Indies and was attached to the civil service there. He became judge, or sheriff, or something of the kind; had been instrumental in quelling a riot of the blacks, and was knighted for it. He married rather late in life, in his forty-first year, a young American lady. This young lady's mother—it is curious how things come about!—was first cousin to John Paul, the Islip lawyer. Lady Fontaine soon persuaded her husband to quit the West Indies for America. Being well off, for he had amassed money, he could do as he pleased; and to America they went with their two daughters. From that time they lived sometimes in America, sometimes in the West Indies: Sir Dace would not quite abandon his old home there. Changes came as the years went on: Lady Fontaine died; Sir Dace lost a good portion of his fortune through some adverse speculation. A disappointed man, he resolved to come to England and settle down on some property that had fallen to him in right of his wife; a small estate called Oxlip Grange, which lay between Islip and Crabb. Any way, old Paul got a letter, saying they were on the road. However, when they arrived, they found that the tenants at Oxlip Grange could not be got to go out of it without proper notice—which anybody but Sir Dace Fontaine would have known to be reasonable. After some cavilling, the tenants agreed to leave at the end of six months; and the Fontaines went into that pretty little place, Maythorn Bank, then to be let furnished, until the time should expire. So there they were, located close to us at Crabb Cot, Sir Dace Fontaine and his two daughters.

Colonel Letsom had included me in the dinner invitation, for which I felt obliged to him: I was curious to see what the Fontaines were like. Tom Coney said one of the girls was beautiful, lovely—like an angel: the other was a little quick, dark young woman, who seemed to have a will of her own.

We reached Colonel Letsom's betimes—neighbourly fashion. In the country you don't rush in when the dinner's being put on the table; you like to get a chat beforehand. The sunbeams were slanting into the drawing-room as we entered it. Four of the Letsoms were present, besides the major, and Herbert Tanerton and his wife, for the throat was better. All of us were talking together when the strangers were announced: Sir Dace Fontaine, Miss Fontaine, and Miss Verena Fontaine.

Sir Dace was a tall, heavy man, with a dark, sallow, and arbitrary face; Miss Fontaine was little and pale; she had smooth black hair, and dark eyes that looked straight out at you. Her small teeth were brilliantly white, her chin was pointed. A particularly calm face altogether, and one that could boast of little beauty—but I rather took to it.

Did you ever see a fairy? Verena Fontaine looked like nothing else. A small, fair, graceful girl, with charming manners and pretty words. She had the true golden hair, that is so beautiful but so rare, delicate features, and laughing eyes blue as the summer sky. I think her beauty and her attractions altogether took some of us by surprise; me for one. Bob Letsom looked fit to eat her. The sisters were dressed alike, in white muslin and pink ribbons.

How we went in to dinner I don't remember, except that Bob and I brought up the rear together. Sir Dace took Mrs. Letsom, I think, and the colonel Mrs. Todhetley; and that beautiful girl, Verena, fell to Tod. Tod! The two girls were about the most self-possessed girls I ever saw; their manners quite American. Not their accent: that was good. Major Letsom and Sir Dace fraternized wonderfully: they discovered that they had once met in the West Indies.

After dinner we had music. The sisters sang a duet, and Mary Ann Letsom a song; and Herbert Tanerton sang, forgetting his throat, Grace playing for him; and they made me sing.

The evening soon passed, and we all left together. It was a warmish night, with a kind of damp smell exhaling from the shrubs and hedges. The young ladies muffled some soft white woollen shawls round their faces, and called our climate a treacherous one. The parson and Grace said good-night, and struck off on the near way to Timberdale; the rest of us kept straight on.

"Why don't your people always live here?" asked Verena of me, as we walked side by side behind the rest. "By something that was said at dinner I gather that you are not here much."

"Mr. Todhetley's principal residence lies at a distance. We only come here occasionally."

"Well, I wish you stayed here always. It would be something to have neighbours close to us. Of course you know the dreadful little cottage we are in—Maythorn Bank?"

"Quite well. It is very pretty, though it is small."

"Small! Accustomed to our large rooms in the western world, it seems to us that we can hardly turn in these. I wish papa had managed better! This country is altogether frightfully dull. My sister tells us that unless things improve she shall take flight back to the States. She could do it," added Verena; "she is twenty-one now, and her own mistress."

I laughed. "Is she obliged to be her own mistress because she is twenty-one?"

"She is her own," said Verena. "She has come into her share of the money mamma left us and can do as she pleases."

"Oh, you were speaking in that sense."

"Partly. Having money, she is not tied. She could go back to-morrow if she liked. We are not bound by your English notions."

"It would not suit our notions at all. English girls cannot travel about alone."

"That comes of their imperfect education. What harm do you suppose could anywhere befall well brought-up girls? We have been self-dependent from childhood; taught to be so. Coral could take care of herself the whole world over, and meet with consideration, wheresoever she might be."

"What do you call her—Coral? It is a very pretty name."

"And coral is her favourite ornament: it suits her pale skin. Her name is really Coralie, but I call her Coral—just as she calls me Vera. Do you like my name—Verena?"

"Very much indeed. Have you read 'Sintram'?"

"'Sintram'!—no," she answered. "Is it a book?"

"A very nice book, indeed, translated from the German. I will lend it you, if you like, Miss Verena."

"Oh, thank you. I am fond of nice books. Coralie does not care for books as I do. But—I want you to tell me," she broke off, turning her fair face to me, the white cloud drawn round it, and her sweet blue eyes laughing and dancing—"I can't quite make out who you are. They are not your father and mother, are they?"—nodding to the Squire and Mrs. Todhetley, who were on ever so far in front with Sir Dace.

"Oh no. I only live with them. I am Johnny Ludlow."

Maythorn Bank had not an extensive correspondence as a rule, but three letters were delivered there the following morning. One of the letters was for Verena: which she crushed into her hand in the passage and ran away with to her room. The others, addressed to Sir Dace, were laid by his own man, Ozias, on the breakfast-table to await him.

"The West Indian mail is in, papa," observed Coralie, beginning to pour out the coffee as her father entered. "It has brought you two letters. I think one of them is from George Bazalgette."

Sir Dace wore a rich red silk dressing-gown, well wadded. A large fire burnt in the grate of the small room. He felt the cold here much. Putting his gold eye-glasses across his nose, as he slowly sat down— all his movements were deliberate—he opened the letter his daughter had specially alluded to, and read the few lines it contained.

"What a short epistle!" exclaimed Coralie.

"George Bazalgette is coming over; he merely writes to tell me so," replied Sir Dace. "Verena," he added, for just then Verena entered and wished him good-morning, with a beaming face, "I have a letter here from George Bazalgette. He is coming to Europe; coming for you."

A defiant look rose to Verena's bright blue eyes. She opened her mouth to answer; paused; and closed it again without speaking. Perhaps she recalled the saying, "Discretion is the better part of valour." It certainly is, when applied to speech.

Breakfast was barely over when Ozias came in again. He had a copper-coloured face, as queer as his name, but he was a faithful, honest servant, and had lived in the family twenty years. The gardener was waiting for instructions about the new flower-beds, he told his master; and Sir Dace went out. It left his daughters at liberty to talk secrets. How pretty the two graceful little figures looked in their simple morning dresses of delicate print, tied with bows of pale green ribbon.

"I told you I knew George Bazalgette would be coming over, Vera," began Coralie. "His letter by the last mail quite plainly intimated that."

Verena tossed her pretty head. "Let him come! He will get his voyage out and home for nothing. I hope he'll be fearfully sea-sick!"

Not to make a mystery of the matter, which we heard all about later, and which, perhaps, led to that most dreadful crime—but I must not talk of that yet. George Bazalgette was a wealthy West Indian planter, and wanted to marry Miss Verena Fontaine. She did not want to marry him, and for the very good reason that she intended to marry somebody else. There had been a little trouble about it with Sir Dace; and alas! there was destined to be a great deal more.

"Shall I tell you what I hope, Vera?" answered Coralie, in her matter-of-fact, unemotional way. "I hope that Edward Pym will never come here, or to Europe at all, to worry you. Better that the sea should swallow him up en voyage."

Verena's beaming face broke into smiles. Her sister's pleasant suggestion went for nothing, for a great joy lay within her.

"Edward Pym has come, Coral. The ship has arrived in port, and he has written to me. See!"

She took the morning's letter from the bosom of her dress, and held it open for Coralie to see the date, "London," and the signature "Edward." Had the writer signed his name in full, it would have been Edward Dace Pym.

"How did he know we were here?" questioned Coralie, in surprise.

"I wrote to tell him."

"Did you know where to write to him?"

"I knew he had sailed from Calcutta in the Rose of Delhi; we all knew that; and I wrote to him to the address of the ship's brokers at Liverpool. The ship has come on to London, it seems, instead of Liverpool, and they must have sent my letter up there."

"If you don't take care, Vera, some trouble will come of this. Papa will never hear of Edward Pym. That's my opinion."

She was as cool as were the cucumbers growing outside in the garden, under the glass shade. Verena was the opposite—all excitement; though she did her best to hide it. Her fingers were restless; her blushes came and went; the sweet words of the short love-letter were dancing in her heart.

"MY DARLING VERA,

"The ship is in; I am in London with her, and I have your dear letter. How I wish I could run down into Worcestershire! That cannot be just yet: our skipper will take care to be absent himself, I expect, and I must stay: he is a regular Martinet as to duty. You will see me the very hour I can get my liberty. How strange it is you should be at that place—Crabb! I believe a sort of aunt of mine lives there; but I have never seen her.

"Ever your true lover,
"EDWARD."

"Who is it—the sort of aunt?" cried Coralie, when Verena had read out the letter; "and what does he mean?"

"Mrs. Letsom, of course. Did you not hear her talking to papa, last night, about her dead sister, who had married Captain Pym?"

"And Edward was the son of Captain Pym's first wife, papa's sister. Then, in point of fact, he is not related to Mrs. Letsom at all. Well, it all happened ages ago," added Coralie, with supreme indifference, "long before our time."

Just so. Edward Pym, grown to manhood now, and chief-mate of the Rose of Delhi, was the son of that Captain Pym and his first wife. When Captain Pym died, a relative of his, who had no children of his own, took to the child, then only five years old, and brought him up. The boy turned out anything but good, and when he was fourteen he ran away to sea. He found he had to stick to the sea, for his offended relative would do no more for him: except that, some years later, when he died, Edward found that he was down for five hundred pounds in his will. Edward stayed on shore to spend it, and then went to sea again, this time as first officer in an American brig. Chance, or something else, took the vessel to the West India Islands, and at one of them he fell in with Sir Dace Fontaine, who was, in fact, his uncle, but who had never taken the smallest thought for him—hardly remembered he had such a nephew—and made acquaintance with his two cousins. He and Verena fell in love with one another; and, on her side, at any rate, it was not the passing fancy sometimes called by the name, but one likely to last for all time. They often met, the young officer having the run of his uncle's house whenever he could get ashore; and Edward, who could be as full of tricks and turns as a fox when it suited his convenience to be so, contrived to put himself into hospital when the brig was about to sail, saying he was sick; so he was left behind. The brig fairly off, Mr. Edward Pym grew well again, and looked to have a good time of idleness and love-making. But he reckoned without his host. A chance word, dropped inadvertently, opened the eyes of Sir Dace to the treason around. The first thing he did was to forbid Mr. Edward Pym his house; the second thing was to take passage with his family for America. Never would he allow his youngest and prettiest and best-loved daughter to become the wife of an ill-conducted, penniless ship's mate; and that man a cousin! The very thought was preposterous! So Edward Pym, thrown upon his beam-ends, joined a vessel bound for Calcutta. Arrived there, he took the post of chief mate on the good ship Rose of Delhi, Captain Tanerton, bound for England.

"What is this nonsense I hear, about your wanting to leave the sea, John?"

The question, put in the Rector of Timberdale's repellent, chilly tone, more intensified when anything displeased him, brought only a smile to the pleasant face of his brother. Ever hopeful, sunny-tempered Jack, had reached the Rectory the previous night to make a short visit. They sat in the cheerful, bow-windowed room, the sun shining on Jack, as some days before it had shone on Grace; the Rector in his easy-chair at the fire.

"Well, I suppose it is only what you say, Herbert—nonsense," answered Jack, who was playing with the little dog, Dash. "I should like to leave the sea well enough, but I don't see my way clear to do it at present."

"Why should you like to leave it?"

"Alice is anxious that I should. She cannot always sail with me now; and there are the little ones to be seen to, you know, Herbert. Her mother is of course—well, very kind, and all that," went on Jack, after an imperceptible pause, "but Alice would prefer to train her children herself; and, to do that, she must remain permanently on shore. It would not be a pleasant life for us, Herbert, she on shore and I at sea."

"Do you ever think of duty, John?"

"Of duty? In what way?"

"When a man has deliberately chosen his calling in life, and spent his first years in it, it is his duty to continue in that calling, and to make the best of it."

"I suppose it is, in a general way," said Jack, all smiles and good-humour. "But—if I could get a living on shore, Herbert, I don't see but what my duty would lie in doing it as much as it now lies at sea."

"You may not see it, John. Chopping and changing often brings a man to poverty."

"Oh, I'd take care, I hope, not to come to poverty. Down, Dash! Had I a farm of two or three hundred acres, I could make it answer well, if any man could. You know what a good farmer I was as a boy, Herbert—in practical knowledge, I mean—and how I loved it. I like the sea very well, but I love farming. It was my born vocation."

"I wish you'd not talk at random!" cried Herbert, fretfully. "Born vocation! You might just as well say you were born to be a mountebank! And where would you get the money to stock a farm of two or three hundred acres? You have put none by, I expect. You never could keep your pence in your pocket when a lad: they were thrown away right and left."

"That's true," laughed Jack. "Other lads used to borrow them. True also that I have not put money by, Herbert. I have not been able to."

"Of course you have not! It wouldn't be you if you had."

"No, Dash, there's not a bit more; you've had it all," cried Jack to the dog. But he, ever generous-natured, did not tell his brother why he had not been able to put by: that the calls made upon him by his wife's mother—Aunt Dean, as they still styled her—were so heavy and so perpetual. She wanted a great deal for herself, and she presented vast claims for the expenses of Jack's two little children, and for the maintenance of her daughter when Alice stayed on shore. Alice whispered to Jack she believed her mother was making a private purse for herself. Good-natured Jack thought it very likely, but he did not stop the supplies. Just as Aunt Dean had been a perpetual drain upon her brother, Jacob Lewis, during his lifetime, so she now drained Jack.

"Then, with no means at command, what utter folly it is for you to think of leaving the sea?" resumed the parson.

"So it is, Herbert," acquiesced Jack. "I assure you I don't think of it."

"Alice does."

"Ay, poor girl, because she wishes it."

"Do you see any chance of leaving it?"

"Not a bit," readily acknowledged Jack.

"Then where's the use of talking about it—of harping upon it?"

"None in the world," said Jack.

"Then we'll drop the subject, if you please," pursued Herbert, forgetting, perhaps, that it was he who introduced it.

"Jump then, Dash! Jump, good little Dash!"

"What a worry you make with that dog, John! Attend to me. I want to know why you came to London instead of to Liverpool."

"She was laid on for London this time," answered Jack.

"Laid on!" ejaculated Herbert, who knew as much about sailor's phrases as he did of Hebrew.

Jack laughed. "The agents in Calcutta chartered the ship for London, freights for that port being higher than for Liverpool. The Rose of Delhi is a free ship."

"Oh," responded Herbert. "I thought perhaps she had changed owners."

"No. But our broker in London is brother to the owners in Liverpool. There are three of them in all. James Freeman is the broker; Charles and Richard are the owners. Rich men they must be!"

"When do you think you shall sail again?"

"It depends upon when they can begin to reload and get the fresh cargo in."

"That does not take long, I suppose," remarked Herbert, slightingly.

"She may be loaded in three days if the cargo is ready and waiting. It may be three weeks if the cargo's not—or more than that."

"And Alice does not go with you?"

Jack shook his head: something like a cloud passed over his fresh, frank face. "No, not this time."

We were all glad to see Jack Tanerton again. He had paid Timberdale but one visit, and that a flying one, since he took command of the Rose of Delhi. It was the old Jack Tanerton, frank of face, hearty of manner, flying to all the nooks and corners of the parish with outstretched hands to rich and poor, with kind words and generous help for the sick and sorrowful: just the same, only with a few more years gone over his head. I don't say but Herbert was also glad to see him; only Herbert never displayed much gladness at anything.

One morning Jack and I chanced to be out together; when, in passing through the green and shady lane, that would be fragrant in summer with wild roses and woodbine, and that skirted Maythorn Bank, we saw some one stooping to peer through the sweetbriar hedge, as if he wanted to see what the house was like, and did not care to look at it openly. He sprang up at sound of our footsteps. It was a slight, handsome young man of five or six-and-twenty, rather under the middle height, with a warm colour, bright dark eyes, and dark whiskers. The gold band on his cap showed that he was a sailor, and he seemed to recognize Jack with a start.

"Good-morning, sir," he cried, hurriedly.

"Is it you, Mr. Pym?—good-morning," returned Jack, in a cool tone. "What are you doing down here?"

"The ship's finished unloading, and is gone into dry dock to be re-coppered, so I've got a holiday," replied the young man: and he walked away with a brisk step, as if not caring to be questioned further.

"Who is he?" I asked, as we went on in the opposite direction.

"My late chief mate: a man named Pym."

"You spoke as if you did not like him, Jack."

"Don't like him at all," said Jack. "My own chief mate left me in Calcutta, to better himself, as the saying runs; he got command of one of our ships whose master had died out there; Pym presented himself to me, and I engaged him. He gave me some trouble on the homeward voyage; drank, was insolent, and would shirk his duty when he could. Once I had to threaten to put him in irons. I shall never allow him to sail with me again—and he knows it."

"What is he here for?"

"Don't know at all," returned Jack. "He can't have come after me, I suppose."

"Has he left the ship?"

"I can't tell. I told the brokers in London I should wish to have another first officer appointed in Pym's place. When they asked why, I only said he and I did not hit it off together very well. I don't care to report ill of the young man; it might damage his prospects; and he may do better with another master than he did with me."

At that moment Pym overtook us, and accosted Jack: saying something about some bales of "jute," which, as I gathered, had constituted part of the cargo.

"Have you got your discharge from the ship, Mr. Pym?" asked Jack, after answering his question about the bales of jute.

"No, sir."

"No!"

"Not yet. I have not applied for it. There's some talk, I fancy, of making Ferrar chief," added Pym. "Until then I keep my post."

The words were not insolent, but the tone had a ring in it that betokened no civility. I thought Pym would have liked to defy Jack had he dared. Jack's voice, as he answered, was a little haughty—and I had never heard that from Jack in all my life.

"I shall not take Ferrar as chief. What are you talking of, Mr. Pym? Ferrar is not qualified."

"Ferrar is qualifying himself now; he is about to pass," retorted Pym. "Good-afternoon, sir."

Had Pym looked back as he turned off, he would have seen Sir Dace Fontaine, who came, in his slow, lumbering manner, round the corner. Jack, who had been introduced to him, stopped to speak. But not a word could Sir Dace answer, for staring at the retreating figure of Pym.

"Does my sight deceive me?" he exclaimed. "Who is that man?"

"His name is Pym," said Jack. "He has been my first mate on board the Rose of Delhi."

Sir Dace Fontaine looked blacker than thunder. "What is he doing down here?"

"I was wondering what," said Jack. "At first I thought he might have come down after me on some errand or other."

Sir Dace said no more. Remarking that we should meet again in the evening, he went his way, and we went ours.

For that evening the Squire gave a dinner, to which the Fontaines were coming, and old Paul the lawyer, and the Letsoms, and the Ashtons from Timberdale Court. Charles Ashton, the parson, was staying with them: he would come in handy for the grace in place of Herbert Tanerton, who had a real sore throat this time, and must stay at home.

But now it should be explained that, up to this time, none of us had the smallest notion that there was anything between Pym and Verena Fontaine, or that Pym was related to Sir Dace. Had Jack known either the one fact or the other, he might not have said what he did at the Squire's dinner-table. Not that he said much.

It occurred during a lull. Sir Dace craned his long and ponderous neck over the table towards Jack.

"Captain Tanerton, were you satisfied with that chief mate of yours, Edward Pym? Did he do his duty as a chief mate ought?"

"Not always, Sir Dace," was Jack's ready answer. "I was not particularly well satisfied with him."

"Will he sail with you again when you go out?"

"No. Not if the decision lies with me."

Sir Dace frowned and drew his neck in again. I fancied he would have been glad to hear that Pym was going out again with Jack—perhaps to be rid of him.

Colonel Letsom spoke up then. "Why do you not like him, Jack?"

"Well, for one thing, I found him deceitful," spoke out Jack, after hesitating a little, and still without any idea that Pym was known to anybody present.

Verena bent forward to speak then from the end of the table, her face all blushes, her tone resentful.

"Perhaps Mr. Pym might say the same thing of you, Captain Tanerton—that you are deceitful?"

"I!" returned Jack, with his frank smile. "No, I don't think he could say that. Whatever other faults I may have, I am straightforward and open: too much so, perhaps, on occasion."

When the ladies left the table, the Squire despatched me with a message to old Thomas about the claret. In the hall, after delivering it, I came upon Verena Fontaine.

"I am going to run home for my music," she said to me, as she put her white shawl on her shoulders. "I forgot to bring it."

"Let me go for you," I said, taking down my hat.

"No, thank you; I must go myself."

"With you, then."

"I wish to go alone," she returned, in a playful tone, but one that had a decisive ring in it. "Stay where you are, if you please, Mr. Johnny Ludlow."

She meant it; I saw that; and I put my hat down and went into the drawing-room. Presently somebody missed her; I said she had gone home to fetch her music.

Upon which they all attacked me for letting her go—for not offering to fetch it for her. Tod and Bob Letsom, who had just come into the room, told me I was not more gallant than a rising bear. I laughed, and did not say what had passed. Mary Ann Letsom plunged into one of her interminable sonatas, and the time slipped on.

"Johnny," whispered the mater to me, "you must go after Verena Fontaine to see what has become of her. You ought not to have allowed her to go out alone."

Truth to say, I was myself beginning to wonder whether she meant to come back at all. Catching up my hat again, I ran off to Maythorn Bank.

Oh! Pacing slowly the shadiest part of the garden there, was Miss Verena, the white shawl muffled round her. Mr. Pym was pacing with her, his face bent down to a level with hers, his arm passed gingerly round her waist.

"I thought they might be sending after me," she cried out, quitting Pym as I went in at the gate. "I will go back with you, Mr. Johnny. Edward, I can't stay another moment," she called back to him; "you see how it is. Yes, I'll be walking in the Ravine to-morrow."

Away she went, with so fleet a step that I had much ado to keep up with her. That was my first enlightenment of the secret treason which was destined to bring forth so terrible an ending.

"You won't tell tales of me, Johnny Ludlow?" she stopped to say, in a beseeching tone, as we reached the gate of Crabb Cot. "See, I have my music now."

"All right, Miss Verena. You may trust me."

"I am sure of that. I read it in your face."

Which might be all very well; but I thought it would be more to the purpose could she have read it in Pym's. Pym's was a handsome face, but not one to be trusted.

She glided into the room behind Thomas and his big tea-tray, seized upon a cup at once, and stood with it as coolly as though she had never been away. Sir Dace, talking near the window with old Paul, looked across at her, but said nothing. I wondered how long they had been in the drawing-room, and whether he had noticed her absence.

It was, I think, the next afternoon but one that I went to Maythorn Bank, and found Jack Tanerton there. The Squire had offered to drive Sir Dace to Worcester, leaving him to fix the day. Sir Dace wrote a note to fix the following day, if that would suit; and the Squire sent me to say it would.

Coralie was in the little drawing-room with Sir Dace, but not Verena. Jack seemed to be quite at home with them; they were talking with animation about some of the ports over the seas, which all three of them knew so well. When I left, Jack came with me, and Sir Dace walked with us to the gate. And there we came upon Mr. Pym and Miss Verena promenading together in the lane as comfortably as you please. You should have seen Sir Dace Fontaine's face. A dark face at all times; frightfully dark then.

Taking Verena by the shoulder, never speaking a word, he marched her in at the gate, and pushed her up the path towards the house. Then he turned round to Pym.

"Mr. Edward Pym," said he, "as I once had occasion to warn you off my premises in the Colonies, I now warn you off these. This is my house, and I forbid you to approach it. I forbid you to attempt to hold intercourse of any kind with my daughters. Do you understand me, sir?"

"Quite so, Uncle Dace," replied the young man: and there was the same covert defiance in his tone that he had used the other day to his captain.

"I should like to know what brings you in this neighbourhood?" continued Sir Dace. "You cannot have any legitimate business here. I recommend you to leave it."

"I will think of it," said Pym, as he lifted his cap to us generally, and went his way.

"What does it mean, Johnny?" spoke Tanerton, breathlessly, when we were alone. "Is Pym making-up to that sweet girl?"

"I fancy so. Wanting to make up, at least."

"Heaven help her, then! It's like his impudence."

"They are first cousins, you see."

"So much the worse. I expect, though, Pym will find his match in Sir Dace. I don't like him, by the way, Johnny."

"Whom? Pym?"

"Sir Dace. I don't like his countenance: there's too much secretiveness in it for me. And in himself too, unless I am mistaken."

"I am sure there is in Pym."

"I hate Pym!" flashed Jack. And at the moment he looked as if he did.

But would he have acknowledged as much, even to me, had he foreseen the cruel fate that was, all too soon, to place Edward Pym beyond the pale of this world's hate?—and the dark trouble it would bring home to himself, John Tanerton?

II

Striding along through South Crabb, and so on down by old Massock's brick-fields, went Sir Dace Fontaine, dark and gloomy. His heavy stick and his heavy tread kept pace together; both might have been the better for a little lightness.

Matters were not going on too smoothly at Maythorn Bank. Seemingly obedient to her father, Verena Fontaine contrived to meet her lover, and did not take extraordinary pains to keep it secret. Sir Dace, watching stealthily, found it out, and felt just about at his wits' end.

He had no power to banish Edward Pym from the place: he had none, one must conclude, to exact submission from Verena. She had observed to me, the first night we met, that American girls grow up to be independent of control in many ways. That is true: and, as it seems to me, they think great guns of themselves for being so.

Sir Dace was beginning to turn his anger on Colonel Letsom. As chance had it, while he strode along this morning, full of wrath, the colonel came in view, turning the corner of the strongest and most savoury brick-yard.

"Why do you harbour that fellow?" broke out Sir Dace, fiercely, without circumlocution of greeting.

"What, young Pym?" cried the little colonel in his mild way, jumping to the other's meaning. "I don't suppose he will stay with us long. He is expecting a summons to join his ship."

"But why do you have him at your house at all?" reiterated Sir Dace, with a thump of his stick. "Why did you take him in?"

"Well, you see, he came down, a stranger, and presented himself to us, calling my wife aunt, though she is not really so, and said he would like to stay a few days with us. We could not turn him away, Sir Dace. In fact we had no objection to his staying; he behaves himself very well. He'll not be here long."

"He has been here a great deal too long," growled Sir Dace; and went on his way muttering.

Nothing came of this complaint of Sir Dace Fontaine's. Edward Pym continued to stay at Crabb, Colonel Letsom not seeing his way clear to send him adrift; perhaps not wanting to. The love-making went on. In the green meadows, where the grass and the sweet wild flowers were springing up, in the Ravine, between its sheltering banks, redolent of romance; or in the triangle, treading underfoot the late primroses and violets—in one or other of these retreats might Mr. Pym and his ladye-love be seen together, listening to the tender vows whispered between them, and to the birds' songs.

Sir Dace, conscious of all this, grew furious, and matters came to a climax. Verena was bold enough to steal out one night to meet Pym for a promenade with him in the moonlight, and Sir Dace came upon them sitting on the stile at the end of the cross lane. He gave it to Pym hot and strong, marched Verena home, and the next day carried both his daughters away from Crabb.

But I ought to mention that I had gone away from Crabb myself before this, and was in London in with Miss Deveen. So that what had been happening lately I only knew by hearsay.

To what part of the world Sir Dace went, was not known. Naturally Crabb was curious upon the point. Just as naturally it was supposed that Pym, having nothing to stay for, would now take his departure. Pym, however, stayed on.

One morning Mr. Pym called at Maythorn Bank. An elderly woman, one Betty Huntsman, who had been employed by the Fontaines as cook, opened the door to him. The coloured man, Ozias, and a maid, Esther, had gone away with the family. It was the second time Mr. Pym had presented himself upon the same errand: to get the address of Sir Dace Fontaine. Betty, obeying her master's orders, had refused it; this time he had come to bribe her. Old Betty, however, an honest, kindly old woman, refused to be bribed.

"I can't do it, sir," she said to Pym. "When the master wrote to give me the address, on account of sending him his foreign letters, he forbade me to disclose it to anybody down here. It is only myself that knows it, sir."

"It is in London; I know that much," affirmed Pym, making a shot at the place, and so far taking in old Betty.

"That much may possibly be known, sir. I cannot tell more."

Back went Pym to Colonel Letsom's. He sat down and wrote a letter in a young lady's hand—for he had all kinds of writing at his fingers' ends—and addressed it to Mrs. Betty Huntsman at Maythorn Bank, Worcestershire. This he enclosed in a bigger envelope, with a few lines from himself, and posted it to London, to one Alfred Saxby, a sailor friend of his. He next, in a careless, off-hand manner, asked Colonel Letsom if he'd mind calling at Maythorn Bank, and asking the old cook there if she could give him her master's address. Oh, Pym was as cunning as a fox, and could lay out his plans artfully. And Colonel Letsom, unsuspicious as the day, and willing to oblige everybody, did call that afternoon to put the question to Betty; but she told him she was not at liberty to give the address.

The following morning, Pym got the summons he had been expecting, to join his ship. The Rose of Delhi was now ready to take in cargo. After swearing a little, down sat Mr. Pym to his desk, and in a shaky hand, to imitate a sick man's, wrote back word that he was ill in bed, but would endeavour to be up in London on the morrow.

And, the morning following this, Mrs. Betty Huntsman got a letter from London.

"London, Thursday.

"DEAR OLD BETTY,

"I am writing to you for papa, who is very poorly indeed. Should Colonel Letsom apply to you for our address here, you are to give it him: papa wishes him to have it. We hope your wrist is better.

"CORALIE FONTAINE."

Betty Huntsman, honest herself, never supposed but the letter was written by Miss Fontaine. By-and-by, there came a ring at the bell.

"My uncle, Colonel Letsom, requested me to call here this morning, as I was passing on my way to Timberdale Rectory," began Mr. Pym; for it was he who rang, and by his authoritative voice and lordly manner, one might have thought he was on board a royal frigate, commanding a cargo of refractory soldiers.

"Yes, sir!" answered Betty, dropping a curtsy.

"Colonel Letsom wants your master's address in London—if you can give it him. He has to write to Sir Dace to-day."

Betty produced a card from her innermost pocket, and showed it to Mr. Pym: who carefully copied down the address.

That he was on his way to Timberdale Rectory, was not a ruse. He went on there through the Ravine at the top of his speed, and asked for Captain Tanerton.

"Have got orders to join ship, sir, and am going up this morning. Any commands?"

"To join what ship?" questioned Jack.

"The Rose of Delhi. She is beginning to load."

Jack paused. "Of course you must go up, as you are sent for. But I don't think you will go out in the Rose of Delhi, Mr. Pym. I should recommend you to look out for another ship."

"Time enough for that, Captain Tanerton, when I get my discharge from the Rose of Delhi: I have not got it yet," returned Pym, who seemed to take a private delight in thwarting his captain.

"Well, I shall be in London myself shortly, and will see about things," spoke Jack.

"Any commands, sir?"

"Not at present."

Taking his leave of Colonel and Mrs. Letsom, and thanking them for their hospitality, Edward Pym departed for London by an afternoon train. He left his promises and vows to the young Letsoms, boys and girls, to come down again at the close of the next voyage, little dreaming, poor ill-fated young man, that he would never go upon another. Captain Tanerton wrote at once to head-quarters in Liverpool, saying he did not wish to retain Pym as chief mate, and would like another one to be appointed. Strolling back to Timberdale Rectory from posting the letter at Salmon's, John Tanerton fell into a brown study.

A curious feeling, against taking Pym out again, lay within him; like an instinct, it seemed; a prevision of warning. Jack was fully conscious of it, though he knew not why it should be there. It was a great deal stronger than could have been prompted by his disapprobation of the man's carelessness in his duties on board.

"I'll go up to London to-morrow," he decided. "Best to do so. Pym means to sail in the Rose of Delhi if he can; just, I expect, because he sees I don't wish him to: the man's nature is as contrary as two sticks. I'll not have him again at any price. Yes, I must go up to-morrow."

"L'homme propose"—we know the proverb. Very much to Jack's surprise, his wife arrived that evening at the Rectory from Liverpool, with her eldest child, Polly. Therefore, Jack did not start for London on the morrow; it would not have been at all polite.

He went up the following week. His first visit was to Eastcheap, in which bustling quarter stood the office of Mr. James Freeman, the ship's broker. After talking a bit about the ship and her cargo, Jack spoke of Pym.

"Has a first officer been appointed in Pym's place?"

"No," said Mr. Freeman. "Pym goes out with you again."

"I told you I did not wish to take Pym again," cried Jack.

"You said something about it, I know, and we thought of putting in the mate from the Star of Lahore; but he wants to keep to his own vessel."

"I won't take Pym."

"But why, Captain Tanerton?"

"We don't get on together. I never had an officer who gave me so much provocation—the Americans would say, who riled me so. I believe the man dislikes me, and for that reason was insubordinate. He may do better in another ship. I am a strict disciplinarian on board."

"Well," carelessly observed the broker, "you will have to make the best of him this voyage, Captain Tanerton. It is decided that he sails with you again."

"Then, don't be surprised if there's murder committed," was Jack's impetuous answer.

And Mr. Freeman stared: and noted the words.

The mid-day sun was shining hotly upon the London pavement, and especially upon the glittering gold band adorning the cap of a lithe, handsome young sailor, who had just got out of a cab, and was striding along as though he wanted to run a race with the clocks. It was Edward Pym: and the reader will please take notice that we have gone back a few days, for this was the day following Pym's arrival in London.

"Halt a step," cried he to himself, his eye catching the name written up at a street corner. "I must be out of my bearings."

Taking from his pocket a piece of paper, he read some words written there. It was no other than the address he had got from Bessy Huntsman the previous day.

"Woburn Place, Russell Square," repeated he. "This is not it. I'll be shot if I know where I am! Can you tell me my way to Woburn Place?" asked he, of a gentleman who was passing.

"Turn to the left; you will soon come to it."

"Thank you," said Pym.

The right house sighted at last, Mr. Pym took his standing in a friendly door-way on the other side of the road, and put himself on the watch. Very much after the fashion of a bailiff's man, who wants to serve a writ.

He glanced up at the windows; he looked down at the doors; he listened to the sound of a church clock striking; he scraped his feet in impatience, now one foot, now the other. Nothing came of it. The rooms behind the curtained windows might be untenanted for all the sign given out to the eager eyes of Mr. Pym.

"Hang it all!" he cried, in an explosion of impatience: and he could have sent the silent dwelling to Jericho.

No man of business likes his time to be wasted: and Mr. Pym could very especially not afford to waste his to-day. For he was supposed to be at St. Katherine's Docks, checking cargo on board the Rose of Delhi. When twelve o'clock struck, the dinner hour, he had made a rush from the ship, telling the foreman of the shed not to ship any more cargo till he came back in half-an-hour, and had come dashing up here in a fleet cab. The half-hour had expired, and another half-hour to it, and it was a great deal more than time to dash back again. If anybody from the office chanced to go down to the ship, what a row there'd be!—and he would probably get his discharge.

He had not been lucky in his journey from Worcestershire the previous day. The train was detained so on the line, through some heavy waggons having come to grief, that he did not reach London till late at night; too late to go down to his lodgings near the docks; so he slept at an hotel. This morning he had reported himself at the broker's office; and Mr. Freeman, after blowing him up for his delay, ordered him on board at once: since they began to load, two days ago now, a clerk from the office had been down on the ship, making up the cargo-books in Pym's place.

"I'll be hanged if I don't believe they must all be dead!" cried Pym, gazing at the house. "Why does not somebody show himself? I can't post the letter—for I know my letters to her are being suppressed. And I dare not leave it at the door myself, lest that cantankerous Ozias should answer me, and hand it to old Dace, instead of to Vera."

Luck at last! The door opened, and a maid-servant came out with a jug, her bonnet thrown on perpendicularly. Mr. Pym kept her in view, and caught her up as she was nearing a public-house.

"You come from Mrs. Ball's, Woburn Place?" said he.

"Yes, sir," answered the girl, doubtfully, rather taken aback at the summary address, but capitulating to the gold-lace band.

"I want you to give this letter privately to Miss Verena Fontaine. When she is quite alone, you understand. And here's half-a-crown, my pretty lass, for your trouble."

The girl touched neither letter nor money. She surreptitiously put her bonnet straight, in her gratified vanity.

"But I can't give it, sir," she said. "Though I'm sure I'd be happy to oblige you if I could. The Miss Fontaines and their papa is not with us now; they've gone away."

"What?" cried Pym, setting his teeth angrily, an expression crossing his face that marred all its good looks. "When did they leave? Where are they gone to?"

"They left yesterday, sir, and they didn't say where. That black servant of theirs and our cook couldn't agree; there was squabbles perpetual. None of us liked him; it don't seem Christian-like to have a black man sitting down to table with you. Mrs. Ball, our missis, she took our part; and the young ladies and their papa they naturally took his part: and so, they left."

"Can I see Mrs. Ball?" asked Pym, after mentally anathematizing servants in general, black and white. "Is she at home?"

"Yes, sir, and she'll see you, I'm sure. She is vexed at their having left."

He dropped the half-crown into the girl's hand, returned the note to his pocket, and went to the house. Mrs. Ball, a talkative, good-humoured woman in a rusty black silk gown, with red cheeks and quick brown eyes, opened the door to him herself.

She invited him in. She would have given him Sir Dace Fontaine's address with all the pleasure in life, if she had it, she said. Sir Dace did not leave it with her. He simply bade her take in any letters that might come, and he would send for them.

"Have you not any notion where they went?—to what part of the town?" asked the discomfited Pym. That little trick he had played Betty Huntsman was of no use to him now.

"Not any. Truth to say, I was too vexed to ask," confessed Mrs. Ball. "I knew nothing about their intention to leave until they were packing up. Sir Dace paid me a week's rent in lieu of warning, and away they went in two cabs. You are related to them, sir? There's a look in your face that Sir Dace has got."

Mr. Pym knitted his brow; he did not take it as a compliment. Many people had seen the same likeness; though he was a handsome young man and Sir Dace an ugly old one.

"If you can get their address, I shall be much obliged to you to keep it for me; I will call again to-morrow evening," were his parting words to the landlady. And he went rattling back to the docks as fast as wheels could take him.

Mr. Pym went up to Woburn Place the following evening accordingly, but the landlady had no news to give him. He went the next evening after, and the next, and the next. All the same. He went so long and to so little purpose that he at last concluded the Fontaines were not in London. Sir Dace neither sent a messenger nor wrote for any letters there might be. Two were waiting for him; no more. Edward Pym and Mrs. Ball became, so to say, quite intimate. She had much sympathy with the poor young man, who wanted to find his relatives before he sailed—and could not.

It may as well be told, not to make an unnecessary mystery of it, that the Fontaines had gone straight to Brighton. At length, however, Mrs. Ball was one day surprised by a visit from Ozias. She never bore malice long, and received him civilly. Her rooms were let again, so she had got over the smart.

"At Brighton!" she exclaimed, when she heard where they had been—for the man had no orders to conceal it. "I thought it strange that your master did not send for his letters. And how are the young ladies? And where are you staying now?"

"The young ladies, they well," answered Ozias. "We stay now at one big house in Marylebone Road. We come up yesterday to this London town: Sir Dace, he find the sea no longer do for him; make him have much bile."

Edward Pym had been in a rage at not finding Verena. Verena, on her part, though rather wondering that she did not hear from him, looked upon his silence as only a matter of precaution. When they were settled at Woburn Place, after leaving Crabb, she had written to Pym, enjoining him not to reply. It might not be safe, she said, for Coralie had gone over to "the enemy," meaning Sir Dace: Edward must contrive to see her when he came to London to join his ship. And when the days went on, and Verena saw nothing of her lover, she supposed he was not yet in London. She went to Brighton supposing the same. But, now that they were back from Brighton, and still neither saw Pym nor heard from him, Verena grew uneasy, fearing that the Rose of Delhi had sailed.

"What a strange thing it is about Edward!" she exclaimed one evening to her sister. "I think he must have sailed. He would be sure to come to us if he were in London."

"How should he know where we are?" dissented Coralie. "For all he can tell, Vera, we may be in the moon."

A look of triumph crossed Vera's face. "He knows the address in Woburn Place, Coral, for I wrote and gave it him: and Mrs. Ball would direct him here. Papa sent Ozias there to-day for his letters; and I know Edward would never cease going there, day by day, to ask for news, until he heard of me."

Coralie laughed softly. Unlocking her writing-case, she displayed a letter that lay snugly between its leaves. It was the one that Vera had written at Woburn Place. Verena turned very angry, but Coralie made light of it.

"As I dare say he has already sailed, I confess my treachery, Vera. It was all done for your good. Better think no more of Edward Pym."

"You wicked thing! You are more cruel than Bluebeard. I shall take means to ascertain whether the Rose of Delhi is gone. Captain Tanerton made a boast that he'd not take Edward out again, but he may not have been able to help himself," pursued Vera, her tone significant. "Edward intended to go in her, and he has a friend at court."

"A friend at court!" repeated Coralie. "What do you mean? Who is it?"

"It is the Freemans out-door manager at Liverpool, and the ship's husband—a Mr. Gould. He came up here when the ship got in, and he and Edward made friends together. The more readily because Gould and Captain Tanerton are not friends. The captain complained to the owners last time of something or other connected with the ship—some bad provisions, I think, that had been put on board, and insisted on its being rectified. As Mr. Gould was responsible, he naturally resented this, and ever since he has been fit to hang Captain Tanerton."

"How do you know all this, Verena?"

"From Edward. He told me at Crabb. Mr. Gould has a great deal more to do with choosing the officers than the Freemans themselves have, and he promised Edward he should remain in the Rose of Delhi."

"It is strange Edward should care to remain in the ship when her commander does not like him," remarked Coralie.

"He stays in because of that—to thwart Tanerton," laughed Verena lightly. "Partly, at least. But he thinks, you see, and I think, that his remaining for two voyages in a ship that has so good a name may tell well for him with papa. Now you know, Coral."

The lovers met. Pym found her out through Mrs. Ball. And Verena, thoroughly independent in her notions, put on her bonnet, and walked with him up and down the Marylebone Road.

"We sail this day week, Vera," he said. "My life has been a torment to me, fearing I should not see you before the ship went out of dock. And, in that case, I don't think I should have gone in her."

"Is it the Rose of Delhi?" asked Vera.

"Of course. I told you Gould would manage it. She is first-rate in every way, and the most comfortable ship I ever was in—barring the skipper."

"You don't like him, I know. And he does not like you."

"I hate and detest him," said Pym warmly—therefore, as the reader must perceive, no love was lost between him and Jack. "He is an awful screw for keeping one to one's duty, and I expect we shall have no end of squalls. Ah, Verena," continued the young man, in a changed tone, "had you only listened to my prayers at Crabb, I need not have sailed again at all."

Mr. Edward Pym was a bold wooer. He had urged Verena to cut the matter short by marrying him at once. She stopped his words.

"I will marry you in twelve months from this, if all goes well, but not before. It is waste of time to speak of it, Edward—as I have told you. Were I to marry without papa's consent—and you know he will not give it—he can take most of the money that came to me from mamma. Only a small income would remain to me. I shall not risk that."

"As if Sir Dace would exact it! He might go into one of his passions at first, but he'd soon come round; he'd not touch your money, Vera." And Edward Pym, in saying this, fully believed it.

"You don't know papa. I have been used to luxuries, Edward, and I could not do without them. What would two hundred pounds a-year be for me—living as I have lived? And for you, also, for you would be my husband? Next May I shall be of age, and my fortune will be safe—all my own."

"A thousand things may happen in a year," grumbled Pym, who was wild to lead an idle life, and hated the discipline on board ship. "The Rose of Delhi may go down, and I with it."

"She has not gone down yet. Why should she go down now?"

"What right had Coralie to intercept your letter?" asked Pym, passing to another phase of his grievances.

"She had no right; but she did it. I asked Esther, our own maid, to run and put it in the post for me. Coralie, coming in from walking, met Esther at the door, saw the letter in her hand, and took it from her, saying she would go back and post it herself. Perhaps Esther suspected something: she did not tell me this. Coralie had the face to tell it me herself yesterday."

"Well, Vera, you should have managed better," returned Pym, feeling frightfully cross.

"Oh, Edward, don't you see how it is?" wailed the girl, in a piteous tone of appeal—"that they are all against me. Or, rather, against you. Papa, Coralie, and Ozias: and I fancy now that Coralie has spoken to Esther. Papa makes them think as he thinks."

"It is a fearful shame. Is this to be our only interview?"

"No," said Vera. "I will see you every day until you sail."

"You may not be able to. We shall be watched, now Coralie has turned against us."

"I will see you every day until you sail," repeated the girl, with impassioned fervour. "Come what may, I will contrive to see you."

In making this promise, Miss Verena Fontaine probably did not understand the demands on a chief mate's time when a ship is getting ready for sea. To rush up from the docks at the mid-day hour, and rush back again in time for work, was not practicable. Pym had done it once; he could not do it twice. Therefore, the only time to be seized upon was after six o'clock, when the Rose of Delhi was left to herself and her watchman for the night, and the dock-gates were shut. This brought it, you see, to about seven o'clock, before Pym could be hovering, like a wandering ghost, up and down the Marylebone Road; for he had to go to his lodgings in Ship Street first and put himself to rights after his day's work, to say nothing of drinking his tea. And seven o'clock was Miss Verena Fontaine's dinner hour. Sir Dace Fontaine's mode of dining was elaborate; and, what with the side-dishes, the puddings and the dessert, it was never over much before nine o'clock.

For two days Verena made her dinner at luncheon. Late dining did not agree with her, she told Coralie, and she should prefer some tea in her room. Coralie watched, and saw her come stealing in each night soon after nine. Until that hour, she had promenaded with Edward Pym in the bustling lighted streets, or in the quieter walks of the Regent's Park. On the third day, Sir Dace told her that she must be in her place at the dinner-table. Verena wondered whether the order emanated from his arbitrary temper, or whether he had any suspicion. So, that evening she dined as usual; and when she and Coralie went into the drawing-room at eight o'clock, she said her head ached, and she should go to bed.

That night there was an explosion. Docked of an hour at the beginning of their interview, the two lovers made up for it by lingering together an hour longer at the end of it. It was striking ten when Verena came in, and found herself confronted by her father. Verena gave Coralie the credit of betraying her, but in that she was wrong. Sir Dace—he might have had his suspicions—suddenly called for a particular duet that was a favourite with his daughters, bade Coralie look it out, and sent up for Verena to come down and sing it. Miss Verena was not to be found, so could not obey.

Sir Dace, I say, met her on the stairs as she came in. He put his hand on her shoulder to turn her footsteps to the drawing-room, and shut the door. Then came the explosion. Verena did not deny that she had been out with Pym. And Sir Dace, in very undrawing-room-like language, swore that she should see Pym no more.

"We have done no harm, papa. We have been to Madame Tussaud's."

"Listen to me, Verena. Attempt to go outside this house again while that villain is in London, and I will carry you off, as I carried you from Crabb. You cannot beard me."

It was not pleasant to look at the face of Sir Dace as he said it. At these moments of excitement, it would take a dark tinge underneath the skin, as if the man, to use Jack Tanerton's expression, had a touch of the tar-brush; and the dark sullen eyes would gleam with a peculiar light, that did not remind one of an angel.

"We saw Henry the Eighth and his six wives," went on Vera. "Jane Seymour looked the nicest."

"How dare you talk gibberish, at a moment like this?" raved Sir Dace. "As to that man, I have cursed him. And you will learn to thank me for it."

Verena turned whiter than a sheet. Her answering words seemed brave enough, but her voice shook as she spoke them.

"Papa, you have no right to interfere with my destiny in life; no, though you are the author of my being. I have promised to be the wife of my cousin Edward, and no earthly authority shall stay me. You may be able to control my movements now by dint of force, for you are stronger than I am; but my turn will come."

"Edward Pym—hang him!—is bad to the backbone."

"I will have him whether he is bad or good," was Verena's mental answer: but she did not say it aloud.

"And I will lock you in your room from this hour, if you dare defy me," hissed Sir Dace.

"I do not defy you, papa. It is your turn, I say; and you have strength and power on your side."

"Take care you do not. It would be the worse for you."

"Very well, papa," sighed Verena. "I cannot help myself now; but in a twelvemonth's time I shall be my own mistress. We shall see then."

Sir Dace looked upon the words as a sort of present concession. He concluded Miss Verena had capitulated and would not again go a-roving. So he did not go the length of locking her in her room.

Verena was mild as milk the next day, and good as gold. She never stirred from the side of Coralie, but sat practising a new netting-stitch, her temper sweet, her face placid. The thought of stealing out again to meet Mr. Pym was apparently further off than Asia.

I have said that I was in London at this time, staying with Miss Deveen. It was curious that I should be so during those dreadful events that were so soon to follow. Connected with the business that kept me and Mr. Brandon in town, was a short visit made us by the Squire. Not that the Squire need have come; writing would have done; but he was nothing loth to do so: and it was lovely weather. He stayed with Mr. Brandon at his hotel in Covent Garden; and we thought he meant to make a week of it. The Squire was as fond of the sights and the shops as any child.

I went down one morning to breakfast with them at the Tavistock, and there met Jack Tanerton. Later, we started to take a look at a famous cricket-match that was being played at Lord's. In crossing the Marylebone Road, we met Sir Dace Fontaine.

His lodgings were close by, he said, and he would have us go in. It was the day I have just told you of; when Verena sat, good as gold, by her sister's side, trying the new netting-stitch.

The girls were in a sort of boudoir, half-way up the stairs. The French would, I suppose, call it the entresol: a warm-looking room, with stained glass in the windows, and a rich coloured carpet. Coralie and Vera were, as usual, dressed alike, in delicate summer-muslins. Vera—how pretty she looked!—had blue ribbon in her hair: her blue eyes laughed at seeing us, a pink flush set off her dimples.

"When do you sail, Captain Tanerton?" abruptly asked Sir Dace, suddenly interrupting the conversation.

"On Thursday, all being well," answered Jack.

"Do you take out the same mate?—that Pym?"

"I believe so; yes, Sir Dace."

We had to go away, or should not find standing-room on the cricket-ground. Sir Dace said he would accompany us, and called out to Ozias to bring his hat. Before the hat came, he thought better of it, and said he would not go; those sights fatigued him. I did not know what had taken place until later, or I might have thought he stayed at home to guard Verena. He gave us a cordial invitation to dinner in the evening, we must all go, he said; and Mr. Brandon was the only one of us who declined.

"I am very busy," said Jack, "but I will contrive to get free by seven this evening."

"Very busy indeed, when you can spend the day at Lord's!" laughed Verena.

"I am not going to Lord's," said Jack. Which was true. "I have come up this way to see an invalid passenger who is going out in my ship."

"Oh," quoth Vera, "I thought what a nice idle time you were having of it. Mind, Johnny Ludlow, that you take me in to dinner to-night. I have something to tell you."

Close upon the dinner-hour named, seven, the Squire and I were again at Sir Dace Fontaine's. Tanerton's cab came dashing up at the same moment. Coralie was in the drawing-room alone, her white dress and herself resplendent in coral ornaments. Sir Dace came in, and the Squire began telling him about the cricket-match, saying he ought to have been there. Presently Sir Dace rang the bell.

"How is it that dinner's late?" he asked sternly of Ozias—for Sir Dace liked to be served to the moment.

"The dinner only wait for Miss Verena, sir," returned Ozias, "She no down yet."

Sir Dace turned round sharply to look at the sofa behind him, where I sat with Coralie, talking in an undertone. He had not noticed, I suppose, but that both sisters were there.

"Let Miss Verena be told that we wait for her," he said, waving his hand to Ozias.

Back came Ozias in a minute or two. "Miss Verena, she no upstairs, sir. She no anywhere."

Of all the frowns that ever made a face ugly, the worst sat on Sir Dace Fontaine's, as he turned to Coralie.

"Have you let her go out?" he asked.

"Why of course she is not out, papa," answered Coralie, calm and smiling as usual.

"Let Esther go into Miss Verena's room, Ozias, and ask her to come down at once."

"Esther go this last time, Miss Coralie. She come down and say, Ozias, Miss Verena no upstairs at all; she go out."

"How dare—" began Sir Dace; but Coralie interrupted him.

"Papa, I will go and see. I am sure Verena cannot be out; I am sure she is not. She went into her room to dress when I went into mine. She came to me while she was dressing asking me to lend her my pearl comb; she had just broken one of the teeth of her own. She meant to come down to dinner then and was dressing for it: she had no thought of going out."

Coralie halted at the door to say all this, and then ran up the stairs. She came down crest-fallen. Verena had stolen a march on them. In Sir Dace Fontaine's passionate anger, he explained the whole to us, taking but a few short sentences to do it. Verena had been beguiled into a marriage engagement with Edward Pym: he, Sir Dace, had forbidden her to go out of the house to meet him; and, as it appeared, she had set his authority at defiance. They were no doubt tramping off now to some place of amusement; a theatre, perhaps: the past evening they had gone to Madame Tussaud's. "Will you take in Miss Fontaine, Squire?" concluded Sir Dace, with never a break between that and the explanation.

How dark and sullen he looked, I can recall even now. Deprived of my promised partner, Verena, I went down alone. Sir Dace following with Jack, into whose arm he put his own.

"I wish you joy of your chief officer, Captain Tanerton!" cried he, a sardonic smile on his lips.

It must have been, I suppose, about nine o'clock. We were all back in the drawing-room, and Coralie had been singing. But somehow the song fell flat; the contretemps about Verena, or perhaps the sullenness it had left on Sir Dace, produced a sense of general discomfort; and nobody asked for another. Coralie took her dainty work-box off a side-table, and sat down by me on the sofa.

"I may as well take up my netting, as not," she said to me in an undertone. "Verena began a new collar to-day—which she will be six months finishing, if she ever finishes it at all. She dislikes the work; I love it." Netting was the work most in vogue at that time. Mrs. Todhetley had just netted herself a cap.

"Do you think we shall see your sister to-night?" I asked of Coralie in a whisper.

"Of course you will, if you don't run away too soon. She'll not come in later than ten o'clock."

"Don't you fancy that it has put out Sir Dace very much?"

Coralie nodded. "It is something new for papa to attempt to control us; and he does not like to find he can't. In this affair I take his part; not Verena's. Edward Pym is not a suitable match for her in any way. For myself, I dislike him."

"I don't much like him, either; and I am sure Captain Tanerton does not. Your sister is in love with him, and can see no fault. Cupid's eyes are blind, you know."

"I don't know it at all," she laughed. "My turn with Cupid has not yet come, Johnny Ludlow. I do not much think Cupid could blind me, though he may be blind himself. If—why, what's this?"

Slowly lifting the lid of the box, which had been resting on her lap unopened, she saw a sealed note there, lying uppermost, above the netting paraphernalia. It was addressed to herself, in Verena's handwriting. Coralie opened it with her usual deliberation.

"DEAR CORALIE,

"As I find you and papa intend to keep me a prisoner, and as I do not choose to be kept a prisoner, and do not think you have any right to exercise this harsh control over me, I am leaving home for a few days. Tell papa that I shall be perfectly safe and well taken care of, even if I could not take care of myself—which I can, as you must know.

"Ever yours,
"VERA."

Coralie laughed just a little. It seemed as if nothing ever put her out: she did know that Verena could, as the note phrased it, take care of herself. She went up to her father, who was standing by the fire talking with the Squire and Tanerton. Sir Dace, fresh from a hot country, was always chilly, as I have said before, and kept up a big fire whether it was warm or cold.

"Papa, here is a note from Verena. I have just found it in my work-box. Would you like to see what she says?"

Sir Dace put his coffee-cup on the mantelpiece, and took the note from Coralie. I never saw any expression like that of his face as he read. I never saw any face go so darkly white. Evidently he did not take the news in the same light way that Coralie did.

A cry broke from him. Staggering back against the shelf, he upset a vase that stood at the corner. A beautiful vase of Worcester china, with a ground of delicate gilt tracery, and a deliciously-painted landscape standing out from it. It was not at the vase, lying in pieces on the fender, we looked, but at Sir Dace. His face was contorted; his eyes were rolling. Tanerton, ever ready, caught his arm.

"Help me to find her, my friends!" he gasped, when the threatened fit had passed. "Help me this night to find my daughter! As sure as we are living, that base man will marry her to-morrow, if we do not, and then it will be too late."

"Goodness bless me, yes!" cried the Squire, brushing his hair the wrong way, his good old red face all excitement, "Let us start at once! Johnny, you come with me. Where can we go first?"

That was the question for them all—where to go? London was a large place; and to set out to look for a young lady in it, not knowing where to look, was as bad as looking for the needle in the bottle of hay.

"She may be at that villain's place," panted Sir Dace, whose breath seemed to be all wrong. "Where does he live? You know, I suppose," appealing to Jack.

"No, I don't," said Jack. "But I can find out. I dare say it is in Ship Street. Most of—"

"Where is Ship Street?" interrupted the Squire, looking more helpless than a lunatic.

"Ship Street, Tower Hill," explained Jack; and I dare say the Squire was as wise as before. "Quite a colony of officers live there, while their vessels are lying in St. Katherine's Docks. Ship Street lies handy, you see; they have to be on board by six in the morning."

"I knew a young fellow who lodged all the way down at Poplar, because it was near to his ship," contended the Squire.

"No doubt. His ship must have been berthed in the East India Docks; they are much further off. I will go away at once, then. But," added Jack, arresting his steps, and turning to Sir Dace, "don't you think it may be as well to question the household? Your daughter may have left some indication of her movements."

Jack's thought was not a bad one. Coralie rang the bell for their own maid, Esther, a dull, silent kind of young woman. But Esther knew nothing. She had not helped Miss Verena to dress that evening, only Miss Coralie. Miss Verena said she did not want her. She believed Maria saw her go out.

Maria, the housemaid, was called: a smart young woman, with curled hair and a pink bow in her cap. Her tale was this. While the young ladies were dressing for dinner, she entered the drawing-room to attend to the fire, and found it very low. She went on her knees to coax it up, when Miss Verena came in in her white petticoat, a little shawl on her neck. She walked straight up to Miss Fontaine's work-box, opened it and shut it, and then went out of the room again.

"Did she speak to you?" asked John Tanerton.

"Yes, sir. Leastways she made just a remark—'What, that fire out again?' she said. That was all, sir."

"Go on," sharply cried Sir Dace.

"About ten minutes later, I was at the front-door, letting out the water-rate—who is sure to call, as my missis told him, at the most ill-convenient time—when Miss Verena came softly down the stairs with her bonnet and mantle on. I felt surprised. 'Don't shut me in, Maria, when I want to go out,' she said to me in a laughing sort of way, and I pulled the door back and begged her pardon. That was all, sir."

"How was she dressed?" asked Coralie.

"I couldn't say," answered the girl; "except that her clothes were dark. Her black veil was down over her face; I noticed that; and she had a little carpet-bag in her hand."

So there we were, no wiser than before. Verena had taken flight, and it was impossible to say whither.

They were for running all over the world. The Squire would have started forthwith, and taken the top of the Monument to begin with. John Tanerton, departing on his search to find Pym's lodgings, found we all meant to attend him, including Ozias.

"Better let me go alone," said Jack. "I am Pym's master at sea, and can perhaps exercise some little authority on shore. Johnny Ludlow can go with me."

"And you, papa, and Mr. Todhetley might pay a visit to Madame Tussaud's," put in Coralie, who had not lost her equanimity the least in the world, seeming to look upon the escapade as more of a joke than otherwise. "They will very probably be found at Madame Tussaud's: it is a safe place of resort when people want to talk secrets and be under shelter."

There might be reason in what Coralie said. Certainly there was no need for a procession of live people and two cabs to invade the regions of Tower Hill. So Jack, buttoning his light over-coat over his dinner toggery, got into a hansom with me, and the two old gentlemen went off to see the kings and queens.

"Drive like the wind," said Jack to the cabman. "No. 23, Ship Street, Tower Hill."

"I thought you did not know his number," I said, as we went skimming over the stones.

"I do not know Pym's: am not sure that he puts up in Ship Street. My second mate, Mark Ferrar, lives at No. 23, and I dare say he can direct me to Pym's."

Mark Ferrar! The name struck on my memory. "Does Ferrar come from Worcester, do you know, Jack? Is he related to the Battleys of Crabb?"

"It is the same," said Jack. "I have heard his history. One of his especial favourites is Mr. Johnny Ludlow."

"How strange!—strange that he should be in your ship! Does he do well? Is he a good sailor?"

"First-rate. Ferrar is really a superior young man, steady and painstaking, and has got on wonderfully. As soon as he qualifies for master, which will be in another year or two, he will be placed in command, unless I am mistaken. Our owners see what he is, and push him forward. They drafted him into my ship two years ago."

How curious it was! Mark Ferrar, the humble charity-boy, the frog, who had won the heart of poor King Sanker, rising thus quickly towards the top of the tree! I had always liked Mark; had seen how trustworthy he was.

Our cab might fly like the wind; but Tower Hill seemed a long way off in spite of it. Dashing into Ship Street at last, I looked about me, and saw a narrow street with narrow houses on either side, narrow doors that somehow did not look upright, and shutters closed before the downstairs windows.

No. 23. Jack got out, and knocked at the door. A young boy opened it, saying he believed Mr. Ferrar was in his parlour.

You had to dive down a step to get into the passage. I followed Jack in. The parlour-door was on the right, and the boy pushed it open. A smart, well-dressed sailor sat at the table, his head bent over books and papers, apparently doing exercises by candle-light.

It was Mark Ferrar. His honest, homely face, with the wide mouth and plain features, looked much the same; but the face was softened into—I had almost said—that of a gentleman. Mark finished the sentence he was writing, looked up, and saw his captain.

"Oh, sir, is it you?" he said, rising. "I beg your pardon."

"Busy at your books, I see, Mr. Ferrar?"

Mark smiled—the great, broad, genuine smile I so well remembered. "I had to put them by for other books, while I was studying to pass for chief, sir. That done, I can get to them again with an easy conscience."

"To be sure. Can you tell me where Mr. Pym lodges?"

"Close by: a few doors lower down. But I can show you the house, sir."

"Have you forgotten me, Mark?" I asked, as he took up his cap to come with us.

An instant's uncertain gaze; the candle was behind him, and my face in the shade. His own face lighted up with a glad light.

"No, sir, that indeed I have not, I can never forget Mr. Johnny Ludlow. But you are about the last person, sir, I should have expected to see here."

In the moment's impulse, he had put out his hand to me; then, remembering, I suppose, what his position was in the old days, drew it back quickly. "I beg your pardon, sir," he said, with the same honest flush that used to be for ever making a scarlet poppy of his face. But I was glad to shake hands with Mark Ferrar.

"How are all your people at Worcester, Mark?" I asked, as we went down the street.

"Quite well, thank you, sir. My old father is hearty yet, and my brother and sister are both married. I went down to see them last week, and stayed a day or two."

The greatest change in Ferrar lay in his diction. He spoke as we spoke. Associating now with men of education, he had taken care to catch up their tone and accent; and he was ever, afloat or ashore, striving to improve himself.

Ferrar opened Pym's door without knocking, dived down the step, for the houses were precisely similar, and entered the parlour. He and Pym occupied the same apartments in each house: the parlour and the little bed-room behind it.

The parlour was in darkness, save for what light came into it from the street gas-lamp, for these shutters were not closed. Ferrar went into the passage and shouted out for the landlady, Mrs. Richenough. I thought it an odd name.

She came in from the kitchen at the end of the passage, carrying a candle. A neat little woman with grey hair and a puckered face; the sleeves of her brown gown were rolled up to the elbows, and she wore a check apron.

"Mr. Pym, sir?" she said, in answer to Ferrar. "He dressed hisself and went out when he'd swallowed down his tea. He always do go out, sir, the minute he's swallowed it."

"Do you expect him back to-night?" questioned Jack.

"Why yes, sir, I suppose so," she answered, "he mostly comes in about eleven."

"Has any young lady been here this evening, ma'am?" blandly continued Jack. "With Mr. Pym?—or to inquire for him?"

Mrs. Richenough resented the question. "A young lady!" she repeated, raising her voice. "Well, I'm sure! what next?"

"Take care: it is our captain who speaks to you," whispered Ferrar in her ear; and the old woman dropped a curtsy to Jack. Captains are captains with the old landladies in Ship Street.

"Mr. Pym's sister—or cousin," amended Jack.

"And it's humbly asking pardon of you, sir. I'm sure I took it to mean one of them fly-away girls that would like to be running after our young officers continual. No, sir; no young lady has been here for Mr. Pym, or with him."

"We can wait a little while to see whether he comes in, I presume, ma'am," said Jack.

Intimating that Mr. Pym's captain was welcome to wait the whole night if he pleased, Mrs. Richenough lighted the lamp that stood on the table, shut the shutters, and made Jack another curtsy as she withdrew.

"Do you wish me to remain, sir?" asked Mark.

"Not at all," was the captain's answer. "There will be a good deal to do to-morrow, Mr. Ferrar: mind you are not late in getting on board."

"No fear, sir," replied Ferrar.

And he left us waiting.

III

The dwellings in Ship Street, Tower Hill, may be regarded as desirable residences by the young merchant-seamen whose vessels are lying in the neighbouring clocks, but they certainly do not possess much attraction for the general eye.

Seated in Edward Pym's parlour, the features of the room gradually impressed themselves upon my mind, and they remain there still. They would have remained, I think, without the dreadful tragedy that was so soon to take place in it. It was weary work waiting. Captain Tanerton, tired with his long and busy day, was nodding asleep in the opposite chair, and I had nothing to do but look about me.

It was a small room, rather shabby, the paper of a greenish cast, the faded carpet originally red: and the bedroom behind, as much as could be seen of it through the half-open door, looked smaller and poorer. The chairs were horsehair, the small table in the middle had a purple cloth on it, on which stood the lamp, that the landlady had just lighted. A carved ivory ornament, representing a procession of priests and singers, probably a present to Mrs. Richenough from some merchant-captain, stood under a glass shade on a bracket against the wall; the mantelpiece was garnished with a looking-glass and some china shepherds and shepherdesses. A monkey-jacket of Pym's lay across the back of a chair; some books and his small desk were on the chiffonier. In the rooms above, as we learnt later, lodged a friend of Pym's, one Alfred Saxby, who was looking out for a third mate's berth.

At last Pym came in. Uncommonly surprised he seemed to see us sitting there, but not at all put out: he thought the captain had come down on some business connected with the ship. Jack quietly opened the ball; saying what he had to say.

"Yes, sir. I do know where Miss Verena Fontaine is, but I decline to say," was Pym's answer when he had listened.

"No, sir, nothing will induce me to say," he added to further remonstrance, "and you cannot compel me. I am under your authority at sea, Captain Tanerton, but I am not on shore—and not at all in regard to my private affairs. Miss Verena Fontaine is under the protection of friends, and that is quite enough."

Enough or not enough, this was the utmost we could get from him. His captain talked, and he talked, each of them in a civilly-cold way; but nothing more satisfactory came of it. Pym wound up by saying the young lady was his cousin, and he could take care of her without being interfered with.

"Do you trust him, Johnny Ludlow?" asked Jack, as we came away.

"I don't trust him on the whole; not a bit of it. But he seems to speak truth in saying she is with friends."

And, as the days went on, bringing no tidings of Verena, Sir Dace Fontaine grew angry as a raging tiger.

When a ship is going out of dock, she is more coquettish than a beauty in her teens. Not in herself, but in her movements. Advertised to sail to-day, you will be told she'll not start until to-morrow; and when to-morrow comes the departure will be put off until the next day, perhaps to the next week.

Thus it was with the Rose of Delhi. From some uncompromising exigencies, whether connected with the cargo, the crew, the brokers, or any other of the unknown mysteries pertaining to ships, the day that was to have witnessed her departure—Thursday—did not witness it. The brokers, Freeman and Co., let it transpire on board that she would go out of dock the next morning. About mid-day Captain Tanerton presented himself at their office in Eastcheap.

"I shall not sail to-morrow—with your permission," said he to Mr. James Freeman.

"Yes, you will—if she's ready," returned the broker. "Gould says she will be."

"Gould may think so; I do not. But, whether she be ready or not, Mr. Freeman, I don't intend to take her out to-morrow."

The words might be decisive words, but the captain's tone was genial as he spoke them, and his frank, pleasant smile sat on his face. Mr. Freeman looked at him. They valued Captain Tanerton as they perhaps valued no other master in their employ, these brothers Freeman; but James had a temper that was especially happy in contradiction.

"I suppose you'd like to say that you won't go out on a Friday!"

"That's just it," said Jack.

"You are superstitious, Captain Tanerton," mocked the broker.

"I am not," answered Jack. "But I sail with those who are. Sailors are more foolish on this point than you can imagine: and I believe—I believe in my conscience—that ships, sailing on a Friday, have come to grief through their crew losing heart. No matter what impediment is met with—bad weather, accidents, what not—the men say at once it's of no use, we sailed on a Friday. They lose their spirit, and their energy with it; and I say, Mr. Freeman, that vessels have been lost through this, which might have otherwise been saved. I will not go out of dock to-morrow; and I refuse to do it in your interest as much as in my own."

"Oh, bother," was all James Freeman rejoined. "You'll have to go if she's ready."

But the words made an impression. James Freeman knew what sailors were nearly as well as Jack knew: and he could not help recalling to memory that beautiful ship of Freeman Brothers, the Lily of Japan. The Lily had been lost only six months ago; and those of her crew, who were saved, religiously stuck to it that the calamity was brought about through having sailed on a Friday.

The present question did not come to an issue. For, on the Friday morning, the Rose of Delhi was not ready for sea; would not be ready that day. On the Saturday morning she was not ready either; and it was finally decided that Monday should be the day of departure. On the Saturday afternoon Captain Tanerton ran down to Timberdale for four-and-twenty hours; Squire Todhetley, his visit to London over, travelling down by the same train.

Verena Fontaine had not yet turned up, and Sir Dace was nearly crazy. Not only was he angry at being thwarted, but one absorbing, special fear lay upon him—that she would come back a married woman. Pym was capable of any sin, he told the Squire and Coralie, even of buying the wedding-ring; and Verena was capable of letting it be put on her finger. "No, papa," dissented Coralie in her equable manner, "Vera is too fond of money and of the good things money buys, to risk the loss of the best part of her fortune. She will not marry Pym until she is of age; be sure of that. When he has sailed she will come home safe and sound, and tell us where she has been."

Captain Tanerton went down, I say, to Timberdale. He stayed at the Rectory with his wife and brother until the Sunday afternoon, and then returned to London. The Rose of Delhi was positively going out on Monday, so he had to be back—and, I may as well say here, that Jack, good-natured Jack, had invited me to go in her as far as Gravesend.

During that brief stay at Timberdale, Jack was not in his usual spirits. His wife, Alice, noticed it, and asked him whether anything was the matter. Not anything whatever, Jack readily answered. In truth there was not. At least, anything he could talk of. A weight lay on his spirits, and he could not account for it. The strong instinct, which had seemed to warn him against sailing with Pym again, had gradually left him since he knew that Pym was to sail, whether or not. In striving to make the best of it, he had thrown off the feeling: and the unaccountable depression that weighed him down could not arise from that cause. It was a strange thing altogether, this; one that never, in all his life, had he had any experience of; but it was not less strange than true.

Monday - The Rose of Delhi lay in her place in the freshness of the sunny morning, making ready to go out of dock with the incoming tide. I went on board betimes: and I thought I had never been in such a bustling scene before. The sailors knew what they were about. I conclude, but to me it seemed all confusion. The captain I could not see anywhere; but his chief officer, Pym, seemed to be more busy than a certain common enemy of ours is said to be in a gale of wind.

"Is the captain not on board?" I asked of Mark Ferrar, as he was whisking past me on deck.

"Oh no, sir; not yet. The captain will not come on board till the last moment—if he does then."

The words took me by surprise. "What do you mean, by saying 'If he does then'?"

"He has so much to do, sir; he is at the office now, signing the bills of lading. If he can't get done in time he will join at Gravesend when we take on some passengers. The captain is not wanted on board when we are going out of dock, Mr. Johnny," added Ferrar, seeing my perplexed look. "The river-pilot takes the ship out."

He pointed to the latter personage, just then making his appearance on deck. I wondered whether all river-pilots were like him. He was broad enough to make two ordinarily stout people; and his voice, from long continuous shouting, had become nothing less than a raven's croak.

At the last moment, when the ship was getting away, and I had given the captain up, he came on board. How glad I was to see his handsome, kindly face!

"I've had a squeak for it, Johnny," he laughed, as he shook my hand: "but I meant to go down with you if I could."

Then came all the noise and stir of getting away: the croaking of the pilot alone distinguishable to my uninitiated ears. "Slack away the stern-line"—he called it starn. "Haul in head-rope." "Here, carpenter, bear a hand, get the cork-fender over the quarter-gallery." "What are you doing aft there?—why don't you slack away that stern-line?" Every other moment it seemed to me that we were going to pitch into the craft in the pool, or they into us. However, we got on without mishap.

Captain Tanerton was crossing the ship, after holding a confab with the pilot, when a young man, whom he did not recognize, stepped aside out of his way, and touched his cap. The captain looked surprised, for the badge on the cap was the one worn by his own officers.

"Who are you?" he asked.

"Mr. Saxby, if you please, sir."

"Mr. Saxby! What do you do here?"

"Third mate, if you please, sir," repeated the young man. "Your third mate, Mr. Jones, met with an accident yesterday; he broke his leg; and my friend, Pym, spoke of me to Mr. Gould."

Captain Tanerton was not only surprised, but vexed. First, for the accident to Jones, who was a very decent young fellow; next, at his being superseded by a stranger, and a friend of Pym's. He put a few questions, found the new man's papers were in order, and so made the best of it.

"You will find me a good and considerate master, Mr. Saxby, if you do your duty with a will," he said in a kind tone.

"I hope I shall, sir; I'll try to," answered the young man.

On we went swimmingly, in the wake of the tug-boat; but this desirable tranquillity was ere long destined to be marred.

On coming up from the state-room, as they called it, after regaling ourselves on a cold collation, the captain was pointing out to me something on shore, when one of the crew approached hastily, and touched his cap. I found it was the carpenter: a steady-looking man, who was fresh to the ship, having joined her half-an-hour before starting.

"Beg pardon, sir," he began. "Might I ask you when this ship was pumped out last?"

"Why, she is never pumped out," replied the captain.

"Well, sir," returned the man, "it came into my head just now to sound her, and I find there's two feet of water in the hold."

"Nonsense," said Jack: "you must be mistaken. Why, she has never made a cupful of water since she was built. We have to put water in her to keep her sweet."

"Any way, sir, there's two feet o' water in her now."

The captain looked at the man steadily for a moment, and then thought it might be as well to verify the assertion—or the contrary—himself, being a practical man. Taking the sounding-rod from the carpenter's hand, he wiped it dry with an old bag lying near, and then proceeded to sound the well.

Quite true: there were two feet of water. No time lost he. Ordering the carpenter to rig the pumps, he called all hands to man them.

For a quarter-of-an-hour, or twenty minutes, the pumps were worked without intermission; then the captain sounded, as before, doing it himself. There was no diminution of water—it stood at the same level as before pumping. Upon that, he and the carpenter went down into the hold, to listen along the ship's sides, and discover, if they could, where the water was coming in. Five minutes later, Jack was on deck again, his face grave.

"It is coming in abreast of the main hatchway on the starboard side; we can hear it distinctly," he said to the pilot. "I must order the ship back again: I think it right to do so." And the broad pilot, who seemed a very taciturn pilot, made no demur to this, except a grunt. So the tug-boat was ordered to turn round and tow us back again.

"Where's Mr. Pym?" cried the captain. "Mr. Pym!"

"Mr. Pym's in the cabin, sir," said the steward, who chanced to be passing.

"In the cabin!" echoed Jack, in an accent that seemed to imply the cabin was not Mr. Pym's proper place just then. "Send him to me, if you please, steward."

"Yes, sir," replied the steward. But he did not obey with the readiness exacted on board ship. He hesitated, as if wanting to say something before turning away.

No Pym came. Jack grew impatient, and called out an order or two. Young Saxby came up, touching his cap, according to rule.

"Do you want me, sir?"

"I want Mr. Pym. He is below. Ask him to come to me instantly."

It brought forth Pym. Jack's head was turned away for a moment, and I saw what he did not. That Pym had a fiery face, and walked as if his limbs were slipping from under him.

"Oh, you are here at last, Mr. Pym—did you not receive my first message?" cried Jack, turning round. "The cargo must be broken out to find the place of leakage. See about it smartly: there's no time to waste."

Pym had caught hold of something at hand to enable him to stand steady. He had lost his wits, that was certain; for he stuttered out an answer to the effect that the cargo might be—hanged.

The captain saw his state then. Feeling a need of renovation possibly, after his morning's exertions, Mr. Pym had been making free, a great deal too much so, with the bottled ale below, and had finished up with brandy-and-water.

The cargo might be hanged!

Captain Tanerton, his brow darkening, spoke a sharp, short, stern reprimand, and ordered Mr. Pym to his cabin.

What could have possessed Pym unless it might be the spirit that was in the brandy, nobody knew. He refused to obey, broke into open defiance, and gave Captain Tanerton sauce to his face.

"Take him below," said the captain quietly, to those who were standing round. "Mr. Ferrar, you will lock Mr. Pym's cabin-door, if you please, and bring me the key."

This was done, and Mr. Pym encaged. He kicked at his cabin-door, and shook it; but he could not escape: he was a prisoner. He swore for a little while at the top of his voice; then he commenced some uproarious singing, and finally fell on his bed and went to sleep.

Hands were set to work to break out the cargo, which they piled on deck; and the source of the leakage was discovered. It seemed a slight thing, after all, to have caused so much commotion—nothing but an old treenail that had not been properly plugged-up. I said so to Ferrar.

"Ah, Mr. Johnny," was Ferrar's answering remark, his face and tone strangely serious, "slight as it may seem to you, it might have sunk us all this night, had we chanced to anchor off Gravesend."

What with the pumps, that were kept at work, and the shifting of the cargo, and the hammering they made in stopping up the leak, we had enough to do this time. And about half-past three o'clock in the afternoon the brave ship, which had gone out so proudly with the tide, got back ignominiously with the end of it, and came to an anchor outside the graving-dock, there not being sufficient water to allow of her entering it. The damage was already three-parts repaired, and the ship would make her final start on the morrow.

"'Twas nothing but a good Providence could have put it into my head to sound the ship, sir," remarked the carpenter, wiping his hot face, as he came on deck for something or other he needed. "But for that, we might none of us have seen the morning's sun."

Jack nodded. These special interpositions of God's good care are not rare, though we do not always recognize them. And yet, but for that return back, the miserable calamity so soon to fall, would not have had the chance to take place.

Captain Tanerton caused himself to be rowed ashore, first of all ordering the door of his prisoner to be unfastened. I got into the waterman's wherry with him, for I had nothing to stay on board for. And a fine ending it was to my day's pleasuring!

"Never mind, Johnny," he said, as we parted. "You can come with us again to-morrow, and I hope we shall have a more lucky start."

Captain Tanerton went straight to the brokers', saw Mr. James Freeman, and told him he would not take out Edward Pym. If he did, the man's fate would probably be that of irons from Gravesend to Calcutta.

And James Freeman, a thorough foe to brandy-and-water when taken at wrong times, listened to reason, and gave not a word of dissent. He there and then made Ferrar chief mate, and put another one second in Ferrar's place; a likely young man in their employ who was waiting for a berth. This perfectly satisfied Captain Tanerton, under the circumstances.

The captain was then rowed back to his ship. By that time it was five o'clock. He told Ferrar of the change; who thanked him heartily, a glow of satisfaction rising to his honest face.

"Where's Pym?" asked the captain. "He must take his things out of the ship."

"Pym is not on board, sir. Soon after you left, he came up and went ashore: he seemed to have pretty nearly slept off the drink. Sir Dace Fontaine is below," added Ferrar, dropping his voice.

"Sir Dace Fontaine! Does he want me?"

"He wanted Mr. Pym, sir. He has been looking into every part of the ship: he is looking still. He fancies his daughter is concealed on board."

"Oh, nonsense!" cried the captain; "he can't fancy that. As if Miss Fontaine would come down here—and board ships!"

"She was on board yesterday, sir."

"What!" cried the captain.

"Mr. Pym brought her on board yesterday afternoon, sir," continued Ferrar, his voice as low as it could well go. "He was showing her about the ship."

"How do you know this, Mr. Ferrar?"

"I was here, sir. Expecting to sail last week, I sent my traps on board. Yesterday, wanting a memorandum-book out of my desk, I came down for it. That's how I saw them."

Captain Tanerton, walking forward to meet Sir Dace, knitted his brow. Was Mr. Pym drawing the careless, light-headed girl into mischief? Sir Dace evidently thought so.

"I tell you, Captain Tanerton, she is quite likely to be on board, concealed as a stow-away," persisted Sir Dace, in answer to the captain's assurance that Verena was not, and could not be in the ship. "When you are safe away from land, she will come out of hiding and they will declare their marriage. That they are married, is only too likely. He brought her on board yesterday afternoon when the ship was lying in St. Katharine's Dock."

"Do you know that he did?" cried Jack, wondering whence Sir Dace got his information.

"I am told so. As I got up your ladder just now I inquired of the first man I saw, whether a young lady was on board. He said no, but that a young lady had come on board with Mr. Pym yesterday afternoon to see the ship. The man was your ship-keeper in dock."

"How did you hear we had got back to-day, Sir Dace?"

"I came down this afternoon to search the ship before she sailed—I was under a misapprehension as to the time of her going out. The first thing I heard was, that the Rose of Delhi had gone and had come back again. Pym is capable, I say, of taking Verena out."

"You may be easy on this point, Sir Dace," returned Jack. "Pym does not go out in the ship: he is superseded." And he gave the heads of what had occurred.

It did not tend to please Sir Dace. Edward Pym on the high seas would be a less formidable adversary than Edward Pym on land: and perhaps in his heart of hearts Sir Dace did not really believe his daughter would become a stow-away.

"Won't you help me to find her? to save her?" gasped Sir Dace, in pitiful entreaty. "With this change—Pym not going out—I know not what trouble he may not draw her into. Coralie says Verena is not married; but I—Heaven help me! I know not what to think. I must find Pym this night and watch his movements, and find her if I can. You must help me."

"I will help you," said warm-hearted Jack—and he clasped hands upon it. "I will undertake to find Pym. And, that your daughter is not on board, Sir Dace, I pass you my word."

Sir Dace stepped into the wherry again, to be rowed ashore and get home to his dinner—ordered that evening for six o'clock. In a short while Jack also quitted the ship, and went to Pym's lodgings in Ship Street. Pym was not there.

Mr. Pym had come in that afternoon, said his landlady, Mrs. Richenough, and startled her out of her seven senses; for, knowing the ship had left with the day's tide, she had supposed Mr. Pym to be then off Gravesend, or thereabouts. He told her the ship had sprung a leak and put back again. Mr. Pym had gone out, she added, after drinking a potful of strong tea.

"To sober him," thought the captain. "Do you expect him back to sleep, Mrs. Richenough?"

"Yes, I do, sir. I took the sheets off his bed this morning, and I've just been and put 'em on again. Mr. Saxby's must be put on too, for he looked in to say he should sleep here."

Where to search for Pym, Jack did not know. Possibly he might have gone back to the ship to offer an apology, now that he was sobered. Jack was bending his steps towards it when he met Ferrar: who told him Pym had not gone back.

Jack put on his considering-cap. He hardly knew what to do, or how to find the fugitives: with Sir Dace, he deemed it highly necessary that Verena should be found.

"Have you anything particular to do to-night, Mr. Ferrar?" he suddenly asked. And Ferrar said he had not.

"Then," continued the captain, "I wish you would search for Pym." And, knowing Ferrar was thoroughly trustworthy, he whispered a few confidential words of Sir Dace Fontaine's fear and trouble. "I am going to look for him myself," added Jack, "though I'm sure I don't know in what quarter. If you do come across him, keep him within view. You can tell him also that his place on the Rose of Delhi is filled up, and he must take his things out of her."

Altogether that had been a somewhat momentous day for Mr. Alfred Saxby—and its events for him were not over yet. He had been appointed to a good ship, and the ship had made a false start, and was back again. An uncle and aunt of his lived at Clapham, and he thought he could not do better than go down there and regale them with the news: we all naturally burn to impart marvels to the world, you know. However, when he reached his relatives' residence, he found they were out; and not long after nine o'clock he was back at Mrs. Richenough's.

"Is Mr. Pym in?" he asked of the landlady; who came forward rubbing her eyes as though she were sleepy, and gave him his candle.

"Oh, he have been in some little time, sir. And a fine row he's been having with his skipper," added Mrs. Richenough, who sometimes came off the high ropes of politeness when she had disposed of her supper beer.

"A row, has he!" returned Saxby. "Does not like to have been superseded," he added to himself. "I must say Pym was a fool to-day—to go and drink, as he did, and to sauce the master."

"Screeching out at one another like mad, they've been," pursued Mrs. Richenough. "He do talk stern, that skipper, for a young man and a good-looking one."

"Is the captain in there now?"

"For all I know. I did think I heard the door shut, but it might have been my fancy. Good-night, sir. Pleasant dreams."

Leaving the candle in Saxby's hands, she returned to her kitchen, which was built out at the back. He halted at the parlour-door to listen. No voices were to be heard then; no sounds.

"Pym may have gone to bed—I dare say his head aches," thought Saxby: and he opened the door to see whether the parlour was empty.

Why! what was it?—what was the matter? The young man took one startled look around and then put down the candle, his heart leaping into his mouth.

The lamp on the table threw its bright light on the little room. Some scuffle appeared to have taken place in it. A chair was overturned; the ivory ornament with its glass shade had been swept from its stand to the floor: and by its side lay Edward Pym—dead.

Mr. Alfred Saxby, third mate of that good ship, the Rose of Delhi, might be a sufficiently self-possessed individual when encountering sudden surprises at sea; but he certainly did not show himself to be so on shore. When the state of affairs had sufficiently impressed itself on his startled senses, he burst out of the room in mortal terror, shouting out "murder."

There was nobody in the house to hear him but Mrs. Richenough. She came forward, slightly overcome by drowsiness; but the sight she saw woke her up effectually.

"Good mercy!" cried she, running to the prostrate man. "Is he dead?"

"He looks dead," shivered Mr. Saxby, hardly knowing whether he was not dead himself.

They raised Pym's head, and put a pillow under it. The landlady wrung her hands.

"We must have a doctor," she cried: "but I can see he is dead. This comes of that quarrel with his captain: I heard them raving frightfully at one another. There has been a scuffle here—see that chair. Oh! and look at my beautiful ivory knocked down!—and the shade all broke to atoms!"

"I'll fetch Mr. Ferrar," cried Saxby, feeling himself rather powerless to act; and with nobody to aid him but the gabbling woman.

Like mad, Saxby tore up the street, burst in at Mark Ferrar's open door and went full butt against Mark himself; who was at the moment turning quickly out of it.

"Take care, Saxby. What are you about?"

"Oh, for Heaven's sake do come, Mr. Ferrar! Pym is dead. He is lying dead on the floor."

The first thing Ferrar did was to scan his junior officer narrowly, wondering whether he could be quite sober. Yes, he seemed to be that; but agitated to trembling, and his face as pale as death. The next minute Ferrar was bending over Pym. Alas, he saw too truly that life was extinct.

"It's his skipper that has done it, sir," repeated the landlady.

"Hush, Mrs. Richenough!" rebuked Ferrar. "Captain Tanerton has not done this."

"But I heard 'em screeching and howling at one another, sir," persisted Mrs. Richenough. "Their quarrel must have come to blows."

"I do not believe it," dissented Ferrar. "Captain Tanerton would not be capable of anything of the kind. Fight with a man who has served under him!—you don't understand things, Mrs. Richenough."

Saxby had run for the nearest medical man. Ferrar ran to find his captain. He knew that Captain Tanerton intended to put up at a small hotel in the Minories for the night.

To this hotel went Ferrar, and found Captain Tanerton. Tired with his evening's search after Pym, the captain was taking some refreshment, before going up to Sir Dace Fontaine's—which he had promised, in Sir Dace's anxiety, to do. He received Ferrar's report—that Pym was dead—with incredulity: did not appear to believe it: but he betrayed no embarrassment, or any other guilty sign.

"Why, I came straight here from Pym," he observed. "It's hardly twenty minutes since I left him. He was all right then—except that he had been having more drink."

"Old Mother Richenough says, sir, that Pym and you had a loud quarrel."

"Say that, does she," returned the captain carelessly. "Her ears must have deceived her, Mr. Ferrar."

"A quarrel and fight she says, sir. I told her I knew better."

Captain Tanerton took his cap and started with Ferrar for Ship Street, plunging into a reverie. Presently he began to speak—as if he wished to account for his own movements.

"When you left me, Mr. Ferrar—you know"—and here he exchanged a significant glance with his new first mate—"I went on to Ship Street, and took a look at Pym's room. A lamp was shining on the table, and his landlady had the window open, closing the shutters. This gave me an opportunity of seeing inside. Pym I saw; but not—not anyone else."

Again Captain Tanerton's tone was significant. Ferrar appeared to understand it perfectly. It looked as though they had some secret understanding between them which they did not care to talk of openly. The captain resumed.

"After fastening the shutters, Mrs. Richenough came to the door—for a breath of air, she remarked, as she saw me: and she positively denied, in answer to my questions, that any young lady was there. Mr. Pym had never had a young lady come after him at all, she protested, whether sister or cousin, or what not."

"Yes, sir," said Ferrar: for the captain had paused.

"I went in, and spoke to Pym. But, I saw in a moment that he had been drinking again. He was not in a state to be reasoned with, or talked to. I asked him but one question, and asked it civilly: would he tell me where Verena Fontaine was. Pym replied in an unwilling tone; he was evidently sulky. Verena Fontaine was at home again with her people; and he had not been able, for that reason, to see her. Thinking the ship had gone away, and he with it, Verena had returned home early in the afternoon. That was the substance of his answer."

"But I—I don't know whether that account can be true, sir," hesitated Ferrar. "I was not sure, you know, sir, that it was the young lady; I said so—"

"Yes, yes, I understood that," interrupted the captain quickly. "Well, it was what Pym said to me," he added, after a pause: "one hardly knows what to believe. However, she was not there, so far as I could ascertain and judge; and I left Pym and came up here to my hotel. I was not two minutes with him."

"Then—did no quarrel take place, sir?" cried Ferrar, thinking of the landlady's story.

"Not an angry word."

At this moment, as they were turning into Ship Street, Saxby, who seemed completely off his head, ran full tilt against Ferrar. It was all over, he cried out in excitement, as he turned back with them: the doctor pronounced Pym to be really dead.

"It is a dreadful thing," said the captain. "And, seemingly, a mysterious one."

"Oh, it is dreadful," asserted young Saxby. "What will poor Miss Verena do? I saw her just now," he added, dropping his voice.

"Saw her where?" asked the captain, taking a step backwards.

"In the place where I've just met you, sir," replied Saxby. "I was running past round the corner into the street, on my way home from Clapham, when a young lady met and passed me, going pretty nearly as quick as I was. She had her face muffled in a black veil, but I am nearly sure it was Miss Verena Fontaine. I thought she must be coming from Pym's lodgings here."

Captain Tanerton and his chief mate exchanged glances of intelligence under the light of the street gas-lamp. The former then turned to Saxby.

"Mr. Saxby," said he, "I would advise you not to mention this little incident. It would not, I am sure, be pleasant to Miss Verena Fontaine's friends to hear of it. And, after all, you are not sure that it was she."

"Very true, sir," replied Saxby. "I'll not speak of it again."

"You hear, sir," answered Ferrar softly, as Saxby stepped on to open the house-door. "This seems to bear out what I said. And, by the way, sir, I also saw—"

"Hush!" cautiously interrupted the captain—for they had reached the door, and Mrs. Richenough stood at it.

And what Mr. Ferrar further saw, whatever it might be, was not heard by Captain Tanerton. There was no present opportunity for private conversation: and Ferrar was away in the morning with the Rose of Delhi.

After parting with Captain Tanerton on leaving the ship, I made my way to the Mansion House, took an omnibus to Covent Garden, and called at the Tavistock to tell Mr. Brandon of the return of the ship. Mr. Brandon kept me to dinner. About eight o'clock I left him, and went to the Marylebone Road to see the Fontaines. Coralie was in the drawing-room alone.

"Is it you, Johnny Ludlow!" she gaily cried, when old Ozias showed me in. "You are as welcome as flowers in May. Here I am, without a soul to speak to. You must have a game at chess with me."

"Your sister is not come home, then?"

"Not she. I thought it likely she would come, as soon as the ship's head was turned seaward—I told you so. But she has not. And now the ship's back again, I hear. A fine time you must have had of it!"

"We just had. But how did you know?"

"From papa. Papa betook himself to the docks this afternoon, to assure himself, I presume, that the Rose of Delhi was gone. And my belief is, Johnny, that he will work himself into a nervous fever," Coralie broke off to say, in her equable way, as she helped me to place the pieces. "When he got there, he found the ship was back again. This put him out a little, as you may judge; and something else put him out more. He heard that Vera went on board with Pym yesterday afternoon when the ship was lying in St. Katherine's Docks. Upon that, what notion do you suppose he took up? I have first move, don't I?"

"Certainly. What notion did he take up?" The reader must remember that I knew nothing of Sir Dace's visit to the ship.

"Why, that Vera might be resolving to convert herself into a stowaway, and go out with Pym and the ship. Poor papa! He went searching all over the vessel. He must be off his head."

"Verena would not do that."

"Do it?" retorted Coralie. "She'd be no more likely to do it than to go up a chimney, as the sweeps do. I told papa so. He brought me this news when he came home to dinner. And he might just as well have stayed away, for all he ate."

Coralie paused to look at her game. I said nothing.

"He could only drink. It was as if he had a fierce thirst upon him. When the sweets came on, he left the table and shut himself in his little library. I sent Ozias to ask if he would have a cup of tea or coffee made; papa swore at poor Ozias, and locked the door upon him. When Verena does appear I'd not say but he'll beat her."

"No, no: not that."

"But, I tell you he is off his head. He is still shut up: and nobody dare go near him when he gets into a fit of temper. It is so silly of papa! Verena is all right. But this disobedience, you see, is something new to him."

"You can't move that bishop. It leaves your king in check."

"So it does. The worst item of news remains behind," added Coralie. "And that is that Pym does not sail with the ship."

"I should not think he would now. Captain Tanerton would not take him."

"Papa told me Captain Tanerton had caused him to be superseded. Was Pym very much the worse for what he took, Johnny? Was he very insolent? You must have seen it all?"

"He had taken quite enough. And he was about as insolent as a man can be."

"Ferrar is appointed to his place, papa says; and a new man to Ferrar's."

"Ferrar is! I am glad of that: very. He deserves to get on."

"But Ferrar is not a gentleman, is he?" objected Coralie.

"Not in one sense. There are gentlemen and gentlemen. Mark Ferrar is very humble as regards birth and bringing-up. His father is a journeyman china-painter at one of the Worcester china-factories; and Mark got his learning at St. Peter's charity-school. But every instinct Mark possesses is that of a refined, kindly, modest gentleman; and he has contrived to improve himself so greatly by dint of study and observation, that he might now pass for a gentleman in any society. Some men, whatever may be their later advantages, can never throw off the common tone and manner of early habits and associations. Ferrar has succeeded in doing it."

"If Pym stays on shore it may bring us further complication," mused Coralie. "I should search for Verena myself then—and search in earnest. Papa and old Ozias have gone about it in anything but a likely manner."

"Have you any notion where she can be?"

"Just the least bit of notion in the world," laughed Coralie. "It flashed across me the other night where she might have hidden herself. I don't know it. I have no particular ground to go upon."

"You did not tell Sir Dace?"

"Not I," lightly answered Coralie. "We two sisters don't interfere with one another's private affairs. I did keep back a letter of Vera's; one she wrote to Pym when we first left home; but I have done so no more. Here comes some tea at last!"

"I should have told," I continued in a low tone. "Or taken means myself to see whether my notion was right or wrong."

"What did it signify?—when Pym was going away in a day or two. Check to you, Johnny Ludlow."

That first game, what with talking and tea-drinking, was a long one. I won it. When Ozias came in for the tea-cups Coralie asked him whether Sir Dace had rung for anything. No, the man answered; most likely his master would remain locked in till bed-time; it was his way when any great thing put him out.

"I don't think I can stay for another game," I said to Coralie, as she began to place the men again.

"Are you in such a hurry?" cried Coralie, glancing round at the clock: which said twenty minutes to ten.

I was not in any hurry at all that night, as regarded myself: I had thought she might not care for me to stay longer. Miss Deveen and Cattledon had gone out to dinner some ten miles away, and were not expected home before midnight. So we began a fresh game.

"Why! that clock must have stopped!"

Chancing to look at it by-and-by, I saw that it stood at the same time—twenty minutes to ten. I took out my watch. It said just ten minutes past ten.

"What does it signify?" said Coralie. "You can stay here till twenty minutes to twelve if you like—and be whirled home in a cab by midnight then."

That was true. If—

"Good gracious!" exclaimed Coralie.

She was looking at the door with surprised eyes. There stood Verena, her bonnet on; evidently just come in.

Verena tripped forward, bent down, and kissed her sister. "Have you been desperately angry, Coral?" she lightly asked, giving me her hand to shake. "I know papa has."

"I have not been angry," was Coralie's equable answer: "but you have acted childishly, Verena. And now, where have you been?"

"Only in Woburn Place, at Mrs. Ball's," said Verena, throwing off her bonnet, and bringing her lovely flushed face close to the light as she sat down. "When I left here that evening—and really, Johnny, I was sorry not to stay and go in to dinner with you," she broke off, with a smile—"I went straight to our old lodgings, to good old Mother Ball. 'They are frightful tyrants at home,' I said to her, 'I'm not sure but they'll serve me as Bluebeard did his wives; and I want to stay with you for a day or two.' There's where I have been all the time, Coral; and I wondered you and papa did not come to look for me."

"It is where I fancied you might be," returned Coral. "But I only thought of it on Saturday night. Does that mean check, Johnny?"

"Check and mate, mademoiselle."

"Oh, how wicked you are!"

"Mrs. Ball has been more careful of me than she'd be of gold," went on Vera, her blue eyes dancing. "The eldest daughter, Louise, is at home now: she teaches music in a school: and, if you'll believe me, Coral, the old mother would never let me stir out without Louise. When Edward Pym came up in the evening to take me for a walk, Louise must go with us. 'I feel responsible to your papa and sister, my dear,' the old woman would say to me. Oh, she was a veritable dragon."

"Was Louise with you when you went on board the Rose of Delhi yesterday afternoon?" cried Coralie, while I began to put away the chessmen.

Verena opened her eyes. "How did you hear of that? No, we tricked Louise for once. Edward had fifty things to say to me, and he wanted me alone. After dinner he proposed that we should go to afternoon service. I made haste, and went out with him, calling to Louise that she'd catch us up before we reached the church, and we ran off in just the contrary direction. "I should like to show you my ship," Edward said; and we went down in an omnibus. Mrs. Ball shook her head when we got back, and said I must never do it again. As if I should have the chance, now Edward's gone!"

Coralie glanced at her. "He is gone, I suppose?"

"Yes," sighed Vera. "The ship left the docks this morning. He took leave of me last night."

Coralie looked doubtful. She glanced again at her sister under her eyelids.

"Then—if Edward Pym is no longer here to take walks with you, Vera, how is it you came home so late to-night?"

"Because I have been to a concert," cried Vera, her tone as gay as a lark's. "Louise and I started to walk here this afternoon. I wanted you to see her; she is really very nice. Coming through Fitzroy Square, she called upon some friends of hers who live there, the Barretts—he is a professor of music. Mrs. Barrett was going to a concert to-night and she said if we would stay she'd take us. So we had tea with her and went to it, and they sent me home in a cab."

"You seem to be taking your pleasure!" remarked Coralie.

"I had such an adventure downstairs," cried Verena, dropping her voice after a pause of thought. "Nearly fell into the arms of papa."

"What—now?"

"Now; two minutes ago. While hesitating whether to softly tinkle the kitchen-bell and smuggle myself in and up to my room, or to storm the house with a bold summons, Ozias drew open the front-door. He looked so glad to see me, poor stupid old fellow. I was talking to him in the passage when I heard papa's cough. 'Oh, hide yourself, Missee Vera,' cried Ozias, 'the master, he so angry;' and away I rushed into papa's little library, seeing the door of it open—"

"He has come out of it, then!" interjected Coralie.

"I thought papa would go upstairs," said Vera. "Instead of that, he came on into the room. I crept behind the old red window-curtains, and—"

"And what?" asked Coralie, for Verena made a sudden pause.

"Groaned out with fright, and nearly betrayed myself," continued Verena. "Papa stared at the curtains as if he thought they were alive, and then and there backed out of the room. Perhaps he feared a ghost was there. He was looking so strange, Coralie."

"All your fault, child. Since the night you went away he has looked more like a maniac than a rational man, and acted like one. I have just said so to Johnny Ludlow."

"Poor papa! I will be good and tractable as an angel now, and make it up to him. And—why, Coralie, here are visitors."

We gazed in surprise. It is not usual to receive calls at bedtime. Ozias stood at the door showing in Captain Tanerton. Behind him was Alfred Saxby.

The captain's manner was curious. No sooner did he set eyes on us than he started back, as if he thought we might bite him.

"Not here. Not the ladies. I told you it was Sir Dace I wanted," he said in quick sentences to Ozias. "Sir Dace alone."

Ozias went back down the stairs, and they after him, and were shown into the library. It was a little room nearly opposite the front-entrance, and underneath the room called the boudoir. You went down a few stairs to it.

Verena turned white. A prevision of evil seized her.

"Something must be the matter," she shivered, laying her hand upon my arm. "Did you notice Captain Tanerton's face? I never saw him look like that. And what does he do here? Where is the ship? And oh, Johnny"—and her voice rose to a shriek—"where's Edward Pym?"

Alas! we soon knew what the matter was—and where Edward Pym was. Dead. Murdered. That's what young Saxby called it. Sir Dace, looking frightfully scared, started with them down to Ship Street. I went also; I could not keep away. George was to sit up for me at home if I were late.

"For," as Miss Deveen had said to me in the morning, laughingly, "there's no telling, Johnny, at what unearthly hour you may get back from Gravesend."

IV

It was a dreadful thing to have happened. Edward Pym found dead; and no one could tell for a certainty who had been the author of the calamity.

He had died of a blow dealt to him, the doctors said: it had struck him behind the left ear. Could it be possible that he had fallen of himself, and struck his head against something in falling, was a question put to the doctors—and it was Captain Tanerton who put it. It perhaps might be possible, the medical men answered, but not at all probable. Mr. Pym could not have inflicted the blow upon himself, and there was no piece of furniture in the room, so far as they saw, that could have caused the injury, even though he had fallen upon it.

The good luck of the Rose of Delhi seemed not to be in the ascendant. Her commander could not sail with her now. Neither could her newly-appointed third mate, Alfred Saxby. So far as might be ascertained at present, Captain Tanerton was the last man who had seen Pym alive; Alfred Saxby had found him dead; therefore their evidence would be required at the official investigation.

Ships, however, cannot be lightly detained in port when their time for sailing comes: and on the day following the events already told of, the Rose of Delhi finally left the docks, all taut and sound, the only one of her old officers, sailing in her, being Mark Ferrar. The brokers were put out frightfully at the detention of Tanerton. A third mate was soon found to replace Saxby: a master not so easily. They put in an elderly man, just come home in command of one of their ships. Put him in for the nonce, hoping Captain Tanerton would be at liberty to join her at Dartmouth, or some other place down channel.

On this same day, Tuesday, the investigation into the events of that fatal Monday, as regarded Edward Pym, was begun. Not the coroner's inquest: that was called for the morrow: but an informal inquiry instituted by the brokers and Sir Dace Fontaine. In a back-room of the office in Eastcheap, the people met; and—I am glad to say—I was one of them, or I could not have told you what passed. Sir Dace sat in the corner, his elbow resting on the desk and his hand partly covering his face. He did not pretend to feel the death as an affectionate uncle would have felt it; still Pym was his nephew, and there could be no mistake that the affair was troubling him.

Mrs. Richenough, clean as a new pin, in her Sunday gown and close bonnet, a puzzled look upon her wrinkled face, told what she knew—and was longer over it than she need have been. Mr. Pym, who lodged in her parlour floor, had left her for good, as she supposed, on the Monday morning, his ship, the Rose of Delhi, being about to go out of dock. Mr. Saxby, who had lodged in the rooms above Mr. Pym, got appointed to the same ship, and he also left. In the afternoon she heard that the ship had got off all right: a workman at the docks told her so. Later, who should come to the door but Mr. Pym—which naturally gave her great surprise. He told her the ship had sprung a leak and had put back; but they should be off again with the next day's tide, and he should have to be abroad precious early in the morning to get the cargo stowed away again—

"What time was this?" interrupted Mr. Freeman.

"About half-past four, I fancy, sir. Mr. Pym spoke rather thick—I saw he had been taking a glass. He bade me make him a big potful of strong tea—which I did at once, having the kettle on the fire. He drank it, and went out."

"Go on, Mrs. Richenough."

"An hour afterwards, or so, his captain called, wanting to know where he was. Of course, sirs, I could not say; except that he had had a big jorum of tea, and was gone out."

Captain Tanerton spoke up to confirm this. "I wanted Pym," he said. "This must have been between half-past five and six o'clock."

"About nine o'clock; or a bit earlier, it might be—I know it was dark and I had finished my supper—Mr. Pym came back," resumed the landlady. "He seemed in an ill-humour, and he had been having more to drink. 'Light my lamp, Mother Richenough,' says he roughly, 'and shut the shutters: I've got a letter to write.' I lighted the lamp, and he got out some paper of his that was left in the table-drawer, and the ink, and sat down. After closing the shutters I went to the front-door, and there I saw Captain Tanerton. He asked me—"

"What did he ask you?" cried Mr. Freeman's lawyer, for she had come to a dead standstill.

"Well, the captain asked me whether any young lady had been there. He had asked the same question afore, sir: Mr. Pym's cousin, or sister, I b'lieve he meant. I told him No, and he went into the parlour to Mr. Pym."

"What then?"

"Well, gentlemen, I went back to my kitchen, and shut myself in by my bit o' fire; and, being all lonely like, I a'most dozed off. Not quite; they made so much noise in the parlour, quarrelling."

"Quarrelling?" cried the lawyer.

"Yes, sir; and were roaring out at one another like wolves. Mr. —"

"Stay a moment, ma'am. How long was it after you admitted Captain Tanerton that you heard this quarrelling?"

"Not above three or four minutes, sir. I'm sure of that. 'Mr. Pym's catching it from his captain, and he is just in the right mood to take it unkindly,' I thought to myself. However, it was no business of mine. The sounds soon ceased, and I was just dozing off again, when Mr. Saxby came home. He went into the parlour to see Mr. Pym, and found him lying dead on the floor."

A silent pause.

"You are sure, ma'am, it was Captain Tanerton who was quarrelling with him?" cried the lawyer, who asked more questions than all the rest put together.

"Of course I am sure," returned Mrs. Richenough. "Why, sir, how could it be anybody else? Hadn't I just let in Captain Tanerton to him? Nobody was there but their two selves."

Naturally the room turned to Jack. He answered the mute appeal very quietly.

"It was not myself that quarrelled with Pym. No angry word of any kind passed between us. Pym had been drinking; Mrs. Richenough is right in that. He was not in a state to be reproved or reasoned with, and I came away at once. I did not stay to sit down."

"You hear this, Mrs. Richenough?"

"Yes, sir, I do; and I am sure the gentleman don't speak or look like one who could do such a deed. But, then, I heard the quarrelling."

An argument indisputable to her own mind. Sir Dace looked up and put a question for the first time. He had listened in silence. His dark face had a wearied look on it, and he spoke hardly above a whisper.

"Did you know the voice to be that of Captain Tanerton, Mistress Landlady? Did you recognize it for his!"

"I knew the voice couldn't be anybody else's, sir. Nobody but the captain was with Mr. Pym."

"I asked you whether you recognized it?" returned Sir Dace, knitting his brow. "Did you know by its tone that it was Captain Tanerton's?"

"Well, no, sir, I did not, if you put it in that way. Captain Tanerton was nearly a stranger to me, and the two shut doors and the passage was between me and him. I had only heard him speak once or twice before, and then in a pleasant, ordinary voice. In this quarrel his voice was raised to a high, rough pitch; and in course I could not know it for his."

"In point of fact, then, it comes to this: You did not recognize the voice for Captain Tanerton's."

"No, sir; not, I say, if you put it in that light."

"Let me put it in this light," was Sir Dace Fontaine's testy rejoinder: "Had three or four people been with Mr. Pym in his parlour, you could not have told whose voice it was quarrelling with him? You would not have known?"

"That is so, sir. But, you see, I knew it was his captain that was with him."

Sir Dace folded his arms and leaned back in his chair, his cross-questioning over. Mrs. Richenough was done with for the present, and Captain Tanerton entered upon his version of the night's events.

"I wished particularly to see Mr. Pym, and went to Ship Street in search of him, as I have already said. He was not there. Later, I went down again—"

"I beg your pardon, Captain Tanerton," interrupted the lawyer; "what time do you make it—that second visit?"

"It must have been nearly nine o'clock. Mr. Pym was at home, and I went into his parlour. He sat at the table writing, or preparing to write. I asked him the question I had come to ask, and he answered me. Scarcely anything more passed between us. He was three-parts tipsy. I had intended to tell him that he was no longer chief mate of my ship—had been superseded; but, seeing his condition, I did not. I can say positively that I was not more than two minutes in the room."

"And you and he did not quarrel?"

"We did not. Neither were our voices raised. It is very probable, in his then condition, that he would have attempted to quarrel had he known he was discharged; but he did not know it. We were perfectly civil to each other; and when I wished him good-night, he came into the passage and shut the front-door after me."

"You left no one with him?"

"No one; so far as I saw. I can answer for it that no one was in the parlour with us: whether any one was in the back room I cannot say. I do not think so."

"After that, Captain Tanerton?"

"After that I went straight to my hotel in the Minories, and ordered tea. While taking it, Mr. Ferrar came in and told me Edward Pym was dead. I could not at first believe it. I went back to Ship Street and found it too true. In as short a time as I could manage it, I went to carry the news to Sir Dace Fontaine, taking young Saxby with me."

Jack had spoken throughout in the ready, unembarrassed manner of one who tells a true tale. But never in all my life had I seen him so quiet and subdued. He was like one who has some great care upon him. The other hearers, not knowing Jack as I knew him, would not notice this; though I cannot answer for it that one of them did not James Freeman. He never took his eyes off Jack all the while; peered at him as if he were a curiosity. It was not an open stare; more of a surreptitious one, taken stealthily from under his eyebrows.

Some testimony as to Pym's movements that afternoon was obtained from Mrs. Ball, the lawyer having already been to Woburn Place to get it. She said that young Pym came to her house between five and six o'clock nearer six than five, she thought, and seemed very much put out and disappointed to find Miss Verena Fontaine had left for her own home. He spoke of the ship's having sprung a leak and put back again, but he believed she would get out again on the morrow. Mrs. Ball did not notice that he had been drinking; but one of her servants met him in the street after he left the house, heard him swearing to himself, and saw him turn into a public-house. If he remained in it until the time he next appeared in Ship Street, his state then was not to be wondered at.

This was about all that had been gathered at present. A great deal of talking took place, but no opinion was expressed by anybody. Time enough for that when the jury met on the morrow. As we were turning out of the back-room, the meeting over, Mr. Freeman put his hand upon Jack, to detain him. Jack, in his turn, detained me.

"Captain Tanerton," he said, in a grave whisper, "do you remember making a remark to me not long ago, in this, my private room—that if we persisted in sending Pym out with you in the ship, there would be murder committed?"

"I believe I do," said Jack, quietly. "They were foolish words, and meant nothing."

"I do not like to remember them," pursued Mr. Freeman. "As things have turned out, it would have been better that you had not used them."

"Perhaps so," answered Jack. "They have done no harm, that I know of."

"They have been singularly verified. The man has been murdered."

"Not on board the Rose of Delhi."

"No. Off it."

"I should rather call it death by misadventure," said Jack, looking calmly at the broker. "At the worst, done in a scuffle; possibly in a fall."

"Most people, as I think you will find, will call it murder, Captain Tanerton."

"I fear they will."

Mr. Freeman stood before Jack, waiting—at least it struck me so—to hear him add, "But I did not commit it"—or words to that effect. I waited too. Jack never spoke them: he remained silent and still. Since the past day his manner had changed. All the light-hearted ease had gone out of it; the sunny temperament seemed exchanged for one of thought and gloom.

Fine tidings to travel down to Timberdale!

On Wednesday, the day following this, the Squire stood at the gate of Crabb Cot after breakfast, looking this way and that. Dark clouds were chasing each other over the face of the sky, now obscuring the sun, now leaving it to shine out with intense fierceness.

"It won't do to-day," cried the Squire. "It's too windy, Joe. The fish would not bite."

"They'd bite fast enough," said Tod, who had set his mind upon a day's fishing, and wanted the Squire to go with him.

"Feel that gust, Joe! Why, if—halloa, here comes Letsom!"

Colonel Letsom was approaching at the pace of a steam-engine, his mild face longer than usual. Tod laughed.

The colonel, never remembering to say How d'ye do, or to shake hands, dragged two letters out of his pocket, all in a flurry.

"Such fearful news, Todhetley!" he exclaimed. "Pym—you remember that poor Pym?"

"What should hinder me?" cried the Squire. "A fine dance we had, looking for him and Verena Fontaine the other night in London! What of Pym!"

"He is dead!" gasped the colonel. "Murdered."

The pater took off his spectacles, thinking they must affect his hearing, and stared.

"And it is thought," added the colonel, "that—that Captain Tanerton did it."

"Good mercy, Letsom! You can't mean it."

Colonel Letsom's answer was to read out portions of the two letters. One of them was written to his daughter Mary Ann by Coralie Fontaine; three sheets full. She gave much the same history of the calamity that has been given above. It could not have been done by any hand but Captain Tanerton's, she said; though of course not intentionally; nobody thought that: her father, Sir Dace, scorned any worse idea. Altogether, it was a dreadful thing; it had struck Verena into a kind of wild despair, and bewildered them all. And in a postscript she added what she had apparently forgotten to say before— that Captain Tanerton denied it.

Tod looked up, a flush on his face. "One thing may be relied upon, colonel—that if Tanerton did do it, he will avow it. He would never deny it."

"This other letter is from Sir Dace," said the colonel, after putting Coralie's aside. And he turned round that we might look over his shoulder while he read it.

It gave a much shorter account than Coralie's; a lighter account, as if he took a less grave view of the affair; and it concluded with these words: "Suspicion lies upon Tanerton. I think unjustly. Allowing that he did do it, it could only have been done by a smartly-provoked blow, devoid of ill-intention. No one knows better than myself how quarrelsome and overbearing that unfortunate young man was. But I, for one, believe what Tanerton says—that he was not even present when it happened. I am inclined to think that Pym, in his unsteady state, must in some way have fallen when alone, and struck his head fatally."

"Sir Dace is right; I'll lay my fortune upon it," cried Tod warmly.

"Don't talk quite so fast about your fortune, Joe; wait till you've got one," rebuked the pater. "I must say it is grievous news, Letsom. It has upset me."

"I am off now to show the letters to Paul," said the colonel. "It will be but neighbourly, as he is a connection of the Fontaines."

Shaking hands, he turned away on the road to Islip. The Squire, leaning on the gate, appeared to be looking after him: in reality he was deep in a brown study.

"Joe," said he, in a tone that had a sound of awe in it, "this is curious, taken in conjunction with what Alice Tanerton told us yesterday morning."

"Well, it does seem rather queer," conceded Tod. "Something like the dream turning up trumps."

"Trumps?" retorted the pater.

"Truth, then. Poor Alice!"

A singular thing had happened. Especially singular, taken in conjunction (as the Squire put it) with this unfortunate news. And when the reader hears the whole, though it won't be just yet, he will be ready to call out, It is not true. But it is true. And this one only fact, with its truth and its singularity, induced me to recount the history.

On Tuesday morning, the day after the calamity in Ship Street—you perceive that we go back a day—the Squire and Tod turned out for a walk. They had no wish to go anywhere in particular, and their steps might just as well have been turned Crabb way as Timberdale way—or, for that matter, any other way. The morning was warm and bright: they strolled towards the Ravine, went through it, and so on to Timberdale.

"We may as well call and see how Herbert Tanerton is, as we are here," remarked the Squire. For Herbert had a touch of hay-fever. He was always getting something or other.

The Rector was better. They found him pottering about his garden; that prolific back-garden from which we once saw—if you don't forget it—poor, honest, simple-minded Jack bringing strawberries on a cabbage-leaf for crafty Aunt Dean. The suspected hay-fever turned out to be a bit of a cold in the head: but the Rector could not have looked more miserable had it been in the heart.

"What's the matter with you now?" cried the Squire, who never gave in to Herbert's fancies.

"Matter enough," he growled in answer: "to have a crew of ridiculous women around you, no better than babies! Here's Alice in a world of a way about Jack, proclaiming that some harm has happened to him."

"What harm? Does she know of any?"

"No, she does not know of any," croaked Herbert, flicking a growing gooseberry off a bush with the rake. "She says a dream disclosed it to her."

The pater stared. Tod threw up his head with a laugh.

"You might have thought she'd got her death-warrant read out to her, so white and trembling did she come down," continued Herbert in an injured tone. "She had dreamt a dream, foreshadowing evil to Jack, she began to tell us—and not a morsel of breakfast could she touch."

"But that's not like Alice," continued the Squire. "She is too sensible: too practical for such folly."

"It's not like any rational woman. And Grace would have condoled with her! Women infect each other."

"What was the dream?"

"Some nonsense or other, you may be sure. I would not let her relate it, to me, or to Grace. Alice burst into tears and called me hard-hearted. I came out here to get away from her."

"For goodness' sake don't let her upset herself over a rubbishing dream, Tanerton," cried the Squire, all sympathy. "She's not strong, you know, just now. I dreamt one night the public hangman was appointed to take my head off; but it is on my shoulders yet. You tell her that."

"Yesterday was the day Jack was to sail," interrupted Tod.

"Of course it was," acquiesced the Rector: "he must be half-way down the channel by this time. If— Here comes Alice!" he broke off. "I shall go. I don't want to hear more of such stuff."

He went on down the garden in a huff, disappearing behind the kidney-beans. Alice, wearing a light print gown and black silk apron, her smooth brown hair glossy as ever, and her open face as pretty, shook hands with them both.

"And what's this we hear about your tormenting yourself over a dream?" blundered the Squire. Though whether it was a blunder to say it, I know not; or whether, but for that, she would have spoken: once the ice is broken, you may plunge in easily. "My dear, I'd not have thought it of you."

Alice's face took a deeper gravity, her eyes a far-off look. "It is quite true, Mr. Todhetley," she sighed. "I have been very much troubled by a dream."

"Tell it us, Alice," said Tod, his whole face in a laugh. "What was it about?"

"That you may ridicule it?" she sighed.

"Yes," he answered. "Ridicule it out of you."

"You cannot do that," was her quiet answer: and Tod told me in later days that it rather took him aback to see her solemn sadness. "I should like to relate it to you, Mr. Todhetley. Herbert would not hear it, or let Grace."

"Herbert's a parson, you know, my dear, and parsons think they ought to be above such things," was the Squire's soothing answer. "If it will ease your mind to tell it me— Here, let us sit down under the pear-tree."

So they sat down on the bench under the blossoms of the pear-tree, the pater admonishing Tod to behave himself; and poor Alice told her dream.

"I thought it was the present time," she began. "This very present day, say, or yesterday; and that Jack was going to sea in command—"

"But, my dear, he always goes in command."

"Of course. But in the dream the point was especially presented to my mind—that he was going out in command. He came to me the morning of the day he was to sail, looking very patient, pale, and sorrowful. It seemed that he and I had had some dispute, causing estrangement, the previous night: it was over then, and I, for one, repented of the coldness."

"Well, Alice?" broke in Tod: for she had stopped, and was gazing out straight before her.

"I wish I could show to you how real all this was," she resumed. "It was more as though I were wide awake, and enacting it. I never had so vivid a dream before; never in all my life."

"But why don't you go on?"

"Somebody had been murdered: some man. I don't know who it was—or where, or how. Jack was suspected. Jack! But it seemed that it could not be brought home to him. We were in a strange town; at least, it was strange to me, though it seemed that I had stayed in it once before, many years ago. Jack was standing before me all this while, you understand, in his sadness and sorrow. It was not he who had told me what had happened. I seemed to have known it already. Everybody knew it, everybody spoke of it, and we were in cruel distress. Suddenly I remembered that when I was in the town the previous time, the man who was murdered had had a bitter quarrel with another man, a gentleman: and a sort of revelation came over me that this gentleman had been the murderer. I went privately to some one who had authority in the ship, and said so; I think her owner. He laughed at me—did I know how high this gentleman was, he asked; the first magnate in the town. That he had done it I felt sure; surer than if I had seen it done; but no one would listen to me—and in the trouble I awoke."

"That's not much to be troubled at," cried the Squire.

"The trouble was terrible; you could not feel such in real life. But I have not told all. Presently I got to sleep again, and found myself in the same dream. I was going through the streets of the town in an open carriage, the ship's owner with me—"

"Was the ship the Rose of Delhi?"

"I don't know. The owner, sitting with me in the carriage, was not either of the owners of the Rose of Delhi, whom I know well; this was a stranger. We were going over a bridge. Walking towards us on the pavement, I saw two gentlemen arm-in-arm: one an officer in a dusky old red uniform and cocked-hat; the other an evil-looking man who wore a long brown coat. He walked along with his eyes on the ground. I knew him by intuition—that it was the man who had had the quarrel years before, and who had done the murder now. 'There's the gentleman you would have accused,' said my companion before I could speak, pointing to this man: 'he stands higher in position than anybody else in the town.' They walked on in their security, and we drove on in our pain. I ought to say in my pain, for I alone felt it. Oh, I cannot tell you what it was—this terrible pain; not felt so much, it seemed, because my husband could not be cleared, as for his sadness and sorrow. Nothing like it, I say, can ever be felt on earth."

"And what else, Alice?"

"That is all," she sighed. "I awoke for good then. But the pain and the fear remain with me."

"Perhaps, child, you are not very well?—been eating green gooseberries, or some such trash. Nothing's more likely to give one bad dreams than unripe fruit."

"Why should the dream have left this impression of evil upon me—this weight of fear?" cried Alice, never so much as hearing the pater's irreverent suggestion. "If it meant nothing, if it were not come as a warning, it would pass from my mind as other dreams pass."

Not knowing what to say to this, the Squire said nothing. He and Tod both saw how useless it would be; no argument could shake her faith in the dream, and the impression it had left.

The Squire, more easily swayed than a child, yet suspecting nothing of the news that was on its way to Timberdale, quitted the Rectory and went home shaking his head. Alice's solemn manner had told upon him. "I can't make much out of the dream, Joe," he remarked, as they walked back through the Ravine; "but I don't say dreams are always to be ridiculed, since we read of dreams sent as warnings in the Bible. Anyhow, I hope Jack will make a good voyage. He has got home safe and sound from other voyages: why should he not from this one?"

Before that day was over, they saw Alice again. She walked over to Crabb Cot in the evening with her little girl—a sprightly child with Jack's own honest and kindly eyes. Alice put a sealed paper into the Squire's hand.

"I know you will think me silly," she said to him, in a low tone: "perhaps gone a little out of my senses; but, as I told you this morning, nothing has ever impressed me so greatly and so unpleasantly as this dream. I cannot get it out of my mind for a moment; every hour, as it goes by, only serves to render it clearer. I have written it down here, every particular, more minutely than I related it to you this morning, and I have sealed it up, you see; and I am come to ask you to keep it. Should my husband ever be accused, it may serve to—"

"Now, child, don't you talk nonsense," interrupted the pater. "Accused of what?"

"I don't know. I wish I did. I hope you will pardon me, Mr. Todhetley," she went on, in deprecation; "but indeed there lies upon me a dread—an apprehension that startles me. I dare say I express myself badly; but it is there. And, do you know, Jack has lately experienced the same sensation; he told me so on Sunday. He said it was like an instinct of coming evil."

"Then that accounts for it," cried the Squire, considerably relieved, and wondering how Jack could be so silly, if she was. "If your husband told you that, Alice, of course the first thing you'd do would be to go and dream of it."

"Perhaps so. What he said made no impression on me; he laughed as he said it: I don't suppose it made much on him. Please keep the paper."

The Squire carried the paper upstairs and locked it up in the little old walnut bureau in his bedroom. He told Alice where he had put it. And she, declining any refreshment, left again with little Polly for Timberdale Rectory.

"Has Herbert come to?" asked Tod laughingly, as he went to open the gate for her.

"Oh dear, no," answered Alice. "He never will, if you mean as to hearing me tell the dream."

They had a hot argument after she left: Mrs. Todhetley maintaining that some dreams were to be regarded as sacred things; while Tod ridiculed them with all his might, asserting that there never had been, and never could be anything in them to affect sensible people. The Squire, now taking one side, now veering to the other, remained in a state of vacillation, something like Mahomet's coffin hovering between earth and heaven.

And, you will now readily understand that when the following morning, Wednesday, Colonel Letsom brought the Squire the news of Pym's death, calling it murder, and that Jack was suspected, and the ship had gone out without him, this dream of Alice Tanerton's took a new and not at all an agreeable prominence. Even Tod, sceptical Tod, allowed that it was "queer."

On this same morning, Wednesday, Alice received a letter from her husband. He spoke of the mishap to the ship, said that she had put back, and had again gone out; he himself being detained in London on business, but he expected to be off in a day or two and join her at some place down channel. But not a word did he say of the cause of his detention, or of the death of Edward Pym. She heard it from others.

With this confirmation, as it seemed, of her dream, Alice took it up more warmly. She went over to the old lawyer at Islip, John Paul, recounted the dream to him, and asked what she was to do. Naturally, old Paul told her "nothing:" and he must have laughed in his sleeve as he said it.

The good ship, Rose of Delhi, finally went away with all her sails set for the East; but John Tanerton went not with her.

The inquest on the unfortunate young man, Pym, was put off from time to time, and prolonged and procrastinated. Captain Tanerton had to wait its pleasure; the ship could not.

The case presented difficulties, and the jury could not see their way to come to a verdict. Matters looked rather black against Captain Tanerton; that was not denied; but not sufficiently black, it would seem, for the law to lay hold of him. At any rate, the law did not. Perhaps the persistent advocacy of Sir Dace Fontaine went some way with the jury. Sir Dace gave it as his strong opinion that his misguided nephew, being the worse for drink, had fallen of himself, probably with his head on the iron fender, and that Captain Tanerton's denial was a strictly true one. The end finally arrived at was—that there was not sufficient evidence to show how the death was caused.

At the close of the investigation Jack went down to Timberdale. Not the open-hearted, ready-handed Jack of the old days, but a subdued, saddened man who seemed to have a care upon him. The foolish speech he had thoughtlessly made to Mr. Freeman preceded him: and Herbert Tanerton—always looking on the darkest side of everything and everybody, considered it a proof that Jack had done the deed.

Timberdale (including Crabb) held opposite opinions; half of it taking Captain Tanerton's side, half the contrary one. As to the Squire, he was more helpless than an old sheep. He had always liked Jack, had believed in him as in one of us: but, you see, when one gets into trouble, faith is apt to waver. A blow, argued the pater in private, is so easily given in the heat of passion.

"A pretty kettle of fish this is," croaked Herbert to Jack, on his brother's arrival.

"Yes, it is," sighed Jack.

"The ship's gone without you, I hear."

"She had to go. Ships cannot be delayed to await the convenience of one man: you must know that, Herbert."

"How came you to do it, John?"

"To do what?" asked Jack. "To stay? It was no fault of mine. I was one of the chief witnesses, and the coroner would not release me."

"You know what I mean. Not that. How came you to do it, I ask?"

"To do what?" repeated Jack.

"Kill Pym."

Jack's face took a terrible shade of pain as he looked at his brother. "I should have thought, Herbert, that you, of all people, might have judged me better than that."

"I don't mean to say you did it deliberately; that you meant to do it," returned the Rector in his coldest manner. "But that was a very awkward threat of yours—that if the brokers persisted in sending Pym out with you, there'd be murder committed. Very incautious!"

"You can't mean what you say; you cannot surely reflect on what you would imply—that I spoke those words with intention!" flashed Jack.

"You did speak them—and they were verified," contended Herbert. Just the same thing, you see, that Mr. Freeman had said to Jack in London. Poor Jack!

"How did you hear that I had said anything of the kind?"

"Somebody wrote it to Timberdale," answered the parson, crustily. There could be no question that the affair had crossed him more than anything that had ever happened in this world. "I think it was Coralie Fontaine."

"I am deeply sorry I ever spoke them, Herbert—as things have turned out."

"No doubt you are. The tongue's an evil and dangerous member. Let us drop the subject: the less it is recurred to now, the better."

Captain Tanerton saw how it was—that all the world suspected him, beginning with his brother.

And he certainly did not do as much to combat the feeling as he might have done. This was noticed. He did not assert his innocence strenuously and earnestly. He said he was not guilty, it's true, but he said it too quietly. A man accused of so terrible a crime would move heaven and earth to prove the charge false—if false it were. Jack denied his guilt, but denied it in a very tame fashion. And this had its effect upon his upholders.

There could be no mistaking that some inward trouble tormented him. His warm, genial manners had given place to thoughtfulness and care. Was Jack guilty?—his best friends acknowledged the doubt now, in the depths of their heart. Herbert Tanerton was worrying himself into a chronic fever: chiefly because disgrace was reflected on his immaculate self, Jack being his brother. Squire Todhetley, meeting Jack one day in Robert Ashton's cornfield, took Jack's hands in his, and whispered that if Jack did strike the blow unwittingly, he knew it was all the fault of that unhappy, cross-grained Pym. In short, the only person who retained full belief in Jack was his wife. Jack had surely done it, said Timberdale under the rose, but done it unintentionally.

Alice related her dream to Jack. Not being given to belief in dreams, Jack thought little of it. Nothing, in fact. It was no big, evil-faced man who harmed Pym, he answered, shaking his head; and he seemed to speak as one who knew.

Timberdale was no longer a pleasant resting-place for John Tanerton, and he quitted it for Liverpool, with Alice and their little girl. Aunt Dean received him coolly and distantly. The misfortune had put her out frightfully: with Jack's income threatened, there would be less for herself to prey upon. She told him to his face that if he wanted to correct Pym, he might have waited till they got out to sea: blows were not thought much of on board ship.

The next day Jack paid a visit to the owners, and resigned his command. For, he was still attached ostensibly to the Rose of Delhi, though another master had temporarily superseded him.

"Why do you do this?" asked Mr. Charles Freeman. "We can put you into another ship, one going on a shorter voyage, and when your own comes home you can take her again."

"No," said Jack. "Many thanks, though, for your confidence in me. All the world seems to believe me guilty. If I were guilty I am not fit to command a ship's crew."

"But you were not guilty?"

More emphatically than Jack had yet spoken upon the affair, he spoke now: and his truthful, candid eyes went straight into those of his questioner.

"I was not. Before Heaven, I say it."

Charles Freeman heaved a sigh of relief. He liked Jack, and the matter had somewhat troubled him.

"Then, Captain Tanerton—I fully believe you—why not reconsider your determination, and remain on active service? The Shamrock is going to Madras; sails in a day or two; and you shall have her. She'll be home again before the Rose of Delhi. For your own sake I think you should do this—to still rancorous tongues."

Jack sighed. "I can't feel free to go," he said. "This suspicion has troubled me more than you can imagine. I must get some employment on shore."

"You should stand up before the world and assert your innocence in this same emphatic manner," returned the owner. "Why have you not done it?"

Jack's voice took a tone of evasion at once. "I have not cared to do it."

Charles Freeman looked at him. A sudden thought flashed into his mind.

"Are you screening some one, Captain Tanerton?"

"How can you ask such a question?" rejoined Jack. But the deep and sudden flush that rose with the words, gave fresh food for speculation to Mr. Freeman. He dropped his voice.

"Surely it was not Sir Dace Fontaine who—who killed him? The uncle and nephew were not on good terms."

Jack's face and voice brightened again—he could answer this with his whole heart. "No, no," he impressively said, "it was not Sir Dace Fontaine. You may at least rely upon that."

When I at length got back to Crabb, the Fontaines were there. After the inquest, they had gone again to Brighton. Poor Verena looked like a ghost, I thought, when I saw her on the Sunday in their pew at church.

"It has been a dreadful thing," I said to her, as we walked on together after service; "but I am sorry to see you look so ill."

"A dreadful thing!—ay, it has, Johnny Ludlow," was her answer, spoken in a wail. "I expect it will kill some of us."

Sir Dace looked ill too. His furtive eyes had glanced hither and thither during the service, like a man who has a scare upon him; but they seemed ever to come back to Verena.

Not another word was said by either of us until we were near the barn. Then Verena spoke.

"Where is John Tanerton?"

"In Liverpool, I hear."

"Poor fellow!"

Her tone was as piteous as her words, as her looks. All the bloom had gone from her pretty face; its lips were white, dry, and trembling. In Coralie there was no change; her smiles were pleasant as ever, her manners as easy. The calamity had evidently passed lightly over her; as I expect most things in life did pass.

Saying good-morning at the turning, Sir Dace and Verena branched off to Maythorn Bank. Coralie lingered yet, talking with Mr. Todhetley.

"My dear, how ill your father is looking!" exclaimed the Squire.

"He does look ill," answered Coralie. "He has never been quite the same since that night in London. He said one day that he could not get the sight of Pym out of his mind—as he saw him lying on the floor in Ship Street."

"It must have been a sad sight."

"Papa is also, I think, anxious about Verena," added Coralie. "She has taken the matter to heart in quite an unnecessary manner; just, I'm sure, as if she intended to die over it. That must vex papa: I see him glancing at her every minute in the day. Oh, I assure you I am the only cheerful one of the family now," concluded Coralie, lightly, as she ran away to catch the others.

That was the last we saw of them that year. On the morrow we left for Dyke Manor.

In the course of the autumn John Tanerton ran up to Timberdale from Liverpool. It had come to his knowledge that the Ash Farm, belonging to Robert Ashton, was to let—Grace had chanced to mention it incidentally when writing to Alice—and poor Jack thought if he could only take it his fortune was made. He was an excellent, practical farmer, and knew he could make it answer. But it would take two or three thousand pounds to stock the Ash Farm, and Jack had not as many available shillings. He asked his brother to lend him the money.

"I always knew you were deficient in common sense," was the Rector's sarcastic rejoinder to the request. "Three thousand pounds! What next?"

"It would be quite safe, Herbert: you know how energetic I am. And I will pay you good interest."

"No doubt you will—when I lend it you. You have a cheek!"

"But—"

"That will do; don't waste breath," interrupted Herbert, cutting him short. And he positively refused the request—refused to listen to another word.

Strolling past Maythorn Bank that same afternoon, very much down in looks and spirits, Jack saw Sir Dace Fontaine. He was leaning over his little gate, looking just as miserable as Jack. For Sir Dace to look out of sorts was nothing unusual; for Jack it was. Sir Dace asked what was amiss: and Jack—candid, free-spoken, open-natured Jack—told of his disappointment in regard to the Ash Farm: his brother not feeling inclined to advance him the necessary money to take it—three thousand pounds.

"I wonder you do not return to the sea, Captain Tanerton," cried Sir Dace.

"I do not care to return to it," was Jack's answer.

"Why?"

"I shall never go to sea again, Sir Dace," he said in his candour.

"Never go to sea again!"

"No. At any rate, not until I am cleared. While this dark cloud of suspicion lies upon me I am not fit to take the command of others. Some windy night insubordinate men might throw the charge in my teeth."

"You are wrong," said Sir Dace, his countenance taking an angry turn. "You know, I presume, your own innocence—and you should act as if you knew it."

He turned back up the path without another word, entered his house, and shut the door. Jack walked slowly on. Presently he heard footsteps behind him, looked round, and saw Verena Fontaine. They had not met since the time of Pym's death, and Jack thought he had never seen such a change in any one. Her bright colour was gone, her cheeks were wasted—a kind of dumb despair sat in her once laughing blue eyes. All Jack's pity—and he had his share of it—went out to her.

"I heard a little of what you said to papa at the garden-gate, Captain Tanerton—not much of it. I was in the arbour. Why is it that you will not yet go to sea again? What is it you wait for?"

"I am waiting until I can stand clear in the eyes of men," answered Jack, candid as usual, but somewhat agitated, as if the topic were a sore one. "No man with a suspicion attaching to him should presume to hold authority over other men."

"I understand you," murmured Verena. "If you stood as free from suspicion with all the world as you are in my heart, and—and"—she paused from emotion—"and I think in my father's also, you would have no cause to hesitate."

Jack took a questioning glance at her; at the sad, eager eyes that were lifted beseechingly to his. "It is kind of you to say so much," he answered. "It struck me at the time of the occurrence that you could not, did not, believe me guilty."

Verena shivered. As if his steady gaze were too much for her, she turned her own aside towards the blue sky.

"Good-bye," she said faintly, putting out her hand. "I only wanted to say this—to let you know that I believe in your innocence."

"Thank you," said Jack, meeting her hand. "It is gratifying to hear that you do me justice."

He walked quietly away. She stood still to watch him. And of all the distressed, sad, aching countenances ever seen in this world, few could have matched that of Miss Verena Fontaine.

V

Spring sunshine, bright and warm to-day, lay on Timberdale. Herbert Tanerton, looking sick and ill, sat on a bench on the front lawn, holding an argument with his wife, shielded from outside gazers by the clump of laurel-trees. We used to say the Rector's illnesses were all fancy and temper; but it seemed to be rather more than that now. Worse tempered he was than ever; Jack's misfortunes and Jack's conduct annoyed him. During the past winter Jack had taken some employment at the Liverpool Docks, in connection with the Messrs. Freeman's ships. Goodness knew of what description it was, Herbert would say, turning up his nose.

A day or two ago Jack made his appearance again at the Rectory; had swooped down upon it without warning or ceremony, just as he had in the autumn. Herbert did not approve of that. He approved still less of the object which had brought Jack at all. Jack was tired of the Liverpool Docks; the work he had to do was not congenial to him; and he had now come to Timberdale to ask Robert Ashton to make him his bailiff. Not being able to take a farm on his own account, Jack thought the next best thing would be to take the management of one. Robert Ashton would be parting with his bailiff at Midsummer, and Jack would like to drop into the post. Anything much less congenial to the Rector's notions, Jack could hardly have pitched upon.

"I can see what it is—Jack is going to be a thorn in my side for ever," the Rector was remarking to his wife, who sat near him, doing some useful work. "He never had any idea of the fitness of things. A bailiff, now!—a servant!"

"I wish you would let him take a farm, Herbert—lend him the money to stock one."

"I know you do; you have said so before."

Grace sighed. But when she had it on her conscience to say a thing she said it.

"Herbert, you know—you know I have never thought it fair that we should enjoy all the income we do; and—"

"What do you mean by 'fair'?" interrupted Herbert. "I only enjoy my own."

"Legally it is yours. Rightly, a large portion of it ought to be Jack's. It does not do us any good, Herbert, this superfluous income; you only put it by. It does not in the slightest degree add to our enjoyment of life."

"Do be quiet, Grace—unless you can talk sense. Jack will get no money from me. He ought to be at sea. What right had he to give it up? The Rose of Delhi is expected back now: let him take her again."

"You know why he will not, Herbert. And he must do something for a living. I wish you would not object to his engaging himself to Robert Ashton. If—"

"Why don't you wish anything else that's lowering and degrading? You are as devoid of common sense as he!" retorted the parson, walking away in a fume.

Matters were in this state when we got back to Crabb Cot; to stop at it for a longer or a shorter period as fate and the painters at Dyke Manor would allow. Jack urging Robert Ashton to promise him the bailiffs post—vacant the next Midsummer; Herbert strenuously objecting to it; and Robert Ashton in a state of dilemma between the two. He would have liked well enough to engage John Tanerton: but he did not like to defy the Rector. When the Squire heard this later, his opinion vacillated, according to custom: now leaning to Herbert's side, now to Jack's. And the Fontaines, we found, were in all the bustle of house-moving. Their own house, Oxlip Grange, being at length ready for them, they were quitting Maythorn Bank.

"Goodness bless me!" cried the Squire, coming in at dusk from a stroll he had taken the evening of our arrival. "I never got such a turn in my life."

"What has given it you, sir?"

"What has given it me, Johnny? why, Sir Dace Fontaine. I never saw any man so changed," he went on, rubbing up his hair. "He looks like a ghost, more than a man."

"Is he ill?"

"He must be ill. Sauntering down that narrow lane by Maythorn Bank, I came upon a tall something mooning along like a walking shadow. I might have taken it for a shadow, but that it lifted its bent head, and threw its staring eyes straight into mine—and I protest that a shadowy sensation crept over myself when I recognized it for Fontaine. You never saw a face so gloomy and wan. How long is it since we saw him, Johnny?"

"About nine months, I think, sir."

"The man must be suffering from a wasting complaint, or else he has some secret care that's fretting him to fiddle-strings. Mark my words, all of you, it is one or the other."

"Dear me!" put in Mrs. Todhetley, full of pity. "I always thought him a gloomy man. Did you ask him whether he was ill?"

"Not I," said the pater: "he gave me no opportunity. Had I been a sheriffs-officer with a writ in my hand he could hardly have turned off shorter. They had moved into the other house that day, he muttered, and he must lock up Maythorn Bank and be after them."

This account of Sir Dace was in a measure cleared up the next morning. Who should come in after breakfast but the surgeon, Cole. Talking of this and that, Sir Dace Fontaine's name came up.

"I am on my way now to Sir Dace; to the new place," cried Cole. "They went into it yesterday. Might have gone in a month ago, but Sir Dace made no move to do it. He seems to have no heart left to do anything; neither heart nor energy."

"I knew he was ill," cried the Squire. "No mistaking that. And now, Cole, what is it that's the matter with him?"

"He shows symptoms of a very serious inward complaint," gravely answered Cole. "A complaint that, if it really does set in, must prove fatal. We have some hopes yet that we shall ward it off. Sir Dace does not think we shall, and is in a rare fright about himself."

"A fright, is he! That's it, then."

"Never saw any man in such a fright before," went on Cole. "Says he's going to die—and he does not want to die."

"I said last night the man was like a walking shadow. And there's a kind of scare in his face."

Cole nodded. "Two or three weeks ago I got a note from him, asking me to call. I found him something like a shadow, as you observe, Squire. The cold weather had kept him indoors, and I had not chanced to see him for some weeks. When Sir Dace told me his symptoms, I suppose I looked grave. Combined with his wasted appearance, they unpleasantly impressed me, and he took alarm. 'The truth,' he said, in his arbitrary way: 'tell me the truth; only that. Conceal nothing.' Well, when a patient adjures me in a solemn manner to tell the truth, I deem it my duty to do so," added Cole, looking up.

"Go on, Cole," cried the Squire, nodding approval.

"I told him the truth, softening it in a degree—that I did not altogether like some of the symptoms, but that I hoped, with skill and care, to get him round again. The same day he sent for Darbyshire of Timberdale, saying we must attend him conjointly, for two heads were better than one. Two days later he sent for somebody else—no other than Mr. Ben Rymer."

We all screamed out in surprise. "Ben Rymer!"

"Ay," said Cole, "Ben Rymer. Ben has got through and is a surgeon now, like the rest of us. And, upon my word, I believe the fellow has his profession thoroughly in hand. He will make a name in the world, the chances for it being afforded him, unless I am mistaken."

Something like moisture stood in the Squire's good old eyes. "If his father, poor Rymer, had but lived to see it!" he softly said. "Anxiety, touching Ben, killed him."

"So we three doctors make a pilgrimage to Sir Dace regularly everyday; sometimes together, sometimes apart," added Cole. "And, of the three of us, I believe the patient likes young Rymer best—has most confidence in him."

"Shall you cure him?"

"Well, we do not yet give up hope. If the disease does set in, it will—"

"What?"

"Run its course quickly."

"An instant yet, Cole," cried the Squire, stopping the surgeon as he was turning away. "You have told us nothing. How does the parish get on?—and the people? How is Letsom?—and Crabb generally? Tanerton—how is he?—and Timberdale? Coming here fresh, we are thirsting for news."

Cole laughed. He knew the pater liked gossip as much as any old woman: and the reader must understand that, as yet, we had not heard any, having reached Crabb Cot late the previous afternoon.

"There is no particular news, Squire," said he. "Letsom is well; so is Crabb. Herbert Tanerton's not well. He is in a crusty way over Jack."

"He is always in a way over something. Where is Jack?"

"Jack's here, at the Rectory; just come to it. Robert Ashton's bailiff is about to take a farm on his own account, and Jack came rushing over from Liverpool to apply for the post."

Tod, who had been too much occupied with his fishing-flies to take much heed before, set up a shrill whistle at this. "How will the parson like that?" he asked.

"The parson does not like it at all. Whether he will succeed in preventing it, is another matter," concluded Cole. And, with that, he made his escape.

Close upon the surgeon's departure, Colonel Letsom came in; he had heard of our arrival. It was a pity, he said, the two brothers should be at variance. Jack wanted the post—he must make a living somehow; and the Rector was in a way over it; not quite mad, but next door to it; Ashton of course not knowing what to do between them. From that subject, he began to speak of the Fontaines.

A West Indian planter, one George Bazalgette, had been over on a visit, he said, and had spent Christmas at Maythorn Bank; his object being to induce Verena to accept him as her husband. Verena would not listen to him, and he wasted his eloquence in vain. She made no hesitation in vowing to him that her affections were buried in the grave of Edward Pym.

"Fontaine told me confidentially in London that he intended she should have Bazalgette," remarked the Squire. "It was the evening we went looking for her at that wax-work place."

"Ay; but Fontaine is changed," returned the colonel: "all his old domineering ways are gone out of him. When Bazalgette was over here, he did not attempt even to persuade her: she must take her own course, he said. So poor Bazalgette went back as he came—wifeless. It was a pity."

"Why?"

"Because this George Bazalgette was a nice fellow," replied Colonel Letsom. "An open-hearted, fine-looking, generous man, and desperately in love with her. Miss Verena will not readily find his compeer in a summer day's march."

"As old as Adam, I suppose, colonel," interjected Tod.

"Yes—if you choose to put Adam's age down at three or four and thirty," laughed the colonel, as he took his leave.

To wait many hours, once she was at Crabb, without laying in a stock of those delectable "family pills," invented by the late Thomas Rymer, would have been quite beyond the philosophy of Mrs. Todhetley. That first morning, not ten minutes after Colonel Letsom left us, taking the Squire with him, she despatched me to Timberdale for a big box of them. Tod would not come: said he had his flies to see to.

Dashing through the Ravine and out on the field beyond it, I came upon Jack Tanerton. Good old Jack! The Squire had said Sir Dace was changed: I saw that Jack was. He looked taller and thinner, and the once beaming face had care upon it.

"Where are you bound for, Jack?"

"Not for any place in particular. Just sauntering about."

"Walk my way, then. I am going to Rymer's."

"It is such nonsense," cried Jack, speaking of his brother, after we had plunged a bit into affairs. "Calling it derogatory, and all the rest of it! I could be just as much of a gentleman as Ashton's bailiff as I am now. Everybody knows me. He gives a good salary, and there's a pretty house; and I have also my own small income. Alice and I and the little ones should be as happy as the day's long. If I give in to Herbert and don't take it, I don't see what I am to turn to."

"But, Jack, why do you give up the sea?" I asked. And Jack told me what he had told others: he should never take command again until he was a free man.

"Don't you think you are letting that past matter hold too great an influence over you?" I presently said. "You must be conscious of your own innocence—and yet you seem as sad and subdued as though you were guilty!"

"I am subdued because other people think me guilty!" he answered. "Changed? I am. It is that which has changed me; not the calamity itself."

"Jack, were I you, I should stand up in the face and eyes of all the world, and say to them, 'Before God, I did not kill Pym.' People would believe you then. But you don't do it."

"I have my reasons for not doing it, Johnny Ludlow. God knows what they are; He knows all things. I dare say I may be set right with the world in time: though I don't see how it is to be done."

A smart young man, a new assistant, was behind the counter at Ben Rymer's, and served me with the pills. Coming out, box in hand, we met Ben himself. I hardly knew him, he was so spruce. His very hair and whiskers were trimmed down to neatness and looked of a more reasonable colour; his red-brown beard was certainly handsome, and his clothes were well cut.

"Why, he has grown into a dandy, Jack," I said, after we had stood a minute or two, talking with the surgeon.

"Yes," said Jack, "he is going in for the proprieties of life now. Ben may make a gentleman yet—and a good man to boot."

That same afternoon, it chanced that the Squire met Ben Rymer. Striding along in his powerful fashion, Ben came full tilt round the sharp corner that makes the turning to the Islip Road, and nearly ran over the pater. Ben had been to Oxlip Grange.

"So, sir," cried the pater, stopping him, "I hear you are in practice now, and intend to become a respectable man. It's time you did."

"Ay, at last," replied Ben good-humouredly. "It is a long lane, Squire, that has no turning."

"Don't you lapse back again, Mr. Ben."

"Not if I know it, sir. I hope I shall not."

"It was anxiety on your score, you know, that troubled your good father's mind in dying."

"If it did not bring his death on," readily conceded Ben, his light tone changing. "I know it all, Squire—and have felt it."

"Look here," cried the Squire, catching at Ben's button-hole, which had a lovely lily-of-the-valley in it, "there was nothing on earth your poor patient father prayed for so earnestly as for your welfare; that you might be saved for time and eternity. Now I don't believe such prayers are ever lost. So you will be helped on your way if you bear steadfastly onwards."

Giving the young man's hand a wring, the Squire turned off on his way. In half-a-minute he was back again.

"Hey, Mr. Benjamin?—here. How is Sir Dace Fontaine? I suppose you have just left him?"

So Ben had to come back at the call. To the pater's surprise he saw his eyes were moist.

"He is worse, sir, to-day; palpably worse."

"Will he get over it?"

Ben gave his head an emphatic shake, which somehow belied his words: "Cole and Darbyshire think there is hope yet, Squire."

"And you do not; that's evident. Well, good-day."

The next move in this veritable drama was the appearance of Alice Tanerton and her six-months-old baby at Timberdale. Looking upon the Rectory as almost her home—it had been Jack's for many years of his life—Alice came to it without the ceremony of invitation: the object of her coming now being to strive to induce Herbert to let her husband engage himself to Robert Ashton. And this visit of Alice's was destined to bring about a most extraordinary event.

One Wednesday evening when Jack and his wife were dining with us—and that troublesome baby, which Alice could not, as it seemed, stir abroad without, was in the nursery squealing—Alice chanced to say that she had to go to Islip the following day, her mother having charged her to see John Paul the lawyer, concerning a little property that she, Aunt Dean, held in Crabb. It would be a tremendously long walk for Alice from Timberdale, especially as she was not looking strong, and Mrs. Todhetley proposed that I should drive her over in the pony-carriage: which Alice jumped at.

Accordingly, the next morning, which was warm and bright, I took the pony-carriage to the Rectory, picked up Alice, and then drove back towards Islip. As we passed Oxlip Grange, which lay in our way, Sir Dace Fontaine was outside in the road, slowly pacing the side-path. I thought I had never seen a man look so ill: so down and gloomy. He raised his eyes, as we came up, to give me a nod. I was nodding back again, when Alice screamed out and startled me. She started the pony too, which sprang on at a tangent.

"Johnny! Johnny Ludlow!" she gasped, her face whiter than death and her lips trembling like an aspen leaf, "did you see that man? Did you see him?"

"Yes. I was nodding to him. What is the matter?"

"It was the man I saw in my dream: the man who had committed the murder in it."

I stared at her, wondering whether she had lost her wits.

"Do you remember the description I gave of that man?" she continued, in excitement. "I do. I wrote it down at the time, and Mr. Todhetley holds it, sealed up. Every word, every particular is in my memory now, as I saw him in my dream. 'A tall, evil-looking, dark man in a long brown coat, who walked with his eyes fixed on the ground.' I tell you, Johnny Ludlow, that is the man."

Her vehemence infected me. I looked round after Sir Dace. He was turning this way now. Certainly the description seemed like enough. His countenance just now did look an evil one; and he was tall and he was dark, and he wore a long brown coat this morning, nearly reaching to his heels, and his eyes were fixed on the ground as he walked.

"But what if his looks do tally with the man you saw in your dream, Alice? What of it?"

"What of it!" she echoed, vehemently. "What of it! Why, don't you see, Johnny Ludlow? This man must have killed Edward Pym."

"Hush, Alice! It is impossible. This is Sir Dace Fontaine."

"I do not care who he is," was her impulsive retort. "As surely as that Heaven is above us, Edward Pym got his death at the hand of this man. My dream revealed it to me."

I might as well have tried to stem a torrent as to argue with her; so I drove on and held my tongue. Arrived at the office of Paul and Chandler, I following her in, leaving a boy with the pony outside. Alice pounced upon old Paul with the assertion: Sir Dace Fontaine was the evil and guilty man she had seen in her dream. Considering that Paul was a sort of cousin to Sir Dace's late wife, this was pretty well. Old Paul stared at her as I had done. Her cheeks were hectic, her eyes wildly earnest. She recalled to the lawyer's memory the dream she had related to him; she asserted in the most unqualified manner that Dace Fontaine was guilty. Tom Chandler, who was old Paul's partner and had married his daughter Emma, came into the room in the middle of it, and took his share of staring.

"It must be investigated," said Alice to them. "Will you undertake it?"

"My dear young lady, one cannot act upon a fancy—a dream," cried old Paul: and there was a curious sound of compassionate pity in his voice, which betrayed to Alice the gratifying fact that he was regarding her as a monomaniac.

"If you will not act, others will," she concluded at last, after exhausting her arguments in vain. And she came away with me in resentment, having totally forgotten all about her mother's business.

To Crabb Cot then—she would go—to take counsel with the Squire. He told her to her face she was worse than a lunatic to suspect Sir Dace; and he would hardly get out the sealed packet at all. It was opened at last, and the dream, as written down in it by herself at the time, read.

"John Tanerton, my husband, was going to sea in command," it began. "He came to me the morning of the day they were to sail, looking very patient, pale and sorrowful: more so than any one, I think, could look in life. He and I seemed to have had some estrangement the previous night that was not remembered by either of us now, and I, for one, repented of it. Somebody was murdered (though I could not tell how this had been revealed to me), some man; Jack was suspected by all people, but they could not bring it home to him. We were in some strange town; strangers in it; though I, as it seemed to me, had been in it once, many years before. All this while, Jack was standing before me in his sadness and sorrow, mutely appealing to me, as it seemed, to clear him. Everybody was talking of it and glancing at us askance, everybody shunned us, and we were in cruel distress. Suddenly I remembered that when I was in the town before, the man now murdered had had a bitter quarrel with another man, a gentleman of note in the town; and a conviction came over me, powerful as a revelation, that it was he who had now committed the murder. I left Jack, and told this to some one connected with the ship, its owner, I think. He laughed at the words, saying that the gentleman I would accuse was of high authority in the town, one of its first magnates. That he had done it, however high he might be, I felt perfectly certain; but nobody would listen to me; nobody would heed so improbable a tale: and, in the trouble this brought me, I awoke. Such trouble! Nothing like it could be felt in real life.

"That was dream the first.

"I lay awake for some little time thinking of it, and then went to sleep again: and this was dream the second.

"The dream seemed to recommence from where it had left off. It was afternoon. I was in a large open carriage, going through the streets of the town, the ship's owner (as I say I think he was) sitting beside me. In passing over a bridge we saw two gentlemen walking towards us arm-in-arm on the footpath, one of them an officer in a dusky old red uniform and cocked hat, the other a tall, evil-looking dark man, who wore a long brown coat and kept his eyes on the ground. Though I had never seen him in my life before, I knew it was the guilty man; he had killed the other, committed the crime in secret: but ere I could speak, he who was sitting with me said, 'There's the gentleman you would have accused this morning. He stands before everybody else in the town. Fancy your accusing him of such a thing!' It seemed to me that I did not answer, could not answer for the pain. That he was guilty I knew, and not

Jack, but I had no means of bringing it home to him. He and the man in uniform walked on in their secure immunity, and I went on in the carriage in my pain. The pain awoke me.

"And now it only remains for me to declare that I have set down this singular dream truthfully, word for word; and I shall seal it up and keep it. It may be of use if any trouble falls upon Jack, as the dream seems to foretell—and of some trouble in store for him he has already felt the shadow. So strangely vivid a dream, and the intense pain it brought and leaves with me, can hardly have visited me for nothing.—ALICE TANERTON."

That was all the paper said. The Squire, poring through his good old spectacles over it, shook his head as Alice pointed out the description of the guilty man, how exactly it tallied with the appearance of Sir Dace Fontaine; but he only repeated Paul the lawyer's words, "One cannot act upon a dream."

"It was Sir Dace; it was Sir Dace," reiterated Alice, clasping her hands piteously. "I am as sure of it as that I hope to go to heaven." And I drove her home in the belief.

There ensued a commotion. Not a commotion to be told to the parish, but a private one amidst ourselves. I never saw a woman in such a fever of excitement as Alice Tanerton was in from that day, or any one take up a matter so warmly.

Captain Tanerton did not adopt her views. He shook his head, and said Sir Dace it could not have been. Sir Dace was at his house in the Marylebone Road at the very hour the calamity happened off Tower Hill. I followed suit, hearing out Jack's word. Was I not at the Marylebone Road that evening myself, playing chess with Coralie?—and was not Sir Dace shut up in his library all the time, and never came out of it?

Alice listened, and looked puzzled to death. But she held to her own opinion. And when a fit of desperate obstinacy takes possession of a woman without rhyme or reason, you cannot shake it. As good try to argue with the whistling wind. She did not pretend to see how it could have been, she said, but Sir Dace was guilty. And she haunted Paul and Chandler's office at Islip, praying them to take the matter up.

At length, to soothe her, and perhaps to prevent her carrying it elsewhere, they promised they would. And of course they had to make some show of doing it.

One evening Tom Chandler came to Crabb Cot and asked to see me alone. "I want you to tell me all the particulars you remember of that fatal night," he began, when I went to him in the Squire's little room. "I have taken down Captain Tanerton's testimony, and I must have yours, Johnny."

"But, are you going to stir in it?"

"We must do something, I suppose. Paul thinks so. I am going to London to-morrow on other matters, and shall use the opportunity to make an inquiry or two. It is rather a strange piece of business altogether," added Mr. Chandler, as he took his place at the table and drew the inkstand towards him. "John Tanerton is innocent. I feel sure of that."

"How strongly Mrs. Tanerton has taken it up!"

"Pretty well for that," answered Tom Chandler, a smile on his good-natured face. "She told us yesterday in the office that it must be the consciousness of guilt which has worried Sir Dace to a skeleton. Now then, we'll begin."

He dotted down my answers to his questions, also what I voluntarily added. Then he took a sheet of paper from his pocket, closely written upon, and compared its statements—they were Tanerton's—with mine. Putting his finger on the paper to mark a place, he looked at me.

"Did Sir Dace speak of Pym or of Captain Tanerton that night, when you were playing chess with Miss Fontaine?"

"Sir Dace did not come into the drawing-room. He had left the dinner-table in a huff to shut himself up in his library, Miss Fontaine said; and he stayed in it."

"Then you did not see Sir Dace at all that night?"

"Oh yes, later—when Captain Tanerton and young Saxby came up to tell him of the death. We then all went down to Ship Street together. You have taken that down."

"True," said Chandler. "Well, I cannot make much out of it as it stands," he concluded, folding the papers and putting them in his pocket-book. "What do you say is the number of the house in the Marylebone Road?"

I told him, and he went away, wishing he could accept my offer of staying to drink tea with us.

"Look here, Chandler," I said to him at the front-door: "why don't you take down Sir Dace Fontaine's evidence, as well as mine and Tanerton's?"

"I have done it," he answered. "I was with Sir Dace to-day. Mrs. Tanerton's suspicions are of course—absurd," he added, making a pause, as if at a loss for a suitable word, "but for her peace of mind, poor lady, we would like to pitch upon the right individual if we can. And as yet he seems to be a myth."

The good ship, Rose of Delhi, came gaily into port, and took up her berth in St. Katharine's Docks as before; for she had been chartered for London. Her owners, the Freemans, wrote at once from Liverpool to Captain Tanerton, begging him to resume command. Jack wrote back, and declined.

How is it that whispers get about! Do the birds in the air carry them?—or the winds of heaven? In some cases it seems impossible that anything else can have done it. Paul and Chandler, John Tanerton and his wife, the Squire and myself: we were the only people cognizant of the new suspicion that Alice was striving to cast on Sir Dace, one and all of us had kept silent lips: and yet, the rumour got abroad. Sir Dace Fontaine was accused of knowing more about Pym's death than he ought to know, and Tom Chandler was in London for the purpose of investigating it. This might not have mattered very much for ordinary ears, but it reached those of Sir Dace.

Coralie Fontaine heard it from Mary Ann Letsom. In Mary Ann's indignation at the report, she spoke it out to Coralie; and Coralie, laughing at the absurdity of the thing, repeated it to Sir Dace. How he received it, or what he said about it, did not transpire.

A stagnant kind of atmosphere seemed to hang over us just then, like the heavy, unnatural calm that precedes the storm. Sir Dace got weaker day by day, more of a shadow; Herbert Tanerton and his brother were still at variance, so far as Jack's future was concerned; and Mr. Chandler seemed to have taken up his abode in London for good.

"Does he never mean to come back?" demanded Alice one day of the Squire: and her lips and cheeks were red with fever as she asked it. The truth was, that some cause of Paul and Chandler's then on at Westminster was prolonging itself out—even when it did begin—unconscionably.

One morning I met Ben Rymer as he was leaving Oxlip Grange. Coralie Fontaine had walked with him to the gate, talking earnestly, their two heads together. Ben shook hands with her and came out, looking as grave as a judge.

"How is Sir Dace?" I asked him. "Getting on?"

"Getting off," responded Ben. "For that's what it will be now; and not long first, unless he mends."

"Is he worse?"

"He is nearly as bad as he can be, to be alive. And yesterday, he must needs go careering off to Islip by himself to transact some business with Paul the lawyer! He was no more fit for it than—than this is," concluded Ben, giving a flick to his silk umbrella as he marched off. Ben went in for silk umbrellas now: in the old days a cotton one would have been too good for him.

"I am so sorry to hear Sir Dace is no better," I said to Coralie Fontaine, who had waited at the gate to speak to me.

Coralie shook her head. Some deep feeling sat in her generally passive face: the tears stood in her eyes.

"Thank you, Johnny Ludlow. It is very sad. I feel sure Mr. Rymer has given up all hope, though he does not say so to me. Verena looks nearly as ill as papa. I wish we had never come to Europe!"

"Sir Dace exerts himself too greatly, Mr. Rymer says."

"Yes; and worries himself also. As if his affairs needed as much as a thought!—I am sure they must be just as straight and smooth as yonder green plain. He had to see Mr. Paul yesterday about some alteration in his will, and went to Islip, instead of sending for Paul here. I thought he would have died when he got home. Papa has a strange restlessness upon him. Good-bye, Johnny. I'd ask you to come in but that things are all so miserable."

It was late in the evening, getting towards bedtime. Mrs. Todhetley had gone upstairs with the face-ache, Tod was over at old Coney's, and I and the Squire were sitting alone, when Thomas surprised us by showing in Tom Chandler. We did not know he was back from London.

"Yes, I got back this evening," said he, as he sat down near the lamp, and spread some papers out on the table. "I am in a bit of a dilemma, Mr. Todhetley; and I am come here at this late hour to put it before you."

Chandler's voice had dropped to a mysterious whisper; his eyes were glancing at the door to make sure it was shut. The Squire pushed up his spectacles and drew his chair nearer. I sat on the opposite side, wondering what was coming.

"That suspicion of Alice Tanerton's—that Sir Dace killed Pym," went on Chandler, his left hand resting on the papers, his eyes on the Squire's. "I think it was a true one."

"A what?" cried the pater.

"A true one. That Sir Dace did kill him."

"Goodness bless me!" gasped the Squire, his good old face taking a lighter tint. "What on earth do you mean, man?"

"Well, I mean just that," answered Chandler. "And I feel myself to be, in consequence, in an uncommonly awkward position. One can't well accuse Sir Dace, a man close upon the grave; and Paul's relative in addition. And yet, Captain Tanerton must be cleared."

"I can't make top or tail of what you mean, Tom Chandler!" cried the Squire, blinking like a bewildered owl. "Don't you think you are dreaming?"

"Wish I was," said Tom, "so far as this business goes. Look here. I'll begin at the beginning and go through the story. You'll understand it then."

"It's more than I do now. Or Johnny, either. Look at him!"

"When Mrs. John Tanerton brought to us that accusation of Sir Dace, on the strength of her dream," began Chandler, after glancing at me, "I thought she must have turned a little crazy. It was a singular dream; there's no denying that; and the exact resemblance to Sir Dace Fontaine of the man she saw in it, was still more singular: so much so, that I could not help being impressed by it. Another thing that strongly impressed me, was Captain Tanerton's testimony: from the moment I heard it and weighed his manner in giving it, I felt sure of his innocence. Revolving these matters in my own mind, I resolved to go to Sir Dace and get him to give me his version of the affair; not in the least endorsing in my own mind her suspicion of him, or hinting at it to him, you understand; simply to get more evidence. I went to Sir Dace, heard what he had to say, and brought away with me a most unpleasant doubt."

"That he was guilty?"

"That he might be. His manner was so confused, himself so agitated when I first spoke. His hands trembled, his lips grew white, He strove to turn it off, saying I had startled him, but I felt a very queer doubt arising in my mind. His narrative had to be drawn from him; it was anything but clear, and full of contradictions. 'Why do you come to me about this?' he asked: 'have you heard anything?' 'I only come to ask you for information,' was my answer: 'Mrs. John Tanerton wants the matter looked into. If her husband is not guilty, he ought to be cleared in the face of the world.' 'Nobody thinks he was guilty,' retorted Sir Dace in a shrill tone of annoyance. 'Nobody was guilty: Pym must have fallen and injured himself.' I came away from the interview, as I tell you, with my doubts very unpleasantly stirred," resumed Chandler; "and it caused me to be more earnest in looking after odds and ends of evidence in London than I otherwise might have been."

"Did you pick up any?"

"Ay, I did. I turned the people at the Marylebone lodgings inside out, so to say; I found out a Mrs. Ball, where Verena Fontaine had hidden herself; and I quite haunted Dame Richenough's in Ship Street, Tower Hill. There I met with Mark Ferrar. A piece of good fortune, for he told me something that—"

"What was it?" gasped the Squire, eagerly.

"Why this—and a most important piece of evidence it is. That night, not many minutes before the fatal accident must have occurred, Ferrar saw Sir Dace Fontaine in Ship Street, watching Pym's room. He was standing in an entry on the opposite side of the street, gazing across at Pym's. This, you perceive, disproves one fact testified to—that Sir Dace spent that evening shut up in his library at home. Instead of that he was absolutely down on the spot."

The Squire rubbed his face like a helpless man. "Why could not Ferrar have said so at the time?" he asked.

"Ferrar attached no importance to it; he thought Sir Dace was but looking over to see whether his daughter was at Pym's. But Ferrar had no opportunity of giving testimony: he sailed away the next morning in the ship. Nothing could exceed his astonishment when I told him in London that Captain Tanerton lay under the suspicion. He has taken Crabb on his way to Worcester to support this testimony if needful, and to impart it privately to Tanerton."

"Well, it all seems a hopeless puzzle to me," returned the pater. "Why on earth did not Jack speak out more freely, and say he was not guilty?"

"I don't know. The fact, that Sir Dace did go out that night," continued Chandler, "was confirmed by one of the maids in the Marylebone Road—Maria; a smart girl with curled hair. She says Sir Dace had not been many minutes in the library that night, to which he went straight from the dinner-table in a passion, when she saw him leave it again, catch up his hat with a jerk as he passed through the hall, and go out at the front-door. It was just after Ozias had been to ask him whether he would take some coffee, and got sent away with a flea in his ear. Whether or not Sir Dace came in during the evening, Maria does not know; he may, or may not, have done so, but she did see him come home in a cab at ten o'clock, or soon after it. She was gossiping with the maids at a house some few doors off, when a cab stopped near to them, Sir Dace got out of it, paid the man, and walked on to his own door. Maria supposed the driver had made a mistake in the number. So you see there can be no doubt that Sir Dace was out that night."

"He was certainly in soon after ten," I remarked. "Verena came home about that time, and she saw him downstairs."

"Don't you bring her name up, Johnny," corrected the Squire. "That young woman led to all the mischief. Running away, as she did—and sending us off to that wax-work show in search of her! Fine figures they cut, some of those dumb things!"

"I found also," resumed Chandler, turning over his papers, on which he had looked from time to time, "that Sir Dace met with one or two slight personal mishaps that night. He sprained his wrist, accounting for it the next morning by saying he had slipped in getting into bed; and he lost a little piece out of his shirt-front."

"Out of his shirt front!"

"Just here," and Chandler touched the middle button of his shirt. "The button-hole and a portion of the linen round it had been torn away. Nothing would have been known of that but for the laundress. She brought the shirt back before putting it into water, lest it should be said she had done it in the washing. Maria remembered this, and told me. A remarkably intelligent girl, that."

"Did Maria—I remember the girl—suspect anything?" asked the Squire.

"Nothing whatever. She does not now; I accounted otherwise for my inquiries. Altogether, what with these facts I have told you, and a few minor items, and Ferrar's evidence, I can draw but one conclusion—that Sir Dace Fontaine killed Pym."

"I never heard such a strange thing!" cried the pater. "And what's to be done?"

"That's the question," said Chandler. "What is to be done?" And he left us with the doubt.

Well, it turned out to be quite true; but I have not space here to go more into detail. Sir Dace Fontaine was guilty, and the dream was a true dream.

"Did you suspect him?" the Squire asked privately of Jack, who was taken into counsel the next day.

"No, I never suspected Sir Dace," Jack answered. "I suspected some one else—Verena."

"No!"

"I did. About half-past eight o'clock that night, Ferrar had seen a young lady—or somebody dressed as one—watching Pym's house from the opposite entry: just where, it now appears, he later saw Sir Dace. Ferrar thought it was Verena Fontaine. A little later, in fact just after the calamity must have occurred, Alfred Saxby also saw a young lady running from the direction of the house, whom he also took to be Verena. Ferrar and I came to the same conclusion—I don't know about Saxby—that Verena must have been present when it happened. I thought that, angry at the state Pym was in, she might have given him a push in her vexation, perhaps inadvertently, and that he fell. Who knew?"

"But Verena was elsewhere that evening, you know; at a concert."

"I knew she said so; but I did not believe it. Of course I know now that both Ferrar and Saxby were mistaken; that it was somebody else they saw, who bore, one must imagine, some general resemblance to her."

"Well, I think you might have known better," cried the Squire.

"Yes, I suppose I ought to. But, before the inquest had terminated, I chanced to be alone with Verena; and her manner—nay, her words, two or three she said—seemed to imply her guilt, and also a consciousness that I must be aware of it. I had no doubt at all from that hour."

"And is it for that reason, consideration for her, that you have partially allowed suspicion to rest upon yourself?" pursued the Squire, hotly.

"Of course. How could I be the means of throwing it upon a defenceless girl?"

"Well, John Tanerton, you are a chivalrous goose!"

"Verena must have known the truth all along."

"That's not probable," contended the Squire. "And Chandler wants to know what is to be done."

"Nothing all all, that I can see," answered Jack. "Sir Dace is not in a condition to have trouble thrown upon him."

Good Jack! generous Jack! There are not many such self-denying spirits in the world.

And what would have been done is beyond guessing, had Sir Dace not solved the difficulty himself. Solved it by dying.

But I must first tell of a little matter that happened. Although we had heard what we had, one could not treat the man cavalierly, and the Squire—just as good at heart as Jack—went up to make inquiries at Oxlip Grange, as usual. One day he and Colonel Letsom strolled up together, and were asked to walk in. Sir Dace wished to see them.

"If ever you saw a living skeleton, it's what he is," cried the Squire to us when he came home. "It is in the nature of the disease, I believe, that he should be. Dress him up in his shroud, and you'd take him for nothing but bones."

Sir Dace was in the easy-chair by his bedroom fire, Coralie sitting with him. By his side stood a round table with papers and letters upon it.

"I am glad you have chanced to call," he said to them, as he sent Coralie away. "I wanted my signature witnessed by some one in influential authority. You are both county magistrates."

"The signature to your will," cried the Squire, falling to that conclusion.

"Not my will," answered Sir Dace. "That is settled."

He turned to the table, his long, emaciated, trembling fingers singling out a document that lay upon it. "This is a declaration," he said, "which I have written out myself, being of sound mind, you perceive, and which I wish to sign in your presence. I testify that every word written in it is truth; I, a dying man, swear that it is so, before God."

His shaky hands scrawled his signature, Dace Fontaine; and the Squire and Colonel Letsom added theirs to it. Sir Dace then sealed up the paper, and made them each affix his seal also. He then tottered to a cabinet standing by the bed's head, and locked it up in it.

"You will know where to find it when I am gone," he said. "I wish some one of you to read it aloud, after the funeral, to those assembled here. When my will shall have been read, then read this."

On the third day after this, at evening, Sir Dace Fontaine died. We heard no more about anything until the day of the funeral, which took place on the following Monday. Sir Dace left a list of those he wished invited to it, and they went. Sir Robert Tenby, Mr. Brandon, Colonel Letsom and his eldest son; the parsons of Timberdale, Crabb, and Islip; the three doctors who had attended him; old Paul and Tom Chandler; Captain Tanerton, and ourselves.

He was buried at Islip, by his own directions. And when we got back to the Grange, after leaving him in the cold churchyard, Mr. Paul read out the will. Coralie and Verena sat in the room in their deep mourning. Coralie's eyes were dry, but Verena sobbed incessantly.

Apart from a few legacies, one of which was to his servant Ozias, his property was left to his two daughters, in equal shares. The chief legacy, a large one, was left to John Tanerton—three thousand pounds. You should have seen Jack's face of astonishment as he heard it. Herbert looked as if he could not believe his ears. And Verena glanced across at Jack with a happy flush.

"Papa charged me, just before he died, to say that a sealed paper of his would be found in his private cabinet, which was to be read out now," spoke Coralie, in the pause which ensued, as old Paul's voice ceased. "He said Colonel Letsom and Mr. Todhetley would know where to find it," she added; breaking down with a sob.

The paper was fetched, and old Paul was requested to read it. So he broke the seals.

You may have guessed what it was: a declaration of his guilt—if guilt it could be called. In a straightforward manner he stated the particulars of that past night: and the following is a summary of them.

Sir Dace went out again that night after dinner, not in secret, or with any idea of secrecy; it simply chanced, he supposed, that no one saw him go. He was too uneasy about Verena to rest; he fully believed her to be with Pym; and he went down to Ship Street. Before entering the street he dismissed the cab, and proceeded cautiously to reconnoitre, believing that if he were seen, Pym would be capable of concealing Verena. After looking about till he was tired, he took up his station opposite Pym's lodgings—which seemed to be empty—and stayed, watching, until close upon nine o'clock, when he saw Pym enter them. Before he had time to go across, the landlady began to close the shutters; while she was doing it, Captain Tanerton came up, and went in. Captain Tanerton came out in a minute or two, and walked quickly back up the street: he, Sir Dace, would have gone after him to ask him whether Verena was indoors with Pym, or not, but the captain's steps were too fleet for him. Sir Dace then crossed over, opened the street-door, and entered Pym's parlour. A short, sharp quarrel ensued. Pym was in liquor, and—consequently—insolent. In the heat of passion Sir Dace—he was a strong man then—seized Pym's arm, and shook him. Pym flew at him in return like a tiger, twisted his wrist round, and tore his shirt. Sir Dace was furious then; he struck him a powerful blow on the head—behind the ear no doubt, as the surgeons testified afterwards—and Pym fell. Leaving him there, Sir Dace quitted the house quietly, never glancing at the thought that the blow could be fatal. But, when seated in a cab on the way home, the idea suddenly occurred to him—what if he had killed Pym? The conviction, though he knew not why, or wherefore, that he had killed him, took hold of him, and he went into his house, a terrified man. The rest was known, the manuscript went on to say. He allowed people to remain in the belief that he had not been out-of-doors that night: though how bitterly he repented not having declared the truth at the time, none could know, save God. He now, a dying man, about to appear before that God, who had been full of mercy to him, declared that this was the whole truth, and he further declared that he had no intention whatever of injuring Pym; all he thought was, to knock him down for his insolence. He hoped the world would forgive him, though he had never forgiven himself; and he prayed his daughters to forgive him, especially Verena. He would counsel her to return to the West Indies, and marry George Bazalgette.

That ended the declaration: and an astounding surprise it must have been to most of the eager listeners. But not one ventured to make any comment on it, good or bad. The legacy to John Tanerton was understood now. Verena crossed the room as we were filing out, and put her two hands into his.

"I have had a dreadful fear upon me that it was papa," she whispered to him, the tears running down her cheeks. "Nay, worse than a fear: a conviction. I think you have had the same, Captain Tanerton, and that you have generously done your best to screen him; and I thank you with my whole heart."

"But, indeed," began Jack—and pulled himself up, short.

"Let me tell you all," said Verena. "I saw papa come in that night: I mean to our lodgings in the Marylebone Road, so I knew he had been out. It was just past ten o'clock: Ozias saw him too—but he is silent and faithful. I did not want papa to see me; fate, I suppose, made me back into that little room, papa's library, until he should have gone upstairs. He did not go up; he came into the room: and I hid myself behind the window curtain. I cannot describe to you how strange papa looked; dreadful; and he groaned and flung up his arms as one does in despair. It frightened me so much that I said nothing to anybody. Still I had not the key to it: I thought it must be about me: and the torn shirt—for I saw that, and saw him button his coat over it—I supposed he had, himself, done accidentally. I drew one of the glass doors softly open, got out that way, and up to the drawing-room. Then you came in with the news of Edward's death. At first, for a day or so, I thought as others did—that suspicion lay on you. But, gradually, all these facts impressed themselves on my mind in their startling reality; and I felt, I saw, it could have been no other than he—my poor father. Oh, Captain Tanerton, forgive him! Forgive me!"

"There's nothing to forgive; I am sorry it has come out now," whispered Jack, deeming it wise to leave it at that, and he stooped and gave her the kiss of peace.

So this was the end of it. Of the affair which had so unpleasantly puzzled the world, and tried Jack.

Jack, loyal, honest-hearted Jack, shook hands with everybody, giving a double shake to Herbert's, and went forthwith down to Liverpool.

"I will take the Rose of Delhi again, now," he said to the Freemans. "For this next voyage, at any rate."

"And for many a one after it, we hope, Captain Tanerton," was their warm answer. And Jack and his bright face went direct from the office to New Brighton, to tell Aunt Dean.

And what became of the Miss Fontaines, you would like to ask? Well, I have not time at present to tell you about Coralie; I don't know when I shall have. But, if you'll believe me, Verena took her father's advice, sailed back over the seas, and married George Bazalgette.

A CURIOUS EXPERIENCE

What I am about to tell of took place during the last year of John Whitney's life, now many years ago. We could never account for it, or understand it: but it occurred (at least, so far as our experience of it went) just as I relate it.

It was not the custom for schools to give a long holiday at Easter then: one week at most. Dr. Frost allowed us from the Thursday in Passion week, to the following Thursday; and many of the boys spent it at school.

Easter was late that year, and the weather lovely. On the Wednesday in Easter week, the Squire and Mrs. Todhetley drove over to spend the day at Whitney Hall, Tod and I being with them. Sir John and Lady Whitney were beginning to be anxious about John's health—their eldest son. He had been ailing since the previous Christmas, and he seemed to grow thinner and weaker. It was so perceptible when he got home from school this Easter, that Sir John put himself into a flurry (he was just like the Squire in that and in many another way), and sent an express to Worcester for Henry Carden, asking him to bring Dr. Hastings with him. They came. John wanted care, they said, and they could not discover any specific disease at present. As to his returning to school, they both thought that question might be left with the boy himself. John told them he should prefer to go back, and laughed a little at this fuss being made over him: he should soon be all right, he said; people were apt to lose strength more or less in the spring. He was sixteen then, a slender, upright boy, with a delicate, thoughtful face, dreamy, grey-blue eyes and brown hair, and he was ever gentle, sweet-tempered, and considerate. Sir John related to the Squire what the doctors had said, avowing that he could not "make much out of it."

In the afternoon, when we were out-of-doors on the lawn in the hot sunshine, listening to the birds singing and the cuckoo calling, Featherston came in, the local doctor, who saw John nearly every day. He was a tall, grey, hard-worked man, with a face of care. After talking a few moments with John and his mother, he turned to the rest of us on the grass. The Squire and Sir John were sitting on a garden bench, some wine and lemonade on a little table between them. Featherston shook hands.

"Will you take some?" asked Sir John.

"I don't mind a glass of lemonade with a dash of sherry in it," answered Featherston, lifting his hat to rub his brow. "I have been walking beyond Goose Brook and back, and upon my word it is as hot as midsummer."

"Ay, it is," assented Sir John. "Help yourself, doctor."

He filled a tumbler with what he wanted, brought it over to the opposite bench, and sat down by Mrs. Todhetley. John and his mother were at the other end of it; I sat on the arm. The rest of them, with Helen and Anna, had gone strolling away; to the North Pole, for all we knew.

"John still says he shall go back to school," began Lady Whitney, to Featherston.

"Ay; to-morrow's the day, isn't it, John? Black Thursday, some of you boys call it."

"I like school," said John.

"Almost a pity, though," continued Featherston, looking up and about him. "To be out at will all day in this soft air, under the blue skies and the sunbeams, might be of more benefit to you, Master John, than being cooped up in a close school-room."

"You hear, John!" cried Lady Whitney. "I wish you would persuade him to take a longer rest at home, Mr. Featherston!"

Mr. Featherston stooped for his tumbler, which he had lodged on the smooth grass, and took another drink before replying. "If you and John would follow my advice, Lady Whitney, I'd give it."

"Yes?" cried she, all eagerness.

"Take John somewhere for a fortnight, and let him go back to school at the end," said the surgeon. "That would do him good."

"Why, of course it would," called out Sir John, who had been listening. "And I say it shall be done. John, my boy, you and your mother shall go to the seaside—to Aberystwith."

"Well, I don't think I should quite say that, Sir John," said Featherston again. "The seaside would be all very well in this warm weather; but it may not last, it may change to cold and frost. I should suggest one of the inland watering-places, as they are called: where there's a Spa, and a Pump Room, and a Parade, and lots of gay company. It would be lively for him, and a thorough change."

"What a nice idea!" cried Lady Whitney, who was the most unsophisticated woman in the world. "Such as Pumpwater."

"Such as Pumpwater: the very place," agreed Featherston. "Well, were I you, my lady, I would try it for a couple of weeks. Let John take a companion with him; one of his schoolfellows. Here's Johnny Ludlow: he might do."

"I'd rather have Johnny Ludlow than any one," said John.

Remarking that his time was up, for a patient waited for him, and that he must leave us to settle the question, Featherston took his departure. But it appeared to be settled already.

"Johnny can go," spoke up the Squire. "The loss of a fortnight's lessons is not much, compared with doing a little service to a friend. Charming spots are those inland watering-places, and Pumpwater is about the best of them all."

"We must take lodgings," said Lady Whitney presently, when they had done expatiating upon the gauds and glories of Pumpwater. "To stay at an hotel would be so noisy; and expensive besides."

"I know of some," cried Mrs. Todhetley, in sudden thought. "If you could get into Miss Gay's rooms, you would be well off. Do you remember them?"—turning to the Squire. "We stayed at her house on our way from—"

"Why, bless me, to be sure I do," he interrupted. "Somebody had given us Miss Gay's address, and we drove straight to it to see if she had rooms at liberty; she had, and took us in at once. We were so comfortable there that we stayed at Pumpwater three days instead of two."

It was hastily decided that Mrs. Todhetley should write to Miss Gay, and she went indoors to do so. All being well, Lady Whitney meant to start on Saturday.

Miss Gay's answer came punctually, reaching Whitney Hall on Friday morning. It was addressed to Mrs. Todhetley, but Lady Whitney, as had been arranged, opened it. Miss Gay wrote that she should be much pleased to receive Lady Whitney. Her house, as it chanced, was then quite empty; a family, who had been with her six weeks, had just left: so Lady Whitney might take her choice of the rooms, which she would keep vacant until Saturday. In conclusion, she begged Mrs. Todhetley to notice that her address was changed. The old house was too small to accommodate the many kind friends who patronized her, and she had moved into a larger house, superior to the other and in the best position.

Thus all things seemed to move smoothly for our expedition; and we departed by train on the Saturday morning for Pumpwater.

It was a handsome house, standing in the high-road, between the parade and the principal street, and rather different from the houses on each side of it, inasmuch as that it was detached and had a narrow slip of gravelled ground in front. In fact, it looked too large and handsome for a lodging-house; and Lady Whitney, regarding it from the fly which had brought us from the station, wondered whether the driver had made a mistake. It was built of red-brick, with white stone facings; the door, set in a pillared portico, stood in the middle, and three rooms, each with a bay-window, lay one above another on both sides.

But in a moment we saw it was all right. A slight, fair woman, in a slate silk gown, came out and announced herself as Miss Gay. She had a mild, pleasant voice, and a mild, pleasant face, with light falling curls, the fashion then for every one, and she wore a lace cap, trimmed with pink. I took to her and to her face at once.

"I am glad to be here," said Lady Whitney, cordially, in answer to Miss Gay's welcome. "Is there any one who can help with the luggage? We have not brought either man or maid-servant."

"Oh dear, yes, my lady. Please let me show you indoors, and then leave all to me. Susannah! Oh, here you are, Susannah! Where's Charity?—my cousin and chief help-mate, my lady."

A tall, dark person, about Miss Gay's own age, which might be forty, wearing brown ribbon in her hair and a purple bow at her throat, dropped a curtsy to Lady Whitney. This was Susannah. She looked strong-minded and capable. Charity, who came running up the kitchen-stairs, was a smiling young woman-servant, with a coarse apron tied round her, and red arms bared to the elbow.

There were four sitting-rooms on the ground-floor: two in front, with their large bay-windows; two at the back, looking out upon some bright, semi-public gardens.

"A delightful house!" exclaimed Lady Whitney to Miss Gay, after she had looked about a little. "I will take one of these front-rooms for our sitting-room," she added, entering, haphazard, the one on the right of the entrance-hall, and putting down her bag and parasol. "This one, I think, Miss Gay."

"Very good, my lady. And will you now be pleased to walk upstairs and fix upon the bedrooms."

Lady Whitney seemed to fancy the front of the house. "This room shall be my son's; and I should like to have the opposite one for myself," she said, rather hesitatingly, knowing they must be the two best chambers of all. "Can I?"

Miss Gay seemed quite willing. We were in the room over our sitting-room on the right of the house looking to the front. The objection, if it could be called one, came from Susannah.

"You can have the other room, certainly, my lady; but I think the young gentleman would find this one noisy, with all the carriages and carts that pass by, night and morning. The back-rooms are much more quiet."

"But I like noise," put in John; "it seems like company to me. If I could do as I would, I'd never sleep in the country."

"One of the back-rooms is very lively, sir; it has a view of the turning to the Pump Room," persisted Susannah, a sort of suppressed eagerness in her tone; and it struck me that she did not want John to have this front-chamber. "I think you would like it best."

"No," said John, turning round from the window, out of which he had been looking, "I will have this. I shall like to watch the shops down that turning opposite, and the people who go into them."

No more was said. John took this chamber, which was over our sitting-room, Lady Whitney had the other front-chamber, and I had a very good one at the back of John's. And thus we settled down.

Pumpwater is a nice place, as you would know if I gave its proper name, bright and gay, and our house was in the best of situations. The principal street, with its handsome shops, lay to our right; the Parade, leading to the Spa and Pump Room, to our left, and company and carriages were continually passing by. We visited some of the shops and took a look at the Pump Room.

In the evening, when tea was over, Miss Gay came in to speak of the breakfast. Lady Whitney asked her to sit down for a little chat. She wanted to ask about the churches.

"What a very nice house this is!" again observed Lady Whitney presently: for the more she saw of it, the better she found it. "You must pay a high rent for it, Miss Gay."

"Not so high as your ladyship might think," was the answer; "not high at all for what it is. I paid sixty pounds for the little house I used to be in, and I pay only seventy for this."

"Only seventy!" echoed Lady Whitney, in surprise. "How is it you get it so cheaply?"

A waggonette, full of people, was passing just then; Miss Gay seemed to want to watch it by before she answered. We were sitting in the dusk with the blinds up.

"For one thing, it had been standing empty for some time, and I suppose Mr. Bone, the agent, was glad to have my offer," replied Miss Gay, who seemed to be as fond of talking as any one else is, once set on. "It had belonged to a good old family, my lady, but they got embarrassed and put it up for sale some six or seven years ago. A Mr. Calson bought it. He had come to Pumpwater about that time from foreign lands; and he and his wife settled down in the house. A puny, weakly little woman she was, who seemed to get weaklier instead of stronger, and in a year or two she died. After her death her husband grew ill; he went away for change of air, and died in London; and the house was left to a little nephew living over in Australia."

"And has the house been vacant ever since?" asked John.

"No, sir. At first it was let furnished, then unfurnished. But it had been vacant some little time when I applied to Mr. Bone. I concluded he thought it better to let it at a low rent than for it to stand empty."

"It must cost you incessant care and trouble, Miss Gay, to conduct a house like this—when you are full," remarked Lady Whitney.

"It does," she answered. "One's work seems never done—and I cannot, at that, give satisfaction to all. Ah, my lady, what a difference there is in people!—you would never think it. Some are so kind and considerate to me, so anxious not to give trouble unduly, and so satisfied with all I do that it is a pleasure to serve them: while others make gratuitous work and trouble from morning till night, and treat me as if I were just a dog under their feet. Of course when we are full I have another servant in, two sometimes."

"Even that must leave a great deal for yourself to do and see to."

"The back is always fitted to the burden," sighed Miss Gay. "My father was a farmer in this county, as his ancestors had been before him, farming his three hundred acres of land, and looked upon as a man of substance. My mother made the butter, saw to the poultry, and superintended her household generally: and we children helped her. Farmers' daughters then did not spend their days in playing the piano and doing fancy work, or expect to be waited upon like ladies born."

"They do now, though," said Lady Whitney.

"So I was ready to turn my hand to anything when hard times came—not that I had thought I should have to do it," continued Miss Gay. "But my father's means dwindled down. Prosperity gave way to adversity. Crops failed; the stock died off; two of my brothers fell into trouble and it cost a mint of money to extricate them. Altogether, when father died, but little of his savings remained to us. Mother took a house in the town here, to let lodgings, and I came with her. She is dead, my lady, and I am left."

The silent tears were running down poor Miss Gay's cheeks.

"It is a life of struggle, I am sure," spoke Lady Whitney, gently. "And not deserved, Miss Gay."

"But there's another life to come," spoke John, in a half-whisper, turning to Miss Gay from the large bay-window. "None of us will be overworked there."

Miss Gay stealthily wiped her cheeks. "I do not repine," she said, humbly. "I have been enabled to rub on and keep my head above water, and to provide little comforts for mother in her need; and I gratefully thank God for it."

The bells of the churches, ringing out at eight o'clock, called us up in the morning. Lady Whitney was downstairs, first. I next. Susannah, who waited upon us, had brought up the breakfast. John followed me in.

"I hope you have slept well, my boy," said Lady Whitney, kissing him. "I have."

"So have I," I put in.

"Then you and the mother make up for me, Johnny," he said; "for I have not slept at all."

"Oh, John!" exclaimed his mother.

"Not a wink all night long," added John. "I can't think what was the matter with me."

Susannah, then stooping to take the sugar-basin out of the side-board, rose, turned sharply round and fixed her eyes on John. So curious an expression was on her face that I could but notice it.

"Do you not think it was the noise, sir?" she said to him. "I knew that room would be too noisy for you."

"Why, the room was as quiet as possible," he answered. "A few carriages rolled by last night—and I liked to hear them; but that was all over before midnight; and I have heard none this morning."

"Well, sir, I'm sure you would be more comfortable in a backroom," contended Susannah.

"It was a strange bed," said John. "I shall sleep all the sounder to-night."

Breakfast was half over when John found he had left his watch upstairs, on the drawers. I went to fetch it.

The door was open, and I stepped to the drawers, which stood just inside. Miss Gay and Susannah were making the bed and talking, too busy to see or hear me. A lot of things lay on the white cloth, and at first I could not see the watch.

"He declares he has not slept at all; not at all," Susannah was saying with emphasis. "If you had only seconded me yesterday, Harriet, they need not have had this room. But you never made a word of objection; you gave in at once."

"Well, I saw no reason to make it," said Miss Gay, mildly. "If I were to give in to your fancies, Susannah, I might as well shut up the room. Visitors must get used to it."

The watch had been partly hidden under one of John's neckties. I caught it up and decamped.

We went to church after breakfast. The first hymn sung was that one beginning, "Brief life."

"Brief life is here our portion;
Brief sorrow, short-lived care.
The life that knows no ending,
The tearless life, is there."

As the verses went on, John touched my elbow: "Miss Gay," he whispered; his eyelashes moist with the melody of the music. I have often thought since that we might have seen by these very moods of John—his thoughts bent upon heaven more than upon earth—that his life was swiftly passing.

There's not much to tell of that Sunday. We dined in the middle of the day; John fell asleep after dinner; and in the evening we attended church again. And I think every one was ready for bed when bedtime came. I know I was.

Therefore it was all the more surprising when, the next morning, John said he had again not slept.

"What, not at all!" exclaimed his mother.

"No, not at all. As I went to bed, so I got up—sleepless."

"I never heard of such a thing!" cried Lady Whitney. "Perhaps, John, you were too tired to sleep?"

"Something of that sort," he answered. "I felt both tired and sleepy when I got into bed; particularly so. But I had no sleep: not a wink. I could not lie still, either; I was frightfully restless all night; just as I was the night before. I suppose it can't be the bed?"

"Is the bed not comfortable?" asked his mother.

"It seems as comfortable a bed as can be when I first lie down in it. And then I grow restless and uneasy."

"It must be the restlessness of extreme fatigue," said Lady Whitney. "I fear the journey was rather too much for you my dear."

"Oh, I shall be all right as soon as I can sleep, mamma."

We had a surprise that morning. John and I were standing before a tart-shop, our eyes glued to the window, when a voice behind us called out, "Don't they look nice, boys!" Turning round, there stood

Henry Carden of Worcester, arm-in-arm with a little white-haired gentleman. Lady Whitney, in at the fishmonger's next door, came out while he was shaking hands with us.

"Dear me!—is it you?" she cried to Mr. Carden.

"Ay," said he in his pleasant manner, "here am I at Pumpwater! Come all this way to spend a couple of days with my old friend: Dr. Tambourine," added the surgeon, introducing him to Lady Whitney. Any way, that was the name she understood him to say. John thought he said Tamarind, and I Carrafin. The street was noisy.

The doctor seemed to be chatty and courteous, a gentleman of the old school. He said his wife should do herself the honour of calling upon Lady Whitney if agreeable; Lady Whitney replied that it would be. He and Mr. Carden, who would be starting for Worcester by train that afternoon, walked with us up the Parade to the Pump Room. How a chance meeting like this in a strange place makes one feel at home in it!

The name turned out to be Parafin. Mrs. Parafin called early in the afternoon, on her way to some entertainment at the Pump Room: a chatty, pleasant woman, younger than her husband. He had retired from practice, and they lived in a white villa outside the town.

And what with looking at the shops, and parading up and down the public walks, and the entertainment at the Pump Room, to which we went with Mrs. Parafin, and all the rest of it, we felt uncommonly sleepy when night came, and were beginning to regard Pumpwater as a sort of Eden.

"Johnny, have you slept?"

I was brushing my hair at the glass, under the morning sun, when John Whitney, half-dressed, and pale and languid, opened my door and thus accosted me.

"Yes; like a top. Why? Is anything the matter, John?"

"See here," said he, sinking into the easy-chair by the fireplace, "it is an odd thing, but I have again not slept. I can't sleep."

I put my back against the dressing-table and stood looking down at him, brush in hand. Not slept again! It was an odd thing.

"But what can be the reason, John?"

"I am beginning to think it must be the room."

"How can it be the room?"

"I don't know. There's nothing the matter with the room that I can see; it seems well-ventilated; the chimney's not stopped up. Yet this is the third night that I cannot get to sleep in it."

"But why can you not get to sleep?" I persisted.

"I say I don't know why. Each night I have been as sleepy as possible; last night I could hardly undress I was so sleepy; but no sooner am I in bed than sleep goes right away from me. Not only that: I grow terribly restless."

Weighing the problem this way and that, an idea struck me.

"John, do you think it is nervousness?"

"How can it be? I never was nervous in my life."

"I mean this: not sleeping the first night, you may have got nervous about it the second and third."

He shook his head. "I have been nothing of the kind, Johnny. But look here: I hardly see what I am to do. I cannot go on like this without sleep; yet, if I tell the mother again, she'll say the air of the place does not suit me and run away from it—"

"Suppose we change rooms to-night, John?" I interrupted. "I can't think but you would sleep here. If you do not, why, it must be the air of Pumpwater, and the sooner you are out of it the better."

"You wouldn't mind changing rooms for one night?" he said, wistfully.

"Mind! Why, I shall be the gainer. Yours is the better room of the two."

At that it was settled; nothing to be said to any one about the bargain. We did not want to be kidnapped out of Pumpwater—and Lady Whitney had promised us a night at the theatre.

Two or three more acquaintances were made, or found out, that day. Old Lady Scott heard of us, and came to call on Lady Whitney; they used to be intimate. She introduced some people at the Pump Room. Altogether, it seemed that we should not lack society.

Night came; and John and I went upstairs together. He undressed in his own room, and I in mine; and then we made the exchange. I saw him into my bed and wished him a good-night.

"Good-night, Johnny," he answered. "I hope you will sleep."

"Little doubt of that, John. I always sleep when I have nothing to trouble me. A very good-night to you."

I had nothing to trouble me, and I was as sleepy as could be; and yet, I did not and could not sleep. I lay quiet as usual after getting into bed, yielding to the expected sleep, and I shut my eyes and never thought but it was coming.

Instead of that, came restlessness. A strange restlessness quite foreign to me, persistent and unaccountable. I tossed and turned from side to side, and I had not had a wink of sleep at day dawn, nor any symptom of it. Was I growing nervous? Had I let the feeling creep over me that I had suggested to John? No; not that I was aware of. What could it be?

Unrefreshed and weary, I got up at the usual hour, and stole silently into the other room. John was in a deep sleep, his calm face lying still upon the pillow. Though I made no noise, my presence awoke him.

"Oh, Johnny!" he exclaimed, "I have had such a night."

"Bad?"

"No; good. I went to sleep at once and never woke till now. It has done me a world of good. And you?"

"I? Oh well, I don't think I slept quite as well as I did here; it was a strange bed," I answered, carelessly.

The next night the same plan was carried out, he taking my bed; I his. And again John slept through it, while I did not sleep at all. I said nothing about it: John Whitney's comfort was of more importance than mine.

The third night came. This night we had been to the theatre, and had laughed ourselves hoarse, and been altogether delighted. No sooner was I in bed, and feeling dead asleep, than the door slowly opened and in came Lady Whitney, a candle in one hand, a wineglass in the other.

"John, my dear," she began, "your tonic was forgotten this evening. I think you had better take it now. Featherston said, you know— Good gracious!" she broke off. "Why, it is Johnny!"

I could hardly speak for laughing, her face presented such a picture of astonishment. Sitting up in bed, I told her all; there was no help for it: that we had exchanged beds, John not having been able to sleep in this one.

"And do you sleep well in it?" she asked.

"No, not yet. But I feel very sleepy to-night, dear Lady Whitney."

"Well, you are a good lad, Johnny, to do this for him; and to say nothing about it," she concluded, as she went away with the candle and the tonic.

Dead sleepy though I was, I could not get to sleep. It would be simply useless to try to describe my sensations. Each succeeding night they had been more marked. A strange, discomforting restlessness pervaded me; a feeling of uneasiness, I could not tell why or wherefore. I saw nothing uncanny, I heard nothing; nevertheless, I felt just as though some uncanny presence was in the room, imparting a sense of semi-terror. Once or twice, when I nearly dozed off from sheer weariness, I started up in real terror, wide awake again, my hair and face damp with a nameless fear.

I told this at breakfast, in answer to Lady Whitney's questions: John confessed that precisely the same sensations had attacked him the three nights he lay in the bed. Lady Whitney declared she never heard the like; and she kept looking at us alternately, as if doubting what could be the matter with us, or whether we had taken scarlet-fever.

On this morning, Friday, a letter came from Sir John, saying that Featherston was coming to Pumpwater. Anxious on the score of his son, he was sending Featherston to see him, and take back a report. "I think he would stay a couple of days if you made it convenient to entertain him, and it would be a little holiday for the poor hard-worked man," wrote Sir John, who was just as kind-hearted as his wife.

"To be sure I will," said Lady Whitney. "He shall have that room; I dare say he won't say he cannot sleep in it: it will be more comfortable for him than getting a bed at an hotel. Susannah shall put a small bed into the back-room for Johnny. And when Featherston is gone, I will take the room myself. I am not like you two silly boys—afraid of lying awake."

Mr. Featherston arrived late that evening, with his grey face of care and his thin frame. He said he could hardly recall the time when he had had as much as two days' holiday, and thanked Lady Whitney for receiving him. That night John and I occupied the back-room, having conducted Featherston in state to the front, with two candles; and both of us slept excellently well.

At breakfast Featherston began talking about the air. He had always believed Pumpwater to have a rather soporific air, but supposed he must be mistaken. Any way, it had kept him awake; and it was not a little that did that for him.

"Did you not sleep well?" asked Lady Whitney.

"I did not sleep at all; did not get a wink of it all night long. Never mind," he added with a good-natured laugh, "I shall sleep all the sounder to-night."

But he did not. The next morning (Sunday) he looked grave and tired, and ate his breakfast almost in silence. When we had finished, he said he should like, with Lady Whitney's permission, to speak to the landlady. Miss Gay came in at once: in a light fresh print gown and black silk apron.

"Ma'am," began Featherston, politely, "something is wrong with that bedroom overhead. What is it?"

"Something wrong, sir?" repeated Miss Gay, her meek face flushing. "Wrong in what way, sir?"

"I don't know," answered Featherston; "I thought perhaps you could tell me: any way, it ought to be seen to. It is something that scares away sleep. I give you my word, ma'am, I never had two such restless nights in succession in all my life. Two such strange nights. It was not only that sleep would not come near me; that's nothing uncommon you may say; but I lay in a state of uneasy, indescribable restlessness. I have examined the room again this morning, and I can see nothing to induce it, yet a cause there must undoubtedly be. The paper is not made of arsenic, I suppose?"

"The paper is pale pink, sir," observed Miss Gay. "I fancy it is the green papers that have arsenic in them."

"Ay; well. I think there must be poison behind the paper; in the paste, say," went on Featherston. "Or perhaps another paper underneath has arsenic in it?"

Miss Gay shook her head, as she stood with her hand on the back of a chair. Lady Whitney had asked her to sit down, but she declined. "When I came into the house six months ago, that room was re-papered, and I saw that the walls were thoroughly scraped. If you think there's anything—anything in the room that prevents people sleeping, and—and could point out what it is, I'm sure, sir, I should be glad to remedy it," said Miss Gay, with uncomfortable hesitation.

But this was just what Featherston, for all he was a doctor, could not point out. That something was amiss with the room, he felt convinced, but he had not discovered what it was, or how it could be remedied.

"After lying in torment half the night, I got up and lighted my candle," said he. "I examined the room and opened the window to let the cool breeze blow in. I could find nothing likely to keep me awake, no stuffed-up chimney, no accumulation of dust, and I shut the window and got into bed again. I was pretty cool by that time and reckoned I should sleep. Not a bit of it, ma'am. I lay more restless than ever, with the same unaccountable feeling of discomfort and depression upon me. Just as I had felt the night before."

"I am very sorry, sir," sighed Miss Gay, taking her hand from the chair to depart. "If the room is close, or anything of that—"

"But it is not close, ma'am. I don't know what it is. And I'm sure I hope you will be able to find it out, and get it remedied," concluded Featherston as she withdrew.

We then told him of our experience, John's and mine. It amazed him. "What an extraordinary thing!" he exclaimed. "One would think the room was haunted."

"Do you believe in haunted rooms, sir?" asked John.

"Well, I suppose such things are," he answered. "Folks say so. If haunted houses exist, why not haunted rooms?"

"It must lie in the Pumpwater air," said Lady Whitney, who was too practical to give in to haunted regions, "and I am very sorry you should have had your two nights' rest spoilt by it, Mr. Featherston. I will take the room myself: nothing keeps me awake."

"Did you ever see a ghost, sir?" asked John.

"No, never. But I know those who have seen them; and I cannot disbelieve what they say. One such story in particular is often in my mind; it was a very strange one."

"Won't you tell it us, Mr. Featherston?"

The doctor only laughed in answer. But after we came out of church, when he was sitting with me and John on the Parade, he told it. And I only wish I had space to relate it here.

He left Pumpwater in the afternoon, and Lady Whitney had the room prepared for her use at once, John moving into hers. So that I had mine to myself again, and the little bed was taken out of it.

The next day was Monday. When Lady Whitney came down in the morning the first thing she told us was, that she had not slept. All the curious symptoms of restless disturbance, of inward agitation, which we had experienced, had visited her.

"I will not give in, my dears," she said, bravely. "It may be, you know, that what I had heard against the room took all sleep out of me, though I was not conscious of it; so I shall keep to it. I must say it is a most comfortable bed."

She "kept" to the room until the Wednesday; three nights in all; getting no sleep. Then she gave in. Occasionally during the third night, when she was dropping asleep from exhaustion, she was startled up from it in sudden terror: terror of she knew not what. Just as it had been with me and with John. On the Wednesday morning she told Susannah that they must give her the back-room opposite mine, and we would abandon that front-room altogether.

"It is just as though there were a ghost in the room," she said to Susannah.

"Perhaps there is, my lady," was Susannah's cool reply.

On the Friday evening Dr. and Mrs. Parafin came in to tea. Our visit would end on the morrow. The old doctor held John before him in the lamplight, and decided that he looked better—that the stay had done him good.

"I am sure it has," assented Lady Whitney. "Just at first I feared he was going backward: but that must have been owing to the sleepless nights."

"Sleepless nights!" echoed the doctor, in a curious tone.

"For the first three nights of our stay here, he never slept; never slept at all. After that—"

"Which room did he occupy?" interrupted the doctor, breathlessly. "Not the one over this?"

"Yes, it was. Why? Do you know anything against it?" questioned Lady Whitney, for she saw Dr. and Mrs. Parafin exchange glances.

"Only this: that I have heard of other people who were unable to sleep in that room," he answered.

"But what can be amiss with the room, Dr. Parafin?"

"Ah," said he, "there you go beyond me. It is, I believe, a fact, a singular fact, that there is something or other in the room which prevents people from sleeping. Friends of ours who lived in the house before Miss Gay took it, ended by shutting the room up."

"Is it haunted, sir?" I asked. "Mr. Featherston thought it might be."

He looked at me and smiled, shaking his head. Mrs. Parafin nodded hers, as much as to say It is.

"No one has been able to get any sleep in that room since the Calsons lived here," said Mrs. Parafin, dropping her voice.

"How very strange!" cried Lady Whitney. "One might think murder had been done in it."

Mrs. Parafin coughed significantly. "The wife died in it," she said. "Some people thought her husband had—had—had at least hastened her death—"

"Hush, Matty!" interposed the doctor, warningly. "It was all rumour, all talk. Nothing was proved—or attempted to be."

"Perhaps there existed no proof," returned Mrs. Parafin. "And if there had—who was there to take it up? She was in her grave, poor woman, and he was left flourishing, master of himself and every one about him. Any way, Thomas, be that as it may, you cannot deny that the room has been like a haunted room since."

Dr. Parafin laughed lightly, objecting to be serious; men are more cautious than women. "I cannot deny that people find themselves unable to sleep in the room; I never heard that it was 'haunted' in any other way," he added, to Lady Whitney. "But there—let us change the subject; we can neither alter the fact nor understand it."

After they left us, Lady Whitney said she should like to ask Miss Gay what her experience of the room had been. But Miss Gay had stepped out to a neighbour's, and Susannah stayed to talk in her place. She could tell us more about it, she said, than Miss Gay.

"I warned my cousin she would do well not to take this house," began Susannah, accepting the chair to which Lady Whitney pointed. "But it is a beautiful house for letting, as you see, my lady, and that and the low rent tempted her. Besides, she did not believe the rumour about the room; she does not believe it fully yet, though it is beginning to worry her: she thinks the inability to sleep must lie in the people themselves."

"It has been an uncanny room since old Calson's wife died in it, has it not, Susannah?" said John, as if in jest. "I suppose he did not murder her?"

"I think he did," whispered Susannah.

The answer sounded so ghostly that it struck us all into silence.

Susannah resumed. "Nobody knew: but one or two suspected. The wife was a poor, timid, gentle creature, worshipping the very ground her husband trod on, yet always in awe of him. She lay in the room, sick, for many many months before she died. Old Sarah—"

"What was her illness?" interrupted Lady Whitney.

"My lady, that is more than I can tell you, more, I fancy, than any one could have told. Old Sarah would often say to me that she did not believe there was any great sickness, only he made it out there was, and persuaded his wife so. He could just wind her round his little finger. The person who attended on her was one Astrea, quite a heathenish name I used to think, and a heathenish woman too; she was copper-coloured, and came with them from abroad. Sarah was in the kitchen, and there was only a man besides. I lived housekeeper at that time with an old lady on the Parade, and I looked in here from time to time to ask after the mistress. Once I was invited by Mr. Calson upstairs to see her, she lay in the room over this; the one that nobody can now sleep in. She looked so pitiful!—her poor, pale, patient face down deep in the pillow. Was she better, I asked; and what was it that ailed her. She thought it was not much beside weakness, she answered, and that she felt a constant nausea; and she was waiting for the warm weather: her dear husband assured her she would be better when that came."

"Was he kind to her, Susannah?"

"He seemed to be, Master Johnny; very kind and attentive indeed. He would sit by the hour together in her room, and give her her medicine, and feed her when she grew too weak to feed herself, and sit up at night with her. A doctor came to see her occasionally; it was said he could not find much the matter with her but debility, and that she seemed to be wasting away. Well, she died, my lady; died quietly in that room; and Calson ordered a grand funeral."

"So did Jonas Chuzzlewit," breathed John.

"Whispers got afloat when she was under ground—not before—that there had been something wrong about her death, that she had not come by it fairly, or by the illness either," continued Susannah. "But they were not spoken openly; under the rose, as may be said; and they died away. Mr. Calson continued to live in the house as before; but he became soon ill. Real sickness, his was, my lady, whatever his wife's might have been. His illness was chiefly on the nerves; he grew frightfully thin; and the setting-in of some grave inward complaint was suspected: so if he did act in any ill manner to his wife it seemed he would not reap long benefit from it. All the medical men in Pumpwater were called to him in succession; but they could not cure him. He kept growing thinner and thinner till he was like a walking shadow. At last he shut up his house and went to London for advice; and there he died, fourteen months after the death of his wife."

"How long was the house kept shut up?" asked Lady Whitney, as Susannah paused.

"About two years, my lady. All his property was willed away to the little son of his brother, who lived over in Australia. Tardy instructions came from thence to Mr. Jermy the lawyer to let the house furnished, and Mr. Jermy put it into the hands of Bone the house-agent. A family took it, but they did not stay: then another family took it, and they did not stay. Each party went to Bone and told him that something was the matter with one of the rooms and nobody could sleep in it. After that, the furniture was sold off, and some people took the house by the year. They did not remain in it six months. Some other people took it then, and they stayed the year, but it was known that they shut up that room. Then the house stayed empty. My cousin, wanting a better house than the one she was in, cast many a longing eye towards it; finding it did not let, she went to Bone and asked him what the rent would be. Seventy pounds to her, he said; and she took it. Of course she had heard about the room, but she did not believe it; she thought, as Mr. Featherston said the other morning, that something must be wrong with the paper, and she had the walls scraped and cleaned and a fresh paper put on."

"And since then—have your lodgers found anything amiss with the room?" questioned Lady Whitney.

"I am bound to say they have, my lady. It has been the same story with them all—not able to get to sleep in it. One gentleman, an old post-captain, after trying it a few nights, went right away from Pumpwater, swearing at the air. But the most singular experience we have had was that of two little girls. They were kept in that room for two nights, and each night they cried and screamed all night long, calling out that they were frightened. Their mother could not account for it; they were not at all timid children, she said, and such a thing had never happened with them before. Altogether, taking one thing with another, I fear, my lady, that something is wrong with the room. Miss Gay sees it now: but she is not superstitious, and she asks what it can be."

Well, that was Susannah's tale: and we carried it away with us on the morrow.

Sir John Whitney found his son looking all the better for his visit to Pumpwater. Temporarily he was so. Temporarily only; not materially: for John died before the year was out.

Have I heard anything of the room since, you would like to ask. Yes, a little. Some eighteen months later, I was halting at Pumpwater for a few hours with the Squire, and ran to the house to see Miss Gay. But the house was empty. A black board stood in front with big white letters on it TO BE LET. Miss Gay had moved into another house facing the Parade.

"It was of no use my trying to stay in it," she said to me, shaking her head. "I moved into the room myself, Master Johnny, after you and my Lady Whitney left, and I am free to confess that I could not sleep. I had Susannah in, and she could not sleep; and, in short, we had to go out of it again. So I shut the room up, sir, until the year had expired, and then I gave up the house. It has not been let since, and people say it is falling into decay."

"Was anything ever seen in the room, Miss Gay?"

"Nothing," she answered, "or heard either; nothing whatever. The room is as nice a room as could be wished for in all respects, light, large, cheerful, and airy; and yet nobody can get to sleep in it. I shall never understand it, sir."

I'm sure I never shall. It remains one of those curious experiences that cannot be solved in this world. But it is none the less true.

ROGER BEVERE

I

"There's trouble everywhere. It attaches itself more or less to all people as they journey through life. Yes, I quite agree with what you say, Squire: that I, a man at my ease in the world and possessing no close ties of my own, ought to be tolerably exempt from care. But I am not so. You have heard of the skeleton in the closet, Johnny Ludlow. Few families are without one. I have mine."

Mr. Brandon nodded to me, as he spoke, over the silver coffee-pot. I had gone to the Tavistock Hotel from Miss Deveen's to breakfast with him and the Squire—who had come up for a week. You have heard of this visit of ours to London before, and there's no need to say more about it here.

The present skeleton in Mr. Brandon's family closet was his nephew, Roger Bevere. The young fellow, now aged twenty-three, had been for some years in London pursuing his medical studies, and giving perpetual trouble to his people in the country. During this present visit Mr. Brandon had been unable to hear of him. Searching here, inquiring there, nothing came of it: Roger seemed to have vanished into air. This morning the post had brought Mr. Brandon a brief note:

"SIR,

"Roger Bevery is lying at No. 60, Gibraltar Terrace (Islington District), with a broken arm.

"Faithfully yours, "T. PITT."

The name was spelt Bevery in the note, you observe. Strangers, deceived by the pronunciation, were apt to write it so.

"Well, this is nice news!" had been Mr. Brandon's comment upon the short note.

"Any way, you will be more at your ease now you have found him," remarked the Squire.

"I don't know that, Todhetley. I have found, it seems, the address of the place where he is lying, but I have not found him. Roger has been going to the bad this many a day; I expect by this time he must be nearing the journey's end."

"It is only a broken arm that he has, sir," I put in, thinking what a gloomy view he was taking of it all. "That is soon cured."

"Don't you speak so confidently, Johnny Ludlow," reproved Mr. Brandon. "We shall find more the matter with Roger than a broken arm; take my word for that. He has been on the wrong tack this long while. A broken arm would not cause him to hide himself—and that's what he must have been doing."

"Some of those hospital students are a wild lot—as I have heard," said the Squire.

Mr. Brandon nodded in answer. "When Roger came from Hampshire to enter on his studies at St. Bartholomew's, he was as pure-hearted, well-intentioned a young fellow as had ever been trained by an anxious mother"—and Mr. Brandon poured a drop more weak tea out of his own tea-pot to cover his emotion. "Fit for heaven, one might have thought: any way, had been put in the road that leads to it. Loose, reckless companions got hold of him, and dragged him down to their evil ways."

Breakfast over, little time was lost in starting to find out Gibraltar Terrace. The cab soon took us to it. Roger had been lying there more than a week. Hastening up that way one evening, on leaving the hospital, to call upon a fellow-student, he was knocked down by a fleet hansom rounding the corner of Gibraltar Terrace. Pitt the doctor happened to be passing at the time, and had him carried into the nearest house: one he had attended patients in before. The landlady, Mrs. Mapping, showed us upstairs.

(And she, poor faded woman, turned out to have been known to the Squire in the days long gone by, when she was pretty little Dorothy Grape. But I have told her story already, and there's no need to allude to it again.)

Roger lay in bed, in a small back-room on the first-floor; a mild, fair, pleasant-looking young man with a white bandage round his head. Mr. Pitt explained that the arm was not absolutely broken, but so much contused and inflamed as to be a worse hurt. This would not have kept him in bed, however, but the head had also been damaged, and fever set in.

"So this is where he has lain, hiding, while I have been ransacking London for him!" remarked Mr. Brandon, who was greatly put out by the whole affair; and perhaps the word "hiding" might have more truth in it than even he suspected.

"When young Scott called last night—a fellow-student of your nephew's who comes to see him and bring him changes of clothes from his lodgings—he said you were making inquiries at the hospital and had left your address," explained Pitt. "So I thought I ought to write to you, sir."

"And I am much obliged to you for doing it, and for your care of him also," said Mr. Brandon.

And presently, when Pitt was leaving, he followed him downstairs to Mrs. Mapping's parlour, to ask whether Roger was in danger.

"I do not apprehend any, now that the fever is subsiding," answered Pitt. "I can say almost surely that none will arise if we can only keep him quiet. That has been the difficulty throughout—his restlessness. It is just as though he had something on his mind."

"What should he have on his mind?" retorted Mr. Brandon, in contention. "Except his sins. And I expect they don't trouble him much."

Pitt laughed a little. "Well, sir, he is not in any danger at present. But if the fever were to come back again—and increase—why, I can't foresee what the result might be."

"Then I shall send for Lady Bevere."

Pitt opened his eyes. "Lady Bevere!" he repeated. "Who is she?"

"Lady Bevere, sir, is Roger's mother and my sister. I shall write to-day."

Mr. Brandon had an appointment with his lawyers that morning and went out with the Squire to keep it, leaving me with the patient. "And take care you don't let him talk, Johnny," was his parting injunction to me. "Keep him perfectly quiet."

That was all very well, and I did my best to obey orders; but Roger would not be kept quiet. He was for ever sighing and starting, now turning to this side, now to that, and throwing his undamaged arm up like a ball at play.

"Is it pain that makes you so restless?" I asked.

"Pain, no," he groaned. "It's the bother. The pain is nothing now to what it was."

"Bother of what?"

"Oh—altogether. I say, what on earth brought Uncle John to London just now?"

"A matter connected with my property. He is my guardian and trustee, you know." To which answer Bevere only groaned again.

After taking a great jorum of beef-tea, which Mrs. Mapping brought up at mid-day, he was lying still and tranquil, when there came a loud knock at the street-door. Steps clattered up the stairs, and a tall, dark-haired young man put his head into the room.

"Bevere, old fellow, how are you? We've been so sorry to hear of your mishap!"

There was nothing alarming in the words and they were spoken gently; or in the visitor either, for he was good-looking; but in a moment Bevere was sitting bolt upright in bed, gazing out in fright as though he saw an apparition.

"What the deuce has brought you here, Lightfoot?" he cried, angrily.

"Came to see how you were getting on, friend," was the light and soothing answer, as the stranger drew near the bed. "Head and arm damaged, I hear."

"Who told you where to find me?"

"Scott. At least, he—"

"Scott's a false knave then! He promised me faithfully not to tell a soul." And Bevere's inflamed face and passionate voice presented a contrast to his usual mild countenance and gentle tones.

"There's no need to excite yourself," said the tall young man, sitting down on the edge of the bed and taking the patient's hand. "Dick Scott let fall a word unawares—that Pitt was attending you. So I came up to Pitt's just now and got the address out of his surgery-boy."

"Who else heard the chance word?"

"No one else. And I'm sure you know that you may trust me. I wanted to ask if I could do anything for you. How frightened you look, old fellow!"

Bevere lay down again, painfully uneasy yet, as was plain to be seen.

"I didn't want any one to find me out here," he said. "If some—some people came, there might be the dickens to pay. And Uncle John is up now, worse luck! He does not understand London ways, and he is the strictest old guy that ever wore silver shoe-buckles—you should see him on state occasions. Ask Johnny Ludlow there whether he is strait-laced or not; he knows. Johnny, this is Charley Lightfoot: one of us at Bart's."

Charley turned to shake hands, saying he had heard of me. He then set himself to soothe Bevere, assuring him he would not tell any one where he was lying, or that he had been to see him.

"Don't mind my temper, old friend," whispered Bevere, repentantly, his blue eyes going out to the other's in sad yearning. "I am a bit tried—as you'd admit, if all were known."

Lightfoot departed. By-and-by the Squire and Mr. Brandon returned, and Mrs. Mapping gave us some lunch in her parlour. When the Squire was ready to leave, I ran up to say good-bye to Roger. He gazed at me questioningly, eyes and cheeks glistening with fever. "Is it true?" he whispered.

"Is what true?"

"That Uncle John has written for my mother?"

"Oh yes, that's true."

"Good Heavens!" murmured Bevere.

"Would you not like to see her?"

"It's not that. She's the best mother living. It is—for fear—I didn't want to be found out lying here," he broke off, "and it seems that all the world is coming. If it gets to certain ears, I'm done for."

Scarlet and more scarlet grew his cheeks. His pulse must have been running up to about a hundred-and-fifty.

"As sure as you are alive, Roger, you'll bring the fever on again!"

"So much the better. I do—save for what I might say in my ravings," he retorted. "So much the better if it carries me off! There'd be an end to it all, then."

"One might think you had a desperate secret on your conscience," I said to him in my surprise. "Had set a house on fire, or something as good."

"And I have a secret; and it's something far more dreadful than setting a house on fire," he avowed, recklessly, in his distress. "And if it should get to the knowledge of Uncle John and the mother—well, I tell you, Johnny Ludlow, I'd rather die than face the shame."

Was he raving now?—as he had been on the verge of it, in the fever, a day or two ago. No, not by the wildest stretch of the fancy could I think so. That he had fallen into some desperate trouble which must be kept secret, if it could be, was all too evident. I thought of fifty things as I went home and could not fix on one of them as likely. Had he robbed the hospital till?—or forged a cheque upon its house-surgeon? The Squire wanted to know why I was so silent.

When I next went to Gibraltar Terrace Lady Bevere was there. Such a nice little woman! Her face was mild, like Roger's, her eyes were blue and kind as his, her tones as genial. As Mary Brandon she had been very pretty, and she was pleasing still.

She had married a lieutenant in the navy, Edmund Bevere. Her people did not like it: navy lieutenants were so poor, they said. He got on better, however, than the Brandons had thought for; got up to be rear-admiral and to be knighted. Then he died; and Lady Bevere was left with a lot of children and not much to bring them up on. I expect it was her brother, Mr. Brandon, who helped to start them all in life. She lived in Hampshire, somewhere near Southsea.

In a day or two, when Roger was better and sat up in blankets in an easy-chair, Mr. Brandon and the Squire began about his shortcomings—deeming him well enough now to be tackled. Mr. Brandon demanded where his lodgings were, for their locality seemed to be a mystery; evidently with a view of calling and putting a few personal questions to the landlady; and Roger had to confess that he had had no particular lodgings lately; he had shared Dick Scott's. This took Mr. Brandon aback. No lodgings of his own!—sharing young Scott's! What was the meaning of it? What did he do with all the money allowed him, if he could not pay for rooms of his own? And to the stern questioning Roger only answered that he and Scott liked to be together. Pitt laughed a little to me when he heard of this, saying Bevere was too clever for the old mentors.

"Why! don't you believe he does live with Scott?" I asked.

"Oh, he may do that; it's likely enough," said Pitt. "But medical students, running their fast career in London, are queer subjects, let me tell you, Johnny Ludlow; they don't care to have their private affairs supervised."

"All of them are not queer—as you call it, Pitt."

"No, indeed," he answered, warmly: "or I don't know what would become of the profession. Many of them are worthy, earnest fellows always, steady as old time. Others pull up when they have had their fling, and make good men: and a few go to the bad altogether."

"In which class do you put Roger Bevere?"

Pitt took a minute to answer. "In the second, I hope," he said. "To speak the truth, Bevere somewhat puzzles me. He seems well-intentioned, anxious, and can't have gone so far but he might pull-up if he could. But—"

"If he could! How do you mean?"

"He has got, I take it, into the toils of a fast, bad set; and he finds their habits too strong to break through. Any way without great difficulty."

"Do you think he—drinks?" I questioned, reluctantly.

"No mistake about that," said Pitt. "Not so sharply as some of them do, but more than is good for him."

I'm sure if Roger's pulling-up depended upon his mother, it would have been done. She was so gentle and loving with him; never finding fault, or speaking a harsh word. Night and morning she sat by the bed, holding his hands in hers, and reading the Psalms to him—or a prayer—or a chapter in the Bible. I can see her now, in her soft black gown and simple little white lace cap, under which her hair was smoothly braided.

Whatever doubts some of us might be entertaining of Roger, nothing unpleasant in regard to him transpired. Dreaded enemies did not find him out, or come to besiege the house; though he never quite lost his undercurrent of uneasiness. He soon began to mend rapidly. Scott visited him every second or third day; he seemed to be fully in his confidence, and they had whisperings together. He was a good-natured, off-hand kind of young man, short and thick-set. I can't say I much cared for him.

The Squire had left London. I remained on with Miss Deveen, and went down to Gibraltar Terrace most days. Lady Bevere was now going home and Mr. Brandon with her. Some trouble had arisen about the lease of her house in Hampshire, which threatened to end in a lawsuit, and she wanted him to see into it. They fixed upon some eligible lodgings for Roger near Russell Square, into which he would move when they left. He was sufficiently well now to go about; and would keep well, Pitt said, if he took care of himself. Lady Bevere held a confidential interview with the landlady, about taking care of her son Roger.

And she gave a last charge to Bevere himself, when taking leave of him the morning of her departure. The cab was at the door to convey her and Mr. Brandon to Waterloo Station, and I was there also, having gone betimes to Gibraltar Terrace to see the last of them.

"For my sake, my dear," pleaded Lady Bevere, holding Roger to her, as the tears ran down her cheeks: "you will do your best to keep straight for my sake!"

"I will, I will, mother," he whispered back in agitation, his own eyes wet; "I will keep as straight as I can." But in his voice there lay, to my ear, a ring of hopeless despair. I don't know whether she detected it.

She turned and took my hands. She and Mr. Brandon had already exacted a promise from me that once a-week at least, so long as I remained in London, I would write to each of them to give news of Roger's welfare.

"You will be sure not to forget it, Johnny? I am very anxious about him—his health—and—and all," she added in a lowered voice. "I am always fearing lest I did not do my duty by my boys. Not but that I ever tried to do it; but somehow I feel that perhaps I might have done it better. Altogether I am full of anxiety for Roger."

"I will be sure to write to you regularly as long as I am near him, dear Lady Bevere."

It was on a Tuesday morning that Lady Bevere and Mr. Brandon left London. In the afternoon Roger was installed in his new lodgings by Mr. Pitt, who had undertaken to see him into them. He had the parlour and the bed-chamber behind it. Very nice rooms they were, the locality and street open and airy; and the landlady, Mrs. Long, was a comfortable, motherly woman. Where his old lodgings had been situated, he had never said even to me: the Squire's opinion was (communicated in confidence to Mr. Brandon), that he had played up "Old Gooseberry" in them, and was afraid to say.

I had meant to go to him on the Wednesday, to see that the bustle of removal had done him no harm; but Miss Deveen wanted me, so I could not. On the Thursday I got a letter from the Squire, telling me to do some business for him at Westminster. It took me the whole of the day: that is, the actual business took about a quarter-of-an-hour, and waiting to see the people (lawyers) took the rest. This brought it, you perceive, to Friday.

On that morning I mounted to the roof of a city omnibus, which set me down not far off the house. Passing the parlour-windows to knock at the door, I saw in one of them a card: "Apartments to let." It was odd, I thought, they should put it in a room that was occupied.

"Can I see Mr. Bevere?" I asked of the servant.

"Mr. Bevere's gone, sir."

"Gone where? Not to the hospital?" For he was not to attempt to go there until the following week.

"He is gone for good, sir," she answered. "He went away in a cab yesterday evening."

Not knowing what to make of this strange news, hardly believing it, I went into the parlour and asked to see the landlady—who came at once. It was quite true: Bevere had left. Mrs. Long, who, though elderly, was plump and kindly, sat down to relate the particulars.

"Mr. Bevere went out yesterday morning, sir, after ordering his dinner—a roast fowl—for the same hour as the day before; two o'clock. It was past three, though, before he came in: and when the girl brought the dinner-tray down, she said Mr. Bevere wanted to speak to me. I came up, and then he told me he was unexpectedly obliged to leave—that he might have to go into the country that night; he didn't yet know. Well, sir, I was a little put out: but what could I say? He paid me what was due and the rent up to the week's end, and began to collect his things together: Sarah saw him cramming them into his new portmanteau when she brought his tea up. And at the close of the evening, between the lights, he had a cab called and went away in it."

"Alone?"

"Quite alone, sir. On the Wednesday afternoon Dr. Pitt came to see him, and that same evening a young man called, who stayed some time; Scott, I think the name was; but nobody at all came yesterday."

"And you do not know where Mr. Bevere is?—where he went to?"

"Why no, sir; he didn't say. The cab might have taken him to one of the railway-stations, for all I can tell. I did not ask questions. Of course it is not pleasant for a lodger to leave you in that sudden manner, before he has well been three days in the house," added Mrs. Long, feelingly, "especially with the neighbours staring out on all sides, and I might have asked him for another week's rent in lieu of proper notice; but I couldn't be hard with a well-mannered, pleasant young gentleman like Mr. Bevere—and with his connections, too. I'm sure when her ladyship came here to fix on the rooms, she was that kind and affable with me I shall never forget it—and talked to me so lovingly about him—and put half-a-crown into Sarah's hand when she left! No, sir, I couldn't be hard upon young Mr. Bevere."

Mrs. Long had told all she knew, and I wished her good-day. Where to now? I deliberated, as I stood on the doorstep. This sudden flight looked as though Roger wanted to avoid people. If any one was in the secret of it, it would be Richard Scott, I thought; and I turned my steps to St. Bartholomew's Hospital.

I suppose I interrupted Scott at some critical performance, for he came to me with his coat-cuffs turned up and no wristbands on.

"Glad to see you, I'm sure," cried he; "thought it might be an out-patient. Bevere?—oh, do you want him?" he ran on, not giving himself time to understand me perfectly, or pretending at it. "Bevere is at his new lodgings near Russell Square. He will not be back here until next week."

"But he is not at his new lodgings," I said. "He has left them."

"Left!" cried Scott, staring.

"Left for good, bag and baggage. Gone altogether."

"Gone where?" asked Scott.

"That's what I have come to ask you. I expect you know."

Scott's face presented a puzzle. I wondered whether he was as innocent as he looked.

"Let us understand one another," said he. "Do you tell me that Bevere has left his new lodgings?"

"He has. He left them last night. Ran away from them, as one may say."

"Why, he had only just got into them! Were the people sharks? I was with him on Wednesday night: he did not complain of anything then."

"He must have left, I fancy, for some private reason of his own. Don't you know where he is gone, Scott? You are generally in his confidence."

"Don't know any more than the dead."

To dispute the declaration was not in my power. Scott seemed utterly surprised, and said he should go to Mrs. Long's the first leisure moment he had, to see if any note or message had been left for him. But I had already put that question to the landlady, and she answered that neither note nor message of any kind had been left for anybody. So there we were, nonplussed, Scott standing with his hands in his pockets. Make the best of it we would, it resolved itself into nothing more than this: Bevere had vanished, leaving no clue.

From thence I made my way to Mr. Pitt's little surgery near Gibraltar Terrace. The doctor was alone in it, and stood compounding pills behind the counter.

"Bevere run away!" he exclaimed at my first words. "Why, what's the meaning of that? I don't know anything about it. I was going to see him this afternoon."

With my arms on the counter, my head bending towards him, I recounted to Pitt the particulars Mrs. Long had given me, and Scott's denial of having any finger in the pie. The doctor gave his head a twist.

"Says he knows no more than the dead, does he! That may be the case; or it may not. Master Richard Scott's assertions go for what they are worth with me where Bevere's concerned: the two are as thick as thieves. I'll find him, if I can. What do you say?—that Bevere would not conceal himself from me? Look here, Johnny Ludlow," continued Pitt rapidly, bringing forward his face till it nearly touched mine, and dropping his voice to a low tone, "that young man must have got into some dangerous trouble, and has to hide himself from the light of day."

Leaving Pitt to make his patients' physic, I went out into the world, not knowing whether to seek for Bevere in this quarter or in that. But, unless I found him, how could I carry out my promise of writing to Lady Bevere?

I told Miss Deveen of my dilemma. She could not help me. No one could help, that I was able to see. There was nothing for it but to wait until the next week, when Bevere might perhaps make his appearance at the hospital. I dropped a note to Scott, asking him to let me know of it if he did.

But of course the chances were that Bevere would not appear at the hospital: with need to keep his head en cachette, he would be no more safe there than in Mrs. Long's rooms: and I might have been hunting for him yet, for aught I can tell, but for coming across Charley Lightfoot.

It was on the following Monday. He was turning out of the railway-station near Miss Deveen's, his uncle, Dr. Lightfoot, being in practice close by. Telling him of Roger Bevere's flight, which he appeared not to have heard of, I asked if he could form any idea where he was likely to have got to.

"Oh, back to the old neighbourhood that he lived in before his accident, most likely," carelessly surmised Lightfoot, who did not seem to think much of the matter.

"And where is that?"

"A goodish distance from here. It is near the Bell-and-Clapper Station on the underground line."

"The Bell-and-Clapper Station!"

Lightfoot laughed. "Ironically called so," he said, "from a bell at the new church close by, that claps away pretty well all day and all night in the public ears."

"Not one of our churches?"

"Calls itself so, I believe. I wouldn't answer for it that its clergy have been licensed by a bishop. Bevere lived somewhere about there; I never was at his place; but you'll easily find it out."

"How? By knocking at people's doors and inquiring for him?"

Lightfoot put on his considering-cap. "If you go to the refreshment-room of the Bell-and-Clapper Station and ask his address of the girls there," said he, "I dare say they can give it you. Bevere used to be uncommonly fond of frequenting their company, I believe."

Running down to the train at once I took a ticket for the Bell-and-Clapper Station, and soon reached it. It was well named: the bell was clanging away with a loud and furious tongue, enough to drive a sick man mad. What a dreadful infliction for the houses near it!

Behind the counter in the refreshment-room stood two damsels, exchanging amenities with a young man who sat smoking a cigar, his legs stretched out at ease. Before I had time to speak, the sound of an up-train was heard; he drank up the contents of a glass that stood at his elbow, and went swiftly out.

It was a pretty looking place: with coloured decanters on its shelves and an array of sparkling glass. The young women wore neat black gowns, and might have looked neat enough altogether but for their monstrous heads of hair. That of one in particular was a sight to be seen, and must have been copied from some extravagant fashion plate. She was dark and handsome, with a high colour and a loud voice, evidently a strong-minded young woman, perfectly able to take care of herself. The other girl was fair, smaller and slighter, with a somewhat delicate face, and a quiet manner.

"Can you give me the address of Mr. Roger Bevere?" I asked of this younger one.

The girl flushed scarlet, and looked at her companion, who looked back again. It was a curious sort of look, as much—I thought—as to say, what are we to do? Then they both looked at me. But neither spoke.

"I am told that Mr. Bevere often comes here, and that you can give me his address."

"Well, sir—I don't think we can," said the younger one, and her speech was quite proper and modest. "We don't know it, do we, Miss Panken?"

"Perhaps you'll first of all tell me who it was that said we could give it you," cried Miss Panken, in tones as strong-minded as herself, and as though she were by a very long way my superior in the world.

"It was one of his fellow-students at the hospital."

"Oh—well—I suppose we can give it you," she concluded. "Here, I'll write it down. Lend me your pencil, Mabel: mine has disappeared. There," handing me the paper, "if he is not there, we can't tell you where he is."

"Roger Bevary, 22, New Crescent," was what she wrote. I thanked her and went out, encountering two or three young men who rushed in from another train and called individually for refreshment.

New Crescent was soon found, but not Bevere. The elderly woman-servant who answered me said Mr. Bevere formerly lived with them, but left about eighteen months back. He had not left the neighbourhood, she thought, as she sometimes met him in it. She saw him only the past Saturday night when she was out on an errand.

"What, this past Saturday!" I exclaimed. "Are you certain?"

"To be sure I am, sir. He was smoking a pipe and looking in at the shop windows. He saw me and said, Good-night, Ann: he was always very pleasant. I thought he looked ill."

Back I went to the refreshment-room. Those girls knew his address well enough, but for some reason would not give it—perhaps by Bevere's orders. Two young men were there now, sipping their beer, or whatever it was, and exchanging compliments with Miss Panken. I spoke to her civilly.

"Mr. Bevere does not live at New Crescent: he left it eighteen months ago. Did you not know that? I think you can give me his address if you will."

She did not answer me at all. It may be bar-room politeness. Regarding me for a full minute superciliously from my head to my boots, she slowly turned her shoulders the other way, and resumed her talk with the customers.

I spoke then to the other, who was wiping glasses. "It is in Mr. Bevere's own interest that I wish to find him; I wish it very particularly indeed. He lives in this neighbourhood; I have heard that: if you can tell me where, I shall be very much obliged to you."

The girl's face looked confused, timid, full of indecision, as if she knew the address but did not know whether to answer or not. By this time I had attracted attention, and silence fell on the room. Strong-minded Miss Panken came to the relief of her companion.

"Did you call for a glass of ale?" she asked me, in a tone of incipient mockery.

"Nor for soda?—nor bitters?—not even cherry-brandy?" she ran on. "No? Then as you don't seem to want anything we supply here, perhaps you'll take yourself off, young man, and leave space for them that do. Fancy this room being open to promiscuous inquirers, and us young ladies being obliged to answer 'em!" added Miss Panken affably to her two friends. "I'd like to see it!"

Having thus put me down and turned her back upon me, I had nothing to wait for, and walked out of the lady's presence. The younger one's eyes followed me with a wistful look. I'm sure she would have given the address had she dared.

After that day, I took to haunt the precincts of the Bell-and-Clapper, believing it to be my only chance of finding Bevere. Scott had a brief note from him, no address to it, stating that he was not yet well enough to resume his duties; and this note Scott forwarded to me. A letter also came to me; from Lady Bevere asking what the matter was that I did not write, and whether Roger was worse. How could I write, unless I found him?

So, all the leisure time that I could improvise I spent round about the Bell-and-Clapper. Not inside the room, amid its manifold attractions: Circe was a wily woman, remember, and pretty bottles are insidious. That particular Circe, also, Miss Panken, might have objected to my company and ordered me out of it.

Up one road, down another, before this row of houses and that, I hovered for ever like a walking ghost. But I saw nothing of Bevere.

Luck favoured me at last. One afternoon towards the end of the week, I was standing opposite the church, watching the half-dozen worshippers straggling into it, for one of its many services, listening to the irritating ding-dong of its bell, and wondering the noise was put up with, when suddenly Richard Scott came running up from the city train. Looking neither to the right nor the left, or he must inevitably have seen me, he made straight for a cross-road, then another, and presently entered one of a row of small houses whose lower rooms were on a level with the ground and the yard or two of square garden that fronted them. "Paradise Place." I followed Scott at a cautious distance.

"Bevere lives there!" quoth I, mentally.

Should I go in at once boldly, and beard him? While deliberating—for somehow it goes against my nature to beard anybody—Scott came striding out and turned off the other way: which led to the shops. I crossed over and went in quietly at the open door.

The parlour, small and shabby as was Mrs. Mapping's in Gibraltar Terrace, was on the left, its door likewise open. Seated at a table, taking his tea, was Roger Bevere; opposite to him, presiding over the ceremonies, sat a lady who must unquestionably have been first-cousin to those damsels at the Bell-and-Clapper, if one might judge by the hair.

"Roger!" I exclaimed. "What a dance you have led us!"

He started up with a scarlet face, his manner strangely confused, his tongue for the moment lost. And then I saw that he was without his coat, and his arm was bandaged.

"I was going to write to you," he said—an excuse invented on the spur of the moment, "I thought to be about before now, but my arm got bad again."

"How was that?"

"Well, I hurt it, and did not pay attention to it. It is properly inflamed now."

I took a seat on the red stuff sofa without being invited, and Bevere dropped into his chair. The lady at the tea-tray had been regarding me with a free, friendly, unabashed gaze. She was a well-grown, attractive young woman, with a saucy face and bright complexion, fine dark eyes, and full red lips. Her abundant hair was of the peculiar and rare colour that some people call red and others gold. As to her manners, they were as assured as Miss Panken's, but a great deal pleasanter. I wondered who she was and what she did there.

"So this is Johnny Ludlow that I've heard tell of!" she exclaimed, catching up my name from Bevere, and sending me a gracious nod. "Shall I give you a cup of tea?"

"No, thank you," was my answer, though all the while as thirsty as a fish, for the afternoon was hot.

"Oh, you had better: don't stand on ceremony," she said, laughing. "There's nothing like a good cup of tea when the throat's dry and the weather's baking. Come! make yourself at home."

"Be quiet, Lizzie," struck in Bevere, his tone ringing with annoyance and pain. "Let Mr. Ludlow do as he pleases." And it struck me that he did not want me to take the tea.

Scott came in then, and looked surprised to see me: he had been out to get something for Bevere's arm. I felt by intuition that he had known where Bevere was all along, that his assumption of ignorance was a pretence. He and the young lady seemed to be upon excellent terms, as though they had been acquainted for ages.

The arm looked very bad: worse than it had at Gibraltar Terrace. I stood by when Scott took off the bandages. He touched it here and there.

"I tell you what, Bevere," he said: "you had better let Pitt see to this again. He got it right before; and—I don't much like the look of it."

"Nonsense!" returned Bevere. "I don't want Pitt here."

"I say nonsense to that," rejoined Scott. "Who's Pitt?—he won't hurt you. No good to think you can shut yourself up in a nutshell—with such an arm as this, and—and—" he glanced at me, as if he would say, "and now Ludlow has found you out."

"You can do as much for the arm as Pitt can," said Bevere, fractiously.

"Perhaps I could: but I don't mean to try. I tell you, Bevere, I do not like the look of it," repeated Scott. "What's more, I, not being a qualified practitioner yet, would not take the responsibility."

"Well, I will go to Pitt to-morrow if I'm no better and can get my coat on," conceded Bevere. "Lizzie, where's the other bandage?"

"Oh, I left it in my room," said Lizzie; and she ran up the stairs in search of it.

So she lived there! Was it her home, I wondered; or Bevere's; or their home conjointly? The two might have vowed eternal friendship and set up housekeeping together on a platonic footing. Curious problems do come into fashion in the great cities of this go-ahead age; perhaps that one had.

Scott finished dressing the arm, giving the patient sundry cautions meanwhile; and I got up to leave. Lizzie had stepped outside and was leaning over the little wooden entrance-gate, chanting a song to herself and gazing up and down the quiet road.

"What am I to say to your mother?" I said to Bevere in a low tone. "You knew I had to write to her."

"Oh, say I am all right," he answered. "I have written to her myself now, and had two letters from her."

"How do the letters come to you? Here?"

"Scott gets them from Mrs. Long's. Johnny"—with a sharp pressure of the hand, and a beseeching look from his troubled blue eyes—"be a good fellow and don't talk. Anywhere."

Giving his hand a reassuring shake, and lifting my hat to the lady at the gate as I passed her, I went away, thinking of this complication and of that. In a minute, Scott overtook me.

"I think you knew where he was, all along," I said to him; "that your ignorance was put on."

"Of course it was," answered Scott, as coolly as you please. "What would you? When a fellow-chum entrusts confidential matters to you and puts you upon your honour, you can't betray him."

"Oh, well, I suppose not. That damsel over there, Scott—is she his sister, or his cousin, or his aunt?"

"You can call her which you like," replied Scott, affably. "Are you very busy this afternoon, Ludlow?"

"I am not busy at all."

"Then I wish you would go to Pitt. I can't spare the time. I've a heap of work on my shoulders to-day: it was only the pressing note I got from Bevere about his arm that brought me out of it. He is getting a bit doubtful himself, you see; and Pitt had better come to it without loss of time."

"Bevere won't thank me for sending Pitt to him. You heard what he said."

"Nonsense as to Bevere's thanks. The arm is worse than he thinks for. In my opinion, he stands a good chance of losing it."

"No!" I exclaimed in dismay. "Lose his arm!"

"Stands a chance of it," repeated Scott. "It will be his own fault. A week yesterday he damaged it again, the evening he came back here, and he has neglected it ever since. You tell Pitt what I say."

"Very well, I will. I suppose the account Bevere gave to his mother and Mr. Brandon—that he had been living lately with you—was all a fable?"

Scott nodded complaisantly, striding along at the pace of a steam-engine. "Just so. He couldn't bring them down upon him here, you know."

I did not exactly know. And thoughts, as the saying runs, are free.

"So he hit upon the fable, as you call it, of saying he had shared my lodgings," continued Scott. "Necessity is a rare incentive to invention."

We had gained the Bell-and-Clapper Station as he spoke: two minutes yet before the train for the city would be in. Scott utilized the minutes by dashing to the bar for a glass of ale, chattering to Miss Panken and the other one while he drank it. Then we both took the train; Scott going back to the hospital— where he fulfilled some official duty beyond that of ordinary student—and I to see after Pitt.

II

Roger Bevere's arm proved obstinate. Swollen and inflamed as I had never seen any arm yet, it induced fever, and he had to take to his bed. Scott, who had his wits about him in most ways, had not spoken a minute too soon, or been mistaken as to the probable danger; while Mr. Pitt told Roger every time he came to dress it, beginning with the first evening, that he deserved all he got for being so foolhardy as to neglect it: as a medical man in embryo, he ought to have foreseen the hazard.

It seemed to me that Roger was just as ill as he was at Gibraltar Terrace, when they sent for his mother: if not worse. Most days I got down to Paradise Place to snatch a look at him. It was not far, taking the underground-railway from Miss Deveen's.

I made the best report I could to Lady Bevere, telling nothing—excepting that the arm was giving a little trouble. If she got to learn the truth about certain things, she would think the letters deceitful. But what else could I do?—I wished with all my heart some one else had to write them. As Scott had said to me about the flitting from Mrs. Long's (the reason for which or necessity, I was not enlightened upon yet), I could not betray Bevere. Pitt assured me that if any unmanageable complications arose with the arm, both Lady Bevere and Mr. Brandon should be at once telegraphed for. A fine complication it would be, of another sort, if they did come! How about Miss Lizzie?

Of all the free-and-easy young women I had ever met with, that same Lizzie was the freest and easiest. Many a time have I wondered Bevere did not order her out of the room when she said audacious things to him or to me—not to say out of the house. He did nothing of the kind; he lay passive as a bird that has had its wings clipped, all spirit gone out of him, and groaning with bodily pain. Why on earth did he allow her to make his house her abode, disturbing it with her noise and her clatter? Why on earth—to go on further—did he rent a house at all, small or large? No one else lived in it, that I saw, except a little maid, in her early teens, to do the work. Later I found I was mistaken: they were only lodgers: an old landlady, lame and quiet, was in the kitchen.

"Looks fearfully bad, don't he?" whispered Lizzie to me on one occasion when he lay asleep, and she came bursting into the room for her bonnet and shawl.

"Yes. Don't you think you could be rather more quiet?"

"As quiet as a lamb, if you like," laughed Lizzie, and crept out on tiptoe. She was always good-humoured.

One afternoon when I went in, Lizzie had a visitor in the parlour. Miss Panken! The two, evidently on terms of close friendship, were laughing and joking frantically; Lizzie's head, with its clouds of red-gold hair, was drawn close to the other head and the mass of black braids adorning it. Miss Panken sat sipping a cup of tea; Lizzie a tumbler of hot water that gave forth a suspicious odour.

"I've got a headache, Mr. Johnny," said she: and I marvelled that she did not, in her impudence, leave the "Mr." out. "Hot gin-and-water is the very best remedy you can take for it."

Shrieks of laughter from both the girls followed me upstairs to Roger's bedside: Miss Panken was relating some joke about her companion, Mabel. Roger said his arm was a trifle better. It always felt so when Pitt had been to it.

"Who is it that's downstairs now?" he asked, fretfully, as the bursts of merriment sounded through the floor. "Sit down, Johnny."

"It's a girl from the Bell-and-Clapper refreshment-room. Miss Panken they call her."

Roger frowned. "I have told Lizzie over and over again that I wouldn't have those girls encouraged here. What can possess her to do it?" And, after saying that, he passed into one of those fits of restlessness that used to attack him at Gibraltar Terrace.

"Look here, Roger," I said, presently, "couldn't you—pull up a bit? Couldn't you put all this nonsense away?"

"Which nonsense?" he retorted.

"What would Mr. Brandon say if he knew it? I'll not speak of your mother. It is not nice, you know; it is not, indeed."

"Can't you speak out?" he returned, with intense irritation. "Put what away?"

"Lizzie."

I spoke the name under my breath, not liking to say it, though I had wanted to for some time. All the anger seemed to go out of Roger. He lay still as death.

"Can't you, Roger?"

"Too late, Johnny," came back the answer in a whisper of pain.

"Why?"

"She is my wife."

I leaped from my chair in a sort of terror. "No, no, Roger, don't say that! It cannot be."

"But it is," he groaned. "These eighteen months past."

I stood dazed; all my senses in a whirl. Roger kept silence, his face turned to the pillow. And the laughter from below came surging up.

I had no heart affection that I was aware of, but I had to press my hand to still its thumping as I leaned over Roger.

"Really married? Surely married?"

"As fast and sure as the registrar could marry us," came the smothered answer. "We did not go to church."

"Oh, Roger! How came you to do it?"

"Because I was a fool."

I sat down again, right back in the chair. Things that had puzzled me before were clearing themselves now. This was the torment that had worried his mind and prolonged, if not induced, the fever, when he first lay ill of the accident; this was the miserable secret that had gone well-nigh to disturb the brain: partly for the incubus the marriage entailed upon him, partly lest it should be found out. It had caused him to invent fables in more ways than one. Not only had he to conceal his proper address from us all when at Gibraltar Terrace, especially from his mother and Mr. Brandon; but he had had to scheme with Scott to keep his wife in ignorance altogether—of his accident and of where he was lying, lest Lizzie should present herself at his bedside. To account for his absence from home, Scott had improvised a story to her of Roger's having been despatched by the hospital authorities to watch a case of illness at a little distance; and Lizzie unsuspiciously supplied Scott with changes of raiment and other things Roger needed from his chest of drawers.

This did for a time. But about the period of Roger's quitting Gibraltar Terrace, Lizzie unfortunately caught up an inkling that she was being deceived. Miss Panken's general acquaintance was numerous, and one day one of them chanced to go into the bar-room of the Bell-and-Clapper, and to mention, incidentally, that Roger Bevere had been run over by a hansom cab, and was lying disabled in some remote doctor's quarters—for that's what Scott told his fellow-students. Madam Lizzie rose in rebellion, accused Scott of being no gentleman, and insisted upon her right to be enlightened. So, to stop her from making her appearance at St. Bartholomew's with inconvenient inquiries, and possibly still more inconvenient revelations, Roger had promptly to quit the new lodgings at Mrs. Long's, and return to the old home near the Bell-and-Clapper. But I did not learn these particulars at first.

"Who knows it, Roger?" I asked, breaking the silence.

"Not one of them but Scott," he answered, supposing I alluded to the hospital. "I see Pitt has his doubts."

"But they know—some of them—that Lizzie is here!"

"Well? So did you, but you did not suspect further. They think of course that—well, there's no help for what they think. When a fellow is in such a position as mine, he has to put up with things as they come. I can't quite ruin myself, Johnny; or let the authorities know what an idiot I've been. Lizzie's aunt knows it; and that's enough at present; and so do those girls at the Bell-and-Clapper—worse luck!"

It was impossible to talk much of it then, at that first disclosure; I wished Roger good-afternoon, and went away in a fever-dream.

My wildest surmises had not pictured this dismal climax. No, never; for all that Mistress Lizzie's left hand displayed a plain gold ring of remarkable thickness. "She would have it thick," Roger said to me later. Poor Roger! poor Roger!

I felt it like a blow—like a blow. No good would ever come of it—to either of them. Worse than no good to him. It was not so much the unsuitableness of the girl's condition to his; it was the girl herself. She would bring him no credit, no comfort as long as she lived: what happiness could he ever find with her? I had grown to like Roger, with all his faults and failings, and it almost seemed to me, in my sorrow for him, as if my own life were blighted.

It might not have been quite so bad—not quite—had Lizzie been a different girl. Modest, yielding, gentle, like that little Mabel I had seen, for instance, learning to adapt her manners to the pattern of her husband's; had she been that, why, in time, perhaps, things might have smoothed down for him. But Lizzie! with her free and loud manners, her off-hand ways, her random speech, her vulgar laughs! Well, well!

How was it possible she had been able to bring her fascinations to bear upon him—he with his refinement? One can but sit down in amazement and ask how, in the name of common-sense, such incongruities happen in the world. She must have tamed down what was objectionable in her to sugar and sweetness while setting her cap at Bevere; while he—he must have been blind, physically and mentally. But no sooner was the marriage over than he awoke to see what he had done for himself. Since then his time had been principally spent in setting up contrivances to keep the truth from becoming known. Mr. Brandon had talked of his skeleton in the closet: he had not dreamt of such a skeleton as this.

"Must have gone in largely for strong waters in those days, and been in a chronic state of imbecility, I should say," observed Pitt, making his comments to me confidentially.

For I had spoken to him of the marriage, finding he knew as much as I did. "I shall never be able to understand it," I said.

"That's easy enough. When Circe and a goose sit down to play chess, no need to speculate which will win the game."

"You speak lightly of it, Mr. Pitt."

"Not particularly. Where's the use of speaking gravely now the deed's done? It is a pity for Bevere; but he is only one young man amidst many such who in one way or another spoil their lives at its threshold. Johnny Ludlow, when I look about me and see the snares spread abroad in this great metropolis by night and by day, and at the crowds of inexperienced lads—they are not much better—who have to run to and fro continually, I marvel that the number of those who lose themselves is not increased tenfold."

He had changed his tone to one solemn enough for a judge.

"I cannot think how he came to do it," I argued. "Or how such a one as Bevere, well-intentioned, well brought up, could have allowed himself to fall into what Mr. Brandon calls loose habits. How came he to take to drinking ways, even in a small degree?"

"The railway refreshment-bars did that for him, I take it," answered Pitt. "He lived up here from the first, by the Bell-and-Clapper, and I suppose found the underground train more convenient than the omnibus. Up he'd rush in a morning to catch—say—the half-past eight train, and would often miss it by half-a-minute. A miss is as good as a mile. Instead of cooling his heels on the draughty and deserted platform, he would turn into the refreshment-room, and find there warmth and sociable company in the shape of pretty girls to chat with: and, if he so minded, a glass of something or other to keep out the cold on a wintry morning."

"As if Bevere would!—at that early hour!"

"Some of them do," affirmed Pitt. "Anyway, that's how Bevere fell into the habit of frequenting the bar-room of the Bell-and-Clapper. It lay so handy, you see; right in his path. He would run into it again of an evening when he returned: he had no home, no friends waiting for him, only lodgings. There—"

"I thought Bevere used to board with a family," I interrupted.

"So he did at first; and very nice people they were: Mr. Brandon took care he should be well placed. That's why Bevere came up this way at all: it was rather far from the hospital, but Mr. Brandon knew the people. In a short time, however, the lady died, the home was broken up, and Bevere then took lodgings on his own account; and so—there was no one to help him keep out of mischief. To go on with what I was saying. He learnt to frequent the bar-room at the Bell-and-Clapper: not only to run into it in a morning, but also on his return in the evening. He had no sociable tea or dinner-table waiting for him, you see, with pleasant faces round it. All the pleasant faces he met were those behind the counter; and there he would stay, talking, laughing, chaffing with the girls, one of whom was Miss Lizzie, goodness knows how long—the places are kept open till midnight."

"It had its attractions for him, I suppose—what with the girls and the bottles."

Pitt nodded. "It has for many a one besides him, Johnny. Roger had to call for drink; possibly without the slightest natural inclination for anything, he had perforce to call for it; he could hardly linger there unless he did. By-and-by, I reckon, he got to like the drink; he acquired the taste for it, you see, and habit soon becomes second nature; one glass became two glasses, two glasses three. This went on for a time. The next act in the young man's drama was, that he allowed himself to glide into an entanglement of some sort with one of the said girls, Miss Lizzie Field, and was drawn in to marry her."

"How have you learnt these particulars?"

"Partly from Scott. They are true. Scott has a married brother living up this way, and is often running up here; indeed at one time he lived with him, and he and Bevere used to go to and fro to St. Bartholomew's in company. Yes," slowly added the doctor, "that refreshment-room has been the bane of Roger Bevere."

"And not of Scott?"

"It did Scott no good; you may take a vow of that. But Scott has some plain, rough common-sense of his own, which kept him from going too far. He may make a good man yet; and a name also, for he possesses all the elements of a skilful surgeon. Bevere succumbed to the seductions of the bar-room, as other foolish young fellows, well-intentioned at heart, but weak in moral strength, have done, and will do again. Irresistible temptations they present, these places, to the young men who have to come in contact with them. If the lads had to go out of their way to seek the temptation, they might never do it; but it lies right in their path, you perceive, and they can't pass it by. Of course I am not speaking of all young men; only of those who are deficient in moral self-control. To some, the Bell-and-Clapper bar-room presents no more attraction than the Bell-and-Clapper Church by its side; or any other of such rooms, either."

"Is there not any remedy for this state of things?"

Pitt shrugged his shoulders. "I suppose not," he said. "Since I pulled up from drinking, I have been unable to see what these underground railway-rooms are needed for: why a man or woman, travelling for half-an-hour, more or less, must needs be provided with places to drink in at both ends of the journey and all the middles. Biscuits and buns are there as well, you may say—serving an excuse perhaps. But for one biscuit called for, there are fifty glasses of ale, or what not. Given the necessity for the rooms," added Pitt, with a laugh, "I should do away with the lady-servers and substitute men; which would put an end to three parts of the attraction. No chance of that reformation."

"Because it would do away with three parts of the custom," I said, echoing his laugh.

"Be you very sure of that, Johnny Ludlow. However, it is no business of mine to find fault with existing customs, seeing that I cannot alter them," concluded the doctor.

What he said set me thinking. Every time I passed by one of these stations, so crowded with the traffic of young city men, and saw the bottles arrayed to charm the sight, their bright colours gleaming and glistening, and looked at the serving-damsels, with their bedecked heads, arrayed to charm also, I knew Pitt must be right. These rooms might bring in grist to their owners' mill; but it struck me that I should not like, when I grew old, to remember that I had owned one.

Roger Bevere's arm began to yield to treatment, but he continued very ill in himself; too ill to get up. Torment of mind and torment of body are a bad complication.

One afternoon when I was sitting with him, sundry quick knocks downstairs threatened to disturb the doze he was falling into—and Pitt had said that sleep to him just now was like gold. I crept away to stop it. In the middle of the parlour, thumping on the floor with her cotton umbrella—a huge green thing that must have been the fellow, when made, to Sairey Gamp's—stood Mrs. Dyke, a stout, good-natured, sensible woman, whom I often saw there. Her husband was a well-to-do coachman, whose first wife had been sister to Lizzie's mother, and this wife was their cousin.

"Where's Lizzie, sir?" she asked. "Out, I suppose?"

"Yes, I think so. I saw her with her bonnet on."

"The girl's out, too, I take it, or she'd have heard me," remarked Mrs. Dyke, as she took her seat on the shabby red sofa, and pushed her bonnet back from her hot and comely face. "And how are we going on up there, sir?"—pointing to the ceiling.

"Very slowly. He cannot get rid of the fever."

She lodged the elegant umbrella against the sofa's arm and turned sideways to face me. I had sat down by the window, not caring to go back and run the risk of disturbing Roger.

"Now come, sir," she said, "let us talk comfortable: you won't mind giving me your opinion, I dare say. I have looked out for an opportunity to ask it: you being what you are, sir, and his good friend. Them two—they don't hit it off well together, do they?"

Knowing she must allude to Bevere and his wife, I had no ready answer at hand. Mrs. Dyke took silence for assent.

"Ah, I see how it is. I thought I must be right; I've thought it for some time. But Lizzie only laughs in my face, when I ask her. There's no happiness between 'em; just the other thing; I told Lizzie so only yesterday. But they can't undo what they have done, and there's nothing left for them, sir, but to make the best of it."

"That's true, Mrs. Dyke. And I think Lizzie might do more towards it than she does. If she would only—"

"Only try to get a bit into his ways and manners and not offend him with hers," put in discerning Mrs. Dyke, when I hesitated, "He is as nice a young gentleman as ever lived, and I believe has the making in him of a good husband. But Lizzie is vulgar and her ways are vulgar; and instead of checking herself and remembering that he is just the opposite, and that naturally it must offend him, she lets herself grow more so day by day. I know what's what, sir, having been used to the ways of gentry when I was a young woman, for I lived cook for some years in a good family."

"Lizzie's ways are so noisy."

"Her ways are noisy and rampagious," assented Mrs. Dyke, "more particularly when she has been at her drops; and noise puts out a sick man."

"Her drops!" I repeated, involuntarily, the word calling up a latent doubt that lay in my mind.

"When girls that have been in busy employment all day and every day, suddenly settle down to idleness, they sometimes slip into this habit or that habit, not altogether good for themselves, which they might never else have had time to think of," remarked Mrs. Dyke. "I've come in here more than once lately and seen Lizzie drinking hot spirits-and-water in the daytime: I know you must have seen the same, sir, or I'd not mention it—and beer she'll take unlimited."

Of course I had seen it.

"I think she must have learnt it at the counter; drinking never was in our family, and I never knew that it was in her father's," continued Mrs. Dyke. "But some of the young women, serving at these bars, get to like the drink through having the sight and smell of it about 'em all day long."

That was more than likely, but I did not say so, not caring to continue that branch of the subject.

"The marriage was a misfortune, Mrs. Dyke."

"For him I suppose you gentlemen consider it was," she answered. "It will be one for her if he should die: she'd have to go back to work again and she has got out o' the trick of it. Ah! she thought grand things of it at first, naturally, marrying a gentleman! But unequal marriages rarely turn out well in the long run. I knew nothing of it till it was done and over, or I should have advised her against it; my husband's place lay in a different part of London then—Eaton Square way. Better, perhaps, for Lizzie had she gone out to service in the country, like her sister."

"Did she always live in London?"

"Dear, no, sir, nor near it; she lived down in Essex with her father and mother. But she came up to London on a visit, and fell in love with the public life, through getting to know a young woman who was in it. Nothing could turn her, once her mind was set upon it; and being sharp and clever, quick at figures, she got taken on at some wine-vaults in the city. After staying there awhile and giving satisfaction, she changed to the refreshment-room at the Bell-and-Clapper. Miss Panken went there soon after, and they grew very intimate. The young girl left, who had been there before her; very pretty she was: I don't know what became of her. At some of the counters they have but one girl; at others, two."

"It is a pity girls should be at them at all—drawing on the young men! I am speaking generally, Mrs. Dyke."

"It is a pity the young men should be so soft as to be drawn on by them—if you'll excuse my saying it, sir," she returned, quickly. "But there—what would you? Human nature's the same all the world over: Jack and Jill. The young men like to talk to the girls, and the girls like very much to talk to the young men. Of course these barmaids lay themselves out to the best advantage, in the doing of their hair and their white frills, and what not, which is human nature again, sir. Look at a young lady in a drawing-room: don't she set herself off when she is expecting the beaux to call?"

Mrs. Dyke paused for want of breath. Her tongue ran on fast, but it told of good sense.

"The barmaids are but like the young ladies, sir; and the young fellows that congregate there get to admire them, while sipping their drops at the counter; if, as I say, they are soft enough. When the girls get hold of one softer than the rest, why, perhaps one of them gets over him so far as to entrap him to give her his name—just as safe as you hook and land a fish."

"And I suppose it has a different termination sometimes?"

Honest Mrs. Dyke shook her head. "We won't talk about that, sir: I can't deny that it may happen once in a way. Not often, let's hope. The young women, as a rule, are well-conducted and respectable: they mostly know how to take care of themselves."

"I should say Miss Panken does."

Mrs. Dyke's broad face shone with merriment. "Ain't she impudent? Oh yes, sir, Polly Panken can take care of herself, never fear. But it's not a good atmosphere for young girls to be in, you see, sir, these public bars; whether it may be only at a railway counter, or at one of them busy taverns in the town, or at the gay places of amusement, the manners and morals of the girls get to be a bit loose, as it were, and they can't help it."

"Or anybody else, I suppose."

"No, sir, not as things are; and it's just a wrong upon them that they should be exposed to it. They'd be safer and quieter in a respectable service, which is the state of life many of 'em were born to—though a few may be superior—and better behaved, too: manners is sure to get a bit corrupted in the public line. But the girls like their liberty; they like the free-and-easy public life and its idleness; they like the flirting and the chaffing and the nonsense that goes on; they like to be dressed up of a day as if they were so many young ladies, their hair done off in bows and curls and frizzes, and their hands in cuffs and lace-edgings; now and then you may see 'em with a ring on. That's a better life, they think, than they'd lead as servants or shop-women, or any of the other callings open to this class of young women: and perhaps it is. It's easier, at any rate. I've heard that some quite superior young people are in it, who might be, or were, governesses, and couldn't find employment, poor young ladies, through the market being so overstocked. Ah, it is a hard thing, sir, for a well-brought-up young woman to find lady-like employment nowadays. One thing is certain," concluded Mrs. Dyke, "that we shall never have a lack of barmaids in this country until a law is passed by the legislature—which, happen, never will be passed—to forbid girls serving in these places. There'd be less foolishness going on then, and a deal less drinking."

These were Pitt's ideas over again.

A loud laugh outside, and Lizzie came running in. "Why, Aunt Dyke, are you there!—entertaining Mr. Johnny Ludlow!" she exclaimed, as she threw herself into a chair. "Well, I never. And what do you two think I am going to do to-morrow?"

"Now just you mind your manners, young woman," advised the aunt.

"I am minding them—don't you begin blowing-up," retorted Lizzie, her face brimming over with good-humour.

"You might have your things stole; you and the girl out together," said Mrs. Dyke.

"There's nothing to steal but chairs and tables. I'm sure I'm much obliged to you both for sitting here to take care of them. You'll never guess what I am going to do," broke off Lizzie, with shrieks of laughter. "I am going to take my old place again at the Bell-and-Clapper, and serve behind the counter for the day: Mabel Falkner wants a holiday. Won't it be fun!"

"Your husband will not let you; he would not like it," I said in my haste, while Mrs. Dyke sat in open-mouthed amazement.

"And I shall put on my old black dress; I've got it yet; and be a regular barmaid again. A lovely costume, that black is!" ironically ran on Lizzie. "Neat and not gaudy, as the devil said when he painted his tail pea-green. You need not look as though you thought I had made acquaintance with him and heard him say it, Mr. Johnny; I only borrowed it from one of Bulwer's novels that I read the other day."

If I did not think that, I thought Madam Lizzie had been making acquaintance this afternoon with something else. "Drops!" as Mrs. Dyke called it.

"There I shall be to-morrow, at the old work, and you can both come and see me at it," said Lizzie. "I'll treat you more civilly, Mr. Johnny, than Polly Panken did."

"But I say that your husband will not allow you to go," I repeated to her.

"Ah, he's in bed," she laughed; "he can't get out of it to stop me."

"You are all on the wrong tack, Lizzie girl," spoke up the aunt, severely. "If you don't mind, it will land you in shoals and quicksands. How dare you think of running counter to what you know your husband's wishes would be?"

She received this with a louder laugh than ever. "He will not know anything about it, Aunt Dyke. Unless Mr. Johnny Ludlow here should tell him. It would not make any difference to me if he did," she concluded, with candour.

And as I felt sure it would not, I held my tongue.

By degrees, as the days went on, Roger got about again, and when I left London he was back at St. Bartholomew's. Other uncanny things had happened to me during this visit of mine, but not one of them brought with it so heavy a weight as the thought of poor Roger Bevere and his blighted life.

"His health may get all right if he will give up drinking," were the last words Pitt said to me. "He has promised to do so."

The weather was cold and wintry as we began our railway journey. From two to three years have gone on, you must please note, since the time told of above. Mr. Brandon was about to spend the Christmas with his sister, Lady Bevere—who had quitted Hampshire and settled not far from Brighton—and she had sent me an invitation to accompany him.

We took the train at Evesham. It was Friday, and the shortest day in the year; St. Thomas, the twenty-first of December. Some people do not care to begin a journey on a Friday, thinking it bodes ill-luck: I might have thought the same had I foreseen what was to happen before we got home again.

London reached, we met Roger Bevere at the Brighton Station, as agreed upon. He was to travel down with us. I had not seen him since the time of his illness in London, except for an hour once when I was in town upon some business for the Squire. Nothing had transpired to his friends, so far as I knew, of the fatal step he had taken; that was a secret still.

I cannot say I much liked Roger's appearance now, as he sat opposite me in the railway-carriage, leaning against the arm of the comfortably-cushioned seat. His fair, pleasant face was gentle as ever, but the once clear blue eyes no longer looked very clear and did not meet ours freely; his hands shook, his fingers were restless. Mr. Brandon did not much like the signs either, to judge by the way he stared at him.

"Have you been well lately, Roger?"

"Oh yes, thank you, Uncle John."

"Well, your looks don't say much for you."

"I am rather hard-worked," said Roger. "London is not a place to grow rosy in."

"Do you like your new work?" continued Mr. Brandon. For Roger had done with St. Bartholomew's Hospital, and was outdoor assistant to a surgeon in private practice, a Mr. Anderson.

"I like it better than the hospital work, Uncle John."

"Ah! A fine idea that was of yours—wanting to set up in practice for yourself the minute you had passed. Your mother did well to send the letter to me and ask my advice. Some of you boys—boys, and no better—fresh from your hospital studies, screw a brass-plate on your door, announcing yourselves to the world as qualified surgeons. A few of you go a step further and add M.D."

"Many of us take our degree as physician at once, Uncle John," said Roger. "It is becoming quite the custom."

"Just so: the custom!" retorted Mr. Brandon, cynically. "Why didn't you do it, and modestly call yourself Dr. Bevere? In my former days, young man, when some ultra-grave ailment necessitated application to a physician, we went to him in all confidence, knowing that he was a man of steady years, of long-tried experience, whose advice was to be relied upon. Now, if you are dying and call in some Dr. So-and-so, you may find him a young fellow of three or four and twenty. As likely as not only an M.B. in reality, who has arrogated to himself the title of Doctor. For I hear some of them do it."

"But they think they have a right to be called so, Uncle John. The question—"

"What right?" sharply demanded Mr. Brandon. "What gives it them?"

"Well—courtesy, I suppose," hesitated Roger.

"Oh," said Mr. Brandon.

I laughed. His tone was so quaint.

"Yes, you may laugh, Johnny Ludlow—showing your thoughtlessness! There'll soon be no modesty left in the world," he continued; "there'll soon be no hard, plodding work. Formerly, men were content to labour on patiently for years, to attain success, whether in fame, fortune, or for a moderate competency. Now they must take a leap into it. Tradespeople retire before middle-age, merchants make colossal fortunes in a decade, and (to leave other anomalies alone) you random young hospital students spring into practice full-fledged M.D.'s."

"The world is changing, Uncle John."

"It is," assented Mr. Brandon. "I'm not sure that we shall know it by-and-by."

From Brighton terminus we had a drive of two or three miles across country to get to Prior's Glebe—as Lady Bevere's house was named. It was old-fashioned and commodious, and stood in a large square garden that was encircled by a thick belt of towering shrubs. Nothing was to be seen around it but a huge stretch of waste land; half a-mile-off, rose a little church and a few scattered cottages. "The girls must find this lively!" exclaimed Roger, taking a comprehensive look about him as we drove up in the twilight.

Lady Bevere, kind, gentle, simple-mannered as ever, received us lovingly. Mr. Brandon kissed her, and she kissed me and Roger. It was the first Christmas Roger had spent at home since rushing into that mad act of his; he had always invented some excuse for declining. The eldest son, Edmund, was in the navy; the second, George, was in the Church; Roger was the third; and the youngest, John, had a post in a merchant's house in Calcutta. Of the four girls, only the eldest, Mary, and the youngest were at home. The little one was named Susan, but they called her Tottams. The other two were on a visit to their aunt, the late Sir Edmund Bevere's sister.

Dinner was waiting when we got in, and I could not snatch half a word with Roger while making ready for it. He and I had two little rooms opening to each other. But when we went upstairs for the night we could talk at will; and I put my candle down on his chest of drawers.

"How are things going with you, Roger?"

"Don't talk of it," he cried, with quite a burst of emotion. "Things cannot be worse than they are."

"I fancy you have not pulled up much, as Pitt used to call it, have you, old friend? Your hands and your face tell tales."

"How can I pull up?" he retorted.

"You promised that you would."

"Ay. Promised! When all the world's against a fellow, he may not be able to keep his promises. Perhaps may not care to."

"How is Lizzie?" I said then, dropping my voice.

"Don't talk of her," repeated Bevere, in a tone of despair; despair if I ever heard it. It shut me up.

"Johnny, I'm nearly done over; sick of it all," he went on. "You don't know what I have to bear."

"Still—as regards yourself, you might pull up," I persisted, for to give in to him, and his mood and his ways, would never do. "You might if you chose, Bevere."

"I suppose I might, if I had any hope. But there's none; none. People tell us that as we make our bed so we must lie upon it. I made mine in an awful fashion years ago, and I must pay the penalty."

"I gather from this—forgive me, Bevere—that you and your wife don't get along together."

"Get along! Things with her are worse than you may think for. She—she—well, she has not done her best to turn out well. Heaven knows I'd have tried my best; the thing was done, and nothing else was left for us: but she has not let me. We are something like cat-and-dog now, and I am not living with her."

"No!"

"That is, I inhabit other lodgings. She is at the old place. I am with a medical man in Bloomsbury, you know. It was necessary for me to be near him, and six months ago I went. Lizzie acquiesced in that; the matter was obvious. I sometimes go to see her; staying, perhaps, from Saturday to Monday, and come away cursing myself."

"Don't. Don't, Bevere."

"She has taken to drink," he whispered, biting his agitated lips. "For pretty near two years now she has not been a day sober. As Heaven hears me, I believe not one day. You may judge what I've had to bear."

"Could nothing be done?"

"I tried to do it, Johnny. I coaxed, persuaded, threatened her by turns, but she would not leave it off. For four months in the autumn of last year, I did not let a drop of anything come into the house; drinking water myself all the while—for her sake. It was of no use: she'd go out and get it: every public-house in the place knows her. I'd come home from the hospital in the evening and find her raving and rushing about the rooms like a mad woman, or else lying incapable on the bed. Believe me, I tried all I could to keep her straight; and Mrs. Dyke, a good, motherly woman, you remember, did her best to help me; but she was too much for both of us, the demon of drink had laid too fast hold of her."

"Does she come bothering you at your new lodgings?"

"She doesn't know where to come," replied Bevere; "I should not dare to tell her. She thinks I am in the doctor's house, and she does not know where that is. I have told her, and her Aunt Dyke has told her, that if ever she attempts to come after me there, I shall stop her allowance. Scott—you remember Richard Scott!"

"Of course."

"Well, Scott lives now near the Bell-and-Clapper: he is with a surgeon there. Scott goes to see her for me once a-week, or so, and brings me news of her. I declare to you, Johnny Ludlow, that when I first catch sight of his face I turn to a cold shiver, dreading what he may have to say. And you talk about pulling up! With such a wife as that, one is thankful to drown care once in a way."

"I—I suppose, Roger, nothing about her has ever come out here?"

He started up, his face on fire. "Johnny, lad, if it came out here—to my mother—to all of them—I should die. Say no more. The case is hopeless, and I am hopeless with it."

Any way, it seemed hopeless to talk further then, and I took up my candle. "Just one more word, Roger: Does Lizzie know you have come down here? She might follow you."

His face took a look of terror. The bare idea scared him. "I say, don't you invent impossible horrors," gasped he. "She couldn't come; she has never heard of the place in connection with me. She has never heard anything about my people, or where they live, or don't live, or whether I have any. Good-night."

"Good-night, Roger."

III

People say you can never sleep well in a strange bed. I know I did not sleep well, but very badly, that first night at Lady Bevere's. It was not the fault of the bed, or of its strangeness; it was Roger's trouble haunting me.

He did not seem to have slept well either, to judge by his looks when I went into his room in the morning. His fair, pleasant face was pale; his lips trembled, the blue eyes had torment in their depths.

"I have had a bad dream," he said, in answer to a remark I made. "An awful dream. It came to me in my last sleep this morning; and morning dreams, they say, come true. I'm afraid I have you to thank for it, Johnny."

"Me!"

"You suggested last night, startling me well-nigh out of my senses by it, that Lizzie might follow me down here. Well, I dreamt she did so. I saw her in the dining-room, haranguing my mother, her red-gold hair streaming over her shoulders and her arms stretched wildly out. Uncle John stood in a corner of the room, looking on."

I felt sorry, and told him so: of course my speaking had prompted the dream. He need not fear. If Lizzie did not know he had come down here, or that his family lived here, or anything about them, she could not follow him.

"You see shadows where no shadows are, Roger."

"When a man spoils his life on its threshold, it is all shadow; past, present, and future."

"Things may mend, you know."

"Mend!" he returned: "how can they mend? They may grow worse; never mend. My existence is one long torment. Day by day I live in dread of what may come: of her bringing down upon herself some public disgrace and my name with it. No living being, man or woman, can imagine what it is to me; the remorse for my folly, the mortification, the shame. I believe honestly that but for a few things instilled into me at my mother's knee in childhood, I should have put an end to myself."

"It is a long lane that has no turning."

"Lanes have different outlets: bad as well as good."

"I think breakfast must be ready, Roger."

"And I started with prospects so fair!" he went on. "Never a thought or wish in my heart but to fulfil honestly the duties that lay in my way to the best of my power, to God and to man. And I should have done it, but for— Johnny Ludlow," he broke off, with a deep breath of emotion, "when I see other young fellows travelling along the same wrong road, once earnest, well-meaning lads as I was, not turning aside of their own wilful, deliberate folly, but ensnared to it by the evil works and ways they encounter in that teeming city, my soul is wrung with pity for them. I sometimes wonder whether God will punish them for what they can hardly avoid; or whether He will not rather let His anger fall on those who throw temptations in their way."

Poor Roger, poor Roger! Mr. Brandon used to talk of the skeleton in his closet: he little suspected how terrible was the skeleton in Roger's.

Lady Bevere kept four servants: for she was no better off, except for a little income that belonged to herself, than is many another admiral's widow. An upper maid, Harriet, who helped to wait, and did sewing: a housemaid and a cook; and an elderly man, Jacob, who had lived with them in the time of Sir Edmund.

During the afternoon of this day, Saturday, Roger and I set off to walk to Brighton with the two girls. Not by the high-road, but by a near way (supposed to cut off half the distance) across a huge, dreary, flat marsh, of which you could see neither the beginning nor the end. In starting, we had reached the gate at the foot of the garden, when Harriet came running down the path. She was a tall, thin, civil young woman, with something in her voice or in her manner of speaking that seemed to my ear familiar, though I knew not how or why.

"Miss Mary," she said, "my lady asks have you taken umbrellas, if you please. She thinks it will snow when the sun goes down."

"Yes, yes; tell mamma we have them," replied Mary: and Harriet ran back.

"How was it the mother came to so lonely a spot as this?" questioned Roger, as we went along, the little one, Tottams, jumping around me. "You girls must find it lively?"

Mary laughed as she answered. "We do find it lively, Roger, and we often ask her why she came. But when mamma and George looked at the place, it was a bright, hot summer's day. They liked it then: it has plenty of rooms in it, you see, though they are old-fashioned; and the rent was so very reasonable. Be quiet, Tottams."

"So reasonable that I should have concluded the place had a ghost in it," said Roger.

"George's curacy was at Brighton in those days, you know, Roger: that is why we came to the neighbourhood."

"And George had left for a better curacy before you had well settled down here! Miss Tottams, if you pull at Johnny Ludlow like that, I shall send you back by yourself."

"True. But we like the place very well now we are used to it, and we know a few nice people. One family—the Archers—we like very much. Six daughters, Roger; one of them, Bessy, would make you a charming wife. You will have to marry, you know, when you set up in practice. They are coming to us next Wednesday evening."

My eye caught Roger's. I did not intend it. Caught the bitter expression in it as he turned away.

Brighton reached, we went on the pier. Then, while they did some commissions for Lady Bevere at various shops, I went to the post-office, to register two letters for Mr. Brandon. Tottams wanted to keep with me, but they took her, saying she'd be too troublesome. The letters registered, I came out of the office, and was turning away, when some one touched me on the arm.

"Mr. Ludlow, I think! How are you?"

To my surprise it was Richard Scott. He seemed equally surprised to see me. I told him I had come down with Roger Bevere to spend Christmas week at Prior's Glebe.

"Lucky fellow!" exclaimed Scott, "I have to go back to London and drudgery this evening: came down with my governor last night for an operation to-day. Glad to say it's all well over."

But a thought had flashed into my mind: I ought not to have said so much. Drawing Scott out of the passing crowd, I spoke.

"Look here, Scott: you must be cautious not to say that Bevere's down here. You must not speak of it."

"Speak where?" asked Scott, turning his head towards me. He had put his arm within mine as we walked along. "Where?"

"Oh—well—up with you, you know—in Bevere's old quarters. Or—or in the railway-room at the Bell-and-Clapper."

Scott laughed. "I understand. Madam Lizzie might be coming after him to his mother's. But—why, what an odd thing!"

Some thought seemed to have struck him suddenly. He paused in his walk as well as in his speech.

"I dare say it was nothing," he added, going on again. "Be at ease as to Bevere, Ludlow. I should as soon think of applying to him a lighted firebrand."

"But what is it you call odd?" I asked, feeling sure that, whatever it might be, it was connected with Bevere.

"Why, this," said Scott. "Last night, when we got here, I left my umbrella in the carriage, having a lot of other things to see to of my own and the governor's. I went back as soon as I found it out, but could hear nothing of it. Just now I went up again and got it"—slightly showing the green silk one he held in his hand. "A train from London came in while I stood there, bringing a heap of passengers. One of them looked like Lizzie."

I could not speak from consternation.

"Having nothing to do while waiting for my umbrella to be brought, I was watching the crowd flock out of the station," continued Scott. "Amidst it I saw a head of red-gold hair, just like Lizzie's. I could not see more of her than that; some other young woman's head was close to hers."

"But do you think it was Lizzie?"

"No, I do not. So little did I think it that it went clean out of my mind until you spoke. It must have been some accidental resemblance; nothing more; red-gold hair is not so very uncommon. There's nothing to bring her down to Brighton."

"Unless she knows that he is here."

"That's impossible."

"What a wretched business it is altogether!"

"You might well say that if you knew all," returned Scott. "She drinks like a fish. Like a fish, I assure you. Twice over she has had a shaking-fit of three days' duration—I suppose you take me, Ludlow—had to be watched in her bed; the last time was not more than a week ago. She'll do for herself, if she goes on. It's an awful clog on Bevere. The marriage in itself was a piece of miserable folly, but if she had been a different sort of woman and kept herself steady and cared for him—"

"The problem to me is, how Bevere could have been led away by such a woman."

"Ah, but you must not judge of that by what she is now. She was a very attractive girl, and kept her manners within bounds. Just the kind of girl that many a silly young ape would lose his head for; and Bevere, I take it, lost his heart as well as his head."

"Did you know of the marriage at the time?"

"Not until after it had taken place."

"They could never have pulled well together as man and wife; two people so opposite as they are."

"No, I fancy not," answered Richard Scott, looking straight out before him, but as though he saw nothing. "She has not tried at it. Once his wife, safe and sure, she thought she had it all her own way—as of course in one sense she had, and could give the reins to her inclination. Nothing that Bevere wanted her to do, would she do. He wished her to give up all acquaintance with the two girls at the Bell-and-Clapper; but not she. He—"

"Is Miss Panken flourishing?"

"Quite," laughed Scott, "The other one came to grief—Mabel Falkner."

"Did she! I thought she seemed rather nice."

"She was a very nice little girl indeed, as modest as Polly Panken is impudent. The one could take care of herself; the other couldn't—or didn't. Well, Mabel fell into trouble, and of course lost her post. Madam Lizzie immediately gave her house-room, setting Bevere, who forbade it, at defiance. What with grief and other disasters, the girl fell sick there; had an illness, and had to be kept I don't know how long. It put Bevere out uncommonly."

"Is this lately?"

"Oh no; last year. Lizzie— By the way," broke off Scott, stopping again and searching his pocket, "I've got a note from her for Bevere. You can give it him."

The words nearly seared away my senses. A note from Lizzie to Bevere! "Why, then, she must know he is here!" I cried.

"You don't understand," quietly said Scott, giving me a note from his pocket-book. "A day or two ago, I met Lizzie near the Bell-and-Clapper. She—"

"She is well enough to be out, then!"

"Yes. At times she is as well as you are. Well, I met her, and she began to give me a message for her husband, which I could not then wait to hear. So she sent this note to me later, to be delivered to him when we next met. I had not time to go to him yesterday, and here the note is still."

It was addressed "Mr. Bevary." I pointed out the name to Scott.

"Does she not know better, think you?"

"Very likely not," he answered. "A wrong letter, more or less, in a name, signifies but little to one of Lizzie's standard of education. It is not often, I expect, she sees the name on paper, or has to write it. Fare you well, Ludlow. Remember me to Bevere."

Scott had hardly disappeared when they met me. I said nothing of having seen him. After treating Tottams to some tarts and a box of bonbons, we set off home again; the winter afternoon was closing, and it was nearly dark when we arrived. Getting Roger into his room, I handed him the note, and told him how I came by it. He showed me the contents.

"DEAR ROGER,

"When you where last at home, you said you should not be able to spend Christmas with me, so I am thinking of trying a little jaunt for myself. I am well now and mean to keep so, and a few days in the country air may help me and set me up prime. I inscribe this to let you know, and also to tell you that I shall pay my journey with the quarter's rent you left, so you must send or bring the sum again. Aunt Dyke has got the rumaticks fine, she can't come bothering me with her lectures quite as persistent as usual. Wishing you the compliments of the season, I remain,

"Your affectionate wife,
"LIZZIE."

"Gone into Essex, I suppose; she has talked sometimes of her cousin there," was all the remark made by Bevere. And he set the note alight, and sent it blazing up the chimney. Of course I did not mention Scott's fancy about the red-gold hair.

Sunday. We crossed the waste land in the morning to the little church I have spoken of. A few cottages stood about it, and a public-house with a big sign, on which was painted a yellow bunch of wheat, and the words The Sheaf o' Corn. It was bitterly cold weather, the wind keen and cutting, the ground a sort of grey-white from a sprinkling of snow that had fallen in the night. I suppose they don't, as a rule, warm these rural churches, from want of means or energy, but I think I never felt a church so cold before. Mr. Brandon said it had given him a chill.

In the evening, after tea, we went to church by moonlight. Not all of us this time. Mr. Brandon stayed away to nurse his chill, and Roger on the plea of headache. The snow was beginning to come down smartly. The little church was lighted with candles stuck in tin sconces nailed to the wall, and was dim enough. Lady Bevere whispered to me that the clergyman had a service elsewhere in the afternoon, so could only hold his own in the evening.

It was snowing with a vengeance when we came out—large flakes half as big as a shilling, and in places already a foot deep. We made the best of our way home, and were white objects when we got there.

"Ah!" remarked Mr. Brandon, "I thought we should have it. Hope the wind will go down a little now."

The girls and their mother went upstairs to take off their cloaks. I asked Mr. Brandon where Roger was. He turned round from his warm seat by the fire to answer me.

"Roger is outside, enjoying the benefit of the snow-storm. That young man has some extraordinary care upon his conscience, Johnny, unless I am mistaken," he added, his thin voice emphatic, his eyes throwing an inquiry into mine.

"Do you fancy he has, sir?" I stammered. At which Mr. Brandon threw a searching look at me, as if he had a mind to tax me with knowing what it was.

"Well, you had better tell him to come in, Johnny."

Roger's great-coat, hanging in the hall, seemed to afford an index that he had not strayed beyond the garden. The snow, coming down so thick and fast but a minute or two ago, had temporarily ceased, following its own capricious fashion, and the moon was bright again. Calling aloud to Roger as I stood on the door-step, and getting no answer, I went out to look for him.

On the side of the garden facing the church, was a little entrance-gate, amid the clusters of laurels and other shrubs. Hearing footsteps approach this, and knowing all were in from church, for the servants got back before we did, I went down the narrow cross-path leading to it, and looked out. It was not Roger, but a woman. A lady, rather, by what the moonbeams displayed of her dress, which looked very smart. As she seemed to be making for the gate, I stepped aside into the shrubs, and peered out over the moor for Roger. The lady gave a sharp ring at the bell, and old Jacob came from the side-door of the house to answer it.

"Is this Prior's Glebe?" she asked—and her voice gave an odd thrill to my pulses, for I thought I recognized it.

"Yes, ma'am," said Jacob.

"Lady Beveer's, I think."

"That's near enough," returned Jacob, familiar with the eccentricities of pronunciation accorded to the name. "What did you please to want?"

"I want Miss Field."

"Miss Field!" echoed the old man.

"Harriet Field. She lives here, don't she? I'd like to see her."

"Oh—Harriet! I'll send her out," said he, turning away.

The more I heard of the voice, the greater grew my dismay. Surely it was that of Roger's wife! Was it really she that Scott had seen at the station? Had she come after Roger? Did she know he was here? I stood back amid the sheltering laurels, hardly daring to breathe. Waiting there, she began a little dance, or shuffle of the feet, perhaps to warm herself, and broke into a verse of a gay song. "As I live, she's not sober!" was the fear that flashed across me. Harriet, her things still on, just as she came in from church, came swiftly to the gate.

"Well, Harriet, how are you?"

"Why, Lizzie!—it's never you!" exclaimed Harriet, after an amazed stare at the visitor.

"Yes, it's me. I thought I'd come over and see you. That old man was polite though, to leave me standing here."

"But where have you come from? And why are you so late?"

"Oh, I'm staying at Brighton; came down on the spree yesterday. I'm late because I lost my way on this precious moor—or whatever it calls itself—and got a mile, or so, too far. When the snow came on—and ain't it getting deep!—I turned into a house to shelter a bit, and here I am. A man that was coming out of church yonder directed me to the place here."

She must have been at The Sheaf o' Corn. What if she had chanced to ask the route of me!

"You got my letter, then, telling you I had left my old place at Worthing, and taken service here," said Harriet.

"I got it safe enough; it was directed to the Bell-and-Clapper room," returned Lizzie. "What a stick of a hand you do write! I couldn't decipher whether your new mistress was Lady Beveen or Lady Beveer. I had thought you never meant to write to me again."

"Well, you know, Lizzie, that quarrel between us years back, after father and mother died, was a bitter one; but I'm sure I don't want to be anything but friendly for the future. You haven't written, either. I never had but that one letter from you, telling me you had got married, and that he was a gentleman."

"And you wrote back asking whether it was true, or whether I had jumped over the broomstick," retorted Lizzie, with a laugh. "You always liked to be polite to me, Harriet."

"Do you ever see Uncle Dyke up in London, Lizzie?"

"And Aunt Dyke too—she's his second, you know. They are both flourishing just now with rheumatism. He has got it in his chest, and she in her knees—tra, la, la, la! I say, are you not going to invite me in?"

Lizzie's conversation had been interspersed with laughs and antics. I saw Harriet look at her keenly. "Was it a public-house you took shelter in, Lizzie?" she asked.

"As if it could have been a private one! That's good."

"Is your husband with you at Brighton? I suppose you are married, Lizzie?"

"As safe as that you are an old maid—or going on for one. My husband's a doctor and can't leave his patients. I came down with a friend of mine, Miss Panken; she has to go back to-night, but I mean to stay over Christmas-Day. I'll tell you all about my husband if you'll be civil enough to take me indoors."

"I can't take you in to-night, Lizzie. It's too late, for one thing, and we must not have visitors on a Sunday. But you can come over to tea to-morrow evening; I'm sure my lady won't object. Come early in the afternoon. And look here," added Harriet, dropping her voice, "don't drink anything beforehand; come quiet and decent."

"Who has been telling you that I do drink?" demanded Lizzie, in a sharp tone.

"Well, nobody has told me. But I can see it. I hope it's not a practice with you; that's all."

"A practice! There you go! It wouldn't be you, Harriet, if you didn't say something unpleasant. One must take a sup of hot liquor when benighted in such freezing snow as this. And I did not put on my warm cloak; it was fine and bright when I started."

"Shall I lend you one? I'll get it in a minute. Or a waterproof?"

"Thanks all the same, no; I shall walk fast, I don't feel cold—and I should only have the trouble of bringing it back to-morrow afternoon. I'll be here by three o'clock. Good-night, Harriet."

"Good-night, Lizzie. Go round to that path that branches off from our front-gate; keep straight on, and you can't miss the way."

I had heard it all; every syllable; unable to help it. The least rustle of the laurels might have betrayed me. Betrayed me to Lizzie.

What a calamity! She did not appear to have come down after Roger, did not appear to know that he was connected with Lady Bevere—or that the names were the same. But at the tea-table the following evening she would inevitably learn all. Servants talk of their masters and their doings. And to hear Roger's name would be ruin.

I found Roger in his chamber. "Uncle Brandon was putting inconvenient questions to me," he said, "so I got away under pretence of looking at the weather. How cold you look, Johnny!"

"I am cold. I went into the garden, looking for you, and I had a fright there."

"Seen a ghost?" returned he, lightly.

"Something worse than a ghost. Roger, I have some disagreeable news for you."

"Eh?—what?" he cried, his fears leaping up: indeed they were very seldom down. "They don't suspect anything, do they? What is it? Why do you beat about the bush?"

"I should like to prepare you. If—"

"Prepare me!" sharply interrupted Roger, his nerves all awry. "Do you think I am a girl? Don't I live always in too much mental excruciation to need preparation for any mortal ill?"

"Well, Lizzie's down here."

In spite of his boast, he turned as white as the counterpane on his bed. I sat down and told him all. His hair grew damp as he listened, his face took the hue of despair.

"Heaven help me!" he gasped.

"I suppose you did not know Harriet was her sister?"

"How was I to know it? Be you very sure Lizzie would not voluntarily proclaim to me that she had a sister in service. What wretched luck! Oh, Johnny, what is to be done?"

"Nothing—that I see. It will be sure to come out over their tea to-morrow. Harriet will say 'Mr. Roger's down here on a visit, and has brought Mr. Johnny Ludlow with him'—just as a little item of gossip. And then—why, then, Lizzie will make but one step of it into the family circle, and say 'Roger is my husband.' It is of no use to mince the matter, Bevere," I added, in answer to a groan of pain; "better look the worst in the face."

The worst was a very hopeless worst. Even if we could find out where she was staying in Brighton, and he or I went to her to try to stop her coming, it would not avail; she would come all the more.

"You don't know her depth," groaned Roger. "She'd put two and two together, and jump to the right conclusion—that it is my home. No, there's nothing that can be done, nothing; events must take their course. Johnny," he passionately added, "I'd rather die than face the shame."

Lady Bevere's voice on the stairs interrupted him. "Roger! Johnny! Why don't you come down? Supper's waiting."

"I can't go down," he whispered.

"You must, Roger. If not, they'll ask the reason why."

A fine state of mental turbulence we were in all day on Monday. Roger dared not stir abroad lest he should meet her and have to bring her home clinging to his coat-tails. Not that much going abroad was practicable, save in the beaten paths. Snow had fallen heavily all night long. But the sky to-day was blue and bright.

With the afternoon began the watching and listening. I wonder whether the reader can picture our mental state? Roger had made a resolve that as soon as Lizzie's foot crossed the threshold, he would disclose all to his mother, forestalling her tale. Indeed, he could do nothing less. Says Lord Byron, "Whatever sky's above me, here's a heart for every fate." I fear we could not then have said the same.

Three o'clock struck. Roger grew pale to the lips as he heard it. I am not sure but I did. Four o'clock struck; and yet she did not come. The suspense, the agony of those few afternoon hours brought enough pain for a lifetime.

At dusk, when she could not have known me at a distance, I went out to reconnoitre, glad to go somewhere or do something, and prowled about under shelter of the dark shrubs, watching the road. She was not in sight anywhere; coming from any part; though I stayed there till I was blue with cold.

"Not in a state to come, I expect," gasped Roger, when I got in, and reported that I could see nothing of her, and found him still sitting over the dining-room fire.

He gave a start as the door was flung open. It was only Harriet, with the tea-tray and candles. We had dined early. George, the clergyman, was expected in the evening, and Lady Bevere thought it would be more sociable if we all took supper with him. Tottams followed the tea-tray, skipping and singing.

"I wish it was Christmas-Eve every day!" cried the child. "Cook's making such a lot of mince pies and cakes in the kitchen."

"Why, dear me, somebody has been drawing the curtains without having shut the shutters first!" exclaimed Harriet, hastening to remedy the mistake.

I could have told her it was Roger. As the daylight faded and the fire brightened, he had shut out the window, lest dreaded eyes should peer through it and see him.

"Your sister's not come yet, Harriet!" said Tottams. For the advent of Harriet's expected visitor was known in the household.

"No, Miss Tottams, she is not," replied Harriet, "I can't think why, unless she was afraid of the snow underfoot."

"There's no snow to hurt along the paths," contended Tottams.

"Perhaps she'd not know that," said Harriet. "But she may come yet; it is only five o'clock—and it's a beautiful moon."

Roger got up to leave the room and met Lady Bevere face to face. She caught sight of the despair on his, for he was off his guard. But off it, or on it, no one could fail to see that he was ill at ease. Some young men might have kept a smooth countenance through it all, for their friends and the world; Roger was sensitive to a degree, refined, thoughtful, and could not hide the signs of conflict.

"What is it that is amiss with him, Johnny?" Lady Bevere said, coming to me as I stood on the hearthrug before the fire, Tottams having disappeared with Harriet. "He looks wretchedly ill; ill with care, as it seems to me; and he cannot eat."

What could I answer? How was it possible, with those kind, candid blue eyes, so like Roger's, looking confidingly into mine, to tell her that nothing was amiss?

"Dear Lady Bevere, do not be troubled," I said at length. "A little matter has been lately annoying Roger in London, and—and—I suppose he cannot forget it down here."

"Is it money trouble?" she asked.

"Not exactly. No; it's not money. Perhaps Roger will tell you himself. But please do not say anything to him unless he does."

"Why cannot you tell me, Johnny?"

Had Madam Lizzie been in the house, rendering discovery inevitable, I would have told her then, and so far spared Roger the pain. But she was not; she might not come; in which case perhaps the disclosure need not be made—or, at any rate, might be staved off to a future time. Lady Bevere held my hands in hers.

"You know what this trouble is, Johnny; all about it?"

"Yes, that's true. But I cannot tell it you. I have no right to."

"I suppose you are right," she sighed. "But oh, my dear, you young people cannot know what such griefs are to a mother's heart; the dread they inflict, the cruel suspense they involve."

And the evening passed on to its close, and Lizzie had not come.

A little circumstance occurred that night, not much to relate, but not pleasant in itself. George, a good-looking young clergyman, got in very late and half-frozen—close upon eleven o'clock. He would not have supper brought back, but said he should be glad of some hot brandy-and-water. The water was brought in and put with the brandy on a side-table. George mixed a glass for himself, and Roger went and mixed one. By-and-bye, when Roger had disposed of that, he went back to mix a second. Mr. Brandon glided up behind him.

"No, Roger, not in your mother's house," he whispered, interposing a hand of authority between Roger and the brandy. "Though you may drink to an unseemly extent in town, you shall not here."

"Roger got some brandy-and-water from mamma this afternoon," volunteered Miss Tottams, dancing up to them. She had been allowed to sit up to help dress the rooms; and, of all little pitchers, she had the sharpest ears. "He said he felt sick, Uncle John."

They came back to the fire and sat down again, Roger looking in truth sick; sick almost unto death.

Mr. Brandon went up to bed; Lady Bevere soon followed, and we began the rooms, Harriet and Jacob coming in to help. Roger exclaimed at the splendid heaps of holly. Of late years he had seen only the poor scraps they get in London.

"A merry Christmas to you, Roger!"

"Don't, Johnny! Better that you should wish me dead."

The bright sun was shining into his room as I entered it on this Christmas morning: Roger stood brushing his hair at the glass. He looked very ill.

"How can I look otherwise?" retorted poor Roger. "Two nights and not a wink of sleep!—nothing but fever and apprehension and intolerable restlessness. And you come wishing me a merry Christmas!"

Well, of course it did sound like a mockery. "I will wish you a happier one for next year, then, Roger. Things may be brighter then."

"How can they be?—with that dreadful weight that I must carry about with me for life? Do you see this?"—sweeping his hand round towards the window.

I saw nothing but the blessed sunlight—and said so.

"That's it," he answered: "that blessed sunlight will bring her here betimes. With a good blinding snowfall, or a pelting downpour of cats and dogs, I might have hoped for a respite. What a Christmas offering for my mother! I say!—don't go away for a minute—did you hear Uncle John last night about the brandy?"

I nodded.

"It is not that I like drink, or care for it for drinking's sake; I declare it to you, Johnny Ludlow; but I take it, and must take it, to drown care. With that extra glass last night, I might have got to sleep—I don't know. Were my mind at ease, I should be as sober as you are."

"But don't you see, Roger, that unless you pull up now, while you can, you may not be able to do it later."

"Oh yes, I see it all," he carelessly said. "Well, it no longer matters much what becomes of me. There's the breakfast-bell. You can go on, Johnny."

The rooms looked like green bowers, for we had not spared either our pains or the holly-branches, and it would have been as happy a Christmas-Day as it was a bright one, but for the sword that was hanging over Roger Bevere's head. Neither he nor I could enjoy it. He declined to go to church with us, saying he felt ill: the truth being that he feared to meet Lizzie. Not to attend divine service on Christmas-Day was regarded by Mr. Brandon as one of the cardinal sins. To my surprise he did not remonstrate with Roger in words: but he looked the more.

Lady Bevere's dinner hour on Christmas-Day was four o'clock, which gave a good long evening. Roger ate some turkey and some plum-pudding, mechanically; his ears were listening for the dreaded sound of the door-bell. We were about half-way through dinner, when there came a peal that shook the house. Lady Bevere started in her chair. I fancy Roger went nearly out of his.

"Why, who can be coming here now—with such a ring as that?" she exclaimed.

"Perhaps it is Harriet's sister!" cried the little girl, in her sharp, quick way. "Do you think it is, Harriet?"

"She's free enough for it," returned Harriet, in a vexed tone. "I told her she might come yesterday, Miss Tottams, my lady permitting it, but I did not tell her she might come to-day."

I glanced at Roger. His knife and fork shook in his hands; his face wore the hue of the grave. I was little less agitated than he.

Another respite. It was only a parcel from the railway-station, which had been delayed in the delivery. And the dinner went on.

And the evening went on too, as the past one went on—undisturbed. Later, when some of us were playing at snap-dragon in the little breakfast-room, Harriet came in to march Miss Tottams off to bed.

"Your sister did not come after all, did she, Harriet?" said Mary.

"No, Miss Mary. She's gone back to London," continued Harriet, after a pause. "Not enough life for her, I dare say, down here."

Roger glanced round. He did not dare ask whether Harriet knew she was gone back, or only supposed it.

Mary laughed. "Fond of life, is she?"

"She always was, Miss Mary. She is married to a gentleman. At least, that is her account of him: he is a medical man, she says. But it may be he is only a medical man's assistant."

"Did she go back yesterday, or to-day?" I inquired, carelessly. "She would have a cold journey."

"Yesterday, if she's gone at all, sir," replied Harriet: "she'd hardly travel on Christmas-Day. If not, she'll be here to-morrow."

Roger groaned—and turned it off with a desperate cough, as though the raisins burnt his throat.

The next day came, Wednesday, again clear, cold, and bright. At breakfast George and Mary agreed to walk to Brighton. "You will come too," said George, looking at us.

I said nothing. Roger shook his head. Of all places in the known world he'd not have ventured into Brighton, and run the risk of meeting her, perambulating its streets.

"No!—why, it will be a glorious walk," remonstrated George.

"Don't care for it this morning," shortly answered Roger. "I'm sure Johnny doesn't."

Mr. Brandon came, if I may so put it, to the rescue. "I shall take a walk myself, and you two may go with me," said he to us. "I should like to see what the country looks like yonder"—pointing to the unknown regions beyond the little church. And as this was just in the opposite direction to Brighton, Roger made no objection, and we set off soon after breakfast. The sky overhead was blue and clear, the snow on the ground dazzlingly white.

The regions beyond the church were the same as these: a long-stretched-out moor of flat dreariness. Mr. Brandon walked on. "We shall come to something or other in time," said he. Walking with him meant walking when he was in the mood for it.

A mile or two onwards, more or less, a small settlement loomed into view, with a pound and a set of rusty stocks, and an old-fashioned inn, its swinging sign, The Rising Sun, as splendid as that other sign nearer Prior's Glebe: and it really appeared to us as if all the inhabitants had turned out to congregate round the inn-door.

"What's to do, I wonder?" cried Mr. Brandon: "seems to be some excitement going on." When near enough he inquired whether anything was amiss, and the whole throng answered together.

A woman had been found that morning frozen to death in the snow, and had been carried into The Rising Sun. A young woman wearing smart clothes, added a labourer, as the rest of the voices died away: got benighted, perhaps, poor thing, and lost her way, and so lay down to die; seemed to have been dead quite a day or two, if not more. The missis at The Sheaf o' Corn yonder had been over, and recognized her as having called in there on Sunday night and had some drink.

Why, as the man spoke, should the dread thought have flashed into my mind—was it Lizzie? Why should it have flashed simultaneously into Roger's? Had Lizzie lost her way that past Sunday night—and sunk down into some sheltered nook to rest awhile, and so sleep and then death overtook her? Roger glanced at me with frightened eyes, a dawn of horror rising to his countenance.

"I will just step in and take a look at her," I said, and bore on steadily for the door of the inn, deaf for once to Mr. Brandon's authoritative call. What did I want looking at dead women, he asked: was the sight so pleasant? No, it was not pleasant, I could have answered him, and I'd rather have gone a mile away from it; but I went in for Roger's sake.

The innkeeper—an elderly man, with a bald head and red nose—came forward, grumbling that for the past hour or two it had been sharp work to keep out the crowd, all agape to see the woman. I asked him to let me see her, assuring him it was not out of idle curiosity that I wished it. Believing me, he acquiesced at once; civilly remarking, as he led the way through the house, that he had sent for the police, and expected them every minute.

On the long table of a bleak-looking outer kitchen, probably used only in summer, lay the dead. I took my look at her.

Yes, it was Lizzie. Looking as peaceful as though she had only just gone to sleep. Poor thing!

"Do you recognize her, sir? Did you think you might?"

I shook my head in answer. It would not have done to acknowledge it. Thanking him, I went out to Roger. Mr. Brandon fired off a tirade of reproaches at me, and said he was glad to see I had turned white.

"Yes," I emphatically whispered to Roger in the midst of it. "Go you in, and satisfy yourself."

Roger disappeared inside the inn. Mr. Brandon was so indignant at the pair of us, that he set off at a sharp pace for home again, I with him, Roger presently catching us up. Twice during the walk, Roger was taken with a shivering-fit, as though sickening for the ague. Mr. Brandon held his tongue then, and recommended him, when we got in, to put himself between some hot blankets.

In the dead woman's pocket was found Harriet Field's address; and a policeman presented himself at Prior's Glebe with the news of the calamity and to ask what Harriet knew of her. Away went Harriet to The Rising Sun, and recognized the dead. It was her sister, she said; she had called to see her on Sunday night, having walked over from Brighton, and must have lost her way on the waste land in returning. What name, was the next question put; and, after a moment's hesitation, Harriet answered "Elizabeth Field." Not feeling altogether sure of the marriage, she said nothing about it.

Will you accuse Roger Bevere of cowardice for holding aloof; for keeping silence? Then you must accuse me for sanctioning it. He could not bring himself to avow all the past shame to his mother. And what end would it answer now if he did?—what good effect to his poor, wretched, foolish wife? None.

"Johnny," he said to me, with a grasp of his fevered hand, "is it wrong to feel as if a great mercy had been vouchsafed me?—is it wicked? Heaven knows, I pity her fate; I would have saved her from it if I could. Just as I'd have kept her from her evil ways, and tried to be a good husband to her—but she would not let me."

They held an inquest upon her next day: or, as the local phraseology of the place put it, "Sat upon the body of Elizabeth Field." The landlady of The Sheaf o' Corn was an important witness.

She testified that the young woman came knocking at the closed door of the inn on the Sunday evening during church time, saying she had lost her way. Nobody was at home but herself and the servant-girl, her husband having gone to church. They let her in. She called for a good drop of drink—brandy-and-water—while sitting there, and was allowed to have it, though it was out of serving hours, as she declared she was perishing with cold. Before eight o'clock, she left, and was away about half-an-hour. Then she came back again, had more to drink, and bought a pint bottle of brandy, to carry, as she told them, home to her lodgings, and she got the girl to draw the cork, saying her rooms did not possess a corkscrew. She took the bottle away with her. Was she tipsy? interposed the coroner at this juncture. Not very, the witness replied, not so tipsy but that she could walk and talk, but she had had quite enough. She went away, and they saw her no more.

Harriet's evidence, next given, did not amount to much. The deceased, her younger sister, had lived for some years in London, but she did not know at what address latterly; she used to serve at a refreshment-bar, but had left it. Until the past Sunday night, when Lizzie called unexpectedly at Prior's Glebe, they had not met for five or six years: it was then arranged that Lizzie should come to drink tea with her the next afternoon: but she never came. Felt convinced that the death was pure accident, through her having lost her way in the snow.

With this opinion the room agreed. Instead of taking the direct path to Brighton, as Harriet had enjoined, she must have turned back The Sheaf o' Corn for more drink. And that she had wandered in a wrong direction, upon quitting it, across the waste land, there could not be any doubt; or that she had sat down, or fallen down, possibly from fatigue, in the drift where she was found. The brandy bottle lay near her, empty. Whether she died of the brandy, or of the exposure to the cold night, might be a question. The jury decided that it was the latter.

And nothing whatever had come out touching Roger.

Harriet had already given orders for a decent funeral, in the neighbouring graveyard. It took place on the afternoon of the following day, Friday. By a curious little coincidence, George Bevere was asked to take the service, the incumbent being ill with a cold. It afforded a pretext for Roger's attending. He and I walked quietly up in the wake of George, and stood at the grave together. Harriet thanked us for it afterwards: she looked upon it as a compliment paid to herself.

"Scott shall forward to her every expense she has been put to as soon as I am back in London," said Roger to me. "He will know how to manage it."

"Shall you tell Mrs. Dyke?"

"To be sure I shall. She is a trustworthy, good woman."

Our time at Prior's Glebe was up, and we took our departure from it on the Saturday morning; another day of intense cold, of dark blue skies, and of bright sunshine. George left with us.

"My dear, you will try—you will try to keep straight, won't you; to be what you ought to be," whispered Lady Bevere in the bustle of starting, as she clasped Roger's hands in the hall, tears falling from her eyes: all just as it was that other time in Gibraltar Terrace. "For my sake, dear; for my sake."

"I shall do now, mother," he whispered back, meeting her gaze through his wet eyelashes, his manner strangely solemn. "God has been very good to me, and I—I will try from henceforth to do my best in all ways."

And Roger kept his word.

KETIRA THE GIPSY

I

"I tell you what it is, Abel. You think of everybody else before yourself. The Squire says there's no sense in it."

"No sense in what, Master Johnny?"

"Why, in supplying those ill-doing Standishes with your substance. Herbs, and honey, and medicine—they are always getting something or other out of you."

"But they generally need it, sir."

"Well, they don't deserve it, you know. The Squire went into a temper to-day, saying the vagabonds ought to be left to starve if they did not choose to work, instead of being helped by the public."

Our hen-roosts had been robbed, and it was pretty certain that one or other of the Standish brothers was the thief. Perhaps all three had a hand in it. Chancing to pass Abel Carew's garden, where he was at work, I turned in to tell him of the raid; and stayed, talking. It was pleasant to sit on the bench outside the cottage-window, and watch him tend his roots and flowers. The air was redolent of perfume; the bees were humming as they sailed in the summer sunshine from herb to herb, flower to flower; the dark blue sky was unclouded.

"Just look at those queer-looking people, Abel! They must be gipsies."

Abel let his hands rest on his rake, and lifted his eyes to the common. Crossing it, came two women, one elderly, one very young—a girl, in fact. Their red cloaks shone in the sun; very coarse and sunburnt straw hats were tied down with red kerchiefs. That they belonged to the gipsy fraternity was apparent at the first glance. Pale olive complexions, the elder one's almost yellow, were lighted up with black eyes of wonderful brilliancy. The young girl was strikingly beautiful; her features clearly cut and delicate, as though carved from marble, her smooth and abundant hair of a purple black. The other's hair was purple black also, and had not a grey thread in it.

"They must be coming to tell our fortunes, Abel," I said jestingly. For the two women seemed to be making direct for the gate.

No answer from Abel, and I turned to look at him. He was gazing at the coming figures with the most intense gaze, a curious expression of inquiring doubt on his face. The rake fell from his hand.

"My search is ended," spoke the woman, halting at the gate, her glittering black eyes scanning him intently. "You are Abel Carew."

"Is it Ketira?" he asked, the words dropping from him in slow hesitation, as he took a step forward.

"Am I so much changed that you need doubt it for a moment?" she returned: and her tone and accent fell soft and liquid; her diction was of the purest, with just the slightest foreign ring in it. "Forty years have rolled on since you and I met, Abel Carew; but I come of a race whose faces do not change. As we are in youth, so we are in age—save for the inevitable traces left by time."

"And this?" questioned Abel, as he looked at the girl and drew back his gate.

"She is Ketira also; my youngest and dearest. The youngest of sixteen children, Abel Carew; and every one of them, save herself, lying under the sod."

"What—dead?" he exclaimed. "Sixteen!"

"Fifteen are dead, and are resting in peace in different lands: ten of them died in infancy ere I had well taken my first look at their little faces. She is the sixteenth. See you the likeness?" added the gipsy, pointing to the girl's face; as she stood, modest and silent, a conscious colour tingeing her olive cheeks, and glancing up now and again through her long black eyelashes at Abel Carew.

"Likeness to you, Ketira?"

"Not to me: though there exists enough of it between us to betray that we are mother and daughter. To him—her father."

And, while Abel was looking at the girl, I looked. And in that moment it struck me that her face bore a remarkable likeness to his own. The features were of the same high-bred cast, pure and refined; you might have said they were made in the same mould.

"I see; yes," said Abel.

"He has been gone, too, this many a year; as you, perhaps, may know, Abel; and is with the rest, waiting for us in the spirit-land. Kettie does not remember him, it is so long ago. There are only she and I left to go now. Kettie—"

She suddenly changed her language to one I did not understand. Neither, as was easy to be seen, did Abel Carew. Whether it was Hebrew, or Egyptian, or any other rare tongue, I knew not; but I had never in my life heard its sounds before.

"I am telling Kettie that in you she may see what her father was—for the likeness in your face and his, allowing for the difference of age, is great."

"Does Kettie not speak English?" inquired Abel.

"Oh yes, I speak it," answered the girl, slightly smiling, and her tones were soft and perfect as those of her mother.

"And where have you been since his death, Ketira? Stationary in Ai—"

He dropped his voice to a whisper at the last word, and I did not catch it. I suppose he did not intend me to.

"Not stationary for long anywhere," she answered, passing into the cottage with a majestic step. I lifted my hat to the women—who, for all their gipsy dress and origin, seemed to command consideration—and made off.

The arrival of these curious people caused some commotion at Church Dykely. It was so rare we had any event to enliven us. They took up their abode in a lonely cottage no better than a hut (one room up and one down) that stood within that lively place, the wilderness on the outskirts of Chanasse Grange; and there they stayed. How they got a living nobody knew: some thought the gipsy must have an income, others that Abel helped them.

"She was very handsome in her youth," he said to me one day, as if he wished to give some explanation of the arrival I had chanced to witness. "Handsomer and finer by far than her daughter is; and one who was very near of kin to me married her—would marry her. She was a born gipsy, of what is called a high-caste tribe."

That was all he said. For Abel's sake, who was so respected, Church Dykely felt inclined to give respect to the women. But, when it was discovered that Ketira would tell the fortune of any one who cared to go surreptitiously to her lonely hut, the respect cooled down. "Ketira the gipsy," she was universally called: nobody knew her by any other name. The fortune-telling came to the ears of Abel, arousing his indignation. He went to Ketira in distress, begging of her to cease such practices—but she waved him majestically out of the hut, and bade him mind his own business. Occasionally the mother and daughter shut up their dwelling and disappeared for weeks together. It was assumed they went to attend fairs and races, camping out with the gipsy fraternity. Kettie at all times and seasons was modest and good; never was an unmaidenly look seen from her, or a bold word heard. In appearance and manner and diction she might have been a born lady, and a high-bred one. Graceful and innocent was Kettie; but heedless and giddy, as girls are apt to be.

"Look there, Johnny!"

We were at Worcester races, walking about on the course. I turned at Tod's words, and saw Ketira the gipsy, her red cloak gleaming in the sun, just as it had gleamed that day, a year before, on Dykely Common. For the past month she had been away, and her cottage shut up.

She stood at the open door of a carriage, reading the hand of the lady inside it. A notable object was Ketira on the course, with her quaint attire, her majestic figure, her fine olive-dark features, and the fire of her brilliant eyes. What good or ill luck she was promising, I know not; but I saw the lady turn pale and snatch her hand away. "You cannot know what you tell me," she cried in a haughty tone, sharp enough and loud enough to be heard.

"Wait and see," rejoined Ketira, turning away.

"So you have come here to see the fun, Ketira," I said to her, as she was brushing by me. During the past year I had seen more of her than many people had, and we had grown familiar; for she, as she once expressed it, "took" to me.

"The fun and the business; the pleasure and the wickedness," she answered, with a sweep of the hand round the course. "There's plenty of it abroad."

"Is Kettie not here?" I asked: and the question made her eyes glare. Though, why, I was at a loss to know, seeing that a race-ground is the legitimate resort of gipsies.

"Kettie! Do you suppose I bring Kettie to these scenes—to be gazed at by this ribald mass?"

"Well, it is a rabble, and a good one," I answered, looking at the crowd.

"Nay, boy," said she, following my glance, "it's not the rabble Kettie need fear, as you count rabble; it's their betters"—swaying her arms towards the carriages, and the dandies, their owners or guests; some of whom were balancing themselves on the steps to talk to the pretty girls within, and some were strolling about the enclosed paddock, forbidden ground but to the "upper few." "Ketira is too fair to be shown to them."

"They would not eat her, Ketira."

"No, they would not eat her," she replied in a dreamy tone, as if her thoughts were elsewhere.

"And I don't see any other harm they could do her, guarded by you."

"Boy," she said, dropping her voice to an impressive whisper, and lightly touching my arm with her yellow hand, "I have read Kettie's fate in the stars, and I see that there is some great and grievous peril approaching her. It may be averted; there's just a chance that it may: meanwhile I am encompassing her about with care, guarding her as the apple of my eye."

"And if it should not be averted?" I asked in the moment's impulse, carried away by the woman's impressive earnestness.

"Then woe be to those who bring the evil upon her!"

"And of what nature is the evil?"

"I know not," she replied, her eyes taking again their dreamy, far-off look. "Woe is me!—for I know it not."

"How do you do, Ludlow? Not here alone, are you?"

A good-looking young fellow, Hyde Stockhausen, had reined in his horse to ask the question: giving at the same time a keen glance to the gipsy woman and then a half-smile at me, as if he suspected I was having my fortune told.

"The rest are on the course somewhere. The Squire is driving old Jacobson about."

As Hyde nodded and rode on, I chanced to see Ketira's face. It was stretched out after him with the most eager gaze on it, a defiant look in her black eyes. I thought Stockhausen must have offended her.

"Do you know him?" I asked involuntarily.

"I never saw him before; but I don't like him," she answered, showing her white and gleaming teeth. "Who is he?"

"His name is Stockhausen."

"I don't like him," she repeated in a muttering tone. "He is an enemy. I don't like his look."

Considering that he was a well-looking man, with a pleasant face and gay blue eyes, a face that no reasonable spirit could take umbrage at, I wondered to hear her say this.

"You must have a peculiar taste in looks, Ketira, to dislike his."

"You don't understand," she said abruptly: and, turning away, disappeared in the throng.

Only once more did I catch sight of Ketira that day. It was at the lower end of Pitchcroft, near the show. She was standing in front of a booth, staring at a group of horsemen who seemed to have met and halted there, one of whom was young Stockhausen. Again the notion crossed me that he must in some way have affronted her. It was on him her eyes were fixed: and in them lay the same curious, defiant expression of antagonism, mingled with fear.

Hyde Stockhausen was the step-son of old Massock of South Crabb. The Stockhausens had a name in Worcestershire for dying off, as I have told the reader before. Hyde's father had proved no exception. After his death the widow married Massock the brickmaker, putting up with the man's vulgarity for the sake of his riches. It took people by surprise: for she had been a lady always, as Miss Hyde and as Mrs. Stockhausen; one might have thought she would rather have put up with a clown from Pershore fair than with Massock the illiterate. Hyde Stockhausen was well educated: his uncle, Tom Hyde the parson, had taken care of that. At twenty-one he came into some money, and at once began to do his best to spend it. He was to have been a parson, but could not get through at Oxford, and gave up trying for it. His uncle quarrelled with him then: he knew Hyde had not tried to pass, and that he openly said nobody should make a parson of him. After the quarrel, Hyde went off to see what the Continent was like. He stayed so long that the world at home thought he was lost. For the past ten or eleven months he had been back at his mother's at South Crabb, knocking about, as Massock phrased it to the Squire one day. Hyde said he was "looking-out" for something to do: but he was quite easy as to the future, feeling sure his old uncle would leave him well off. Parson Hyde had never married; and had plenty of money to bequeath to somebody. As to Hyde's own money, that had nearly come to an end.

Naturally old Massock (an ill-conditioned kind of man) grew impatient over this state of things, reproaching Hyde with his idle habits, which were a bad example for his own sons. And only just before this very day that we were on Worcester racecourse, rumours reached Church Dykely that Stockhausen was coming over to settle there and superintend certain fields of brick-making, which Massock had recently purchased and commenced working. As if Massock could not have kept himself and his bricks at South Crabb! But it was hardly likely that Hyde, really a gentleman, would take to brick-making.

We did not know much of him. His connection with Massock had kept people aloof. Many who would have been glad enough to make friends with Hyde would not do it as long as he had his home at Massock's. His mother's strange and fatal marriage with the man (fatal as regarded her place in society) told upon Hyde, and there's no doubt he must have felt the smart.

The rumour proved to be correct. Hyde Stockhausen took up his abode at Church Dykely, as overseer, or clerk, or manager—whatever might be the right term for it—of the men employed in his step-father's brick operations. The pretty little house, called Virginia Cottage, owned by Henry Rimmer, which had the Virginia creeper trailing up its red walls, and flowers clustering in its productive garden, was furnished for him; and Hyde installed himself in it as thoroughly and completely as though he had entered on brick-making for life. Some people laughed. "But it's only while I am turning myself round," he said, one day, to the Squire.

Hyde soon got acquainted with Church Dykely, and would drop into people's houses of an evening, laughing over his occupation, and saying he should be able to make bricks himself in time. His chief work seemed to be in standing about the brick-yard watching the men, and in writing and book-keeping at home. Old Massock made his appearance once a month, when accounts and such-like items were gone over between them.

When it was that Hyde first got on speaking terms with Kettie, or where, or how, I cannot tell. So far as I know, nobody could tell. It was late in the autumn when Ketira and her daughter came back to their hut; and by the following early spring some of us had grown accustomed to seeing Hyde and Kettie together in an evening, snatching a short whisper or a five-minutes' walk. In March, I think it was, she and Ketira went away again, and returned in May.

The twenty-ninth of May was at that time kept as a holiday in Worcestershire, though it has dropped out of use as such in late years. In Worcester itself there was a grand procession, which country people went in to see, and a special service in the cathedral. We had service also at Church Dykely, and the villagers adorned their front-doors with immense oak boughs, sprays of which we young ones wore in our jackets, the oak-balls and leaves gilded. I remember one year that the big bough (almost a tree) which Henry Rimmer had hoisted over his sign, the "Silver Bear," came to grief. Whether Rimmer had not secured it as firmly as usual, or that the cords were rotten, down came the huge bough with a crash on old Mr. Stirling's head, who chanced to be coming out of the inn. He went on at Rimmer finely, vowing his neck was broken, and that Rimmer ought to be hung up there himself.

On this twenty-ninth of May I met Kettie. It was on the common, near Abel Carew's. Kettie had caught up the fashion of the place, and wore a little spray of oak peeping out from between the folds of her red cloak. And I may as well say that neither she nor her mother ever went out without the cloak. In cold and heat, in rain and sunshine, the red cloak was worn out-of-doors.

"Are you making holiday to-day, Kettie?"

"Not more than usual; all days are the same to us," she answered, in her sweet, soft voice, and with the slightly foreign accent that attended the speech of both. But Kettie had it more strongly than her mother.

"You have not gilded your oak-ball."

Kettie glanced down at the one ball, nestling amid its green leaves. "I had no gilding to put on it, Mr. Johnny."

"No! I have some in my pocket. Let me gild it for you."

Her teeth shone like pearls as she smiled and held out the spray. How beautiful she was! with those delicate features and the large dark eyes!—eyes that were softer than Ketira's. Taking the little paper book from my pocket, and some of the gilt leaf from between its tissue leaves, I wetted the oak-ball and gilded it. Kettie watched intently.

"Where did you get it all from?" she asked, meaning the gilt leaf.

"I bought it at Hewitt's. Don't you know the shop? A stationer's; next door to Pettipher the druggist's. Hewitt does no end of a trade in these leaves on the twenty-ninth of May."

"Did you buy it to gild oak-balls for yourself, sir?"

"For the young ones at home: Hugh and Lena. There it is, Kettie."

Had it been a ball of solid gold that I put into her hand, instead of a gilded oak-ball, Kettie could not have shown more intense delight. Her cheeks flushed; the wonderful brilliancy that joy brought to her eyes caused my own eyes to turn away. For her eighteen years she was childish in some things; very much so, considering the experience that her wandering life must (as one would suppose) have brought her. In replacing the spray within her cloak, Kettie dropped something out of her hand—apparently a small box folded in paper. I picked it up.

"Is it a fairing, Kettie? But this is not fair time."

"It is—I forget the name," she replied, looking at me and hesitating. "My mother is ill; the pains are in her shoulder again; and my uncle Abel has given me this to rub upon it, the same that did her good before. I cannot just call the name to mind in the English tongue."

"Say it in your own."

She spoke a very outlandish word, laughed, and turned red again. Certainly there never lived a more modest girl than Kettie.

"Is it liniment?—ointment?"

"Yes, it is that, the last," she said: "Abel calls it so. I thank you for what you have done for me, sir. Good-day."

To show so much gratitude for that foolish bit of gilt leaf on her oak-ball! It illumined every line of her face. I liked Kettie: liked her for her innocent simplicity. Had she not been a gipsy, many a gentleman might have been proud to make her his wife.

Close upon that, it was known that Ketira was laid up with rheumatism. The weather came in hot, and the days went on: and Kettie and Hyde were now and then seen together.

One evening, on leaving Mrs. Scott's, where we had been to arrange with Sam to go fishing with us on the morrow, Tod said he would invite Hyde Stockhausen to be of the party; so we took Virginia Cottage on our road home, and asked for Hyde.

"Not at home!" retorted Tod, resenting the old woman's answer, as though it had been a personal affront. "Where is he?"

"Master Hyde has only just stepped out, sir; twenty minutes ago, or so," said she, pleadingly excusing the fact. Which was but natural: she had been Hyde's nurse when he was a child; and had now come here to do for him. "I dare say, sir, he be only walking about a bit, to get the fresh air."

Tod whistled some bars of a tune thoughtfully. He did not like to be crossed.

"Well, look here, Mrs. Preen," said he. "Some of us are going to fish in the long pond on Mr. Jacobson's grounds to-morrow: tell Mr. Hyde that if he would like to join us, I shall be happy to see him. Breakfast, half-past eight o'clock; sharp."

In turning out beyond the garden, I could not help noticing how pretty and romantic was the scene. A good many trees grew about that part, thick enough almost for a wood in places; and the light and shade, cast by the moon on the grass amidst them, had quite a weird appearance. It was a bright night; the moon high in the sky.

"Is that Hyde?" cried Tod.

Halting for a moment in doubt, he peered out over the field to the distance. Some one was leisurely pacing under the opposite trees. Two people, I thought: but they were completely in the shade.

"I think it is Hyde, Tod. Somebody is with him."

"Just wait another instant, lad, and they'll be in that patch of moonlight by the turning."

But they did not go into that patch of moonlight. Just before they reached it (and the two figures were plain enough now) they turned back again and took the narrow inlet that led to Oxlip Dell. Whoever it was with Hyde had a hooded cloak on. Was it a red one? Tod laughed.

"Oh, by George, here's fun! He has got Kettie out for a moonlight stroll. Let's go and ask them how they enjoy it."

"Hyde might not like us to."

"There you are again, Johnny, with your queer scruples! Stuff and nonsense! Stockhausen can't have anything to say to Kettie that all the world may not hear. I want to tell him about to-morrow."

Tod made off across the grass for the inlet, I after him. Yes, there they were, promenading Oxlip Dell in the flickering light, now in the shade, now in the brightest of the moonbeams; Hyde's arm hugging her red cloak.

Tod gave a grunt of displeasure. "Stockhausen must be doing it for pastime," he said; "but he ought not to be so thoughtless. Ketira the gipsy would give the girl a shaking if she knew: she—"

The words came to an abrupt ending. There stood Ketira herself.

She was at the extreme end of the inlet amid the trees, holding on by the trunk of one, round which her head was cautiously pushed to view the promenaders. Comparatively speaking, it was dark just here; but I could see the strangely-wild look in the gipsy's eyes: the woe-begone expression of her remarkable face.

"It is coming," she said, apparently in answer to Tod's remarks, which she could not have failed to hear. "It is coming quickly."

"What is coming?" I asked.

"The fate in store for her. And it's worse than death."

"If you don't like her to walk out by moonlight, why not keep her in?—not that there can be any harm in it," interposed Tod. "If you don't approve of her being friendly with Hyde Stockhausen," he went on after a pause, for Ketira made no answer, "why don't you put a stop to it?"

"Because she has her mother's spirit and her mother's will" cried Ketira. "And she likes to have her own way: and I fear, woe's me! that if I forced her to mine, things might become worse than they are even now: that she might take some fatal step."

"I am going home," said Tod at this juncture, perhaps fancying the matter was getting complicated: and, of all things, he hated complications. "Good-night, old lady. We heard you were in bed with rheumatism."

He set off back, up the narrow inlet. I said I'd catch him up: and stayed behind for a last word with Ketira.

"What did you mean by a fatal step?"

"That she might leave me and seek the protection of the Tribe. We have had words about this. Kettie says little, but I see the signs of determination in her silent face. 'I will not have you meet or speak to that man,' I said to her this morning—for she was out with him last evening also. She made me no reply: but—you see—how she has obeyed! Her heart's life has been awakened, and by him. There's only one object to whom she clings now in all the whole earth; and that is to him. I am nothing."

"He will not bring any great harm upon her: you need not fear that of Hyde Stockhausen."

"Did I say he would?" she answered fiercely, her black eyes glaring and gleaming. "But he will bring sorrow on her and rend her heart-strings. A man's fancies are light as the summer wind, fickle as the ocean waves: but when a woman loves it is for life; sometimes for death."

Hyde and Kettie had disappeared at the upper end of the dell, taking the way that in a minute or two would bring them out in the open fields. Ketira turned back along the narrow path, and I with her.

"I knew he would bring some ill upon me, that first moment when I saw him on Worcester race-ground," resumed Ketira in a low tone of pain. "Instinct warned me that he was an enemy. And what ill can be like that of stealing my young child's heart! Once a girl's heart is taken—and taken but to be toyed with, to be flung back at will—her day-dreams in this life are over."

Emerging into the open ground, the first thing we saw was the pair of lovers about to part. They were standing face to face: Hyde held both her hands while speaking his last words, and then bent suddenly down, as if to whisper them. Ketira gave a sharp cry at that, perhaps she fancied he was stealing a kiss, and lifted her right hand menacingly. The girl ran swiftly in the direction of her home—which was not far off—and Hyde strode, not much less quickly, towards his. Ketira stood as still as a stone image, watching him till he disappeared within his gate.

"There's no harm in it," I persuasively said, sorry to see her so full of trouble. But she was as one who heard not.

"No harm at all, Ketira. I dare answer for it that a score of lads and lasses are out. Why should we not walk in the moonlight as well as the sunlight? For my part, I should call it a shame to stay indoors on this glorious night."

"An enemy, an enemy! A grand gentleman, who will leave her to pine her heart away! What kind of man is he, that Hyde Stockhausen?" she continued, turning to me fiercely.

"Kind of man? A pleasant one. I have not heard any ill of him."

"Rich?"

"No. Perhaps he will be rich some time. He makes bricks, you know, now. That is, he superintends the men."

"Yes, I know," she answered: and I don't suppose there was much connected with Hyde she did not know. Looking this way, looking that, she at length began to walk, slowly and painfully, towards Hyde's gate. The thought had crossed me—why did she not take Kettie away on one of their long expeditions, if she dreaded him so much. But the rheumatism lay upon her still too heavily.

Flinging open the gate, she went across the garden, not making for the proper entrance, but for a lighted room, whose French-window stood open to the ground. Hyde was there, just sitting down to supper.

"Come in with me," she said, turning her head round to beckon me on.

But I did not choose to go in. It was no affair of mine that I should beard Hyde in his den. Very astonished indeed must he have been, when she glided in at the window, and stood before him. I saw him rise from his chair; I saw the astounded look of old Deborah Preen when she came in with his supper ale in a jug.

What they said to one another, I know not. I did not wish to listen: though it was only natural I should stay to see the play out. Just as natural as it was for Preen to come stealing round through the kidney beans to the front-garden, an anxious look on her face.

"What does that old gipsy woman want with the young master, Mr. Ludlow? Is he having his fortune told?"

"I shouldn't wonder. Wish some good genius would tell mine!"

The interview seemed to have been short and sharp. Ketira was coming out again. Hyde followed her to the window. Both were talking at once, and the tail of the dispute reached our ears.

"I repeat to you that you are totally mistaken," Hyde was saying. "I have no 'designs,' as you put it, on your daughter, good or bad; no design whatever. She is perfectly free to go her own way, for me. My good woman, you have no cause to adjure me in that solemn manner. Sacred? 'Under Heaven's protection?' Well, so she may be. I hope she is. Why should I wish to hinder it? I don't wish to, I don't intend to. You need not glare so."

Ketira, outside the window now, turned and faced him, her great eyes fixed on him, her hand raised in menace.

"Do not forget that. I have warned you, Hyde Stockhausen. By the Great Power that regulates all things, human and divine, I affirm that I speak the truth. If harm in any shape or of any kind comes to my child, my dear one, my only one, through you, it will cost you more than you would now care to have foretold."

"Bless my heart!" faintly ejaculated old Preen. And she drew away, and backed for shelter into the bean rows.

Ketira brushed against me as she passed, taking no notice whatever; left the garden, and limped away. Hyde saw me swinging through the gate.

"Are you there, Johnny?" he said, coming forward. "Did you hear that old gipsy woman?" And in a few words I told him all about it.

"Such a fuss for nothing!" he exclaimed. "I'm sure I wish no ill to the girl. Kettie's very nice; bright as the day: and I thought no more harm of strolling a bit with her in the moonlight than I should think it if she were my sister."

"But she is not your sister, you see, Hyde. And old Ketira does not like it."

"I'll take precious good care to keep Kettie at arm's-length for the future; make you very sure of that," he said, in a short, fractious tone. "I don't care to be blamed for nothing. Tell Todhetley I can't spare the time to go fishing to-morrow—wish I could. Good-night."

A fine commotion. Church Dykely up in arms. Kettie had disappeared.

About a fortnight had gone on since the above night, during which period Ketira's rheumatism took so obstinate a turn that she had the felicity of keeping her bed. And one morning, upon Duffham's chancing to pay his visit to her before breakfast, for he was passing the hut on his way home from an early patient, he found the gipsy up and dressed, and just as wild as a lioness rampant. Kettie had gone away in the night.

"Where's she gone to?" naturally asked Duffham, leaning on his cane, and watching the poor woman; who was whirling about like one demented, her rheumatism forgotten.

"Ah, where's she gone to?—where?" raved old Ketira. "When I lay down last night, leaving her to put the plates away and to follow me up when she had done it, I dropped asleep at once. All night long I never woke; the pain was easier, all but gone, and I had been well-nigh worn out with it. 'Why, what's the time, Kettie?' I said to her in our own tongue, when I opened my eyes and saw the sun was high. She did not answer, and I supposed she had gone down to get the breakfast. I called, and called; in vain. I began to put my clothes on; and then I found that she had not lain down that night; and—woe's me! she's gone."

Duffham could not make anything of it; it was less in his line than rheumatism and broken legs. Being sharp-set for his breakfast, he came away, telling Ketira he would see her again by-and-by.

And, shortly afterwards, he chanced to meet her. Coming out on his round of visits, he encountered Ketira near Virginia Cottage. She had been making a call on Hyde Stockhausen.

"He baffles me," she said to the doctor: and Duffham thought if ever a woman's face had the expression "baffled" plainly written on it, Ketira's had then. "I don't know what to make of him. His speech is fair: but—there's the instinct lying in my heart."

"Why, you don't suppose, do you, that Mr. Stockhausen has stolen the child?" questioned Duffham, after a good pause of thought.

"And by whom do you suppose the child has been stolen, if not by him?" retorted the gipsy.

"Nay," said Duffham, "I should say she has not been stolen at all. It is difficult to steal girls of her age, remember. Last night was fine; the stars were bright as silver: perhaps, tempted by it, she went out a-roaming, and you will see her back in the course of the day."

"I suspect him," repeated Ketira, her great black eyes flashing their anger on Hyde's cottage. "He acts cleverly; but, I suspect him."

Drawing her scarlet cloak higher on her shoulders, she bent her steps towards Oxlip Dell. Duffham was turning on his way, when old Abel Crew came up. We called him "Crew," you know, at Church Dykely.

"Are you looking for Kettie?" questioned Duffham.

"I don't know where to look for her," was Abel's answer. "This morning I was out before sunrise searching for rare herbs: the round I took was an unusually large one, but I did not see anything of the child. Ketira suspects that Mr. Stockhausen must know where she is."

"And do you suspect he does?"

"It is a question that I cannot answer, even to my own mind," replied Abel. "That they were sometimes seen talking and walking together, is certain; and, so far, he may be open to suspicion. But, sir, I know nothing else against him, and I cannot think he would wish to hurt her. I am on my way to ask him."

Interested by this time in the drama, Duffham followed Abel to Virginia Cottage. Hyde Stockhausen was in the little den that he made his counting-house, adding up columns of figures in a ledger, and stared considerably upon being thus pounced upon.

"I wonder what next!" he burst forth, turning crusty before Abel had got out half a sentence. "That confounded old gipsy has just been here with her abuse; and now you have come! She has accused me of I know not what all."

"Of spiriting away her daughter," put in Duffham; who was standing back against the shelves.

"But I have not done it," spluttered Hyde, talking too fast for convenience in his passion. "If I had spirited her away, as you call it, here she would be. Where could I spirit her to?—up into the air, or below the ground?"

"That's just the question—where is she?" rejoined Duffham, gently swaying his big cane.

"How should I know where she is?" retorted Hyde. "If I had 'spirited' her away—I must say I like that word!—here she'd be. Do you suppose I have got her in my house?—or down at the brick-kilns?"

Abel, since his first checked sentence, had been standing quietly and thoughtfully, giving his whole attention to Hyde, as if wanting to see what he was made of. For the second time he essayed to speak.

"You see, sir, we do not know that she is not here. We have your word for it; but—"

"Then you had better look," interrupted Hyde, adding something about "insolence" under his breath. "Search the house. You are welcome to. Mr. Duffham can show you about it; he knows all its turnings and windings."

What could have been in old Abel's thoughts did not appear on the surface; but he left the room with just a word of respectful apology for accepting the offer. Hyde, who had made it at random in his passion, never supposing it would be caught at, threw back his head disdainfully, and sent a contemptuous word after him. But when Duffham moved off in the same direction, he was utterly surprised.

"Are you going to search?"

"I thought you meant me to be his pilot," said Duffham, as cool as you please. "There's not much to be seen. I expect, but the chairs and tables."

Any way, Kettie was not to be seen. The house was but a small one, with no surreptitious closets or cupboards, or other hiding-places. All the rooms and passages stood open to the morning sun, and never a suspicious thing was in them.

Hyde had settled to his accounts again when they got back. He did not condescend to turn his head or notice the offenders any way. Abel waited a moment, and then spoke.

"It may seem to you that I have done a discourteous thing in availing myself of your offer, Mr. Stockhausen; if so, I crave your pardon for it. Sir, you cannot imagine how seriously this disappearance of the child is affecting her mother. Let it plead my excuse."

"It cannot excuse your suspicion of me," returned Hyde, pausing for a moment in his adding up.

"In all the ends of this wide earth there lies not elsewhere a shadow of clue to any motive for her departure. At least, none that we can gather. The only ground for thinking of you, sir, is that you and she have been friendly. For all our sakes, Mr. Stockhausen, I trust that she will be found, and the mystery cleared up."

"Don't you think you had better have the brick-kilns visited—as well as my house?" sarcastically asked Hyde. But Abel, making no rejoinder, save a civil good-morning, departed.

"And now I'll go," said Duffham.

"The sooner the better," retorted Hyde, taking a penful of ink and splashing some of it on the floor.

"There's no cause for you to put yourself out, young man."

"I think there is cause," flashed Hyde. "When you can come to my house with such an accusation as this!—and insolently search it!"

"The searching was the result of your own proposal. As to an accusation, none has been made in my hearing. Kettie has mysteriously disappeared, and it is only natural her people should wish to know where she is, and to look for her. You take up the matter in a wrong light, Mr. Hyde."

"I don't know anything of Kettie"—in an injured tone; "I don't want to. It's rather hard to have her vagaries put upon my back."

"Well, you have only to tell them you don't in an honest manner; I dare say they'll believe you. Abel Carew is one of the most reasonable men I ever knew; sensible, too. Try and find the child yourself; help them to do it, if you can see a clue; make common cause with them."

"You would not like to be told that you had 'spirited' somebody away, more than I like it," grumbled Hyde; who, thoroughly put out, was hard to bring round. "I'm sure you are as likely to turn kidnapper as I am. It must be a good two weeks since anybody saw me speak to the girl."

"I shall have my patients thinking I am kidnapped if I don't get off to them," cried Duffham. "Mrs. Godfrey's ill, and she is the very essence of impatience. Good-day."

Thoroughly at home in the house, Duffham made no ceremony of departing by the back-door, it being more convenient for the road he was going. Deborah Preen was washing endive at the pump in the yard. She turned round to address Duffham as he was passing.

"Has the master spoke to you about his throat, sir?"

"No," said Duffham, halting. "What is amiss with his throat?"

"He has been given to sore throats all his life, Dr. Duffham. Many's the time I have had him laid up with them when he was a child. Yesterday he was quite bad with one, sir; and so he is this morning."

"Perhaps that's why he's cross," remarked Duffham.

"Cross! and enough to make him cross!" returned she, taking up the implication warmly. "I ask your pard'n, sir, for speaking so to you; but I'd like to know what gentleman could help being cross when that yellow gipsy comes to attack him with her slanderous tongue, and say to him, Have you come across to my hut in the night and stole my daughter out of it?"

"You think your master did not go across and commit the theft?"

"I know he did not," was Preen's indignant answer. "He never stirred out of his own home, sir, all last night; he was nursing his throat indoors. At ten o'clock he went to bed, and I took him up a posset after he was in it. Well, sir, I was uneasy, for I don't like these sore throats, and between two and three o'clock I crept into his room and found him sleeping quietly; and I was in again this morning and woke him up with a cup o' tea."

"A pretty good proof that he did not go out," said Duffham.

"He never was as much as out of his bed, sir. The man that sleeps indoors locked up the house last night, and opened it again this morning. Ketira the gipsy would be in gaol if she got her deservings!"

"I wonder where the rest of us would be if we got ours!" quoth Duffham. "I suppose I had better go back and take a look at this throat!"

To see the miserable distress of Ketira that day, and the despair upon her face as she dodged about between Virginia Cottage and the brickfields, was like a gloomy picture.

"Do you remember telling me once that you feared Kettie might run away to the tribe?" I asked, meeting her on one of these wanderings in the afternoon. "Perhaps that is where she is gone?"

The suggestion seemed to offend her mortally. "Boy, I know better," she said, facing round upon me fiercely. "With the tribe she would be safe, and I at rest. The stars never deceive me."

And, when the sun went down that night and the stars came out, the environs of Virginia Cottage were still haunted by Ketira the gipsy.

You would not have known the place again. Virginia Cottage, the unpretending little homestead, had been converted into a mansion. Hyde Stockhausen had built a new wing at one end, and a conservatory at the other; and had put pillars before the rustic porch, over which the Virginia creeper climbed.

We heard last month about Ketira the gipsy: and of the unaccountable disappearance of her daughter, Kettie; and of the indignant anger displayed by Hyde Stockhausen when it was suggested that he might have kidnapped her. Curiously enough, within a few days of that time, Hyde himself disappeared from Church Dykely: not in the mysterious manner that Kettie had, but openly and with intention.

The inducing cause of Hyde's leaving, as was stated and believed, was a quarrel with his step-father, Massock. It chanced that the monthly settling-day, connected with the brickfields, fell just after Kettie vanished. Massock came over for it as usual, and was overbearing as usual; and perhaps Hyde, already in a state of inward irritation, was less forbearing than usual. Any way, ill-words arose between them. Massock accused Hyde of neglecting his interests, and of being too much of a gentleman to look after the work and the men. Hyde retorted: one word led to another, and there ensued a serious quarrel. The upshot was, that Hyde threw up his post. Vowing he would never again have anything to do with old Massock or his precious bricks as long as he lived, he packed up a small portmanteau and quitted Church Dykely there and then, to the intense tribulation of his ancient nurse and servant, Deborah Preen.

"Leave him alone," said Massock roughly. "He'll be back safe enough in a day or two."

"Where is he gone?" asked Ketira the gipsy: who, hovering still around Virginia Cottage, had seen Hyde's exit with his portmanteau.

Massock stared at her, and at her red cloak: she had penetrated to his presence to ask the question. He had never before seen Ketira; never heard of her.

"What is it to you?" he demanded, in his coarse manner. "Who are you? Do you come here to tell his fortune? Be off, old witch!"

"His fortune may be told sooner than you care to hear it—if you are anything to him," was the gipsy's answer. And that same night she quitted Church Dykely herself, wandering away to be lost in the "wide wide world."

Massock's opinion, that Hyde would return in a day or two, proved to be a mistaken one. Rimmer, at the Silver Bear, got a letter from a lawyer in Worcester, asking him to release Mr. Stockhausen from Virginia Cottage—which Hyde had taken for three years. But, this, Rimmer refused to do. So Hyde had to make the best of his bargain: and every quarter, as the quarters went on, the rent was punctually remitted to Henry Rimmer by the lawyer: who gave, however, no clue to his client's place of abode. It was said that Hyde had been reconciled to his uncle, Parson Hyde (now getting into his dotage), and was by him supplied with funds.

One fine evening, however, in the late spring, when not very far short of a twelvemonth had elapsed, Hyde astonished Deborah Preen by his return. After a fit of crying, to show her joy, Deborah brought him in some supper and stood by while he ate it, telling him the news of what had transpired in the village since he left.

"Are those beautiful brickfields being worked still?" he asked.

"'Deed but they are then, Master Hyde. A sight o' bricks seems to be made at 'em. Pitt the foreman, he have took your place as manager, sir, and keeps the accounts."

"Good luck to him!" said Hyde, drinking a glass of ale. "That queer old lady in the red cloak: what has become of her?"

"What, that gipsy hag?" cried Preen. "She's dead, sir."

"Dead!"

"Yes, sir, dead: and a good riddance, too. She went away the very night you went, Mr. Hyde, and never came back again. A week or two ago Abel Carew got news that she was dead."

(Shortly before this, some wandering gipsies had set up their camp within a mile or two of Church Dykely. Abel Carew, never having had news of Ketira since her departure, went to them to make inquiries. At first the gipsies seemed not to understand of whom he was speaking; but upon his making Ketira clear to them, they told him she had been dead about a month; of her daughter, Kettie, they knew nothing.)

"She's not much loss," observed Hyde in answer to Deborah: and his face took a brighter look, as though the news were a relief—Preen noticed it. "The old gipsy was as mad as a March hare."

"And ten times more troublesome than one," put in Preen. "Be you come home to stay, master?"

"I dare say I shall," replied Hyde. "As good settle down here as elsewhere: and there'd be no fun in paying two rents."

So we had Hyde Stockhausen amidst us once more. He did not intend to take up with brickmaking again, but to live as a gentleman. His uncle made him an allowance, and he was going to be married. Abel Carew questioned him about Kettie one day when they met on the common, asking whether he had seen her. Never, was the reply of Hyde. So that what with the girl's prolonged disappearance and her mother's death, it was assumed that we had done with the two gipsies for ever.

Hyde was engaged to a Miss Peyton. A young lady just left an orphan, whom he had met only six weeks ago at some seaside place. He had fallen in love with her at first sight, and she with him. She had two or three hundred a-year: and Hyde, there was little doubt, would come into all his uncle's money; so he saw no reason why he should not make Virginia Cottage comfortable for her, and went off to the Silver Bear, to talk to Henry Rimmer about it.

The result was, that improvements were put in hand without delay. A wing (consisting of a handsome drawing-room downstairs, and a bed and dressing-room above) was added to the cottage on one side; on the other side, Hyde built a conservatory. The house was also generally embellished and set in order, and some new furniture brought in. And I think if ever workmen worked quickly, these did; for the alterations seemed no sooner to be begun than they were done.

"So you have sown your wild oats, Master Hyde," remarked the Squire one day in passing, as he stood to watch the finishing touches, then being put to the outside of the house.

"Don't know that I ever had many to sow, sir," said Hyde, nodding to me.

"And what sort of a young lady is this wife that you are about to bring home?" went on the pater.

Hyde's face took a warm flush and his lips parted with a half-smile; which proved what she was to him. "You will see, sir," he said in answer.

"When is the wedding to be?"

"This day week."

"This day week!" echoed the Squire, surprised: and Hyde, who seemed to have spoken incautiously, looked vexed.

"I did not intend to say as much; my thoughts were elsewhere," he observed. "Don't mention it again, Mr. Todhetley. Even old Deborah has not been told."

"I'll take care, lad. But it is known all over the place that the wedding is close at hand."

"Yes: but not the day."

"When do you go away for it?"

"On Saturday."

"Well, good luck to you, lad! By the way, Hyde," continued the Squire, "what did they do about that drain in the yard? Put a new pipe?"

"Yes," said Hyde, "and they have made a very good job of it. Will you come and see it?"

Pipes and drains held no attraction for me. While the pater went through the house to the yard, I strolled outside the front-gate and across to the little coppice to wait for him. It was shady there: the hot midsummer sun was ablaze to-day.

And I declare that a feather might almost have knocked me down. There, amidst the trees of the coppice, like a picture framed round by green leaves, stood Ketira the gipsy. Or Ketira's ghost.

Believing that she was dead and buried, I might have believed it to be the latter, but for the red cloth cloak: that was real. She was staring at Hyde's house with all the fire of her glittering eyes, looking as though she were consumed by some inward fever.

"Who lives there now?" she abruptly asked me without any other greeting, pointing her yellow forefinger at the house.

"The cottage was empty ever so long," I carelessly said, some instinct prompting me not to tell too much. "Lately the workmen have been making alterations in it. How is Kettie? Have you found her?"

She lifted her two hands aloft with a gesture of despair: but left me unanswered. "These alterations: by whom are they made?"

But the sight of the Squire, coming forth alone, served as an excuse for my making off. I gave her a parting nod, saying I was glad to see her again in the land of the living.

"Ketira the gipsy is here, sir."

"No!" cried the pater in amazement. "Why do you say that, Johnny?"

"She is here in the coppice."

"Nonsense, lad! Ketira's dead, you know."

"But I have just seen her, and spoken to her."

"Then what did those gipsy-tramps mean by telling Abel Carew that she had died?" cried the Squire explosively, as he marched across the few yards of greensward towards the coppice.

"Abel did not feel quite sure at the time that he and they were not talking of two persons. That must have been the case, sir."

We were too late. Ketira was already half-way along the path that led to the common: no doubt on her road to pay a visit to Abel Carew. And I can only relate what passed there at second hand. Between ourselves, Ketira was no favourite of his.

He was at his early dinner of bread-and-butter and salad when she walked in and astonished him. Abel, getting over his surprise, invited her to partake of the meal; but she just waved her hand in refusal, as much as to say that she was superior to dinner and dinner-eating.

"Have you found Kettie?" was his next question.

"It is the first time a search of mine ever failed," she replied, beginning to pace the little room in agitation, just as a tiger paces its confined cage. "I have given myself neither rest nor peace since I set out upon it; but it has not brought me tidings of my child."

"It must have been a weary task for you, Ketira. I wish you would break bread with me."

"I was helped."

"Helped!" repeated Abel. "Helped by what?"

"I know not yet, whether angel or devil. It has been one or the other:—according as he has, or has not, played me false."

"As who has played you false?"

"Of whom do you suppose I speak but him?" she retorted, standing to confront Abel with her deep eyes. "Hyde Stockhausen has in some subtle manner evaded me: but I shall find him yet."

"Hyde Stockhausen is back here," quietly observed Abel.

"Back here! Then it is no false instinct that has led me here," she added in a low tone, apparently communing with herself. "Is Ketira with him?"

"No, no," said Abel, vexed at the question. "Kettie has never come back to the place since she left it."

"When did he come?"

"It must be about two months ago."

"He is in the same dwelling-house as before! For what is he making it so grand?"

"It is said to be against his marriage."

"His marriage with Ketira?"

"With a Miss Peyton; some young lady he has met. Why do you bring up Ketira's name in conjunction with this matter—or with him?"

She turned to the open casement, and stood there, as if to inhale the sweet scent of Abel's flowers, and listen to the hum of his bees. Her face was working, her strange eyes were gleaming, her hands were clasped to pain.

"I know what I know, Abel Carew. Let him look to it if he brings home any other wife than my Ketira."

"Nay," remonstrated peaceful old Abel. "Because a young man has whispered pretty words in a maiden's ear, and given her, it may be, a moonlight kiss, that does not bind him to marry her."

"And would I have wished to bind him had it ended there?" flashed the gipsy. "No; I should have been thankful that it had so ended. I hated him from the first."

"You have no proof that it did not so end, Ketira."

"No proof; none," she assented. "No tangible proof that I could give to you, her father's brother, or to others. But the proof lies in the fatal signs that show themselves to me continually, and in the unerring instinct of my own heart. If the man puts another into the place that ought to be hers, let him look to it."

"You may be mistaken, Ketira. I know not what the signs you speak of can be: they may show themselves to you but to mislead; and nothing is more deceptive than the fancies of one's imagination.

Be it as it may, vengeance does not belong to us. Do not you put yourself forward to work young Stockhausen ill."

"I work him ill!" retorted the gipsy. "You are mistaking me altogether. It is not I who shall work it. I only see it—and foretell it."

"Nay, why speak so strangely, Ketira? It cannot be that you—"

"Abel Carew, talk not to me of matters that you do not understand," she interrupted. "I know what I know. Things that I am able to see are hidden from you."

He shook his head. "It is wrong to speak so of Hyde Stockhausen—or of any one. He may be as innocent in the matter as you or I."

"But I tell you that he is not. And the conviction of it lies here"—striking herself fiercely on the breast.

Abel sighed, and began to put his dinner-plates together. He could not make any impression upon her, or on the notion she had taken up.

"Do you know what it is to have a breaking heart, Abel Carew?" she asked, her voice taking a softer tone that seemed to change it into a piteous wailing. "A broken heart one can bear; for all struggle is over, and one has but to put one's head down on the green earth and die. But a breaking heart means continuous suffering; a perpetual torture that slowly saps away the life; a never-ending ache of soul and of spirit, than which nothing in this world can be so hard to battle with. And for twelve months now this anguish has been mine!"

Poor Ketira! Mistaken or not mistaken, there could be no question that her trouble was grievous to bear; the suspense, in which her days were passed, well-nigh unendurable.

This, that I have told, occurred on Thursday morning. Ketira quitted Abel Carew only to bend her steps back towards Virginia Cottage, and stayed hovering around the house that day and the next. One or another, passing, saw her watching it perpetually, herself partly hidden. Now peeping out from the little coppice; now tramping quickly past the gate, as though she were starting off on a three-mile walk; now stealing to the back of the house, to gaze at the windows. There she might be seen, in one place or another, like a haunting red dragon: her object, as was supposed, being to get speech of Hyde Stockhausen. She did not succeed. Twice she went boldly to the door, knocked, and asked for him. Deborah Preen slammed it in her face. It was thought that Hyde, who then knew of her return and that the report of her death was false, must be on the watch also, to avoid her. If he wanted to go abroad and she was posted at the back, he slipped out in front: when he wished to get in again and caught sight of her red cloak illumining the coppice, he made a dash in at the back-gate, and was lost amid the kidney beans.

By this time the state of affairs was known to Church Dykely: a rare dish of nuts for the quiet place to crack. Those of us who possessed liberty made pleas for passing by Virginia Cottage to see the fun. Not that there was much to see, except a glimpse of the red cloak in this odd spot or in that.

"Stockhausen must be silly!" cried the Squire. "Why does he not openly see the poor woman and inquire what it is she wants with him? The idea of his shunning her in this absurd way! What does he mean by it, I wonder?"

Now, before telling more, I wish to halt and say a word. That much ridicule will be cast on this story by the intelligent reader, is as sure as that apples grow in summer. Nevertheless, I am but relating what took place. Certain things in it were curiously strange; not at all explainable hitherto: possibly never to be explained. I chanced to be personally mixed up with it, so to say, in a degree; from its beginning, when Ketira and her daughter first appeared at Abel Carew's, to its ending, which has yet to be told. For that much I can vouch—I mean what I was present at. But you need not accord belief to the whole, unless you like.

Chance, and nothing else, caused me to be sent over this same evening to Mr. Duffham's. It was Friday, you understand; and the eve of the day Hyde Stockhausen would depart preparatory to his marriage. One of our maids had been ailing for some days with what was thought to be a bad cold: as she did not get better, but grew more feverish, Mrs. Todhetley decided to send for the doctor, if only as a measure of precaution.

"You can go over to Mr. Duffham's for me, Johnny," she said, as we got up from tea—which meal was generally taken at the manor close upon dinner, somewhat after the fashion that the French take their tasse de café. "Ask him if he will be so kind as to call in to see Ann when he is out to-morrow morning."

Nothing loth was I. The evening was glorious, tempting the world out-of-doors, calm and beautiful, but very hot yet. The direct way to Duffham's from our house was not by Virginia Cottage: but, as a matter of course, I took it. Going along at tip-top speed until I came within sight of it, I then slackened to a snail's pace, the better to take observations.

There's an old saying, that virtue is its own reward. If any virtue existed in my choosing this circuitous and agreeable route, I can only say that for once the promise was at fault, for I was not rewarded. Were Hyde Stockhausen's house a prison, it could not have been much more closely shut up. The windows were closed on that lovely midsummer night; the doors looked tight as wax. Not a glimpse could I catch of as much as the bow of Deborah Preen's mob-cap atop of the short bedroom blinds; and Hyde might have been over in Africa for all that could be seen of him.

Neither (for a wonder) was there any trace of Ketira the gipsy. Her red cloak was nowhere. Had she obtained speech of Hyde, and so terminated her watch, or had she given it up in despair? Any way, there was nothing to reward me for having come that much out of my road, and I went on, whistling dolorously.

But, hardly had I got past the premises and was well on the field-path beyond, when I met Duffham. Giving him the message from home, which he said he would attend to, I enlarged on the disappointment just experienced in seeing nothing of anybody.

"Shut up like a jail, is it?" quoth Duffham. "I have just had a note from Stockhausen, asking me to call there. His throat's troubling him again, he says: wants me to give him something that will cure him by to-morrow."

I had turned with the doctor, and went walking with him up the garden, listening to what he said. But I meant to leave him when we reached the door. He began trying it. It was fastened inside.

"I dare say you can come in and see Hyde, Johnny. What do you want with him?"

"Not much; only to wish him good luck."

"Is your master afraid of thieves that he bolts his doors?" cried Duffham to old Preen when she let us in.

"'Twas me fastened it, sir; not master," was her reply. "That gipsy wretch have been about yesterday and to-day, wanting to get in. I've got my silver about, and don't want it stolen. Mr. Hyde's mother and Massock have been here to dinner; they've not long gone."

Decanters and fruit stood on the table before Hyde. He started up to shake hands, appearing very much elated. Duffham, more experienced than I, saw that he had been taking quite enough wine.

"So you have had your stepfather here!" was one of the doctor's first remarks. "Been making up the quarrel, I suppose."

"He came of his own accord; I didn't invite him," said Hyde, laughing. "My mother wrote me word that they were coming—to give me their good wishes for the future."

"Just what Johnny Ludlow here says he wants to give," said Duffham: though I didn't see that he need have brought my words up, and made a fellow feel shy.

"Then, by Jove, you shall drink them in champagne!" exclaimed Hyde. He caught up a bottle of champagne that stood under the sideboard, from which the wire had been removed, and would have cut the string but for the restraining hand of Duffham.

"No, Hyde; you have had rather too much as it is."

"I swear to you that I have not had a spoonful. It has not been opened, you see. My mother refused it, and Massock does not care for champagne: he likes something heavier."

"If you have not taken champagne, you have taken other wine."

"Sherry at dinner, and port since," laughed Hyde.

"And more of it than is good for you."

"When Massock sits down to port wine he drinks like a fish," returned Hyde, still laughing. "Of course I had to make a show of drinking with him. I wished the port at Hanover."

By a dexterous movement, he caught up a knife and cut the string. Out shot the cork with a bang, and he filled three of the tumblers that stood on the sideboard with wine and froth—one for each of us. "Your health, doctor," nodded he, and tossed off his own.

"It will not do your throat good," said Duffham, angrily. "Let me look at the throat."

"Not until you and Johnny have wished me luck."

We did it, and drank the wine. Duffham examined the throat; and told Hyde, for his consolation, that it was not in a state to be trifled with.

"Oh, it's nothing," said Hyde carelessly. "But I don't want it to be bad to-morrow when I travel, and I thought perhaps you might be able to give me something or other to set it to rights to-night. I start at ten to-morrow morning."

"Sore throats are not cured so easily," retorted Duffham. "You must have taken cold."

Telling him he would send in a gargle and a cooling draught, and that he was to go to bed soon, Duffham rose to leave. Hyde opened the glass-doors of the room that we might pass out that way, and stepped over the threshold with us. Talking with Duffham, he strolled onwards towards the gate.

"About three weeks, I suppose," he said, in answer to the query of how long he meant to be away. "If Mabel—"

Gliding out of the bushy laurels on one side the path, and planting herself right in front of us, came Ketira the gipsy. Her face looked yellower than ever in the twilight of the summer's evening; her piercing black eyes fiercer. Hyde was taken aback by the unexpected encounter. He started a step back.

"Where's my daughter, Hyde Stockhausen?"

"Go away," he said, in the contemptuous tone one might use to a dog. "I don't know anything of your daughter."

"Only tell me where she is, that I may find her. I ask no more."

"I tell you that I do not know anything of her. You must be mad to think it. Get along with you!"

"Hyde Stockhausen, you lie. You do know where she is; you know that it is with you she has been. Heaven hears me say it: deny it if you dare."

His face looked whiter than death. Just for an instant he seemed unable to speak. Ketira changed her tone to one of plaintive wailing.

"She was my one little ewe lamb. What had she or I done to you that you should come as a spoiler to the fold? I prayed you not. Make her your wife, and I will yet bless you. It is not too late. Do not break her heart and mine."

Hyde had had time to rally his courage. A man full of wine can generally call some up, even in the most embarrassing of situations. He scornfully asked the gipsy whether she had come out of Bedlam. Ketira saw how hard he was—that there was no hope.

"It is said that you depart to-morrow to bring home a bride, Hyde Stockhausen. I counsel you not to do it. For your own sake, and for the young woman's sake, I bid you beware. The marriage will not bring good to you or to her."

That put Hyde in a towering passion. His words came out with a splutter as he spurned her from him.

"Cease your folly, you senseless old beldame! Do you dare to threaten me? Take yourself out of my sight instantly, before I fetch my horsewhip. And, if ever you attempt to molest me again, I will have you sent to the treadmill."

Ketira stood looking at him while he spoke, never moving an inch. As his voice died away she lifted her forefinger in warning. And anything more impressive than her voice, than her whole manner—anything more startlingly defiant than her countenance, I never wish to see.

"It is well; I go. But listen to me, Hyde Stockhausen; mark what I say. Only three times shall you see me again in life. But each one of those times you shall have cause to remember; and after the last of them you will not need to see me more."

It was a strange threat. That she made it, Duffham could, to this day, corroborate. Pulling her red cloak about her shoulders, she went swiftly through the gate, and disappeared within the opposite coppice.

Hyde smiled; his good humour was returning to him. One can be brave enough when an enemy turns tail.

"Idiotic old Egyptian!" he exclaimed lightly. "What on earth ever made her take the fancy into her head, that I knew what became of Kettie, I can't imagine. I wonder, Duffham, some of you people in authority here don't get her confined as a lunatic!"

"We must first of all find that she is a lunatic," was Duffham's dry rejoinder.

"Why, what else is she?"

"Not that."

"She is; and a dangerous one," retorted Hyde.

"Nonsense, man! Gipsies have queer ways and notions; and—and—are not to be judged altogether as other people," added the doctor, finishing off (as it struck me) with different words from those he had been about to say. "Good-night; and don't take any more of that champagne."

Hyde returned indoors, and we walked away, not seeing a sign of the red cloak anywhere.

"I must say I should not like to be attacked in this manner, were I Hyde," I remarked to Duffham. "How obstinate the old gipsy is!"

"Ah," replied Duffham. "I'd sooner believe her than him."

The words surprised me, and I turned to him quickly. "Why do you say that, sir?"

"Because I do say it, Johnny," was the unsatisfactory answer. "And now good-evening to you, lad, for I must send the physic in."

"Just a word, please, Mr. Duffham. Do you know where that poor Kettie is?—and did you know that Hyde Stockhausen stole her?"

"No, to both your questions, Johnny Ludlow."

Everybody liked Hyde's wife. A fragile girl with a weak voice, who looked as if a strong wind would blow her away. Duffham feared she was not strong enough to make old days.

Virginia Cottage flourished. Parson Hyde had died and left all his fortune to Hyde: who had now nothing to do but take care of his wife and his money, and enjoy life. Before the next summer came round, Hyde had a son and heir. A fine little shaver, with blue eyes like Hyde's, and good lungs. His mother was a long while getting about again: and then she looked like a shadow, and had a short, hacking kind of cough. Hyde wore a grave face at times, and would say he wished Mabel could get strong.

But Hyde was regarded with less favour than formerly. People did not scruple to call him "villain." And one Sunday, when Mr. Holland told us in his sermon that man's heart was deceitful above all things and desperately wicked, the congregation wondered whether he meant it especially for Stockhausen. For the truth had come out.

When Hyde departed to keep his marriage engagement, Ketira the gipsy had again disappeared from Church Dykely. In less than a month afterwards, Abel Carew received a letter from her. She had found Kettie: and she had found that her own instincts against Hyde Stockhausen were not mistaken ones. For all his seeming fair face and his indignant denials, it was he who had been the thief.

"Of all brazen-faced knaves, that Stockhausen must be the worst!—an adept in cunning, a lying hypocrite!" exploded the Squire.

"I suspected him at the time," said Duffham.

"You did! What were your grounds for it?"

"I had no particular grounds. His manner did not appear to me to be satisfactory; that was all. Of course I was not sure."

"He is a base man," concluded the Squire. And from that time he turned the cold shoulder on Hyde.

But time is a sure healer of wounds; a softener of resentment. As it passed on, we began to forget Hyde's dark points, and to remember his good qualities. Any way, Ketira the gipsy and Ketira's daughter passed out of memory, just as they had passed out of sight.

Suddenly we heard that Abel Carew was preparing to go on a journey. I went off to ask him where he was bound for.

"I am going to see them, Master Johnny," he replied. "I don't know how they are off, sir, and it is my duty to see. The child is ill: and I fear they may be wanting assistance, which Ketira is too proud to write and ask for."

"Kettie ill! What is the matter with her?"

Abel shook his head. "I shall know more when I get there, sir."

Abel Carew locked up his cottage and began his pilgrimage into Hertfordshire with a staff and a wallet, intending to walk all the way. In a fortnight he was back again, bringing with him a long face.

"It is sad to see the child," he said to me, as I sat in his room listening to the news. "She is no more like the bonnie Kettie that we knew here, than a dead girl's like a living one. Worn out, bent and silent, she sits, day after day and week after week, and her mother cannot rouse her. She has sat so all along."

"But what is the matter with her?"

"She is slowly dying, sir."

"What of?"

"A broken heart."

"Oh dear!" said I; believing I knew who had broken it.

"Yes," said Abel, "he. He won her heart's best love, Master Johnny, and she pines for him yet. Ketira says it was his marriage that struck her the death-blow. A few weeks she may still linger, but they won't be many."

Very sorry did I feel to hear it: for Ketira's sake as well as Kettie's. The remembrance of the day I had gilded the oak-ball, and her wonderful gratitude for it, came flashing back to me.

And there's nothing more to add to this digression. Except that Kettie died.

The tidings did not appear to affect Hyde Stockhausen. All his thoughts were given to his wife and child. Old Abel had never reproached him by as much as a word: if by chance they met, Abel avoided looking at him, or turned off another way.

When the baby was six months old and began to cut his teeth, he did not appear inclined to do it kindly. He grew thin and cross; and the parents, who seemed to think no baby ever born could come up to this one, began to be anxious. Hyde worshipped the child ridiculously.

"The boy will do well enough if he does not get convulsions," Duffham said in semi-confidence to some people over his surgery counter. "If they come on—why, I can't answer for what the result might be. Fat? Yes, he is a great deal too fat: they feed him up so."

The surgeon was sitting by his parlour-fire one snowy evening shortly after this, when Stockhausen burst upon him in a fine state of agitation; arms working, breath gone. The baby was in a fit.

"Come, come; don't you give way," cried the doctor, believing Hyde was going into a fit on his own account. "We'll see."

Out of one convulsion into another went the child that night: but in a few days it was better; thought to be getting well. Mr. and Mrs. Stockhausen in consequence felt themselves in the seventh heaven.

"The danger is quite past," observed Hyde, walking down the snowy path with Duffham, one morning when the doctor had been paying a visit; and Hyde rubbed his hands in gleeful relief, for he had been like a crazed lunatic while the child lay ill. "Duffham, if that child had died, I think I should have died."

"Not a bit of it," said Duffham. "You are made of tougher stuff."

He was about to open the garden-gate as he spoke. But, suddenly appearing there to confront them stood Ketira the gipsy. A moment's startled pause ensued. Duffham spoke kindly to her. Hyde recoiled a step or two; as if the sight had frightened him.

"You may well start back," she said to the latter, taking no notice of Duffham's civility. "I told you, you should not see me many times in life, Hyde Stockhausen, but that when you did, I should be the harbinger of evil. Go home, and meet it."

Turning off under the garden-hedge, without another word, she disappeared from their view as suddenly as she had come into it. Hyde Stockhausen made a feint of laughing.

"The woman is more mad than ever," he said. "Decidedly, Duffham, she ought to be in confinement."

Never an assenting syllable gave Duffham. He was looking as stern as a judge. "What's that?" he suddenly exclaimed, turning sharply to the house.

A maid-servant was flying down the path. Deborah Preen stood at the door, crying and calling as if in some dire calamity. Hyde rushed towards her, asking what was amiss. Duffham followed more slowly. The baby had got another attack of convulsions.

And this time it was for death.

When these events were happening, Great Malvern was not the overgrown, fashionable place it is now; but a quiet little spot with only a few houses in it, chiefly clustering under the highest of the hills. Amid these houses, one bright May day, Hyde Stockhausen went, seeking lodgings.

Hyde had not died of the loss of the baby. For here he was, alive and well, nearly eighteen months afterwards. That it had been a sharp trial for him nobody doubted; and for his wife also. And when a second baby came to replace the first, it brought them no good, for it did not live a week.

That was in March: two months ago: and ever since Mrs. Stockhausen had been hovering between this world and the next. A fever and other ailments had taken what little strength she had out of her. This, to Hyde Stockhausen, was a worse affliction than even the loss of the children, for she was to him as the very apple of his eye. When somewhat improving, the doctors recommended Malvern. So Hyde had brought her to it with a nurse and old Deborah; and had left them at the Crown Hotel while he looked for lodgings.

He found them in one of the houses down by the abbey. Some nice rooms, quite suitable. And to them his wife was taken. For a very few days afterwards she seemed to be getting better: and then all the bad symptoms returned. A doctor was called in. He feared she might not rally again; that the extreme debility might prevent it: and he said as much to Hyde in private.

Anything more unreasonable than the spirit in which Hyde met this, the Malvern doctor had never seen.

"You are a fool," said Hyde. "Begging your pardon, sir, I should think you don't know your profession. My wife is fifty pounds better than she was at Church Dykely. How can you take upon yourself to say she will not rally?"

"I said she might not," replied the surgeon, who happened to possess a temper mild as milk. "I hope she will with all my heart. I shall do my best to bring it about."

It was an anxious time. Mrs. Stockhausen fluctuated greatly: to-day able to sit up in an easy-chair; to-morrow too exhausted to be lifted out of bed. But, one morning she did seem to be ever so much better. Her cheeks were pink, her lips had a smile.

"Ah," said the doctor cheerfully when he went in, "we shall do now, I hope. You are up early to-day."

"I felt so much better that I wanted to get up and surprise you," she answered in quite a strong voice—for her. "And it was so warm, and the world looked so beautiful. I should like to be able to mount one of those donkeys and go up the hill. Hyde says that the view, even from St. Ann's well, is charming."

"So it is," assented the surgeon. "Have you never seen it?"

"No, I have not been to Malvern before."

This was the first day of June. Hyde would not forget the date to the last hour of his life. It was hot summer weather: the sun came in at the open window, touching her hair and her pale forehead as she lay back in the easy-chair after the doctor left; a canary at a neighbouring house was singing sweetly; the majestic hills, with their light and shade, looked closer even than they were in reality. Hyde began to lower the blind.

"Don't, please, Hyde."

"But, my darling, the sun will soon be in your eyes."

"I shall like it. Is it not a lovely day! I think it is that which has put new life into me."

"And we shall soon have you up the hill, where we can sit and look all over everywhere. On one or two occasions, when the atmosphere was rarefied to an unusual degree, I have caught the silver line of the Bristol Channel."

"How pleasant it will be, Hyde! To sit there with you, and to know that I am getting well!"

Early in the afternoon, when Mabel lay down to rest, Hyde went strolling up the hill, for the first time since his present stay at Malvern. He got as far as St. Ann's; drank a tumbler of the water, and then paced about, hither and thither, to the right and left, not intending to ascend higher that day. If he went to the summit, Mabel might be awake before he got home again; and he would not have lost five minutes of her waking moments for a mine of gold. Looking at his watch, he sat down on a bench that was backed by some dark trees.

"Yes," he mused, "it will be delightful to sit about here with Mabel, and show her the different points of interest in the landscape. Worcester Cathedral, and St. Andrew's Spire; and the Bristol—"

Some stir behind caused him to turn his head. The words froze on his tongue. There stood Ketira the gipsy. She had been sitting or lying amidst the trees, wrapped in her red cloak. Hyde's look of startled dread was manifest. She saw it; and accosted him.

"We meet again, Hyde Stockhausen. Ah, you have cause to fear!—your face may well whiten to the shivering hue of snow at sight of me! You are alone in the world now—as you left my daughter to be. Once more we shall see one another. Till then farewell."

Recovering his equanimity when left alone, Hyde betook himself down the zig-zag path towards the village, calling the gipsy all the wicked names in the dictionary, and feeling tempted to give her into custody.

At his home, he was met by a commotion. The nurse wore a scared face; Deborah Preen, wringing her hands, burst out sobbing.

Mabel was dead. Had died in a fainting-fit.

Leaving his wife in her grave at Malvern, Hyde Stockhausen returned to Church Dykely. We hardly knew him.

A more changed man than Hyde was from that time the world has never seen. He walked about like a melancholy maniac, hands in his coat-pockets, eyes on the ground, steps dragging; looking just like one who has some great remorse lying upon his conscience and is being consumed by the past. The most wonderful thing in the eyes of Church Dykely was, that he grew religious: came to church twice on Sunday, stayed for the Sacrament, was good to the poor, gentle and kindly to all. Mr. Holland observed to the Squire that Stockhausen had become a true Christian. He made his will, and altogether seemed to be tired of life.

"Go you, Johnny, and ask him to come over to us sometimes in an evening; tell him it will be a break to his loneliness," said the Squire to me one day. "Now that the poor fellow is ill and repentant, we must let bygones be bygones. I hear that Abel Carew spent half-an-hour sociably with him yesterday."

I went off as directed. Summer had come round again, for more than a year had now passed since Mabel's death, and the Virginia creeper on the cottage walls was all alight with red flowers. Hyde was pacing his garden in front of it, his head bent.

"Is it you, Johnny?" he said, in the patient, gentle tone he now always used, as he held his hand out. He was more like a shadow than a man; his face drawn and long, his blue eyes large and dark and sad.

"We should be so glad if you would come," I added, after giving the message. "Mrs. Todhetley says you make yourself too much of a stranger. Will you come this evening?"

He shook his head slightly, clasping my hand the while, his own feeling like a burning coal, and smiling the sweetest and saddest smile.

"You are all too good for me; too considerate; better far than I deserve. No, I cannot come to you this evening, Johnny: I have not the spirits for it; hardly the strength. But I will come one evening if I can. Thank them all, Johnny, for me."

And he did come. But he could not speak much above a whisper, so weak and hollow had his voice grown. And of all the humble-minded, kindly-spirited individuals that ever sat at our tea-table, the chiefest was Hyde Stockhausen.

"I fear he is going the way of all the Stockhausens," said Mrs. Todhetley afterwards. "But what a beautiful frame of mind he is in!"

"Beautiful, you call it!" cried the pater. "The man seems to me to be eating his heart out in some impossible atonement. Had I set fire to the church and burnt up all the congregation, I don't think it could have subdued me to that extent."

Of all places, where should I next meet Hyde but at Worcester races! We knew that he had been worse lately, that his mother had come to Virginia Cottage to be with him at the last, and that there was no further hope. Therefore, to see Hyde this afternoon, perched on a tall horse on Pitchcroft, looked more like magic than reality.

"You at the races, Hyde!"

"Yes; but not for pleasure," he answered, smiling faintly; and looking so shadowy and weak that it was a marvel how he could stick on the horse. "I am in search of one who is growing too fond of these scenes. I want to find him—and to say a few last words to him."

"If you mean Jim Massock"—for I thought it could be nobody but young Jim—"I saw him yonder, down by the shows. He was drinking porter outside a booth. How are you, Hyde?"

"Oh, getting on slowly," he said, with a peculiar smile.

"Getting on! It looks to me to be the other way."

Turning his horse quickly round, after nodding to me, in the direction of the shows and drinking booths, he nearly turned it upon a tall, gaunt skeleton in a red cloak—Ketira the gipsy. She must have sprung out of the crowd.

But oh, how ill she looked! Hyde was strangely altered; but not as she was. The yellow face was shrivelled and shrunken, the fire had left her eyes. Hyde checked his horse; but the animal turned restive. He controlled it with his hand, and sat still before Ketira.

"Yes, look at me," she burst forth. "For the last time. The end is close at hand both for you and for me. We shall meet Kettie where we are going."

He leaned from his horse to speak to her: his voice a low sad wail, his words apparently those of deprecating prayer. Ketira heard him quietly to the end, gazing into his face, and then slowly turned away.

"Fare you well, Hyde Stockhausen. Farewell for ever."

Before leaving the course Hyde had an accident. While talking to Jim Massock, some drums and trumpets struck up their noise at a neighbouring show; the horse started violently, and Hyde was thrown. He thought he was not much hurt and mounted again.

"What else could you expect?" demanded Duffham, when Hyde got back to Virginia Cottage. "You have not strength to sit a donkey, and you must go careering off to Worcester races on a fiery horse!"

But the fall had done Hyde some inward damage, and it hastened the end. He died that day week.

"Some men's sins go before them to Judgment, and some follow after," solemnly said Mr. Holland the next Sunday from the pulpit. "He who is gone from among us had taken his to his Saviour—and he is now at rest."

"All chance and coincidence," pronounced Duffham, talking over the strange threat of Ketira the gipsy and its stranger working out. "Yes; chance, I say, each of the three times. The woman, happening to be at hand, must have known by common report that the child was in peril; she may have learnt at Malvern that the wife was dying; and any goose with eyes in its head might have read coming death on his face that afternoon on Pitchcroft. That's all about it, Johnny."

Very probably. The reader can exercise his own judgment. I only know it all happened.

THE CURATE OF ST MATTHEW'S

I

"No, Johnny Ludlow, I shall not stay at home, and have the deeds sent up and down by post. I know what lawyers are; so will you, some time: this letter to be read and answered to-day; that paper to be digested and despatched back to-morrow—anything to enchance their bill of costs. I intend to be in London, on the spot; and so will you be, Mr. Johnny."

So said Mr. Brandon to me, as we sat in the bay-window at Crabb Cot, at which place we were staying. I was willing enough to go to London; liked the prospect beyond everything; but he was not well, and I thought of the trouble to him.

"Of course, sir, if you consider it necessary we should be there. But—"

"Now, Johnny Ludlow, I have told you my decision," he interrupted, cutting me short in all the determination of his squeaky little voice. "You go with me to London, sir, and we start on Monday morning next; and I dare say we shall be kept there a week. I know what lawyers are."

This happened when I came of age, twenty-one; but I should not be of age as to my property for four more years: until then, Mr. Brandon remained my arbitrary guardian and trustee, just as strictly as he had been. Arbitrary so far as doing the right thing as trustee went, not suffering me, or any one else, to squander a shilling. One small bit of property fell to me now; a farm; and old Brandon was making as much legal commotion over the transfer of it from his custody to mine, as though it had been veined with gold. For this purpose, to execute the deeds of transfer, he meant to take up his quarters in London, to be on the spot with the lawyers who had it in hand, and to carry me up with him.

And what great events trivial chances bring about! Chances, as they are called. These "chances" are all in the hands of one Divine Ruler, who is ever shaping them to further His own wise ends. But for my going to London that time and staying there—however, I'll not let the cat out of the bag.

He stayed with us at Crabb Cot until the Monday, when we started for London; the Squire and Tod coming to the station to see us off. Mr. Brandon wore a nankeen suit, and had a green veil in readiness. A green veil, if you'll believe me! The sun was under a cloud just then; had been for the best part of the morning; but if it came out fiercely—Tod threw up his arms behind old Brandon's back, and gave me a grin and a whisper.

"I wouldn't be you for something, Johnny; he'll be taken for a lunatic."

"And mind you take care of yourself, sir," put in the Squire, to me. "London is a dreadful place; full of temptations; and you are but an inexperienced boy, Johnny. Be cautious and watchful, lad; don't pick up any strange acquaintances in the streets; sharpers are on the watch to get you into conversation, and then swindle you out of all the money in your pockets. Be sure don't forget the little hamper for Miss Deveen; and—"

The puffing of the engine, as we started, drowned the rest. We reached Paddington, smoothly and safely—and old Brandon did not once put on the veil. He took a cab to the Tavistock Hotel, and I another cab to Miss Deveen's.

For she had asked me to stay with her. Hearing of my probable visit to town through a letter of Helen Whitney's, she, ever kind, wrote at once, saying, if I did go, I must make her house my home for the time, and that it would be a most delightful relief to the stagnation she and Miss Cattledon had been lately enjoying. Of course that was just her pleasant way of putting it.

The house looked just as it used to look; the clustering trees of the north-western suburb were as green and grateful to the tired eye as of yore; and Miss Deveen, in grey satin, received me with the same glad smile. I knew I was a favourite of hers; she once said there were few people in the world she liked as well as she liked me—which made me feel proud and grateful. "I should leave you a fortune, Johnny," she said to me that same day, "but that I know you have plenty of your own." And I begged her not to do anything of the kind; not to think of it: she must know a great many people to whom her money would be a Godsend. She laughed at my earnestness, and told me I should be unselfish to the end.

We spent a quiet evening. The grey-haired curate, Mr. Lake, who had come in the first evening I ever spent at Miss Deveen's, years ago, came in again by invitation. "He is so modest," she had said to me, in those long-past years, "he never comes without being invited:" and he was modest still. His hair had been chestnut-coloured once; it was half grey and half chestnut now; and his face and voice were gentle, and his manners kindly. Cattledon was displaying her most gracious behaviour, and thinnest waist; one of the roses I had brought up with the strawberries was sticking out of the body of her green silk gown. For at least half-a-dozen years she had been setting her cap at the curate—and I think she must have been endowed with supreme patience.

"If you do not particularly want me this morning, Miss Deveen, I think I will go over to service."

It was the next morning, and after breakfast. Cattledon had been downstairs, giving the orders for dinner—and said this on her return. Every morning she went through the ceremony of asking whether she was wanted, before attiring herself for church.

"Not I," cried Miss Deveen, with a half-smile. "Go, and welcome, Jemima!"

I stood at the window listening to the ting-tang: the bell of St. Matthew's Church could be called nothing else: and watched her pick her way across the road, just deluged by the water-cart. She wore a striped fawn-coloured gown, cut straight up and down, which made her look all the thinner, and a straw bonnet and white veil. The church was on the other side of the wide road, lower down, but within view. Some stragglers went into it with Cattledon; not many.

"Does it pay to hold the daily morning service?"

"Pay?" repeated Miss Deveen, looking at me with an arch smile. And I felt ashamed of my inadvertent, hasty word.

"I mean, is the congregation sufficient to repay the trouble?"

"The congregation, Johnny, usually consists of some twenty people, a few more, or a few less, as may chance; and they are all young ladies," she added, the smile deepening to a laugh. "At least, unmarried ones; some are as old as Miss Cattledon. Two of them are widows of thirty-five: they are especially constant in attendance."

"They go after the curate," I said, laughing with Miss Deveen. "One year when Mr. Holland was ill, down with us, he had to take on a curate, and the young ladies ran after him."

"Yes, Johnny, the young ladies go after the curates; we have two of them. Mr. Lake is the permanent curate; he has been here, oh, twelve or thirteen years. He does the chief work, in the church and out of it; we have a great many poor, as I think you know. The other curate is changed at least every year, and is generally a young deacon, fresh from college. Our Rector is fond of giving young men their title to orders. The young fellow we have now is a nobleman's grandson, with more money in his pocket to waste on light gloves and hair-wash than poor Mr. Lake dare spend on all his living."

"Mr. Lake seems to be a very good man."

"A better man never lived," returned Miss Deveen warmly, as she got up from the note she was writing, and came to my side. "Self-denying, anxious, painstaking; a true follower of his Master, a Christian to the very depths of his heart. He is one of those unobtrusive men whose merits are kept hidden from the world in general, who are content to work on patiently and silently in their path of duty, looking for no promotion, no reward here, because it seems to lie so very far away from their track."

"Is Mr. Lake poor?"

"Mr. Lake has just one hundred pounds a-year, Johnny. It was what Mr. Selwyn offered him when he first came, and it has never been increased. William Lake told me one day," added Miss Deveen, "that he thought the hundred a-year riches then. He was not a very young man; turned thirty; but his stipend in the country had been only fifty pounds a-year. To have it doubled all at once, no doubt did seem like riches."

"Why does not the Rector raise it?"

"The Rector says he can't afford to do it. I believe Mr. Lake once plucked up courage to ask him for a small increase: but it was of no use. The living is worth six hundred a-year, out of which the senior curate's stipend has to be paid; and Mr. Selwyn's family is expensive. His two sons are just leaving college. So, poor Mr. Lake has just plodded on with his hundred a-year, and made it do. The Rector wishes he could raise it; he knows his worth. During this prolonged illness of Mr. Selwyn's he has been most indefatigable."

"Is Mr. Selwyn ill?"

"Not very ill, but ailing. He has been so for two years. He generally preaches on a Sunday morning, but that is about all the duty he has been able to take. Mr. Lake is virtually the incumbent; he does everything, in the church and out of it."

"Without the pay," I remarked.

"Without the pay, Johnny. His hundred a-year, however, seems to suffice him. He never grumbles at it, never complains, is always contented and cheerful: and no doubt will be contented with it to the end."

"But—if he has no more than that, and no expectation of more, how is it that the ladies run after him? They can't expect him to marry upon a hundred a-year."

"My dear Johnny, let a clergyman possess nothing but the white surplice on his back, the ladies would trot at his heels all the same. It comes naturally to them. They trust to future luck, you see; promotion is always possible, and they reckon upon it. I'm sure the way Mr. Lake gets run after is as good as a play. This young lady sends him a pair of slippers, her own work; that one embroiders a cushion for him: Cattledon painted a velvet fire-screen for him last year—'Oriental tinting.' You never saw a screen so gorgeous."

"Do you think he has—has—any idea of Miss Cattledon?"

"Just as much as he has of me," cried Miss Deveen. "He is kind and polite to her; as he is, naturally, to every one; but you may rely upon it he never gave her a word or a look that would be construed into anything warmer."

"How silly she must be!"

"Not more silly than the rest are. It is a mania, Johnny, and they all go in for it. Jemima Cattledon—stupid old thing!—cherishes hopes of Mr. Lake: a dozen others cherish the same. Most of them are worse than she is, for they course about the parish after him all day long. Cattledon never does that: with all her zeal, she does not forget that she is a gentlewoman; she meets him here, at my house, and she goes to church to see and hear him, but she does not race after him."

"Do you think he is aware of all this pursuit?"

"Well, he must be, in a degree; William Lake is not a simpleton. But the very hopelessness of his being able to marry must in his mind act as a counterbalance, and cause him to look upon it as a harmless pastime. How could he think any one of them in earnest, remembering his poor hundred pounds a-year?"

Thus talking, the time slipped on, until we saw the congregation coming out of church. The service had taken just three-quarters-of-an-hour.

"Young Chisholm has been reading the prayers to-day; I am sure of that," remarked Miss Deveen. "He gabbles them over as fast as a parrot."

The ladies congregated within the porch, and without: ostensibly to exchange compliments with one another; in reality to wait for the curates. The two appeared together: Mr. Lake quiet and thoughtful; Mr. Chisholm, a very tall, slim, empty-headed young fellow, smiling here, and shaking hands there, and ready to chatter with the lot.

For full five minutes they remained stationary. Some important subject of conversation had evidently been started, for they stood around Mr. Lake, listening to something he was saying. The pew-opener, a woman in a muslin cap, and the bell-ringer, an old man in a battered hat, halted on the outskirts of the throng.

"One or other of those damsels is sure to invent some grave question to discuss with him," laughed Miss Deveen. "Perhaps Betty Smith has been breaking out again. She gives more trouble, with her alternate repentings and her lapsings to the tap-room, than all the rest of the old women put together."

Presently the group dispersed; some going one way, some another. Young Chisholm walked off at a smart pace, as if he meant to make a round of morning calls; the elder curate and Miss Cattledon crossed the road together.

"His way home lies past our house," remarked Miss Deveen, "so that he often does cross the road with her. He lives at Mrs. Topcroft's."

"Mrs. Topcroft's! What a curious name."

"So it is, Johnny. But she is a curiously good woman—in my opinion; worth her weight in gold. Those young ladies yonder turn up their noses at her, calling her a 'lodging-letter.' They are jealous; that's the truth; jealous of her daughter, Emma Topcroft. Cattledon, I know, thinks the young girl the one chief rival to be feared."

Mr. Lake passed the garden with a bow, raising his hat to Miss Deveen; and Cattledon came in.

I went off, as quick as an omnibus could take me, to the Tavistock, being rather behind time, and preparing for a blowing-up from Mr. Brandon in consequence.

"Are you Mr. Ludlow, sir?" asked the waiter.

"Yes."

"Then Mr. Brandon left word that he was going down to Lincoln's Inn, sir; and if he is not back here at one o'clock precisely, I was to say that you needn't come down again till to-morrow morning at ten."

I went into the Strand, and amused myself with looking at the shops, getting back to the hotel a few minutes after one. No; Mr. Brandon had not come in. All I could do was to leave Miss Deveen's note of invitation to dine with her—that day, or any other day that might be more convenient, or every day—and tell the man to be sure to give it him.

Then I went into the National Gallery, after getting some Bath buns at a pastrycook's. It was between five and six when I returned to Miss Deveen's. Her carriage had just driven up; she and Cattledon were alighting from it.

"I have a little commission to do yet at one of the shops in the neighbourhood, and I may as well go about it now," remarked Miss Deveen. "Will you go with me, Johnny?"

Of course I said I would go; and Miss Cattledon was sent indoors to fetch a small paper parcel that lay on the table in the blue room.

"It contains the patterns of some sewing silks that I want to get," she added to me, as we stood waiting on the door-steps. "If—"

At that moment, out burst the ting-tang. Miss Deveen suddenly broke off what she was saying, and turned to look at the church.

"Do they have service at this hour?" I asked.

"Hush, Johnny! That bell is not going for service. Some one must be dead."

In truth, I heard that, even as she spoke. Three times three it struck out, followed by the sharp, quick strokes.

"That's the passing-bell!" exclaimed Cattledon, coming quickly from the hall with the little packet in her hand. "Who can be dead? It hardly rings out once in a year."

For, it appeared, the bell at St. Matthew's did not in general toll for the dead: was not expected to do so. Our bell at Church Dykely rang for any one who could pay for it.

Waiting there on the steps, we saw Mr. Lake coming from the direction of the church. Miss Deveen walked down the broad path of her small front-garden, and stood at the gate to wait for him.

"Who is it?" she asked.

"Oh, it is a grievous thing!" he cried, in answer, his gentle face pale, his blue eyes suppressing their tears. "It is no other than my dear Rector; my many years' friend!"

"The Rector!" gasped Miss Deveen.

"Indeed it is. The complaint he suffered from has increased its symptoms lately, but no one thought of attaching to them the slightest danger. At two o'clock to-day he sent for me, saying he felt very ill. I found him so when I got there; ill, and troubled. He had taken a turn for the worse; and death—death," added Mr. Lake, pausing to command his voice, "was coming on rapidly."

Miss Deveen had turned as white as her point-lace collar.

"He was troubled, you say?" she asked.

"In such a case as this—meeting death face to face unexpectedly—it is hardly possible not to be troubled, however truly we may have lived in preparation for it," answered the sad, soft voice of the curate. "Mr. Selwyn's chief perplexity lay in the fact that he had not settled his worldly affairs."

"Do you mean, not made his will?"

"Just so," nodded Mr. Lake; "he had meant to do so, he said to me, but had put it off from time to time. We got a lawyer in, and it was soon done; and—and—I stayed on with him afterwards to the end."

"Oh dear, it is a piteous tale," sighed Miss Deveen. "And his wife and daughters are away!"

"They went to Oxford last Saturday for a week; and the two sons are there, as you know. No one thought seriously of his illness. Even this morning, when I called upon him after breakfast, though he said he was not feeling well, and did not look well, such a thing as danger never occurred to me. And now he is dead!"

Never did a parson's death cause such a stir in a parish as poor Mr. Selwyn's did in this. A lively commotion set in. People flew about to one another's houses like chips in a gale of wind. Not only was the sorrow to himself to be discussed, but the uncertainty as to what would happen now. Some six months previously a church not far off, St. Peter's, which had rejoiced in three energetic curates, and as many daily services, suddenly changed its incumbent; the new one proved to be an elderly man with wife and children, who did all the duty himself, and cut off the curates and the week-day prayers. What if the like calamity should happen to St. Matthew's!

I was away most of the following day with Mr. Brandon, so was not in the thick of it, but the loss was made up for in the evening.

"Of course it is impossible to say who will get the living," cried Mrs. Jonas, one of the two widows already mentioned, who had been dining with Miss Deveen. "I know who ought to—and that is our dear Mr. Lake."

"'Oughts' don't go for much in this world," growled Dr. Galliard, a sterling man, in spite of his gruffness. He had recently brought Cattledon out of a bilious attack, and ran in this evening to see whether the cure lasted. "They go for nothing in the matter of Church patronage," continued he. "If Lake had his deserts, he'd be made incumbent of this living to-morrow: but he is as likely to get it as I am to get the Lord Chancellor's seals."

"Who would have done as Mr. Lake has done—given himself up solely and wholly to the duties of the church and the poor, for more years than I can count?" contended Mrs. Jonas, who was rich and positive, and wore this evening a black gauze dress, set off with purple grapes, and a spray of purple grapes in her black hair. "I say the living is due to him, and the Lord Chancellor ought to present him with it."

Dr. Galliard gave a short laugh. He was a widower, and immensely popular, nearly as much so as Mr. Lake. "Did you ever know a curate succeed to a living under the circumstances?" he demanded. "The Lord Chancellor has enough friends of his own, waiting to snap up anything that falls; be sure of that, Mrs. Jonas."

"Some dean will get it, I shouldn't wonder," cried Cattledon. For at this time we were in the prime old days when a Church dignitary might hold half-a-dozen snug things, if he could drop into them.

"Just so; a dean or some other luminary," nodded the doctor. "It is the province of great divines to shine like lights in the world, and of curates to toil on in obscurity. Well—God sees all things: and what is wrong in this world may be set right in the next."

"You speak of the Lord Chancellor," quietly put in Miss Deveen: "the living is not in his gift."

"Never said it was—was speaking generally," returned the doctor. "The patron of the living is some other great man, nobleman, or what not, living down in the country."

"In Staffordshire, I think," said Miss Deveen, with hesitation, not being sure of her memory. "He is a baronet, I believe; but I forget his name."

"All the same, ma'am: there's no more chance for poor Lake with him than with the Lord Chancellor," returned Dr. Galliard. "Private patrons are worse beset, when a piece of preferment falls in, than even public ones."

"Suppose the parish were to get up a petition, setting forth Mr. Lake's merits and claims, and present it to the patron?" suggested Mrs. Jonas. "Not, I dare say, that it would be of much use."

"Not the slightest use; you may rely upon that," spoke the doctor, in his decisive way. "Lake's best chance is to get taken on by the new man, and stand out for a higher salary."

Certainly it seemed to be his best and only chance of getting any good out of the matter. But it was just as likely he would be turned adrift.

The next day we met Mrs. Jonas in the King's Road. She had rather a down look as she accosted Miss Deveen.

"No one seems willing to bestir themselves about a petition; they say it is so very hopeless. And there's a rumour abroad that the living is already given away."

"To whom is it given?" asked Miss Deveen.

"Well, not to a Very Reverend Dean, as Miss Cattledon suggested last night, but to some one as bad—or good: one of the Canons of St. Paul's. I dare say it's true. How hard it is on Mr. Lake! How hard it must seem to him!"

"He may stay here as curate, then."

"Never you expect that," contended Mrs. Jonas, her face reddening with her zeal. "These cathedral luminaries have invariably lots of their own circle to provide for."

"Do you not think it will seem hard on Mr. Lake?" I said to Miss Deveen, as we left the little widow, and walked on.

"I do, Johnny Ludlow. I do think he ought to have it; that in right and justice no one has so great a claim to it as he," she impressively answered. "But, as Dr. Galliard says, 'oughts' go for nothing in Church patronage. William Lake is a good, earnest, intellectual man; he has grown grey in the service of the parish, and yet, now that the living is vacant, he has no more chance of it than that silly young Chisholm has—not half as much, I dare say, if the young fellow were only in priest's orders. It is but a common case: scores of curates who have to work on, neglected, to their lives' end could testify to it. Here we are, Johnny. This is Mrs. Topcroft's."

Knocking at the house-door—a small house standing ever so far back from the road—we were shown by a young servant into a pleasant parlour. Emma Topcroft, a merry, bright, laughing girl, of eighteen or nineteen, sat there at work with silks and black velvet. If I had the choice given me between her and Miss Cattledon, thought I, as Mr. Lake seems to have, I know which of the two I should choose.

"Mamma is making a rice-pudding in the kitchen," she said, spreading her work out on the table for Miss Deveen to see.

"You are doing it very nicely, Emma. And I have brought you the fresh silks. I could not get them before: they had to send the patterns into town. Is the other screen begun?"

"Oh yes; and half done," answered Emma, briskly, as she opened the drawer of a-work-table, and began unfolding another square of velvet from its tissue paper. "I do the sober colours in both screens first, and leave the bright ones till last. Here's the mother."

Mrs. Topcroft came in, turning down her sleeves at the wrist; a little woman, quite elderly. I liked her the moment I saw her. She was homely and motherly, with the voice and manners of a lady.

"I came to bring Emma the silks, and to see how the work was getting on," said Miss Deveen as she shook hands. "And what a grievous thing this is about Mr. Selwyn!"

Mrs. Topcroft lifted her hands pityingly. "It has made Mr. Lake quite ill," she answered; "I can see it. And"—dropping her voice—"they say there will be little, or nothing, for Mrs. Selwyn and the children."

"Yes, there will; though perhaps not much," corrected Miss Deveen. "Mrs. Selwyn has two hundred a-year of her own. I happen to know it."

"I am very thankful to hear that: we were fearing the worst. I wonder," added Mrs. Topcroft, "if this will take Mr. Lake from us?"

"Probably. We cannot tell yet. People are saying he ought to have the living if it went by merit: but there's not any hope of that."

"Not any," acquiesced Mrs. Topcroft, shaking her head. "It does seem unjust: that a clergyman should wear out all his best days toiling for a church, and be passed over at last as not worth a consideration."

"It is the way of the world."

"No one knows his worth," went on Mrs. Topcroft, "So patient, so good, so self-denying; and so anxious for the poor and sick, and for all the ill-doers who seem to be going wrong. I don't believe there are many men in this world so good as he. All he can scrape and save out of his narrow income he gives away, denying himself necessaries to be able to do it: Mr. Selwyn, you know, has given nothing. It has been said he grudged even the communion money."

That was Mrs. Topcroft's report of Mr. Lake; and she ought to know. He had boarded with her long enough. He had the bedroom over the best parlour; and the little den of a back-parlour was given over to his own use, in which he saw his parishioners and wrote his sermons.

"They come from the same village in the West of England," said Miss Deveen to me as we walked homewards. "Mr. Lake's father was curate of the place, and Mrs. Topcroft's people are the doctors: her brothers are in practice there now. When she was left a widow upon a very slender income, and settled down in this little house, Mr. Lake came to board with her. He pays a guinea a-week only; but Mrs. Topcroft has told me that it pays her amply, and she could not have got along without it. The housekeeping is, of necessity, economical: and that suits the pocket on both sides."

"I like Mrs. Topcroft. And she seems quite a lady, though she is poor."

"She is quite a lady, Johnny. Her husband was a civil engineer, very clever: but for his early death he might have become as renowned as his master, Sir John Rennie. The son; he is several years older than

Emma; is in the same profession, steady and diligent, and he gains a fair salary now, which of course helps his mother. He is at home night and morning."

"Do you suppose that Mr. Lake thinks of Emma?"

Miss Deveen laughed—as if the matter were a standing joke in her mind. "I do not suppose it, Johnny. I never saw the smallest cause to lead me to suppose it: she is too much of a child. Such a thing never would have been thought of but for the jealous suspicions of the parish—I mean of course our young ladies in it. Because Emma Topcroft is a nice-looking and attractive girl, and because Mr. Lake lives in her companionship, these young women must needs get up the notion. And they despise the Topcrofts accordingly, and turn the cold shoulder on them."

It had struck me that Emma Topcroft must be doing those screens for Miss Deveen. I asked her.

"She is doing them for me in one sense, Johnny," was the answer. "Being an individual of note, you see"—and Miss Deveen laughed again—"that is, my income being known to be a good one, and being magnified by the public into something fabulous, I have to pay the penalty of greatness. Hardly a week passes but I am solicited to become the patroness of some bazaar, not to speak of other charities, or at least to contribute articles for sale. So I buy materials and get Emma Topcroft to convert them into nicknacks. Working flowers upon velvet for banner-screens, as she is doing now; or painting flowers upon cardboard for baskets or boxes, which she does nicely, and various other things. Two ends are thus served: Emma makes a pretty little income, nearly enough for her clothes, and the bazaars get the work when it is finished, and sell it for their own benefit."

"It is very good of you, Miss Deveen."

"Good! Nay, don't say that, Johnny," she continued, in a reproving tone. "Those whom Heaven has blessed with ample means must remember that they will have to render an account of their stewardship. Trifles, such as these, are but odds and ends, not to be thought of, beside what I ought to do—and try to do."

That same evening Mr. Lake came in, unexpectedly. He called to say that the funeral was fixed for Saturday, and that a portion of the burial-service would be read in the church here, before starting for the cemetery: Mrs. Selwyn wished it so.

"I hear that the parish began to indulge a hope that you would be allowed to succeed Mr. Selwyn," Miss Deveen observed to him as he was leaving; "but—"

"I!" he exclaimed, interrupting her in genuine surprise, a transient flush rising to his face. "What, succeed to the living! How could any one think of such a thing for a moment? Why, Miss Deveen, I do not possess any interest: not the slightest in the world. I do not even know Sir Robert Tenby. It is not likely that he has ever heard my name."

"Sir Robert Tenby!" I cried, pricking up my ears. "Is Sir Robert Tenby the patron?"

"Yes. His seat is in Worcestershire?"

"Do you know him, Johnny?" asked Miss Deveen.

"A little; not much. Bellwood is near Crabb Cot. I used often to see his wife when she was Anne Lewis: we were great friends. She was a very nice girl."

"A girl, Johnny! Is she younger than he is?"

"Young enough to be his daughter."

"But I was about to say," added Miss Deveen to the curate, "that I fear there can be no chance for you, if this report, that the living is already given away, be correct. I wish it had been otherwise."

"There could be no chance for me in any case, dear Miss Deveen; there's no chance for any one so unknown and obscure as I am," he returned, suppressing a sigh as he shook her hand. "Thank you all the same for your kind wishes."

How long I lay awake that night I don't care to recall. An extraordinary idea had taken possession of me. If some one would only tell Sir Robert Tenby of the merits of this good man, he might be so impressed as to give him the living. We were not sure about the Canon of St. Paul's: he might be a myth, as far as our church went.

Yes, these ideas were all very well; but who would presume to do it? The mice, you know, wanted to bell the cat, but none of them could be got to undertake the task.

Down I went in the morning to Mr. Brandon as soon as breakfast was over. I found him in his sitting-room at his breakfast: dry toast, and tea without milk; a yellow silk handkerchief thrown cornerwise over his head, and his face looking green. He had a bilious attack coming on, he said, and thought he had taken a slight cold.

Now I don't want to disparage Mr. Brandon's merits. In some things he was as good as gold. But when he fell into these fanciful attacks he was not practically worth a rush. It was hardly a propitious moment for the scheme I had in my head; but, unfortunately, there was no time to lose: I must speak then, or not at all. Down I sat, and told my tale. Old Brandon, sipping his tea by spoonfuls, listened, and stared at me with his little eyes.

"And you have been getting up in your brain the Utopian scheme that Sir Robert Tenby would put this curate into the living! and want me to propose it to him! Is that what you mean, young man?"

"Yes, sir. Sir Robert would listen to you. You are friendly with him, and he is in town. Won't you, please, do it?"

"Not if I know it, Johnny Ludlow. Solicit Robert Tenby to give the living to a man I never heard of: a man I know nothing about! What notions you pick up!"

"Mr. Lake is so good and so painstaking," I urged. "He has been working all these years—"

"You have said all that before," interrupted old Brandon, shifting the silk handkerchief on his head more to one side. "I can't answer for it, you know. And, if I could, I should not consider myself justified in troubling Sir Robert."

"What I thought was this, sir: that, if he got to know all Mr. Lake is, he might be glad to give him the living: glad of an opportunity to do a good and kind act. I did not think of your asking him to give the living; only to tell him of Mr. Lake, and what he has done, and been. He lives only in Upper Brook Street. It would not be far for you to go, sir."

"I should not go if he lived here at the next door, Johnny Ludlow: should not be justified in going on such an errand. Go yourself."

"I don't like to, sir."

"He wouldn't eat you; he'd only laugh at you. Robert Tenby would excuse in a silly lad what he might deem impertinence from me. There, Johnny; let it end."

And there it had to end. When old Brandon took up an idea he was hard as adamant.

I stood at the hotel door, wishing I could screw up courage to call at Sir Robert's, but shrinking from it terribly. Then I thought of poor Mr. Lake, and that there was no one else to tell about him; and at last I started, for Upper Brook Street.

"Is Lady Tenby at home?" I asked, when I got to the door.

"Yes, sir." And the man showed me into a room where Lady Tenby sat, teaching her little boy to walk.

She was just the same kind and simple-mannered woman that she had been as Anne Lewis. Putting both her hands into mine, she said how glad she was to see me in London, and held out the child to be kissed. I explained my errand, and my unwillingness to come; saying I could venture to tell her all about it better than I could tell Sir Robert.

She laughed merrily. "He is not any more formidable than I am, Johnny; he is not the least bit so in the world. You shall see whether he is"—opening the door of the next room. "Robert," she called out in glee, "Johnny Ludlow is here, and is saying you are an ogre. He wants to tell you something, and can't pluck up courage to do it."

Sir Robert Tenby came in, the Times in his hand, and a smile on his face: the same kind, rugged, homely face that I knew well. He shook hands with me, asking if I wanted his interest to be made prime-minister.

And somehow, what with their kindness and their thorough, cordial homeliness, I lost my fears. In two minutes I had plunged into the tale, Sir Robert sitting near me with his elbow on the table, and Anne beside him, her quiet baby on her knee.

"I thought it so great a pity, sir, that you should not hear about Mr. Lake: how hard he has worked for years, and what a good and self-denying man he is," I concluded at last, after telling what Miss Deveen thought of him, and what Mrs. Topcroft said. "Not, of course, that I could presume to suggest such a thing, sir, as that you should bestow upon him the living—only to let you know there was a man so deserving, if—if it was not given already. It is said in the parish that the living is given."

"Is this Mr. Lake a good preacher?" asked Sir Robert, when I paused.

"They say he is one of the best and most earnest of preachers, sir. I have not heard him; Mr. Selwyn generally preached."

"Does he know of your application to me?"

"Why, no, Sir Robert, of course not! I could not have had the face to tell any one I as much as wished to make it. Except Mr. Brandon. I spoke to him because I wanted him to come instead of me."

Sir Robert smiled. "And he would not come, I suppose?"

"Oh dear, no: he asked me whether I thought we lived in Utopia. He said I might come if I chose—that what would be only laughed at in a silly boy like me, might be deemed impertinence in him."

The interview came to an end. Anne said she hoped I should dine with them while I was in town—and Mr. Brandon also, Sir Robert added; and with that I came out. Came out just as wise as I had gone in; for never a word of hope did Sir Robert give. For all he intimated to the contrary, the living might be already in the hands of the Canon of St. Paul's.

Two events happened the next day, Saturday. The funeral of the Rector, and the departure of Miss Cattledon for Chelmsford, in Essex. An aunt of hers who lived there was taken dangerously ill, and sent for her by telegram. Mr. Brandon came up to dine with us in the evening— But that's neither here nor there.

I sat in Miss Deveen's pew at church with herself on the Sunday morning; she wore black silk out of respect to the late Rector. Mr. Lake and the young deacon, who had a luxuriant crop of yellow hair, had put on black gloves. The church was full; all the world and his wife seemed to have come to it; and the parsons' surplices stood on end with starch.

Mr. Lake was in the reading-desk; it caused, I think, some surprise—could that yellow-haired nonentity of a young dandy be going to preach? He stood at the communion-table, looking interesting, and evidently suffering from a frightful cold: which cold, as we found later, was the reason that Mr. Lake took nearly all the service himself.

What a contrast they were! The simpering, empty-faced young deacon, who was tall and slender as a lamp-post, and had really not much more brains than one; and the thoughtful, earnest, middle-aged priest, with the sad look on his gentle face. Nothing could be more impressive than his reading of the prayers; they were prayed, not read: and his voice was one of those persuasive, musical voices you don't often hear. If Sir Robert Tenby could but hear this reading! I sighed, as Mr. Lake went through the Litany.

Hardly had the thought crossed my mind, when some commotion in the church caused most of us to turn round: a lady was fainting. But for that, I might never have seen what I did see. In the next pew, right behind ours, sat Sir Robert and Lady Tenby. So surprised was I that I could not for the moment believe my eyes, and simply stared at them. Anne caught the look, and smiled at me.

Was it a good omen? I took it to be one. If Sir Robert had no thought of Mr. Lake, or if the living was already given to that canon, why should he have come all this way to hear him? I recalled the Sunday, years ago now, when Sir Robert had sat in his own pew at Timberdale, listening attentively to Herbert Tanerton's reading and preaching, deliberating within his mind—I know I thought so then—whether he should bestow upon him the living of Timberdale, or not; whether Herbert was worthy of it. Sir Robert did give it to him: and I somehow took it for an earnest that he might give this one to Mr. Lake.

Meanwhile Mr. Lake ascended the pulpit-stairs in his black gown, and began his sermon: supremely unconscious that the patron of the church was just in front of him, looking and listening. No one present knew Sir Robert and Lady Tenby.

You should have heard that sermon: all its earnest eloquence, its sound piety, its practical application, and its quiet, impressive delivery. It was not exactly a funeral sermon; but when he spoke of the late Rector, who had been so unexpectedly taken away, and whose place in this world could know him no more, hardly a dry eye was in the church: and if he himself had not once or twice paused to call up his equanimity, his own eyes would not have been dry, either. I was glad Sir Robert heard it. It was a sermon to be remembered for all time.

Miss Deveen waited in her pew until the people had mostly gone; she did not like being in a crowd. The Tenbys waited also. In the porch Anne put her hand upon my arm, speaking in a whisper.

"That is Miss Deveen, I suppose, Johnny? What a nice face she has! What a fine, handsome woman she is! How good she looks!"

"She is good; very. I wish I might introduce her to you."

"That's just what I was going to ask you to do, Johnny. My husband would like to speak with her."

I did it outside in the churchyard. After speaking together for a minute or two, Miss Deveen invited them to step into her house, pointing to it that they might see it was close by. Sir Robert walked on by her side, I behind with Anne. An open carriage was pacing in the road, the servants wearing the Tenby livery: people turned to look at it, wondering whose grand carriage it was. As we went slowly onwards Mr. Lake overtook us. He did not stop, only lifted his hat to Miss Deveen in passing: but she arrested him to ask after Mrs. Selwyn.

"Oh, she is very ill, very sad," he answered, in a tone as if the sorrow were his own. "And at present I fear there's nothing for her but to bear; to bear as she best may: not yet can she open her heart to consolation."

Miss Deveen said no more, and he walked on. It struck me she had only stopped him that Sir Robert might see him face to face. Being a shrewd woman, it could not be but that she argued good from this unexpected visit. And she knew I had been to them.

They would not stay to take lunch; which was on the table when we went in. Anne said she must get home to her baby: not the young shaver I saw; a little girl a month or two old. Sir Robert spared a few minutes to shut himself up in the drawing-room with Miss Deveen; and then the carriage whirled them off.

"I hope he was asking you about Mr. Lake?" I said impulsively.

"That is just what he was asking, Johnny," replied Miss Deveen. "He came here this morning, intending to question me. He is very favourably impressed with William Lake; I can see that: and he said he had never heard a better sermon, rarely one as good."

"I dare say that canon of St. Paul's is all an invention! Perhaps Mrs. Jonas went to sleep and dreamt it."

"It is certainly not fact," laughed Miss Deveen. "Sir Robert tells me he does not as much as know any one of the canons by sight."

"He did not tell you he should give it to Mr. Lake?"

"No, Johnny: neither did he give me any grounds for supposing that he would. He is a very cautious man; I can see that; conscientiously wishing to do right, and act for the best. We must say nothing of this abroad, remember."

The Reverend William Lake sat down to his breakfast on Monday morning, as the clock was striking half-past nine. He had been called out to baptize a sick baby and pray by its dying mother. Pouring himself out a cup of tea, buttering his first slice of dry toast, and cracking his egg, for that's what his breakfast consisted of, he took up a letter lying on the table, which had come by the morning post. Opening it presently, he found it to contain a request from Sir Robert Tenby that he would call upon him that morning at eleven o'clock, in Upper Brook Street.

"Sir Robert Tenby cannot know of our daily service," thought the clergyman, after reading the note twice over, and wondering what he was wanted for; he having no knowledge of the tide of affairs: no more notion that Sir Robert had been at the church the previous day than that the man in the moon was there. "I must ask Chisholm to take the service this morning."

Accordingly, his breakfast over, and a sprucer coat put on, he went to the deacon's lodgings—handsome rooms in a good house. That young divine was just beginning breakfast, the table being laid with toasted ham and poached eggs, and potted meats, and hot, buttered muffins, and all kinds of nice things, presenting a contrast to the frugal one Mr. Lake had just got up from.

"Took an extra snooze in bed to nurse myself," cried the young man, in half-apology for the lateness of the meal, as he poured out a frothing cup of chocolate. "My cold?—oh, it's better."

"I am glad of that," said Sir. Lake. "I want you to take the service this morning."

"What, do it all!"

"If you will be so good. I have a note here from Sir Robert Tenby, asking me to call upon him at eleven o'clock. I can't think what he wants."

"Sir Robert Tenby? That's the patron! Oh, I dare say it's only to talk about the Selwyns; or to tell you to take the duty until some one's appointed to the living."

"Ay," replied Mr. Lake. And he had no other thought, no idea of self-benefit, when he started off to walk to Upper Brook Street.

An hour later, seated in Sir Robert's library, enlightenment came to him. After talking with him for some time, questioning him of his Church views and principles, hearing somewhat of his past career and of what he had formerly done at Cambridge, to all of which he gave answers that were especially pleasing to the patron's ear, Sir Robert imparted to him the astounding fact that he—he!—was to be the new Rector.

William Lake sat, the picture of astonishment, wondering whether his ears were playing him false.

"I!" he exclaimed, scarcely above his breath. "I never thought of myself. I can hardly believe—believe—pardon me, Sir Robert—is there no mistake?"

"No mistake so far as I am concerned," replied Sir Robert, suppressing a smile. "I have heard of your many years' services at St. Matthew's, and of your worth. I do not think I could bestow it upon one who deserves it better than you—if as well. The living is yours, if you will accept it."

"You are very kind, sir," gasped the curate, not in the least recovering his senses. "May I presume to ask who it is that has been so kind as to speak of me?"

"The person from whom I first heard of you was young Johnny Ludlow," smiled Sir Robert. "Mr. Johnny presented himself to me here last Friday, in a state of mental commotion, not having been able to get any one else to come, evidently thinking, though not saying, that I should commit an act of singular injustice if the living did not find its way to one who, by dint of his hard and earnest work, so richly deserved it."

The tears stood in William Lake's eyes. "I can only thank you, sir, truly and fervently. I have no other means of testifying my gratitude—save by striving ever to do my duty untiringly, under my Lord and Master."

"I am sure you will do it," spoke Sir Robert, impulsively—and he was not a man of impulse in general. "You are not a married man, I believe?"

A faint red light came into the curate's cheeks. "I have not had the means to marry, Sir Robert. It has seemed to me, until this morning, that I never should have them."

"Well, you can marry now," was the laughing rejoinder; "I dare say you will." And the faint light deepened to scarlet, as the curate heard it.

"Shall you give him the living, Robert?" asked Anne, when Mr. Lake had departed.

"Yes, love."

II

When lawyers get a case into their hands, no living conjurer can divine when their clients will get it out again. The hardest problem in Euclid was never more difficult to solve than that. Mr. Brandon came up to town on the Monday morning, bringing me with him; he thought we might be detained a few days, a week at the utmost; yet the second week was now passing, and nothing had been done; our business seemed to be no forwarder than it was at the beginning. The men of law in Lincoln's Inn laid the blame on the conveyancers; the conveyancers laid it on the lawyers. Any way, the upshot was the same—we were kept in London. The fact to myself was uncommonly pleasant, though it might be less so to Mr. Brandon.

The astounding news—that the Reverend William Lake was to have St. Matthew's—and the return of Miss Cattledon from her visit to the sick lady at Chelmsford, rejoiced the ears and eyes of the parish on one and the same day. It was a Wednesday. Miss Cattledon got home in time for dinner, bringing word that her relative was better.

"Has anything been heard about the living?" she inquired, sitting, bonnet in hand, before going up to dress.

Miss Deveen shook her head. In point of fact, we had heard nothing at all of Sir Robert Tenby or his intentions since Mr. Lake's interview with him, and she was not going to tell Cattledon of that, or of Sir Robert's visit on the Sunday.

But, as it appeared, the decision had been made public that afternoon, putting the whole parish into a ferment. Dinner was barely over when Dr. Galliard rushed in with the news.

"Only think of it!" he cried. "Such a piece of justice was never heard of before. Poor Lake has not the smallest interest in the world; and how Sir Robert Tenby came to pick him out is just a marvel. Such a stir it is causing! It's said—I don't know with what truth—that he came up here on Sunday morning to hear Lake preach. Mrs. Herriker saw a fine barouche draw up, high-stepping horses and powdered servants; a lady and gentleman got out of it and entered the church. It is thought now they might have been Sir Robert and Lady Tenby."

"I shouldn't wonder but they were," remarked Miss Deveen.

"Has Mr. Lake really had the living given to him?" questioned Cattledon, her eyes open with surprise, her thin throat and waist all in a tremor, and unable to touch another strawberry.

"Really and truly," replied the doctor. "Chisholm tells me he has just seen the letter appointing him to it."

"Dear me!" cried Cattledon, quite faintly. "Dear me! How very thankful we all ought to be—for Mr. Lake's sake."

"I dare say he is thankful," returned the doctor, swallowing down the rest of his glass of wine, and preparing to leave. "Thank you, no, Miss Deveen; I can't stay longer: I have one or two sick patients on my hands to-night, and must go to them—and I promised Mrs. Selwyn to look in upon her. Poor thing! this terrible loss has made her really ill. By-the-by," he added, turning round on his way from the room, "have you heard that she has decided upon her plans, and thinks of leaving shortly?"

"No—has she?" returned Miss Deveen.

"Best thing for her, too—to be up and doing. She has the chance of taking to a little boys' preparatory school at Brighton; small and select, as the advertisements have it. Some relative of hers has kept it hitherto, has made money by it, and is retiring—"

"Will Mrs. Selwyn like that—to be a schoolmistress?" interrupted Cattledon, craning her neck.

"Rather than vegetate upon her small pittance," returned the doctor briskly. "She is an active, capable woman; has all her senses about her. Better teach little boys, and live and dress well, than enjoy a solitary joint of meat once a-week and a turned gown once a-year—eh, Johnny Ludlow?"

He caught up his hat, and went out in a bustle. I laughed. Miss Deveen nodded approvingly; not at my laugh, but at Mrs. Selwyn's resolution.

The stir abroad might have been pretty brisk that evening; we had Dr. Galliard's word for it: it could have been nothing to what set in the next day. The poor, meek curate—who, however good he might have been to run after, could hardly have been looked upon as an eligible, bonâ-fide prospect—suddenly converted into a rich Rector: six hundred a-year and a parsonage to flourish in! All the ladies, elder and younger, went into a delightful waking-sleep and dreamed dreams.

"Such a mercy!" was the cry; "such a mercy! We might have had some dreadful old drony man here, who does not believe in daily services, and wears a wig on his bald head. Now Mr. Lake, though his hair is getting a little grey, has a most luxuriant and curly crop of it. Beautiful whiskers too."

It was little Daisy Dutton said that, meeting us in the Park road; she was too young and frivolous to know better. Miss Deveen shook her head at her, and Daisy ran on with a laugh. We were on our way to Mrs. Topcroft's, some hitch having arisen about the frames for Emma's screens.

Emma was out, however; and Mrs. Topcroft came forward with tears in her eyes.

"I can hardly help crying since I heard it," she said, taking her handkerchief out of the pocket of her black silk apron. "It must be such a reward to him after his years of work—and to have come so unsought—so unexpectedly! I am sure Sir Robert Tenby must be a good man."

"I think he is one," said Miss Deveen.

"Mr. Lake deserves his recompense," went on Mrs. Topcroft. "No one can know it as I do. Poor Mr. Selwyn knew—but he is gone. I think God's hand must have been in this," she reverently added. "These good and earnest ministers deserve to be placed in power for the sake of those over whom they have charge. I have nothing to say against Mr. Selwyn, but I am sure the parish will find a blessing in Mr. Lake."

"You will lose him," remarked Miss Deveen.

"Yes, and I am sorry for it; but I should be selfish indeed to think of that. About the screens," continued Mrs. Topcroft; "perhaps you would like to see them—I am sorry Emma is out. One, I know, is finished."

Not being especially interested in the screens, I stepped into the garden, and so strolled round to the back of the house. In the little den of a room, close to the open window, sat Mr. Lake writing. He stood up when he saw me and held out his hand.

"It is, I believe, to you that I am indebted for the gift bestowed upon me," he said in a low tone of emotion, as he clasped my hand, and a wave of feeling swept over his face. "How came you to think of me—to be so kind? I cannot thank you as I ought."

"Oh, it's nothing; indeed, I did nothing—so to say," I stammered, quite taken aback. "I heard people say what a pity it was you stood no chance of the living, after working so hard in it all these years; so, as I knew Sir Robert, and knew very well Lady Tenby, I thought it would do no harm if I just told them of it."

"And it has borne fruit. And very grateful I am: to you, and to Sir Robert—and to One who holds all things, great and small, in His hands. Do you know," he added, smiling at me and changing his tone to a lighter one, "it seems to me nothing less than a romance."

This was Thursday. The next day Mr. Lake paid a visit to the bishop—perhaps to go through some formality connected with his appointment, but I don't know—and on the following Sunday morning he "read himself in." No mistake about his being the Rector, after that. It was a lovely day, and Mr. Brandon came up in time for service. After he knew all about it—that I had actually gone to Sir Robert, and that Mr. Lake had the living—he asked me five or six hundred questions, as though he were interested, and now he had come up to hear him preach.

You should have seen how crowded the church was. The ladies were in full force and flutter. Cattledon got herself up in a new bonnet; some of them had new rigging altogether. Each individual damsel looked upon the Rector as her especial prize, sure to be her own. Mr. Lake did every scrap of the duty himself, including the reading of the articles; that delightful young deacon's cold had taken a turn for the worse, through going to a water-party, and he simply couldn't hear himself speak. Poor Mrs. Selwyn and her daughter sat in their pew to-day, sad as the crape robes they wore.

Did you ever feel nervous when some one belonging to you is going to preach—lest he should not come up to expectation, or break down, or anything of that sort? Mr. Lake did not belong to me, but a nervous feeling came over me as he went into the pulpit. For Mr. Brandon was there with his critical ears. I had boasted to him of Mr. Lake's preaching; and felt sensitively anxious that it should not fall short.

I need not have feared. It was a very short sermon, the services had been so long, but wonderfully beautiful. You might have heard a pin drop in the church, and old Brandon himself never stirred hand or foot. At the end of the pew sat he, I next to him; his eyes fixed on the preacher, his attitude that of one who is absorbed in what he hears. Just a few words Mr. Lake spoke of himself, of the new relation between himself and his hearers; very quiet, modest words hearing the ring of truth and good-fellowship.

"That man would do his duty in whatever position of life he might be placed," pronounced old Brandon, as we got out. "Robert Tenby's choice has been a good and wise one."

"Thanks to Johnny Ludlow, here," said Miss Deveen, laughing.

"I don't say but what Johnny Ludlow has his head on his shoulders the right way. He means to do well always, I believe; and does do it sometimes."

Which I am sure was wonderful praise, conceded by old Brandon, calling to my face no end of a colour. And, if you'll believe me, he put his arm within mine; a thing he had never done before; and walked so across the churchyard.

The next week was a busy one. What with Mrs. Selwyn's preparations for going away, and what with the commotion caused by the new state of things, the parish had plenty on its hands. Mr. Lake had begged Mrs. Selwyn not to quit the Rectory until it should be quite and entirely convenient to her; if he got into it six or twelve months hence, he kindly urged, it would be time enough for him. But Mrs. Selwyn, while thanking him for his consideration, knowing how earnestly he meant it, showed him that she was obliged to go. She had taken to the school at Brighton, and had to enter upon it as speedily as might be. A few days afterwards she had vacated the Rectory, and her furniture was packed into vans to be carried away. Some women went into the empty house to clean it down; that it might be made ready for its new tenant. Poor Mr. Selwyn had repaired and decorated the house only the previous year, little thinking his tenure of it would be so short.

Then began the fun. The polite attentions to Mr. Lake, as curate, had been remarkable; to Mr. Lake, as Rector, they were unique. Mrs. Topcroft's door was besieged with notes and parcels. The notes contained invitations to teas and dinners, the parcels small offerings to himself. A person about to set up housekeeping naturally wants all kinds of articles; and the ladies of St. Matthew's were eager to supply contributions. Slippers fell to a discount, purses and silk watch-guards ditto. More useful things replaced them. Ornamental baskets for the mantelpiece, little match-boxes done in various devices, card-racks hastily painted, serviette rings composed of coloured beads, pincushions and scent-mats for the dressing-table, with lots more things that I can't remember. These were all got up on the spur of the moment; more elaborate presents, that might take weeks to complete, were put in hand. In vain Mr. Lake entreated them not to do these things; not to send anything; not to trouble themselves about him, assuring them it made him most uncomfortable; that he preferred not to receive presents of any kind: and he said it so emphatically, they might see he was in earnest. All the same. He might as well have talked to the moon. The ladies laughed, and worked on.

"Mrs. Topcroft, I think you had better refuse to take the parcels in," he said to her one day, when a huge packet had arrived, which proved to be a market-basket, sent conjointly by three old maiden sisters. "I don't wish to be rude, or do anything that would hurt kind people's feelings: but, upon my word, I should like to send all the things back again with thanks."

"They would put them into the empty Rectory if I did not take them in," returned Mrs. Topcroft. "The only way to stop it is to talk to the ladies yourself. Senseless girls!"

Mr. Lake did talk—as well, and as impressively as he knew how. It made not the slightest impression; and the small presents flocked in as before. Mrs. Jonas did not brew a "blessed great jug of camomile-tea," as did one of the admirers of Mr. Weller, the elder; but she did brew some "ginger-cordial," from a valued receipt of her late husband, the colonel, and sent it, corked up in two ornamental bottles, with her best regards. The other widow, Mrs. Herriker, was embroidering a magnificent table-cover, working against time.

We had the felicity of tasting the ginger-cordial. Mrs. Jonas gave a small "at home," and brought out a bottle of it as we were leaving. Cattledon sniffed at her liqueur-glass surreptitiously before drinking it.

"The chief ingredient in that stuff is rum," she avowed to me as we walked home, stretching up her neck in displeasure. "Pine-apple rum! My nose could not be mistaken."

"The cordial was very good," I answered. "Rum's not a bad thing, Miss Cattledon."

"Not at all bad, Johnny," laughed Miss Deveen. "An old sailor-uncle of mine, who had been round the world and back again more times than he could count, looked upon it as the panacea for all earthly ills."

"Any way, before I would lay myself out to catch Mr. Lake, as that widow woman does, and as some others are doing, I would hide my head for ever," retorted Cattledon. And, to give her her due, though she did look upon the parson as safe to fall to her own lot, she did not fish for him. No presents, large or small, went out from her hands.

That week we dined in Upper Brook Street. Miss Deveen, Mr. Brandon, the new Rector, and I; and two strange ladies whom we did not previously know. Mr. Brandon took Anne in to dinner; she put me on her left hand at table, and told me she and Sir Robert hoped I should often go to see them at Bellwood.

"My husband has taken such a fancy to you, Johnny," she whispered. "He does rather take likes and dislikes to people—just as I know you do. He says he took a great liking to me the first time he ever spoke to me. Do you remember it, Johnny?—you were present. We were kneeling in the parlour at Maythorn Bank. You were deep in that child's book of mine, 'Les contes de ma bonne,' and I had those cuttings of plants, which I had brought from France, spread out on newspapers on the carpet, when Sir Robert came in at the glass-doors. That was the first time he spoke to me; but he had seen me at Timberdale Church the previous day. Papa and I and you walked over there: and a very hot day it was, I remember."

"That Sir Robert should take a liking to you, Anne, was only a matter of course; other people have done the same," I said, calling her "Anne" unconsciously, my thoughts back in the past. "But I don't understand why he should take a liking to me."

"Don't you?" she returned. "I can tell you that he has taken it—a wonderful liking. Why, Johnny, if my little baby-girl were twenty years older, you would only need to ask and have her. I'm not sure but he'd offer her to you without asking."

We both laughed so, she and I, that Sir Robert looked down the table, inquiring what our mirth was. Anne answered that she would not forget to tell him later.

"So mind, Johnny, that you come to Bellwood as often as you please whenever you are staying at Crabb Cot. Robert and I would both like it."

And perhaps I may as well mention here that, although the business which had brought Mr. Brandon to London was concluded, he did not go home. When that event would take place, or how long it would be, appeared to be hidden in the archives of the future. For a certain matter had arisen to detain him.

Mr. Brandon had a nephew in town, a young medical student, of whom you once heard him say that he was "going to the bad." By what we learnt now, the young fellow appeared to have gone to it; and Mr. Brandon's prolonged stay was connected with this.

"I shall see you into a train at Paddington, Johnny," he said to me, "and you must make your way home alone. For all I know, I may be kept here for weeks."

But Miss Deveen would not hear of this. "Mr. Brandon remains on for his own business, Johnny, and you shall remain for my pleasure," she said to me in her warm manner. "I had meant to ask Mr. Brandon to leave you behind him."

And that is how I was enabled to see the play played out between the ladies and the new Rector. I did wonder which of them would win the prize; I would not have betted upon Cattledon. It also caused me to see something of another play that was being played in London just then; not a comedy but a tragedy. A fatal tragedy, which I may tell of sometime.

All unexpectedly a most distressing rumour set in; and though none knew whence it arose, a conviction of its truth took the parish by storm. Mr. Lake was about to be married! Distressing it was, and no mistake: for each individual lady had good cause to know that she was not the chosen bride, being unpleasantly conscious that Mr. Lake had not asked her to be.

Green-eyed jealousy seized upon the community. They were ready to rend one another's veils. The young ladies vowed it must be one or other of those two designing widows; Mrs. Jonas and Mrs. Herriker, on their parts, decided it was one of those minxes of girls. What with lady-like innuendos pitched at each other personally, and sharp hints levelled apparently at the air, all of which provoked retort, the true state of the case disclosed itself pretty clearly to the public—that neither widows nor maidens were being thought of by Mr. Lake.

And yet—that the parson had marriage in view seemed to be certain; the way in which he was furnishing his house proved it. No end of things were going into it—at least, if vigilant eyes might be believed—that could be of no use to a bachelor-parson. There must be a lady in the case—and Mr. Lake had not a sister.

With this apparent proof of what was in the wind, and with the conviction that not one of themselves had been solicited to share his hearth and home—as the widow Herriker poetically put it—the world was at a nonplus; though polite hostilities were not much less freely exchanged. Suddenly the general ill-feeling ceased. One and all metaphorically shook hands and made common cause together. A frightful conviction had set in—it must be Emma Topcroft.

Miss Cattledon was the first to scent the fox. Cattledon herself. She—but I had better tell it in order.

It was Monday morning, and we were at breakfast: Cattledon pouring out the coffee, and taking anxious glances upwards through the open window between whiles. What could be seen of the sky was blue enough, but clouds, some dark, some light, were passing rapidly over it.

"Are you fearing it will rain, Miss Cattledon?"

"I am, Johnny Ludlow. I thought," she added, turning to Miss Deveen, "of going after that chair this morning, if you have no objection, and do not want me."

"Go by all means," returned Miss Deveen. "It is time the chair went, Jemima, if it is to go at all. Take Johnny with you: he would like the expedition. As for myself, I have letters to write that will occupy me the whole morning."

Miss Cattledon wished to buy an easy-chair that would be comfortable for an aged invalid: her sick aunt at Chelmsford. But, as Miss Cattledon's purse was not as large as her merits, she meant to get a second-hand chair: which are often just as good as new. Dr. Galliard, who knew all about invalid-chairs and everything else, advised her to go to a certain shop in Oxford Street, where they sold most kinds of furniture, old and new. So we agreed to go this same morning. Cattledon, however, would not miss the morning service; trust her for that.

"It might do you no harm to attend for once, Johnny Ludlow."

Thus admonished, I went over with her, and reaped the benefit of the young deacon's ministry. Mr. Lake did not make his appearance at all: quite an unusual omission. I don't think it pleased Cattledon.

"We had better start at once, Johnny Ludlow," she said to me as we came out; and her tone might have turned the very sweetest of cream to curds and whey. "Look at those clouds! I believe it is going to rain."

So we made our way to an omnibus, then on the point of starting, got in, and were set down at the shop in Oxford Street. Cattledon described what she wanted; and the young man invited us to walk upstairs.

Dodging our way dexterously through the things that crowded the shop, and up the narrow staircase, we reached a room that seemed, at first sight, big enough to hold half the furniture in London.

"This way, ma'am," said the young man who had marshalled us up. "Invalid-chairs," he called out, turning us over to another young man, who came forward—and shot downstairs again himself.

Cattledon picked her way in and out amidst the things, I following. Half-way down the room she stopped to admire a tall, inlaid cabinet, that looked very beautiful.

"I never come to these places without longing to be rich," she whispered to me with a sigh, as she walked on. "One of the pleasantest interludes in life, Johnny Ludlow, must be to have a good house to furnish and plenty of money to— Dear me!"

The extreme surprise of the exclamation following the break off, caused me to look round. We were passing a side opening, or wing of the room; a wing that seemed to be filled with bedsteads and bedding. Critically examining one of the largest of these identical bedsteads stood the Reverend William Lake and Emma Topcroft.

So entranced was Cattledon that she never moved hand or foot, simply stood still and gazed. They, absorbed in their business, did not see us. The parson seemed to be trying the strength of the iron, shaking it with his hand; Emma was poking and patting at the mattress.

"Good Heavens!" faintly ejaculated Cattledon; and she looked as if about to faint.

"The washhand-stands are round this way, and the chests of drawers also," was called out at this juncture from some unknown region, and I knew the voice to be Mrs. Topcroft's. "You had better come if you have fixed upon the beds. The double stands look extremely convenient."

Cattledon turned back the way she had come, and stalked along, her head in the air. Straight down the stairs went she, without vouchsafing a word to the wondering attendant.

"But, madam, is there not anything I can show you?" he inquired, arresting her.

"No, young man, not anything. I made a mistake in coming here."

The young man looked at the other young man down in the shop, and tapped his finger on his forehead suggestively. They thought her crazy.

"Barefaced effrontery!" I heard her ejaculate to herself: and I knew she did not allude to the young men. But never a word to me spoke she.

Peering about, on this side the street and on that, she espied another furniture shop, and went into it. Here she found the chair she wanted; paid for it, and gave directions for it to be sent to Chelmsford.

That what we had witnessed could have but one meaning—the speedy marriage of Mr. Lake with Emma Topcroft—Cattledon looked upon as a dead certainty. Had an astrologer who foretells the future come forth to read the story differently, Cattledon would have turned a deaf ear. Mrs. Jonas happened to be sitting with Miss Deveen when we arrived home; and Cattledon, in the fulness of her outraged heart, let out what she had seen. She had felt so sure of Mr. Lake!

Naturally, as Mrs. Jonas agreed, it could have but one meaning. She took it up accordingly, and hastened forth to tell it. Ere the sun went down, it was known from one end of the parish to the other that Emma Topcroft was to be Mrs. Lake.

"A crafty, wicked hussy!" cried a chorus of tongues. "She, with that other woman, her mother, to teach her, has cast her spells over the poor weak man, and he has been unable to escape!"

Of course it did seem like it. It continued to seem like it as the week went on. Never a day dawned but the parson and Emma went to town by an omnibus, looking at things in this mart, buying in that. It became known that they had chosen the carpets: Brussels for the sitting-rooms, colour green; drugget for the bed-chambers, Turkey pattern: Mrs. Jonas fished it out. How that impudent girl could have the face to go with him upon such errands, the parish could not understand. It's true Mrs. Topcroft always made one of the party, but what of that?

Could anything be done? Any means devised to arrest the heresy and save him from his dreadful fate? Sitting nose and knees together at one another's houses, their cherished work all thrown aside, the ladies congregated daily to debate the question. They did not quite see their way clear to warning the parson that Emma was neither more nor less than a Mephistopheles in petticoats. They would have assured herself of the fact with the greatest pleasure had that been of any use. How sly he was, too— quite unworthy of his cloth! While making believe to be a poor man, he must have been putting by a nice nest-egg; else how could he buy all that furniture?

Soon another phase of the affair set in: one that puzzled them exceedingly. It came about through an ebullition of temper.

Mrs. Jonas had occasion to call upon the Rector one afternoon, concerning some trouble that turned up in the parish: she being a district visitor and presiding at the mothers' meetings. Mr. Lake was not at home. Emma sat in the parlour alone stitching away at new table-cloths and sheets.

"He and mamma went out together after dinner," said Emma, leaving her work to hand a chair to Mrs. Jonas. "I should not wonder if they are gone to the house. The carpets were to be laid down to-day."

She looked full at Mrs. Jonas as she said it, never blushing, never faltering. What with the bold avowal, what with the sight of the sheets and the table-linen, and what with the wretched condition of affairs, the disappointment at heart, the discomfort altogether, Mrs. Jonas lost her temper.

"How dare you stand there with a bold face and acknowledge such a thing to me, you unmaidenly girl?" cried the widow, her anger bubbling over as she dashed away the offered chair. "The mischief you are doing poor Mr. Lake is enough, without boasting of it."

"Good gracious!" exclaimed Emma, opening her eyes wide, and feeling more inclined to laugh than to cry, for her mood was ever sunny, "what am I doing to him?"

How Mrs. Jonas spoke out all that was in her mind, she could never afterwards recall. Emma Topcroft, gazing and listening, could not remain ignorant of her supposed fault now; and she burst into a fit of laughter. Mrs. Jonas longed to box her ears. She regarded it as the very incarnation of impudence.

"Marry me! Me! Mr. Lake! My goodness!—what can have put such a thing into all your heads?" cried Emma, in a rapture of mirth. "Why, he is forty-five if he's a day! He wouldn't think of me: he couldn't. He came here when I was a little child: he does not look upon me as much else yet. Well, I never!"

And the words came out in so impromptu a fashion, the surprise was so honestly genuine, that Mrs. Jonas saw there must be a mistake somewhere. She took the rejected chair then, her fears relieved, her tones softened, and began casting matters about in her mind; still not seeing any way out of them.

"Is it your mother he is going to marry?" cried she, the lame solution presenting itself to her thoughts, and speaking it out on the spur of the moment. It was Emma's turn to be vexed now.

"Oh, Mrs. Jonas, how can you!" she cried with spirit. "My poor old mother!" And somehow Mrs. Jonas felt humiliated, and bit her lips in vexation at having spoken at all.

"He evidently is going to be married," she urged presently, returning to the charge.

"He is not going to marry me," said Emma, threading her needle. "Or to marry my mother either. I can say no more than that."

"You have been going to London with him to choose some furniture: bedsteads, and carpets and things," contended Mrs. Jonas.

"Mamma has gone with him to choose it all: Mr. Lake would have been finely taken in, with his inexperience. As to me, I wanted to go too, and they let me. They said it would be as well that young eyes should see as well as theirs, especially the colours of the carpets and the patterns of the crockery-ware."

"What a misapprehension it has been!" gasped Mrs. Jonas.

"Quite so—if you mean about me," agreed Emma. "I like Mr. Lake very much; I respect him above every one in the world; but for anything else—such a notion never entered my head: and I am sure it would not enter his."

Mrs. Jonas, bewildered, but intensely relieved, wished Emma good-afternoon civilly, and went away to enlighten the world. A reaction set in: hopes rose again to fever heat. If it was neither Emma Topcroft nor her mother, why, it must be somebody else, argued the ladies, old and young, and perhaps she was not chosen yet: and the next day they were running about the parish more than ever.

Seated in her drawing-room, in her own particular elbow-chair, in the twilight of the summer's evening, was Miss Deveen. Near to her, telling a history, his voice low, his conscious face slightly flushed, sat the Rector of St. Matthew's. The scent from the garden flowers came pleasantly in at the open window; the moon, high in the heavens, was tinting the trees with her silvery light. One might have taken them for two lovers, sitting there to exchange vows, and going in for romance.

Miss Deveen was at home alone. I was escorting that other estimable lady to a "penny-reading" in the adjoining district, St. Jude's, at which the clergy of the neighbourhood were expected to gather in full force, including the Rector of St. Matthew's. It was a special reading, sixpence admission, got up for the benefit of St. Jude's vestry fire-stove, which wanted replacing with a new one. Our parish, including Cattledon, took up the cause with zeal, and would not have missed the reading for the world. We flocked to it in numbers.

Disappointment was in store for some of us, however, for the Rector of St. Matthew's did not appear. He called, instead, on Miss Deveen, confessing that he had hoped to find her alone, and to get half-an-hour's conversation with her: he had been wishing for it for some time, as he had a tale to tell.

It was a tale of love. Miss Deveen, listening to it in the soft twilight, could but admire the man's constancy of heart and his marvellous patience.

In the West of England, where he had been curate before coming to London, he had been very intimate with the Gibson family—the medical people of the place. The two brothers were in partnership, James and Edward Gibson. Their father had retired upon a bare competence, for village doctors don't often make fortunes, leaving the practice to these two sons. The rest of his sons and daughters were out in the world—Mrs. Topcroft was one of them. William Lake's father had been the incumbent of this parish, and the Lakes and the Gibsons were ever close friends. The incumbent died; another parson was appointed to the living; and subsequently William Lake became the new parson's curate, upon the enjoyable stipend of fifty pounds a-year. How ridiculously improvident it was of the curate and Emily Gibson to fall in love with one another, wisdom could testify. They did; and there was an end of it, and went in for all kinds of rose-coloured visions after the fashion of such-like poor mortals in this lower world. And when he was appointed to the curacy of St. Matthew's in London, upon a whole one hundred pounds a-year, these two people thought Dame Fortune was opening her favours upon them. They plighted their troth solemnly, and exchanged broken sixpences.

Mr. Lake was thirty-one years of age then, and Emily was nineteen. He counted forty-five now, and she thirty-three. Thirty-three! Daisy Dutton would have tossed her little impertinent head, and classed Miss Gibson with the old ladies at the Alms Houses, who were verging on ninety.

Fourteen summers had drifted by since that troth-plighting; and the lovers had been living—well, not exactly upon hope, for hope seemed to have died out completely; and certainly not upon love, for they did not meet: better say, upon disappointment. Emily, the eldest daughter of the younger of the two brothers, was but one of several children, and her father had no fortune to give her. She kept the house, her mother being dead, and saw to the younger children, patiently training and teaching them. And any chance of brighter prospects appeared to be so very hopeless, that she had long ago ceased to look for it.

As to William Lake, coming up to London full of hope with his rise in life, he soon found realization not answer to expectation. He found that a hundred a-year in the metropolis, did not go so very much further than his fifty pounds went in the cheap and remote village. Whether he and Emily had indulged a hope of setting up housekeeping on the hundred a-year, they best knew; it might be good in theory, it was not to be accomplished in practice. It's true that money went further in those days than it goes in these; still, without taking into calculation future incidental expenses that marriage might bring in its train, they were not silly enough to risk it.

When William Lake had been five years at St. Matthew's, and found he remained just as he was, making both ends meet upon the pay, and saw no prospect of being anywhere else to the end, or of gaining more, he wrote to release Emily from her engagement. The heartache at this was great on both sides, not to be got over lightly. Emily did not rebel; did not remonstrate. A sensible, good, self-enduring girl, she would not for the world have crossed him, or added to his care; if he thought it right that they should no longer be bound to one another, it was not for her to think differently. So the plighted troth was recalled and the broken sixpences were despatched back again. Speaking in theory, that is, you understand: practically, I don't in the least know whether the sixpences were returned or kept. It must have been a farce altogether, taken at the best: for they had just gone on silently caring for each other; patiently bearing—perhaps in a corner of their hearts even slightly hoping—all through these later years.

Miss Deveen drew a deep breath as the Rector's voice died away in the stillness of the room. What a number of these long-enduring, silently-borne cases the world could tell of, and how deeply she pitied them, was very present to her then.

"You are not affronted at my disclosing all this so fully, Miss Deveen?" he asked, misled by her silence. "I wished to—"

"Affronted!" she interposed. "Nay, how could I be? I am lost in the deep sympathy I feel—with you and with Emily Gibson. What a trial it has been!—how hopeless it must have appeared. You will marry now."

"Yes. I could not bring myself to disclose this abroad prematurely," he added; "though perhaps I ought to have done it before beginning to furnish the house. I find that some of my friends, suspecting something from that fact, have been wondering whether I was thinking of Emma Topcroft. Though indeed I feel quite ashamed to repeat to you any idea that is so obviously absurd, poor child!"

Miss Deveen laughed. "How did you hear that?" she asked.

"From Emma herself. She heard of it from—from—Mrs. Jonas, I think—and repeated it to me, and to her mother, in the highest state of glee. To Emma, it seemed only fun: she is young and thoughtless."

"I conclude Emma has known of your engagement?"

"Only lately. Mrs. Topcroft knew of it from the beginning: Emily is her niece. She knew also that I released Emily from the engagement years ago, and she thought I did rightly, my future being so hopeless. But how very silly people must be to suppose I could think of that child Emma! I must set them right."

"Never mind the people," cried Miss Deveen. "Don't set them right until you feel quite inclined to do so. As to that, I believe Emma has done it already. How long is it that you and Emily have waited for one another?"

"Fourteen years."

"Fourteen years! It seems half a lifetime. Do not let another day go on, Mr. Lake; marry at once."

"That was one of the points on which I wished to ask your opinion," he rejoined, his tones hesitating, his face shrinking from the moonlight. "Do you think it would be wrong of me to marry—almost directly? Would it be at all unseemly?"

"Wrong? Unseemly?" cried Miss Deveen. "In what way?"

"I hardly know. It may appear to the parish so very hurried. And it is so short a time since my kind Rector died."

"Never mind the parish," reiterated Miss Deveen. "The parish would fight at your marriage, though it were put off for a twelvemonth; be sure of that. As to Mr. Selwyn, he was no relative of yours. Surely you have waited long enough! Were I your promised wife, sir, I wouldn't have you at all unless you married me to-morrow morning."

They both laughed a little. "Why should the parish fight at my marriage, Miss Deveen?" he suddenly asked.

"Why?" she repeated; thinking how utterly void of conceit he was, how unconscious he had been all along in his modesty. "Oh, people always grumble at everything, you know. If you were to remain single, they would say you ought to marry; and if you marry, they will think you might as well have remained single. Don't trouble your head about the parish, and don't tell any one a syllable beforehand if you'd rather not. I shouldn't."

"You have been so very kind to me always, Miss Deveen, and I have felt more grateful than I can say. I hope—I hope you will like my wife. I hope you will allow me to bring her here, and introduce her to you."

"I like her already," said Miss Deveen. "As to your bringing her here, if she lived near enough you should both come here to your wedding-breakfast. What a probation it has been!"

The tears stood in his grey eyes. "Yes, it has been that; a trial hardly to be imagined. I don't think we quite lost heart, either she or I. Not that we have ever looked to so bright an ending as this; but we knew that God saw all things, and we were content to leave ourselves in His hands."

"I am sure that she is good and estimable! One to be loved."

"Indeed she is. Few are like her."

"Have you never met—all these fourteen years?"

"Yes; three or four times. When I have been able to take a holiday I have gone down there to my old Rector; he was always glad to see me. It has not been often, as you know," he added. "Mr. Selwyn could not spare me."

"I know," said Miss Deveen. "He took all the holidays, and you all the work."

"He and his family seemed to need them," spoke the clergyman from his unselfish heart. "Latterly, when Emily and I have met, we have only allowed it to be as strangers."

"Not quite as strangers, surely!"

"No, no; I used the word thoughtlessly. I ought to have said as friends."

"Will you pardon me for the question I am about to ask you, and not attribute it to impertinent curiosity?" resumed Miss Deveen. "How have you found the money to furnish your house? Or are you doing it on credit?"

His whole face lighted up with smiles. "The money is Emily's, dear Miss Deveen. Her father, Edward Gibson, sent me his cheque for three hundred pounds, saying it was all he should be able to do for her, but he hoped it might be enough for the furniture."

Miss Deveen took his hands in hers as he rose to leave. "I wish you both all the happiness that the world can give," she said, in her earnest tones. "And I think—I feel sure—Heaven's blessing will rest upon you."

We turned out from the penny-reading like bees from a hive, openly wondering what could have become of Mr. Lake. Mrs. Jonas hoped his head was not splitting—she had seen him talking to Miss Cattledon long enough in the afternoon in that hot King's Road to bring on a sunstroke. Upon which Cattledon retorted that the ginger-cordial might have disagreed with him. With the clearing up as to Emma Topcroft, these slight amenities had recommenced.

Miss Deveen sat reading by lamp-light when we arrived home. Taking off her spectacles, she began asking us about the penny-reading; but never a hint gave she that she had had a visitor.

Close upon this Mr. Lake took a week's holiday, leaving that interesting young deacon as his substitute, and a brother Rector to preach on the Sunday morning. No one could divine what on earth he had gone out for, as Mrs. Herriker put it, or what part of the world he had betaken himself to. Miss Deveen kept counsel; Mrs. Topcroft and Emma never opened their lips.

The frightful truth came out one morning, striking the parish all of a heap. They read it in the Times, amongst the marriages. "The Reverend William Lake, Rector of St. Matthew's, to Emily Mary, eldest daughter of Edward Gibson, Member of the Royal College of Surgeons." Indignation set in.

"I have heard of gay deceivers," gasped Miss Barlow, who was at the least as old as Cattledon, and sat in the churchwarden's pew at church, "but I never did hear of deceit such as this. And for a clergyman to be guilty of it!"

"I'm glad I sent him a doll," giggled Daisy Dutton. "I dare say it is a doll he has gone and married."

This was said in the porch, after morning prayers. Whilst they were all at it, talking as fast as they could talk, Emma Topcroft chanced to pass. They pounced upon her forthwith.

"Married! Oh yes, of course he is married; and they are coming home on Saturday," said Emma, in response.

"Is she a doll?" cried Daisy.

"She is the nicest girl you ever saw," returned Emma; "though of course not much of a girl now; and they have waited for one another fourteen years."

Fourteen years! Thoughts went back, in mortification, to slippers and cushions. Mrs. Jonas cast regrets to her ginger-cordial.

"Of course he has a right to be engaged—and to have slyly kept it to himself, making believe he was a free man: but to go off surreptitiously to his wedding without a word to any one!—I don't know what he may call it," panted Mrs. Herriker, in virtuous indignation, "I call it conduct unbefitting a gentleman. He could have done no less had he been going to his hanging."

"He would have liked to speak, I think, but could not get up courage for it; he is the shyest man possible," cried Emma. "But he did not go off surreptitiously: some people knew of it. Miss Deveen knew—and Dr. Galliard knew—and we knew—and I feel nearly sure Mr. Chisholm knew, he simpered so the other day when he called for the books. I dare say Johnny Ludlow knew."

All which was so much martyrdom to Jemima Cattledon, listening with a face of vinegar. Miss Deveen!—and Johnny Ludlow!—and those Topcrofts!—while she had been kept in the dark! She jerked up her skirts to cross the wet road, inwardly vowing never to put faith in surpliced man again.

We went to church on Sunday morning to the sound of the ting-tang. Mr. Lake, looking calm and cool as usual, was stepping into the reading-desk: in the Rector's pew sat a quiet-looking and quietly dressed young lady with what Miss Deveen called, then and afterwards, a sweet face. Daisy Dutton took a violent fancy to her at first-sight: truth to say, so did I.

Our parish—the small knot of week-day church-goers in it—could not get over it at all. Moreover, just at this time they lost Mr. Chisholm, whose year was up. Some of them "went over" to St. Jude's in a body; that church having recently set up daily services, and a most desirable new curate who could "intone." "As if we would attend that slow old St. Matthew's now, to hear that slow old parson Lake!" cried Mrs. Herriker, craning her neck disparagingly.

The disparagement did not affect William Lake. He proved as indefatigable as Rector as he had been as curate, earning the golden opinions he deserved. And he and his wife were happy.

But he would persist in declaring that all the good which had come to him was owing to me; that but for my visit to London at that critical time, Sir Robert Tenby would never have heard there was such a man as himself in the world.

"It is true, Johnny," said Miss Deveen. "But you were only the humble instrument in the hand of God."

MRS CRAMP'S TENANT

I

It was autumn weather, and we had just arrived at Crabb Cot. When you have been away from a familiar place, whether it may be only for days, or whether it may be for weeks or months or years, you are eager on returning to it to learn what has transpired during your absence, concerning friends or enemies, the parish or the public.

Bob Letsom ran in that first evening, and we had him to ourselves; the Squire and Mrs. Todhetley were still in the dining-room. I asked after Coralie Fontaine.

"Oh, Coralie's all right," said he.

"Do the old ladies go on at her still?" cried Tod.

Bob laughed. "I think they've stopped that, finding it hopeless."

When Sir Dace Fontaine died, now eighteen months ago, the two girls, Coralie and Verena, were left alone. Verena shortly went back to the West Indies to marry George Bazalgette, Coralie remained at Oxlip Grange. Upon that, all the old ladies in the place, as Tod had ungallantly put it, beginning with Bob's mother, set on to lecture her: telling her she must not continue to live alone, she must take a companion of mature age. Why must she not live alone, Coralie returned: she had old Ozias to protect her from robbers, and her maid-servants to see to her clothes and her comforts. Because it was not proper, said the old ladies. Coralie laughed at that, and told them not to be afraid; she could take care of herself. And apparently she did. She had learnt to be independent in America; could not be brought to understand English stiffness and English pride: and she would go off to London and elsewhere for a week or two at a time, just as though she had been sixty years of age.

"I have an idea she will not be Coralie Fontaine much longer," continued Letsom.

"Who will she be, then?"

"Coralie Rymer."

"You can't mean that she is going to take up with Ben!"

"Well, I fancy so. Some of us thought they were making up to one another before Sir Dace died—when Ben was attending him. Don't you recollect how much old Fontaine liked Ben?—he'd have had him by his side always. Ben's getting on like a house on fire; has unusual skill in surgery and is wonderful at operations: he performed a very critical one upon old Massock this summer, and the man is about again as sturdy and impudent as ever."

"Does Ben live down here entirely?"

"He goes up to London between whiles—in pursuit of his studies and the degrees he means to take. He is there now. Oh, he'll get on. You'll see."

"Well, what else, Letsom?" cried Tod. "You have told us no news about anybody yet."

"Because there's none to tell."

"How do those two old dames get on—the Dennets?"

"Oh, they are gone off to some baths in Germany for a twelvemonth, with suppressed gout, and their house is let to a mysterious tenant."

"Mysterious in what way?"

"Well, nobody sees her, and she keeps the doors bolted and barred. The Dennets left it all in Mrs. Cramp's hands, being intimate with her, for they started in a hurry, and she put it into a new agent's hands at Worcester, and he put an advertisement in the papers. Some lady answered it, a stranger; she agreed to all conditions by letter, took possession of the house, and has shut herself up as if something uncanny were inside it. Mrs. Cramp does not like it at all; and queer rumours are beginning to go about."

"What's her name?"

"Nobody knows."

The house spoken of was North Villa, where Jacob Chandler used to live. When the Chandlers went down in the world it was taken on lease by the Miss Dennets, two steady middle-aged sisters.

The first visit we paid the following morning was to Oxlip Grange, to see Coralie. Meeting the Squire on the way he said he would go with us. North Villa lies not far from us, soon after you turn into the Islip Road, and the Grange is about a quarter-of-a-mile farther on. I took a good stare at the villa in passing. Two of the upstairs windows were open, but the mysterious tenant was not to be seen.

Old Ozias was in the Grange garden, helping the gardener; it was how he professed to fill up his time; and the door was opened by a tall, smart maid, with curled hair and pink bows in her cap. Where had I seen her? Why, at the lodgings in the Marylebone Road in London! She was Maria, who had been housemaid there during the enacting of that tragedy.

Coralie Fontaine sat in her pretty parlour, one opening from the large drawing-room, flirting a paper hand-screen between her face and the fire, which she would have, as Sir Dace used to, whether it might be cold weather or hot. Small and pale, her black hair smooth and silky, her dark eyes meeting ours honestly, her chin pointed, her pretty teeth white, she was not a whit changed. Her morning dress was white, with scarlet ribbons, and she was downright glad to see us. The Squire inquired after Verena.

"She is quite well," replied Coralie. "At least, she would be but for grumbling."

"What has she to grumble about, my dear?"

"Nothing," said Coralie.

"Then why does she do it? Dear me! Is her husband not kind to her?"

Coralie laughed at the notion. "He is too kind, Mr. Todhetley. Kindness to people is George Bazalgette's weakness, especially to Verena. Her grievance lies in George's sister, Magnolia Bazalgette."

"What a splendacious name!" interrupted Tod. "Magnolia!"

"She was named after the estate, Magnolia Range, a very beautiful place and one of the finest properties on the island," said Coralie. "Magnolia lives with George, it was always her home, you see; and Verena does not take kindly to her. She complains that Magnolia domineers over the household and over herself. It is just one of Verena's silly fancies; she always wants to be first and foremost; and I have written her one or two sharp letters."

"Coralie," I said here, "is not the girl, who showed us in, Maria?—she who used to live in those lodgings in London?"

Coralie nodded. "The last time I was staying in London, Maria came to me, saying she had left her place and was in want of one. I engaged her at once. I like the girl."

"She is an uncommonly smart girl in the way of curls and caps," remarked Tod.

"I like smart people about me," laughed Coralie.

Who should come in then but Mrs. Cramp. She was smart. A flounced gown of shiny material, green in one light, red in another, and a purple bonnet with white strings. She was Stephen Cramp's widow, formerly Mary Ann Chandler; her speech was honest and homely, and her comely face wore a look of perplexity.

"I don't much like the look of things down yonder," she began, nodding her head in the direction of North Villa and as she sat down her flounces went up, displaying her white cotton stockings and low, tied shoes. "I have been calling there again, and I can't get in."

"Nobody can get in," said Coralie.

"They have put a chain on the door, and they answer people through it. No chain was ever there before, as long as I have known the house. I paid no attention to the things people were saying," continued Mrs. Cramp; "but I did not much like something I heard last night. I'll see the lady, I said to myself this morning, and down to the house I went, walked up the garden, and—"

"But what is it that people have been saying, Mrs. Cramp?" struck in the Squire. "These boys have heard something or other."

"What's said is, that there's something queer about the lady," replied Mrs. Cramp. "I can't make it out myself, Squire. Some people say she's pig-faced."

"Pig-faced!"

"Well, they do. Last night I heard she was black. And, putting two and two together, as one can't help doing in such a case, I don't like that report at all."

The Squire stared—and began thinking. He believed he knew what Mrs. Cramp meant.

"Well, I went there, and rang," she resumed. "And they opened the door a couple of inches and talked to me over the chain: some sour-faced woman-servant of middle age. I told her I had come to see my tenant—her mistress; she answered that her mistress could not be seen, and shut the door in my face."

Mrs. Cramp untied her white satin bonnet-strings, tilted back her bonnet, caught up the painted fan, fellow to the one Coralie was handling, and fanned herself while she talked.

"As long as it was said the lady was pig-faced and hid herself from people's eyes accordingly, I thought little of it, you understand, Squire; but if she is black, that's a different matter. It sets one fearing that some scandal may come of it. The Miss Dennets would drop down in a fit on the spot if they heard that person had got into their house."

Coralie laughed.

"Ah, my dear, you careless young people make jokes of things that would fret us old ones to fiddle-strings," reproved Mrs. Cramp. "The four Indians may be with her, you know, and most likely are, concealed in cupboards. You don't know what such desperate characters might do—break into your house here some dark night and kill you in your bed. It is not a pleasant thing, is it, Squire?"

"That it's not, if it be as you put it," assented he, growing hot.

"Look here, Mrs. Cramp," interposed Tod. "If the lady has never been seen, how can it be known she is black, or pig-faced?"

"I've never treated the pig-faced report as anything but rubbish," answered Mrs. Cramp; "but I'll tell you, Mr. Joseph, how it has come out that she's black. I heard from Susan Dennet yesterday morning, and she asked whether any letters were lying at home for her or Mary. So I sent my servant Peggy last evening to inquire—a stupid thing of a girl she is, comes from over beyond Bromyard. Peggy went to the kitchen-door—and they have a chain there as well as to the other—and was told that no letters had come for the Miss Dennets. It was growing dark, and Peggy, who had never been on the premises before, mistook the path, and turned into one that took her to the latticed arbour. Many a time have I sat there in poor Jacob's days, with the Malvern Hills in the distance."

"So have I, Mary Ann," added the Squire, calling her unconsciously by her Christian name, his thoughts back in the time when they were boy and girl together.

"Peggy found her mistake then, and was turning back, when there stood in her path a black woman, who must have followed her down: black face, black hands, all black. What's more, she was wrapped round in yellow; a shroud, Peggy declares, but the girl was quite beyond herself with fright, and could not be expected to know shrouds from cloaks in the twilight. The woman stood stock still, never speaking, only staring; and Peggy tore back in her terror, and fell into the arms of a railway-porter, just then bringing a parcel from the station. 'Goodness help us!' she shrieked out, 'there's a blackamore in the path yonder:' and the girl came home more dead than alive. That is how I've learnt the mysterious lady is black," summed up Mrs. Cramp; "and knowing what we do know, I don't like it."

Neither did the Squire. And Mrs. Cramp departed in a flutter. We all liked her, in spite of her white stockings and shoes.

Some few months before this, a party of strangers appeared one morning at Worcester, and took handsome lodgings there. Four fashionable-looking gentlemen, with dark skins and darker hair; natives, apparently, of some remote quarter of the globe, say Asia or Africa, whose inhabitants are of a fine copper colour; and one lady, understood to be their sister, who was darker than they were—almost quite black. Two rather elderly and very respectable English servants, man and wife, were in their train. They lived well, these people, regardless of cost: had sumptuous dishes on their table, choice fruits, hot-house flowers. They made no acquaintance whatever in the town, rarely went abroad on foot, but took an airing most days in a large old rumbling open barouche, supplied by the livery stables. Worcester, not less alive to curiosity than is any other city, grew to be all excitement over these people, watched their movements with admiration, and called them "The Indians." The lady was seen in the barouche but once, enveloped in a voluminous yellow mantle, the hood of which was drawn over her face. It transpired that she was not in good health, and one evening, when she had a fainting-fit, a doctor was called in to her. His report to the town the next day was that she was really a coloured woman, very much darker than her brothers, with the manners and culture of a lady, but strikingly reserved. After a sojourn of about two months, the party, servants and all, quitted their lodgings, giving the landlady only an hour's notice, to spend, as they gave out, a week at Malvern. They paid their bill in full, asked permission to leave two or three of their heaviest trunks with her, and departed.

But they did not go to Malvern. It was not discovered where they did go. Nothing more was seen of them; nothing certain heard. The trunks they had left proved to be empty; some accounts owing in the town came in to be paid. All this looked curious. By-and-by a frightful rumour arose—that these people had been mixed up in some dreadful crime: one report said forgery, another murder. It was affirmed that Scotland Yard had been looking for them for months, and that they had disguised themselves as Indians (to quote the word Worcester used) to avert detection. But some observant individuals maintained that they were Indians (to use the word again), that no disguise or making-up could have converted their faces to what they were. Nothing more had as yet been heard of them, saving that a sum of money, enough to cover the small amount of debts left behind, was transmitted to the landlady anonymously. Excitement had not yet absolutely died away in the town. It was popularly supposed that the Indians were lying concealed in some safe hiding-place, perhaps not far distant.

And now, having disclosed this strange episode, the fame of which had gone about the county, you will be able to understand Mrs. Cramp's consternation. It appeared to be only too probable that the hiding-place was North Villa: of the lady in the yellow mantle, at any rate, whether her four brothers were with her or not.

II

I sat, perched on the fence of the opposite field, as though waiting for some one, whistling softly, and taking crafty looks at North Villa, for our curiosity as to its doings grew with the days, when a fine, broad-shouldered, well-dressed gentleman came striding along the road, flicking his cane.

"Well, Johnny!"

At the first moment I did not know him, I really did not; he looked too grand a gentleman for Benjamin Rymer, too handsome. It was Ben, however. The improvement in him had been going on gradually for some years now; and Ben, in looks, in manner, ay, and in conduct, could hold his own with the best in the land.

"I did not know you were down here," I said, meeting his offered hand. Time was when he would not have presumed to hold out his hand to me unsolicited, boy though I was in those old days: he might have thought nothing of offering it to a nabob now.

"I got down yesterday," said Ben. "Glad enough to have taken my M.D., and to have done with London."

"I thought you did not mean to take a physician's degree."

"I did not, as I chiefly go in for surgery. But when I considered that my life will probably be spent in this country place, almost as a general practitioner, I thought it best to take it. It gives one a standing, you see, Ludlow. And so," he added laughing, "I am Dr. Rymer. What are you sitting here for, Johnny? Watching that house?"

"Have you heard about it?" I asked.

"Coralie—Miss Fontaine—told me of it when I was with her last evening. Is there anything to be seen?"

"Nothing at all. I have been here for twenty minutes and have not caught a glimpse of any one, black or white. Yesterday, when Salmon's boy took some grocery there, he saw the black lady peeping at him behind the blind."

"It seems a strange affair altogether," remarked Ben. "The sudden appearance of the people at Worcester, that was strange, as was their sudden disappearance. If it be in truth they who are hiding themselves here, I can't say much for their wisdom: they are too near to the old scene."

"I wonder you don't set up in London," I said to Ben as we walked onwards.

"It is what I should like to do of all things," he replied in a tone of eagerness, "and confine my practice wholly to surgery. But my home must be here. Circumstances are stronger than we are."

"Will it be at Oxlip Grange?" I quietly asked.

Ben turned his head to study my face, and what he read there told tales. "I see," he said, "you know. Yes, it will be at Oxlip Grange. That has been settled a long while past."

"I wish you every happiness; all good luck."

"Thank you, Johnny."

We were nearing the place in question when Mrs. Cramp turned out of its small iron gate, that stood beside the ornamental large ones, in her bewitching costume of green and purple. "And how are you, Mr. Benjamin?" she asked. "Come down for good?"

"Yes."

"And he is Dr. Rymer now, Mrs. Cramp," I added.

"I am glad to hear it," said she warmly, "and I'll shake your hand on the strength of it," and she gave his hand a hearty shake. "At one time you said you never would take a doctor's degree."

"So I did," said Ben. "But somebody wished me to take it."

"Your mother, I guess,"—though, for my part, I did not suppose it was his mother. "Any way, you'll do well now."

"I hope so," answered Ben. "You look fluttered, Mrs. Cramp."

"I'm more fluttered than I care to be; I am living in a chronic state of flutter," avowed Mrs. Cramp. "It's over that tenant of mine; that woman down yonder," pointing towards North Villa.

"Why should you flutter yourself over her?" he remonstrated. "She is not your tenant."

"Indeed but she is my tenant. To all intents and purposes she is my tenant. The Miss Dennets left the house in my hands."

"How was it you did not have references with her, Mrs. Cramp?"

"That donkey of an agent never asked for any," retorted she. "He was thrown off his guard, he says, by her sending him the first month's rent in advance, and telling him she had only one or two old servants, and no children, and the furniture would be as much cared for as if it were made of gold. Last night she sends to me the advance rent for next month, though it's not due for two days yet, and that has fluttered me, I can tell you, Mr. Benjamin, for I was hoping she wouldn't pay, and that I might be able to get her out. I am now going there with the receipt, and to try again to get to see her: the woman who left the money never waited for one. Afraid of being catechised, I take it."

Picking up her green skirts she sailed down the road. Coralie Fontaine was leaning over the little gate, and opened it as we approached. A beautiful cashmere shawl, all scarlet and gold, contrasted with her white dress, and her drooping gold ear-drops glittered in the autumn sun. She made a dainty picture, and I saw Dr. Benjamin's enraptured eyes meet hers. If they were not over head and ears in love with one another, never you trust me again.

"Mrs. Cramp is in a way," cried Coralie, as we strolled with her up the garden, amidst its old-fashioned flowers, all bloom and sweetness. "I'm sure that black lady is as good as a play to us."

"News came to me this morning from my sister," said Benjamin. "She and the Archdeacon are coming home; he has not been well, and has six months' leave of absence."

"Do they bring the children?" asked Coralie.

"As if they'd leave them! Why, Coralie, those two small damsels are the very light of Margaret's eyes—to judge by her letters; and of Sale's too, I shouldn't wonder. Margaret asks me to take lodgings for them. I think Mrs. Boughton's might be large enough—where Sale lodged in the old days."

"Lodgings!" indignantly exclaimed Coralie. "I do think you Europeans, you English, are the most inhospitable race on the face of the earth! Your only sister, whom you have not seen for years, of whom you are very fond, is coming back to her native place with her husband and children for a temporary stay, and you can talk of putting them into lodgings? For shame, Benjamin!"

"But what else am I to do?" questioned he, good-humouredly laughing at her. "I have only one bedroom and one sitting-room of my own, the two about as large as a good-sized clothes-closet; I cannot invite a man and his wife and two children to share them, and he an archdeacon! There wouldn't be space to turn round in."

"Let them come here," said Coralie.

"Thank you," he said, after a few moments' hesitation: and it struck me he might be foreseeing difficulties. "But—they will not be here just yet."

He had some patients at Islip, and went on there; I said adieu to Coralie and walked homewards, thinking of the ups and downs of life. Presently Mrs. Cramp's green gown loomed into view; her face red, her bonnet awry. I saw she had not met with any luck.

"No, I have not," she said. "I walked up into their porch as bold as you please, Johnny Ludlow, and I knocked and I rang, letting 'em think it was the Queen come, if they would. And when the woman with the sour face opened the door an inch, she just took the receipt from me; but as to seeing her mistress, I might as well have asked to see the moon. And I heard a scuffle, as if people were listening. Oh, it's those Indians: trust me for that."

Away she went, without further ceremony, and I went back to the ups and downs of earthly life.

It was not so very long ago that Thomas Rymer had lain on his death-bed, brought to it by the troubles of the world, and by the anxiety for his children, for whom no career seemed to present itself, saving that of hard, mean, hopeless drudgery: if not something worse for Benjamin. But how things had changed! Benjamin, pulling himself up from his ill-doings, was—what he was. A man respected; clever, distinguished, with probably a great career of usefulness before him, and about to be married to a charming girl of large fortune. While Margaret, whom her father had so loved, so pitied, was the wife of a man high in the Church, and happy as a queen. For, as you have gathered, the Reverend Isaac Sale, who had given up Herbert Tanerton's humble curacy to go out as chaplain to the Bahama Islands, had been made an archdeacon. Ups and downs, ups and downs! they make the sum and substance of existence. Glancing at the blue sky, over which fleecy white clouds were softly drifting, I lost myself in wondering whether Thomas Rymer could look down and still see his children here.

The chemist's shop at Timberdale had been sold by Benjamin Rymer to the smart young man who had carried it on during his absences, one James Boom, said to be Scotch. Benjamin had his rooms there at present; good-sized closets, he has just called them; and took his meals with Mr. Boom. Mrs. Rymer, the mother (having appropriated all the purchase-money), had set up her home in Birmingham amidst her old friends and relatives, and Benjamin had covenanted to allow her money yearly from his practice.

Public commotion increased. It spread to Oxlip Grange. One night, Ozias was sitting back amidst the laurels at the side of the house to smoke his pipe, when Maria came out to ask him what he had done with the best tea-tray, which they couldn't find. As she stood a moment while he reflected, there came two figures softly creeping round from the front—women. One wore a close bonnet and full dark cloak, the other was altogether enveloped in some shapeless garment that might be yellow by daylight, out of which a jet-black face and jet-black hands shone conspicuously in the rays of the stars. Maria, very much frightened, grasped hold of the old man's shoulder.

The pipe trembled in his hand: he had a mortal dread of assassins and housebreakers. "No speaky, no speaky," whispered he. "We watch, you and me. They come hurt Missee."

The figures made for the lighted window of the large drawing-room, which was at the end of this side of the house. Coralie was sitting alone within it, expecting visitors to tea. The blind was not drawn quite down, and they stooped to peer in, and remained there as if glued to the window. Maria could stand it no longer, but in creeping away, she rustled the laurels frightfully: we are sure to make the most noise, you know, when we want to be silent. The women looked round, and there came from them a rattling hiss, like that of a snake. With a scream, Maria made for the refuge of the kitchen-door; Ozias flew after her, dropping his pipe.

It must have disturbed the women. For just about then, when the Squire, holding my arm, arrived at Miss Fontaine's gate, they were coming out: two disguised figures, who went swiftly down the road.

"Mercy be good to us!" cried the Squire, aghast. He had drawn back in politeness to let them pass through the gate, and had found the black face come nearly into contact with his own. "Johnny, lad, that must be Mrs. Cramp's tenant and her servant!"

They brushed past Mrs. Todhetley coming along with Tod. Maria and Ozias were in the drawing-room when we got in, talking like wild things. The other guests soon arrived, Dr. Rymer, Mrs. Cramp, and Tom Chandler and his wife from Islip. Ozias gave an opinion that Missee (meaning Coralie) was about to be assassinated in her bed.

At this Coralie laughed. She had no fear, but she did not like it. "I cannot see what they could possibly want, looking in at me!" she cried. "It was very rude."

"They want Missee's diamonds," spoke Ozias. "Missee got great lot beauty diamonds, lot other beauty jewels; black woman come in this night—next night—after night—who know which—and smother Missee and take dem all."

Poor Mrs. Cramp, sitting in the biggest arm-chair, her sandalled shoes stretched on a footstool, was quite taken out of herself with dismay. The Squire rubbed his face incessantly, asking what was to be done. Dr. Rymer said nothing in regard to what was to be done; but he gave his head an emphatic nod, as if he knew.

The next morning he presented himself at North Villa, and asked to see its tenant. The woman-servant denied him—over the chain. Ben insisted upon his card and his request being taken in. After a battle of words, she took them in, shutting the door in his face the while; and the doctor cooled his heels in the porch for five minutes. As she drew the door open again, he caught sight of a black face twisted round the sitting-room door-post to peep at him, a black hand, with rings on it, grasping it. She saw him looking at her, and disappeared like a shot. The message brought out by the servant was that her mistress was an invalid, unable to see visitors: if Dr. Rymer had any business with her, he must be good enough to convey it by letter.

"Very well," said the doctor, in his decisive way: "I warn you and your mistress not again to intrude on Miss Fontaine's premises, as you did last night. If you do, you must take the consequences."

At this, the woman stared as if it were so much Greek to her. She answered that she had not been on Miss Fontaine's premises, then or ever; had not been out-of-doors at all the previous night. And Ben thought by her tone she was speaking truth.

"It was one of those Indian brothers disguised in a cloak and bonnet," said we all when we heard this. And Coralie's servants took to watching through the livelong night at the upper windows, turn and turn about, growing thin from dread of the assassins.

Altogether, what with one small item and another, Mrs. Cramp's tenant kept us alive. A belief had prevailed that the woman-servant was the same who had attended the Indians; but this was dispelled. A housemaid of ours, Nancy, a flighty sort of girl, often in hot water with her elders thereby, whose last service had been with old Lawyer Cockermouth, at Worcester, was out on an errand when she met this woman and recognized her for an old acquaintance. During Nancy's service with the lawyer she had been there as the cook-housekeeper.

"It is Sarah Stone, ma'am, and nobody else!" cried Nancy, running in to tell the news to Mrs. Todhetley. "She left for her temper, soon after I left; I heard say that old Miss Cockermouth wouldn't put up with it any longer."

"Are you sure it is the same, Nancy?" asked Mrs Todhetley.

"Why, ma'am, I know Sarah Stone as well as I know my own mother. 'What, is it you that's living here with that there black lady?' I says to her. 'What is it to you whether I'm living with a black lady or a white 'un,' she answers me, crustily: 'just mind your own affairs, Nancy Dell.' 'Well,' says I, 'there's a pretty talk about her; it's not me that would like to serve a wild Indian'—and that set Sarah Stone off at a strapping pace, ma'am."

Thus things went on. North Villa seeming to grow more isolated day by day, and its inmates more mysterious. When the rent for the next month was nearly due, Mrs. Cramp found it left at her house as before: and poor Mrs. Cramp felt fit to have a fever.

One evening, early in November, Mr. Cole, the surgeon of Crabb, was seen to go into North Villa. He was seen to go again the following morning, and again in the afternoon, and again in the evening. It transpired that the black lady was alarmingly ill.

Naturally, it put the parish up in arms. We made a rush for Cole, wanting to ask him five hundred things. Cole, skimming along the ground like a lamplighter, avoided us all; and the first to succeed in pouncing upon him was Miss Timmens, the schoolmistress. Very downright and honest, she was in the habit of calling a spade a spade, and poured out her questions one upon another. They had met by the yellow barn.

"Well, no," answers Cole, when he could get a word in, "I don't think that any murderer is at North Villa; do not see one about, but there's a baby." "A baby!" shrieks Miss Timmens, as she pushed back the bunches of black curls from her thin cheeks with their chronic redness, "a baby!" "Yes, a baby," says Cole, "a new baby." "Good mercy!" cries she, "a baby! a black baby! Is it a boy or a girl, Mr. Cole?" "It's a boy," says Cole. "Good mercy! a black boy!—what an extraordinary sight it must be!" Cole says nothing to this; only looks at her as meek as a lamb. "And now, between ourselves, doctor," goes on Miss Timmens, confidentially, "did you see the Indians there?—those men?" "Did not see any man at all," answers Cole, "saw no sign of a man being there." "Ah, of course they'd take their precautions to keep out of sight," nodded Miss Timmens, thinking old Cole uncommonly stupid to-day. "And how do you relish attending on a black patient, doctor? And what's she like?" "Why," answers Cole, "black patients are much the same as white ones; have the same number of arms and legs and fingers." "Oh, indeed," says Miss Timmens, quite sharply; and she wishes Cole good-day. And that was the best that could be got out of Cole.

The doctor's visits were watched with the most intense interest; three times a-day at first, then twice a-day, then once; and then they ceased altogether.

"Black lady on her legs again?" says Ben Rymer, meeting Cole about this time. "Quite so," answers Cole. "Mind that you get paid, sir," says Ben, with a laugh. "No need to mind that," returns Cole, "five sovereigns were put into my hand when the child was born." "By the black lady?" asks Ben, opening his eyes: for two guineas was the crack fee in our parts. "Yes, it was the black lady who gave it me," says Cole with emphasis: "and that, she took care to say, was not to include subsequent attendance. Wish you the same luck in your next case, Rymer."

Rymer thanked him and went off laughing. He was getting on in his practice like a house on fire, his fame rising daily.

"How do you like it—his setting up here?" confidentially questioned the Squire of Darbyshire, the doctor at Timberdale.

"Plenty of room for both of us," replied Darbyshire, "and I am not as young as I was. It rather strikes me, though, Squire, it is not exactly at Timberdale that Rymer will pitch his tent."

The next exciting event had nothing to do with North Villa. It was the arrival of Archdeacon Sale with his wife and children. They did not go to Coralie's. Herbert Tanerton opened his heart, and carried them off to the Rectory from the railway-station. That was so like Herbert! Had Sale remained a poor curate he might have gone to the workhouse and taken Margaret with him; being an archdeacon Herbert chose to make much of him. Margaret was not altered, she was loving and gentle as ever; with the same nice face, and poor Thomas Rymer's sad, sweet eyes shining from it.

Of course the first thing confided to the Bahama travellers was the mystery at North Villa. The Archdeacon took a sensible view of it. "As long as the black lady does not molest you," he said, "why trouble yourselves about her?"

After that we had a bit of a lull. Nothing exciting occurred. Saving a report that two of the Indians were seen taking the air in the garden of North Villa, each with a formidable stick in his hand. But it turned out that they were two tramps who had gone in to beg.

III

I thought it would have come to a quarrel. The Squire maintained his view and Coralie maintained hers. They talked at each other daily, neither giving way.

Christmas-Day was approaching, and it had pleased Miss Fontaine to project a sumptuous dinner for it, to be given at Oxlip Grange to all her special friends. The Squire protested he never heard of anything so unreasonable. He did not dine out of his own house on Christmas-Day, and she must come to Crabb Cot.

The third week in December had set in, when one evening, as we rose from table, the Squire impulsively declared he would go and finally have it out with her.

Meaning Coralie. Settling himself into his great-coat, he called to me to go after him. In the Islip Road we overtook Cole, walking fast also. He had been sent for to the baby at North Villa, he said; and we left him at the gate.

Coralie was in her favourite little parlour, reading by lamplight. The Squire sat down by the fire in a flutter, and began remonstrating about the Christmas dinner. Coralie only laughed.

"It is unreasonable, dear Mr. Todhetley, even to propose our going to you. Think of the number! I wish to have everybody. The Archdeacon and his wife, and Dr. Rymer, and Mrs. Cramp, and the Letsoms, and Tom Chandler and Emma, and of course, her father, old Mr. Paul, as he is some relation of mine, and— Why, that's a carriage driving up! I wonder who has come to-night?"

Another minute, and old Ozias rushed in with a beaming face, hardly able to get his words out for excitement.

"Oh, Missee, Missee, it Massa George; come all over wide seas from home,"—and there entered a fine man with a frank and handsome face—George Bazalgette.

"Where's Verena?" he exclaimed, after kissing Coralie and shaking hands genially with the Squire, though they had never met before.

Coralie looked surprised. "Verena?" she repeated. "Is she not with you?"

"She is not with me; I wish she was. Where is she, Coralie?"

"But how should I know where she is?" retorted Coralie, looking up at Mr. Bazalgette.

"Is she not staying with you? Did she not come over to you?"

"Certainly not," said Coralie. "I have not seen Verena since she went out, sixteen months ago. Neither have I heard from her lately. What is it that you mean, George?"

George Bazalgette stood back against the book-case, and told us what he meant. Some weeks ago—nay, months—upon returning to Magnolia Range after a week's absence at his other estate across the country, he found Verena flown. She left a note for him, saying she did not get on well with Magnolia, and was going to stay a little while with Mrs. Dickson. He felt hurt that Verena had not spoken openly to him about Magnolia, but glad that she should have the change, as she had not been well of late. Mrs. Dickson was his aunt and lived in a particularly healthy part of one of the adjoining islands. Time passed on; he wrote to Verena, but received no answer to his letters, and he concluded she was so put out with Magnolia that she would not write. By-and-by he thought it was time to see after her, and journeyed to Mrs. Dickson's. Mrs. Dickson was absent, gone to stay with some friends at St. Thomas, and the servants did not know when she would return. He supposed, as a matter of course, that she had taken Verena with her, and went back home. Still the time passed; no news of Verena, no letters, and he proceeded again to Mrs. Dickson's. Then, to his unbounded astonishment, he found that Verena had only stayed with her one week, and had taken the mail-packet for Southampton on her way to stay with her sister at Oxlip Grange. Giving a blessing to Mrs. Dickson for not having written to inform him of all this, and for having kept his letters to Verena by that young lady's arbitrary command, he came off at once to England.

"Good gracious!" exclaimed Coralie. "She did not come here."

The fine colour on George Bazalgette's face, which retained its freshness though he did live in a hot climate, lost its brightness.

"She would be the least likely to come here, of all places," pursued Coralie. "In the last answer I ever sent her, after a letter of complaints to me, hinting that she thought of coming here for a time, I scolded her sharply and assured her I should despatch her back to you the next day."

"What am I to do?" he exclaimed. "Where look for her?"

Not caring to intrude longer, we took our departure, the Squire shaking his head dubiously over Mrs. George Bazalgette's vagaries. "It was the same thing," he said, "when she was Verena Fontaine, as you remember, Johnny, and what a good fellow her husband seems to be.—Halloa! Why, that's Cole again!"

He was coming out of North Villa. "You are back soon!" he cried. And we told him of the arrival of George Bazalgette.

Cole seemed to stare with all his eyes as he listened. I could see them in the starlight. "What will he do if he can't find her here?" he asked of me. "Do you know, Johnny Ludlow?"

"Go back by the first and fleetest ship to turn Mrs. Dickson inside-out. He thinks she and Verena have played him a trick in letting him come over. How did you find the black baby?"

"Found nothing the matter with it," growled Cole. "These young mothers are so fanciful!"

We left him standing against the gate, supposing that he had to go higher up. And what happened then, I can only tell you by hearsay.

Cole, propping his back against the spikes, turned his face up to the stars, as if he were taking counsel of them. Counsel he needed from somebody or something, for he was in a dilemma.

"Well, I'll chance it," he thought, when he had got pretty cold. "It seems the right thing to do."

Walking briskly to Oxlip Grange, he asked to see Mr. Bazalgette; and after whispering a few words into that gentleman's ear, brought him out to North Villa. "You stand behind me, so as not to be seen," he directed, ringing the bell.

"I'm coming in again," said he to Sarah Stone, when she pulled the door back about an inch. So she undid the chain; the doctor was privileged, and he slipped in, Mr. Bazalgette behind him. Sarah, the faithful, was for showing fight.

"It is all right," said Cole. "Not yet, sir"—putting out his arm to bar Mr. Bazalgette's passage. "You go in first, to your mistress, Sarah, and say that a gentleman is waiting to see her: just landed from the West Indies."

But the commotion had attracted attention, and a young lady, not black, but charmingly white, appeared at the parlour-door, a black head behind her.

"George!" she shrieked. And the next moment flew into his arms, sobbing and crying, and kissing him. Cole decamped.

That past evening in November, when Cole received a message that his services were needed at North Villa, he went expecting to be introduced to a black lady. A black lady in truth showed him in; or, to be correct, a lady's black attendant, and he saw—Verena Fontaine.

That is, Verena Bazalgette. She put Cole upon his honour, not to disclose her secret, and told him a long string of her sister-in-law's iniquities, as touching lecturing and domineering, and that she had left home intending to come over for a time to Coralie. Whilst staying with Mrs. Dickson before sailing, a letter was forwarded to her from Magnolia Grange. It was from Coralie; and it convinced Verena that Coralie's would be no safe refuge, that she would be sent out of it at once back to her husband. She sailed, as projected, allowing Mrs. Dickson to think she was still coming to her sister. Upon landing at Southampton she went on to a small respectable inn at Worcester, avoiding the larger hotels lest she should meet people who knew her. Seeing the advertisement of North Villa to let, she wrote to the agent, and secured it. To be near Coralie seemed like a protection, though she might not go to her. Next she answered an advertisement from a cook (inserted by Sarah Stone), and engaged her, binding her to secrecy. The woman, though of crusty temper, was honest and trustworthy, and espoused the cause of her young mistress, and was zealously true to her. She carried in to her the various reports that were abroad, of the Indians and the black lady, and all the rest of it; causing Verena bursts of laughter, the only divertisement she had in her imprisoned life: she did not dare to go out lest she should be recognized and the news carried to Coralie. Dalla, a faithful native servant who had been left in the West Indies and returned to Verena when she married George Bazalgette, attended her on her solitary voyage. She it was who was black, not Verena. And the night they stole into the premises of Oxlip Grange it was done with the hope of getting a sly peep at Coralie's face; both of them were longing for it. Hearing the stir in the shrubs, Dalla had hissed; her thoughts were back in her own land, and it was her mode of startling away four-footed night animals there.

George Bazalgette was very angry with his wife, more especially so at her having absented herself at that uncertain time, and he declared to her that he would put her away from him for good if ever she attempted such a thing again. With tears enough to float a ship, Verena gave him her solemn promise that she never would leave him again. Never again: she had been too miserable this time, and the baby had nearly frightened her to death, for she had not expected him so soon and had meant to go back for it.

The Squire could not hold out now, and the Christmas dinner was at Coralie's. We went over to Timberdale Church in the morning, a lot of us, to hear the Archdeacon preach. Herbert gave up the pulpit to him, taking the prayers himself. He was a plain little man, as you knew before, and he gave us a plain sermon, but it was one of those that are worth their weight in gold. Lady Tenby whispered that to me as we came out. "And oh, Johnny," she said, "we are so glad he has got on! We always liked Isaac Sale."

It was a grand dinner-party, though not as many were present as Coralie wanted. The Letsoms did not care to leave their own fireside, or old Paul, or the Chandlers. Verena was the life of it, laughing and joking and parading about with her baby, who had been christened "George" the day before, Mrs. Cramp having been asked to be its godmother.

"Which I think was very pretty of them, Mr. Johnny," she said to me after dinner; "and I'm proud of standing to it."

"It was in recompense for the worry I've given you, you dear old thing!" whispered Verena, as she pulled Mrs. Cramp's chair backwards and kissed her motherly forehead. "You'll never have such a tenant again—for worry."

"Never, I hope, please Heaven!" assented Mrs. Cramp. "And I'm sure I shall never see a black woman without shivering. Now, my dear, you just put my chair down; you'll have me backwards. Hold it, will you, Mr. Johnny!"

"What dishes of talk you'll get up about me with Susan Dennet!" went on Verena, the chair still tilted. "We are going back home the beginning of the year, do you know. George got his letters to-day."

"And what about that young lady over there—that Miss Magnolia?" asked Mrs. Cramp.

Verena let the chair fall in ecstasy, and her tone was brimful of delight. "Oh, that's the best news of all! Magnolia is going to be married: she only waits for George to get back to give her away. I must say this is a delightful Christmas-Day!"

On the thirty-first of December, the last day in the year, Coralie was married to Dr. Rymer. Archdeacon Sale, being Benjamin's brother-in-law, came over to Islip Church to tie the knot. Her brother-in-law, George Bazalgette, gave her away. The breakfast was held at Coralie's, Verena presiding in sky-blue satin.

And amidst the company was a lady some of us had not expected to see—Mrs. Rymer. She had scarlet ringlets (white feathers setting them off to-day) and might be vulgar to her fingers'-ends, but she was Benjamin's mother, and Coralie had privately sent for her.

"You have my best wishes, Mr. Benjamin," said the Squire, drawing Ben aside while Coralie was putting on her travelling attire; "and I'd be glad with all my heart had your father lived to see it."

"So should I be, Squire."

"Look here," whispered the Squire, holding him by the button-hole, "did you ever tell her of that— that—you know—that past trouble?"

"Of the bank-note, you mean," said Ben. "I told her of that long ago, and everything else that could tell against me. Believe me, Mr. Todhetley, though my faults were many in the days gone by, I could not act dishonourably by my dear wife; no, nor by any one else now."

The Squire nodded with a beaming face, and pressed Ben's hand.

"And let me thank you now, sir, for your long-continued kindness, your expressions of esteem for my poor father and of goodwill to me," said Ben, with emotion. "I have not talked of it, but I have felt it."

They started away in their new close carriage, amidst a shower of rice and old shoes; and we finished up the revels in the evening with a dance and a fiddle, the Squire leading out Mrs. Cramp. Then came a cold supper.

The noise had reached its height, and the champagne was going about, when the Squire interrupted with a "Hush, hush!" and the babel ceased. The clock on the mantelpiece was striking twelve. As the last stroke vibrated on the air, its echo alone breaking the silence, the Squire rose and lifted his hands—

"A Happy New Year to us all, my friends! May God send His best blessings with it!"

It may as well be added, in the interests of peace and quietness, that those Indians had not committed any crime at all; it had been invented by rumour, as Worcester discovered later. They were only inoffensive strangers, travelling about to see the land.

MRS HENRY WOOD (aka ELLEN WOOD) – A CONCISE BIBLIOGRAPHY

Danesbury House (1860)
East Lynne (1861)
The Elchester College Boys (1861)
A Life's Secret (1862)
Mrs. Halliburton's Troubles (1862)
The Channings (1862)
The Foggy Night at Offord: A Christmas Gift for the Lancashire Fund (1863)
The Shadow of Ashlydyat (1863)
Verner's Pride (1863)
Lord Oakburn's Daughters (1864)
Oswald Cray (1864)
Trevlyn Hold; or, Squire Trevlyn's Heir (1864)
William Allair; or, Running away to Sea (1864)
Mildred Arkell: A Novel (1865)
The Argosy (1865)
Elster's Folly: A Novel (1866)
St. Martin's Eve: A Novel (1866)
Lady Adelaide's Oath (1867)
Orville College: A Story (1867)
The Ghost of the Hollow Field (1867)
Anne Hereford: A Novel (1868)
Castle Wafer; or, The Plain Gold Ring (1868)
The Red Court Farm: A Novel (1868)
Roland Yorke: A Novel (1869)
Bessy Rane: A Novel (1870)
George Canterbury's Will (1870)
Dene Hollow (1871)
Within the Maze: A Novel (1872)
The Master of Greylands (1872)
Johnny Ludlow (1874)
Bessy Wells (1875)
Told in the Twilight: Containing 'Parkwater' and nine short stories (1875)
Adam Grainger: A Tale (1876)
Edina (1876)
Our Children (1876)
Parkwater: With four other tales (1876)
Pomeroy Abbey (1878)
Lady Adelaide (1879)
Johnny Ludlow, Second Series (1880)
A Tale of Sin and Other Tales (1881)

Court Netherleigh: A Novel (1881)
About Ourselves (1883)
Johnny Ludlow. Third Series (1885)
Lady Grace and Other Stories (1887)
The Story of Charles Strange (1888)
Featherston's Story. A Tale by Johnny Ludlow (1889)
The Unholy Wish and Other Stories (1890)
The House of Halliwell. A Novel (1890)
Ashley and Other Stories (1897)
Victor Serenus (1898)
Johnny Ludlow. Fifth series (1899)
Johnny Ludlow. Sixth series (1899)

Translations
Les Channing. Traduit de l'Anglais par Mme Abric-Encontre (1864)
Les Filles de Lord Oakburn: Roman traduit de l'anglais par L. Bochet (1876)
La Gloire des Verner: Roman traduit de l'anglais par L. de L'Estrive (1878)
Le Serment de Lady Adelaïde: Roman traduit de l'anglais par Léon Bochet (1878)